LEAGUE OF ELDER
The Belmont Saga

SANDS OF THE SOLAR EMPIRE
AGAINST THE DRURIES

REN GARCIA

Also by Ren Garcia

The League of Elder Series:
Sygillis of Metatron
The Hazards of the Old Ones

The Temple of the Exploding Head Trilogy:
The Dead Held Hands
The Machine
The Temple of the Exploding Head

The Belmont Saga:
Sands of the Solar Empire
Against the Druries

The Shadow tech Goddess Series:
The Shadow tech Goddess
Stenibelle
Kat

The House of Bloodstein:
Perlamum
Mentralysis

Collected Works:
The Temple of the Exploding Head Omnibus
The Belmont Saga

Non-Fiction by Ren Garcia:
10 Weeks at Chanute

For more please visit: www.thetempleoftheexlodinghead.com

Table of Contents

Book I
Sands of the Solar Empire

Part 1—The Admiral's Pleasure

Part 2—All That Resists Him

Part 3—The Demon That Came For His Soul

Book II
Against the Druries

Part 1—The Sisters' Fist

Part 2—The Woman in Gray

Part 3—The Pilgrims of Merian

Book I
Sands of the Solar Empire

For Corina Emilia
--You'll always be my Big 'Sis

I—The *Seeker*

The Admiralty of the 3rd Fleet had a rare situation on their hands—what to do with the *Seeker*.

Officially designated Main Fleet Vessel 4562, she was a forty year old *Straylight*-class Warbird, P2 variant, hailing from the old glory days of the League/Xaphan conflict, when fighting the Xaphans was honorable and romantic. The *Seeker*, once the pride of the Fleet, had been in the thick of countless battles and quests, always triumphant.

But, times change, and the *Seeker's* best days appeared to be behind her. Things were deteriorating quickly. Her current captain, Lord Gona of St. Paris, was suddenly retiring to the rolling hills of Remnath—his hastily penned resignation mentioned something about taking up wine-making at his sprawling estate—and her captain's chair, therefore, was open.

Captain Gona wasn't the only prominent officer leaving the *Seeker* in a hurry. The engineer informed the 3rd Fleet Admiralty that he too was stepping down at once. He gave them no particular reason. He quickly Appointed to another ship and was gone.

The same with the boatswain. Even the cook, a Chef Parsley, stepped aside, put his boots on the ground and opened a restaurant in Saga.

Finally, the *Seeker's* crew began filtering away, hooking onto other vessels as fast as they could get them, like rats scurrying away from a burning building.

Such a mass exodus from a once-great ship never looked good out in the public. Officers, cooks, and crew normally didn't flee from a prominent Warbird like the *Seeker*, a veteran of Mirendra, a veteran of Two-Pitch Nebula—there must be some scandalous reason as to why, and the Admiralty, knowing how the gossip-mill could easily begin to turn, scrambled to keep the matter quiet.

Very quickly, the *Seeker* was an abandoned hulk, running lonely in the low polar orbit assigned to her.

Lord Milos of Probert, the Fleet's chief engineer, was flown aboard the ship to give her a good sounding; perhaps the reason why everybody wanted to leave would make itself plainly known in short order. Perhaps there was some insidious gas present aboard the ship addling the crew's wits, or some undetected radiation causing the problem. Certainly Probert would get to the bottom of it.

He assessed the status and condition of the *Seeker* with his usual terse and blunt authority.

Significant wear metal fatigue in J's 27 through 45—the "neck" of the ship. Most, if not all, of the structural components, including custom-crafted parts and linkages, shall need replacing in dry dock. Cause: age of the ship.

Stellar mach coils 1, 2, 3, 4, 5, 6 and 7 are tach'ed out and require replacing, as standard Fleet maintenance procedures demand. As before, additional time in dry dock shall be required to perform the engine refit.

Battle Shot batteries 2 through 14, starboard-side and 10 through 17, port side, are badly overdue for replacement, both through wear of use and a lack of suitable ordinance to arm them. As the Seeker *does not have the capacity for a thermoplant powerful enough to make use of modern Sar-Beam weaponry, the batteries will need to be replaced and refitted by hand with a team of master armorers custom assembling each unit. Assessment: Possible, but ruinously expensive.*

Probert discovered no odd gases or radiations aboard the *Seeker*, just an old, lonely ship whose grocery list of urgent needs was long and costly.

A final note on Lord Probert's report was interesting, though rather out-of-character for the renowned Fleet engineer who normally stuck to cold, stark facts and calculated data. He said the *Seeker* had a strange "feel" to it as he prowled the decks, and it wasn't due to gas or radiation.

Ship's haunted, he said in so many words. In interviewing Captain Gona, the engineer, the boatswain and the cook, the Admiralty got a similar story— the ship was beset by moaning demons and bad dreams. To serve aboard the ship was unbearable, and, all of them agreed they would never set foot aboard her again.

So, there the Admirals were with a decrepit forty year old Warbird that needed a large amount of expensive refitting to keep space-worthy, and, apparently, required an exorcism as well—just think of the scandal *that* would make.

Scuttle her, melt the *Seeker* down, and recast her as something useful; that seemed the clear course of action. However, because the *Seeker* was a fairly well-known and well-thought-of ship, the Admiralty couldn't simply tow her to the Fleet scrap yards at Kana X4 and make her disappear. Though having fallen into obscurity as of late, she had fought a great deal of battles with the Xaphans over the years and come through unvanquished, with the famed Captain Davage in command and his fighting countess, Sygillis of Blanchefort, sitting at his side. Also, the Sisterhood of Light, a highly influential sect the Fleet was always attempting to please, was very fond of the *Seeker* due to their past association with it.

"How is the *Seeker*," the Sisterhood often asked when they visited the Fleet. It was, quite probably, the only ship in the active Fleet they knew by name, and it was those casual but frequent inquires that help put a shield over the old ship that no other vessel could enjoy.

So, what to do with the *Seeker*?

In a virtual no-win situation, the Admiralty decided to raise the captain's chair of the *Seeker* to an open debate one last time, Free Boot style as sometimes was still done; in doing so, they could have time to grease up the Sisterhood and any others who had a fondness for the *Seeker*—let them know, at a measured pace, that the famed ship was getting too old and dangerous to keep in service. That way, she could slowly fade away, and those who loved her could accept it as what must be.

The great days of the *Seeker* were clearly well behind her.

So, using the vague and contentious Free Boot system from the old days of the Fleet, the *Seeker's* chair was put up on the blocks. Anybody wanting the chair could simply present themselves and prove their merits. That person had to have a good sponsor, connections, a grand House behind them and, best of all, the willing coin to repair her. The pickings, however, might prove to be slim. Most of the young hopefuls coming up through the ranks of the Fleet and League Society wanted the captain's chair of newer ships, either right off the blocks awaiting a christening, or fairly new, just needing a coat of paint.

The Admiralty knew that few would want a once great Warbird with only a few years of service life left that needed an expensive dry docking and was rumored to be haunted.

So, who was it to be? Who would come and save the *Seeker,* with all the aches and pains and ghosts that came with her?

II—THE APPOINTMENT

The day of days had arrived. Paymaster Stenstrom, Lord of Belmont-South Tyrol, was to face Appointment as captain of the old Main Fleet Vessel, *Seeker*.

He sat in a small holding room at the Main Fleet complex in Armenelos. The room smelled of fine food; a lavish breakfast had been brought in earlier by the Fleet orderlies.

A big breakfast served to an appointment candidate was tradition, for once he or she stepped out onto the red velvet and pooled light of the Admiralty floor, one could expect to be there all day and not have the opportunity to eat again until late evening. A hearty breakfast was meant to sustain the candidate for that prolonged period of time. Stenstrom, so far, had only picked at the plate of eggs and bacon, hashed potatoes, airy pancakes and ham set before him. He'd spread a bit of marmalade on a slice of toasted bread and ate it, but that was all so far.

Stenstrom wasn't alone in the holding room; he had esteemed company. Captain Davage, the Lord of Blanchefort, was his sponsor for this Appointment and was to offer the opening remarks on the floor. Davage was the *Seeker*'s original and most famous captain, a fighting captain from the north and the scourge of the Xaphan hoards. He sat at the table regal in his Fleet uniform, blue-haired with his longish locks tied back in a tail, Vith-style. His glinting CARG sat saddled at his waist.

Stenstrom paced the room like a beast.

"One thing you need to know, Bel, is that the Admiralty floor is rung out. I'm certain you share telepathy with select people—I do. I share a deep telepathy with my countess, sometimes with my first officer, but that's all, for I've always believed that one's mind should be private. I don't even share telepathy with my children; however, the Admiralty floor is designed to pierce your mind. You shall hear many voices in your head. Sometimes it can be

difficult to know when one is speaking, or simply thinking, so be ready for that. It can be overwhelming. Keep your stray thoughts in a bag, as they say, for the Admirals shall hear them."

Davage took a drink of his coffee. "You need to sit down and eat your breakfast. You've a long day ahead of you." Davage's easy manner and soothing voice helped calm Stenstrom. He was a good friend.

"I know, Dav," Stenstrom replied. "I'm simply ready to get out there and begin. I've been waiting for this day for a long time."

Davage smiled. "Do the thing with your hands, again. Come on, let's see it."

Stenstrom laughed and raised his hands, showing them, palms forward, to Davage. "Are you ready?"

Davage nodded.

In a quick movement, Stenstrom waved his hands. Where a moment earlier they were empty, now there were several brightly colored balls held between his fingers. He waved his hands again, and the balls vanished, replaced by a small golden locket. Davage clapped. "By Creation, how do you do that, Bel?"

Stenstrom chuckled. "Family secret, just one of the many skills my mother taught me. I'm certain you could Sight me and find out for yourself how I do it."

"I could, I could," Davage said. "But that would kill the fun, I think, ruin the mystery. I suppose I really don't want to know."

Stenstrom opened the locket he'd produced out of thin air and gazed at the picture within. He set it down on the table next to his plate and began eating.

Davage took another sip of coffee. "What do you have there, Bel?" he asked.

Stenstrom blushed. "Oh, it's a picture of Lilly, a Lady of Gamboa."

Davage leaned forward. "May I?"

Stenstrom slid the locket to him and Davage took a look. "My, what a very beautiful young lady—most striking. Is she your betrothed?"

"Yes and no. She's a good friend, I suppose. She painted this portrait herself—she's a fine artist. I think painted pictures have more life for me than a holo or vid. She painted this picture just for me—there's a bit of her soul in it, I think."

Davage smiled. "A sentiment I share, though I have no hand-painted lockets of my countess—Syg can't paint. So, she's just a good friend then, this Lilly of Gamboa?"

Stenstrom began eating his eggs. "It's rather complicated. We fell in love several years ago; it was my mother's doing. She arranged for us to meet, and, oddly enough, it worked out, though I usually resisted my mother's attempts to pair me up with somebody. I asked for her hand, but, she, being a heady lady, didn't offer hers in return. Instead, she offered a compromise. She noted how young we both are, how we have seen little of the League around us. She offered five years—five years for both of us to explore and see what's out there, free of strings or entanglements. If, at the end of five years, we still love each other, then we will present ourselves to the League and be wed."

"I see," Davage said. "What a wise lady she is. And what are your thoughts?"

"We've a year to go. I've been around, obviously. I went to school in Bern and became a Paymaster, sailing the heavens, mostly with you, but I've not yet met her equal, and I doubt I will. I'm ready for Lilly. I wish she were here with me, this very day."

"And how does she feel?"

Stenstrom thought a moment. "I really don't know, I've not heard from her in some time; my letters go unanswered, my coms and vids unopened. Perhaps she's moved on, though I continue to have hope." He noted his attire. "Lilly helped me pick out my 'fighting' uniform here: my shirt, boots, pants, and this coat that I love so much."

Davage finished his coffee. "Yes, that coat…" he said, eyeing it hanging over the chair. "If I may offer a bit of sound advice, I would use the time given to you as best you can. You have five years—use it, let your heart soar. The last thing you will want is to look back some day and say 'I had five years, and I wasted it.' That will simply lead to regret."

An old fashioned clock hanging near the door chimed.

Davage stood and approached the seated Stenstrom. "Ah, it's almost time. You finish your breakfast and listen carefully to what I have to say. Despite what you might soon be hearing upon the floor, this Appointment is decided. It's done. You, Bel, shall be the next bonded captain of the *Seeker*. This debate is simply a reason for the Admirals to put on their uniforms and their hose and throw their weight around. An Appointment, especially an Appointment to the Captain's seat of a Main Fleet Vessel, is something they live for. An Appointment to a boatswain's chair or an engineer's chair is one thing—those are skilled, highly technical positions requiring a great deal of documentable craft and experience, and involves material that the Admirals have little or no knowledge of. Those are fairly cut and dry. A Free Boot Captain's chair, well now, that's an entirely different beast. *Anybody* can debate to a Captain's chair in such a situation, and, therefore, the Admirals are given leave to pick apart a candidate and discard them as they wish. However, despite their bluster, there are certain guidelines which they follow to a point, and, if you meet those guidelines, they are going to Appoint you, no matter how ugly the proceedings get. I know their guidelines, and you meet them all."

Stenstrom swallowed his eggs. "What are they?"

"Oh, the usual Society nonsense mostly. See, in theory, any man or woman may present themselves as a candidate to a Free Boot Captain's chair. In reality, only a select few may be successfully Appointed. First, a candidate needs a suitable sponsor. I am your sponsor, and proudly so, so that's that. Next, they look at your pedigree—who are you, where you come from—that's important to them. If you come from some seedy Calvert line, or worse, then that's a big black mark. Fear not; your pedigree is firm. You are the next Lord of Belmont-South Tyrol, a fine-standing Zenon House, and the Admiralty simply loves Ze-

Captain Davage, Lord of Blanchefort

nons—loves them. Secondly, your mother, Lady Jubilee, is of the House of Tyrol, a wondrous Esther line."

Stenstrom stopped eating. "Dav, the Sisters have secretly investigated my mother and her House of Tyrol on suspicion of sorcery, black magic and demon-summoning several times in the recent past prior to her death. And, she was under Wirguild for nearly ninety years prior to that."

"Yes, Elders rest her soul. Well, the Sisters, as far as I'm aware, did not issue any public edicts, condemnations, or statements on that matter regarding your mother; therefore, I wouldn't give tongue to it on the debating floor if I were you. So, as I said, your pedigree is confirmed. Again, anything other than Calvert and the like and you're fine. Next, the Admirals look at familiar standing."

"And that is?"

"If the Admirals are to be given any credit, they do give hard work, accomplishment and seniority its proper due. Fleet crewmen who work their way up the chain are often rewarded—look at me. I started as a junior helmsman of a barely space-worthy *Webber*-ship, and look where I ended up. The Admiralty appreciates such things. Now, you do not have any direct familiar standing; however, you have an abundance of indirect. Your father, Lord Stenstrom the Older, has been the captain of the *Caroline* for nineteen appointments—he's a beloved Fleet captain, any Admiral would say so, and, you, as his son, inherit a good deal of that positive will automatically. That alone is enough to check off on the Admiral's familiar standing point."

"I wish my father could be here today."

"No family members allowed, unfortunately."

"What about my service as a Fleet Paymaster?"

"That, Bel, is a negative. Don't get me wrong. A Paymaster is a well-regarded occupation. However, I can't think of any Paymasters currently in command of a Fleet vessel, Warbird or otherwise. Paymasters generally aren't associated with the command chair. They are thought of as little men, sitting in a stuffy office somewhere, counting beans, observing transactions, and cutting checks. And, to that point, the Admiralty is going to want to know why you became a Fleet Paymaster and not an active crewman or officer."

Stenstrom put his fork down and smiled. "Shall I tell them why, Dav?"

"The truth? Absolutely not! The truth, if I recall correctly, involves some sort of black magic ritual, robed, oiled females, and a heated knife plunged in your heart under a blood moon. That does not need to be spoken of on the debating floor. For the love of the Elders, think up a tawdry, mundane lie and stick to it. Don't dwell on it in your thoughts either, for the Admirals shall hear them on the floor. Make your lie and your thoughts as boring as possible so that the point will be forgotten and moved on from for lack of interest. So, discounting the Paymaster connection, your father's status shall grant you more than enough familiar standing to make the Admiral's list. There's one final category that the Admirals look at with high regard."

"And that is?"

"Money, Bel. The Admirals always cater to Lords and Ladies who can offer up a brick of pledged cash."

"I've got one hundred thousand Belmont sesterces to offer up, and quite a bit more in reserve."

"Yes," Davage replied. "Enough said."

The clock began chiming steadily. Davage looked up. "It's near time. Come, let's get you ready."

Stenstrom stood up from the table and wiped his lips. Davage approached and looked him over. "Let me straighten your shirt." He busily began fussing with his frilly white shirt and complicated buttons.

"Now, there are a few more things before we head out. As captain of a Main Fleet Vessel, you're going to have to keep a few rules in mind. I'll tell you what they are, and they might sound a bit contradictory, but hear me out. One, a Warbird captain, as you are about to become, *never* takes an order from an admiral who is not within one hundred thousand stellar miles of his position."

"Never?"

"Never. One of the reasons the Fleet has been so successful over the years is because we follow the principles given to us by the Elders. And the Elders never said anything about taking orders from a far-flung Admiral on the other side of League space, a person who has been promoted to their level of incompetence and who has no idea what your situation is. There are a handful of fighting Admirals out there, Admiral Carfax coming closest to my mind, and in war-situations you have to listen to them. However, discounting those select situations, it's the captain, sitting there in the heat of battle who makes the decisions and calls the shots. Waiting for an Admiral to make a decision for you will get you and your crew killed. You know the man who replaced me on the *Seeker's* chair?"

"Captain Gona of St. Paris?"

"Yes, Captain Gona. He's gone off, retiring. He's going to ferment grapes and make wine at his Remnath home I hear tell, hence the *Seeker's* empty chair. Good for him. I am certain there are plenty of people who love Captain Gona; unfortunately, none of them may be counted as Fleet captains."

"Why?"

"Because he was considered a bore, an Admiral's man. He listened to the Admirals, took their advice, and played taxi to them. He ferried them around the League and sat at their beck and call."

"Is that bad?"

Davage picked up Stenstrom's pistols, two old-fashioned lock-style pistols with well-worn wooden stocks and handed them to him. Stenstrom slid them into either side of his green sash, the stocks jutting out.

"It's terrible," Davage said continuing. "Captain Gona took a proud Warbird like the *Seeker,* my *Seeker,* and turned her into a lowly carrier pigeon, hauling freight and serving as Admiral Pax's personal chariot. As captain, you're going to be seeing a lot of tags and callouts for Admirals wanting this and Admirals wanting that—do not fall for any of it. Admiral Pax is notorious for doing so. He'll send a blunt call out: 'I want the *Seeker* to pick me up and take me to Planet X over here.' He'll make it sound quite important. He'll even issue threats and post warnings on what would happen should the *Seeker* not show up. You must take steps to ignore his bravado. There are two questions you have to ask yourself when considering ferrying an Admiral: One—does the Admiral have a sufficient amount of breathable air available to him? Two—does the Admiral have a quantity of untainted food and potable water to sustain him? If the answer to both of those questions is 'Yes,' then let the Admiral sit on his doffed-out ass and await the arrival of a scout ship as he is supposed to. Scout ships have to follow the Admiral's orders; you do not. You've got a Main Fleet Warbird, and you're sitting on it. That makes you immune to an Admiral's orders unless he's within one hundred thousand stellar miles of your position, and do not forget that; therefore, it is often wise to know an Admiral's itinerary when he's out in the League and avoid those places where he'll be at all costs. If you let the Admiralty in, if you play nurse-maid to them too often, you are done as a Warbird captain. You will belong to them. You have to stand up and be blunt and rather merciless in your rebuff right from the go."

Stenstrom laughed. "I see. I'll remember that. What's the second rule?"

Davage picked up Stenstrom's heavy green coat. "When in the Fleet HQ, you have to respect the Admiralty. You have to bite your tongue, play their game, and abide by their rules. Here, we are in the Fleet—here we have to play nice. I sound pretty rotten towards the Admirals, and, given some of the things they do, they deserve it, but truth be told, they've got a hard job. For many, they are the face of the Fleet to the League. They have to maintain relations, secure monies, which is an endless task, maintain the ships, and find the best people to fill the chairs when they come open. Here, you have to give them their due." Davage looked at Stenstrom's coat. "This coat you wear is not playing nice. The Admirals will pick up on it and give you no peace."

Stenstrom put his coat on. It was a beautiful coat: dark hunter green, silver and gold embroidery, and the letters HRN standing out in silver on the collar. Stenstrom took his locket and placed it in a pocket inside the coat's breast. "Lilly picked this coat out for me. We were in Minz when she found it. I adore my coat," he said. "It makes me feel close to her."

"I advise you wear something else. Something … less inflammatory."

"As you said, I have to stand up to the Admirals. I shall do so with my coat if I must. It's just a coat." He put on his huge triangle hat and adjusted it.

"Yes, just a coat. And it'll be just a piece of rotten fruit that comes raining down on you and your HRN coat. The Admirals pay for the right to throw things down onto the debating floor. It's a traditional way of making a fervent point—this coat will give them their monies' worth, I fear."

Davage then took the black, silk mask Stenstrom was wearing and straightened it. Stenstrom's blue eyes sparkled through the holes. Davage shook his head. "You know, the first time I saw you wearing a mask, I honestly didn't know what to think. I recall having you clapped in irons and I thought 'Who in Creation is this fellow?'"

"Just something I have to endure. I promised my mother I'd never endanger myself—she tended to be a worry-wart. This mask protects me from all things she conjured at me before she died. Elders rest her soul."

"She sent demons at you with the thought of keeping you safe?"

"Yes."

"And you're certain you cannot take it off, if only for a few hours?"

"If I do, the Admirals shall get to watch me die upon their floor. Remove my mask and the charms within, and I die."

Davage clapped him on the shoulder. "So be it. Just be ready to be rather inconvenienced this afternoon."

The clock stopped, and the door opened. An adjutant stood in the doorway. "Sirs, the gallery is assembled. The Admiralty awaits."

Davage turned to the adjutant. "Thank you, we're coming."

Side by side, they left the room and began the short walk to the Admiralty floor. Stenstrom, fully decked out, could see the red carpeting and pools of circular light waiting ahead. He could see the elevated gallery, dark, full of indistinct movement.

"Oh, Lt. Kilos wanted me to relay you a message, Bel," Davage said. "I believe she said she wants you to: 'Knock `em dead'. She also wanted me to give you a little love tap across the jaw for her, but I think we can dispense with that for now. She, like Syg and me, are all very proud of you."

Stenstrom laughed.

Davage spoke again as they walked. "You know, Bel, the *Seeker*'s over forty years old—that's pretty veteran for a Main Fleet Vessel that's seen a lot of action—most Warbirds cycle into the smelter long before that, and, I must say, I put her through my fair share of hell. But, no matter what, she always came through, always found the strength to get me, and Syg, and my crew home. Lord Milos of Probert, the designer of the *Seeker* and a good friend of mine, has always scoffed at the notion that these huge birds, these great ships he designed, have a soul, that we in the Fleet Captaincy are too sentimental assigning a great machine with feelings and a soul. Lord Probert is wrong, Bel; the *Seeker* has a soul and a heart to match. Captain Gona took away much of the honor she'd acquired, took away part of her soul. Give it back to her, Bel—she deserves it. Make her into a great Warbird again, and she'll never let you down."

✶ ✶ ✶ ✶ ✶

As Davage had predicted, the Admiralty floor rang out with thought. Voices filled Stenstrom's head, turning the whole place into a surreal, noisy dream bathed in red carpet.

I'm hungry.

Did you see that beautiful woman in the lobby?

Do my leggings make me look fat?

Who's this fellow we're looking at today?

Down on the red carpet in a pool of sterile light, he sat in the ornate chair as the Appointment began. Lord Davage stood before the gallery and made his opening remarks.

That's Captain Davage down there. Oh, look at him ...

Did he say Paymaster? The Appointee is a Paymaster?

He's a Paymaster...

Paymaster?

Who's his mother, again?

Oh, he's a handsome fellow, do you see?

What's he wearing? Is that a mask, or a trick of the light?

Stenstrom watched Davage as he easily commanded the floor. His lovely Fleet uniform, his collar speckled with gold stars and ivy, his blue Vith hair tied in a bow as they did it in the north, his heavy CARG flashing at his side. Stenstrom didn't have the Sight like Davage did. Under the lights high over-head, he couldn't see much in the crowd, he just knew there were a lot of people up there, rustling around, raining their thoughts down on him.

Lord Davage disarmed the Admirals to a large extent. He spoke rath-er eloquently, describing Lord Stenstrom's upbringing and pedigree in the House of Belmont-South Tyrol, his mother's status as a lady of Tyrol, and, most importantly, his father's legendary status as captain of the *Caroline,* for over nineteen appointments. That was a bedrock list of endorsements.

I played golf with Captain Stenstrom last week. ...or did I? Who was that?

Are Tyrols of Esther or Barrow stock?

The Admirals muttered to themselves—very impressive. Lord Davage spoke well, as always, and brought up a number of excellent points.

And then there was money, which always impressed the Admiralty. Lords and Ladies with ready cash were always looked upon with regard. The Fleet, mighty and graceful, was fueled primarily by privately donated monies. New ships, new research, new appointments, were all incredibly expensive, and the lord or lady who could offer up a healthy sum was always a welcome sight. Again, the Admiralty was impressed and de-fanged.

He's got how much??

Belmont sesterces? How do those exchange into Grenville solaris? Wow!

We can renovate the eastern Fleet wing with that.

With Davage having thoroughly greased the Admirals, the remaining part of the Appointment should be a breeze, what with pedigree, familial connections, a stately mother, a legendary father and tons of ready cash, Lord Stenstrom should be an easy shoe-in.

But then, Lord Davage had to sit down, and Lord Stenstrom himself stood and took the floor to be interviewed. That's when the fireworks began.

Lord Stenstrom was a commandingly tall figure. He towered over the tall Lord Blanchefort. He certainly looked the part.

Look how tall.

He's a bean pole.

Is that a uniform he's wearing? Paymasters aren't supposed to wear uniforms.

From somewhere in the gallery, an Admiral spoke, or did he?

"Lord Belmont," came the voice. "How long have you been a Fleet Paymaster?"

Stenstrom cleared his throat. "Three years, good sir. I was trained in Bern."

"And where did you receive your tenure for admission into the IBBAANA Brotherhood?"

Stenstrom considered his response. "Calvert."

"Calvert, I see. And, aboard what ships did you serve?"

"The *Sandwich*, sir, a frigate, followed by the *New Faith*."

The gallery rustled.

"And, you have not been involved, as a crewman or an officer, in either the Stellar Fleet or Marines?"

"No, great sir."

But, he's wearing a uniform.

It's a lovely uniform.

"Lord Belmont," the Admiral continued, "you stand before us wishing to assume the captain's chair of a Main Fleet Vessel, a Warbird, yet you have created a career for yourself as a Paymaster and not as an officer or crewman. We wish to know why this is the case."

Tell a tawdry lie, Davage had said. Stenstrom thought a bit of truth would be better.

"My late mother, fearing for my father's safety through his years of service in the Fleet, wished me to practice a more sedate career. I became a Paymaster. I honored her request."

"Your mother?"

"Yes sir. One should honor their mother."

The thoughts rolled in.

I hate my mother.

Perhaps he's a grand Nancy-Boy.

Oh stop it—he appears to be a good boy.

"A fine sentiment. And, of course, Paymasters are an honored addition to our spaceward ships. But, what good can cash-shucking, and coin rumbling do you in asserting your merits as a ship's captain?"

"I commanded the *New Faith* for a time during the Kestral Affair, with glowing after commentary from Captain Davage."

Stenstrom stepped forward—the HRN on his collar glinted in the light.

Hold up—what is that?

HRN??

What is 'that' doing on the Admiralty floor?

The gallery was beginning to froth. "Good Lord Belmont, what, pray, are you wearing?"

"Pardon?"

"Your coat? Where did you get that coat?"

Stenstrom looked at his sleeves. "I purchased it on the open market. I fail to see what relevance my coat has in this matter."

"That coat, sir, is the costume of the Hoban Royal Navy. Perhaps you've heard of them."

Miss, I'll have a bushel here. Fruit, make it rotten!

He's wearing a Hoban Royal Navy coat?

Fruit! Give me fruit to throw!!

Stenstrom was starting to feel he should have listened to Davage. "I have heard of them, after a fashion. I am not overly versed in their exploits. I simply liked the coat, so I bought it."

The Admiral spoke again. "Allow me to fill you in, sir. The Hoban Royal Navy was a far-flung assemblage of drunken yachtsmen who thought to take it upon themselves to post the defense of Hoban, in hopes of polishing their prestige and supplanting the Fleet in the region. That coat you're wearing is one of many such costumes they chose to wear. A question, sir, know you the rank of the coat you're wearing?"

"I'm afraid I do not. Again, I am not well-versed in the organization."

"Grand Plantain, sir. You are wearing the coat of a Grand Plantain—the ranks of the Hoban Royal Navy were designated in fruits. Yet another 'good idea' those fellows had."

Grand Plantain?

He's a big banana, haha!

Look at the banana!

I am going to cast a fruit at him, to make him feel at home. Ya!

An apple came down from the gallery and landed nearby.

Stenstrom found himself becoming rather annoyed. His tongue began to wag. "Your pardon, Admirals, a plantain is most decidedly *not* a banana."

So, he's a chef as well as a lily-livered accountant, is he?

Here, Paymaster, file this rotten orange in an appropriate place!

A smelly orange came down and whizzed over Stenstrom's head. Captain Davage sat there off to the side and drank a coffee, nonplussed.

"Your late mother, Lady Jubilee, may her soul rest at peace, was a lady of Tyrol—that has been previously established," the Admiral said.

"Yes, and what of it?"

"House Tyrol has established roots and ties with the House of Croatoa. House Croatoa is prominent with the current governing body of Hoban. It is that body that formulated the Hoban Royal Navy and unleashed it upon space."

"Irrelevant, sir. Again, neither I, nor my departed mother, have ties to the Hoban Royal Navy—I simply liked the coat."

The Admiral who had been speaking continued. "Regardless, sir, you come before us, a green-fisted clerk wearing the trappings of a clown, and, I must know, for I can bear it no longer, why in Creation are you wearing a mask?"

The rest of the gallery began barking.

"Are you scarred?"

"Are you monstrous?"

"Remove your mask, banana-boy!"

"Give us your coat, so we may burn it!"

"I'll wager you are hideous!"

"How may we take you seriously, sir?" an Admiral from the gallery spoke. "Attired in a fool's coat, and that stupendous mask? Why wear you such a thing?"

By this point in the interrogation, Stenstrom was feeling good and salty. "Because I choose to. Because a great personal hero of mine, Lord Terrance of Walther, wore a mask."

"Lord Terrance of Walther was mad, a vigilant and censured by the Sisterhood for his bravado. You choose such a man as your inspiration?"

"I do. The Sisters were incorrect in their assessment. What tea-drinking female or insipid bed-wetter serves as your inspiration, sir?"

"Hooah!" the Admirals cried in reproach. "Hooah!"

The proceedings had degenerated into a name-calling and humiliation fest—not an uncommon thing during a contentious appointment.

Stenstrom removed his hat and pulled his mask off. There he was, a handsome, blue-eyed, black-haired Lord of Belmont. Mixed into his hair were slight wisps of silver—a gift from his mother's Tyrol stock.

He began to feel the familiar tug on his soul and quickly put the mask back on. He was enraged. "Standing here, I feel myself as a twelve-point buck upon the path!" he shouted into the crowd.

"Were you a twelve-point buck, at least you would have some use!" an Admiral yelled back.

Another outraged Admiral spoke up. "The Lord Belmont must think us sorry or half-witted to ever contemplate him sitting upon the *Seeker's* chair."

"Do not speak of me as if I am dead, sir!" he replied. "I am not dead—I stand before you. I am alive, sir. I'm alive!"

The gallery again stirred. "That… has yet to be determined. You have no experience, and apparently no sense."

"Again, I commanded the *New Faith* during the Kestral Affair and am proud to say I did well."

"You used your Hoban Royal Navy coat to keep the Captain's seat warm, whilst he defended his ship from a cowardly, implacable enemy!"

"Ah," Stenstrom cried. "Cowardly … a true buzz-word here in the Admiralty."

Oh dear … Davage sat there and shook his head.

Get me a bushel!

Somebody threw a head of cabbage down and got Stenstrom in the shoulder.

Huzzah—right in the face! A fine cabbage cast!

Stenstrom picked it up and started to throw it back into the gallery. A small adjutant ran up to him and held out a collection basket.

Stenstrom got out his money purse and put the whole thing into the collection basket.

He's throwing!

Stenstrom threw the cabbage back into the gallery. Soon the adjutant returned with a basket full of vegetables. Grabbing two hand's worth, Stenstrom started throwing in earnest.

I'm hit! Ah me, I'm hit!

By thunder, he'll be a pair of tongs short of a salad when I'm finished with him.

Gah!—I just hit Admiral Veng in the back of the head. Apologies, Admiral!

The gallery howled and returned the favor.

✳ ✳ ✳ ✳ ✳

Lord Davage sat there and sighed. What was the point of all of this—the appointment was decided and this sorry carnival was simply a side-oddity.

A lemon came down; he ducked.

Davage stood, kicking his chair away with force where it toppled over. "ENOUGH!" he shouted, his Vith voice filling the gallery. The cascade of fruits and vegetables from the stands stopped. Stenstrom stood there with two fistfuls of cabbage, ready to let them loose. "What, may I ask, is the point of all of this? You know, as well as I, that this Appointment is decided. You, Admirals, have opened the *Seeker's* chair Free boot style and have invited an open appointment. Lord Belmont, despite his Hoban Royal Navy coat, is well-suited to take the chair, and he meets all of your criteria. Additionally I am personally vouching for his skill and his pending success. I gave him my ship in a time of great need, and I felt perfectly at ease doing so. You have no other willing to take the time and spend the coin to sit upon the *Seeker's* chair. Let us see reason here and set to the hard work ahead."

There was a bit of muttering, but the food-throwing stopped, and the rest of the Appointment passed with much less drama.

Let him have the chair, and pay his coin. See if he keeps it.

We can make things rather difficult for him ...

Welcome to the Fleet ... Captain Stenstrom ... for as long as that lasts.

✳ ✳ ✳ ✳ ✳

Several hours later, Stenstrom sent a Com home to his father. He'd been Appointed as captain of the *Seeker.*

III—An Open Letter from the Fiend of Calvert to the Mad Lord of Walther

Published February 32, 003119ax—Synthnet (St. Edmunds)

I am he who was known as the Fiend of Calvert. I trawled the streets and wharfs there, shutting the eyes of drunks, abusers, frauds and fallen men. As rats are occasionally cleaned from the sewers and other places of refuse, I cleaned the Calvert streets of Elder scum.

I should be praised. I should be given a key to the city.

Instead, I was grievously wounded by the coward who calls himself the Mad Lord of Walther. He fell upon me from behind, applied a harassing wound, and then chased me cross the rooftops, laughing throughout the entire ordeal. Though pained, I managed to escape and had to spend a significant amount of time convalescing the injury he so cowardly inflicted upon me.

Meanwhile, the filth in Calvert festers and grows afresh. Without the cat to keep the mice thinned, they overrun.

I have read your memoirs, Mad Lord. A fanciful bit of fiction, I must say. You claim that I am a lady, that you saw me as a woman in gray. I can assure you, sir, I am no woman. Would a woman be capable of doing what I have done?

If you would care to prove that YOU are no woman, sir, I challenge you to meet me in Calvert, and we may settle our dispute once and for all. Fail to meet me, and I might choose to call on Calvert afresh and resume my art at long last, as there are many throats there needing cutting.

This time you shall not catch me unawares.

Signed
??????????, the Fiend of Calvert

IV—TWINS

The heart of the League consists mostly of two planets: Kana and Onaris. There are many more League worlds that have been added over the years, but Kana and Onaris are the principles, the bastions of the League—like two great rocks facing each other on a vast beach. Other rocks might someday be washed up or eroded into view, but these two were the originals, and all others came later.

They are, in the cosmic scheme of things, neighbors in space—twins almost. To a fast Fleet ship, traveling the distance from Kana to Onaris can, depending on the time of the year, take less than a day, perhaps a little more if the ship is in no hurry. Slower ships, like Fleet merchant-men, frigates, and private vessels might make the trip in two days, perhaps three if they were particularly slow.

Moving through the patrolled lanes between the two planets is like nothing—hardly a thought went into it. It was a boring trip, a maudlin one at that. Modern vessels, even the unsightly rusty ones, could move at colossal speed, luxurious in safety and all the comforts of home.

Kana and Onaris: two great rocks facing each other on a celestial beach, awash in the surf and bound together by cosmic sand.

Consider this, though: take away those modern ships, take away that speed and technology, and suddenly the small space between the two planets widens into a dark gulf full of the foreboding and the unknown—the grains of sand on the beach separating the two rocks now insurmountable and endless.

Kana is the third planet in the Beta Terragrin system, orbiting an energetic G class star, warm and yellow.

.4 light years away is Onaris, the tenth planet in the Nu Torriander system, its star a larger A-class globe the Browns called "Ole Scrub" with an outlying class-2 dwarf star companion not far away. Orbiting two slots down from Onaris is Bazz, a Terraformed newcomer. Being so far from Ole Scrub,

Bazz had pretty tough winters, but was baked hard in the summer from the dwarf star they called "Lil' White-Face." As summers and winters on Bazz depended on planetary positioning rather than rotational tilt, the whole planet was in winter or in summer at once. An extreme place, lots of misfits went to Bazz—the frontier. Lots of people with things to hide went to Bazz in the old EX days before the Xaphans left.

Kana and Onaris: .4 light years apart. That is quite a lot of empty space between the two, space that isn't really all that empty. The League engineers have charts and maps detailing the mundane stellar bodies lying between Kana and Onaris: nebulas, comets, asteroid fields, clouds of frozen methane and the like. However, most League charts center on the shipping lanes, the direct path ships use to make the journey from Kana to Onaris and back. Go off the shipping lanes and one enters the wild lands—the unknown where the small spaces truly become huge and engulfing. None other than local dare-devils and old hermits riding the frontier past Druries Belt truly knew what was there, and nobody else really cared. What difference did it make? Here and there—gone in a blink and a surge of speed.

The "sands" of the Solar Empire, forever vast and unknown, stepped over with speedy ships moving entirely too fast to see what was there.

Coat of Arms of Belmont-South Tyrol

PART 1
THE ADMIRAL'S PLEASURE

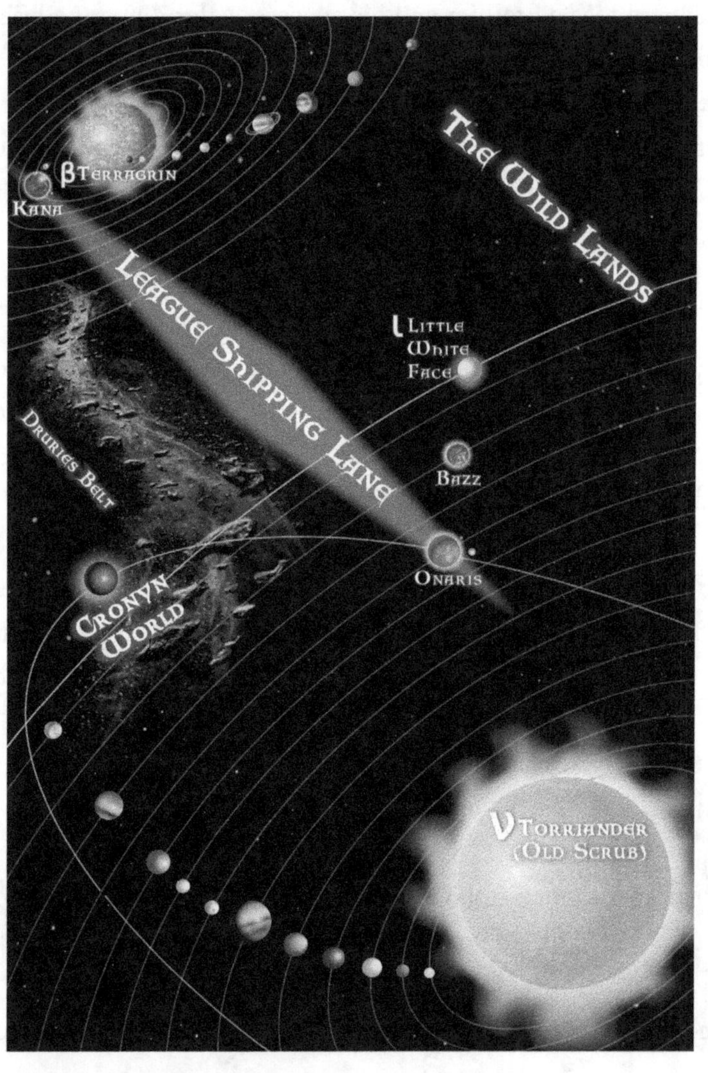

1
—The Old Dream—

The day before he was to take command of his vessel, Stenstrom returned to his ancestral manor south of Tyrol by the sea. His father was there and so were many of his twenty-nine sisters. They sat in the great dining room his mother once loved and toasted to him and his success. After dinner he briefly went out to the hill across the lane and stood in front of his mother's gravestone.

After all this time, he still missed her.

That evening he sat in his father's study with his two favorite sisters, Lyra and Virginia. His father had been a Fleet Captain on the Warbird *Caroline* for decades, and Stenstrom intently listened to his advice.

His father, giddy with excitement, thoroughly briefed his son on what to expect in the days ahead.

"You have an old ship to nurse back to fighting health. She's a good ship, a strong ship. I expect the next few months shall be rather sedate as you settle into command and oversee the *Seeker's* refits. Be certain to take an active role in the refits—do not allow some Admiral or Fleet engineer to run the whole thing un-tempered. Assert your command as captain from day one. Put your nose into places where it might not belong. Do not be afraid to ruffle feathers and stand tip-to-tip with those prima-donnas. Next, you shall need to recruit an engineer and a boatswain. Again, do not allow the Admiralty to select one for you—be bold, be aggressive. Go out and make your pitch to those you feel you can trust. If you wish it, I have a list of names that I think would make fine additions. Take them as you wish."

"Thank you, Father."

Stenstrom the Older stood and poured four glasses of fine brandy. "Here's some of the good stuff. To my son, Lord Stenstrom, captain of the *Seeker.*"

"To Bel, my favorite brother!" Lyra said.

"I hope you'll let me come aboard and cook for you and your crew sometime, Bel," Virginia said

Stenstrom laughed. "My mouth is already watering."

They clinked their glasses and drank. "Ah," Stenstrom the Older said, knocking it back. "Though your mother protested and inconvenienced you as only she could, I am certain she would have been so proud of you today, as I am. Your mother loved you very much, and as you are well aware, that love carried with it a bit of an ordeal. Your mother could be overbearing, but she never meant anything not in your best interest. All in all—I think it made you a better man, better ready to lead."

Stenstrom stood there and remembered his departed mother. "Elders rest her soul." The four of them were quiet for a moment.

He truly wished his mother could be here to see what he'd become.

That night he slept in his boyhood bedroom. He had a troubling dream that night—one of those select dreams that reoccurs periodically throughout one's life. This was a dream he first had as a little boy, and it never failed to come back to him before momentous occasions, like this one.

He dreamed of himself as a little boy, barely ten years old. He was playing in a vast sand pit behind his family manor along with Lyra and Virginia. Under the warm sun of the afternoon, his black-haired sister Lyra played in the sand along with him. Virginia sat nearby stuffing her face with something from the kitchens, watching them play. Virginia, with her mottled head of silver/black hair, was not near as tomboyish as Lyra was.

Laughing, he and Lyra wrestled in the sand. Lyra was several years older than he was, and much bigger. She got him in a headlock and then threw him to the other side of the sand pit. He could remember the feeling of flying through the air, a brief look at the sky as he fell into the unbroken sand. The puffy clouds. And he always recalled seeing stars out on the horizon in a squarish constellation, even though it was broad daylight. The stars shone clearly.

His dream was always the same: the sand, his sisters, the wrestling, the stars. He hit the sand, and then, as always, the dream became muddled.

There was a great clamor. Something hidden in the sand jumped out with terrifying speed.

There was a SNAP!

In his dream, he could see his two sisters standing there, Lyra in the sand with him and Virginia nearby. They were both staring at him. Virginia dropped the thing she was eating; it plopped into the sand. Her mouth was full of food, but she didn't chew.

Lyra then turned and ran. "Momma, Momma!" she screamed. Virginia just stood there open-mouthed.

As always, the last thing he could remember at the end of the dream was Lyra returning to the play area, leading Mother by her hand.

"Bel? BEL!" his mother screamed. "BEL!"

And that was all he could ever remember. That was the end of the dream. Whenever he had that old dream, it stayed with him all day long, just on the outskirts of his thoughts, lingering.

He sighed and tried to put the dream out of his head. He dressed, said goodbye to his father and sisters, and headed south to begin his new life as Fleet captain.

2

—St. Porter's Day—

Stenstrom arrived at the sprawling Fleet headquarters in the Zenon city of Armenelos bright and early to perform a series of perfunctory administrative duties and take command of his ship. It had been a month since his contentious appointment with the Admiralty. His mentor, Lord Davage, had long taken his leave and returned to his ship and his loving countess.

He had an appointment with Admiral Derlith, of the 3rd Fleet. He expected it to be a formality, for that's all it should be; after that, he could be introduced to his ship: the *Seeker*. As he walked through the massive marble corridors framed with statuary under towering rotundas and lush botanicals, he was surprised how largely empty the complex was—he'd certainly expected it to be much more bustling. In the broad common areas, many of the little shops and eateries were closed, vendor stalls were covered with tarps, and the cantinas were also not open.

Ah! Of course, it was St. Porter's Day! Stenstrom had completely forgotten. St. Porter's Day was a special holiday celebrated throughout the League. It was a day to express good will to one's fellows and make new friends. It was said a friend or new love made on St. Porter's Day was a friend or love for life.

With a quick movement of his hand, he produced his small golden locket. He opened it, and there was Lilly's radiant face painted in genius strokes, fresh and reassuring.

Fatefully, he had also met her on St. Porter's Day, four years ago.

He gave Lilly-in-the-locket one last smile, and put her back into his coat. Today was going to be amazing. This was his day at last.

Stenstrom took a moment and found a free terminal and sent a com home to Tyrol. There, he greeted his father and his sister Lyra and wished them good fortune, as was customary on St. Porter's Day. They were all smiles and wanted to know how things were progressing.

"Hasn't really started yet," he replied. "I just got here." He wrapped up the communication, sat a moment, and then sent a Com to Lilly in far away Gamboa. He wanted to see her. He wanted to tell her he loved her, at the very least he hoped for a hearty "good luck" from her.

He waited, not expecting the Com to be answered; Lilly hadn't been responding to any of his Coms lately.

The Com connected, he was elated. "Lilly!' he cried, "it is I, Stenstrom."

The image at the far end of the Com was hazy and indistinct, full of rattlings and odd sounds. He thought he saw a point of light, like a lantern light appear in the distance and then the Com broke. The screen went black.

He thought to re-send the Com, but checked his time-piece and thought better of it.

Admiral Derlith awaited.

He stood and continued on his way through the near empty complex to the environs of the 3rd Fleet in the back quarter of the building.

He felt confident. Good things were supposed to happen on St. Porter's Day.

The area was set up as a series of small structures and landscaped courtyards mixed in with thick greenery from the Great Armenelos Forest which wasn't far away. It was so quiet today he could almost hear the trees growing and sopping up moisture. Stenstrom made his way through the maze of walks and passages and finally found the heavy oak door emblazoned with a brass sign reading: ADMIRAL DERLITH.

Stenstrom knocked loudly on the door with the meaty part of his fist.

After a few moments, the door swung open. A meek, small-shouldered fellow stood there. He was decked out in the uniform of a Fleet adjutant, the personal assistant of a higher ranking officer. He wore an elaborate dark blue coat embroidered with silver stitching with a relentlessly frilly white shirt underneath. He wore dark blue knee britches, with white leggings and a buckled pair of black shoes. His hat was large and plumed.

He was a mousy fellow, short of stature and sloped of shoulder. His costume looked rather large on him as well. His hair was a bright banana blonde under his large blue hat.

"Are you Paymaster Stenstrom?" he asked quietly.

"I am. I have an appointment to see Admiral Derlith."

The small man swung the door wide and gestured for him to enter. "Yes, thank you, sir. Right this way."

The man led him through several courtyards and then into a small but lavishly furnished office. Inside, an iron-haired man in an admiral's uniform sat behind a desk. He gave Stenstrom a quick glance and didn't stand or stop what he was doing.

"Sit down," he said in a terse voice.

Stenstrom sat down and waited. The admiral was busy doing something at his desk; what it was Stenstrom really couldn't tell. He appeared to be speaking to somebody, his voice muffled by a directed Com cone.

Stenstrom could make out a few words, though he tried not to eavesdrop.

"Yes, he's here now. It's all arranged."

The adjutant came in a moment later with a coffee service on a silver tray. Leaning over the table, his face close to the cups, he made the admiral a coffee and set it on his desk.

The admiral took a drink. "Josephus," he said. "This is cold."

"Beg your pardon, Admiral," he said and quickly left with the pot.

Without looking at Stenstrom, the Admiral spoke. "You have secured appointment to the captain's chair of the Main Fleet Vessel *Seeker*. You pledged, at the time of your appointment, one hundred thousand Belmont sesterces to be used to fund the refitting of the vessel, as it is in need in several key areas, per Fleet regulations. We have received your pledge, and all is well in that regard. At the present time, your appointment status is marked: Provisional. As you may be aware, there are a number of pre-conditions that must be met for that appointment to be validated and made permanent, or Bonded as we say in the Fleet. They are as follows: One, you must board your vessel no later than 22 bells standard today—failure to do so shall revoke your appointment. Two, your first mission must be at the pleasure of the Admiralty—in this case, my pleasure as the *Seeker* is my ship. You will undertake a mission that I shall give to you, and you must complete it; otherwise, again, your appointment shall be revoked, and you will not be Bonded."

Stenstrom knew all of that. He had, at that time, nine bells to board the

Seeker, and then the mission, the "Admiral's Pleasure" as it was known, was usually some tawdry, perfunctory exercise that was more tedious than challenging.

"I see," he said. "Thank you. And what is the nature of my mission?"

Josephus, the tiny adjutant, returned and prepared another cup of coffee for the Admiral from a steaming hot pot. He took it and casually began sipping. "Why can't you ever give me coffee like this the first time around, Josephus? This is more like it."

"I am sorry, Admiral," he said. "Paymaster, may I offer you a cup?"

Stenstrom smiled at him. "Thank you, I'm fine."

The Admiral finished his cup. "Your mission, Lord Belmont, shall be the following: In Warehouse 87 at the far end of the Fleet complex is a crate of fine, six-year-old Remnath brandy fermented at my very own home in the hills of Remnath. My House is known for its fine grape brandy. You are to take the brandy to a grand ball that is to be thrown by Admiral Pax at Fleet annex Teflegar-Martin II on the planet Bazz. The brandy is to be served to the Admiralty after the main feast has been enjoyed. The ball shall take place on September 32nd—that will give you twelve days to deliver the cargo."

"Twelve days to go to Bazz? Is that all, sir?" Stenstrom asked. A trip to Bazz, at a leisurely rate, should take no more than two.

"Yes, that is all. Recall, your appointment is at peril. You now have less than eight and a half bells to formally board the *Seeker*, and you have twelve days to deliver the goods to Bazz."

Admiral Derlith then returned to whatever it was he was doing. Without a further word the meeting was over.

Stenstrom stood and took his leave. On his way out, he passed Josephus, who was busy preparing a snack for the Admiral. He appeared to be having issues seeing what he was doing.

"Is there anything else I can do for you, Paymaster?" he asked looking up from his work, a mustard-loaded spreading knife perched in his small hand.

"No, I'm fine. Thank you, and Happy Porter's Day to you, my friend."

Josephus lit up. "And to you, sir. Good luck and safe journey."

Stenstrom tipped his hat, then made to leave.

"Sir?" Josephus said, calling out to him.

Stenstrom turned. The adjutant appeared to want to say something but had second thoughts. "Again, good luck, and be bold."

Stenstrom smiled. "I shall do so, sir. Thank you."

He left the courtyard and made his way through the vast complex to the warehouses at the far end—it was a good, brisk walk that took about thirty minutes. As before, he met few people along the way, even less so as the day wore on.

He got to the correct warehouse—Number 87—and tried the door.

It was locked. A sign posted on the door read:

CLOSED FOR ST. PORTER'S DAY. WILL RE-OPEN STANDARD
HOURS 9/21.

Hmmmm.

Stenstrom stood there and thought. This could be a bit tougher than he first imagined. With the place virtually deserted for the holiday, how was he to secure, load and transport his cargo to the *Seeker?* Another problem immediately entered his mind—how was he going to get to the *Seeker* in the first place? He was no pilot. He needed somebody to fly him there, and the pickings here at Fleet appeared to be slim at best. There literally was nobody around to fly him up.

The enormity of the problem hit him fully.

Admiral Derlith …

He spun about in frustration. He'd paid his money. Now Admiral Derlith was going to see to it that he failed his appointment by plunking him square in the middle of a paid holiday. The man was apparently quite sly.

He could, should things get ugly, call up to the *Seeker* and have them send a Ripcar down for him, but that would be embarrassing. He hoped the situation wouldn't come to that.

Stenstrom took his hat off and wiped his brow. He supposed he could simply send a Com to his father, or to his mentor and sponsor, Lord Davage, and they would sort everything out. One or two heated Coms to the Admiralty, and this puerile attempt to drum him off the *Seeker's* chair before he'd even had a chance to sit upon it would be quashed—cold.

But, should he do that, he would be partially validating the Admiral's low opinion of him. They had set obstacles before him, and now it was time to conquer them unassisted.

So be it. The loins were about to be girded.

Airship conceptual designs for Sands cover

3

—Tyrol Sorcery—

He tried the warehouse door—again, it was locked. So, thusly inconvenienced and all alone by design, he determined that he was given lease to use any method necessary to accomplish his goal.

So, what was he to do? Unlike his father and Captain Davage, he had no Gifts of the Mind, the fantastic abilities people from the north and from Zenon could do; his mother's Tyrol stock had suppressed it in him. Neither he nor his twenty-nine sisters could perform the Gifts of the Mind.

But, that didn't mean he was helpless here. Far from it. Training he had, nine years of it, in topics unspoken outside of Tyrol. He pushed up the sleeves of his coat and made ready. It was time to make good use of the skills his mother had taught him.

He could, drawing upon his training as a sorcerer, take command of this situation in any number of ways. For the simple task of opening the door to the warehouse, naught but a bit of slight-of-hand should suffice.

He produced, as if by conjuration, an elaborate set of manual and magnetic lock picks. He'd fully inherited his mother's dexterous hands, and his skill at producing hand-held items out of thin air was impressive. Mother had trained him well.

The lock to the warehouse was a simple manual type. Since nobody was around, there was no need to be sly about it. He selected a Raven's Tooth manual pick, inserted it, and tested around a bit, his trained fingers feeling the internal landscape of the lock through the shaft of the pick.

Voices. People approached.

Stenstrom ceased his work and stepped away.

Two Marines came into the area and stopped near the entrance to the warehouse. "This the door?" one Marine asked.

"Yep."

"I don't see anybody, do you?"

The other Marine looked around. "Nope."

Stenstrom was standing right there not ten feet away—yet another one of the skills that Mother had taught him—to melt into the shadows and be unseen. Stenstrom was adept at it. He leaned against the warehouse and waited for them to leave.

One of the Marines tried the door. "Locked up tight. What are we doing here again?"

"Got a report of a suspicious person snooping about."

"I don't see anybody. Let's to the canteen and set to it. It's St. Porter's Day for Creation's sake."

The other Marine looked around again and adjusted his cap. "All right, I'm satisfied. Let's log our report and be off."

Stenstrom stifled a yawn as the second Marine pulled his communicator. "Base," he said.

"Go ahead," came a reply.

"Base, A-1, investigating report of an unauthorized person skulking about Fleet Warehouse 87. We have investigated and have determined there are no unauthorized persons about. We are quitting the area."

"Negative," came the reply. "Accomplish standard Fret scan."

The two Marines winced. One of them got out a small device with a fold-down screen. He adjusted the screen and pressed buttons. "Well, go on!" he said to the other Marine. "Start spraying!"

The other Marine produced a small gray can from his coat and started moving about the face of the warehouse, spraying a thick, hanging mist from the can. He came within a few feet of Stenstrom, getting him in the face with the spray—it smelled like peaches.

The Marine holding the device waved it around. "I'm not detecting any hint of use of Gifts here. No Wafting, no Cloaks. I see a fading bit of heat near the door, but that's all. Probably just someone stopping by forgetting it's the holiday."

"May we please be off then?" the Marine holding the can asked.

"Base, A1," the first Marine said, putting his device away. "Fret scan complete—no activity detected. We are retiring from the area."

"Acknowledged." With that, the Marine put his communicator back into his coat, and the both of them walked away.

A moment later, Stenstrom returned to the door and continued his work. He slid the pick back in and, with a satisfying "click", the door opened. It was easy. Mother would be proud. He plunged inside.

Within was a vast warehouse. It was quite dark and Stenstrom could see the blinking lights of motion sensors placed at regular intervals. Again, falling upon his skills, he walked into the interior of the warehouse, his smooth, shadow movements not triggering the sensors.

He quickly produced a yellow Holystone. He gave it a shake, and it began to glow in his hand. Holding it up, he could see well enough to make his way about. Unlike many warehouses he'd seen before, which were dusty, cobwebbed places, this one was clean and tidy, full of knick-knacks and trinkets. He found several partitioned areas which were labeled with what, he guessed, were the names of various admirals: Pax, Scy, Garth, Riddle, and finally, Derlith. This warehouse must be where the admirals stash their booty. Rummaging through the Derlith area, Stenstrom found a large crate labeled: BAZZ. Struggling, he pulled it out of its place. He found a pry bar and opened the crate. Inside, cushioned in a nest of soft straw were twelve black bottles of brandy, sealed with wax and labeled with a black covering. Satisfied, he put the lid back on the crate. Testing the crate's weight, he discovered it was too heavy to lift and carry. He looked around.

At the far wall was a float lift.

Making his way through the dark warehouse, he found the float lift was off and locked down.

Out came the lock picks again; this time a magnetic Sarah's Rage pick did the trick, and the float came to life. Fiddling around with the controls, Stenstrom brought it under heel. After a bit of doing, he managed to get the crate on the lift and, floating on air, dragged it out of the warehouse and back down the hall.

One obstacle down.

4

—PRIVATE TAARA—

Following the signs, he then made his way to the ship park, which consisted of a control desk, a large hangar, and an open-air yard, twinkling with running lights. He needed a transport or Ripcar to take him up to the *Seeker*. By this point, he was down to about six bells. A slow Ripcar could get to the *Seeker* in about ten minutes.

As he feared, the ship park was virtually empty—the control desk sat unattended. Outside in the yard, crickets chirped.

Nearby in an alcove, a lonely Marine girl, decked out in her fine red coat, stood guard in front of the bust of a stern-faced admiral mounted on a fluted column. The Marine had short black hair that was tucked up into her cap. Slung across her shoulder was a strummer, a large, mostly ceremonial rifle that the Marines used in large, important places such as Fleet HQ. It was an impressive-looking weapon that had virtually no firepower—it was just for show. Holstered at her waist was the real thing—a jutting, black SK pistol that had a large enough caliber to knock down a brick wall.

Hanging around her neck was a sign on a string. The sign read "MOM" in a harsh, hand-written scrawl.

She saw Stenstrom and burst into a smile. "Hi!" she said in an energetic voice. She then stiffened and adjusted her posture. "I mean, good evening, sir," she said in a much more formal tone, eyeballing his coat and hat.

"Hello," he replied. "I need immediate uplift to the *Seeker*. I understand I may request a transport in this area."

"Nobody's here, sir," she said, doggedly standing next to the sour-faced marble bust. "Everybody's gone home for the holiday, I think. I'm really sorry—they'll be back first thing at six bells. If you want to get some rest in the meantime, you can go to billeting, as I think they're pretty empty today."

Stenstrom looked at her standing there by the bust. "What are you do-

ing?" he asked.

"Me? I'm guarding the statue of Admiral Pax here."

"You're guarding a bust?"

"No, I'm guarding the statue," she said, pointing at it. "That's what they said. After I messed up the surprise inspection and got everybody in trouble, they said: 'Guard Admiral Pax with your life until we come to fetch you.' So, here I am."

Stenstrom gazed at the sign hanging around her neck. "What's that sign?"

She blushed. "Oh, I sort of forgot about that. It means 'Maiden of Misery'—that's what my unit calls me, since I mess things up all the time. I have to wear it all day today."

"That's not very nice."

She shrugged.

He looked around, seeing no one other than her. "Well, 'Mom', you're sure there isn't anyone who can help me?"

"Nope, I mean yep. Nobody until six bells."

Stenstrom winced. Six bells was no good. Six bells was eight bells past his deadline. With nothing else to do, he determined to return to the Admiral's area and demand an extension, as he was clearly being set up to fail in a big way.

As the Marine guard stared at him, he considered his options. The last recourse he had was to do something considered rather embarrassing. He would have to call up to the *Seeker* and have them send a Ripcar down. It was a humbling thing to have to ask his new charge for a lift, but he, by this point, truly didn't care. He needed to be on that ship. Let Derlith and his lot have their laugh; it made no difference to him.

The Marine looked at him carefully, puzzled by his coat. "What sort of uniform is that?" she asked. "I thought you were an admiral or something at first, but that's not an admiral's uniform. Now that I look on it, I don't know what it is. What's HRN mean?"

"It's a long story," he said.

"Is that a mask you're wearing? I can't really see clearly from over here, but it looks like you're wearing a small mask—like a robber."

Stenstrom shook his head. "I'm not a robber, though I rather feel like one at the moment."

She leaned up against the bust and adjusted her sign. "Hey, mister, may I trouble you for a moment? I can't leave my post until I'm relieved, and I'm terribly hungry. They've left me out here all bloody day. Could I possibly ask you to go and get me something from the cafeteria?"

"Are you allowed to eat while on guard duty?"

She thought a moment. "Well, sure. I mean I'm not in some elite guard unit, and I'm not exactly guarding some rare treasure either—I'm stuck here guarding an ugly stone face when I should be at the bars celebrating the holiday. I don't think anybody would be going out with me anyway though. My barracks is pretty sore at me right now." The lettering on the sign she was wearing glinted in the light.

"I'm in a bit of a rush … I'm sorry, I don't know your name."

"Taara. Private Taara de la Anderson. I'm from Bazz—ever been to Bazz?"

Bazz… If only.

"No, no I haven't. Well, Private Taara, I am in a rush and I don't think I've the time. I'm sorry."

She nodded and looked a bit deflated. The stern carved face of Admiral Pax stared over her shoulder.

Stenstrom began pulling the crate away, and looked back. He saw the poor girl standing there lonely and hungry in her red Marine uniform and her sign hanging at her neck. He supposed a bit of good fellowship couldn't hurt. It might even create some good karma. It was St. Porter's Day after all.

"Stand fast, Private Taara, and I'll be right back with something for you."

She lit up. "Wow, thank you, sir! I really appreciate it!"

"Watch my crate, will you?" he called.

"I will, and thanks again!"

Stenstrom walked down the hallway to a small nearby cafeteria. The place was mostly empty, and most of the usual hot items served weren't being offered—only a modest skeleton crew was present. Stenstrom selected a turkey sandwich and a side of bagged Kelsos. He didn't know what she drank, and, as she looked fairly young, he picked her out a can of red Gasol.

Poor kid, he thought as he gathered her food; from Bazz, she said— probably impoverished, probably had no choice but be a Marine. Probably one of those common types who roll through their lives hardly making a mark on anyone or anything.

Quickly, he returned to the ship park and gave Private Taara her meal.

"Thank you so much, sir," she said, unwrapping her sandwich.

"I wasn't sure what you liked, so I did my best."

"Hey," she said smiling, "as I always say: 'just eat, man—just eat.'" She took off her large strummer and held it out. "Could you hold this for a moment?"

Stenstrom snickered and took it—not really a spit-n-polish Marine, was she? Private Taara then seated herself beneath Admiral Pax's chin. "Please," she said, "what's your name, mister?"

"Paymaster Stenstrom, Lord of Belmont. I am the newly appointed commander of the *Seeker.*"

"I wish I was from a neat Kanan House with all those fancy titles, but I'm just a kid from Bazz."

"Well, 'kid from Bazz,' have you had a moment to speak to your family today for the holiday?"

"I have—thanks! You're such a nice fellow. I am very pleased, sir, and, again, thank you for your kindness!"

Stenstrom looked at her. She had the sort of face that one didn't give much regard to at first—she was cute, nothing more. But, the longer one stared at her, the better looking she got. She was actually extremely attractive, in a tom-boyish sort of way.

"Well, I'm off to contact the *Seeker*. I suppose I'll have to ask them for a Ripcar to be sent down." He tipped his hat and prepared to collect his crate.

Taara took a drink from her Gasol and suddenly had a thought. "Did you say the ship you're wanting to contact is the *Seeker*, sir?"

"I did."

She thought a moment, took a look around to see if anybody was coming, then made her way to the control desk and opened a terminal. "I thought I heard the *Seeker* is abandoned. Yes, it says right here that the *Seeker* was half-scuttled last week and is in terminal."

"In terminal? What does that mean?"

"I think it means she's in a decaying orbit." Taara looked proud. "You pick up a few things being posted here. Yes, and take a look—Fleetcom says a reclamation team has been dispatched for two days hence to board and correct her orbit—I guess they're pretty concerned about it. She was then scheduled to make berth in dry-dock 186 for a partial refit."

Stenstrom was getting angry. "And who ordered the *Seeker* half-scuttled? Let me guess … Admiral Derlith, yes?"

Taara toyed about with her terminal. "Yep, Admiral Derlith. That's what it says right here. So, I guess the *Seeker* is abandoned right now. I guess there's nobody up there to send a Ripcar down for you."

Stenstrom drew one of his pistols in a froth. He held it for a moment then slid it back into his sash.

"I'm really sorry," she said.

He shook his head. "Well, Private, I suppose there's a sign around my neck as well, just can't see it as easily."

She appeared sympathetic. "I know how that feels. Listen, for what it's worth, when my shift ends, I'll get you a drink at the canteen—might make you feel better. Would you like that?"

He sighed. "Thanks. If you could please watch my crate," he said, his voice shaking. "I shall be back. I've a few words to say to Admiral Derlith." Stenstrom stormed away.

"Happy Porter's Day!" Taara called to him as he left. "My offer still stands if you change your mind!"

"And to you," he replied. Though this was turning into a real gut-grinder of a day, Private Taara's cheerful demeanor made him feel a bit better.

5

—A-Ram—

Stenstrom made his way back to Admiral Derlith's complex. It was getting late in the evening, and the sky was fading to early starlight.

When he got to the door, he banged on it hard.

After a time, the small, blonde-headed adjutant opened the door. He was wearing white gloves and holding a tarnished sponge that stank of silver polish. "Paymaster Stenstrom, well met again, sir," he said.

"Where is Admiral Derlith? I must see him."

"Admiral Derlith has left the complex for the weekend."

Stenstrom pushed his way into the anti-chamber. The adjutant had been polishing a silver tea set; the room smelled of the labor. He had the holo-terminal on his desk opened up and was reading several postings in overly-large text, as if he had trouble seeing normal-sized text.

Stenstrom was in a good lather. "I see! Well then, you may tell that scoundrel that he has not heard the last of Stenstrom, Lord of Belmont! I shall be back! I shall reappoint to the *Seeker*'s chair, and next time he'll not have a convenient holiday and a half-scuttled ship to foil my appointment!"

The adjutant stood there holding his sponge, his holo-terminal spinning around him. Stenstrom took a glance at the large-printed wording. It said:

AN OPEN LETTER FROM THE FIEND OF CALVERT

"The Fiend of Calvert?" Stenstrom asked, forgetting his anger for the moment.

The adjutant smiled. "Oh, it's a hobby of mine. I remember as a boy I was really scared of the Fiend of Calvert, as he terrorized the streets. I've made it my interest to collect as much information on his crimes as possible and see if I can determine his identity. I've all sorts of theories and what not.

He was never caught."

"I heard he was dead."

"No, no," he said shaking his head. "The Fiend of Calvert is not dead."

The adjutant took off his gloves and cleaned his hands with a cloth. "I'm sorry about this situation," he said. "Sir, is there anything I might help you with?"

Stenstrom looked at the small, slope-shouldered fellow. "I have five bells to board the *Seeker*. As this place is currently a holiday-riddled tomb and the *Seeker* is abandoned, I have no way to board her in time. Then, after that impossible task is completed, I am to deliver a crate of his cheaply-made brandy to Bazz, twelve days hence. Again, as the *Seeker* is half taken apart, I don't see her going anywhere in under a month."

Stenstrom removed his hat. "I'm sorry. I didn't mean to fill your ear." He could see himself reflected in the surface of the shiny tea set, wearing his mask and his HRN coat. The Marine girl Taara was right: he did look like a masked robber. "You do good work, sir," he said. "Again, I'm sorry to barge in here and trouble you."

The adjutant appeared sympathetic. "I heard the Admiral speaking to his peers regarding a 'fine deception' he had just accomplished. He—he was feeling rather proud of himself."

Stenstrom lightly clapped him on the shoulder. "Perhaps Admiral Derlith is the Fiend of Calvert, ever thought of that? Well, let him have his fun for the moment; again, I'll be back and Hell shall be coming with me."

Stenstrom turned to leave.

"Sir?" the adjutant said, switching off the holo-terminal. "I can get you to the *Seeker*. I can fly."

"You?" Stenstrom gave him the once-over. A rather small fellow, no taller than 5'4, slight of build, and that bright head of blonde hair—rather ridiculous.

But who was he to judge; he was wearing a mask and a Hoban Royal Navy coat. "You can fly, sir?"

"I can. Been flying all my life. I never could pass the Fleet or Marine standards for flight school because I have a fair amount of myopia, which isn't correctible by surgery, and my body is of a type that rejects Bio-plants. So, here I am, polishing silver, making coffee, and reading old press releases about the Fiend of Calvert. Stuck here on the ground when I belong in the air."

"Can you see properly to fly then?"

The adjutant reached into his coat and pulled out a thick set of glasses. "I can with these. With these I can see as well as anybody. The Admiral doesn't let me wear them when he's around. He says they're too ugly."

Stenstrom smiled. "You'll do, then. Come with me."

Smiling, the adjutant put his glasses on and followed Stenstrom at a brisk pace out of the area.

"Your name is Josephus, is that correct?" Stenstrom asked on the hoof.

"Yes, but I hate that name, and the Admiral knows it. I am Josephus, Lord of A-Ram. Please, just call me A-Ram. Have you ever heard of the House of A-Ram? It's a Calvert House."

"Sorry, no. I haven't. Well, A-Ram, good to know you. I am Stenstrom, Lord of Belmont-South Tyrol. Just call me Bel."

He held his hand out, and they shook hands. It seems he'd made a friend—perhaps the day wasn't a total loss.

Before long, they arrived back at the ship park. Private Taara had finished her meal and was glad to see him. "You're back!" she said in her happy voice, still standing by the bust.

"I am, and I've found a pilot. I would like to requisition a transport for immediate passage to the *Seeker*."

Taara looked around. "Oh, ok … Where's the pilot?"

"I'm the pilot," A-Ram said.

Taara giggled. "I'm sorry, sir. It's just that you're dressed like an Admiral's secretary."

"That's adjutant … private," A-Ram replied.

"Ah, ok," she replied.

"He was an adjutant this morning, but, as of this moment, he's a pilot," Stenstrom said. "He's been promoted."

Taara looked at him. "Aren't you the guy who's always getting yelled at by that gray-haired Admiral? You are, right?"

A-Ram approached Taara. "I'm still an officer, private, and perhaps a small bit of decorum might …" He stopped in mid-sentence and stared at her. "Don't I know you?" he asked, giving her a full appraisal. "You seem familiar to me."

Taara shrugged. "Well, maybe. Do you hang out at the Marine cantina? Oh! Do you go to the fights every weekend?"

"No, I do not go to the fights."

"Then, I'm not sure where you've seen me—I'm big into the fights."

Taara smiled and gave A-Ram a tap on one of his slight shoulders. "Bet I could beat you at arm-wrestling. What's your name?"

"A-Ram, and you could not," he replied, taking note of the sign hanging around her neck.

Stenstrom stepped in. "And I'll wager I could beat the both of you at once. A contest for another time. Private Taara, we need to get to the *Seeker* as quickly as possible and need to req out a ship."

Taara was a bit saddened. "Sir, I would love to help you, but I can't req you out a ship—I'm just a guard. And, I'm not supposed to do or touch anything other than guard this statue right here." She pointed at Admiral Pax' bust. It scowled out from its alcove.

Stenstrom walked around the desk. Behind was the entrance to the main hangar where dozens of transports were kept.

He tried the door—it was locked.

"Sir, that's not going to help you," Taara called to him.

Out came the lock picks and soon Stenstrom had the door wide open.

He stepped in. The hangar was empty.

"That's what I was trying to tell you. All the transports have been sent to Provst for a cleaning. They're due to be back at six bells."

Again, Stenstrom drew his pistol in frustration.

"I'm sorry," Taara said.

They looked around. "I see a group of Suborbitals over there, parked on the lawn," A-Ram remarked. "We don't need to req those; all we have to do is sign for one."

Taara saw the line of sharp blue Suborbitals parked a short walk away on the green. "You … want to use a Suborbital to mount a ship in orbit? Suborbitals aren't supposed to go into orbit, hence the name, right? Isn't that dangerous?"

"Only if you don't know what you're doing."

She thought about that remark for a moment. "Oh, ok."

They signed for Suborbital 10 and quickly began loading the crate onto it.

As they did, a second Marine arrived, and Private Taara handed the fellow her strummer. She then made her way over to them. "Well, I've been relieved—the guy's statue will just have to get along fine without me now. I just wanted to say good luck, before I head back to my barracks. And, I really enjoyed meeting you two today—you seem like good guys to me. If you two weren't in such a rush, I'd invite you down to the canteen with me to hang out."

"We'll take a pass on that, Private," A-Ram said. "Perhaps next time."

Stenstrom shook her hand as he climbed in. She gave A-Ram another shove. "You're not getting out of the arm-wrestling thing, little guy. We'll do it when you get back."

"Umm, certainly," A-Ram said, climbing in.

She turned, thought it over for a second, and then turned back. "Listen, I know enough to understand that what you're about to do is very dangerous. Additionally, the *Seeker* is in a bad terminal and is currently uninhabited. How are you going to open the bay doors?"

"I suppose we'll just figure that out when we get to it," Stenstrom said, strapping in.

Taara appeared conflicted. "Listen, I'm off for the next few days. No doubt you two will need a hand if you do get aboard, and I'd like to come along. I've never been aboard a fighting starship before. It sounds like fun, and I've got nothing better to do. Of course, I'll bet you two an ale in the canteen that we'll get no higher than fifty thousand feet before we up and turn around."

A-Ram popped his thick glasses back on. "That's a sure bet," he said looking rather bug-eyed.

Taara smiled and tossed her "MOM" sign aside. She readied to enter the craft. "Oh, wait!" she said. She ran back to the desk and disappeared into the hangar—she and the Marine guard exchanging a few disparaging words as she did so, the guard pointing at the discarded sign. A few moments later, she re-appeared carrying three small devices. She exchanged more angry words with the Marine and then offered him some sort of obscene Bazz hand gesture. She popped into the back couch and buckled up. With that, A-Ram sealed the hatches and smoothly lifted the small ship up and away from the Fleet complex into the early evening sky.

"What do you have there?" Stenstrom asked Taara as he settled into his seat.

"Aquanaughts," she said. "So we can breathe … just in case I lose my bet."

Moving fast, A-Ram climbed in a southerly direction, heading for the south pole, the Suborbital moving effortlessly under his control. "I know how Fleetcom likes to orbit starships. Those listed as half-scuttled are assigned a low polar orbit in Zone A. The *Seeker* should be tucked nice and neat in one of them."

They climbed high above the clouds and the Suborbital's engines, starving for air, began to rev to red.

"Look!" A-Ram cried. "There it is."

Stenstrom and Taara looked up. High overhead they saw a bright, fast moving star, heading from south to north. It appeared on the horizon, streaked past them, and then disappeared to the north.

A-Ram struggled with the controls. "She's really moving. I'd also say she's about twenty thousand feet above us still. We'll have to pick up some speed, close the vents, and pray we have enough momentum to reach the ship. We're only going to have one chance at this."

"See, I told you it would be tough sledding in a Suborbital. They weren't kidding around when they named 'em," Taara said.

A-Ram punished the struggling Suborbital, clawing for altitude.

Overhead, the star of the *Seeker* got ever brighter as the Suborbital closed the distance. Through the windscreen, which was rapidly frosting up, they could just begin to see vague detail through the brightness, like looking at a distant planet through a telescope. Also, the *Seeker* appeared to be slowing down as it rose and fell—the Suborbital steadily picking up and matching speed.

"It's really getting cold in here," Taara said as she rubbed her sleeves. She passed out the Aquanaughts, and they put them in their mouths, Taara helping A-Ram with his.

Sucking on his Aquanaught, A-Ram pulled a lever and shut the outside vents. He also enabled a green counter reader: 60:00. "All right, it's now or never," he said with a muffled voice. "I think I've got the trajectory and speed figured out. Bel, I'm going to release the timer. When the counter reads zero,

I'm going to pull up hard. We should slide right in behind the *Seeker* where we can try to open a bay with the grapplers and get in."

He watched the now huge star of the *Seeker* disappear beyond the horizon, and then he released the timer. It began counting down.

The gauges spun, the engines, starving for air, all red-lined and sputtered.

"Zero, A-Ram!" Stenstrom said. "Pull it!"

He pulled back hard, and the Suborbital lurched up. They felt the sickening release as gravity fell away, and the pale blue sky faded to black.

In front of them, the huge mass of the *Seeker* came hurtling into view. It was tumbling in its orbit, spiraling slowly from wingtip to wingtip.

"See, look at it roll," Taara said through her Aquanaught. "Its orbit is terminal. I think it got clipped by an old weather sat a few days ago and busted open a thruster."

The great ship looked like a bird shot dead on the wing. All of its lights were off, and the massive forward sensor was quiet.

Stenstrom gazed at it with wonder. Rolling, tumbling, in desperate shape—that was still his ship.

His ship.

"I don't think we can do this with the *Seeker* rolling like that. We won't be able to dock," A-Ram said.

"Can we start heading down, then?" Taara asked, clutching her coat. "It's freezing in here, and these Aquanaughts will only last a few more minutes."

Stenstrom stared at the ship. "Look there," he said. "Look to that large window in the aft tower section—that's the main mess I think. The way the ship's rolling, that window, centrally located near the pivot point, is hardly moving."

"And so?" A-Ram said.

"So, just crash us through it. Once we're inside, the blast shutters should close, or I'll seal the breach myself and send the bill for its repair to Admiral Derlith."

"Seal it? With what?" A-Ram asked.

"Holystones. You'll see. So, go ahead, A-Ram, just plow into it."

Taara shivered. "You guys can let me back down any time now."

A-Ram pushed his glasses back and punched it. He maneuvered past the rolling wings and made a bead for the large mess hall window spinning ahead like the center of a tire—not taking his eyes off it.

With a bang, the engines went out for want of air. They drifted ahead.

A-Ram pointed the nose at the spinning window as his controls, designed for atmospheric use, gave way.

CRASH!!

The Suborbital plowed through the large window, smashed through the debris of chairs and tables within the mess, and slammed into the far wall, partially going through it. The decompression instantly began pulling the furniture out of the mess, and even began tugging on the Suborbital.

The cracked hatch of the Suborbital flew off and was sucked out into space.

A-Ram, though he was strapped in, was so slight of frame that he was pulled through his straps and out toward the window. "Where's the shutters?" he gasped.

Stenstrom caught and held him fast by the wrist. He flapped up and down in the suction.

Taara leaned forward and grabbed onto A-Ram's arm as well. His aquanaught was sucked out of his mouth and through the window. He screamed in pain.

"Taara, you got him?" Stenstrom roared.

"I got him!"

"I'm going to let go and seal the breach! You ready?"

"I'm ready!"

Stenstrom let go, waved his hands, and three lime green balls appeared between his fingers. They were instantly sucked away, past A-Ram, toward the blown out window. The balls hit the window frame and burst into what looked like a huge spider web. The window, now partially blocked, lost a fair bit of suction. A-Ram fell to the floor with a thud.

Stenstrom surged out of the wrecked Suborbital and, standing, he produced several more lime green Holystones and threw them at the window. Before long, the breach was covered.

The ship, somewhat belatedly, reacted to the depressurization and the blast shutters closed with a clang behind the webbing.

He stood A-Ram up. "You all right? Is everyone all right?"

A bit shaky, A-Ram nodded, and Taara bounced out of the craft, clearly fine. They looked around and noted the damage. The mess was a mess. The Suborbital was done—this flight into low orbit would be its last. Stenstrom and Taara pulled the cargo of brandy out of the wreck of the Suborbital and looked it over. Inside, several of the bottles were cracked.

A-Ram, who had managed to hold onto his hat, rummaged through the crate. "Looks to be we've got nine bottles left. Bel, did the Admiral say how many bottles you were to bring to Bazz?"

"I don't recall him mentioning a specific number. He just said get the brandy there."

A-Ram arranged the bottles on the floor in neat rows. "Well then, that's in our favor. Since he was mum on that point, all we really need is one bottle."

There was no power in the ship. The Grav Pack was still functioning— it worked on a redundant, solar-powered system so it was usually the only thing working on a stripped-out ship, besides the emergency shutters and a tad bit of convection heat to keep the miles of pipes from bursting. Using the chronometer on the Suborbital, Stenstrom made a recording and beamed it to Admiral Derlith's holomail.

He had boarded the *Seeker* with minutes to spare.

They made their way to a nearby Ripcar Bay that was clear. Taara disappeared and returned some time later with a few bagged snacks and cans of flat Gasol. "This was all I could find." Sitting Indian-style, they ate in the dark, softly lit by a few Holystones and using the Admiral's brandy crate as a makeshift table.

"This is kind of cool," Taara said, "sitting here in the dark with two handsome fellows." Taara, apparently a bubbly person, raised her can of warm Gasol. "To Stenstrom, Lord of Belmont-South ... whatever. Here's to your first day of command."

A-Ram smiled and raised his can. "I concur."

Stenstrom laughed and clicked his can with theirs, making his Gasol fizz. "And here's to good friends. As they say, a friend made on St. Porter's Day is a friend indeed."

As they sat there in the dark eating their unappealing meal, a bond was formed between these three people: Stenstrom, A-Ram and Taara. As Stenstrom said, a friend made on St. Porter's Day was a friend for life.

Such a thought could never have been truer.

6

—The MOLLY—

Now that they were aboard the *Seeker*—what was next? The ship, with the exception of working gravity and a little heat, was dead and only had a few days left before its decaying orbit became critical and then entered the atmosphere as a flaming ball of wreckage.

"A reclamation team is coming in from Planet Fall, Bel," A-Ram said. "I recall seeing the order on the Admiral's desk. Either tomorrow or the next day—everything's in a bit of limbo due to the holiday. If they enter the ship, by Fleet rule, all appointments are cancelled. You cannot be bonded as captain if they board."

"Then we need to be well out of here prior to their arrival."

"'Scuse me," Taara said. "The ship's dead. Her engines were removed and hauled out for scrap—I saw it on the roster a few days ago."

The three of them were trying to pry one of the central corridor hatchway doors open with a pole-like strut they had salvaged from the Suborbital. They were hoping to reach the bridge. There, they could assess the situation and, with luck, right the ship. The door stubbornly held shut—they strained and sweated.

"Your boy, A-Ram, Admiral Derlith, had this episode planned out well, didn't he? Bloody holidays! All I have to do is get a stinking crate of brandy to Bazz for an Admiral's party—but look—the *Seeker's* not going anywhere, is it?" Stenstrom wiped his brow. "And I'll wager that brandy is gut-wrenchingly bad, as well."

"I've heard the Admiral produces a very fine brandy," A-Ram replied. "Never tried it myself, but that's what I've heard."

Taara had her Marine coat off and was straining on the pole, her little hands gripped on hard. "Why … drink brandy when a good honey ale is … available? Huh?" She let go of the pole and stared at the unmovable door.

"Elder's Balls, this thing is a pain. Well, why not use our heads here. You boarded the *Seeker*, so that part's taken care of. Why not just hire a ship to transport the brandy to Bazz? Heck, a slow stumblebum transport out of Armenelos would have it there in three or four days, and you've got twelve."

The hatch gave a metallic groan. Encouraged, they strained harder.

"No," A-Ram said, sweating on the pole. "Won't work—the Admiral's got us covered. By order, the *Seeker* has to deliver the goods. And, having a devious mind, he even wrote in verbiage stating that the *Seeker* in particular has to deliver it. Not a model of the *Seeker* sitting on another ship, and not another ship named *Seeker*—this one, and under its own power, no towing or barging." A-Ram released the pole, flexed his aching fingers, and tried again.

"The Admiral appears dead set against me commanding this ship, doesn't he? He welcomed my money with a smile, but, for the rest of it, I'm on the quits," Stenstrom said.

A-Ram let go of the pole. "That coat you wear really got to him. The Admiralty hates the Hoban Royal Navy, certainly you were aware of that. May I ask, why did you wear it to your appointment?"

Stenstrom looked down at his coat. "Because I like it. Because Lilly picked it out for me. Its Hoban Royal Navy connection is irrelevant."

"Who's Lilly?" Taara asked.

"A dear friend of mine."

"Friend? … Girlfriend?"

"If you like. Regarding my coat, my sponsor, Lord Davage, asked that I not wear it—apparently sensing the Admiral's hatred for the group."

"You shouldn't have worn it?" Taara asked.

Stenstrom thought a moment. "I suppose not. I guess I wanted to get their attention, to make a splash. I didn't give them their due in their place of reverence, and look where I am."

He looked around. "All of this is my fault."

A-Ram continued on the pole. "I … don't know if it was just the coat. One of the Admiral's hangers-on seems to have a firm agenda against you."

Stenstrom let go of the pole. "Against me?"

"Yes, I'm not sure who has it in for you or why, but your name's been kicked around quite a bit as of late."

Taara clapped Stenstrom on the shoulder. "Ah, don't worry about that stuff. Things will work out, you'll see. Put a bold face on it, that's what we do on Bazz." She grabbed the pole and began straining again.

The hatch groaned. "Oh … oh, I think we've got it!" Taara cried.

The hatch gave and opened with a clank. Beyond was a dark expanse of corridor stretching off into the distance. They all huffed and puffed; the effort to get the hatch open had been considerable.

"That was a chore." A-Ram peered into the dark. "Bel, I thought the ship was abandoned."

"It is," Stenstrom said trying to pull the pole from its place—it was rooted fast.

"Well, I know I saw somebody standing there in the dark, just now."

"What?" Taara said looking through the hatch. "I don't see anybody."

Stenstrom, holding the pole, stepped through. "I agree. There is nobody here but the three of us."

They all went through into the dark beyond—the air was heavy and stale. A-Ram appeared apprehensive.

"We're going to have to take a good hard look at life support," Stenstrom said. "The air's already getting a little bad."

He waved his hand producing three yellow Holystones. He shook them and they lit up in a yellowish glow. He then handed one each to Taara and A-Ram. "These are cool," Taara said holding hers in her palm. "You're just full of surprises. I like that."

A-Ram shook his Holystone up. He gasped.

"Did you see that?"

"See what?"

"I saw someone moving into the dark—just now! I saw a hint of a passing cloak and the bend of a knee!"

Stenstrom stepped forward. "Hello! Anybody there? Make yourself known!"

No answer.

"Where did you see this person?"

"Just there!" A-Ram said, pointing.

Taara stepped out into the dark, waving her Holystone around, her long black sideburns jangling about her head. "I don't see nobody."

Stenstrom joined her, seeing nothing. "I think your imagination is getting to you, A-Ram. There's nobody here."

A-Ram laughed and felt silly. "Certainly you're right. Sorry."

They made their way down the section, their heels clicking on the metal floor boards.

"Hey, Bel, what's that?" A-Ram asked, pointing.

Lying on the floor in the center of the corridor was a small white envelope. A-Ram stepped up to it and shined his Holystone, illuminating a black flowing script written across its face in an elegant hand. "This letter is addressed to me," he stated.

"To you?"

"Yes."

"Did you know anybody aboard the *Seeker* from the previous crew?"

"Not that I can think of."

Stenstrom approached and leaned over the letter. It read:

to: STENSTROM, LORD OF BELMONT-SOUTH TYROL

"A-Ram," he said flatly, "this letter is addressed to me, not you."

"No, it's addressed to me, Bel I can read, you know."

Stenstrom waved his hand and produced a small chest. He opened the lid, popped the letter in and shut it.

"What are you doing," A-Ram asked.

"I'm putting this letter away for safe keeping. We need to focus on getting to the bridge for the time being." He waved his hands and the chest with the letter resting within, vanished. "We'll examine it in further detail later when time allows."

Not far down the corridor, another hatch emerged in the dim yellow light. Apparently all of the hatches were sealed. All three of them groaned.

"The bridge is several levels up and probably twelve hundred feet away from us with about fifty hatches in between. We'll never get there like this. We need power," A-Ram said. "I'm dreading the prospect of manually opening another hatch."

"You know anything about *Straylight* ships?" Stenstrom asked.

"A little bit," A-Ram said.

"Not a thing," Taara said. "I'm just a grunt."

They approached the next hatch. Stenstrom tested it and it held fast. He sighed in frustration. "Let's have that pole and put our backs into it."

From behind them, toward the aft of the ship, came a distinct groan.

"What was that?" Taara asked.

"Just the ship, the superstructure torquing about," Stenstrom said.

"Ok," she replied. "Didn't sound like metal to me though. Sounded like a person."

"Don't be silly."

They turned back to the locked hatch, and Stenstrom fished the pole into the base. As he strained on the pole, he heard the distinct sound of rapid footsteps approaching, thumping on metal.

Bump ... Bump ... Bump ... Bump ...

"Who's running?" he asked, drawing his NTH pistols. A-Ram stood there rather ashen, and Taara drew her SK.

"Gods," A-Ram said, "I've heard footsteps like that before when I was a boy. It was the Fiend of Calvert running across my rooftop."

"I heard something that time, but I don't see anything," Taara replied.

"It's the Fiend. He's on the ship with us. Perhaps he's the one who left me the letter?"

"Oh please, A-Ram—listen to yourself," Stenstrom reproached. "There is nobody other than us on this ship." He placed his pistols back in their sash.

Stenstrom held his glowing holystone up. "See? Nothing, there's nothing. Just our imaginations. Come on, let's get this hatch open."

Dubious, A-Ram crowded in near Stenstrom and grabbed the pole, tugging on it.

As they began to work on the hatch, a new sound emerged. It was a harsh sound, a grating of metal on metal culminating in an abrupt SNAP! SNAP!

Stenstrom released the pole and stood upright. He was most familiar with the sound.

SNAP! SNAP!

Just like from his old dream. The sound moved up and down his spine, unsettling him.

"Do you all hear that?" he asked.

"Yeah," Taara replied. "Sounds creepy. So what are we going to do? And, you're right about the air, Bel; it's already going foul. Maybe we're all hallucinating or something."

Stenstrom stood there listening.

"Bel?"

He pulled himself from his thoughts. "I'm sorry. We must to the bridge. I suppose we'll figure something out from there."

A-Ram released the pole. "I think it's time to play seriously." He unbuttoned his white shirt and reached in. A moment later he pulled out a gold necklace that he'd been wearing and showed it to them. "Here—I think this might help."

"What's that?" Taara asked.

A-Ram held up a charm in the shape of a freshwater fish.

"Is that a guppy?" Taara asked.

"What are we looking at here, A-Ram?" Stenstrom asked.

"This, Bel, is the MOLLY. It's the LosCapricos weapon of my House. Do you know what it does?"

"No."

"It allows one to do things one wouldn't ordinarily be able to do, and to know things one shouldn't know."

Taara looked at it with interest. "What? The fish does that? You're pulling my leg."

"No—I'm serious. With the MOLLY, I can do and know all sorts of things."

Stenstrom was skeptical. "Sounds too good to be true. Have you ever used it to discover the identity of the Fiend of Calvert?"

He laughed. "No—it doesn't work too well on abstract things like that— it's great for technical matters and physical feats. It does have a few pretty severe drawbacks, however."

"And they are?"

A-Ram blushed. "Well, for one thing, you have to register with the Sisterhood before you use it—they keep a close eye on such things. Also—and I've never witnessed this myself— they say if you use the MOLLY too much, there are repercussions. I'm told that a demon will come for your soul."

"A demon? Is that true?"

"Again, I've not seen it myself. I've never used it for much other than small things." A-Ram laughed. "I used it to win an eating contest once, and that's about it."

Taara laughed. "Did you register with the Sisters for that?"

"Sure did."

"You Kanans, man—wow!"

"So, you're saying you happen to have a mystical familial item that can work near miracles, but, if you use it too much some vile entity will come to claim your soul?"

"Yes, that is correct."

"Well then, Fate works wonders on St. Porter's Day, A-Ram. Remember this?" he said, pulling one of his pistols out of his sash.

Stenstrom's weapon looked like an ancient lock-style pistol. It had a smooth iron barrel with a worn walnut stock inlaid with gothic golden lines. "This is the NTH, the LosCapricos weapon of my family," he said.

"Looks old," Taara said.

"It is old, comes down from my Belmont stock. Though it doesn't look like much, the NTH can kill anything with one shot—people, ghosts, robots, monsters, unsubstantial entities, and demons as well. I've used it to kill demons before, lots of times."

"You've fought demons?" Taara said.

"Sure have. My mother used to like to summon demons at me all the time. I've killed a lot of demons with these. Believe me, these things work. You do not want to get shot with an NTH."

"Why would your mom do that?" Taara asked.

"Because she was a Tyrol and a sorceress. Sorceresses don't play around."

A-Ram studied the pistol. "So, I take it your thought is for me to use the MOLLY with abandon, and then when the demon comes to take my soul, you'll shoot it dead with this pistol."

"Sounds like a good plan to me. I'll shoot the demon dead, and I'll shoot the Fiend too if he shows."

He looked dubious. "I don't know."

Taara laughed. "Well, heck, I'll do it! I'm not scared. Bel here will look out for me, right? Give me that thing!"

A-Ram shook his head and handed her the MOLLY. She quickly put it on and stuffed it under her shirt.

"So, how does it work?"

A-Ram puzzled for a moment. "Well, it's hard to explain. You just do what it is you want to do. It's like moving your arm—how do you explain how to move your arm—you just do it. But, what about the Sisters? They'll get mad if we use it and not register first."

"Well," Stenstrom said. "Seeing as how there don't appear to be any Sisters around, and our Com facilities are probably working as well as life support right now how about we'll let them know first thing once we're on Bazz? I'm certain they won't mind."

A-Ram was dubious and, after a bout of inner turmoil, nodded. "Yes, yes, I imagine that will be fine."

"All right," Taara said. She turned to Stenstrom. "You got me, Bel?"

He raised his NTH and cocked the ancient-looking hammer. "I'm ready."

Taara took a deep breath and pulled her Marine cap off. She was deceptively good-looking: short black hair, fine brown eyes. A pair of sickle-like black sideburns came rolling out to rest on her shoulders.

"What are these pieces of hair you're wearing?" A-Ram asked regarding her sideburns. "Is that common on Bazz?"

Taara appeared to be lost in thought. "What? These are Mollocks. They mean I'm not married. Men on Bazz like to know where they stand with women they don't know. Want to get married, A-Ram? If so, I'll cut them off and give them to you. That's how we do it."

A-Ram giggled.

Taara, wearing the MOLLY, looked around the darkened corridor.

"Anything happening?" Stenstrom asked.

Taara scratched her head and pointed to the hatch. "Well, the first thing we need to do is check up on life support, then get the ship out of this list. The wingtip roll isn't serious. It's the nose-down list she's in that's troubling. We have approximately thirty-two, point six-four hours until she begins entering the atmosphere. Worse, we have approximately nineteen, point six two-eight hours before the Fleet reclamation team arrives from Planet Fall to recover the vessel—the scouting vessel *Demophalon John* is en route and under orders. Their boarding the ship will instantly cost Bel his appointment per Fleet rule—that is the main thing."

Stenstrom smiled. "Pretty impressive, Taara. How are you knowing all that?"

"No clue—I just do. Cool, isn't it?" She suddenly pointed at Stenstrom. "Someone very dear to you is on that ship."

"What?" Stenstrom asked.

Taara blinked. Her sideburns jangled. "What'd I say?"

"You said someone very dear to me is on the scouting ship that's coming for us."

"I did?"

"Yes. I don't think I know anybody on the *Demophalon John*."

"I don't remember saying that."

A-Ram chuckled. "That's the MOLLY playing tricks on you. Happens sometimes. So then," he said, "how are we going to get the *Seeker* out of its terminal orbit?"

Taara walked down the corridor. "We're going to go three sections forward to access point J-91. We shall then enter J-91 and crawl five hundred feet forward until we arrive at engineering carbuncle 2. Once there, we will shunt eleven percent of the grav-pack's stored solar power to the outboard wing thrusters where we will stop the lateral roll. Using the same technique, we will then thrust the nose upward and climb to one-hundred seventy-four thousand feet where we will enter a standard D-Zone parking orbit right down the middle, and, thus, the crisis shall be averted. That's what the reclamation team is planning to do."

Taara shook her head and grinned. "Wow! Who just said that?"

"You did. What about life support?" A-Ram asked.

"We can check its levels, but there's not much we can do to get it going without engine power."

Stenstrom tossed her short black hair.

"Oh come on, Bel. Give 'em a tug."

"Pardon?"

"My Mollocks. Give 'em a yank. I love that."

Stenstrom took her long sideburns and gave them a quick tug. Taara grinned.

"A-Ram, when should we expect our supernatural visit from the demon?" he asked, his NTH pistol at the ready.

"After she's done."

They walked to the next hatch, and A-Ram and Stenstrom started pulling on it again with the pole.

"No, no, fellas, look ..." Taara casually approached a side panel, opened it, and pulled a small lever. The hatch opened easily. "See, it's easy if you know what to do."

"That would have been nice to know a while ago," Stenstrom said with disgust, discarding the pole with a clank.

They made their way forward two more sections and found access point J-91. Taara pulled the cover off and slid into the small space, using her fingers to pull herself ahead.

She abruptly came back out. "You guys hear a fire? I hear fire—cracking, popping."

"I don't hear anything," Stenstrom said. "Do you, A-Ram?"

"No."

Taara shrugged it off and re-entered the access point. Shaking a fresh Holystone, Stenstrom followed, with A-Ram last. Looking at the bottoms of Taara's boots and the holstered muzzle of her SK, he crawled along after her, ready to use his NTH should a demon pop up. The noise the rolling ship was making was pronounced in the tight confines of the tube. Stenstrom could hear a steady "buuuuuuurrrrrrrrr" as the ship creaked relentlessly.

But then, he thought he heard the sound change. Suddenly the creaking became: "bbbbeeeeeeelllllmmmmmmmoooooonnnnnnnnnttttttttttttttttttt …"

And that wasn't all. Stenstrom thought he could hear the sounds of people talking beyond, footsteps, a distant pounding, and, most disturbingly, a slight laugh.

"Shhh," he said. "You hear laughing, A-Ram?"

"No."

Stenstrom was relieved. "Good. I must be hearing things."

"I hear screaming," A-Ram said.

✳ ✳ ✳ ✳ ✳

Sometime later, they crawled to Engineering Carbuncle 2. Stenstrom had spent a fair amount of time on starships, but he had never seen anything like it to this point. It was a cluster of ducts, cable trunks, connectors, and valves—it was like looking at a partially dissected elbow-joint, with all sorts of systems running here and there. Taara was already busy unplugging thick cables from an open access point.

"What do you have here?" he asked her.

"These are the power cables for the grav pack. Solar energy comes in, and is stored in the central grid, where it's then distributed throughout the ship via these cables. Right now, Section 84 in the rear of the ship is without gravity as I've unplugged it. I'm going to take this power and run it over here to the outboard thrusters." She blinked and smiled. "Boy—I'm probably really MOLLYing this all up, aren't I? Better not go anywhere with those pistols, Bel, since I'll probably have a whole slew of demons after me before long."

A-Ram came into the carbuncle. "That was horrible," he said, his leggings grimy from the crawl. "There is somebody back there; I know it."

Taara pulled the cable and plugged it into a connector hidden by a mass of wires. "There," she said. "The wing thrusters should now have power—not much, as the grav-pack doesn't store a whole lot of juice, but it should be just enough to ease us out of the roll."

Stenstrom gave her a pat on the shoulder. "Great work, Taara. So, what's next?"

"Next, we have to make our way to the bridge and give the wheel a yank. That should do it."

"What about life support?" A-Ram asked.

"According to these gauges, it's not bad. The ship isn't generating any fresh air, but a craft this size, fully pressurized, will have enough air to last the three of us quite awhile. It might not smell all that great, but it'll do."

A-Ram looked around. "Let's get started—and let none of us get separated until the issue with the demon—and the Fiend— has been resolved. And I don't think it's as easy to kill off a demon as you think it is, Bel. They can be pretty clever, so I'm told."

They made their way from the carbuncle to the main corridor. Opening the hatches one by one, they made the long trip into the frontal section of the ship. They opened a lift door and, using a set of service rungs, began climbing.

"How far up is the Bridge?" Stenstrom asked.

"Four decks," Taara replied.

In the drafty, dark lift shaft, they heard more noise coming up from below. "Did you hear that?" Stenstrom asked, pulling his NTH.

They heard, in the distance, a thin voice saying: "...*Taara... Taara...*"

"Oh, that's creepy," she remarked. She appeared remarkably calm despite the circumstances.

Stenstrom felt very concerned for her. "Taara, I shouldn't have let you do this. I should have done it."

"Why—I'm not scared. I wanted to do it. Beside, you'll protect me, should I need it, right? Let 'em groan all they want."

Stenstrom was impressed by her courage.

They continued climbing a few more decks and then opened the door to the Bridge.

The Bridge.

Stenstrom had a quick flash in his head, of the old days of the *Seeker*. The white-shirted crewmen manning their posts; the bustle, the excitement. Countess Sygillis of Blanchefort in her elegant gown sitting in the command chair (shoeless as always, no doubt), and Captain Davage prowling behind ever ready to grab the helm. He could hear the voices, the shouted orders. He savored the thought.

The Bridge was a good place where great things had happened.

Wait!

One of his Holystones designed to detect danger began rattling in his HRN pocket. Something was waiting for them here on the Bridge. "You two wait here a moment. I want to check the Bridge and make sure it's safe. There might be some floorboards missing or dangling wires still carrying a charge. Give me a moment."

Taara and A-Ram waited in the lift shaft as Stenstrom stepped onto the Bridge. It was incredibly dark. Even with his Holystone see could see very little. It was like a wall of darkness inhabited the Bridge.

"How's it look?" Taara asked from the shaft.

"Just a moment."

He checked his HRN to see which Holystone was rattling. It was his Astral Plane detector, and that gave him great pause as he'd had a number of encounters with the Astral Plane throughout his life and none of them had been pleasant. He reached into his HRN and pulled out several blue Holystones which could block the Astral Plane and close any doors to it that might be open. He tossed them into the dark and they scattered. He wondered—if the Astral Plane was contaminating the Bridge, could it also have been responsible for all the odd things they'd experienced since boarding the *Seeker?*

The voices?

The strange sounds and glimpses of people hiding in the dark?

Odd letters seemingly left out for their very own eyes?

The Astral Plane did play havoc on one's perceptions, his mother had taught him that.

The blue Holystone effect was immediate. The wall of inky blackness pulled back. He saw all sorts of things as the blue Holystones did their work. He saw sprays of momentary color, and caught glimpses of metal things laid out on the Bridge floor, things with hinges and gleaming jagged teeth, like a cruel trap meant to snare a large animal. There was a vortex of movement and the Astral Plane shut. His detector went quiet.

All clear. It was dark, but his Holystone lit it up in soft light. He carefully stepped out, looking for traps.

"Are we good, Bel?" Taara asked.

He trudged about, not finding anything further. The blue Holystones worked. He'd have to add a few more protections later once they were settled. "Yes, I think so. Come on in."

They stepped in. Save for the yellowish light from their Holystones, the bridge was in pitch dark. Detail emerged as they walked in. The sensing positions were covered with tarps, the navigator's chair was covered with debris, and the Ops panel was removed. The Missive's station was still intact. Braided wire and bits of wall material lay about on the floor. The emergency lights, long since drained, lurked in the corners.

Someone had trapped the Bridge.

Hints of movement. A-Ram was certain he'd seen someone.

Stenstrom's thoughts were dark: *Somebody trapped the ship. Who could have done this?*

The helm wheel emerged from the dark. It was turning slightly to the starboard, moving with the ship's roll. He walked up to it and gently touched its worn surface. "Captain Davage once held this in his hand," he said with awe. "The wonders he once worked with this wheel."

A-Ram approached it. He looked at the wheel—eager. "May I?" he asked.

Stenstrom stepped back, and A-Ram planted his feet.

"My whole life, I've always wanted to hold one of these for real—it was a dream I had."

Stenstrom bowed. "Dream no more, A-Ram. Do your thing; the helm is yours."

He smiled and put his hands on the wheel. He took a deep breath. "What are your orders, Captain?"

Stenstrom blushed. "Taara, which way are we rolling?"

"To the starboard," she said, rooting around near the vacant Ops station. "Three quarter's roll per minute."

"Very well, roll three-quarters to port and ease us out."

"Aye, sir. Rolling three quarters to port," he said.

He turned the wheel, fought with it for a moment, and then eased the roll to a stop. "That was a lot harder than I thought it would be. There's a ton of resistance."

"The ship's not working right now, silly," Taara said. "Get a working ship, and it'll move like glass."

With A-Ram standing behind the wheel, Stenstrom and Taara surveyed the bridge.

"Well, the Ops panels are gone, along with Navigation. The Missive's station appears fine, and the sensing arrays appear to still be here, as they are rather obsolete, and it looks like the plumbing's out in Captain's Office—I mean—your office, Bel."

"Looks like we'll have a long walk to use the bathroom for now. What else do we have?"

Taara flopped down into the Missive's chair. "That's it—ship's pretty much dead. The gas-compression engines are still here, but without the SM coils to power them, they're not much use. At least it's quiet in here, and the air's not too stale yet."

"Do we have Com at all?"

"No way."

Stenstrom shook his head. "Well, here we are. It's not much at present, but it'll have to do until we get to Bazz. We have the whole ship to spread out in, but I advise we stay together until I can kill the demon coming for Taara's soul."

"Thanks," Taara said.

"Don't forget about the Fiend, Bel," A-Ram added.

"How could I forget? Taara, you can have my office to sleep in until we get matters sorted out."

"I'm not some tea-drinker from Kana, Bel. I don't need a room to myself. I can handle the two of you."

He laughed. "Fine then. So, let's to it. Let's get the ship out of this list."

Painting of Private Taara de la Anderson, by Lord A-Ram

7

—LT. GWENDOLYN—

The *Seeker* was now in a high Zone D parking orbit, safely pulled away from the slow, rolling dive it had found itself in. The demon that was supposedly coming for Taara's soul still hadn't shown, and Stenstrom wished for it to come so they could get its killing over with.

Since arresting the decaying orbit, they had managed to get a little power to the bridge by denying gravitational service to some of the rear areas of the ship. They now had dim lights, partial forward and ventral sensing, and port and starboard roll. They also had a feeble stream of stale air pushing in at 1/24th life support from a ventilator.

They also got the backup com system running.

It wasn't long before a message came chattering in.

Appearing dimly in the flickering Holo-cone was a stern-looking woman dressed in a lady's Fleet Tremblar uniform. From what Stenstrom could see, she was a rugged woman with dark brown hair tightly pulled back under her smallish hat. She had a strong chin and a big forehead with either gray or green eyes. Very attractive, in a husky, solid sort of way. Behind her, crewmen bustled about. She stood with polished grace and had a long rapier-like weapon hanging at her side.

She spoke, her voice slightly garbled from the low power of the com.

"Are you Paymaster Stenstrom, Lord of Belmont?"

Stenstrom, unlike the famous Captain Davage who rarely sat in the Captain's chair, liked the chair, so he dramatically sat down in a flutter of his HRN coat and cleared his throat. "Aye, I am. Belmont-South Tyrol to be precise. Well met. And you are?"

"Lt. Gwendolyn, Lady of Prentiss, commanding officer of the scouting ship *Demophalon John*. What is your situation, sir? Fleetcom is very worried about you."

Stenstrom looked around and leaned forward. "Are they? Half-scuttled, that is our situation, as well they should know."

"What is the status of your life support, please?"

Stenstrom took a deep breath. "A little stale, but not bad."

Lt. Gwendolyn tried to look around, but apparently could see little through the poor connection. "Paymaster, my Hospitaler has a few important questions for you, if you would be so kind."

A female Hospitaler, wearing the usual black and silver uniform of a Samaritan, pushed her way into the Holo-cone. She, like the captain, was a solid-looking lady with blond hair twisted into a number of long, sinuous braids decorated with beads. Her silver helmet, winged in the usual fashion, sat askew on her head. "Paymaster Stenstrom, well met. I am Morgan-Jeterix of the Ephysians, Lady of Thompson, Grand Order of Hospitalers. Might I say I had the honor of serving with your father for a time—truly a goodly and honorable man. It has been my goal to make your acquaintance for some time now."

"Thank you, ma'am," Stenstrom replied.

Lt. Gwendolyn appeared impatient. "Please get on with it, Morgan," she said.

Morgan shot her a look. "I wish to ask you a few questions, as, without proper life support, you can quickly become addled with brain asphyxia and not even know it. I want to assess your current medical situation."

"Very well, please ask your questions," Stenstrom said.

"What year were you born, sir?"

"03192ax," Stenstrom quickly replied.

"What is your birth date?"

"December 17th."

Morgan noted a few things down on a pad. "Are you feeling out of sorts at all?"

"No, not really."

"Are you …"

Gwendolyn pushed her way back into the screen. "Thank you, Morgan. As you can see, the Paymaster appears, for the moment, to be fine." She turned to him. "I am relieved to see that you are unharmed. I also see that you managed to get your half-scuttled ship out of its terminal orbit and park at standard altitude for dry-docking, an impressive accomplishment considering the state of your vessel. Please be advised that we shall rendezvous with you in approximately seven hours. At that time, myself and my team shall board the ship and safe-tow it to Dry Dock 186 to begin its repairs."

"The repairs that I am paying for, yes?"

"I am not aware of such things, sir. To continue, at that time we shall rescue you and your people and take you back down to Fleet."

Stenstrom smiled. "Good Lt," he said.

"That's *captain,* if you please," she corrected. "I am the commanding officer of this vessel and I insist proper protocol be observed."

"Yes, thank you. As you can see, Captain, we here on the *Seeker* are in weather shape and have no need of rescue. We are a Warbird on the wing. I have been recently appointed to the chair of the *Seeker* and have been tasked to go at speed to Bazz on the orders of Admiral Derlith. I intend to fulfill that mission."

Lt. Gwendolyn sighed. She put her hand on the hilt of her sword. "Paymaster, I appreciate your position, and am sorry that my presence aboard the ship shall cause your appointment to be rendered void. However, your safety, and that of those with you, is currently my responsibility, and I intend to deliver you and anybody else present on the *Seeker,* to the shore immediately. Am I clear, sir? I hate to be blunt and the bearer of bad news, but there it is. If it is any consolation to you, sir, I shall be glad to make a recommendation to the Admiralty regarding your inventiveness and tenacity in this matter. It is certainly to be commended."

"Thank you," Stenstrom said. "The Admiralty certainly has a keen eye for such things, do they not? And, please, allow me to be clear to you as well, Captain. I have a mission to accomplish, for my chair's sake, and I shall carry it out. You needn't hurry to our position, as we shall not be here upon your arrival."

Gwendolyn approached the Holo-Cone, filling it up. It was hard to judge how big she was, but she looked to be rather tall and solidly built. Stenstrom mused that, if she smiled, she would most probably be very attractive—but her face was set in a stern frown. "According to my logs, you have two unauthorized persons aboard your vessel. She snapped her fingers, and someone handed her a report. She looked at it. "Where is Fleet Adjutant Lt. Josephus, Lord of A-Ram?"

"Here, ma'am," A-Ram piped from behind the helm.

Gwendolyn glanced at him. "I know you, sir, do I not? Yes, yes of course, I've seen you in Admiral Derlith's office. Well met. Sir, you are considered absent from your duties—which is a serious charge. The Admiral is very concerned about you and is graciously willing to forget this matter, but I must have you to his side with all speed."

"Lord A-Ram no longer is in the employ of Admiral Derlith, and he is no longer an Adjutant," Stenstrom said. "I have duly appropriated him, as is my right as ship's commander. Lord A-Ram is now my Master Helmsman."

"What?" Captain Gwendolyn said, shocked.

"I have appointed Lord A-Ram as my Master Helmsman."

"Paymaster, he is an adjutant—an assistant, a helper, and, if my memory is clear, he can barely see two feet in front of his face. Lord A-Ram, I do not mean to belittle you, but …"

"Then why do so?" Stenstrom said, jumping in. "He had the skill and the raw nerve to fly me in a Suborbital onto a dead ship in space. You claim he can't see—perhaps it is you and everybody else at Fleet who cannot see, for there was an unnoticed treasure in your midst the whole time, and I have stolen him away and given him his due at long last."

Gwendolyn sighed. "I am not certain what relevance that has in this conversation, Paymaster. Lord A-Ram shall be returned to the Admiral's office at once."

"Yes, where he may get a badly sore elbow polishing the Admiral's silver. By hook or by crook, Captain, I shall have a crew," Stenstrom replied. "Admiral Derlith has made no other choice possible. This man was wasted in that office and routinely humiliated by an arrogant Admiral. Here he is a Master Helmsman and greatly appreciated."

Gwendolyn shot him an increasingly dirty look. "I see. And where is Private Taara de la Anderson, of the 110th Marines?"

Taara stepped forward and nodded. "That's me."

Gwendolyn turned to her. "You, Private, are officially AWOL from your barracks. I am compelled to inform you that I must take you into custody at once. Adjutant Josephus, will you please take Private Taara to the brig and await my arrival. Is that understood?"

"The brig currently has no gravity, ma'am," Taara chirped.

"Then select a suitable quarters and take her there. Once inside, she is not to emerge until I arrive."

Shrugging, A-Ram began moving in Taara's direction.

Stenstrom got a tad annoyed himself. A-Ram showed every sign of cracking and giving in to Lt. Gwendolyn. A-Ram was used to following orders without much question, and Stenstrom had to intervene. "Stand fast, A-Ram. Let's show a bit of style here, yes?" He turned back to Gwendolyn. "Perhaps you've cotton in your ears, Captain, or that tight bun you've imprisoned your hair in has restricted the blood flow to your brain," he said. "Lord A-Ram is under my command, not yours; therefore, stop issuing him orders."

A-Ram resumed his position behind the helm, dwarfed by it. He looked like he wished to be elsewhere.

Gwendolyn's eyes flashed.

"And," Stenstrom continued, "you will be happy to note that I have appointed Private Taara as my first officer, again as is my right. The *Seeker* has a long tradition of Marines serving as first officer: Lt. Kilos of the 12th Marines, and Lt. Verlin of the 53rd have served this ship proudly, and I wish to carry on said tradition. I am sorry for the confusion. If Admiral Derlith had left me a ship not in pieces, I would have Commed down the required communication hours ago. Perhaps you could do it for me, since you appear to have command of a nice, working scouting ship."

Gwendolyn was shocked. "A … *private* … as a first officer? Paymaster, such a thing is not done …"

"It is now, and Private Taara shall serve me and this ship well."

She shook her head. "Paymaster, I am sorry, I am overriding your appointment. Adjutant Josephus, please take Private Taara into custody, immediately."

Again, A-Ram began moving from behind the helm.

"A-Ram, stand fast and buckle up! Captain, you are not issuing me or my crew orders, and you've naught but the temerity to attempt to do so."

Gwendolyn became rather perturbed. "Paymaster, when I board your vessel and take command, you and I are going to have a short but rather vigorous talk in the gym regarding seniority and proper etiquette, and I warn you, sir, I am a champion boxer."

"I've no doubt, the heavyweight division, yes?" Stenstrom said—Gwendolyn's mouth dropped open in shock at the slap. Taara and Morgan, on the screen, laughed.

Stenstrom stood and approached the Holo-cone. He was standing nose to nose with Lt. Gwendolyn. "Captain, it appears we are both victims of circumstance here—there's no need for us to work against each other. Please, allow me to complete my mission, and then I shall gladly allow you to board the ship and complete yours."

"I have my orders, sir—and you have yours. Please listen carefully: I order you to remain on station and await my arrival, where I, and my team, shall board the ship post haste. At that time, I shall relieve you of your command, take Private Taara into custody, and return Adjutant Josephus to the Fleet. Then, I shall escort you to the gym where I shall gladly relieve you of your teeth. Take your pick—boxing, wrestling, sambo, or a good old-fashioned, bare-knuckle fight—it's up to you!"

"Captain, I will remind you that you are in command of a scouting ship. I am sitting on a Main Fleet Warbird, such as it is, and, therefore, your orders are nullified. And, by the by, should you choose to take a swing at me, be it known that I shall swing back with the utmost vigor. Lady or not, girl or not, I shall put you on the floor."

"My orders come from Admiral Derlith!"

"As do mine!"

Gwendolyn took her hat off, and her dark brown hair spilled out. "You have seven hours, Paymaster. If you are not where you are supposed to be when I come for you, then it's war between us, sir, and it will be a war that you shall lose in earnest!"

"Very well—then it is war. You have thrown down the gauntlet, and I am picking it up and slapping your punch-riddled face with it. If only to cause you the maximum level of annoyance, I am going to Bazz. Stenstrom out!"

Gwendolyn looked like she was about to explode when the screen went off.

A-Ram shook his head.

"That was cool, Bel!" Taara cried. "You really know how to tweak a person off. She looked really, really pissed." Taara gave him a shove. "Am I really your first officer?"

"If you want it."

Taara gave him a grand hug.

A-Ram was skeptical. "That was a fine show of bravado Bel, but the fact remains we're stuck here in orbit. We've no drive engines and are dead in our tracks. Likewise, you're going to be finding yourself in quite a fistfight once Captain Gwendolyn boards the ship," he said.

"Am I?"

"Oh, yes. She's one of Admiral Derlith's favorites—his niece I think. And yes, she was the Fleet's boxing champion in her weight class four years running, ladies division—and it wasn't the heavyweight class either. She's also really good at wrestling and sambo, for what that's worth. She has a fast right hook and a mean streak to match, so I'm told."

"What else?"

"That's about all I know. She was often in attendance in the Admiral's office. She was always quite nice to me—but then again I never slapped her in the face right in front of her crew, either."

"Oh, you're too kind, A-Ram. I'm certain she'll get over it."

"If you're going to fight, I want to be there to watch," Taara said.

Stenstrom walked to the back of the bridge. "Taara, I'm not going to beat up a helpless woman."

"She didn't look helpless to me. I'll bet she could take you—heck I'll bet I could take you too! You never want to fight a girl from Bazz."

Stenstrom ignored her. "So, if only to avoid an embarrassing session of fisticuffs in the gym, we have seven hours to not be here. What are our options? How are we going to do this?"

"We can't use power from the grav packs, Bel," Taara said, still all MOL-LYed up. "That won't break us out of orbit—we won't be able to generate the altitude or the velocity. We have gas compression engines but no coils to run them—and they don't function in space anyway. We have no motive power, plain and simple."

Stenstrom tapped his chin and thought. "I was thinking, with the *Seeker* abandoned and mostly stripped, she's carrying much less weight than she normally would, and, therefore, the amount of thrust required to drive her will be greatly reduced, am I correct?"

"Well sure. Still, we would need a 770 coil, at least," Taara said, impressed by her own knowledge that she shouldn't have.

"If memory serves, a 770 coil is pretty big. All I'm talking is enough thrust to get us away from Kana and on our way to Bazz."

They sat silent for a moment.

"A standard T-60 transport has a fair amount of thrust. If you have five or six of those clamped onto the hull, that would limp us out of orbit, I should think," A-Ram added.

Taara suddenly seemed inspired. She went to the Fore Sensing station and peered into the viewer. "We have a slow tap into Fleetcom's database. Let me just fiddle about with this here for a sec … and, there we go!"

"What are you looking up?" Stenstrom asked.

"I had a thought. Yes, look here—Dry Dock 275. I recall the clerks at the hangar talking about an old tach-Scout ship that's currently docked there for a refit, so I looked it up. Here it is, the *Westminster,* an old *Belleraphon*-class scouting vessel."

"Go on, Taara, what are your thoughts?"

"I'm thinking we up-thrust out of this polar orbit and synch-up with Dry Dock 275. I think, if we reroute enough power, we'll just be able to reach Dry Dock altitude. And, better yet, the *Westminster* will fit nicely into Ripcar Bay 5. We'll put her in there, clamp her down nice and snug, then we'll just drop containment and fire her engines. That should get us out of here in a hurry."

"Ripcar Bay 5?" A-Ram said. "That's a forward-facing bay. We'll be flying backwards."

"So?" Taara replied.

Stenstrom smiled. "And, I would imagine that there is naught but a minimal crew up there on Dry Dock 275, what with the holiday and all."

A-Ram shuffled his feet. "I don't like this, Bel. We're talking about stealing a Fleet vessel."

"Oh, come on, A-Ram—I prefer the term *commandeering.* We're talking about *commandeering* a Fleet vessel."

"The Fleet is going to rain all over us," A-Ram replied.

"Are they? The Admirals make the rules down there in Armenelos, but let them enforce them up here in space. Right? The Fleet Captaincy, should they get wind of this ridiculous situation, is going to be pretty sore—not at us, but at the Admiralty. I can drop names with the best of them—my father,

Captain Davage, and more. Captain Davage told me himself—a Fleet captain is expected to be bold and tenacious at all times, and that's exactly how we're conducting ourselves in carrying out our mission. Taara, how much altitude do we need?"

"Dry Dock 275 is in the second shell of Zone B, about another fifteen thousand feet straight up. Good thing too—if she were in the third or fourth shells, we wouldn't be able to generate the velocity to reach her."

A-Ram sulked behind the wheel. "We're going to get into trouble."

"Look, we get into trouble—I'll buy our way out of it. Money talks, A-Ram, never forget that. I can buy Barr and mouthpieces that'll have the Fleet's head spinning. Besides, we're going to bring the *Westminster* back nice and neat after we've delivered our bloody brandy to Bazz. No harm done, so, with that in mind, let's make ready to up-thrust and do this."

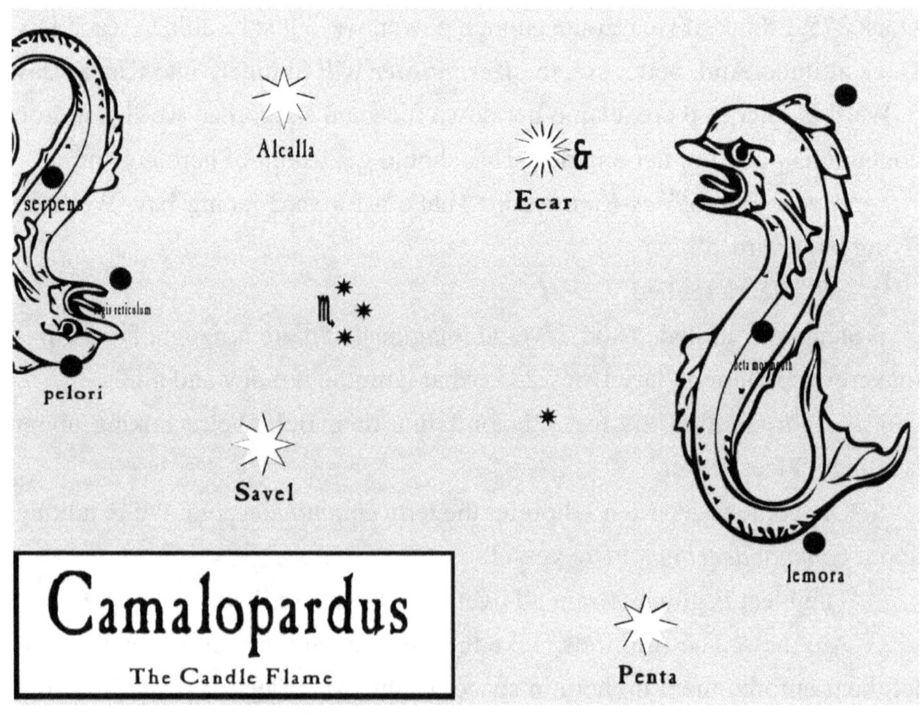

8

—The *Westminster*—

Slowly, the *Seeker* ascended several thousand feet. If the various sensors and automated equipment on the bridge had been functioning, they would have been hearing all sorts of claxons and buoys complaining about proximity violations and the like. However, the *Seeker's* bridge was blissfully quiet.

Soon, on the jumpy holo-cone, the rib-cage of Dry Dock 275 appeared in the distance. It was mostly empty; the only ship within was the tiny, bullet-shaped hull of the *Westminster*.

Carefully, A-Ram slid the *Seeker* to the aft docking collar, and the three of them made their slow way out of the ship.

The clean, fresh air and bright lights of the Dry Dock was a real treat after the darkness and stale, smelly air they'd been breathing. They were met by a single Marine and an angry yardmaster.

"Didn't you get my Com? You're in the wrong Dry Dock! The *Seeker's* scheduled to make berth in Dry Dock 186 a few days hence. You need to get your tub out of here now!"

"Actually sir—I'm sorry—what is your name?" Stenstrom said.

"Senior Yardmaster Piro."

"I see. Well, Senior Yardmaster Piro, we're not staying, obviously. We're just here to pick up the *Westminster*—her presence is required on Bazz for a few days, then we'll have her right back just like we found her."

Piro was dumbfounded. "You're taking the *Westminster?* First I've heard of it. The *Westminster* is scheduled, after her refit, to go to Tantan and serve the Fleet office there. I'm going to get some confirmation. Sgt. Laval, would you mind so much?"

The Marine drew his SK and pointed it at them.

"I'd get your hands up in plain sight and keep them there, if I were you, right now," Piro said walking into his office.

Stenstrom smiled and raised his hands. "Oh, indeed." He glanced at A-Ram and Taara. "Come on, you two, get your hands up. Let's all be friends, shall we?"

A-Ram and Taara raised their hands. The Marine reached out and took Taara's SK. He then pulled Stenstrom's NTH pistols and set them aside. "I'm sorry about this," he said. "I'm certain it's just a mix up. Happens all the time."

"Yes, just a mix up. Sgt., you forgot something," Stenstrom said.

"Sir?" the Marine responded.

Stenstrom waved his fingers and a pink Holystone appeared in his hand. "Holystone," he said. "I always carry a bunch."

"Thank you, sir," the Marine replied. He reached up and took the stone. He instantly fell into a rather stupefied state. He toppled over, and Stenstrom caught him and eased him down. "Pink Holystone works every time. You'll have a nice little dream, Sgt., then you'll be just fine."

Taara put her hands down and walked into the Yardmaster's office.

There was a struggle from within.

Somebody hit the floor with a crash.

Stenstrom and A-Ram came in. Taara was dragging the Yardmaster's unconscious body away from his chair. "Taara, was knocking this man out really necessary?"

"Yes, Bel, it was. He's fine—he'll just have to live with the notion that he got knocked out by a girl is all. I'm certain that's not a tidbit he'll be sharing with his friends any time soon."

Stenstrom produced another pink Holystone and stuck it in Piro's hand.

They then scoured the Dry Dock, looking for anything they might have a use for. They found several crates of insta-meals which they loaded onto the *Westminster*, along with a few boxes of bottled water, four pressure suits with ten hours of air each, three portable generators, two Holo-terms, a Macon air condenser, a Havelock mag system, along with yards of cabling, and some hand-tooling, should it be needed.

They then piled into the *Westminster* and A-Ram fired it up. The transport was rather bullet-shaped with a fairly spacious cargo area and pilot's seat.

A-Ram strapped himself into the pilot's chair and pressed buttons on the organ-like panels in front of him. "Oh, after the Suborbital and the *Seeker's* dead helm, this is like flying a dream," he raved as he pulled away from the dock. "These older engines aren't good for much, but they do generate a lot of work-heavy thrust. We'll break orbit no problem once we get her strapped down."

Taara was amazed. "How do you know how to do all of this stuff—got another MOLLY on you somewhere?"

"No," he laughed. "Lots and lots of un-logged time in the simulators. I'm up on all these old ships. I used to go in them every day, and escape out the front hatch when somebody came in. I would have gotten into loads of trouble if they caught me in there." He looked at Taara's dangling Mollocks. "May I?"

"Oh, sure! Tug away."

A-Ram reached over and gave her two quick tugs on the sideburns.

"That's the spirit! See, this is fun! I love you guys already!"

They had the foresight to pre-open the doors to Ripcar bay 5, and A-Ram carefully slid the *Westminster* in—it was a tight fit. They then donned their newly acquired pressure suits and went out. They hard docked the *Westminster's* landing skids and bolted her down as tightly as they could. Taara, still using the MOLLY with abandon, ran a controller cable from the central node of the transport to a junction nearby. "This way," she explained over the suit's Com, "we'll have control over the ship from the bridge and not have to have somebody actually in the *Westminster* doing the flying." It took awhile, bumbling around in her pressure suit, but she finally got it set up. Taara also connected several power cables to the *Westminster's* generators and shunted the power, allowing the *Seeker* to make use of it.

Their tasks done, they gathered their booty from the Dry Dock and collected it in a cargo net. They then did a short space walk to the adjacent Ripcar bay where they manually entered.

"Well," Taara said getting out of her pressure suit, her short black hair a mess. "That Dry Dock was like a big old grocery store, wasn't it? Look at all this stuff we just stole. This is great!"

"We're going to need to be getting out of here post haste. The pinkies should be wearing off on those two shortly," Stenstrom said.

"You're just pissing people off left and right today, aren't you, Bel?" she added.

They returned to the bridge and set up two of the generators—it took awhile hoisting them up the empty lift shaft with ropes until Taara had the bright idea to cut the gravity in the area, allowing the heavy equipment to float up—that was some inspired stuff. The lights came on and the whole place seemed a tad cheerier. They also set up the Macon, and it began producing fresh, clean air.

A-Ram took the helm, and Stenstrom ordered the *Seeker* backed out of the Dry Dock. The *Westminster* fired, and off they went.

The Westminster

9

—STOP THE *SEEKER*—

Aboard the *Demophalon John*, Lt. Gwendolyn walked through the tight corridors of the ship and headed to her quarters. Her crew, though efficient and polite, gave her plenty of space as she prowled the halls. Nobody said anything to her as she passed by either; they sunk into the walls, trying to be quiet and unnoticed.

Yesterday was St. Porter's Day. She would have forgotten all together, but she overheard several of her crew wishing each other well.

Nobody gave her the "Happy Porter's Day" greeting.

Nobody wanted to get on her bad side or risk provoking the Grizzly Bear, the Snapping Turtle, the Angry Mountain; that's what the crew called her—she'd heard all the various names whispered in the mess and in the corridors.

Her crew, in short, was quite terrified of Lt. Gwendolyn, Lady of Prentiss.

Not only was she mean as a snake and pugnacious to boot, she had the connections in the Admiralty to really make things unpleasant for a poor junior officer or crewman—there were all sorts of rotten duties and crap postings awaiting just such an unfortunate soul. She was even known to K-List crew for even minor offences, sending them and their careers into pure Fleet purgatory that few ever emerged from.

The closest thing she had to a friend was Morgan-Jeterix, the ship's Hospitaler, and why not? Being a Hospitaler, Morgan was immune to the captain's fits of temper and threats of detail or demotion. And, though the crew had never seen such a thing, Morgan-Jeterix could probably out-fight Lt. Gwendolyn if push came to shove—nobody could fight like a Hospitaler. But even with Morgan-Jeterix, their professional relationship was off and on, and they certainly didn't do much together during their off-hours. Gwendolyn didn't approve of Morgan's rather flashy, habits.

Clearly, nobody really liked Lt. Gwendolyn much.

She wondered why sometimes. Sure, she demanded a lot from her crew. Sure, she went by the book. Sure, she could have a hot temper, and sometimes she went off at the mouth, but many captains did, and they had the love of the crew. Why didn't she? Why didn't she have a friend aboard? Why did she eat her meals alone and spend all of her free time in her quarters?

She opened the door to her small cabin and stepped in. She removed her hat and let her long, coffee-brown hair out of its confining bun. She took off her gun belt and hung it from a peg, her family FEDULA, long and rapier-like, glinting in the soft light. Her feet were killing her; she pulled off her Fleet boots that went up to her knees and took a seat. She'd had a long day.

She looked around. Being the captain of a *Tekel*-class scout ship, her quarters were the largest on the ship, yet they were rather small, just big enough for a table, a bathroom and a small bed; still, they were quite luxurious compared to what everybody else got bunked-in together. She didn't need a whole lot of room though. Her quarters were shockingly sterile and devoid of personal mementos and decorations.

A cold room for a well-known cold person.

She liked many of the ancient card games that were once played, and was quite good at them. She had several hand-made, hand-painted decks that were worth quite a bit of money. They were her most prized and sentimental possessions beyond her FEDULA, given to her by her grandfather.

She knew by heart dozens of games, but, mostly, she played solitary ones. Nobody wanted to sit down and play a hand of cards with the Grizzly Bear.

Might get eaten ...

She took out one of her decks and sat down at the table, shuffling the cards around. She dealt eight cards for herself, and eight for a person across the table who wasn't there.

Her lonely thoughts began to spin.

Paymaster Stenstrom, Lord of Belmont ...

She understood how the Paymaster felt. Her mission, on the orders of Admiral Derlith himself, will cost him his chair. He had rubbed the Admiralty the wrong way during his Appointment, and they were going to make him suffer for it. He wouldn't be the first person they cheated out of a captain's chair.

Stenstrom, Lord of Belmont. That was a name she heard from time to time, growing up in the House of Prentiss. When her aunt, a thin, unsmiling woman, came for a visit, she would sit in the parlor and talk with venom about someone named Stenstrom, Lord of Belmont, and his mother—a woman whom her aunt hated above all others.

The words her aunt spoke were ugly and cold, driven by a confined, animal-like fury, all directed at some woman from Tyrol and her son.

And then, many times, her aunt called out for her in a callow voice: *"Gwendolyn!"*

She didn't want to go into her presence. She was frightened of her aunt, but was drawn, and couldn't help herself.

"Gwendolyn! Come here!" Sometimes she heard that voice in her nightmares:

Gggggggggggwendolynnnnnnnnnn!!

Many times, she was stopped half-way by her uncle, Derlith. "Come on, Gwen, let's go outside and get some air," or "Let's put the gloves on and go a round or two—show me what you got." Many times, her uncle saved her having to go before her aunt.

Occasionally, he wasn't there to help her, and she had to go in and see her aunt. She remembered seeing the thin, bent form sitting in the parlor, waiting for her. She never remembered what happened after that—it was blacked out in her mind.

So, there he was, Paymaster Stenstrom, a man with enemies all over the place. She wondered if he was aware of all the various people who hated him from afar.

Gwendolyn didn't hate him. As a girl, she had harbored a vague curiosity about the fellow: what he was like, how he looked, what he had done to deserve her aunt's considerable scorn. She was certain he was only a year or two older than she was—he was just a little boy as her aunt spewed her venom—what could he possibly have done?

No, she didn't hate him at all …

But, she had her orders to take him into custody. Unlike the commander of a Warbird like the *Seeker,* a scout-ship captain had to follow orders from the Admiralty. She had no choice.

She was under orders, but that didn't mean she had to like them.

She had the whole thing pictured out in her head. After she'd accomplished her mission, she had planned to take Paymaster Stenstrom into a quiet cafeteria at Fleet—there was one in the western wing of the complex that she favored—sit him down at a quiet table, and explain. He would, no doubt, be rather surly, perhaps pouting and nostalgic. She imagined herself being unusually patient and accommodating, listening to Lord Belmont cry in his beer. Since he'd been personally sponsored by the great Captain Davage, a man respected by all, then he must be of good quality; he had to be. She planned to stick up for him, to come charging to his rescue and offer him help. She'd read Davage's report regarding Lord Stenstrom's performance during the Kestral Affair. He did very well, very well indeed, so, apparently, he was cut from command cloth. Surely some ship out there in the whole of the Fleet could use such a fellow, maybe not a Warbird, maybe something smaller, but she planned to help him in any way she could.

She wondered how her aunt would react to such a display—probably not well, though Gwendolyn frankly didn't care what her aunt thought. She was no longer a frightened child, and this was none of her aunt's business.

She imagined herself with all sorts of questions, sitting there in the cafeteria with him. A drab cafeteria in the middle of Fleet could hardly been considered a romantic place, but, in her practical and undecorated mind, it might as well have been a garden full of roses. Just she and Paymaster Stenstrom, sitting with their trays, absorbed in discovering each other.

Her questions were many. So, why a Paymaster? Why didn't he simply join the Fleet? He wears a Hoban Royal Navy coat—so he must have some hankering for it, some longing. Why did he choose such an odd route?

And, why the mask? Was he simply an eccentric lord from Belmont. Was he scarred, or was there some other reason for wearing it?

Why?

She wondered what he looked like without it—just like one of those cleverly wrapped presents she used to get on Nether Day, one that was obscured just enough to keep her from knowing what it was—to whet one's appetite to get it unwrapped and find out what was underneath.

Her fantasy continued. As the lunch went on, she had planned to tell him that she would do what she could to help him re-appoint to another ship. She wanted to make amends. And he would see reason and accept, warmly shaking her hand, and then she would get out her decks, push their trays aside, and they'd play cards. They'd play for hours, both of them laughing and talking with abandon, the cards going *fnap … fnap* on the tabletop.

In her mind, she had Paymaster Stenstrom, Lord of Belmont—the man in the mask and the HRN coat—penciled in as a friend, perhaps more. Surely he, like her, was a misfit too.

But then, of course, the Grizzly Bear struck.

He annoyed her during their initial meeting—worse, he infuriated her.

Yes, I can see that—heavyweight division …

What a cruel thing to say—in front of her crew. Morgan laughed—everybody laughed. And, of course, she saw red and went off at the mouth. What had she expected from him—her mission was to remove him of his brand new command. The idyllic and fanciful lunch shared in the Fleet cafeteria that she had hoped for began to seem more and more impossible.

Now, after her performance earlier, she'd committed herself to getting into a brawl with him, and all the good will she'd built up in her mind was temporarily forgotten. She had been furious. If she could have, she would have fought him right there and then. There's that temper again, and the willingness to attempt bodily harm upon another.

Getting into a fight with Paymaster Stenstrom, whether the man could properly defend himself or not—it hadn't mattered to her. Maybe her crew was right to be afraid of her after all.

* * * * *

She was a Prentiss, a long-standing noble family from Zenon, their holdings not too terribly far from the ancestral Belmont holdings in the more southern city of Brynthia, if she wasn't mistaken. Unlike other Zenon Girls, who tended to be quite petite, ladies from Prentiss were large in stature—not fat or overweight, just broad-shouldered, tall and dense. Gwendolyn had six sisters, all like her, but, of all of them, she was the biggest and probably had the most vile temper and the sharpest tongue. Her tongue, in fact, had knocked her right out of the prolific Zenon social scene that her sisters participated so readily in. Though not very old, she was already considered a spinster; most of the eligible lords, looking to find a lady, denounced Gwendolyn of Prentiss as not worth the trouble, and they conducted their search in less volatile pastures. Such fiery ladies were often known as "Black Widows" in League society. Vith ladies were often labeled Black Widows, and sometimes Barrows and Calverts, but almost never Zenons. Sometimes Black Widows were a commodity—interested gentlemen occasionally finding them alluring and irresistible, like hunting for a dangerous animal that could lash out and bite. Yet, in her case, her stature and undeniably volcanic nature kept even the brave at bay.

Fortunately for her, getting married wasn't foremost on her mind. She wanted to educate herself and become something other than the trophy wife on display in a grand sitting room other Zenon Girls dreamed of being. She saw the League around her and wanted to participate, to make her mark and leave an impression. She went to school in Arden, earning an **Ev** degree as an engineer of stellar mechanics—the only Zenon Girl in her class. She did, in fact, have a solid head on her shoulders.

She was also a favorite of one of her uncles on her mother's side, Lord Derlith of Cone, an Admiral in the Stellar Fleet—the younger brother of the mean old aunt she and her sisters were so afraid of. He always thought Gwendolyn had a good head and a stout heart, top among her sisters, though she clearly needed to work on her manners and her social skills. Like most of the Cones, her uncle had the sort of domineering personality that put a stopper on her temper—squelched it before it could top off and really come to a boil. And he genuinely appeared to be fond of his niece. He was patient with her, guiding her throughout her formative years. As an outlet for her energy and to help teach her discipline and respect, he introduced her to contact sports, which wasn't a pursuit proper Zenon Girls usually chose to indulge in, but Gwendolyn was certainly not a standard Zenon Girl. She took up boxing at first, and had an immediate talent for it. Her size and density were a big help. Soon, she began branching out—taking up wrestling and sambo as well.

Such "vulgar" sports weren't in big demand on Kana, so her uncle took her to Onaris every year to compete, and she won a number of tournaments there over time.

He helped her gain admission to the Fleet and guided her quickly through the ranks, Gwendolyn eventually becoming the commanding officer of a scouting ship under his direct command, though engineering appeared to be her true calling. After guiding the *Demophalon John* for a few years, she should easily appoint as either the engineer or captain for some Main Fleet Vessel. She'd heard that he did quite a lot for her behind the scenes, managing to push aside some of the less flattering notes that began bubbling up regarding her behavior: unruly, ill mannered, bad tempered … few command "intangibles" and disliked by her crew.

"Not to worry, Gwen," he often told her. "Leave all that to me."

After she had time to cool off and reflect, she once again found herself admiring this man whom most of the Admiralty wished to see fail—this upstart Paymaster from Tyrol who Free Booted his way onto the chair of a Main Fleet Vessel. Look what he'd accomplished. He had been able to get aboard an abandoned ship in orbit using a Suborbital craft, and he had managed to get two total strangers to help him along the way, at great risk to themselves. She wondered if she could have done the same thing, if she could have gotten anyone to assist her in such a fashion. She rather doubted it.

She looked at the cards across the table. "I'm sorry for today—I'd hoped to get off on a better footing. Friends?" she said hopefully.

As she sat there waiting for the cards to answer, her Com chattered.

"Com," she said in her husky voice.

"Com here, Captain. Message from Fleet, Admiral Derlith."

"Aye, Com, I'll take it here."

She took a moment, straightened her hair, and accepted the message. On her Com screen, the stern, iron-haired image of Admiral Derlith appeared.

"Evening, sir," she said. "Well met."

The Admiral didn't mince words. "Gwendolyn, there has been a change in plans regarding the *Seeker.*"

The Admiral was always very informal with her. He was her uncle, after all.

She was elated. "I see. We were at three hours, twenty-two minutes until our link-up with her, sir."

"The *Seeker* is no longer in orbit around Kana."

"What?"

"Yes, Paymaster Stenstrom and his band of pirates are cutting a notorious swath across the face of the Fleet. Seems the good Paymaster took it upon himself to appropriate the tach-scout ship *Westminster* from Dry Dock 275, and is using her as a drive engine. Two hours ago, he broke orbit and is on a slow-speed course to Bazz by way of Onaris."

Gwendolyn absorbed the news. "I see," she said again.

"In light of this development, your mission has changed. You are to intercept the *Seeker,* board her, and deliver Paymaster Stenstrom, Adjutant Josephus, Lord of A-Ram, and Marine Private Taara de la Anderson back to Fleet immediately. There, they shall face any number of charges and fines. You are authorized to disable the *Seeker* in any manner you see fit to safely accomplish your mission, though I bade you to be mindful of Fleet assets and protect them as best you can. I trust to your good judgment. Am I clear?"

Gwendolyn's elation fell. "Admiral," she said, "I request that another perform this task—I do not feel up to it."

"There is no other that I trust for such a mission. We cannot tag out a Main Fleet Warbird for this task, as it shall then be out of the Admiralty and a matter of public record. The Paymaster, should such a thing come out, might garner sympathy in the court of public opinion throughout the ranks and manage to get out of this situation enhanced. He might even find help—as no doubt, his father or Captain Davage or any other ship's captain with a sabre to rattle would come to his aid should his plight become known. We must keep a tight lid on this, Gwendolyn. I want this matter kept on the hush, and I want that animal from Tyrol before me in irons. We want to rip that mask from his foolish Belmont face and tear that coat right off him. And, for that we need you."

"Who, pray, is *'we,'* Admiral?"

"Never mind. Just get him here on the quick."

She closed her eyes. "Admiral, what is to be done with Paymaster Stenstrom?"

"Let us be creative here for a moment. Stockade is an obvious punishment. Work detail, throw him on the Bag for all to gawk at, possible imprisonment, and censure from the Fleet and the Sisters are likely. And surely, a date with the sonic lash would be in order."

She sat there for a moment.

"Can I count on you, Gwen?"

"Uncle, were you aware that Adjutant Josephus is an accomplished pilot?"

"Josephus? My Josephus? Of course not! The man can barely see and is afraid of his own shadow. He often scares himself into a state with all the research he does on that Calvert Fiend maniac."

"Apparently, he can see well enough to fly a Suborbital onto a wrecked ship in orbit. Apparently he has more skill and more guts than you gave him notice for."

"What does that have to do with your orders, Gwendolyn? When you bring Josephus back here, maybe I'll have a talk with him and flush out these skills that I did not know he had. Perhaps I can introduce him to the right folk. In any event, I need you to put this Paymaster's captaincy to a quick end. Again I'll ask, can I count on you, Gwen?"

She nodded. "Yes, yes Uncle, of course."

"That's a good lady. We'll speak again soon. Please be safe and ensure the unharmed return of Josephus and Private Taara. If you have to get rough with the Paymaster, feel free—just remember, I want that coat. Derlith out."

The screen went black.

Gwendolyn sat there for a moment. She sighed and collected the cards sitting on the table. She arranged them back into an orderly deck. "Com," she said in her usual gruff voice.

"Com here, Captain."

"Com, there's been a change in plans. The *Seeker* has broken orbit around Kana and is headed for Bazz. We are to intercept her at once, board her, and return all persons within to Fleet with all speed. Send to navigation to lay in an adjusted course."

"Aye, ma'am."

"Also, inform the boatswain that I want the Christmas guns checked and made ready to be run out."

The Com paused. "The … guns, ma'am?"

"Did I stutter?"

"No, ma'am."

"Are you incapable of following my orders?"

"No, ma'am!"

"Then carry them out. I'll not repeat them, and I'll expect the boatswain's report in short order."

"Aye, ma'am."

The Com went off. She sat there at the table. Outside she could hear the occasional chattering of crewmen as they passed by. She looked at the empty chair on the other side of the table.

There was nobody there, and there probably never would be. That cafeteria at Fleet was, more and more, an idyllic place she could now never go.

PART 2
ALL THAT RESISTS HIM

The Lady in Grey

1

—A Remarkable Birth—

"So, where're you guys from?" Taara asked. She was sitting at the Missive's chair eating an insta-meal, her feet propped up on the panel. "I'm from the west continent of Bazz, a little village called Dyson-Clampton. Villages on Bazz always have two names—don't ask me why— they just do. Ever heard of it?"

Stenstrom sat down in his chair. "No. I'm afraid I don't know all that much about Bazz. It sounds like a charming place."

"Charming? Nothing charming about it. It's hot in the summer and way cold in the winter; still, it's home."

"I've heard the bugs on Bazz are massive and not to be trifled with," A-Ram said from the helm.

"They sure are big. And mean too. Everything's mean on Bazz. Look at me—I'm mean." She unbuttoned her Marine vest and got comfortable.

Stenstrom laughed. "What's your family do?"

"Well, since you asked, I'll tell you. My mom's a fruit vendor—Galacas mostly when they're in season. My dad and my uncles distil Zemuda. You like Zemuda?"

"I heard it gives you a hangover."

"It can if you're not used to it, and it stops you up pretty good—you never get used to that. Wish we had some right now."

"I like Zemuda," A-Ram said, "in a blue cochina. Very tasty drink."

Taara turned her nose up at the thought. "So, A-Ram, what about you? Where do you come from?" she asked.

He turned the wheel a bit. "From St. Edmund's, a little fishing city south of the forest. A-Ram's a Calvert House. Neither one of you have probably ever been to Calvert."

"I've been to Calvert, and St. Edmund's myself many times," Stenstrom replied.

"You have?"

"Yes. I suppose your being from Calvert is why your thoughts dwell on the Fiend of Calvert so much."

Taara put her fork down and turned to them. "Ok, since I'm not a local, who is the Fiend of Calvert? Can you clue me?"

A-Ram spoke up. "The Fiend of Calvert is a maniac who terrorized the whole of the Calvert region twenty-five years ago."

"Let me guess. He killed ladies, courtesans, that sort of thing?" she asked.

"No, he killed sailors, merchants, drunks—pretty much any dirty man roaming about on the streets was fair game. Since he killed shadowy, down-trodden sorts, nobody really did much about it for a long time, and to this day nobody knows for certain how many people he did away with. After several years of this activity, the riff-raff had had it, and they marched on Calvert Square, demanding justice. The Fiend was like a ghost; nobody could get him, not even the Gifted inspectors from the north they brought in."

"So, what happened?"

"A vigilant from the east called the Mad Lord of Walther came and de-feated the Fiend, and he hasn't been heard from since," A-Ram said.

"He killed the Fiend," Stenstrom said.

"No, he didn't kill him," A-Ram said. "The Fiend escaped, fleeing across the rooftops of Calvert. You know, my room in our house was on the top floor. The night the Mad Lord defeated the Fiend, I was just a kid. I distinctly re-member lying in my bed hearing footsteps on the roof—*bump, bump, bump, bump*—running across to the adjacent house. That was the Fiend fleeing with the Mad Lord in pursuit. Gives me chills when I think how close I was to him. He ran across my rooftop with me only feet away."

"You sure it's a 'he', A-Ram?" Stenstrom asked. "I heard the Fiend was a woman."

"Oh, that old theory again? It's been debunked by Lord Roderick of Dee."

Stenstrom was about to say something when Taara butted in. "What does your family do, A-Ram?" she asked, trying to change the subject, bored with it.

"Fishing and canning mostly. I never liked the sea much. Flying's another story. My brother had an old 22-Merc Suborbital. I got it going when I was young, and that's what I learned to fly on. I love to fly."

"How many brothers and sisters do you have? I've got one—one brother, and we fight all the time," Taara said, seemingly enjoying the *get to know you* session.

"Eight," A-Ram said. "Five brothers and three sisters. I'm the youngest—my mother had a hard time with me and could have no more afterwards. My oldest brother Ephelrood is the pride of our family. He married a Caroline."

Stenstrom thought a moment. "A Caroline—you mean a lady from the House of Caroline? They're Xaphans aren't they?"

A-Ram beamed. "They are. There's an old story about the Carolines that my brother heard of and put to the test. The story goes that, if you venture out to the ruins of Caroline manor bearing gifts and wait there in the moonlight, then you may be rewarded—a Caroline Lady might just pop out of nowhere."

"So, your brother went out and waited amongst the ruins of an abandoned manor with gifts, and a woman just appeared?"

"That's right. Her name is Lady Ezthold. It's a very romantic tale." A-Ram appeared rather envious.

"Hmmm," Stenstrom said. "A-Ram, does the word 'Carofab' mean anything to you?"

"No. Why?"

Stenstrom wanted to say something, but he held his tongue. "Never mind."

"My brother," A-Ram continued. Not only did he have the good fortune to marry a Caroline, but he also had the distinction of participating in the Sister's Program once."

"The Sister's Program?" Stenstrom asked. "Only once? You've never participated, A-Ram?"

A-Ram blushed a little. "Our family—the Sisters normally don't pay us any mind. Calverts—they just don't seem to like us much." He appeared curious. "Bel, have you participated ... with the Sisters, I mean? Belmont is a

Zenon House, is that right? Zenons are usually favored amongst the Sisters."

"Yes, A-Ram, it is. And, to answer the first part of your question, I have."

A-Ram stood there behind the wheel—clearly wanting to know more. Taara smiled. "Bel, I think A-Ram's pretty keen on this Sister thing. I think he wants to know how many times you've corked a Sister and is afraid to come out and ask. That right, A-Ram?"

He didn't reply.

"Well," Stenstrom replied. "I've never thought about it in quite that fashion, Taara, but I've participated twenty-seven times."

"Twenty-seven!" A-Ram exclaimed, spitting. "Twenty-seven times? You, by yourself, have nearly quadrupled the output of the entire A-Ram line with the Sisters since it was patented years ago. Why so many?"

"I don't know. I … really don't. They just come. They come often."

Taara laughed. "Ha! I'll bet they do!"

Stenstrom knew why—he knew perfectly well; he simply didn't want to say. Being spurned by the Sisters was a bad slap and public humiliation that A-Ram appeared to feel quite strongly about. Programmability, as it was called, meant a lot in the League. He looked devastated.

Taara tried to change the subject. "So, Bel, what about you? Where are you from?"

"Tyrol."

"Where's that—I don't know Kana much."

"Esther region, by the sea."

"What's your dad do?"

"He's a Fleet captain. He's commanded the Warbird *Caroline* since before I was born. And no, before you ask, his ship, the *Caroline,* has nothing to do with the House of Caroline previously mentioned."

"Why are you a Paymaster then, Bel?" A-Ram asked. "Why—what with your father and all, and apparently the Sisters approve of you," he said with a touch of bitterness. "Admiral Derlith at first could not for the life of him figure out why you didn't simply join the Fleet. He was certain you had some sort of criminal past and was determined to uncover it."

"Really?"

"Yes. He says you're a sorcerer—is that true?"

"I've been trained as a Tyrol sorcerer, yes."

Taara was fascinated. "What does that mean?"

"Not much— it means I have various skills which come in handy every so often."

Taara stared at him. "Do something?"

"Oh, please …"

"Come on, Bel, do something," she persisted.

"Like what?"

"I don't know, anything."

Stenstrom thought a moment. "All right. Taara, pretend I'm a bad guy. Get the drop on me with your SK."

"You want me to draw on you?"

"Sure."

"Wait a moment." Taara pulled her SK , unloaded the mag, and checked the chamber. She seemed satisfied. "Ok, Bel, you ready?"

"Ready."

In a blur Taara pulled her SK. "Ok, you're covered, I …" Taara looked around. "Bel? Bel … where'd you go?"

His chair was suddenly empty. She shot up and touched his chair. "You invisible or something?"

"Nope," came his voice from the other side of the bridge.

She whirled around. "Where are you, Bel?"

"Right behind you."

She turned and there he was, back in his chair.

"Wow!" she said poking him in the shoulder to see if he was real. "Did you see that, A-Ram?"

"I did. Very impressive."

Taara poked him again. "How'd you do that?"

"Sorry, I can't tell—that's a sorcerer's first rule."

"You know what you could do on Bazz with skills like that?"

Stenstrom laughed. She returned to her chair and remagged her SK. "So, Bel, you sneaky guy you, why did you become a Paymaster?"

"It's a difficult story."

"Seems to me we've got nothing but time," she said, taking her Marine coat off and loosening her boots. "You guys mind if I take my boots off—they're killing me."

Stenstrom sat there—contemplating his life.

With two thuds, Taara's boots bounced to the floor. "So, what about your mom then? What about her?"

My mother...

"My mother's dead, passed away. She was a socialite; she had no particular profession. She raised me and my twenty-nine sisters, as our father was often at sea."

"Twenty-nine sisters?" A-Ram asked. "No brothers? That's odd."

Yes, yes it is.

The questions kept coming and Stenstrom, sitting in his chair, fell into nostalgia as he listened to A-Ram and Taara.

Bad birth ... *A-Ram had a bad birth.*

Mother/Father ...

Sisters. *The Sisters spurned him.*

The House of Caroline ... A-Ram's brother married a Caroline from nowhere. Carofab. A fraud?

Zemuda ...

Sorcerer ... *Tyrol sorcery is forbidden.*

Paymaster ... *Your father's a great captain. Why are you a Paymaster? Why??*

How had he come to this place?

✶ ✶ ✶ ✶ ✶

"Push! For your baby's life, you must push!!"

Lady Jubilee of Belmont-South Tyrol, sweating and near-delusional, was in dire trouble.

She previously had twenty-nine children. She'd never had a problem carrying or delivering any of them. She could typically wear her expensive gowns all the way up to the end, then, lying on a Tyrol altar, her child would literally fly out of her.

The one she was presently in the middle of delivering was her thirtieth. It had been a rather difficult pregnancy, the two-year period laced with bouts of angina, bleeding, pain, and periods of madness and raving—an odd case to be sure. And the delivery itself was proving to be a challenge, the Tyrol altar beneath her staining with blood, salty fluids and sweat. Five Sisters of the highest order presided over the delivery and appeared concerned. They struggled to save the life of the baby. The Sisters normally showed little emotion, but, in this case, they were clearly frantic.

Lady Jubilee and her partially delivered child were both dying.

With no Marines present, the Sisters had no way to speak with Lord and Lady Belmont. However, their thoughts seemed most plain.

"Push, damn you, Tyrol woman! Push, or we shall tear you apart to get at the child. The child shall live—you are of no concern!!"

"Push!!"

Two years prior, when Lady Jubilee, normally such a vibrant and powerful woman, began showing signs of sickness in her thirtieth pregnancy, her Lord Stenstrom became quite concerned, as any husband would for his wife. He took time away from his duties as captain of the Main Fleet Vessel *Caroline* to personally tend to her. Seeing her in the early stages of deterioration, he took his lady to see the Hospitalers in Tyrol for help, and they were perplexed.

At first they simply thought Jubilee's age was playing a factor—she was over two hundred years old, after all. However, after testing, the Hospitalers determined Lady Jubilee was in model shape. She was fit, typically plump in a modest way as was her body-type, and extremely healthy—a standard Elder woman.

They tested her for signs of sickness or poisoning—nothing could be found. Still, her symptoms were clear: she writhed in bouts of invasive pain, she fell into madness and began to walk a road of slow deterioration that could lead to her eventual death—all the signs were there.

Stumped, the Hospitalers noted everything unusual and pertinent about the lady that they could use to aid in their analysis. Her hair was a bright silver in color—Pewterlock, the shade was called in the east, a trademark of her House Tyrol heritage. Lady Jubilee had a number of vices. She liked to indulge in smoking as was the fashion in the Esther region, and not simply the demure, tiny cigarettes mounted on a stick as ladies often enjoyed; rather, she smoked a large, home-made coal that was almost large enough to be considered a cigar. She smoked them quite often; however, she had given the habit up for her pregnancy—she was loudly eager to take it back up again as soon as she delivered. She also enjoyed the occasional stiff drink, not fruity cocktails, but good, stiff "men's drinks"—but again had given the practice up for her pregnancy. She was medium-sized for an Esther woman and carried a bit of extra weight, but nothing so excessive that might explain her symptoms.

The Hospitalers also shared with her their pre-natal assessment of the child: a boy, a fairly big one. Though lacking an heir, Lord Stenstrom was reserved at the news of a boy-child. He had twenty-nine daughters, and twelve of them had false-indicated as a boy, so he wasn't holding his breath.

Fearing for her, the Hospitalers, seeing no other course, thought the safest thing would be to terminate the pregnancy—Lady Jubilee's welfare was possibly at stake. Though Lord and Lady Belmont already had twenty-nine children, they didn't want, if at all possible, to give up on the child and decided to go to the Sisterhood of Light for help. Such a visit was their last choice, for Lady Jubilee's House of Tyrol was historically not close to the Sisters for a number of reasons—still, this was for their unborn child.

They visited the Sister's research facility at Valenhelm and, though graciously welcomed, they got the usual Sisterhood treatment—a smiling disinterest. The Sisters, being the Sisters, had little time for such a mundane thing as a troubled pregnancy. They took the test results the Hospitalers had given them and promised to go over the findings and reply in short order.

In other words, the Sisters weren't going to help them.

So, they returned to their holdings in Tyrol, and Lady Jubilee continued to suffer, her symptoms becoming severe to the point of her being bed-ridden, her husband and her children sitting at her side in their grand bedroom trying to keep her spirits up.

Time passed, and Lady Jubilee fell into protracted madness, eyes blank, hands trembling. Fearing for his wife, Lord Stenstrom Commed the Hospitalers: please, save his Lady, he said to them frantically over the Com.

End the pregnancy. Save her life.

The Hospitalers arrived the next day from their sanctum in Tyrol, ready to perform the unhappy procedure.

A contingent of Sisters also arrived.

Although they, on the surface, behaved in their usual demure fashion, the Sisters nevertheless appeared a bit anxious—a bit windblown. They intercepted the Hospitalers and, after a lengthy meeting with them and Lord Stenstrom, insisted that the pregnancy continue.

The Hospitalers objected—Lady Jubilee was clearly in dire straits. She had twenty-nine children, and sadly, the thirtieth should be terminated.

The Sisters insisted they be allowed to take action. They went into her room and closed the door. When they emerged some time later, they announced the lady and her unborn child were both fine.

Lord Stenstrom went to Jubilee's side. There she was, resting in bed on a mound of pillows, a little sweaty, but otherwise doing much better than she had been.

"My Lord, my Lord …" she said softly.

Whatever the Sisters did behind the closed door of the bedroom, it was effective; her sanity was restored, her pain managed.

The Hospitalers demanded to examine Lady Jubilee. The Sisters dismissed them outright.

After that, the Sisters became quite interested in Lady Jubilee's pregnancy. They remained in close attendance, visiting often, monitoring Lady Jubilee's progress, and eventually took up temporary residence in a chapel on the green, so that they could stay close by should their help be needed at a moment's notice. Their protracted presence was galling, not only for Lady Jubilee, but for the people and Lords of Tyrol, for the Sisters were considered a prying and dangerous nuisance in the region. The Tyrols as a people and the Sisters had never been close.

The thing Lady Jubilee had dreaded was finally at hand …

Lord Stenstrom sat by Lady Jubilee's bedside. The grand bedroom room was decorated in old Tyrol signets and inlaid mosaic. Through the many windows, afternoon sun filtered in along with the steady gritty sound of the surf from the sea.

Two Sisters sat nearby, each flanked with their usual Marines. The Sisters were asking a series of probing questions, and there appeared to be no way of getting out of it.

Lady Jubilee did not want to answer questions from the Sisters. She had many secrets.

Lord Stenstrom, feeling the tension in the room, tried to break the ice and send the conversation down a suitable path. "Great Sisters, may I offer a thought regarding my Lady's condition?"

"You may, of course, Lord Belmont," a Marine said.

"There is a long-standing Wirguild placed upon my Lady's head. Perhaps her condition is a result of that death-mark."

"We are aware of the Wirguild placed upon the Lady Jubilee's head. We have determined that no provable malfeasance or similar activities have been acted upon her in such regard."

Lord Stenstrom nodded. "I see, I see …"

The Sisters turned to Lady Jubilee. "You are in your final weeks of pregnancy, Lady Jubilee," a Marine said for one of the Sisters. "Your distress and continued symptoms are caused by an unusually high demand made upon your body by your unborn child. We have not seen the like in some time. We have, through herbal, botanical and chemical remedies, arrested the problem and you shall carry your child to term without fear or further worry, provided you allow us to continue your treatment."

"We are grateful, Great Sisters," Lord Stenstrom replied.

"We have questions, for both of you, and desire an honest discourse. You need not fear or be modest in this. We simply need all information possible to ensure our diagnosis is sound and our prescribed treatment appropriate."

Sounded reasonable enough.

Lady Jubilee resisted. She did not want to answer questions from the Sisters. She had secrets, many secrets.

They instantly detected this, easily reading her surface thoughts "We care not for your Tyrol ancestry. We are aware that we are not trusted or, for that matter, well-liked in this area. We know the ancient Tyrol lords did not love the Elders. You need not fear—our interest in this matter lies solely with your unborn child. Any secrets or breaches of Elder law committed by you or your House are of no concern at this time."

Stenstrom and Lady Jubilee looked at each other and clasped hands, the both of them dreading what was to come.

The Sisters began. "The condition of your child does not look to us to be natural. Did either of you take, or otherwise indulge in, anything unusual prior to the conception of this child?" the Sisters asked them. "Please be honest."

As per usual, the Sisters were grappled into their minds, taking their answers both by ear, and directly from their thoughts. Lying would be pointless, and might possibly provoke more questions.

Jubilee swallowed. "I … took an herbal fertility mixture, to promote my body's ability to bear children, as I am getting rather old. I have often done so."

The Sisters noted her admission. "Your body is fully healthy and your age is of no concern. Such an herbal remedy shall, as we understand, promote the production of triple X chromosomes, and most certainly ensure that you shall bear a girl-child. You must have been taking this remedy for some time, as we see you have twenty-nine daughters, and no sons—a statistical impossibility, as Lord Belmont is perfectly virile and his Y counts are normal."

"Clearly," she replied.

"Where did you get this herbal fertility remedy?" a Sister asked.

Jubilee was uncomfortable. "It is a family remedy. I made it myself."

"We see," the Marine said for a Sister. "And you are skilled in the herbal arts?"

"I … have some skill, yes."

The Sisters didn't react. "In a normal situation, we would be interested in learning more of this herbal remedy, to test and determine if it is safe and legal for practical use; however, what is done is done. Again, as previously stated, we shall confine ourselves to observation and treatment in this matter."

Jubilee was relieved.

The Sisters turned to Stenstrom. "And you, sir?"

Stenstrom cleared his throat. He felt the Sisters' collective gaze cutting into him deep. He spoke. "Before our latest pregnancy, I … purchased a serum which was purported to promote the creation of a child with admirable genes.”

The Sisters noted his comments. “And you wished for a boy-child, yes?”

“Yes, I have made no secret of that. Our House needs an heir.”

Jubilee turned to her husband. She looked like she wanted to say something but held her tongue.

“You wish to add something, Lady Jubilee?” one of the Marines asked.

She faded back into the pillows and said nothing.

The Sisters continued. “And where did you acquire this serum, Lord Belmont?”

“Bazz—it was sold to me by a reputable pharmacy and vigorously argued as safe.”

The Sisters noted his admission in their usual fashion, displaying little emotion one way or the other. “We have heard of such things and know the potion you speak of. This Bazz potion … it shall certainly guarantee you the birth of a boy-child. Are we correct?”

“That is its promised effect, yes.”

Again, Jubilee looked like she wanted to have a private word with her husband, but she couldn’t with the Sisters present.

“And that was all you took, Lord Belmont?”

“Yes.”

“We have detected certain other compounds present in Lady Jubilee’s body—we believe that the potion you took on Bazz was tainted somehow.”

“Tainted? The Hospitalers detected no poisons or taints.”

“Indeed, we have knowledge the Hospitalers do not, but no matter. We have arrested its effects as best we can.”

The interview went on. They insisted nothing was wrong, either with herself or her unborn child and that the herbals and serums they took, even with the odd taint, should not prove harmful. They prescribed a revised retinue of herbal treatments, which appeared to calm her symptoms, and took their leave.

She was in her final weeks of pregnancy.

✶　✶　✶　✶　✶

“Push! Push, woman, push! By the Elders, to protect this child, we shall

dash you aside without hesitation!"

Jubilee screamed, the altar beneath her dripping with dark blood. Lord Stenstrom took her hand and whispered in her ear. "Push, my lady, push. Our child is almost born."

"Something's wrong—something's wrong! She's tearing me apart!"

"Our baby is almost born. Just a little more."

"I can't!"

The Sisters had enough. Their actions clearly indicated that they had little care or sympathy for Lady Jubilee. It was the child they wanted.

They TKed into her, wrenching her flesh aside without regard or mercy.

Jubilee arched her back and uttered a cry of anguish that was soul-shattering.

Through torn flesh and shattered bone, their child was free of her womb. Held aloft by the Sisters, it took its first breath and cried.

✷　✷　✷　✷　✷

When Jubilee awoke some time later, she discovered the Sisters had departed. The Hospitalers were back. They had labored through the night to save her life, for, as she was later told, the Sisters had nearly torn her apart and left her for dead.

They had worked hard, and she was out of danger. She was a strong woman.

"Child? Where's our child? Where is she?"

The Hospitalers and Lord Stenstrom leaned over her. "The child is fine. Our son is fine, Jubilee," Lord Stenstrom said.

Her eyes, previously heavy-lidded and bleary, snapped open with fury. "Son? A son!" she said, trying to sit up, her voice ragged. "There will be no sons—I have told you that! I have told you that!"

The Hospitalers were shocked. "Lady Jubilee, please try to calm yourself."

"Keep out of this!" She pointed at Lord Stenstrom. "When you are no longer at peril, then you shall have a son—not before!"

"There will be no more children for you, Lady Jubilee. To save you, we had to remove your womb," a Hospitaler said. Lady Jubilee was shocked at the news. Womb gone—no more children? How could this be? Her bearing completely changed. Though she had now thirty children, the fact she could have no more filled her with such loss. "No sons for us ... No sons for my Lord ..." she moaned. The Hospitalers must surely think her mad.

Lord Stenstrom went to the nearby crib and picked up a bundle of blankets. "Here, Jubilee, see our son."

She scowled, regaining her fury. "I'll murder this infant before I've a chance to become devoted to him, you watch! You watch! I'll not be heartbroken! I'll not attend his funeral as I shall yours!"

The Hospitalers stood there, not quite knowing what to make of this display.

But, Lord Stenstrom, holding the perfect baby boy in his arms knelt down and showed him to Jubilee. She looked at the bundle and gasped with joy, her fury instantly forgotten.

"Look, look at our son."

"Our son ..."

Their perfect baby boy. All it took was one look.

2

—The House of Belmont-South Tyrol,—

Lady Jubilee of Tyrol hailed from the eastern Esther city of the same name. Although officially of Esther stock and occupying Esther lands to the northeast, the Tyrols had always considered themselves a separate tribe—the eighth tribe as they liked to say descended from the lost Tartans of old. During the time of the Elders, they mostly shunned the star-faring activities the Vith, Esthers, Remnaths and Zenons took up with relish, contenting themselves to stay in the eastern reaches of Esther, avoiding the stars and concerning themselves with things considered forbidden. They were a silver-haired, smoky people, divested in things arcane and non-Elder. There were supposedly mystical schools located somewhere in the craggy city that taught Black Magic, various sorceries, forbidden chemistries, dark herbals and other questionable subjects to their students, so much so that the Sisters often visited the region hoping to discover more about these alleged schools and what was taught there. The Lords of the City, however, were charming and quick-tongued, always able to side-track the Sisters and allay their sundry fears and suspicions. Tyrol was such a pretty place by the sea, the people silver-haired and lively, and, therefore, what bad things could possibly be going on under all that splendor?

The third daughter of seven, Lady Jubilee of House Tyrol was reputed to be a top graduate of one of those hidden schools of sorcery. It was said she knew how to brew poisons, cast spells, summon demons, construct death totems, and other such blasphemies that, should the Sisters become aware, were crimes punishable by death. She was medium-sized, fair-skinned and a tad plump in an attractive way. She bucked tradition and wore her silver Pewterlock hair short with a large, rather pronounced "swoop" of bangs parted on the side—her short hair becoming her personal trademark, making her instantly recognizable wherever she went. She had numerous "trademarks"—

her short hair being one and her rather inflated bowling average being another. Carrying a 260-280 average, she was said to have bowled two consecutive 300 games. Not to be outdone, her brash, confrontational nature was another notable trademark she bore. In her youth she was a feisty, rather catty woman, often feuding with this lady or that over minor slights and perceived insults, and was not above threatening to cast the occasional spell or curse to intimidate a rival or make her point clear. Lady Sephla of Cone once went to the Sisters complaining of an attack of warts—and that Lady Jubilee of Tyrol had done it via arcane methods. A great deal of angry letters and venomous encounters were exchanged after that incident, Lady Sephla demanding justice and hoping to see Lady Jubilee bending in the stocks for a day or two. Jubilee seldom allowed an occasion to pass without making her thoughts on Lady Sephla plainly known whether at home or in public, and she even bedded down her betrothed and wrote all about his various carnal strengths and shortcomings in the local postings.

... terrible kisser. Tiny cowleg ...

Lady Jubilee wasn't above a bit of harlotry to humiliate a rival.

Still, unpleasantness aside, Jubilee could be winsome and rather fetching and had the face of an angel with the demeanor to match—case in point—the day she met her husband to be.

St Gala's Veil. She was enjoying a fabulous Nether Day ball in the city of Jacarta with several of her sisters. She'd had several dances with various gentlemen and excused herself to take a short rest. Smoking her usual cigarette behind the cover of a convenient potted plant, she overheard Lady Sephla of Cone's younger sister, Vendra, excitedly speaking to her circle of Ballwig friends regarding a handsome young gentleman of whom she was very keen on. She had invited the fellow, Lord Stenstrom of Belmont, to the ball via correspondence and was positively taken with him. She announced to her friends that she was instantly in love. And they clapped and congratulated her.

Jubilee listened to all this and crushed out her cigarette. A churlish wave passed over her. Where was this man the foolish Vendra of Cone was babbling over—this Lord Stenstrom of Belmont? She was going to steal him away from her, feed him, drink him, possibly bed him, and make a point of being loud about it. Let Vendra's sister wail to the Sisters about that!

With bad intentions, she ventured out into the ball to perform her dirty work.

She spied about, trying to seek him out of the crowd.

Where was he, she didn't know. She had to ask. A gentleman pointed him out. He was standing over there ...

Over there.

Oh my...

Just look at him ...

Lady Jubilee stopped in her tracks.

There was Lord Stenstrom of Belmont, the sixth son of a prominent Zenon House, standing by the tables, dressed in a Fleet uniform and framed in blue, getting punch for Lady Vendra. It was said she instantly fell in love with the handsome fellow at that moment, open mouthed and heart-struck. What began as a tawdry ploy to humiliate a rival's sister, became the first moment of the rest of her life.

As per usual with Lady Jubilee, none of her exploits could pass without hints of sorcery or under-handed doings floating about. She got him away from Lady Vendra, turning on all of the considerable charm she possessed, casually engaging him, pulling him into privacy. A momentary word became a protracted aside, an innocent inquiry, and then a dance across the floor. It was said by her rivals that she put something in Lord Stenstrom's drink that night, or cast him a potent spell. In any event, after their first dance together, Lord Stenstrom lost his heart to Lady Jubilee of Tyrol, their glittering night of dancing turning into a lifetime of love and devotion, as he soon made her his lady.

$$* \quad * \quad * \quad * \quad *$$

The enemies Lady Jubilee made that night at St Gala's Veil were many and persistent. No longer was she engaged in social cattiness with a foolish rival, for this was now a matter of the heart and Lady Vendra of Cone became not just a social enemy, but a mortal one as well.

But, as time would tell, Lady Vendra would not vent her rage on Lady Jubilee herself, but on those she loved.

$$* \quad * \quad * \quad * \quad *$$

It was a usual custom for the lady to relocate to the House of the lord she'd married. However, Lady Jubilee couldn't bear to leave her beloved Tyrol, and her father Carjil, a lord swimming in Tyrol money, put up a fair fortune to renovate an old Merian monastery complex south of the city, complete with gardens, chapels and ballrooms, and offered it to the new couple as a gift. The estate was sprawling with a view of the sea and the secluded, breathtaking monastery, freshly rebuilt and ready to accommodate, was truly lovely. Lord Stenstrom, upon touring the rolling, wooded grounds, agreed it was a fabulous home and promptly relocated from his traditional lands near Brynthia on the flowing banks of the Great Blue Pierce River in Zenon. There they began their life together, the brand new Belmont-South Tyrol branch.

3

—THE WIRGUILD—

The courier rode up the sea-side lane. He arrived in a grand afternoon procession of float cars from the League offices in Armenelos. He and his vast entourage were admitted to the manor grounds and, while they waited outside, the courier was allowed to await the Lady in the parlor.

"Great Lady," the courier said in his polished burr as Lady Jubilee entered the parlor holding her new baby daughter Beryla in her arms. "Well met. I am Lord Marist of Grenville. I have come to your wondrous home by the sea bearing an official dispatch from the League Ex-Commons. The nature of the dispatch compels me to deliver it in person."

It had been a little over two years since Lady Jubilee met her Lord Belmont. After a whirlwind romance, where she was promptly impregnated, they made lavish plans to be married. Several months later, a daughter was born to them.

Lady Jubilee, still carrying her baby, approached him, and he bowed. "Good sir, you are most welcome here. Our home is honored with your presence. I shall be pleased to hear your dispatch."

Lord Grenville bowed again. "I am compelled to deliver it to both yourself and Lord Belmont. Both must hear the dispatch."

"Lord Belmont is at sea in his Fleet ship. He is not here."

"I am aware of Lord Belmont's important duties in space. I have a portable Com, directly fed into the League's communication network. With your permission, we may make use of it to contact Lord Belmont directly."

Lady Jubilee approved, and Lord Grenville pulled the tiny Com from his coat and set it up. Soon, the flickering image of Lord Stenstrom loomed in holographics.

Lord Grenville then pulled a scroll from his coat and began his oratory in a singing, joyous voice. "I, Lord Marist of Grenville, am here in the presence of Lord and Lady Belmont-South Tyrol bearing an official dispatch from the League ex-Commons on behalf of the Sisterhood of Light. I am compelled to inform your Greatness, Lady Jubilee of Belmont-South Tyrol, with Lord Stenstrom of Belmont-South Tyrol in attendance, that a legal Wirguild has been issued and approved against the Lady Jubilee."

On the Com, Lord Stenstrom appeared shocked. "A Wirguild?"

"Yes, my lord. A Wirguild is a public declaration of revenge against an individual Household or against a single person. The Sisterhood of Light holds the final say to whether a Wirguild is accepted and made legal or not accepted and therefore rejected. The League Ex-Commons is then tasked with formally informing the parties involved."

"I am aware of that, sir. Who is issuing the Wirguild?" Stenstrom asked.

Jubilee cleared her throat and shuffled uncomfortably. Baby Beryla gurgled.

More singing from Lord Grenville. "The Wirguild has been issued by the Lady Vendra, fourth daughter of the fabulous House of Cone, against the Lady Jubilee of Belmont-South Tyrol."

Lord Stenstrom was beside himself. "Why in the Name of Creation does Lady Vendra of Cone wish Wirguild against my wife?"

"The Lady Vendra wishes it known to all that the Lady Jubilee of Belmont-South Tyrol, with malice and intent, did willfully steal a man for whom Lady Vendra of Cone did announce her love."

"Love? Is she referring to me? That cannot be—I barely know Lady Vendra and have only met her in person once. And, by the by, that was over two bloody years ago!"

"A Wirguild, sir, is not something that is happened upon quickly or without considerable debate. There are appointments to be made, visits to the various strongholds, and cases for and against to be argued before the Sisterhood. Yea, two years is a rather speedy process for a Wirguild to be duly delivered. And, it is here at last." Marist began singing again. "Be it also known that the Lady Vendra did firstly submit a Wirguild against the entire House of Belmont-South Tyrol, but such request was denied by the Sisterhood. This Wirguild is between the Lady Vendra and the Lady Jubilee alone. If Lady Vendra should take revenge against any other of the Household, she shall be in contempt of the law and appropriate action shall be taken against her. I do bade you, Lady Jubilee, to be at your guard and defend yourself appropriately at all times."

After a little more discourse, Lord Grenville gave the Wirguild scroll to Lady Jubilee and took his leave, his mission completed.

Two days later, Lord Stenstrom returned home—he taking a leave of absence from his post.

He was irate. "Why, Jubilee, does Lady Vendra wish to do you harm? I would think, of any of us, she has cause to be angry with me. We had been introduced via correspondence by my late mother Caroline. The Cones are a fine family from Jacarta in Remnath, which isn't too far from our traditional home in Brynthia. We got on well via correspondence—she seemed a delightful young lady. She invited me to a Nether Day ball in Falz. We had only just met, when you caught my eye, and I discarded her for you. Therefore, if that is what she is angry over, then I should sit down and talk with her."

Jubilee sat there, fidgeting with a cigarette. She fumbled with it, eventually tearing the paper, the tobacco spilling out. "My love, she has good cause to be angry with me."

She took a deep breath and started. "I have been a social rival of her older sister, Lady Sephla, for many years. It's just nonsense, a snide comment here, a social slap there—I don't know who started it or when, but we have been at each other's throats in such a fashion for years. At the Nether Day ball, I was sitting with my cigarette, and, over my shoulder, I could hear Lady Vendra talking to her Ballwig friends. She was very excited. She was talking about you, how it was love at first sight for her. And then I, remembering my rivalry with Lady Sephla, decided to steal you, just to humiliate her."

"Why would you do such a childish, catty thing?" he asked.

"I don't know—that's just what we do—it's almost expected. Sephla did the same thing to my sister Charity on Saluting Day with her fellow several years back—they even got caught in the cloakroom with their knickers down. It didn't occur to me not to try and humiliate her sister."

Stenstrom cupped his face with his hands and listened. "Go on," he said.

Jubilee crushed the remains of the cigarette up in her fist. "Oh, darling, though I started it with all the wrong intentions, the moment I saw you standing there, I fell in love with you too. Everything I said to you at that time, and ever since, has been genuine."

They said a few more words, and Lord Stenstrom forgave Lady Jubilee and took her into his arms.

She then went on to assure him that she could take care of herself; still, Lord Stenstrom took an extended leave of absence from the Fleet and stayed home—ready to defend his wife at all costs.

The days and weeks passed. Nothing unusual happened. As the Cones were from far away Remnath, there was little to no chance of Lady Jubilee happening upon her in the street. There was one story of the two of them being invited to the same Ballwig party in the city of Jacarta. They saw each other, had a few words, and excused themselves. According to the story, they were found on a secluded terrace, Lady Vendra brandishing a pair of long, sharpened hair-pins and Jubilee holding several daggers between her fingers. They appeared to be ready to begin a mortal contest. Interrupted, the two quickly put their weapons away and exited in opposite directions. After that, Lord Stenstrom wrote Lady Vendra a letter stating that what happened at the Nether Day ball was his fault and to forgive Lady Jubilee, but he received no reply.

Shortly after, Lady Jubilee received word that Lady Vendra had tried to kill herself. Having survived her suicide attempt, she had been declared mad and taken away to live out her life in a convent somewhere in the backwater of the League. With Vendra gone off, nothing more happened, the stir the Wirguild caused seemed to have blown over, and life began to return to normal at Belmont Manor.

Except for one small thing.

Lady Jubilee was a consummate worrier—she always had been, and that feature of her personality only got worse after being wed and subjected to the Wirguild. She didn't fret much for herself, as she was more than capable of properly defending against an attack should defending be needed. But, for those unfortunate enough to bear the brunt of her love, she could be unreasonably smothering.

With Lady Vendra's Wirguild lingering in the nether reaches of her mind, Jubilee began looking at everything twice, examining hard to see if any hidden threat existed—regardless of the fact that Vendra was sequestered in a distant convent and insane. Anything, no matter how small or innocent, could be laced with hidden traps and subtle danger. Lady Vendra could have helpers carrying on for her despite her condition.

And she laid a vice down, on both her husband and her growing pool of daughters.

She considered her husband. Lord Belmont was an officer in the Stellar Fleet, a Com Officer of great regard, and was nearly ready to face Appointment to a brand new *Webber*-class starship being assembled in Provst. When her husband got the Appointment at last, Jubilee was excited and rather proud of her handsome husband, as she should be. She bragged to her circle of friends about what her husband has accomplished and how his future was bright. But then, her friends began telling her how dangerous it was being in the Stellar Fleet, how the Xaphans were an implacable enemy, and how many husbands and wives set out in their graceful ships, never to return. She sat there listening, fanning herself, feeling a tightening in her chest as they went on and on.

Hijackings

Abductions

Battles

Spontaneous hull breach

Decompression

Micro-meteors

Micro-Frags

Metal Fatigue

Mid-Space Collision

Stellar Mach

Stellar Mach Dampening

Atomization due to Stellar Mach

Xaphans

Moorlands

Radiation

X-Rays

G-Rays

N-Rays

Spoilt food

Stellar Mach sickness

Stellar Mach Madness

Gift-Valve

Blood bending

Spacing

Boarding

Mutiny

Revolt

Insurrection

Infection

Scurvy

Buggery

Slavery

When they finished the dire list, Lady Jubilee was near ready to pass out with fright. She had no idea Fleet-work was so dangerous. It was said that her arch-enemy, the Lady Vendra of Cone, had—prior to her madness—greased Jubilee's friends to fill her ear full of sordid tales of Fleet work and space travel, playing on her fears, hoping she would do something drastic.

And she did.

Jubilee listened to all the tales and was terrified. She begged her husband to reconsider, to quit the Fleet and do something else—anything. She pleaded with him.

He laughed and assured her he would be fine. What's more, he wanted to honor his beloved wife by naming his new ship after her, for it had not yet been christened.

She flatly refused, so he named it the *Caroline,* after his departed mother and began his long career as a captain in the Fleet.

The years rolled by. Lady Jubilee heard through the gossip circles that Lady Vendra was back on Kana, released from the convent and in her right mind afresh.

The Wirguild was on—it had to be. The world seemed a dangerous place to her all of a sudden. Here were Xaphans and battles in space, and there was this maniac she heard of to the south in Calvert—some person slaying the detritus of the wharfs. All these things played on her mind and made her fear.

Soon after, there was "The Incident" which really pushed Lady Jubilee over the edge regarding her husband's occupation. She was delighted when he returned home to Belmont Manor early, his old ship *Amazing* needing a bit of scheduled refitting, which worked out well because the *Caroline* was soon to be ready to launch.

But then she began hearing stories of what really happened to cause *Amazing* to come home early: his ship came upon a derelict in space, sending out a coded distress signal. They responded, investigating in kind.

The derelict was filled with shaddout explosives that ignited, destroying the derelict and slightly damaging *Amazing* in the process, wounding several crew.

Explosives?

In her mind, this incident could mean only one thing—the Wirguild. An attempt had been made on her husband's life; she was certain of it. She went to the Sisters, and they rebuffed her—there was no proof Lady Vendra of Cone had anything to do with the matter. She then confronted Lord Stenstrom and he laughed it off. It was a Xaphan ship they'd come across—they often have a great deal of explosive ordinance aboard. Nothing to worry about.

Nothing to worry about?

4

—A Need for a Son—

And Lady Jubilee fell into a protracted state of mourning, always expecting her husband to fall, to die in space. She took to wearing black on days when he had to leave with his ship.

However—Captain Stenstrom was a good captain, a skilled captain. He endured and never fell despite many adventures in space.

In a puerile attempt to blackmail Lord Stenstrom out of the stars, Lady Jubilee decided to use their children against him. "You wish an heir, my love? When you place your feet upon the ground for good, then you can expect a son, an heir to all we have. Until such time, you will have Belmont daughters."

It was said that the lady, falling back on her alleged sorcerer's knowledge, had learned various arcane methods of preselecting the sex of her children, as in the manner the Black Hats can do, and that she was determined to have girls, to keep them from following their father to the stars—more things for her to worry about. The fact that there were great numbers of ladies in the Fleet serving right next to her husband didn't occur to her. Jubilee expected ladies to behave just like she did: to have no profession; to sit in social circles; to bowl, to smoke; and, whenever possible, to create gossip. Many in and around Tyrol speculated on the method Jubilee used to prevent the creation of a son: potions, poisons, complicated spells, enchanted items—the list went on and on.

In any event, whatever she was doing worked, eventually racking up twenty-nine daughters as Lord Stenstrom re-appointed to his ship time and time again. Lord Stenstrom, though, was delighted with his daughters, and he loved all of them as they grew into lovely ladies and went their own way. But, as the decades passed and he began to get older, the pressures of succession began to present themselves. They had all sorts of callers at the manor, including demure cousins and discreet distant relatives, friends of friends, even the Lords of the city of Tyrol; each wanted to discuss what was to be done with the holdings of Belmont-South Tyrol should no heir be born.

Everybody, it seemed, was lining up to carve the estate into small lucrative pieces, and nobody wanted to be forgotten or left out. There were already twenty-nine daughters and no sons, and surely none of the latter could be expected by this point. With no heir, all they had would be lost. All their property and wealth would be redistributed to any game enough to step up and seize it, and their twenty-nine daughters could expect nothing; such was the time-honored but rather unfair custom of succession in the League.

Lord Stenstrom, under pressure, began railing Lady Jubilee for a son— the House of Belmont South-Tyrol, needed an heir; otherwise, their branch would fall. If only for their daughters' sakes, they needed a son to protect their assets.

But Lady Jubilee, the most stubborn woman in Tyrol, would not budge.

No sons, no lost coffins to cry over. The day he left the Fleet, that's when House Belmont South-Tyrol, would have its heir, not before.

But apparently, Lord Stenstrom had learned a thing or two himself in his travels. It was said he received a mysterious letter on gray paper one day in his Fleet bag, one with no return stamp. It was said the letter detailed how Lady Jubilee had been taking some sort of homemade potion to prevent the creation of a male child through the years, and that she had no intention of discontinuing its use until he retired from the Fleet. If he ever wanted a son and secure the succession of his household, he would have to fight fire with fire.

Go to Bazz; the letter said, *seek the Elixir of the Gods and you shall have your son.*

And Lord Stenstrom did just that. On Bazz, he discovered a local pharmacy selling a mystical substance that would, in essence, super-charge his Belmont seed, adding wings to his male YY sperm and lead weights to the female XX. Additionally, these "God Sperm" would be packed with nothing but Stenstrom's best: his courage, his brains, his tenacity, and so on. Paying a healthy price in Bazz credits, Stenstrom took the vial and left the pharmacy. He returned to his ship and downed the potion, feeling quite invigorated afterwards.

He would later hear that the pharmacy burned to the ground shortly after he made his purchase.

So, thusly armed with a loin full of "God Sperm", the next time he took his loving, silver-haired lady to bed, something remarkable happened—a battle was waged within her womb, Lady Jubilee's herbal-enhanced male-killing eggs against Lord Stenstrom's "God Sperm."

Apparently, the God Sperm carried the field as, two years later after a very difficult pregnancy, Stenstrom the Younger was born.

* * * * *

Stenstrom the Younger was a delightful boy; everybody thought so, including his army of older sisters, most old enough themselves to be his mother, and the younger ones as well. Dark-haired in the Belmont fashion, bright and smiling, he lit up Lady Jubilee, she sitting and watching him play with his two next youngest sisters, Virginia and Lyra, for hours on end in the nursery and about the grounds.

Circumstance, though, appeared to be conspiring against Lady Jubilee and her new son. The Wirguild of old was still in effect, and with the birth of her son, Lady Jubilee saw sinister conspiracies and hidden threats floating about the manor more than ever. She was convinced Lady Vendra in far away Remnath was at it again in earnest, and, even though the Wirguild was legally only for Lady Jubilee, as with *Amazing* decades before, it appeared she was going to come at her infant son, as that's what would hurt Lady Jubilee and the House of Belmont-South Tyrol the most.

Apparently Lady Vendra was quite patient—she'd waited over eighty years.

One evening, Lady Jubilee found a poisonous wasp in Stenstrom's nursery, placed there in a glass vial through the window. She had a terrible nightmare of a spring-loaded, iron-jawed trap lurking beneath the sands of her son's play area. She awoke from bed and ran to the play area, finding nothing, but was certain she'd seen the outline of it in the sand—that it had been there and been removed.

Then, one afternoon, it happened. Her son was abducted. Lady Jubilee had taken her daughters Virginia and Lyra, along with the toddler Stenstrom, to the city to see a childrens' play in the park. Virginia wanted some candy from an inviting stand. Lady Jubilee turned away for a brief moment to get it for her, and, when she turned back again, Stenstrom was gone, the remains of a Waft cloud quickly dissipating in front of his stroller.

A crowd gathered as Jubilee screamed for help. A hastily organized search of the nearby city streets found nothing.

Lady Jubilee took her daughters and went straight home to get her coach. She was going west to Remnath, to face Lady Vendra of Cone and kill her— perhaps she hadn't given her enough credit for holding a deadly grudge. Perhaps she should have done this years ago. And if her son had been harmed in the least, if one hair was out-of-place, she would kill every last one of them, including hangers-on, servants, passing associates and family pets.

When she got to the manor, she was surprised to find a contingent of Sisters waiting for her.

Her son was happily playing at their feet.

The Sisters told her that they had, in fact, listened to her pleas regarding Lady Vendra's improper conduct and been diligently monitoring the situation. By attempting to abduct her son, Lady Vendra had violated the terms of her Wirguild; therefore, it was immediately revoked, and Lady Vendra had been taken into custody and was to be punished in an undisclosed location.

The Sisters, through their Marines, told her they were glad they could help, and that her son was a joyous, beautiful boy and a testament to the virility of House Belmont-South Tyrol.

Jubilee was elated for the praise and took her son into her arms. She never had much good to say about the Sisters, and they'd nearly been her death during her pregnancy, but they had come to her son's aid. "Whatever we have is yours, Great Sisters, for my son's life."

"Thank you, Great Lady," they replied. "We shall remember that ..."

5

—THE RUINS OF CAROLINE—

Belmont Manor was divided into several wings. Stenstrom and several of his sisters lived in the east wing, and his parents, along with any of his remaining older sisters, lived in the northern. As he steadily grew and became more aware of his surroundings, one thing was made perfectly clear—the manor home and the grounds surrounding it comprised his entire universe, and that universe was sternly ruled by an implacable all-knowing, all seeing goddess.

His mother.

Sitting at the grand table for meals, Stenstrom usually sat toward the back end where he could see outside through the Merian arches to the hillside beyond. His two favorite sisters, Lyra and Virginia, usually sat with him. The rest of his sisters appeared like adults to him, like their mother—regal, elegantly dressed in their Belmont-South Tyrol gowns, their various heads of styled hair a mixture of Pewterlock, half-Pewterlock (black and silver), and black. One of his sisters, Ione, had blonde hair, the burnished color of a golden candlestick, and nobody was quite sure how that happened. Ione was a blonde oddity at mother's black and silver table.

As Stenstrom grew old enough to understand the goings on around him, he soon discovered that, though he had a great many sisters and only one mother, she was equally disruptive in all their lives. Mother, by herself, surrounded every one of them in a smothering embrace, and the situation, though apparently harmonious on the surface, was anything but.

The game was played many times over the years, with any of a number of his sisters sitting at one side of the board, and his mother, the grand-master, sitting alone at the other.

He recalled his sister Celesta sitting there properly with knife and fork in hand, her hair a gloriously shiny shade of Pewterlock. "Mother, I hate you," she said quietly.

"Is that a fact, Celesta? And no, you shall not marry that fool from Tuk. Whoever heard of such a thing?"

Celesta sat there stiff as a board, posture perfect, hair perfect, with only her trembling utensils held in white-knuckle fingers betraying the rage she was feeling within.

His sister Nylar, sometime later: "Mother I wish to go to the schools in Vithland …"

"And why do you want to go to the schools in Vithland?"

"I wish to learn mathematics. I believe I would excel at such a course of study."

"I will not have a mathematician for a daughter."

"But I have already filled out the required forms and passed the necessary entry exams. Please, Mother."

"No, Nylar, and that is all, least you wish to face the knife."

Knife and fork trembled in her hands as well.

And on and on it went, each sister being foiled in one manner or another by their omnipresent mother. Of course, there were the short-lived rebellions, the minor schisms—the empty chairs at the table from time to time, Stenstrom's sister, the radiant Calami, being the most persistent at trying to escape, at running away. Her chair was frequently empty at the table, but always—always, there was the flash of smoke, the clap of thunder, and there was Calami, dazed, bewildered, with a travelling hat tied to her head, often holding small suitcases and other baggage.

Always, there was the whirling about and shrieking in frustrated rage, usually right in front of everybody at the table. "Right on time," Mother said. "Come, remove your hat and eat your dinner, young lady—we shall discuss this in more depth later."

Stenstrom came to learn there was no escaping mother—run wherever you wanted, hide wherever you liked, mother would find you and have you home in a literal flash of smoke. He had no idea how mother accomplished the things that she did—but she did, the proof was at the dinner table—an empty chair at the beginning of the meal, an enraged, trembling sister occupying it by the end.

Mother was everywhere in the manor—almost as if she were the manor—a living, silver-haired embodiment of the house. She could move silently, and she could vanish from sight and pop up out of nowhere at any given time. The shadows in the manor and on the grounds were full of mother—she could emerge out of any one of them whenever she wished.

Stenstrom and Lyra often played in the old Merian ruins dotting the grounds, looking through the old telescopes and old astronomical instruments left there.

"What are these things for?" Stenstrom would ask, putting his eye to the viewfinder.

And mother's voice would answer. "They are for seeing the star that only the Merians can see. A star that doesn't exist."

And there she was, like a ghost.

Yet, however stern and unbending Mother was, she was also loving and nurturing, having equal time for all her thirty children. There was enough time in the day to tend to her children—mother would stop time and make the day longer if need be, such was her power, he thought.

He recalled seeing his sister Calami—yes, that same Calami who often tried to run away, Calami the rebel, Calami who said she hated Mother—weeping into her chest, sobbing over a man who had jilted her. "There, there," Mother said holding her heart-broken daughter. "There, there ..."

✳ ✳ ✳ ✳ ✳

"Tighter! By Creation, make it tighter!" Stenstrom heard coming from his sister's room as he walked down the corridor. He was on the prowl for Lyra—that little tart. She had gotten him into a painful wrestling hold and made him say "uncle!" earlier in the day and he was going to get her back.

The door to his sister Constance's room was ajar, and a yellow beam of light came spilling out. He peeked in.

Inside was Constance's large bedroom with an open terrace and a view of the sea. Constance was sitting at her parlor, apparently getting ready for a night out. His other sisters Jonnia and Ione—the weird blonde-headed sister—were there attending to her. Jonnia was working on Constance's hair, and Ione was pulling on the strings of a tight corset, squeezing Constance into a painful, sunk-in hourglass shape.

A holo-terminal image spun on the boudoir—the image of an oddly dressed, green-haired woman was illuminated there.

Ah!—there were Virginia and Lyra sitting cross-legged on the floor watching.

He crept up and got Lyra from behind, pulling her backwards. She managed to turn around and they were arm in arm, grunting, rolling about on the floor. Though Lyra was several years older, Stenstrom had matured to the point where she couldn't muscle him around anymore. He pinned her down, though she struggled fiercely.

Constance turned to them. "Will you two cut it out!" she hissed. "If you want to fight, go outside into the hallway and fight. This is important."

Stenstrom had a powerful respect and a bit of awe for his sister Constance. She was seven sisters down the line and, to him appeared as a fully grown woman. She was tall and broad-shouldered and carried herself in a distinctive manner. He let Lyra go and they seated themselves next to Virginia, who was eating from a bowl of fruit. She offered a piece or two to Stenstrom and he took them.

"What are you doing?" he asked as Ione continued pulling on Constance's corset.

"I'm leaving," she said. "I'm going Carofab."

"What? Why?"

She sighed, both from Stenstrom's question and from the tightening of the corset. "Because ... I need ... to go. I need to be my ... own person. I've had … enough. Gah!!"

Stenstrom gazed at Constance. She looked odd. Jonnia had made her face up in thick white makeup, especially around the eyes, which were heavily highlighted in black. Her cheeks also were deeply rouged. Her Pewterlock hair was pulled into a strange style and painted a distinct shade of fern green. She appeared to be making herself up in the image of the green-haired girl floating on the holo-terminal.

Ione, her foot placed at the small of Constance's back, tied off the corset. Gasping slightly, Constance stepped into a black silk garter inlaid with sequins. She pulled it up to mid-thigh and arranged it.

"What's that thing?" Stenstrom asked.

"It's my attempt to duplicate a VERY MARY."

"A VERY MARY?"

"You're full of questions tonight, aren't you, little brother?" she said.

Ione then fetched Constance's gown. As she put it on, Stenstrom could see the frilly, somewhat garish gown wasn't what his sisters usually wore. It was outrageous and strange in a trashy, post-modern style Mother would never approve of. Again, just like the holo-terminal image.

"Before you ask, this is a Caroline gown, Bel," she said, touching up the black makeup around her eyes. "I've spent months putting it together."

"What's a Caroline?"

"An old House that went Xaphan long ago. Their ruins still stand to the west in the Halalands. As the story goes, every so often, a Caroline maiden will simply pop up out of the blue amid their ruins. That's the VERY MARY—that's how it works. If a Carline maiden gets into trouble somewhere, the VERY MARY zaps them back safe and sound to their ancestral grounds. Gentlemen seeking a bride often go there bearing gifts, hoping to encounter one. I'm going out there tonight and I'm going to win a love—I am going to go Carofab. I'm going to pass myself off as a Caroline maiden. According to the 2-6-10 spy network, I understand Lord Trevor of Howell shall be out there tonight, and I am going to meet him amid the ruins, disguised as a Caroline."

"What if a real Caroline lady shows up? I heard that actually does happen sometimes," Ione said, tying up Constance's gown.

"Then Lord Trevor will get a lovely show—I'll scratch her eyes out right in front of him if I have to."

Constance stood, looking odd and rather austere in her Caroline gown, weird hair and heavy makeup. "All right, I think I'm ready." She shook her hand and produced, out of thin air, a small, round mirror. She looked herself over. "Yes, yes, I am ready. Oh, this is so exciting!"

Stenstrom was confused. "So, you said you want to be your own person?"

"Yes."

"So, you're going to do that by pretending to be somebody else?"

Constance stopped and thought a moment. "I am going to be my own person … by … pretending to be someone who *doesn't* have our mother. How about that?"

That made sense to him. "Oh," he said.

Constance went to Ione and hugged her. She moved on to Jonnia and hugged her too.

"Mother will not allow this," Stenstrom said. "She'll have you back here in no time."

Constance turned to Stenstrom. "Will she?" She pointed to the door. "Look there."

Stenstrom turned to the door. When he looked back, Constance was gone—vanished.

"Constance?" he asked.

"I can do what Mother can do, Bel," came her voice from behind him. *"And, I know all her tricks—I know how to avoid the Maidens."*

He looked behind and there was nothing there. He felt a hand touch his shoulder and there she was, all strange-looking again.

She smiled, knelt down as best she could and gave Stenstrom, Lyra and Virginia a common hug. "Oh, you three little sprouts, how I love you. Be good to each other, and don't let Mother put an end to all of your dreams. Promise me that."

"When will we see you again, Constance?" Virginia asked.

"I don't know. If all goes well, possibly never."

With that, Constance vanished again. Her voice called back on a cloud.

"Farewell ..."

✳   ✳   ✳   ✳   ✳

Constance's sad parting was a bit overly-dramatic, as Stenstrom soon learned. He would see his big sister Constance again, many times, she sitting at the table on holidays and at other times with her new husband, Lord Trevor of Howell. Though he heard that Mother had been enraged at Constance's antics—passing herself of as a wayward Xaphan maiden—she apparently found favor with Constance's bold inventiveness, and Lord Trevor was welcomed to the family warmly.

In later years, Stenstrom would wonder if Lord Trevor ever realized that his Lady Constance, the woman who appeared before him in the ruins of Caroline manor was not, in fact, a Caroline. He had to, as he didn't seem to be a complete idiot. He wondered if it really mattered. He'd gone out there to find love, and his mission had been accomplished.

The Ruins of Caroline

6

—The Blood Promise—

Lady Jubilee was a smothering blanket, protecting Stenstrom from every harm and perceived threat she could. It could have been that Lady Jubilee, in her fearful mind, was seeing things that weren't there. She continued to see threats coming for her son left and right, from the incarcerated Lady Vendra. If Lady Vendra's hope was to create uncertainty, unrest and panic in Lady Jubilee's mind, then she had succeeded. That had to be the most fiendish revenge of all.

Under Jubilee's watchful gaze, Stenstrom grew into a strong boy, bright-eyed and eager to meet the world around him. Though he was several years younger than Virginia and Lyra, he was fully able to keep up with them, his body and face only marginally addled with the childhood Puffies. Lyra, a certified tomboy and self-proclaimed 'Son of Belmont-South Tyrol' at first resented Stenstrom, loudly denouncing him as a fraud and an intruder. However, as he began to show his prowess, Lyra warmed to her brother and accepted him as "one of the guys."

Stenstrom grew up in a virtual bubble. Smothered by his fearful mother, all he knew was the confines of Belmont Manor and its lands. He rarely got to see the city hugging the coast to the north, and almost never was placed around children his own age. He knew his mother and father, his older sisters, Virginia and Lyra, and the house staff, and that was all.

They were the only people inhabiting his lavish but rather small world.

One thing soon became very clear, something his mother could not hold back: Stenstrom had inherited his father's love of adventure. He and his sister Lyra loved watching the vids and posts of bold men and women doing grand things. They thrilled to stories of adventure and quest. They followed the exploits of the colorful vigilant from Rustam—the Mad Lord of Walther, a man of apparent skill and power who took things into his own hands without waiting for the Sisters to tell him to act.

And, they turned to gaze at the stars and all the possibilities that were there. Using the Merian telescopes placed about the manor grounds, he and Lyra often gazed at the stars. They thrilled whenever they caught a glimpse of a Fleet vessel in their viewfinder, watching it soar, off to wherever.

Looking up into the sky—there was freedom, a place where their father sailed. They made a wager between them as to which would become a Fleet captain first, Lyra or Stenstrom.

And there was the steady stream of gifts that flowed in. Pint-sized Fleet coats, hats, leggings, boots, buckles, toy weapons—the works; certainly gifts from his father in space, hoping that his son would want to follow him some-day. There were models too—of the *Caroline*, a proud *Straylight*–class War-bird, the second to bear the name. There were small toothpick models, large dura-plas ones, even holo-projections with controllers. Lyra and Stenstrom tore into them, putting the clothing on and marching about the manor like lit-tle captains, their holo-*Carolines* soaring through the halls. Lord Stenstrom's son and his tom-boy daughter both had their hearts set on joining the Fleet.

Oddly, one summer when he was nine, Lyra stopped talking about joining the Fleet and sailing the stars. She also stopped looking through the telescopes and wrestling with him in the sand pit. She began wearing gowns—some-thing she'd always resisted. What had gotten into her, Stenstrom wondered.

He didn't have long to find out.

SNAP!!

He had that dream again, of sand and something terrible jumping out of it. The dream of his sisters staring at him open-mouthed. The dream of his terrified, screaming mother.

Bel!!

Stenstrom the Younger was roughly pulled from his sleep by several people dressed in black robes.

"What's this?" he said, trying to wake up. In the dark he could see the Fleet coat and hat that he had been wearing before going to bed thrown over a chair.

Even though he was only nine years old, he was strong—strong enough to wrestle Lyra full out and hold his own though she was five years older. He struggled.

A cloying mist was sprayed into his face. Immediately his strength drained away from him and he fell limp.

Though their faces were covered, he recognized a few of them as he was carried from his bed—Jen, the maid, Laurie, the cook, and Lyra, his sister.

Lyra?

"… sis …" he managed to say.

"Don't struggle, Bel," Lyra whispered. "Just relax; it's going to be all right, I promise."

Saying nothing further, they dragged him through the interior of the manor, and out into the gardens and pebbled walks.

A fire burned ahead.

They entered a courtyard centered with a large fountain. A brass tripod was set-up in front of the fountain basin, and a fire burned in the tripod's pot. Tending the reddish fire, fueled by various oils and fats, was a robed woman.

He was thrown down to the pebbles. As he watched, the woman picked up a knife and plunged the curved blade into the fire.

When the blade began glowing a rosy red, she pulled it out and approached.

The woman was slight and plump, and her hair was a lilting shade of silver. It was his mother.

It was Lady Jubilee.

He was lifted up off the pebbles and carried before her.

She held the sizzling knife up and let him see it.

"We are not here to harm you, my beloved son," she said in a monotone, her voice amplified in the moonlight. "Rather, we wish to protect you. To save you from death. You will make a promise right now—a Tyrol Blood Promise. You will promise that you shall never become an officer or a crewman in the Stellar Fleet. As you make this promise, I shall cut you with this knife. If, you are true to your word, and promise truthfully, you shall feel no pain, and you shall suffer no injury. Should you break this promise, now or in the future, this wound shall burst open, and that shall be your end. I wish you suffer no harm, either by this knife, or by the perils of the Stellar Fleet. I wish to save you, my son."

She showed it to him again—curved and sizzling. "Are you ready?"

Held in place, drugged, he could do nothing but meekly nod.

Several hands undid his nightclothes and bared his chest.

His mother then reached out and applied the knife to her son's chest. "Will you promise, Stenstrom, my only son, that you will never become a member of the Stellar Fleet, as either officer or crewman, as your father has been?"

He looked down as far as he could. He felt no pain, but it looked to all the world that his mother had every bit of that sizzling knife plunged into his chest, right in the vicinity of his heart.

"Do you promise?" she said again.

In his chest, he could feel the beginnings of heat and pain.

"Yes, Mother, I promise. I promise. Please …"

She moved the knife down the length of his chest, finally drawing it out near his belly button.

He felt dizzy and fell to the pebbles, where his robed sister came to his side and helped pick him up.

Jubilee took the knife and put it back into the fire. A line of robed figures emerged from the dark. They were carrying armfuls of bundled clothing: his Fleet coats, hats, shirts, pants. Everything. They threw them into the fountain's basin, making a little mountain. They also tossed in his models of the *Caroline*.

His mother pointed at the pile, and it caught flames, the orange tongues of fire and smoke leaping up into the night, burning cloth and melting the models.

She watched the pile burn for a bit, then turned to him. "Now, I can rest," she said and kissed him on the cheek. "Lyra, take him back to his bed and stay with him through the night. I shall conclude the ritual here and join you in the morning. Watch over him and call for me should anything happen."

Stenstrom was dragged back to his bed where Lyra tucked him in and sat by his side. Through his window, his could see the bonfire of all his stuff out in the gardens.

It was a rough night for him. Stenstrom developed a sickness—an unheard of thing for an Elder—and he sweated into a fever dream.

"How … how could M-Mother do this to me?" he stammered, sweating through his sheets.

Lyra sat at his side and wiped his brow. "Because she loves you. It's her way of trying to keep you safe. You're not the only one who's had a knife plunged into your heart. She does that to all of us. And, this won't be the last time you'll be put to The Promise. As she finds things out, if you go off and do something she doesn't like, she'll drag you back out there again and add onto it—she'll update The Promise. I've been out there four times already."

"My d-dreams. I w-wanted to soar, like f-father."

"And so did I …" Her hand went to her chest.

Lyra kissed him on the forehead, and they watched the fire—both of their dreams turned to smoke. "There's always ways around things, Bel. It might not be what you were expecting or hoping for, but something's always just around the corner. You'll see."

Stenstrom fell into a jumpy sleep, his sister sitting with him all night.

SNAP!! came his dream again—this time a drug-induced nightmare.

SNAP!!

7

—THE WOMAN IN GRAY—

He had a small bundle of items laid out on his bed; a change of clothes, some of his favorite mementos, and a few bites of food. He took the items and placed them in a small backpack.

Stenstrom was taking a page out of his older sister's book; he was running away from home.

His head full of strange, rebellious thoughts, he was determined to see something of the world, to set out on his own. This manor and its grounds were all he knew—was the whole world; yet, with the memory of the knife entering his chest, "home" began to feel confined and smothering.

Home is where you can dream, and then have those dreams quickly taken away in a bit of oil and the soft glow of a fire.

He was nearly finished packing.

"What are you doing?" came a voice.

He jumped out of his skin with fright. He whirled around. Standing in the open doorway was his sister Virginia. She was leaning in, holding a bowl of snacks with both hands. Her messy head of Half Pewterlock hair made interesting marbled streak patterns on her head.

"You scared the life out of me!" he gasped.

"Sorry—what are you doing?"

He returned to his work as she came to his side, still holding her bowl of food.

"I'm leaving."

"Why?"

He felt a momentary sting—the knife in his chest. "Because I don't want to be here anymore."

He finished packing and walked out of his room, Virginia following. "Where are you going?"

"The city."

"And then what?"

They spilled out in into the night, the dewy grass crinkling under their feet. "Why are you plaguing me with questions? I'm going to the city, and then I'm going to vanish into it, just like the Mad Lord of Walther."

"The who? Aren't you at least going to say goodbye to Mother?"

"Creation no—are you mad? How far would I get if she knew what I'm planning?"

They reached the pebbled walk near the familiar Merian ruins, and Stenstrom turned south, his pack slung over his shoulder.

"What about Lyra? Don't you want to say goodbye to her? She's going to be upset."

He hesitated. "Yes, but … you tell her for me, sis. Tell her I love her, and not to worry."

Virginia looked sad. "I love you, Bel."

He gave her a hug, and she almost dropped her bowl. "Love you too, sis." He started walking south.

"Bel, you said you're going to the city, right?"

"Yes," he said on the hoof.

"Well, you're going the wrong way. The city is that way," she said pointing to the north.

Annoyed, he stopped, turned, and started walking north, moving past her as he did. "I know that," he said.

He moved down the walk, passing all the old haunts of his childhood, the places where he, Lyra and Virginia played and crested a low hill. Beyond, the coastline stretched out in the dark blues and pearly grays of night, heading northwest in a rocky curve. About a mile away, straddling the coast and the swampy interior was a huddled, semi-lit collection of stony buildings—the southern proper of Tyrol. As he walked, the city unfolded in front of him in little stages—scattered buildings, a few outlying streets, all mostly dark under the moonlight. Looking back, he could see the manor sitting in the dale, lit up in cheery yellow window light. He could see his room from where he was standing—his bed was there, his toys, his sisters. All he knew was back there in a rectangle of yellow light.

He had a sudden urge to go back. Overhead, a blinking vessel of some sort rumbled by, winged, lit-up, whistling. It banked inland and disappeared, gone as quickly as it came. He was reminded of the Fleet, of the stars, and of the knife in his chest.

He turned back toward the dark mosaic of Tyrol ahead and continued.

He eventually reached the outskirts of the city where the pebbled walk gave way to a wider cobbled street. The whole cityscape around him was relentlessly dark and deserted, the houses and other assorted buildings mostly lightless and without noise. The street he walked was deserted. He wondered, in his child's mind, why it was so dark—why he appeared to be the only living soul around. Shouldn't it be more lively? Shouldn't there be people? He looked up—the night sky appeared odd, littered with stars in unfamiliar constellations.

He thought he heard something, a slight breaking of twig or stirring of rock. He turned to see what had made the noise.

Crouching near a small house on the other side of the street was a shape, like that of a small person pushed up against the wall of the house. The shape sat there, looking at him intently.

"Hello?" he said, surprised at the sound of his own voice, at the loudness of it.

Testing his own courage, he walked across the street toward the figure. "What are you doing there?" he asked.

The figure didn't move, nor did it speak.

As he neared, a storm of some sort, a sudden gust of wind mixed with grit and swirling debris, welled up from the house. Stenstrom coughed and covered his eyes. He gasped for air and quickly stumbled away from the house as fast as he could. After several steps, the cloud of wind and grit abated, and he could breathe. He looked back once and could clearly see a boiling ball of churned-up debris moving down the street away from him. The figure he'd seen hiding against the side of the house was gone.

Astonished, he continued northward, shaken from his encounter with … whatever it was. He approached a small park that was dark and partially wooded. He wanted to find someplace to sit down—to consider his poorly thought out escape attempt. He hadn't expected the world to be so dark and lonely—so full of strange winds and unusual stars. He didn't know what to make of the world. He wandered into the park to gather his wits.

He found a large statue of a fox, carved in a cat-like sitting position, its head pointed upward to gaze at the sky.

Sitting next to the statue, he saw the slight figure of a slender woman.

"Hello?" he asked, remembering his encounter with the thing near the house. Could this person be real?

The woman slowly lifted her head. "Good morning," she said quietly, her voice inflected with an odd accent. "What is a little boy like you doing out all alone at this hour? Please come here."

The woman was sitting on a small bench to the left of the fox statue. It was difficult to see in the dim moonlight, but she appeared to be wearing a gray ladies suit of some sort, with a knee-length skirt. Her slender legs were crossed, and she wore a pair of button-up boots. Her face was thin, with a pair of thoughtful eyes and a pointy chin. A large, flat-brimmed hat sat next to her on the bench. She appeared frail, and slightly bent.

She looked at him. "Why are you out here all alone?"

"I'm running away from home," he said. Having had little contact with strangers, and having been taught to never lie, it didn't occur to him not to answer the woman truthfully.

It also didn't occur to him to not be completely trusting.

"So, your mother does not know where you are?"

"I don't think so. That's the whole point."

The woman reached into the lining of her suit. She appeared momentarily saddened. She pulled her hand back out.

She was holding a knife. Stenstrom stared at it in horror.

"I'm so sorry," she said. "You are such a handsome young fellow—I see so much of your father in your face."

He backed away. "What are you going to do with that knife?" he stammered.

"I'm going to kill you with it," she said standing up. "I've been waiting for you for a long time, to come walking down that road. Please, do not make this harder than it has to be. I truly do not wish to make you suffer any more than is necessary."

He turned to run. The park was alive with shapes—men all around emerging from behind the trees. They were dirty and mangy. They looked to him like the vids of sailors and pirates he and Lyra liked to watch.

"There is no place for you to go," the woman said walking toward him. She raised the knife over her head. "Again, I'm so sorry …"

He backed up against a tree. The woman approached, the knife gleaming.

Thinking fast, Stenstrom changed his tactics. He ran to her and put his arms around her thin waist. "Please don't hurt me."

The woman hesitated. "I … I remember holding you when you were just a little baby, those chubby cheeks, those wonderful bright eyes. I couldn't do it then. I should have, but I didn't. And now here we are …"

"You … you needn't do this. What have I done to deserve this?"

Her free hand came down and lifted his chin. "You haven't done anything. This is a closed circle that we are trapped in, and there is no way out of it. I'm sorry."

She reared back, knife gleaming.

Something appeared next to him in a cloud of black veils. Something breezy kissed him on the cheek.

"No!"

✶ ✶ ✶ ✶ ✶

Stenstrom rose in a gasp. He was in his bed, his room smothered in a layer of night mixed with starlight.

He was in his pajamas. His toys were neatly arranged in the corner. There was no lonely road, no Fox Park, no Woman in Gray.

Through the window he recognized the usual constellations that came out this time of year. All seemed normal.

He lay back and pulled the sheets up to his chin.

What a terrible nightmare.

8

—The Mad Lord of Walther—

When Stenstrom was ten years old, he and his entire family went into the Barbary North Esther city of Rustam for a family gathering. His mother's side of the family had a grand get-together every five years to celebrate the ongoing history of the Tyrol line, to sing their historical praises and confirm once again why Tyrols are Tyrols and not simply an off-shoot of the standard Esther line. His immediate family was fairly large, consisting of his parents, himself, and his twenty-nine sisters, coupled with his aunts, uncles, brothers-in-law, and cousins, creating a veritable army of people to seat and feed. The Tyrols had rented the entire Labyrinth of Rustam for the event, a place of vast gardens and twisting, hedged corridors.

From barely having contact with anyone outside of Belmont Manor to suddenly being thrust into a swarming mass of people, the get-together was bewildering for Stenstrom. Most of his sisters he barely knew—they were much older, had married and moved on long before he came around, and he only saw them on holidays and special events, like this one. He was closest to his youngest sisters, Lyra and Virginia. Lyra had a lovely head of dark black Belmont hair like he did, while Virginia had Half Pewterlock hair, a mixed head of black and Tyrol Pewterlock which reminded Stenstrom of a marble cake.

They sat outdoors in the maze of gardens and hedges, enjoying the mild Rustam weather. Music played, and people laughed as the afternoon wore on. There were many tables set up in the sprawling gardens of the labyrinth to accommodate the near thousand assembled Tyrols. An army of staff moved about attending the people. Stenstrom, wearing his finest little boy clothes, sat at a huge feasting table in the center of the labyrinth with nearly fifty of his sisters, brothers-in-law, and cousins. His parents weren't at that particular table, and he hadn't seen them in some time—he assumed they were off, mingling with other family members. Stenstrom sat somewhere in the middle of the table, flanked by Lyra and Virginia. Lyra's plate was only partially filled as she looked about trying to see if she could recall the names of all these people she barely knew. "There's Celesta over there," she said. "And I think that's her husband. What's his name?"

"I don't know," Stenstrom replied.

Virginia was fully tucked into her heavily-loaded plate of food and wasn't listening. She leaned over her plate, a huge bib was stuffed into her gown.

These Tyrol get-togethers were normally rather dull—just a lot of people eating and talking. However, it wasn't long before the proceedings were rudely interrupted.

A group of armed men appeared from nowhere, Wafting in and covering the hedged exits. They pointed all manner of swords and pistols at the people seated at the table. The staff, that happened to be around, hit the deck and put their hands over their heads.

The band stopped playing. Someone screamed for help.

The sky grew odd, turned a frightening blackish-blue color, and soundless lightning flashed.

"*Shhh, quiet,*" came a commanding voice in a hard Dirge. "*Don't move… Don't move.*" The screams muffled and then stopped all together. The Dirge kept them quiet and still; all those seated at the table appearing as unwilling statuary.

With that, the leader of the villains Wafted in with aplomb. He was a broad, portly man wearing a red coat and a garish hat. His thick, black beard looked like it was composed of animal fur rather than mere facial hair. He looked about and smiled.

"Afternoon, darlings," he said in a flamboyant accent. "I hate to be a bore, but we are to be robbing you of your valuables. I promised my mistress I would be paying the lot of you a visit—she was most keen on it in fact."

"It's Lord Sedgwick of Kold," Lyra mouthed under her breath, unable to fully move or speak under the influence of the Dirge. "The Pirate of Remnath."

Virginia was frozen opened-mouthed, with a forkful of saucy meat halted in mid-flight on its way to her mouth. "What's he want with us?" she mumbled.

Somebody else arrived, a tall woman wearing gray ladies garments and slim, button-up boots. She didn't Waft in, rather she *walked* in from far away, it seemed, across the dark sky, arriving like a goddess. Stenstrom didn't understand what he was seeing. Things didn't quite make sense—time and distance were distorted. The woman's face was mostly obscured by her large, flat-brimmed hat. Stenstrom could see hints of a pointy chin, but that was about it.

He'd seen her before, in a dream, he thought.

She looked around and spoke in a ghostly voice. "He's here, at this table. Fetch him for me. I want him alive!" Lord Sedgwick listened to her instructions intently.

She then walked away, again covering miles across the odd sky, and was gone. When she left, the sky cleared and things appeared to melt back into normalcy—except for Lord Sedgwick's armed pirates roaming about.

Sedgwick pushed his hat away and wiped his beefy brow. "Well, there you have it. Therefore, we're to be robbing the lot of you, and kidnapping someone in particular. We shan't inconvenience you any longer than necessary, but make no mistake, 'Puddings'; do not attempt any heroic use of weapon or Gifts, I warn you. I would hate to have to shed blood here today."

Lord Sedgwick's men fanned out and, holding open bags, began taking items of value, removing rings, necklaces, brooches, watches and anything else they could find that looked valuable. They also leaned over and inspected the faces of all the young men seated at the table.

"Who're we a-lookin' for, Sedge?" one of them called out.

"A boy, should be around ten or twelve, I think. Look for the Puffy ones."

The men began searching anew, carefully inspecting all the young boys.

<Mother! Mother, help us!> his sister Lyra tried to send via telepathy, calling for help.

<Now, now,> came a reply. *<Let's keep this amongst ourselves, shall we?>* It was Lord Sedgwick—he had intercepted her thoughts.

Lyra fumed.

The passing tide of ruffians approached, robbing some, pawing others.

They were just a few place settings down.

"Check that kid there!" one of them said, pointing as he worked to get a large ring off one of his sister's fingers.

The dirty brute turned to Stenstrom.

There was a blast from the near end of the labyrinth. A man appeared in a cloud of wind. He was wearing a blue and green coat, black pantaloons, black bucket boots with spurs, and a Vith-style triangle hat.

Lyra and Stenstrom, unable to move their heads, turned their eyes to him.

The man was wearing a jeweled mask over a well-trimmed mustache. "Dear Sedgwick," he said in a proud voice. "This is a low, even for you, interrupting these good people's dinner."

It's the Mad Lord of Walther, Stenstrom thought. He and Lyra had thrilled to his exploits in the vids and posts for years. He was a notable vigilant from the west, and here he was, in the flesh.

Sedgwick grimaced. "Everywhere I go, I find you close behind, Walther, sniffing my wind! Kill him!" he yelled to his underlings. "Kill this fool, dead, dead, dead!"

They dropped what they were doing, produced a rusty assortment of weapons, and attacked with a shout.

The Mad Lord smiled and threw himself into action. *"Hide, you people!"* he said in commanding Dirge. *"Protect yourselves!"*

"No, stay where you are," Kold Dirged back.

Stenstrom felt sick as the two Dirges clashed and competed in his head.

"I said hide—and that's final!" the Mad Lord's Dirge ripped into their heads as he clashed steel with the first of many henchmen to reach him.

They were free. Stenstrom was seized by his collar and pulled under the table by his sister Lyra. Virginia landed at his side with a *"whuff!"* still wearing her bib. The whole family had thusly taken refuge. Stenstrom couldn't see much under the table. He saw many pairs of booted and shoed feet moving about in confusion, some running in various directions, others Wafting in and out in a cloud. He could hear weapons discharging, shouts and curses, and steel clashing. He could see the Mad Lord's spurred boots mixed in with the other pairs. He could taste the dust that was being kicked up.

A pair of boots suddenly were yanked out of sight, followed by a rough crash onto the tabletop above them. A limp hand bounced into view, lightly clutching a Hit-6 fraglock pistol. Lyra quickly grabbed it and placed it in her sash.

People Wafted in and out in sprays of wind. Men collapsed—some apparently pummeled, others shot or stabbed by the Mad Lord.

The sound of fists crunching into faces and biting steel echoed.

Shoed feet approached at a run. "Gah! Take hostages—kill a few!" a henchman yelled. He looked under the table; there was his wide-eyed, scruffy face. "Wait—he's here! Here's the kid we're lookin' for!" he said as he reached out for Stenstrom.

Lyra pulled the gun from her sash and shot the man in the chest.

Another henchman arrived and knelt down. "What'd you say, Tort?" he cried. He saw Stenstrom. "Ahhh!" he gurgled as Lyra again fired her gun. The pirate fell next to the first man. She put two protective arms around Stenstrom and Virginia, ready to fend off any further attacks.

"You people could help me, you know!" came a Dirge from the Mad Lord.

Now that they were Dirged free by the Mad Lord, lots of daggers were flying around the yard, sent flying by Stenstrom's older sisters, as well as gun fire and sword-play from his brothers-in-law and cousins.

"Damn you lot! Damn you!" Kold cried as a cloud of daggers flew in his direction. He Wafted away, leaving his men to their fate.

Eventually, after a good deal of jostling about and noise, things got quiet in a hurry. Pockets of fallen men lay everywhere. Men babbled in pain; some called for their mothers.

"Hold fast, you!" somebody said.

"Oh, do drop your weapons and sit down will you!" the Mad Lord Dirged.

All around, people dropped their weapons and plopped down to the ground as ordered, nobody able to match the Mad Lord's Dirge.

A single pair of boots approached the table, spurs jingling with each step.

The man knelt down, the leather of his boots creaking.

There he was, the Mad Lord of Walther, hardly even out of breath after all that ruckus. He inspected the dead henchmen. Finally: "Everyone all right under here?"

Stenstrom looked at him: the hat, the mask, the glittering eyes, the handsome face underneath.

Stenstrom thought: *He's not a man—he's a machine—a robot, look!* For a moment, the Mad Lord's face appeared gilded and jeweled, like a high-quality mannequin made of delicate silver and bits of inlaid gold. But, after a second glance, the Mad Lord appeared as nothing more than flesh and blood.

"What are these contretemps?" Lyra gasped. "Where are the Sisters? This is an outrage!"

"It comes with the territory, my lady." He kicked at the dead henchmen. "Did you do that?"

"I did."

"Well done. You Tyrols are always full of surprises. You and your lot fought well. I'll ask again, are the three of you all right?"

"Yes, yes, we're fine," Lyra said, holding onto Stenstrom. "They were after my brother!"

"Were they?" The Mad Lord looked at Stenstrom and did a double-take. Something about the young lad appeared to have gotten his attention. He shook his head and smiled. "Well, what do you know? You're a fine fellow. What's your name?"

"Stenstrom," he replied quietly.

"Well, Lord Stenstrom, keep a clear head and grow up fast, will you? I'm getting too old for this."

"What in the name of Creation is that supposed to mean?" Lyra said, protective of her brother.

The Mad Lord stood. "It means exactly what I said. Good day."

And he vanished with a mighty blast as a crowd of shouting people and their mother and father arrived through the hedge.

Terrance, The Mad Lord of Walther

9

—The Black Maidens—

Immediately after the incident at Rustam Labyrinth with Lord Sedgwick of Kold, Mother's demeanor became even more frantic than normal.

He overheard his mother and father talking in the parlor the next evening.

"The Wirguild is on in earnest, and she is coming at our children! Our children!"

"No, no, I heard she is mortally sick ... on her death bed."

"Then, she has helpers, assassins. We have to take steps! I will take steps!"

The next morning, Stenstrom, Lyra and Virginia were taken down to a small Merian ruin near an outcropping of rock.

Mother was solemn. "The attack on us at Rustam has proved to me that the enemies of our House are many, and will not hesitate to come at you, our children. Therefore, it is time to begin your training. Lyra has some pre-indoctrination to it, so she is a little ahead."

"What training?" Virginia asked.

"Training in matters not spoken of outside of these grounds. Tyrol sorcery."

She laughed. "My friends in the city told me Tyrol sorcery is a myth."

Mother raised her hands and shook them. Six silver daggers appeared between her fingers. She approached Virginia and held them to her throat. "And, are these not real, my daughter?"

She shook her hands again, and the daggers vanished. "As I have done for your sisters before, I will teach you as well. When you have mastered these skills, never again will you be defenseless; never will you be disarmed. You shall walk unseen. No lock shall hold you, and no truth shall bind you."

She produced out of thin air several brightly colored balls. One was magenta purple, one was speckled silver, and the last was solid black.

"What are those?" Stenstrom asked.

"Holystones," Mother said. "I am determining if we are being watched."

She placed the Holystones on the flat surface of one of the Merian telescopes. She watched them for a moment—they just sat there, glinting in the afternoon sun.

Stenstrom stared at the Holystones—they almost looked good enough to eat, like large gumballs. Far away, someone trimmed the lawns west of the manor.

"Good," she said at last, apparently satisfied. She produced an odd-looking key and thrust it into a hidden slot in the rock face. A narrow door opened, sliding inward. "Through here," she said leading them down into the darkness beyond. "Be careful with your footing."

"Where, where are we going?" Virginia asked hesitant of the dark.

"The culverts. They run for miles. They once were just below the surface, taking the drainage water from the Estherlands to the sea. Now, they lay covered up in layers of modern stone and metal framing and are forgotten, the water long since dried up. It is here in these trackless forgotten spaces that I shall teach you all you need know."

"Like Constance?" Stenstrom asked, recalling Constance's seemingly mystical abilities on the night she went Carofab.

"Indeed."

They made their way down a narrow stone staircase, the air quickly becoming cool and damp. Light blossomed—Mother was holding something in her hand that created a soft yellow light. "Continue down. Quickly. No dawdling!"

Stenstrom could see a vast artificial cavern stretching off into the gloom as they exited the staircase. The floor was a flat 'U'-shaped basin about two hundred feet wide. The roof, about twenty feet above them, was a confusion of metal lattice and buttress work. It was amazingly quiet in the depths.

Feet crunching on grit and crushed stone, they walked into the dark for a ways until they came upon a small area that had been cleared out. Stone slabs were arranged in a circle. A line of several large chests sat in the darkness nearby.

"You will find several robes in the first chest on the left. I want you to put them on."

Lyra opened the chest and pulled out three white robes. She passed them out and they scattered into the darkness and changed. When they returned, Mother was sitting on a slab, smoking her usual cigarette, her face lit-up in the orange glow of her coal. Her hand was shaking. They seated themselves around her, and she began.

"You must know by now that your mother has made enemies over the years, some more dangerous than others. I believe these enemies are seeking to harm me through you."

"You're talking about Lord Sedgwick of Kold—the man who attacked us in the labyrinth?" Lyra asked.

"Yes, and perhaps others as well."

"We aren't helpless, Mother," Lyra said.

"Are you? You've no idea what awaits beyond the safety of the manor grounds. It's time to grow up and face the world, and you must have these skills."

"Again, Mother," Virginia said, uncharacteristically defiant. "They say there is no such thing as Tyrol sorcery."

Mother smiled and took a pull from her cigarette. Stenstrom looked at the glow of the coal, orange-red in the dark.

Suddenly, mother vanished.

"Mother?" he said, his voice lost in the quiet vastness of the culvert.

"They know nothing in the city," they heard Mother's voice say, from the shadows. They looked around.

And there was Mother again, sitting right where she was previously. "As I was saying, you three have much to train."

She set up a brass tripod with a pot hanging under it and started a fire. She tossed in a handful of something granular, and the fire leapt up, turning purple. "You shall learn the ways of nature and of the elements, how they relate, how they react with one another—and I'm not simply talking about chemistry. I'm talking about herbalism, cabalism—all the things of the hidden natural world that the Sisters seem to find so repugnant. I am going to teach you skills that shall protect you. You will learn to walk unseen, past both living and non-living eyes. No lock shall hold you; no locked door shall hinder you as well. So, it is time to begin. First, I am going to introduce you to some friends that you all shall soon become very familiar with. I am going to summon spirits that will guard and keep you safe."

"What spirits?" Lyra asked.

Mother smoked her cigarette. "Spirits your elder sisters are quite familiar with, some more than others. Have you ever wondered why we have no expensive security system installed here in our home? Have you ever considered why we have no private army at hire prowling the grounds as other Houses do? That is because we have something better, more seeing, more tireless. We have the Black Maidens. They are manifestations of spirits of the air. They hover over our grounds, seeing everything. Additionally, they are wonderful chaperones. Once summoned, they will follow you wherever you go, and should you need instant assistance, or should I feel you are in danger, they will spirit you away, back home to me. You three have not vexed me much, however, I've been using them on your rebellious sisters for years."

Mother continued. "I shall require a bit of your blood. All of you, I need blood for the summoning. Now, pay attention, the Black Maidens are given lease to locate your position via smell and sight. They can detect you at great distances via smell, and then hone-in precisely by using sight. If your face is covered, they shall not be able to see you. Remember that—your face must be uncovered."

Stenstrom stirred. "Mother, is this really necessary?"

She put her cigarette down and held out a small bowl. "Yes it is. Now, Bel, I shall demonstrate. Give me a bit of your blood."

He took the bowl. Mother produced a dagger and cut him in the arm. He bled into the bowl for a few moments, and she handed him a cloth to tend to his cut. Virginia, watching this, appeared horrified about having to cut herself. Lyra was nonplussed.

Mother added various herbs, salts and metals to the bowl of Stenstrom's blood. She poured the contents into a pot and began stirring. "This process is very delicate—the potential to go wrong is high. What you want is a Black Maiden—and they are fairly harmless."

As Mother stirred, a cloud of steamy smoke issued from the pot. It coalesced into the form of a tall, gaunt, and pale maiden with a sunken face. She wore gossamer veils of black that floated about her on phantom winds. She drifted about, tilting one way, then another. "Please sit next to my son," Mother said.

The Black Maiden looked at Stenstrom and, in a lilting fashion, sat next to him.

"See, perfectly harmless and submissive." Mother crushed out her cigarette. Her tone became dark. "Now, prepare yourselves ..."

The three sat there looking at the ghostly form sitting next to Stenstrom.

Mother continued. "There are other things protecting our House beyond mere Black Maidens. Something cruel and utterly evil. When a Black Maiden encounters someone hostile on our grounds, they summon what I am about to show you. I am going to let you see, so that you will know the difference. Dredged up from the shadow-lands, from the lightless places, are the Soul Devourers, hungry, restless, always seeking their next soul to eat."

Jubilee added something to the pot and the smoke coming out of it became dense and choking. They coughed, sickened with it.

Something rose up in the distance, backlit in a brackish unlight. It appeared to be a naked female rising up with a ballerina's grace, her lean body perfectly formed.

She raised her head. There was no face there, just a huge mouth full of chattering teeth and a seeking, serpent-like tongue.

Virginia, and even Lyra, screamed.

"There is my son," Jubilee said quietly.

The Soul Devourer raised her arms and clenched her hands into grasping claws.

"You may have him."

The creature shouted with feral passion and sprinted toward Stenstrom, eager to tear into him. "YOOOOOUUUUURRR SOUUUUULLLLLLLLL!!" she wailed.

Stenstrom sat there, horrified. Lyra dashed in front of him, ready to stand and fight the unholy thing.

Mother sat there, allowing it to approach. Then she said: "Save my son," and the Black Maiden leaned over and kissed Stenstrom on the cheek.

He was instantly teleported home. He spun about. He was all alone in his room.

Unused back cover concept, by Carol Phillips

10

—His Greatest Enemy—

They sat in the stony darkness of the culvert. Stenstrom was wearing the now familiar white robes. His sisters Virginia and Lyra wore the same. Their training had been going on at a steady rate for nine years, around the calendar without protracted pause. He was now nineteen years old.

Their mother, sitting before them, wore black robes. As usual, Mother slowly smoked a large cigarette with a burning ember that sizzled with every pull.

This old culvert, once flowing with drainage waters from the interior swamps of Esther, became like a second home. They sat in a semicircle in the quiet dark with all manner of arcane flotsam from their years of study scattered around them. There were tripods full of boiling oils and gels heated with purple, red and blue flames. Mortar and pestles, aromatic with the crushed remains of herbs and rare salts, sat pushed aside along with various scrolls and books opened to mystical pages. The books were thick, made of hide and stout vellum, each page meticulously hand copied from mother's originals. Over the past nine years, they'd worked hard, writing down the knowledge Mother shared with them, and each student now had a small library of arcane learning written by their own hand. Lady Lyra's books were very studious and similar to Mother's. Stenstrom's were craftier with generous hand-drawn art, and Lady Virginia's were overflowing with expanded insets and detailed, step-by-step instructions. Near Lady Jubilee was a holo-pedestal—the cheery image of Lord Stenstrom the Older slowly spun, something she always kept near her when he was away on his Fleet vessel that she hated.

Lady Jubilee was, as before, putting her life in jeopardy—she was teaching her children the shadowy and seldom spoken of subject of Tyrol Sorcery, an offense not easily forgiven by the Sisterhood of Light should it become known. Lady Jubilee, as she often said, didn't care about the Sisters and potential punishments that could be in the offing; her children needed these skills and they would have them—the repercussions to herself would be dealt with at another time.

"Now, do it again," she said, her voice echoing around the vastness of the culvert. All heads turned to Virginia as she raised her hands. Virginia had inherited a body shape very similar to Mother's, and therefore was a tad plump in her robes. She shook her hands and, in a blur, two bright blue balls appeared between her fingers.

Jubilee was elated and critical at the same time. "Decent technique, Virginia, but slow hand speed," she said, pointing with her cigarette, the ember making a reddish trail as she moved it about. "I could see how you did that, even in the dark here. You must practice with your dexterity—I have told you so before. Let me see one of your Holystones, please," she said.

Virginia handed one of them to her. She looked at it in the dim light. "There are a number of imperfections in the plaster casing—and it's too thick in spots—it will be difficult to break." She cast the Holystone away, where it bounced off of a stone slab and didn't crack open.

"I expect better next time. It should be hard enough for safe handling, yet thin enough to crack open with the slightest of tosses."

Even in the dark, Stenstrom could see Virginia flushing up a bit.

"Now, Virginia, come here and turn around."

Virginia was shy and apprehensive. "Mother, I'm not ready."

"Come here, Virginia! By Creation, you're as timid and uncoordinated as your sister Deneba was years before."

She slowly stood and approached her mother.

"Turn around."

Virginia winced and turned around. There was a small "click," the sound made loud in the quiet culvert, as Virginia's wrists were bound with a stout set of manacles.

"Now, get out of them, Virginia!"

As Virginia struggled, Mother turned her attention to Lyra. "Lyra has long completed her training. Watch her skill and technique."

Lyra pushed back the sleeves of her white robes and displayed her hands. In a blur, she had six Tyrol MARZABLE daggers nested between her fingers.

Mother was clearly impressed.

"Well done, Lyra!" She reached out and took one of the daggers. "See, impeccable balance. This is what you two have to do." She held it by the tip and sent it tumbling into a solid rock face where it buried to the hilt with a thud. "We often forget the LosCapricos weapon of my family—the MARZABLE, your father's NTH pistol being a bit flashier. But, do not forget your Tyrol heritage and the MARZABLE dagger that comes with it. Make it well and keep it hidden, and you will never run out of them—you will never be disarmed."

Virginia cried out and fell over, her wrists still hopelessly shackled, her robed butt slightly sticking up in the air as she struggled. "I can't, Mother, I can't get out!"

"You have much to train, young lady. Slow hands, thick fingers—you require improvement in every category of the art. Lyra, please save your sister."

Lyra scooted over and reached out. Virginia disappeared.

"Leave me alone!" they heard her voice say.

Mother looked around and pulled on her cigarette. "I will stand corrected, Virginia. You have mastered the art of walking in the shadows—yes, you do that quite well."

There was a clatter off in the darkness. "Oww!" they heard her cry. "These damn things!"

Mother laughed. "Virginia, come back here, and Lyra will take them off."

Virginia re-emerged a moment later, still hopelessly shackled. Lyra approached her, and in an effortless movement had the manacles off.

Jubilee took a pull from her cigarette. "We shall discuss this development in further detail later, young lady," she said to Virginia. "Now, Lyra, shackle your brother."

Lyra smiled and approached. Stenstrom calmly turned and let her put them on.

"Do not be kind to your brother, Lyra. Make them tight."

Lyra squeezed and the manacles clicked tightly into place. She then resumed her seat.

"You forgot something, Lyra," Stenstrom said.

"What did I forget, Bel?"

"These." Stenstrom held out the manacles and handed them to her. She gasped at the speed and ease with which he'd escaped them.

Jubilee sat there in silence, her cigarette glowing brightly. "Now, Bel, I wish to see your MARZABLE."

He shrugged and felt on-the-spot. "I'm not finished with it, Mother."

She held her hand out and motioned with her fingers. He hesitated, then pulled the small silver dagger from the folds of his robes. It had a classic stiletto handle with a tapering blade, sharpened on both sides. He had stained the handle black and embossed tiny stars at regular intervals.

Lady Jubilee carefully inspected the dagger, testing its weight, trying its balance. "Bel, I don't see anything wrong with this MARZABLE—it looks completed to me. I'm very pleased."

Jubilee smiled and gazed at him with a mother's pride. She handed it back to him, where he returned it to the folds of his robes.

"Now, turn it into many."

He raised his hands. He shook them, and six identical daggers appeared between his fingers.

She approved with a nod, as did Lyra. Virginia stewed a bit. "And your Holystones? Let's see those."

Stenstrom shook his hands and the daggers vanished, replaced by four shiny balls of pastel green.

Mother took one and looked at the surface—it was like an enameled ping pong ball. She hauled back and threw it. It smashed against a stone slab and burst into a confusion of spider webs.

"Excellent, Bel—well made!"

Jubilee looked over her shoulder. "Now, Bel, for your final test of the day, I wish you to get up and start walking."

"Walking? Where, Mother?" he asked.

Jubilee pointed into the darkness of the culvert beyond. "That way."

Confused, Stenstrom stood, straightened his robes, and started walking. The stone floor of the culvert was strewn with old pebbles and other bits of wash once carried along by the swamp run-off, and he crunched with every step.

The culvert was vast, stretching off into the dark for as far as his straining eyes could see.

He had no idea how far he had walked when he barely heard his sister Lyra cry out: "Come back, Bel!"

He turned and made his slow way back, seeing nothing at first, then the low purple glow of the tripods came into view along with the three huddled shapes of his mother and two sisters.

When he returned, his mother looked up at him. "Do you know what your trouble is, Bel?"

"No, Mother," he replied.

"You're too compliant. I ask you to walk off into the dark, and you do so without a question." Jubilee turned to his sister, Lyra. "Lyra! Get up and start walking!"

"Why would I want to do that, Mother?"

Jubilee smiled. "You see, Bel—your sister didn't simply take a bizarre order, and nor should you. Are you afraid of me, my son?"

"Mother, you have put me to the knife three times by my latest counting and …"

"There is occasion for the knife, Bel, and there is time when you need to be a man. I have put you to the knife because I love you. I love my children beyond all reason. I have taught you my secrets, and I have made you strong, fully able to see to yourself. Now, with your skills fully matured, I do not have to worry about you quite so much. I would wager your skills against anybody's—Gifted or not, Blue or not. You're a good son, Bel, but I want you to stop being such a good son all of the time. I want you to resist my demands—confound me, challenge me. Look at your sisters before you— they challenged me, and yet they still sit at our family table. Though I am your mother, consider me your enemy. Consider me your greatest, most vile enemy. Henceforth, I shall attempt to confound you and set you to my will. I want you to resist—to confound me in turn. Thus, using your wits, I shall make you strong. Nothing more than your best effort do I expect of you. To give you the will to become your own man—that is the final bit of sorcery I have to teach you, for you have mastered all else."

Jubilee leaned back. "So, Bel, I want you to get up and start walking."

He sat there a moment, then got up and again started walking down the culvert.

After a minute or so, he heard his mother's voice. "Come back, Bel!"

This time, he kept on walking into the deep dark of the culvert.

"Bel!" he heard from far away, but he didn't listen, he kept on going.

After a time of wandering through the dark, he decided he'd gone far enough and turned to go back, but quickly found he was quite lost—he had no idea which way he'd come from. "Mother?" he cried. "Mother!"

No answer.

He spun around, not really sure what to do. He couldn't see a thing, and he had no Holystones on him that would make light.

He heard a sound. It was a soft hiss, like the grating of small bits of dry rock rubbing together. It seemed to be coming from far away, but was rapidly approaching.

He felt he was in terrible danger. He backed away. He felt something dry and abrasive wrap around his ankle, like a coiling snake made of sand or grit. He tried to free himself, but whatever it was had him tight.

He heard something. He heard: *"...belllllllllll..."* in a sort of grating moan.

His first inclination was to panic; however, he managed to recall his untested training. He shook his hand and created three MARZABLE daggers. He quickly let two fly. He could hear the creature moving around his throws in a gritty, snakelike undulation. The MARZABLES bounced off the stone floor of the culvert with a clatter. He heard the unseen creature tittering slightly, as if it were toying with him.

He lined up his third dagger and let it fly. It hit something.

Stenstrom was seized about the waist and held fast for a moment—it felt like a soft beach full of sand—and then it gave him a firm shove, sending him sprawling. He lost his footing and roughly fell to the ground.

Something metallic clattered in front of him—his MARZABLE, returned to him, by the creature?

"...bye...bye..." it hissed. He heard something sliding away in a gritty fuss, and then it was gone.

Three globes of light approached. "Bel!" came his mother's shaking voice, his sisters close by.

★ ★ ★ ★ ★

"Boy, Mother was mad," Lyra said snickering.

Stenstrom, Lyra, and Virginia sat in their favorite Merian ruin down the hillside. Virginia fumbled with her gown.

"She said to resist, so I resisted."

"I don't think she expected you to resist quite so quickly," Virginia said. She shook her hands and nothing happened. "Why am I so bad at this? I don't understand!"

"Keep your hands closer to your chest," Stenstrom said, trying to help with her form.

Virginia got frustrated and vanished into the shadows.

"Virginia, come back here, please," Stenstrom said.

"No! I'm terrible!" came her voice from nowhere.

"Get back here!" Lyra said, annoyed.

Virginia reappeared like nothing, still holding her hands in the same position.

"Thank you," Stenstrom said. "So, what are we to infer from this? Is Mother going to allow us a bit of roam from now on?"

"Perhaps, but I doubt it," Lyra said adjusting Virginia's foot placement. "She might say she wants us to spread our wings, but I don't know if I believe her. I think she's going to sic the Black Maidens on us anytime she wants us home. She's done it before."

"She used them on me last month," Virginia said, readying her hands for another try. "I was visiting at the House of Copperwell when, out of nowhere, a Black Maiden appeared, kissed me on the cheek, and teleported me straight home. It was galling, and a little embarrassing."

"I don't know about you, but I am tired of being sequestered," Lyra said. "I want to stretch out, see the cities, and find a love on my own. Those Black Maidens shall make it impossible—she'll have us back here on a whim."

Stenstrom reached into Virginia's gown. "Don't put your MARZABLE there; it's too difficult to extract. Here is better." He adjusted it.

"Thanks, Bel."

He stepped back and leaned against the old, weathered telescope. "I know almost nothing of the cities, or of the people in them. You two are my best friends. I have no others."

Lyra approached him. "And in that Mother has done you a disservice. How are you to properly interact with your fellows if you've rarely been allowed to do so? There's a big world out there beyond these manor grounds."

"And I've seen almost nothing of it."

Virginia lifted her hands to try again. "Watch your hands," Lyra said. "Now breathe and produce them."

Lyra looked at Stenstrom. "I'm afraid, when you do get out, you're going to be horribly unprepared, have no idea how to act, and probably will get homesick."

"I think you'll do just fine, Bel," Virginia said. She shook her hands. Again nothing happened.

"Not on the upstroke, Sis. On the down stroke. Try again," he said.

"You two and Mother make this look so easy," she said, flustered.

Lyra began toying with the telescope and swung it around to look at the smaller moon Solon which was high to the south. "I've been looking through these old Merian telescopes since I was a child. I've never seen anything other than the ordinary."

"What?" Virginia asked as she flexed her fingers and prepared herself.

"That funny star the Merians say is out there. I've never seen it. How do you hide a star? It cannot exist. The Merians have been deluding themselves, just like we have been."

"How so?" Virginia asked.

"That we'd ever get to live a life that we truly wanted, free of knives and Black Maidens," Lyra said.

Virginia shook her hands and produced one knife between her fingers. "Ah!" she cried in triumph. "For one thing, Lyra, you're looking for the Merian's star in the wrong place."

"What do you mean?"

"You've got the telescope pointing to the south. The star is over there," she said pointing with the dagger to the north-west."

Stenstrom and Lyra looked at each other. "Come again?"

"That big, funny star over there. The yellow one with the red cloud swirling around it, plain as can be. Right over there! Don't you see it?"

Stenstrom and Lyra looked to the north-west and saw nothing but the afternoon sky.

"You see a large yellow star over there?" Stenstrom asked, shading his eyes, seeing nothing.

"Yes," Virginia replied.

"How is it you see a large yellow star to the north-west?" Lyra asked.

"How is it you do not?" she replied. She shook her hands, and her dagger vanished.

11

—The NTH—

Stenstrom the Older was home for the holidays. It was always a happy time when father was home—Mother had a rare light in her eye as she hung on his arm like a school girl. The family together at last.

✳ ✳ ✳ ✳ ✳

Father pulled the old wooden chest off the shelf in his private study. He held it happily for a moment, and then set it down on the desktop.

Stenstrom the Younger sat in the chair opposite him. His sister Lyra sat in another chair nearby. She was in a lovely Belmont gown—that's all she wore anymore.

"Do you know what's in this chest, Bel?" Father asked.

He looked at the chest. "No, Father, I don't."

"A bit of your heritage," he said.

Stenstrom the Older opened the lid. Inside the felt-lined chest were two rather ancient-looking flint-lock pistols. Bel and Lyra leaned forward to get a better look.

The two pistols were mostly made of smooth wood, stained an old reddish-brown and curved in a gentle fashion, like a lazy "j." The stocks were pitted with age, dotted with imperfections. The bases of the grips were capped with ornate brass bulbs, inlaid with fine filigree of gold, silver and lapis. The barrel was, apparently, a simple iron tube that was banded at regular lengths with gold, holding it fast on the stock. It had a large and elaborate hammer mechanism. The hammer was shaped like a large steel "S." The base of the "S" was attached to the pistol via a large, button-like black screw. The top of the "S" held a cherry-red stone of some kind locked in place with a screw vise.

"I think it's time I gave you these, Bel. I've been meaning to for some time, but didn't have the occasion. The NTH pistols have been a Belmont family tradition since the time of the Elders. This set once belonged to Haveral, your grandfather, a great man of Zenon. Now, they belong to you."

Stenstrom sat there and looked at them. Lyra reached into the chest and pulled one out. She held it out to him. "Go ahead, Bel, take it."

He took the pistol and was surprised how heavy it was. He thought about his sister sitting there in her gown. "Father—Lyra is elder; she should have these."

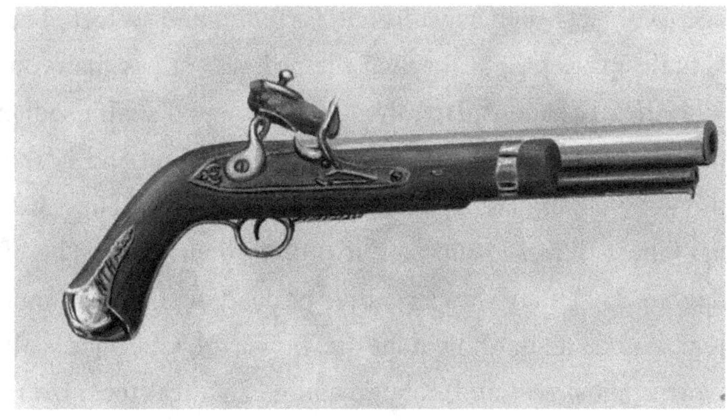

She smiled and shook her head. "I can't use these, Bel." She pulled the other one out of the chest and cocked the hammer with a fussy, springy-sounding click. She aimed at the far wall and pulled the trigger. The large hammer swung around in a dramatic fashion and clanked into the breech.

Nothing happened.

"The NTH pistol only works for men, Bel," Stenstrom the Older said. "There are a number of LosCapricos weapons that are gender-specific one way or the other—the NTH is one of them. Our family being an old Zenon line, the ladies were traditionally expected to be rather demure and above such things as brandishing a firearm—thus the classical image of a Zenon-girl."

Lyra smiled. "It's fine, Bel—take them. None of the elder sisters wanted them. I once had hopes of offering these to my son one day, but these are yours by right."

Bel took the second NTH, the two of them heavy and solid.

"What can you tell me about the NTHs, Bel? What do you know about them?"

He thought a moment. "They are able to destroy nearly anything they hit. They do a great deal of damage, if my reading is correct."

Lord Stenstrom laughed. "Incorrect. That's called a 'Rumalore'—a ruse. Every LosCapricos weapon has to be registered with the Sisterhood of Light, and the Sisters have an exact description of what the weapon does. A Rumalore is a false description that has been registered and is made generally known to the League, though the Sisters know it to be false. The Rumalore for the NTHs is the amount of damage they do—the NTHs actually do no damage to objects such as walls and furniture and so forth because the NTH shot actually passes right through them. I will stress that you take extreme care with these weapons, Bel, though I know you shall use them in a responsible manner. These pistols might look rather quaint and nostalgic, but know you this—they can slay anything set against them. They are sometimes known as 'Ghost-Slayers,' and they live up to their name. They function to the Nth degree. They may slay any, alive or dead, real, unreal, intangible, or incorporeal, and no matter how huge and powerful. One shot is all it takes. They also work against armored, robotic and mechanical foes. Do not expect any large hole or damage to be created, and there is no wounding either—hit a target and they simply fall over and die. I can personally vouch for their power. I've slain creatures with one shot that a fully loaded Marine S/K could do nothing with. I've slain ghosts as well—fear not the supernatural. The range of this weapon is roughly three hundred yards."

Stenstrom the Older pointed at the red stone held in the hammer's vice. "There is some maintenance that goes along with these. The red stone there—that is a cinnabar. You must have a sharpened bit of cinnabar to enter the chamber; otherwise, the NTH will not fire. Cinnabar, as you might know from your studies, is rather toxic and creates mercury if crushed, so, handle it as infrequently as possible. Occasionally, the cinnabar will crack with use and will be rendered useless. It shall then have to be replaced. I have a whole case full of replacement loads, so you shan't have to worry about that for some time to come. As long as you have a whole piece of cinnabar, the NTH shall fire."

Stenstrom the Older smiled. "I've always found it odd that the NTH requires a red stone to fire, yet creates a glowing green blast—rather interesting I might say."

Stenstrom sat with the pistols. He was troubled.

"Why the long face, Bel?" Lyra asked.

"I still feel you have been slighted."

She laughed. "You've always been such a thoughtful young fellow."

Stenstrom slid the two NTHs into his sash. He was struck with inspiration. "I know. Father, will you promise that, when the time comes, you will give your set to Lyra, so that she may in turn offer them to her future son as she wanted to."

Stenstrom the Older leaned back in his chair. "Would that arrangement please you, Lyra?"

She blushed. "Yes, Father. My brother is always thinking of me."

She pinched his cheek and gave him a hug.

"Then it's settled, Lyra. You shall have my set of NTHs to present to my grandson when the time is right. As for now, Bel, let these NTHs keep you safe from any that might wish to harm you."

Initial back cover sketch, by Carol Phillips

12

—THE DEATH OF THE MAD LORD—

Stenstrom was looking all over for his sisters. Lyra was nowhere to be found, and neither was Virginia. Virginia usually wasn't too hard to find—she could usually be found in or near the kitchens, either eating or making something to eat. She was actually a pretty decent cook.

But, today, she wasn't there. He roamed the manor, all their usual haunts empty.

On a lark, he went to the other side of the manor, in parts where he and his sisters rarely went.

He thought he heard something.

"How could they? How could they?" he heard his sister's voice.

He went into the library. Virginia and Lyra were sitting by an open holo-terminal. Lyra was in tears, Virginia was comforting her.

"What's wrong?" Stenstrom asked walking into the library. "I've been looking all over for you two."

Lyra didn't respond; she continued weeping. Virginia looked back. "Sorry, Bel," she said.

Stenstrom came to their side and put his hand on Lyra's shoulder. "You're sobbing like they cancelled Nether Day," he said cheerfully. Lyra didn't respond.

Floating in front of them was a posting. "Are you crying about the news?" he said knocking her in the shoulder again.

The Posting read:

VIGILANT FROM THE EAST SLAIN BY THE SISTERHOOD OF LIGHT

RUSTAM (Synthnet) —Terrance, Lord of Walther, also known locally as the "Mad Lord of Walther" was killed by the Sisterhood of Light

Sunday evening. Declared a public menace after engaging in a horrific and damaging battle in Rustam with Sedgwick, Lord of Kold, the self-styled "Pirate of Remnath", the Sisters presided over the evacuation of Rustam and were instrumental in ensuring the safety of the citizenry. In said battle, Lord Walther allegedly killed Lord Kold and was wanted for immediate questioning by the local authorities. He refused to turn himself in, and the Remnath magistrate declared *Prata-Envita,* a writ granting unquestioned authority to the Sisterhood to handle the matter. The Sisterhood censured Lord Walther and seized his holdings, pending results of an investigation. After repeatedly being asked to surrender, Lord Walther refused, making his slow way south toward a heavily populated area. The Sisters then slew him outside of Rustam, as confirmed by local authorities. The Sisters had nothing further to add on the slaying.

Although considered a vigilant and was openly censured by the Sisterhood on many occasions, Lord Walther was well-liked in the Green Sabre area of Esther for his repeated and well-documented acts of heroism and bravery. Lord Walther is best known across Kana for his uncovering of the "City of the Dead" in Remnath and his defeating of the Fiend of Calvert twenty years ago.

A vigil has been organized at the site of Lord Walther's former holdings and in Rustam by the local citizenry, to both celebrate his life and decry the Sisterhood, whom they claim "murdered" Lord Walther.

Stenstrom read the posting and couldn't believe it. The Mad Lord, an object of his fascination since he was a child, dead …

He recalled his handsome face in Rustam, at the Tyrol dinner, and his actions. He was a good man.

He was a good man.

Stenstrom joined his sister in sadness.

13

—Lillian of Gamboa—

"Father, we have discussed this," Stenstrom the younger said as the two walked the south gardens. The Belmont-South Tyrol manor, once a Merian monastery, sat on a hillside in the distance. With its random placement of white, black and red bricks, its exterior often reminded Stenstrom of a vast gingerbread house covered with candies. Surrounding the manor were mystic walks lined with pergolas and primitive-looking observatories full of star-watching equipment. They were scattered about the hillside and gardens, some in ruin, others used as landscaping features. The Merians once used the equipment to gaze out at their mythical Star of Merian—one that only they could see. Stenstrom and his sister sometimes tried to use the equipment to locate this mythical star, but could never see anything. Virginia said she could see it to the northwest, but he never saw anything but empty sky.

Far away he could hear the waves of the Sea of Esther crashing into the rocky beach.

Stenstrom was incensed; Mother had trucked in yet another young lady for him to meet, an annoying habit she'd acquired.

Lord Stenstrom the Older laughed as they walked the lovely paths. "I know we have; however, it means a great deal to your mother. And, besides, it's St. Porter's Day—good things are supposed to happen on St. Porter's Day."

"Happy coincidence—clever of her to arrange it that way. Mother has been trying to control every aspect of my life since before I can remember. Additionally, per her insistence and direction, I am to defy her wishes and make my own choices. Therefore, as before, I will not see this woman."

"Your mother might seem a bit overbearing, and in some aspects she certainly can be; even so, she does it because she loves you. And, as an added bonus, I think you might like this one—got spirit, I think."

Stenstrom the Younger shrugged. "So, who is it today, just out of curiosity?" he asked.

"A lovely young lady from Esther, Lillian of Gamboa."

"Her, again?"

"I know what you're thinking—many of the Gamboa ilk have made a name for themselves for being rather homely and uninteresting, but this one seems a tad different. I saw her get out of the coach myself as she arrived—she's pretty and seems a vibrant young lady. Let's take your mother out of the equation for a moment, shall we? She's come all this way across the marshes—the least you can do is spend a moment with her and determine for yourself if you wish to get to know her better or not. It's not her fault you and your mother have this on-going contest to one-up the other."

Stenstrom shook his head. "True, but out of sheer principle, I'm not going in there. Mother has to learn that I am not interested in her continued efforts to locate me a bride."

"She's done that for all the children. She's paired off at least ten of your sisters and …"

There was a crack of thunder. As they walked the garden path, the weather began to quickly turn. The clouds grew angry and a strong wind kicked up from the sea.

"I wasn't aware of any storms in the forecast for today."

The two Stenstroms held their hats. This was no usual spring up of bad weather. The clouds banged into each other like two opposing armies and were red-rimmed. The center of the conflagration seemed to be right over their heads.

Sorcery was involved; Stenstrom knew it. Suddenly a thick, reaching fog sprang up.

"Father?" Stenstrom said groping about. "Father!" No reply came.

He whirled around in the fog. This was his mother's doing, and he could expect anything to come running out of the mist, ready to put him to yet another dangerous trial. It was amazing to him how many times his mother mortgaged his soul to simply prove a point, sending a rotting host of minor demons after him, knowing full well he could get rid of them easily with his NTHs—weapons that could slay anything set before him.

The problem today was that he didn't have his NTHs—they had been missing from their felt-lined box that morning.

Mother …

He thought he could hear the babbling of a creek, and smell the stagnant odor of dirty water and drenched mud—odd, there was no creek in the area.

A few feet distant in the thick fog, he saw it—the tepid banks of a creek that had appeared from nowhere. Something swam in it—something with red, beady eyes that watched him intently from the calm water's surface.

A huge, demonic creature in the form of a giant catfish came leaping out of the creek with a drenched roar. It leaned on its fins, clambering toward Stenstrom in a malevolent fashion. The demon fish was a skillet-full of clashing colors. Its scales were a mottled mixture of awful greens and dead ochres, stretched out over a backdrop of blazing, sun-burned red. Its fins were mostly the same shade of blazing red webbing over a scalloped rib-work of black, over-sized fish bones, ending in rather lethal-looking spines. Its reaching whiskers moved about, like a slimy moustache. Its catfish mouth was enormous and glowed slightly from the reddish tint within as if a great fire burned inside.

"Morning, Lord Belmont!" it said. *"I have been summoned to ensure you don't forget to go see your lady friend today! Fail to keep your appointment, and I get to eat you! Isn't that lovely?"*

* * * * *

Lady Jubilee had, for many years, attempted to pair her son, Stenstrom the Younger, to various ladies of standing whom she deemed worthy. One of her favorite social functions was pairing her children off to the various offspring of Great Houses she favored. As Stenstrom was her only son, she threw herself into his pairing with unusual gusto. As per everything Lady Jubilee did, she was very exacting, and rather unflattering in her appraisals of potential candidates, having sullied and greatly angered various Houses with her blunt assessments and quick dismissals. She was looking for an impeccable pedigree, a comely bearing and a high degree of knowledge in the finer things and social graces. Most importantly, Lady Jubilee was looking for a grounded, mundane woman: no Gifts of the Mind, no telepathy and no knowledge of sorcery; she thought it important to counter-balance her son's sorcerous training. As such she ruled out the heroic Vith with their Gifts and a good many of the Zenons as well. She wanted a nice safe Halagirl, or a trusty, earthy Esther woman. She was no longer on speaking terms with several Great Houses whom she'd so insulted. She nearly touched off a disturbing social incident when she publically proclaimed that no Houses of Barrow stock were to be considered for her son: the Dares, Cottens and Tuks reacting strenuously with a fruitless letter-writing campaign to counter her position. Sorry—no Barrows, Vith, Zenons, Calverts or Remnaths. And no Ballwigs either—she didn't trust their intentions (being a founding member of the Ballwigs herself, she knew the unflattering way they tended to treat gentlemen).

Nothing out of the ordinary for her son.

It was quite a shame that she was mortal enemies with the Cones of Remnath (having suspected them of repeatedly trying to murder and abduct her son throughout his early youth), for they had several daughters of fine quality that met her criteria nicely—truly regrettable.

When a potential candidate did emerge who happened to pass all of Lady Jubilee's standards, she would be invited to visit the Belmont-South Tyrol estate and be introduced to Lord Stenstrom the Younger. Normally, the lady would be given a fine breakfast, and then asked to wait in a large ballroom on the north manor grounds called the Chalk House for its white limestone walls. Then, Stenstrom the Younger would be summoned and entreated to go into the Chalk House and see if a rapport was struck.

Stenstrom, however, was on a vendetta in this matter. He was bound and determined to show his mother up—as she fervently requested. She herself asked him to not be such a compliant young man—to thwart her will and set himself against her—though she never failed to get angry when he made a showing of such independence. Many times, he would not go into the Chalk House at all simply to annoy and embarrass his mother; many times he avoided it and allowed the poor lady within to sit all day unattended—she a victim of their ongoing struggle. Other times, he would take one look at the woman sitting there in her gown and walk right back out.

As Stenstrom knew, Lillian of Gamboa, a fine Esther woman, had been asked to House Belmont several times. She was reputed to be a bright young lady, the tenth of fifteen Gamboa children. Usually attired in festive pastels, she was a tallish girl, blonde-headed and blue eyed. She was a noted painter and sculptress with a lovely eye for color and form. Some of her more ambitious works had sold for a fair amount of money and critical acclaim, and she had a small but burgeoning gallery in Gamboa where her works were admired by all.

Lady Jubilee had taken a great liking to Lady Lillian. She personally visited her at her home in Gamboa, had stood in her gallery and marveled at the fabulous works of art she had created, and was generally taken with the lovely young lady. This woman was perfect, so grounded and pretty, so mundane. Lady Jubilee wanted a mundane woman for her son, to keep him properly balanced. When dealing with the arcane, it was a simple matter to become lost in it. Having a decidedly non-arcane companion, specifically a spouse, would provide him with the grounding he needed.

And Lillian of Gamboa seemed perfect. Stately and prim, talented and artistic, but rather dry and humorless, she would do well for her son. Lady Jubilee happily showed her pictures and holo-vids of her son Stenstrom and was pleased that Lillian found him handsome.

So, with a hopeful spirit and an open mind, Lillian boarded her House transport and made the trip across the marshes of Esther to Tyrol to meet Stenstrom the Younger. She certainly didn't quite know what to expect, but she was apparently game to give it a try.

The afternoon came and went. Stenstrom never showed up. Lillian sat in the huge, empty Chalk House all afternoon, alone.

Lady Jubilee's rage afterwards was memorable. *"How could you let that woman sit there unattended?"*

"I did not wish to see her."

"I do not care about your wishes in this matter! You've your House and your name to consider!"

After a vigorous set of apologies from Lady Jubilee, Lady Lillian agreed to give it another go. She said there had been a scheduling error, and that it had been her fault. She begged Lady Lillian to forgive her and please grace them with her presence a second time. Lady Jubilee, with her short head of Pewterlock Tyrol hair swooped in the front, was, above all things, quite ingratiating when she wanted to be, and Lady Lillian forgave the first incident. Not being one to hold a grudge or allow an honest mistake to go unforgiven, Lady Lillian agreed, and again made the trip to Tyrol to meet Lord Stenstrom.

Again, he was a no show. Sitting there alone in the Chalk House a second time, the table full of elegant treats, she sat there in her teal gown and felt humiliated.

Again, she returned to Gamboa—this time in quite a huff.

Again there was a dreadful row that evening in Belmont Manor.

"I am considering making you a guest of our dungeon, boy, or worse!"

"Mother—you yourself have insisted that I confound your various machinations with wit and stratagem. Be relentless, you stated. What think you of it?"

"So I did. Very well, such a position shall force me to take drastic measures! Be at your guard and do not forget that you've only yourself to blame for the consequences!"

Again Lady Jubilee contacted Lillian of Gamboa full of apologies and, this time, said that Lord Stenstrom had been called away at the last moment on urgent business in Tyrol.

Via correspondence, Lillian informed Lady Jubilee that she wished nothing further to do with the House of Belmont and that was that. She then went on a rather scathing letter-writing campaign letting any who would listen know how she was treated at the House of Belmont-South Tyrol.

But, apparently, time heals all, and eventually Lady Lillian sent Lady Jubilee an unsolicited correspondence stating she would forgive the first two incidents and, for a third time, agreed to meet Lord Stenstrom. She wrote it was becoming a matter of pride for her—she would make this foolish Belmont Lord see her, by Creation. She was determined.

Full of thanks and promises of a memorable afternoon, Lady Jubilee made the required preparations.

Sitting there in the Chalk House a third time, Lady Lillian waited.

This time Lord Stenstrom showed.

✶ ✶ ✶ ✶ ✶

Stenstrom ran for his soul—the demon in hot pursuit. For being, quite

literally, a fish out of water, the demon covered the ground rather well, pulling itself along on its fins and grabbing passing trees and other large objects for leverage with its whiskers, leaving a definite trail of slime as it went. The beast was clearly steering him toward the Chalk House and the lovely lady waiting within.

Not having his NTHs to dispatch the beast, and seeing no other choice, Stenstrom made a break for it. He flew into the Chalk House and slammed the door shut, rattling it in its frame. Outside he could hear the maelstrom of wind and angry smoke. He thought he could vaguely hear the demon tittering about, waiting for him. If he came out of that ballroom alone, the demon would have its prize.

"Come out here, Lord Belmont! I have been promised your flesh!"

This time his mother's sorcery had gone too far.

He turned and looked into the interior. The Chalk House was a large, gilded ballroom used for select occasions: Nether Day, Valentine's Day, and other special events. It had been made especially for Lord Stenstrom and Lady Jubilee, being built on the site of an old Merian altar. It was rather modest in size as far as grand League ballrooms went, but it could still hold several hundred people rather comfortably. The floor was made of rare woods from Hoban, and the walls were covered in fine pink and yellow silk paper— his mother had designed the print herself. When she wasn't busy summoning demons and plunging knives into his chest, his mother had a delicate touch for decorating. The four massive chandeliers hanging over the ballroom floor were priceless.

Lady Jubilee had good taste.

Sitting erect on a padded couch at the far end of the hall was a slender young woman wearing a festive pink gown. She had golden blonde hair that was done up in a partial bun, with long, slightly curled tendrils hanging down past the nape of her neck. Her face was nicely painted, her bare back was provocatively curved and her blue eyes sparkled. She looked at him quietly.

Stenstrom was wearing a dark green Belmont coat with a pair of gold knee britches and a pair of shined Tyrol-style boots.

So, what to pick—the lady or the demon? He could go back outside and fight the demon, and he would probably figure out a way to win, or, he could stay and speak with the young lady, offer his apologies, and escort her back to the manor house, where the demon would be dispelled. But then, he would be caving-in to his mother's wishes, and that prospect galled him.

After a few seconds of introspection, he chose the lady—seemed the more sensible of the two—this whole situation was, in fact, not her fault. He removed his hat and approached. Her eyes were locked on him; he could feel them all the way across the room.

"My Lady," he said in a cheerful voice, still somewhat out of breath. "I am sorry that my mother has wasted your time today, and on other occasions previously. She is determined to locate me a bride, and I have repeatedly informed her that I shall discover one on my own. I am sorry you have been inconvenienced today. Please, allow me to escort you back to the manor."

Lady Lillian said nothing, and slowly stood.

"Good sir," she said after a lengthy pause. "This is my third visit to House Belmont. This is the third time I have journeyed across the marshes of Esther to come and make your acquaintance. I have been told, by the Great Lady Jubilee, that there was a scheduling misadventure upon my first visit, and an urgent matter that required your immediate attention on my second."

She paused. "I am to infer that the Great Lady misspoke herself? There was no scheduling issue, was there? You were not called away on urgent business the second time, were you? I would appreciate an honest answer."

Stenstrom looked down at the fine, wood floor. Perhaps he should have selected the demon after all. "You are correct, my lady."

"You simply did not wish to come in and see me, is that it?"

Stenstrom blushed. "Yes, my lady. I am sorry. Again, it has nothing to do with you. It's an issue I have with my mother. I would like to offer my apologies."

Lady Lillian seemed to tense up. "I am not interested in an apology, sir." She reached down behind the couch and drew a long, slim rapier. "Have you a weapon?"

Stenstrom was shocked. "I do not. You wish to have a duel, my lady?"

"I do. I have been repeatedly insulted. I came here in good faith, to meet a promising young gentleman, whom I found rather handsome. Now, sir, I will have satisfaction."

She began walking forward, her blue eyes flashing.

"I do not have a weapon."

"Then I shall simply deal you a minor wound and take my leave. I shall not be back, as you have proved yourself a lout and a bore."

Stenstrom was stung. "I am neither a lout or a bore. I am offended."

Lillian raised her rapier and thrust, rather skillfully. "Then I suggest you defend yourself."

Stenstrom side-stepped her thrust and attempted to grab her by the shoulders.

She Wafted away with a gritty blast, rocking the chandelier. She appeared at the far end of the ballroom.

Gifts? She has Vith Gifts—Stenstrom was impressed.

"I have been thoroughly trained by my brothers and my father," she called out, her voice echoing across the ballroom. "I am your match and more. I suggest you simply take my satisfaction the way that a man does, then I shall depart. Fall on the floor and bleed, sir, and I shall be appeased."

Stenstrom looked to the door.

"Come out here, Belmont!" he thought he heard the demon yell. *"Heheheheh …"*

He raised his left hand. With a vigorous bit of sleight-of-hand, four brightly colored stones appeared between his fingers.

"Do you know what these are?" he asked. "These are Holystones, and they may be cast for a variety of effects. Please lower your weapon."

Lillian was undeterred. "I do not believe in Tyrol magic," she said side-stepping to her right.

"Nor do I," Stenstrom said. "However, here they are. I can blind you with them or make you sneeze, or ruin your gown. Please lower your weapon. I have wronged you, I readily admit it, and wish to apologize."

"Where's my apology, Belmont, for my empty belly?" the demon roared.

Lillian feinted to her right then applied a thrust, getting him slightly in the coat. "I entreat you to use them, sir," she said. "Use your stones. Do something with them!"

Stenstrom took a teal one and threw it to the floor where it burst in a noisy flash.

Lillian covered her eyes. "How dare you!" she cried, still covering her eyes.

There was a huge crash of stone and glass.

The demon had broken into the ballroom.

"Hahaha! I'm not going to have come all this way from the pit of hell only to return to my poisoned stream with an empty stomach!"

"You stated your pre-conditions! I have not violated them!"

"I care not! I was summoned, and therefore, treachery was summoned. I want you in my rotten belly! And, I think I'll eat her too!"

The demon, bounding on its fins and slashing with its catfish whiskers, pulled itself with a fuss into the ballroom.

Lillian stood there with her sword and was horrified. "What in the Name of Creation?"

Stenstrom threw a gray Holystone at the demon where it burst into a grainy cloud around the demon's catfish face. It got the stuff in its gills and sneezed. It then cleared its gills with a blast of mucous dripping down the wallpaper.

"So, a little pepper with my dinner. That's fine!"

Lillian backed away from the creature into the ballroom. She was incensed. "So, you scoundrel, it took a summoned demon to get you in here with me today, did it?"

The demon lunged. Stenstrom backed into a corner and threw a sky blue Holystone and hit it in the head. The demon immediately was covered in polka-dots.

Roaring with anger, it shot out with its whiskers and got Lillian around the waist. She dropped her rapier with a wood and metal clatter/thud. It opened its huge mouth to swallow her.

Stenstrom shook his hand and threw six MARZABLE daggers at the fiend, getting it in its bony fish head.

It turned to Stenstrom with incredible speed, opened wide, and swallowed him whole.

As he slid down the smelly, rotten gullet, a flash of cold steel suddenly ripped in. Lillian, with her little rapier, sliced the demon in two separating its head from its body where it vanished back to wherever it came from with a cry of misery.

Stenstrom, covered in blood and slime, came climbing out of the remains.

Lillian, holding her gory rapier, raised it. "I am going to make you wish you'd selected the demon today, Lord of Pigs!" she said.

She charged forward and was met with a freezing cascade of iced punch that had been set out on the table. Stenstrom, still dripping with demon slime and stinking of innards, was holding the now empty punch bowl.

Lillian stood there open-mouthed. Her face and gown covered in red punch, bits of pink shaved ice trailing down the stainless blade of her rapier, mixing with the demon's blood in a dripping pool at her feet. She was aghast. "V-villain …" she piped.

They stood there looking at each other, Stenstrom holding the punch bowl and Lillian, wide-eyed, her blue eyes standing out like two aqua-marine wheels on a snowy pink landscape, punch dripping off her.

"Quite a pity," he said still holding the bowl, "I was hoping to have a refreshing glass of punch just now after such vigorous activity."

Lillian smiled a little and gave a short laugh. "And I usually enjoy my fish lightly breaded and seasoned with a hint of lemon."

Soon, they both laughed in earnest.

Stenstrom, slimy, took Lillian, dripping, by the hand and they went back to the manor on the hill to get her out of her wet, stained gown and he out of his ruined clothes. There, she changed into a robe, and her gown was taken away to be cleaned by the staff. They chatted for the rest of the afternoon on the terrace overlooking the sea and enjoyed a well-made lunch.

The air cleared and an experience shared, they warmed to each other. Despite himself and his desire to humble his mother, Stenstrom found this spirited woman from Gamboa to be well worth the adventure and the "I told you so" he was sure to hear. She had proven that she was fiery, skilled, Gifted, had a backbone, and had a sense of humor as well—all things Stenstrom found very admirable.

"I'm sorry I chose to avoid you on your first two trips—look what company I missed out on," Stenstrom said eating his lunch.

Lilly sat there in her fluffy robe and smiled. "I'm glad I came again, and I'm glad I didn't stab you in the heart with my sword."

Stenstrom thought about her rapier. "That was quite a blow you struck to the demon."

"It's the MARTIN, the LosCapricos weapon of my family."

"I'm not familiar with that one."

"It works just like a rapier, except when you get really mad; then it always cuts the head off the victim."

"Gods—"

"It's all right. I wasn't going to chop your head off, though I sort of wanted to at first."

✷ ✷ ✷ ✷ ✷

"I told you so!"

It was an amazing summer. Lillian of Gamboa was a grand hit around the Belmont Manor.

"And you liked her, truly?" Lady Jubilee said, walking arm in arm through the garden paths with her son. For once they weren't fighting about something—they talked about Lilly. Lady Jubilee was all smiles—something that didn't happen often.

"I did, Mother. She was beautiful, and she had spirit to match."

"Wonderful. You see, I have good taste. I would not have invited some awful bore or society fool to our home to dally with my son. I was certain you would find favor with her."

Stenstrom looked down at his mother: silver-hair, sparkly eyes, a bright smile. "I wonder though, was it really necessary to summon a demon?"

"A demon? Why, I'm sure I don't know what you're talking about."

"The big, scary catfish you summoned to tear my soul apart. He half destroyed the Chalk House."

They stopped, and Jubilee put her hands on Stenstrom's face. "I care not about the antics that went on in the Chalk House between the two of you— that can be fixed. My son, the last thing in the world I would want is for a demon to feast upon your soul. I have been guilty of subjecting you to bizarre things and putting you to steps I'm certain other young men have not had to face. The love of a Tyrolese mother can be severe."

They reached the end of the path. Ahead, a coach came into view, floating down the lane.

"I have had the good fortune to have thirty wonderful children: twenty-nine daughters, and one fine son. I can't imagine life without any of you. Perhaps I am over-protective. Perhaps I impose my will on you too much. There are times when I am in the wrong, and need to be told as much—your father is good for that. Of course, he's out chasing the stars again."

The coach stopped at the gate, and Lillian of Gamboa got out, lit-up in a fine teal gown and holding a small matching parasol to keep her out of the hot sun.

"But, sometimes, I am right."

Lilly saw him and waved. He waved back.

"I told you so."

$$* \quad * \quad * \quad * \quad *$$

Lilly's skill as a painter was obvious. She stood by the large canvas holding the brush. She looked at her subject with a careful eye. She mixed her paints and smoothed them onto the canvas with easy, learned strokes.

She was painting a portrait of Stenstrom. She had been planning to give it to him as a future birthday present. She refused to let him see it. It was going to be a surprise.

Stenstrom was lying there in the garden, naked, watching her paint. "I hope you're not planning on giving me a nude portrait, Lilly. I might have a hard time finding a place to hang it."

Lilly was also naked. "It's not a nude, silly."

They'd been lovers for some time now. Their rocky start well past them, their relationship quickly had escalated into a passionate one.

Stenstrom lay back and looked at her naked body, partially obscured by the large canvas. "So, Lilly, would you really have stuck me with your sword upon our first meeting?"

"Oh, yes. I was hurt, and angry. I wanted you to acknowledge me, so, yes—I think I would have stabbed you—not to kill, if that means anything to you. I would have simply dealt you an agonizing wound."

She put her brush down and joined him on the couch. "I'm glad I didn't. I'm glad we were able to find each at last. It was worth the wait."

They gazed at each other in the fading afternoon light. "I'm settled, Lilly. I would like to announce ourselves. I am happy with you, and want no other."

She closed her eyes. "Me, the first Countess of Belmont-South Tyrol?"

"Would you accept such a distinction?"

She lay back and thought a moment. "Right now, at this moment, yes—yes I would. Gladly. But…"

"But?"

"Just look at us, Bel. We're both still so young. There is so much we haven't seen or done. There is a whole League out there, and beyond. If we committed to each other now, what if something else came around the corner? I'm not saying something will, I just want us both to know for certain."

She saw the disappointment in Stenstrom's face. "Oh, darling—please. I don't mean it as a rebuke or rejection. I just want the both of us to be assured that, when we commit to each other, that there will be no *maybe's* and *what if's*. I mean, how much do you really know about me?"

"I know all I need to."

"You should be careful with that, Bel. We all have our secrets, and I certainly have my share." She took him into her arms. "Here's what I propose. Let us take five years. During that time, we may both choose to explore the world and the League at large as we will. If in that time we find something different or new, we may be free to explore it. I pray such a thing doesn't happen, but I cannot predict the future. I simply want it to be that when I give my heart to you, or you give yours to me, there will never be any question that we were meant for each other."

"I don't want anybody else, Lilly."

She kissed him. "I pray that, at the end of five years, you still feel the same way. I don't want to lose you either." She took a deep breath. "So, is this what it feels like to be in love? It's wondrous. I don't want it to stop."

"Then let us present ourselves."

She lay back. "No, Bel—five years. Please, that is what I must ask of you."

Stenstrom got up and approached the painting. "No, no, no," Lilly said. "You promised not to look." She laid back, her naked breasts pointing up at the sky. "I have a gift for you, Bel, I've been wanting to give it to you for some time now.

She placed a small golden locket on a delicate chain in the dimple between her beasts and waited for him to take it. He picked it up. "May I open it?" he asked.

"Of course."

Inside was a tiny picture of Lilly's golden face, hand-painted and meticulous. "Did you paint this, Lilly?"

"I did, Bel. I've been working on it for some time. I wanted it to be perfect before I gave it to you. Do you like it?"

"I love it. I'll carry it with me always."

Lilly beamed.

He turned, cradling the locket in his hand and went to fetch his clothes. A few minutes later, partially dressed, he returned.

Lilly lay prone on the couch.

"Lilly, will you stay for dinner this evening, I …"

Lilly was gone. In her place was an intricate sculpture of her nude body in sand, perfect in every detail. Everything about it was perfect, the shape of her face, the curve of her legs, her soft, delicate feet.

Lilly often did this—disappearing at a moment's notice and leaving behind a wonderful sculpture of her likeness in sand. It amazed him how fast she could put these sculptures together—such care and detail—surely such a thing should take hours, but he'd been gone only a few minutes.

The canvas of his portrait was gone too.

Written in sand near her head in a fine cursive hand was: "Bye, bye …" That was another thing Lilly did on her departures. *"Bye … bye …"*

Oh Lilly, he thought. He always felt so sad when she abruptly left like this. He got out the locket and stared at her beautiful face. "Bye, Lilly. Don't be long."

Five years—a lot of things can happen in five years.

✳ ✳ ✳ ✳ ✳

Though he could probably expect to see much less of Lilly around, she would, nevertheless, come to dominate his thoughts and his doings. Just as Stenstrom began to emerge from his mother's wing and openly challenge her, he replaced one domineering woman with another—Lilly.

Everything that happened from then on out she had a hand in determining. Just like she could sculpt a statue of sand with effortless ease, she could sculpt him too.

Five years …

14
—A Question of Occupation—

There was an unspoken disconnect rumbling around Belmont Manor. It had been there for years, and was largely—and wisely—undiscussed.

The disconnect: what sort of occupation would Stenstrom the Younger be allowed to pursue as he matured into a young man. Such a topic was new around the House with Stenstrom being the only son of Belmont. Lady Jubilee assumed that all of her daughters would simply become ladies, countesses and socialites, like she was. Only a few of her daughters, Lady Celesta and Nylar, for example, and more recently, Lady Lyra, had openly antagonized Lady Jubilee on the matter and promptly found themselves outside in the moonlit garden under the knife.

As for Lord Stenstrom the Younger, clearly, his father wanted him to join the Fleet and clearly Lady Jubilee did not.

Lord Stenstrom at one time was rather keen on the idea. He sent his young son all sorts of Fleet memorabilia to fill his thoughts, and spun grand tales of his adventures when he was in attendance at home—both Stenstrom and Lyra soaking them up eagerly. Lady Jubilee frowned on the subject, her hatred of the Fleet most clear.

To further push the matter, Captain Stenstrom took his son on a trip to Onaris aboard his vessel, the *Caroline,* when he was nine—his first trip into space. It was just a quick run to gather supplies, a task great Warbirds normally didn't partake in; however, Captain Stenstrom was eager for a chance to take his son on a brief introductory spin around the stars.

He hoped more would follow.

Stenstrom the Younger was intoxicated with the whole thing: the launch from Esther Bay, listening to his father command the ship, barking out orders, and watching the bridge crew follow them without pause or question. Sitting in his office, the ship under full sail, he looked out the window at the dark gallery of space moving by.

"Do you see that great glowing thread stretching off into the distance, my son," he asked.

"I do, father," Stenstrom the Younger said, his face pushed up against the glass. "What is it?"

"It's a cloud of gas called Druries Belt—just a harmless oddity one finds while at sea. There are many such things, each more wondrous than the previous, all just waiting to be discovered."

"When will we arrive at Onaris?" Stenstrom the Younger asked.

"Oh, in just a few hours."

"What's out there?'

"Here—nothing, just a bit of empty space between Kana and Onaris. Pay it no mind. There's nothing out there except Druries Belt and some drifting ice."

When they returned to Tyrol, Lady Jubilee was incensed, and though she was missing her usual cigarette, she smoked nonetheless.

That was the first time he ever heard his parents engage in a bitter, shouting argument, their voices exchanging back and forth through the halls of the old monastery, he covering his ears so as not to hear the hurtful words being hurled at each other.

As time passed, Stenstrom the Older's zeal diminished a bit. He never saw his son wearing any of the clothes he sent home to him, never saw him playing with the toys and models he'd bought. Perhaps he really didn't have an interest in it after all.

So, what was he to do? He was getting older and the question could be ignored no longer.

The question of Stenstrom's future occupation, the thing Lord Stenstrom and Lady Jubilee always had avoided discussing at any length, finally came to a boil one day when Stenstrom the Younger was seventeen. Lord Stenstrom again took his son for a ride to Onaris, this time bringing Lady Lyra along as well. As he had when he was younger, Stenstrom was full of excitement—so was Lyra. This time, Lord Stenstrom put it to them directly.

"So, would either of you like to join the Fleet, sail the stars with your old man? There is a place waiting for either or both of you. Many clamor for such an opportunity, I beg you not to waste it."

Both of them looked at each other and respectfully said, "No."

"But why—you both seem to love it. I don't understand."

Stenstrom the Younger spoke up: "Mother will not allow it, and has seen to it."

Ah—Stenstrom the Older now understood.

They returned to Belmont Manor the next day. It was time of the Yearly Reasoning, when a League Auditor from the city of Armenelos came to check the House of Belmont's assets and determine if enough tax had been paid—it was a dreary and sometimes infuriating exercise to have to go through.

The auditor, a Lord Belamy of Koff—a small, meek man from the League office, sat there going through all of House Belmont's assets as Lady Jubilee and Lord Stenstrom had a raging fight all around him.

"I have told you that our son will not join the Fleet and have nothing to do with it! I have made that most clear, have I not?" she shouted. "They call you Stenstrom the Brave. Instead, they should call you 'Stenstrom the Deaf', or 'Stenstrom the Forgetful'!"

He returned the favor. "How about these appellations, madam: 'Stenstrom the Pained'. 'Stenstrom the Encumbered', and 'Stenstrom the Determined'! Jubilee, you cannot protect our son so; he has all of the tools needed to be a fine officer in the Fleet, and should be permitted to make his own choices as he sees fit. He loved his trip to Onaris—he has a passion for faring the stars—just as I do. I know he does!"

"We are under Wirguild!"

"The Wirguild is suspended, and has been for years! There's glory to be had for him in the Fleet!"

"And death and destruction and pain for his mother!"

"You are talking nonsense!"

Lord Koff continued checking his papers, trying to blend in with the tabletop. In all his travels, he'd clearly never seen a Lord and Lady behave so.

"He has a world of choices before him—just not the Fleet! Not the Stars! I forbid it! Additionally, I have set him to the Blood Promise—he has promised not to join the Fleet."

Ah—so there it was—there it was. She and her damned rituals. Her su-

perstitions. Stenstrom slammed his hand down on the table, causing Lord Koff's terminal to jump.

"That is a piece of Tyrol nonsense! How could you do such a thing to our son?" he roared.

"I have protected our children from all that may harm them—I have stood guard over their souls, and the Blood Promise is part of that protection! It is my guarantee!"

"Tyrol nonsense!"

"Tyrol nonsense, is it? I should turn you into a fly and swat you flat right now for your temerity!" Jubilee shouted back.

"I wish you would—I truly do! You have been threatening to transform me into this creature or that for years. Go ahead! Do it! End my suffering!"

Amid this thunderstorm, Lord Koff meekly spoke up. "My Lord, might I command your attention for a moment?"

Lady Jubilee turned her fury to Lord Koff, her eyes smoldering. "You!" she spat. "What, in the Name of Creation, do you want?"

Lord Koff trembled under her gaze. "My Lady, I have some figures that I would like to go over with you. I feel, and the data support it, that there has been an underpayment to the League …"

"An underpayment?"

"Yes, Great Lady …"

"AN UNDERPAYMENT?"

Lord Stenstrom approached and looked at Lord Koff's figures. He threw his hands up. "Yes, yes, I agree. I will authorize a payment to you, Lord Koff, this very moment."

His gaze went to Lady Jubilee. "I will go and get the funds. I find the company in this room fairly distasteful at present."

Lady Jubilee watched him exit and lit a fresh cigarette.

Lord Koff tapped his keys. "I certainly hope Lord Belmont understands there shall be additional fees and penalties for the tardy nature of the payment."

Lady Jubilee appeared not to care about taxes and money at the moment. "The hallmark of any sound relationship, Lord Koff, is the ability to fight with vigor with the one you love and make up later, would you not agree?"

"I… well, I…"

She began to choke up a little and pulled from her cigarette to hide it. "We often fight about this and that, and never fail to properly make up. This time will be no different. I love that man—cherish him. That's why I act as I do. He and our children, that's why I care so much."

She pulled herself from her reflections. She turned back to Lord Koff. She looked at the little man sitting there with his terminal and papers, and she sneered with disdain. "You sir, you are an accountant, correct?"

"Yes, Great Lady. I am a fully accredited accountant for the League and a proud member of the IBBAANA brotherhood."

"Truth be told? How nice. And this 'Banana' organization you mentioned, that is some sort of accountant gathering, yes?"

"IBBAANA, Great Lady, and yes, it is a proud brotherhood of accountants and other similar occupations."

"I see. And, have you ever been shot at?"

"What? Shot at? No, Great Lady."

"Have you ever faced death in space?"

"In space? No, Great Lady."

"Has an accountant ever died of botulism?"

"What? Well, I …"

She leaned down and gritted her teeth. "And, do you not believe that I could turn you into a fly, should I so choose to do so?"

Lord Koff sweated. "I … do not know, Great Lady."

Jubilee intimidated Lord Koff for a few minutes more; then Lord Stenstrom returned with a chest of coins.

"An accountant!" she declared as Lord Stenstrom sorted through the coins. "Our son shall become an accountant and join the—the ..." Jubilee snapped her fingers in Lord Koff's face. "What is the name of that insipid brotherhood you grovel in fealty to, sir?"

"What? The IBBAANA, is that what you are referring to? I do not gro—"

"Yes, yes, the 'BANANA'—our son shall belong to such an organization and elevate it to new heights." Jubilee pointed at Lord Koff. "Just like this insignificant man sitting right here! And to ensure such a thing, I shall put him to the Promise."

Lord Koff was open-mouthed in outrage. "Insignificant?" he sputtered.

Stenstrom threw down the chest. "You will force our son into mediocrity? You will force upon him the life of a faceless Hack?"

"Mediocrity?" Koff shouted with indignation. "Faceless Hack?"

"If it ensures a long, uneventful life for our son, then yes I will!"

Lord Koff, a partially forgotten man in the midst of this row, opened his coat and pulled out a holo pedestal. He set it on the table and turned it on. Soon the flickering images of a number of young people began floating about the room. "I will have you know, Great Lady Jubilee, that I am the proud father of fifteen wonderful children. I am not insignificant."

Jubilee stopped shouting at her husband and looked at the smiling images orbiting around his head.

"I see," she said studying them. "And did you have any children that lived, Lord Koff?"

"Lady Jubilee!" Lord Stenstrom said, aghast, dropping his coins. "Where are your manners?"

"Manners be damned! Behold these tawdry waifs, with naught to look at but this man's bald head as he stumbles home after yet another uneventful day. At least they may expect no harm to come to their father. That is what I crave for our son—a simple, uneventful life, free of danger. And that, by Creation, is what he shall have!"

15

—Favored of the Sisters—

Shortly after the big row with Lord Stenstrom, Lady Jubilee was distressed to learn that a contingent of Sisters was coming west from Valenhelm to pay her a visit.

The Sisters always made her nervous. What did they want? More importantly: *what did they know?*

Their intentions soon became clear. With Lady Jubilee and Stenstrom the Younger sitting in the parlor, the group of ten Sisters laid it out for them with uncharacteristic haste and frankness. The Sisters didn't seem to care about Lady Jubilee at all—it was her son they were interested in.

"We have watched your growth, Lord Stenstrom, with great interest. You have matured into an admirable young man," the prim Marine said.

"Thank you, Great Sister."

"We shall be blunt, as we are certain your time is short, as is ours. We wish you to participate in our Program, sir. You have been found to be of fine lineage, and you would honor us with your participation."

Stenstrom was nervous. He knew of the Sister's "Program," where they invited select males throughout the League to inseminate fertile Sisters. He'd heard it was a complicated procedure, requiring many visits and a lengthy negotiation, and to be selected was an honor.

He didn't feel honored. He felt rushed and on-the-spot. He looked to his mother. "Mother, I …"

"This request does not concern your mother, the Great Lady Jubilee. She has no say in your response, either yes or no. Please refer your answer to us."

Stenstrom didn't know what to say or do.

Jubilee spoke up. "Sisters, this is most irregular. Normally, a House may expect a reception and proper sitting before …"

"This is hardly, regular, Lady Jubilee. Do not forget that it was we who saved your son's life on repeated occasions. We expect a small recompense for our assistance."

Lady Jubilee forgotten, they gazed at Stenstrom. "We require an answer, sir. The matter is completely voluntary, and you shall not offend us in any case. Therefore, what say you?"

Stenstrom wanted his mother to answer. "I … perhaps I am a bit too young. I might better serve you in a year or so, when I am more mature."

"You are optimally mature at present, Lord Belmont, hence our presence in your wonderful home. Again, what is your answer?"

Their eyes bored into him.

He swallowed. "Regretfully, I …"

"We certainly hope you will accept our offer. We would leave here … most disappointed otherwise. We would not wish to have to investigate your mother's doings at length. It would pain us to discover that she was engaging in anything … forbidden."

Lady Jubilee stood. "Do not threaten my son! I care not what you do to me! My son is …"

"Sit … down…" the Marine said in a quiet but commanding tone, the Sisters' eyes flaring. Jubilee sat, unable to match the iron wall of their will.

Stenstrom, fearing for his mother, spoke. "Yes, Great Sisters, I accept!"

Jubilee was panicked. "Bel, don't …"

"I accept! I accept! Please, I shall participate!"

The Sisters were silent a moment. Then: "We are most pleased."

Stenstrom felt awkward. "I am not informed regarding what shall happen next. I do not know what is expected of me. Who am I to … assist in this matter?"

The Sisters smiled. "Why, all of us, Lord Belmont. 'Tis a great honor we pay you. And you need not fear—we shall handle this and take a good treatment of you."

They turned to Lady Jubilee. "Get out," the Marines said.

Lady Jubilee was silent and rather helpless in her own home. There was nothing she could do. She stood and left the parlor.

The Sisters then took command of Lord Stenstrom, rendering him helpless within his own body.

He had a vague memory of being led into a guest bedroom. He remembered something about being pushed against the wall, strong arms around him and the softness of heated skin pressed against his.

He thought he recalled the sting of primal release, over and over.

And when it was finished, they left as quickly as they came.

But, it wouldn't be long before they returned. Again and again, a roomful of Sisters demanding servicing, always the same.

Always the implied threats.

✶ ✶ ✶ ✶ ✶

"They come, all the time, Lilly. What am I supposed to do?"

Lilly sat there with him in the moonlight, her arms around him. "Isn't participating in the Sisters' Program a great honor?"

"Yes, so I'm told, but this many times? And they threaten my mother if I show the slightest inclination to resist."

Lilly thought a bit. "Obviously you have something they desperately want. There have been instances in the past where the Sisters have taken particular shines to certain League men—why is not plainly clear. The Sisters are inscrutable. It seems to me that, if you weren't here anymore, they might leave you and your mother alone."

"What do you mean?"

"I mean even the Sisters are supposed to conform with social protocols. Having you service them so often actually violates some of those protocols—they are supposed to 'spread it around,' if you follow my meaning. And, they are supposed to schedule their Program over several visits—not just show up unannounced and demand servicing. I'm afraid with you hidden behind the walls of Belmont Manor and out of the League's eye, they may do as they please."

"So, what am I to do?"

"I think it's time you left home, Bel. Get out, and see the world. If you were out in a public place and not secluded at home, the Sisters would have a much harder time getting to you. Out in the public you are protected—the Sisters could not simply ride in and take you whenever they want."

"What sort of public place?"

"School. University. There are many to choose from."

"I don't want to go to school, Lilly. According to Mother, the only course of study I'm permitted to follow is accounting, and that sounds like a slow death to me."

"Really? Does your mother dominate you so?"

Stenstrom looked at his chest and remembered the searing knife that was plunged into it.

You will study nothing in the schools but accounting ...

"Yes ..."

"Your course of study is really quite pointless, Bel—what difference will it make? Go to school and study accounting—do as little as possible to pass your courses if the subject matter bores you. There, you shall be out in public and shielded from the Sisters. Additionally, I think you need to blossom as a person. You are secluded here in this manor—you see nobody, you talk to no one other than your parents and your sisters and me. You need to get out and interact. School's great for that."

"Why don't you come to school with me?"

"Shall we go over this again, Bel? We have our five years—they have just begun. Fear not—I will come and see you often, and I shall write constantly. Our hearts will not be far."

16

—THE ASTRAL TRAVELER—

With a fair amount of trepidation, Stenstrom enrolled in the University of Bern far to the west in Vithland. The University of Bern was a rich, well-known school across the League. Not a school known for sciences, as the University of Arden was, or a liberal arts school like the University of Dee, Bern was best known as a trade and business school. Many of the most successful traders and merchants across the League were alumni of the U of B.

As typical, his House spared little expense for his maintenance and board. They bought him a lovely terraced apartment on a green near the university grounds complete with several guestrooms so that they could visit often. They furnished the apartment with fine things and filled his closets with the best clothing.

Though Stenstrom dreamed of leaving home often when he was younger, to be free of his mother's leash, he immediately found himself badly homesick in his lovely apartment. He recalled many of his sisters, loudly rebellious at home, bemoaning their freedom, clamoring to take flight, found themselves right back at home of their own volition once they came of age. He recalled his sister Lenta actually came to live at home even after she had been wed, she and her husband moving into her old bedroom—Belmont Manor was a nest that was soul-shattering to walk away from. There were also Calami, Phaedra, Kormanda and Io who were often in attendance at home for months at a time.

Lilly was right. The grounds of his South-Tyrol home and his family were all he'd ever known. He realized he truly didn't have a friend in the world, and didn't have the first clue as to go about making one. He'd been taught to look at people twice, to mistrust and suspect treachery. The trusting little boy who was almost killed in the Fox Park in Tyrol was gone. Strangers, he had learned, were the enemy, in the employ of the enemy and doing the work of the enemy—whoever that was.

From his terrace, he could see the school and the city buildings of Bern not far away. He saw the students coming and going and the floating traffic moving in an orderly fashion down the street. He saw groups of students milling about, laughing, talking, and interacting with each other in a simple yet utterly alien fashion for him. None of his mother's sorcery had prepared him for this, to be a simple student, to be a citizen of the League. He saw young ladies in gowns of all kinds from all over the League. He saw young gentlemen wearing clothing in the style of Vith, Remnath, Zenon, and Hala.

And he felt completely alone in his somber Tyrol clothes, having little if any idea how to go out and fit in.

The last time he'd been truly out of his own was the Fox Park debacle—which he still didn't know if that had been real or simply an elaborate dream. He nearly hit the Com and called home for Mother to come and get him.

After a bit of inner turmoil, he decided to go out and walk about the campus, get a feel for the place. He had to remember that he was no longer a little boy marching down the road with his possessions in a sack; he was no longer helpless.

He walked down the stairs of his building and made his way onto the green, passing many groups of people. He felt out of place in his Tyrol clothes, not seeing anybody else in the familiar Tyrol jacket, leggings and boots. The people seemed friendly enough as he wandered down the green, the ladies curtsying and the gentlemen tipping their hats. He thought to introduce himself several times, to strike up a conversation, but found himself with nothing to say and on the defensive.

He continued on, eventually wandering deep into the mass of tightly packed campus buildings.

He noticed his surroundings change a little; everything seemed dark and quiet. He looked up at the early evening sky—it wasn't a Kanan sky, it was something else, a negative image of what it should be, peppered with unusual stars. He heard a strange wind and odd sounds. After another few moments, the sky reverted to its normal cheery blue.

He remembered a strange sky like that, from his Fox Park dream and from the incident at Rustam Labyrinth. After nine years of arcane study, he knew what it might be—the Astral Plane, a sort of pocket dimension that was always there but seldom noticed. It tended to warp the perceptions of any in close proximity to it, and therefore mundane things might appear unusual, such as the sky. The Astral Plane was difficult to access, daunting to navigate, and dangerous to traverse. According to his mother, the Sisters made Astral travel illegal centuries ago, though the Xaphans sometimes still used it at their peril.

Something had just opened a threshold to the Astral Plane, and then closed it. Part of him, still reminiscing in the Fox Park dream, wanted to run home and hide. The new man in him, however, refused. He would stand and face whatever it was.

Something approached him from behind. He quickly turned.

A lady wearing a summer gown beneath a knit sweater stood there—surprised by his abrupt turn. "Oh," she said, hand over her heart. "You startled me."

Stenstrom looked her over. She seemed innocent enough. "Your pardon," he said.

She stood there for an awkward moment. "This is my first year, and I was just exploring the grounds. Are you new here too?"

Stenstrom didn't answer. She awaited a reply, and, when one didn't come, she rocked back and forth uncomfortably. "Ummm, my name is Corvene of Dan. I was trying to locate the student union, and I thought to have a bite of dinner there. This campus is quite large. Would you care to join me? Perhaps we could locate it together."

"No."

She blushed and adjusted the sleeves of her sweater. "Well. Sorry then. Please, have a good evening." She walked past him and continued around the side of the building.

He felt a little crass for treating the girl in such a manner, and had a thought to follow her around the building and apologize. Still, someone or something had just opened an Astral Plane threshold in the immediate area near enough to warp his perceptions, and her arrival seemed awfully well-timed.

He had a sudden feeling that he was in danger. Quickly, he faded into the shadows and hid by the side of the building.

Someone came around the corner of the building just then. It was her—she'd returned. She walked right past where Stenstrom was hiding and looked around. "Sir?" she said. "Sir, are you still here?"

He noted she bore an odd smell with her this time—not perfume, but something basic and primal. She smelled like a dog in heat, and he found himself drawn to it; aroused by it. She panned around, clearly wondering where he had gone. She walked to the building's edge and looked some more, her neck bending from one side to the other.

What was that smell? It was now more of a stench, filling his nostrils. He could barely contain himself.

Her bearing changed. She straightened, seemed angry, poised and rather sinister. She dug through her bag and produced a smoky vial from within along with a small copper sphere. She set the sphere on the ground, unstoppered the vial and poured out its contents, covering the sphere. She stood over it waiting for something to happen.

The sphere twitched all on its own and began rolling in his direction, picking up steady speed until it rolled off the walk into the shrubs nearby.

The woman looked in his direction, not seeing him, but seemingly knowing he was there. She slowly reached back into her bag and, when she pulled her hand back out, she wore a form-fitting metal assembly around her knuckles. It appeared to be some sort of weapon.

Stenstrom shook his hand, producing his MARZABLE.

He and the woman were engaged in a tense standoff, neither flinching, both ready to strike.

At that moment, warning sirens went off all around campus. The skies darkened and through the clouds came the terrifying rope-like tongue of a cyclone. It had appeared from nowhere and threatened to touch ground right in the middle of the campus. Students from all over scattered for cover.

The woman looked up, saw the cyclone and scowled. She got something out of her sweater, and a gaping hole in the universe opened in front of her.

The Astral Plane, he was sure of it. Things got dark, and the sky changed once again into a nightmare of itself.

She had just opened a door to the Astral Plane. She took one last look in his direction, turned, and walked up the steps of a long bridge, her movements exaggerated, and she walked away into unfathomable chaos, her strides stretching off into the distance.

The Astral door closed. He just caught a glimpse of the lady moving down the bridge as the threshold sealed behind her. She was no longer wearing a gown and a sweater. She was wearing a gray suit and a broad-brimmed hat.

And the frightening cyclone overhead that had everyone on the campus scrambling dissipated and vanished just as quickly as it had come.

✶ ✶ ✶ ✶ ✶*

Since the incident with the Astral traveler, he'd been doing research into the topic of the Astral Plane. He finally found interesting reading.

PLANAR BRIDGE

(qv: teleportation device) Any of a number of devices/artifacts used for rapid travel through the Astral Plane. The existence of the Astral Plane and its exact nature is currently in dispute and no effort has been made to further the technology within League space. The Planar Bridge was first developed by the Xaphan branch of the House of Conwell in 00002ax when it was discovered the Type II world they settled on was a Planar World often lapsing in and out of the Astral Plane. The Astral Bridge is an arcane pendant capable of opening a threshold to the Astral Plane and could be programmed to transport the user to a predetermined location. The assumed nature of Astral travel minimizes the considerations of speed and distance. Bearing is critical and any slight deviation can cause an Astral traveler using the bridge to become hopelessly lost. One of the effects of opening a threshold to the Astral Plane by way of Planar Bridge is the tendency to pull nearby objects into the Astral plane where they are lost forever. The effects upon perception for those near the open threshold is said to vary. The Sisterhood of Light successfully blocked many key points of interest from Astral incursion in 00021ax, thus rendering the use of the Planar Bridge for military purposes moot.

Interesting. So, given this information, he assumed that the woman whom he met on the green weeks earlier was using a Planar Bridge to travel via the Astral Plane. It made sense. Given the odd appearance of the sky and the gray clothing she was revealed to be wearing, he assumed that she was the same woman who attacked him in the Fox Park, and again at the Labyrinth of Rustam as a boy.

Whoever she was, she was persistent.

He set to work, using his array of arcane books and knowledge. He knew from his reading that Planar Bridges were fairly easy to block. He created a number of cyan Holystones made of jasmine, carbolyte and wormwood. Such Holystones would prevent the incursion of thresholds from the Astral Plane and provide him protection. He then set them all over his apartment and all about the university, hiding them in gutters, alcoves, rooftops and anywhere else he could find where they would be safe. He cleaned out a local silver shop of candlesticks, ashtrays curios, and other such items and used them to create a whole retinue of arcane devices and aids designed to detect the presence of the Astral Plane. Thus armed and never without his NTHs and MARZABLE, he could feel reasonably secure that whoever this woman was, she could no longer simply step out of thin air on a Planar Bridge, and he should be able to detect the Astral Plane upon her should she come at him in disguise.

He stayed wary, examining any who came near twice and three times, always waiting for his arcane Astral Plane detectors to come to life.

They never did.

As the semester began and he settled into school, no further incidents were noted and, though never forgotten, the matter fell farther and farther back into his thoughts.

17

—The Bones Club—

One thing that Stenstrom could count on when he was really feeling blue was either an appearance in person or a letter from Lilly. It seemed she could read his thoughts and his state of mind from far away in Gamboa and always came to his spiritual rescue.

Today was no different.

Sitting merrily in his stack of daily posts was a letter in a square envelope, scented with a touch of lavender. Great Lords and Ladies always corresponded in hand-written letters—they were so much more personal and heart-felt than a holo-post or insta-type.

Stenstrom savored the letter for a moment before opening it.

It said:

I've being thinking of you lately. I always think of you, but more so as of recently. I hear from your mother that you are all alone down there at school. She tells me you've not made any friends.

When I suggested our five year hiatus, I never intended for you to become a hermit. I wish you to take this time that we agreed upon and use it to your advantage—live, see what's out there. And, should your travels bring you into the arms of another, then that is something that I shall have to accept. I wished for this time, and you are blameless in whatever comes of it.

I have taken the liberty of making some inquiries for you. I certainly hope you will not be angry with me, and I hope you shall keep to an open mind and do a good effort to make friends. If only for me then, please try to enjoy yourself.

Thinking of you, as always…
Lilly

Stenstrom read the letter several times and replied. He wrote her that he would do as she asked and not go out of his way to be a hermit. If only for her, he would try to enjoy himself and make a friend or two.

What could it hurt?

After lunch the next day, Stenstrom retired to the library to study for a pending exam. Characteristically, he was behind on his studies, but didn't feel overly put off—a bout of furious cramming and he should be up-to-date without undo fuss.

And, characteristically, he sat at the large table alone. Lilly's concern for him passed through his thoughts, but he didn't have time at present to be sociable. It was second nature to avoid strangers and sit by himself—he still really didn't have the first clue how to go about making a friend.

But, all that had to wait because his studies were in peril. He had a selection of books piled in front of him and several holo-term cones floating about for additional research. He was so behind.

Before long, two people approached his table and stood there.

A smallish gentleman in a sumptuous gold and green coat and a skinny lady in a brown gown hovered over his table, staring at him. The woman, her brown hair pulled away from her face and laced into a long, single braid, cooled herself with a black silk fan. She wore fingerless lacy black gloves.

They stood there for what seemed like a long stretch of time.

Eventually, Stenstrom pushed his books aside and looked up, feeling his personal space invaded in a big way. "What's this all about?" he asked.

The pair took Stenstrom's question as an invitation, and they sat down, pulling their chairs out with a draggy, woody fuss that leapt across the open air of the library. The gentleman drew a small silver case from his coat pocket and opened it. Neatly housed within the case was a line of slim cigarettes, leafed in a natural brown color. The gentleman took one out, tapped it on his sleeve, and held it aloft, as if expecting Stenstrom to offer a light.

"I do not have a lighter, if that's what you're hoping for," he said.

The woman lifted her slender hand and, with her thumb and forefinger, pinched down on the end of the cigarette. After a moment a thin trail of smoke curled through her fingers. She slowly let go, and his cigarette was fully lit.

Some sort of sorcery or hidden technology in her palm or on the pads of her fingers—Stenstrom was unimpressed. He returned to his reading.

The fellow in the gold jacket took a puff and let the smoke come out his nostrils, the delicate gray feathers of smoke rising up toward the distant ceiling, getting lost in the wood paneling.

Stenstrom didn't indulge in smoking, but he found the soft, woodsy smell of the smoke pleasant enough.

"I don't believe smoking's allowed in the library," Stenstrom quietly remarked, looking up from his books.

The gentleman smiled slightly and continued smoking, enjoying his cigarette with deliberate slowness, pull after pull.

Finally, as his coal began to fizzle, he spoke. "Are you Stenstrom, Lord of Belmont-South Tyrol?" he asked in a smooth tone.

"I could say no," he replied, "but I'm fairly sure you already know who I am."

"True enough. I am Bannaster, Lord of Tartan, and this lovely lady with me is Alitrix, Lady of Zama."

The woman smiled and ripped her fan. "I am of the Hoban Zamas, sir, not the wild Onaris Zamas. That is a common misconception." Apparently, she found that an important distinction to make plain right off the bat. She gestured with her fan as she spoke.

"Great!" Stenstrom said. "Glad to know you. Now, I have a pile of studying to catch up on, so if you don't mind, could you two please push off?"

Lord Bannaster was unfazed. "We have an opening in an exclusive club that we belong to. You have been highly recommended, and we wish to invite you to join us this evening. I guarantee there will be rich foods, entertainments, and feats of mind and body to freeze your blood. Only the best people shall be there."

"Really?" Stenstrom replied, uninterested.

Lady Alitrix spoke in a greasy accent. "Are you willing to place your soul at risk? Are you willing to face the Sisters' wrath? If you have courage, if you call yourself a man, meet us at this address tonight." She placed a small card onto the tabletop and slid it toward him. "Only those of good blood may join—that shall be your first test."

"Test?" Stenstrom blurted out. "As in the test I'm going to fail if you both don't clear my space."

The two of them stood and walked away, the wooden floor of the library creaking under foot as they went.

Stenstrom thanked Creation for their departure and continued with his reading. After a bit, his curiosity got the better of him—that damn card sitting there on the table. It might as well have been a crowd of people, a flashing light, or a blaring noise, for the card troubled his thoughts and made studying impossible. He picked the card up and had a look at it.

It was blank, just an ivory white card with a faint smell of myrrh.

✶　✶　✶　✶　✶

Stenstrom was annoyed and rather unhappy about his visitors in the library. Though he sat there all afternoon, he got relatively little studying done.

He returned to his apartment, tossed his things aside and sat there—as Lilly's letter had noted, he was alone and had no friends to call on. His last visitor was his sister Lyra. It was always good seeing her, and, in fact, the bed in the guestroom where she had slept was still unmade.

He felt quite lonely all of a sudden, the fine walls of the apartment closing in around him. He longed for home, for Mother, and for Lilly. He got Lilly's letter out and read it again.

I have taken the liberty of making some inquiries for you. I certainly hope you will not be angry with me...

He wondered—were the two bores from the library, Lord Bannaster and Lady Alitrix, responding to an inquiry Lilly had made on his behalf? They had to have been—so, in such an instance, he couldn't be overly sore at them for disrupting his study session. They had, after a fashion, been invited into his presence.

Maybe they were friends with Lilly. Maybe they would tell her that he was a cold fish.

Or, maybe they were in association with the woman in gray: the Astral Traveler.

He went through his books and picked up the scented card Lady Alitrix had given him. Again, it was nothing more than a plain white card—no embossing, holo-triggers, 4-D tattoos or stamping. He had created several simple tools capable of detecting the presence of the Astral Plane. The most effective was a hollow, silver pyramid filled with certain salts and minerals that he had gathered. If the two of them had recently been to the Astral Plane, he should be able to determine that—the components within the pyramid would react and rattle about inside. He ran the smooth bottom of the pyramid over the face of the card.

Nothing happened. The card had not recently been to the Astral Plane.

Determined to be safe, he lost interest in it. He tossed it aside; he had no time for such intrigues.

He put his pyramid away. He sat down.

The clock near the door ticked. Through the window, he could hear traffic floating down the street.

He thought about it some more. Lilly asked him to try and make friends. Lilly had taken the time to reach out for him and start the process; Bannaster and Alitrix—an odd sort, but still.

He picked the card back up. "All right, Lilly, for you, I'll give it a go," he said into the air.

He looked at it—plain and white—what was he supposed to deduce from it? He considered Lord Bannaster and Lady Alitrix, two obviously gentile types who enjoyed a spot of mystery and gothic flaunt in their stuffy, blue society circle. They encoded this card with information of some sort, and he was supposed to be suitably mystified and would have to labor to discover its secret, matching his wits against theirs. It was a tawdry game he truly didn't feel like playing, but, for Lilly ...

He took the card into the bathroom and held it up to the bright lights, hoping something would be revealed. Nothing was.

He looked at it in the mirror, again nothing. He held it under the faucet and ran the water over it—nothing.

He thought about Lady Alitrix's parting words:

"Only those of good blood may join—that shall be your first test."

Blood ...

Oh dear—the thought crossed his mind that he might actually have to smear blood on this card, and some cryptic lettering might react and show up. Bannaster and Alitrix seemed slightly off-putting, and they appeared to have a thirst to boldly break little rules that had no punishable consequences, as with Bannaster's smoking in the library.

Stenstrom sighed, cleaned off his shaving razor, and cut his finger. He squeezed the small cut and allowed several drops to fall on the card.

Something appeared on the face of the card. He rubbed the blood around. *"22 Stang at 24 bells"* it read.

Stenstrom stood there on the deserted street holding the bloody card. 22 Stang—here was the place. The building was a neo-Remnath design, being constructed of grayish sandstone in a boxy footprint, boldly windowed and framed, with a domed roof of metal and glass popping out of the center. In front of the building was a gated yard landscaped in low hedges and beds of colorful flowers.

Number 22 was placed at the wooded end of a quiet side street named "Stang," just off the main drag in downtown Bern, about twenty minutes walk from the university. Surrounding the street on all sides were the capped domes and tall, squarish buildings of Bern, lit up in the evening air. An orderly string of quiet residences lined the street, and, though there was a large bustle of activity at the mouth of the street (traffic coming and going, blinking lights from the shops, people walking), its tree-lined lengthy interior was rather sleepy.

He was dressed in his best: a fine gray Tyrol coat and shirt, black knee britches, and his beloved, Tyrol boots shined to perfection. Tyrol boots sometimes caused a stir in Bern for they, at first glance, looked rather like Hala ranchers' boots. They had a very elongated toe area and always had a mix of leather and metal, the finest using generous amounts of silver, gold and copper at the ankle and the tip. They looked like boots from a suit of armor.

The rustic stocks of his dual NTH pistols stuck out of his sash, and the MARZABLE was hidden, untraceable somewhere in the folds of his clothing. As usual, he was hatless, his wavy, black Belmont hair combed and cut short.

Also hidden in his coat was a special white Holystone—one that would warn him should any Astral travelers become present.

He grappled with his thoughts a moment and truly wished to be elsewhere. Again, Lilly won out—he imagined the door to 22 Stang swinging open and lovely Lilly coming out, bounding down the steps in her festive gown and parasol to great him. He went through the gate, climbed the marble stairs, and tried the main door.

It was locked. He banged on it with his fist.

After a minute or so, the door unlatched and slowly swung inward. A thin man in servant's attire stood within. He gazed at Stenstrom impassively. "Do you have your invitation?"

Invitation? Stenstrom didn't have an invitation—only this bloody card. He held it out. The servant took it and opened the door wide. "If you please," he said, motioning for Stenstrom to enter.

He walked in. The interior of the building was well appointed, scented in the savory aroma of expensive foods and knee-deep in idle chatter. Fine lengths of polished granite and marble lined the floors and the walls. Rich fabrics draped the walls, and vast hangings decorated quiet sitting rooms. Young people, all dressed in their best, roamed about, holding drinks and smoking scented cigarettes. They turned and looked at Stenstrom as he passed, neither approving or disapproving of his presence.

"May I check your weapons, sir?" the servant asked. "They shall be well cared for and returned to you as the evening concludes. It is a House rule. I shall request our attendants polish and clean them for you."

Stenstrom pulled the NTHs out of his sash, pocketed the cinnabar strikers to prevent an accidental misfire, and handed them over.

"Thank you, sir. Do you have anything else?"

"No," he lied, knowing full well he had his MARZABLE hidden in his coat.

The servant placed the NTHs on a small table and produced a scanner. "May I? Again, it is a matter of House procedure."

Stenstrom raised his arms and the servant waved the scanner about his chest and legs. He knew the scanner could never locate the mystical MARZABLE.

The servant seemed satisfied and put the scanner away. "This way, please," he said. Stenstrom followed him through a maze of sitting rooms and luxurious halls. A steady stream of foods and drinks came and went from the kitchens as they walked deeper into the building.

Stenstrom knew what this was: an exclusive club—a den of the rich. His mother and father had belonged to such clubs at various times. He remembered bits and pieces of St Gala's Veil, a fabulous ballroom in Jakarta where his mother was an important member of the group of ladies known as the Ballwigs. Lavish and expensive, the people there like gods, it was just like this, a place to pay extravagant dues and sit with other rich people, talking about nothing and feeling superior.

The servant led Stenstrom away from the main area to a large, oaken door carved with some type of sunburst design. He opened it with a creak, and motioned for Stenstrom to enter.

At the end of a short, dark corridor was a circular room about sixty feet in circumference, domed, about three stories high. The curving walls were painted a lightless sooty black and were lined all around with books and various arcane decorations. The walls were so black and lusterless that it looked as if a fire had raged in the room at some point and turned all into cinders. All the sounds of people talking and moving about elsewhere in the building were hushed into dank silence.

Above, two evenly-spaced wooden catwalks ringed the room and, beyond that, the glass dome at the top admitted starlight from outside. Shadowy hints of telescopes and other astronomical equipment were placed all around the dome. He'd seen the dome from outside—this must be the very center of the building. At floor level, axes and halberds, morning stars, and pikes of various sizes hung on the walls, giving the place a torture-chamber sort of feel. There was a hint of incense floating about, and its woody smell quickly became unpleasant in his nostrils. The floor was a smooth green marble with a golden design hammered into the center.

It was an odd design. He looked at it further as he stepped in.

It was a Xaphan symbol.

Four people sat spaced out along the perimeter of the wall. They sat in the shadows in large, throne-like gothic chairs—two gentlemen and two ladies.

He noticed all four were wearing black from tip to top: black coats, black gowns, black shirts, black shoes. And, not only that, they had painted their faces and hands black so that the only thing that stood out on them was their well-cared for teeth and their eyes—blues, browns and greens on beds of white.

One of them spoke. "Good evening, Lord Belmont. This is our sanctum sanctorum—the heart of our club. Here your soul is at risk."

"Is it?" Stenstrom replied.

"As you have probably guessed, this is an exclusive club. The best of everything can be had here … should you pass muster."

"Here, we do things abhorrent to the Sisterhood," someone else said. "Here, we openly mock them, and deliberately violate their tenets. We are not afraid. Here we do what we will. Here, we are free."

"I see."

"We know your mother's House of Tyrol is on the Sisters' list, for sorcery. We find favor with that. That makes you of interest to us. We would, if you pass our tests, like you to join our club. It is an exclusive offer, and not presented to many."

Stenstrom looked around. "No thanks. I'll have a pass."

One of the women smiled, her white teeth lighting up as if back-lit. "Are you afraid of the Sisters? Are you afraid for your soul?" Her accent was heavy and slightly unpleasant.

He thought of the Sisters, coming to him, their fingers digging into his flesh, their legs around him …

"I have nothing for or against the Sisters," he said. "And there is nothing here that endangers my soul. This is a place of theatre, dramatics, spoiled indulgence and fathers' wealth ill-spent to entertain wayward children."

The woman laughed. "Allow us to put your courage to the test." She produced a black box which she placed on the floor. With a flick of her wrist, the box slid across the floor on its own accord and stopped a few feet in front of him.

The box gave a shudder. He sensed danger and backed up a step or two.

The box lid opened, and a spindly black leg popped out, padded and spider-like, followed by a second, then a third. Each leg was quite a bit larger than the box that had been confining it.

Soon, ten, black legs waved in the air, followed by a hairy bloated body and glittering, jewel-like eyes.

"Have you ever been to Onaris, Lord Stenstrom?" the woman asked, watching the creature emerge from the box. "If you have, then you might have encountered one of these before—it's a demonweb, and I assure you it is quite poisonous and rather bad-tempered."

Stenstrom looked at it with horror: huge, bloated, with a leg span nearing four feet and a belly sac full of searing poison.

"I thought you said you were from Hoban," he said to the woman, who was clearly Lady Alitrix from the library. She cocked her head and gave a slight titter. She raised her hand again and, either through TK, some arcane method, or cleverly hidden technology, began pushing the huge demonweb toward him without touching it.

It didn't like being pushed and reared up aggressively, exposing its coiled-up fangs. It hissed slightly.

Stenstrom replied in kind. He waved his hands and produced two lime green Holystones, and two red ones. He threw a green one at the terrifying creature and webbed it up solid, its legs flexing feebly as it tried to free itself.

Stenstrom then threw a red Holystone, and the webbing caught fire, flames licking up toward the distant ceiling, the room soon full of the smell of roasted demonweb.

The four people in black then clapped in approval. "Well done, Lord Stenstrom. Well done. We had been told that you can create Holystones in the fashion of Tyrol sorcery, and that such things are forbidden by the Sisterhood."

Stenstrom headed for the door. "Yes, and with that I bid you farewell. I wish nothing to do with this club or you lot in particular."

Lady Alitrix waved her hand and the door locked with a heavy click. "But, you've only just arrived ..."

He tried the door and it was locked tight.

One of the gentlemen in black stood, wound back and threw something which spiraled through the air. A rectangular card impacted the door frame near Stenstrom's face and stuck fast in the wood. The card was adorned with several colorful numbers and letters:

"The night has only just begun, Lord Belmont. We insist you share it with us," Lady Alitrix said.

After a moment, using tools unseen and speed unheard of, he had the lock picked, and the heavy door swung open. He marched out.

A trapdoor opened beneath him, and he fell down a slide, plunging into pitch black, emerging in a rather shapeless cave-like room that looked like a dungeon. The irregular walls were made of boulder-like, black rock mortared with ash cement. Five archways, each barred by a stout portcullis, led off in different directions.

In the center of the room was a lone figure standing in white.

"Be our guest, Lord Belmont," came Lady Alitrix's accented voice from above. "However, you shan't wish to stay for long."

He could hear and smell gas entering the chamber from hidden nozzles at various locations. He ran to one of the archways and looked through the portcullis. He could see a passage leading off in some twisting direction before it shortly disappeared into darkness. Stenstrom could feel a breeze passing through the bars. He rattled the portcullis—it was solid and locked to the ground.

"Pick a way out, but be warned: only one way leads to a happy ending."

Covering his mouth with his sleeve, he ran to the figure in white in the center of the room. It appeared to be a Sister. She was in white robes, head-dressed in the usual fashion. She stood silently pointing at one of the archways.

"Sister, Sister?" he said through his sleeve.

She didn't respond. Upon closer inspection, she was a well-made, fully dressed life-sized dummy.

The gas was quickly getting into his head. He ran to the archway the dummy was pointing at. It was an archway guarded by a solidly placed locked portcullis. Again, a twisting passageway beyond led off into the cool darkness and disappeared.

He looked around, trying to figure some way out of this.

Beyond the portcullis, about four feet away, he noticed a panel had been cut into the stony wall. A large round button painted bright orange sat in the center of the panel. The button must open the portcullis.

He reached out for it, but it was well beyond his grasp. He shook his hand and produced a MARZABLE. He lined up the shot and threw, hitting the button easily.

The portcullis quickly rose up into a slot in the ceiling.

Coughing, he made his way into the twisting passageway beyond. He could feel a stiff breeze pulling on him from around the bend.

Stenstrom saw something carved on the floor as he took his first step. It was "IV", the ancient numerology for the number 4.

He suddenly felt an extreme sense of danger. Lady Alitrix and her lot seemed to have a great apathy for the Sisters. Here was a dummy of a Sister pointing at an archway labeled IV; therefore, he reasoned, this door was probably not the way to go to get Lady Alitrix's "happy ending." Something really bad must be waiting for him at the end of this passage.

Holding his breath, he took a quick glance around. He saw, carved into the floor before the other archways: I, II, III, and V.

He recalled the card the gentleman had thrown into the door frame. The card must contain a clue as to which archway he was supposed to take. He recalled seeing I, II, III, IV, V, along with some other lettering. The IV had a star next to it, if he was remembering correctly. The V had a *"P,"* and the rest had *"m*'s."

The gas was clogging his brain.

He didn't have any time to bat this around. IV must be a starting point of some sort, hence the star. V was also different somehow with its *"P."* It made sense to him to add V to IV, five "plus" four, giving him nine. Obviously there was no archway labeled nine, so he assumed the rest of the numbers with the "m's" might mean to subtract; III, "minus" II, minus I from nine was three.

He moved to the archway labeled III. That must be the correct way to go.

Wait …

Didn't one of the numbers have two "m's" next to it? That might indicate that that number needed to be subtracted from twice.

Which one was it?

It was I or II—he was sure of it.

It was I—it had to be I. Then, if his gas-clouded reasoning was correct, the archway he wanted was II.

He didn't give himself any time to mull it over. He went to the II archway, produced another MARZABLE, hit the button, and the portcullis rose up into the ceiling.

He ran into the narrow, twisting corridor and went around the bend.

He was instantly sucked off his feet by a powerful updraft and pulled through a dark hole in the ceiling. He seemed to be going up for a time in a twisting fashion, and then started going down.

He emerged through a small door and landed in a sea of pillows. He looked around. He was in a richly furnished room lying on a vast couch. The room was lit in pleasing yellow light and soft music played. On the other side of the room, a great number of people stood holding drinks and smoking slim cigarettes. The four people in black he'd seen in the sanctum sanctorum stood at the front. They were wiping the black paint from their faces.

After a moment, somebody said "Bravo!" and everybody clapped.

Stenstrom pushed the pillows aside. "What is this?" he demanded, his brain hurting a little from the gas.

Lady Alitrix, her face free of black paint, and her accent gone, spoke. "You pass, Lord Belmont. You passed our test, and well done! You are truly full of surprises!"

"You tried to murder me tonight—a demonweb, a gas-filled dungeon!"

"The demonweb is a very convincing and very expensive robot we use. We call him Arthur and he's been 'killed' lots of times in the past. The gas in the dungeon is a harmless sedative—it might have caused you a bit of a headache later on should you have not escaped."

"And the alternate routes out of the dungeon, what of those?"

"Oh, one of them leads to a lesser, Outer Sanctum room somewhere here in the building—you would have been 'in', but you would have been in an inferior circle. The rest head out into the alley—one of them, the worst one, lands you in a dumpster full of food refuse."

"Number four, is that the one?"

"I believe so, yes. Should you have taken any of the alley ones, you would not have been offered a membership in our club." She smiled brightly. "You, however, picked the good door—you made it to the Inner Sanctum. I had a feeling you would be successful and was pulling for you."

Lord Bannaster stepped forward. "We do enjoy a bit of theatricality from time to time. We enjoy challenging each other—but all in good fun, if you've the intellect to appreciate it. We must say, we were talking before you arrived—we have no idea how you did some of the things you accomplished tonight, most impressive. We've heard about Tyrol sorcery of course, but to see it firsthand, to witness it in action—remarkable! People usually slay Arthur with a weapon pulled from the wall, or with Vith Gifts—we've seen those on occasion. But you—you actually appeared to conjure Holystones from thin air! And the locked door—you were supposed to fall through a trap door *inside* the sanctum sanctorum, but you got through it so fast we had to use the extra one outside the door. Again a spectacular display."

"And the locked portcullis? How was I to open those without sorcery?"

Lady Alitrix sat down next to him. Her real voice was rather pleasing, and, smiling, she was a beautiful young woman. "Well, you could have made ample use of the mannequin of the Sister in the dungeon. You could have ripped her arms or legs off and stuck them through the bars, or, if you had given her a vigorous inspection, you would have found that she is held upright with a long stick which you could have pulled up out of the floor and run through the portcullis to press the button. Again, you did something we've never seen before."

"We call her Alice," Lord Bannaster said.

"And I suppose the 'Stick up the Sister's butt' is a metaphorical reference to your continued disdain for the Sisterhood?"

Lady Alitrix smiled. "I guess so, yes—excellent point! So, Lord Belmont, we would like to invite you to join the Inner Sanctum of the Bones Club. It's a large club—this simply being the Bern Chapter. There are chapters all over the League. Here, we gather often to delight each other, help each other when it's needed, and, on occasion, to challenge one another with intrigues—all in good fun. Helps keep the mind sharp. When you're a member of the Bones Club, you may rest assured that, wherever you go, you have friends waiting for you."

She looked at him hopefully. "So, what do you say? We'd love to have you."

Stenstrom's first inclination was to walk out and leave these people behind. However, in reviewing the events of the evening, he had to admit he had fun—these people had him completely fooled. He could picture himself bringing Lilly here.

"Sure, why not? And call me Bel. All my friends do."

✶　✶　✶　✶　✶

Stenstrom made great strides as the year progressed. No longer an aloof, friendless man about the school, he was now a well-liked and active member of the Bones Club. He even participated in the selection ritual, painting and dressing himself in black and sitting in the sanctum sanctorum, as various candidates came and went, sometimes using his Tyrol sorcery to liven things up. He was amazed how few people actually made it through the process, almost all either ending up in the alley or curling up and becoming incapacitated in the dungeon, unable to choose an exit.

He had a new best friend as well—Lady Alitrix. She was like a dual person—in the Bones Club, she was rather cool and sultry, exuding confidence and wit. She asked him to show her his skills and was amazed how he could make things appear and disappear with only a shake of his hand. Even up close, watching intently, she had no idea how he did it. She wanted to know, but he was mum.

Never tell … his mother's voice rang in his head. *Never give up your secrets.*

Away from the club, however, out in the school, she was timid, shy, and uncertain. She cried out for attention and positive reinforcement, becoming almost sick with worry when she didn't get it.

They became lovers at her suggestion one evening as they gazed through the telescopes at the top of the sanctum's dome; just a bit of harmless fun between friends, no entanglements, no expectations. Just two people enjoying each other; that's what she said.

Lady Alitrix' thinly veiled insecurities came shining through as they made love.

"Do you like that? Do you like that?" she often said, seeking affirmation throughout the encounter.

After the first awkward session, Stenstrom was certain Lady Alitrix wouldn't want to repeat it—she seemed to not have enjoyed a moment. But, she kept coming back for more—always insistent and demanding, quickly fading to lost and fragile as the deed wore on. She liked, most of all, to go into the "dungeon" and have sex on the stony floor with the dummy "Alice" watching.

One thing that was always a given, at least in Stenstrom's mind, was that when Lilly came calling, Alitrix would have to retreat. They were, after all, just friends. And, for a time Alitrix was agreeable, disappearing without a second word whenever Lilly chose to grace him with an appearance. After a year or so, Alitrix began to change her tune a little. She once suggested she be allowed to accompany him and Lilly during her visits—she'd be quiet, simply a friend hanging about, and Stenstrom agreed. However, the two ladies quickly began sniping at each other.

"Is this 'person' someone you are experimenting with, Bel?" Lilly asked, rather bluntly.

"What we share together is none of your business," Alitrix said.

"Quite true; nevertheless, I'd hope, Bel, you might select someone a little more to your level."

Alitrix blushed and was clearly hurt. "What do you mean?"

"I mean, look at you. Rather scrawny and not overly pretty—and clearly not a great intellect or wit either, like a little puppy dog nipping at his heels. Making love to a handsome man like Bel must be … humbling for you, at best."

Alitrix sat there and shivered. Stenstrom had never heard Lilly speak so cruelly.

18

—THE PAYMASTER SOLUTION—

Stenstrom had cast aside all of his old inhibitions. He'd gone his whole life with virtually no friends—his parents, and his two youngest sisters were all the people he knew. Thus far, in the Bones Club he found himself being liked, accepted, and he functioned as a vibrant member. He often invited his sisters Virginia and Lyra to his club meetings, and was delighted when they were able to come, for seeing the two of them mingling and enjoying themselves made him feel good. As Lilly had hoped, he was finally enjoying himself, out every evening with his new friends, Alitrix being his closest.

And, his encounter with the Astral Traveler was a mere distant memory—his various warnings and protections went unused.

All of the old baggage he carried with him was, for the most part, gone.

Except for one thing.

Many members of the club often arrived at 22 Stang wearing brand new Fleet uniforms—they having been newly admitted. Stenstrom looked at them, wearing the fine blue coats and hats he knew so well, and all of his old dreams returned. His desire to soar the stars and see what was there had never really left him—just been beaten into place by a knife in his chest.

Listening to his friends chatter about what ship they had joined and where they were going made him maudlin—sometimes even angry.

What was he to do?

$$\star \quad \star \quad \star \quad \star \quad \star$$

A knock came at the door of his apartment. Stenstrom had quit 22 Stang early that evening, feeling rather sorry for himself as he listened to Lord Wills of Narrow talk of shipping out on the Fleet scouting ship *Centerville* at term's end. He'd felt rather jealous.

He assumed it was Alitrix, come to see what was wrong with him.

Stenstrom opened the door, and there was Lilly, elegant in her pink Gamboa gown and parasol. "Hello, Bel," she said, all smiles.

Stenstrom hadn't expected her, but, as usual, Lilly came and went as her whims dictated.

And she was always welcome.

They embraced warmly in the hallway, and then kissed. "Is this a bad time?" she asked. "Is your little puppy dog here?"

"That's not a nice thing to say, Lilly."

"No, I suppose it isn't. I'm sorry."

They sat down and caught up. He told her that he now had many friends, mostly from the Bones Club, that Lilly had suggested he join. He told her about the dark, posh confines of that exclusive club, where he did many silly things that the others in the group thought were shocking—'look', they gasped, 'look what he just did', and the Sisters would be outraged.

Lilly clapped and listened, glad her Bel was making friends and enjoying himself. "The Bones Club, though a bit off-putting at first, is a fine club to be in. All of the best people belong to it—you'll find wherever you go, you'll have friends from the club waiting for you. I knew you would spread your wings there."

Still, he couldn't hide anything from Lilly. "You outwardly appear to be in fine spirits, but you can't hide anything from me. I can tell something is troubling you—tell me, please. I'm here just for you."

Stenstrom laughed and shook his head. "Nothing goes past your notice, does it? Just silliness really. I saw some of my friends at the club had joined the Fleet. They were wearing their newly fitted uniforms and discussing the ships they were soon to join. I felt left out. I felt jealous. I don't know, Lilly. Sometimes I have thoughts of clearing out of school all together, leaving Kana and heading to who knows where." He laughed. "I'm sorry—just dreams I used to have."

They stepped into the apartment, Lilly hugging him tightly. He could hear her heart beat, and he thought it an odd chain—Alitrix drawing strength from him, and he drawing strength from Lilly, one person feeding on the next.

Lilly was the perfect tonic for his soul; with a fresh dose of Lilly he could go on, do his schooling, entertain his new friends, and become the dreary, land-locked man his mother had envisioned for him.

That evening, Lilly put an odd seed into his head.

They finished the fine meal that Stenstrom had brought in from the kitchens of the Bones Club—room service yet another perk of membership—and asked if Lilly wanted to step out, to see Bern, possibly enjoy a theater or go to 22 Stang and sit.

Instead, they fell into each other's arms and retired to his bedroom.

"So, just who is this Lady Alitrix?" Lilly asked as they lay together in the dark, entwined.

"A friend," Stenstrom said in return.

Lilly considered the thought. "I did tell you that you are free to seek your heart; still, I cannot help but feel a little jealous," she said. "That girl certainly didn't seem up to your level. I almost thought to challenge her."

"Challenge her? You mean to a duel?" He was alarmed.

"Yes, but don't worry. I'm not going to hurt her."

"She is a fine person and I cherish her friendship. So, if you feel that strongly are you prepared to end this five year experiment, Lilly?"

She thought about it. "Frankly, I am a bit put off, but our experiment shall continue. How could you ever take me seriously should I do such a thing over a bland little person like Lady Alitrix of Zama."

Stenstrom was shocked. "Zama—did I mention she was of the House of Zama? I don't recall doing so."

"You didn't. I make it a point to know your doings. I might warn you that girls from Onaris might diminish your House, should you choose to pursue her further."

"She claims she is of the Hoban Zamas, not the Onaris Zamas."

"She's lying."

Stenstrom tried to disengage, but Lilly held him fast. "I'll pose a question that you once asked me, Lilly. Are you enjoying this time apart? Are you seeing anyone?" he asked.

"I'm not really looking."

"Are you wasting your five years? These are the years you asked for, remember?"

"Yes, I remember, but I'm not going out of my way to find somebody else, either. I never meant for these five years to serve as a replacement for you, Bel—I simply wanted to see if, in the natural course of events, something else came along. So far, nothing has."

She tried to change the subject. "How are your studies coming along?"

"Fine. I'm not really interested in studying accounting. I'm sure you know that."

"I listened to you this evening, lamenting your friends, lamenting the Fleet. If you wish to soar the stars in a Fleet ship so badly, Bel, then why don't you?"

"You know full well why. That door has been shut to me."

Lilly jumped out of bed and went to the desk. Her slender naked body glistened in the pearly moonlight coming in through the window. "Where are you going?" he asked.

She turned on the holo-terminal and rejoined him in bed as a carousel of lights began jumping out of it and swirling around the room. "You know, Bel, if you have any faults, I'd say one of them is too heavy a reliance on conventional thinking."

"Conventional thinking?"

"In some ways, you're the fastest thinker I've ever seen—when properly tasked and motivated. In other instances regarding your mother, like this one, you are guilty of very uninspired thought. There're ways around everything, if you want something badly enough."

She paused a moment, her face full of longing. "Look at me; there is something that I want very badly and am currently taking steps to see that I get it."

"Oh, and what is that?"

She reached out with her foot and manipulated the holographic glyph controls. "Let's focus on you for the moment, Bel, and not worry about me, shall we? Let's see …" She worked the floating glyph with her foot, moving it about. Soon a banner popped up.

"What do you have there?" Stenstrom leaned over to look at it as it danced around the room.

It read:

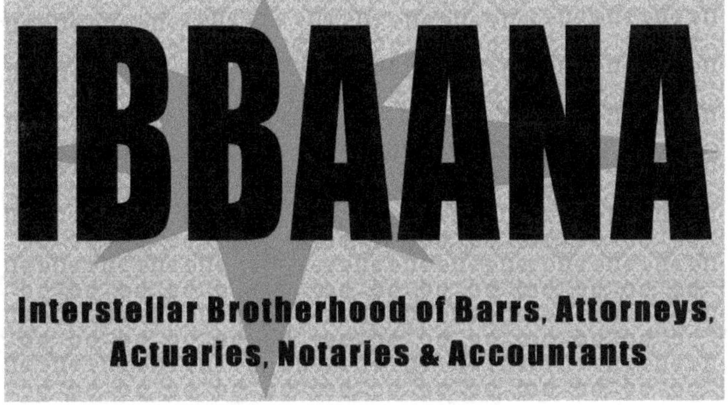

"What's this?"

"The IBBAANA."

"I think my mother's mentioned something about this organization. I truly had no interest."

"You should listen to your mother in this case. The IBBAANA is your ticket to the stars," she said happily. "And, more than that, it's your ticket to glory."

Stenstrom sat up from the bed and looked at the banner. It was a dry, uninteresting posting. He saw nothing of glory or honor in the drab, business-like construction of the holo.

Barrs ...

Actuaries ...

Notaries ...

Attorneys ... Good Creation.

"All right, Lilly, out with it. What's on your mind?"

"If you peruse the rather dry subject matter of this posting, you'll see that all sorts of occupations are covered by this society ... including this one ... Let's see ..." She highlighted a notice with her foot, and it jumped to the forefront. Stenstrom squinted to read it.

"Fleet Paymaster?"

"Yes, indeed," she said with a hint of triumph. "Sounds impressive, doesn't it: Fleet Paymaster. I've been doing some research. Every Fleet vessel manning fifty or more souls is required, by rule, to carry a Paymaster. A

Paymaster is basically a third party who arbitrates the dispersement of funds to the officers and crew. The Paymaster also ensures that all parties entitled to pays from the vessel in question are properly and timely compensated."

"It sounds like a do-nothing to me."

"Well, that's what it is, Bel. But, it's a shipboard do-nothing. You'd be on a ship, but you wouldn't be in the Fleet officially; you'd be a shipboard civilian. See, you've got to learn to be sneaky."

Stenstrom thought about it and the notion began to take flight in his head. "My father's never mentioned anything about Fleet Paymasters before."

"It's not a prestigious thing, and your father, being ship's captain, probably never really dealt with the shipboard Paymaster much—it's more of a clerical thing, probably something the boatswain had to deal with most often."

"Lilly, you really sound like you know what you're talking about."

"I always make it my business to know what I'm talking about."

Stenstrom began reading the notice. His promise to his mother stated he would never join the Fleet as either an officer or a crewman, and she'd updated the Promise over the years. She'd added: the Stellar Marines, the Merchant Marines, Space Traders and Astro-Tenders—anything she had heard of requiring frequent space travel she knifed out of him. And, there was one thing she had knifed *into* him: *accountant.*

But, all of his promises failed to include a shipboard civilian accountant—Mother hadn't thought of that. Perhaps Lilly was onto something. He continued to read, saw the requirements, and his heart sunk.

"No, no, Lilly—look here. You didn't read carefully enough. To be a Fleet Paymaster, you have to be an attorney."

"Ah, Bel, it appears *you* didn't read carefully enough. True, most Fleet Paymasters are attorneys, but, if you read here, (she pointed at a line of text with her foot) an accountant of ten years or more tenure with experience in public financial arbitration may also qualify as a Fleet Paymaster. I mean, to do this job, all you need is a pulse, an impartial mind, and a bit of bookkeeping skills."

Stenstrom snorted. "Lilly, I'm not even graduated yet—I have zero tenure, and I've never arbitrated a public financial deal."

Lilly kissed him on the cheek. "Again, Bel—think creatively. Your lack of experience and tenure is nothing that a few Belmont sesterces placed snuggly in the right pockets won't fix. Come on, Bel—are you so innocent you won't up and bribe a fellow or two? A good, well-thought out bribe can be a noble thing."

Stenstrom sat up and thought about it. Bribe someone? In all his wranglings with his mother in their game of brinkmanship, he had never considered trying something underhanded or unethical. In his mind, the only way to play the game was to play above board.

"I … can't bribe somebody, Lilly—that's unethical."

Lilly pulled him back down and lay on top of him. "What a virtuous young man you are, Bel. Consider this though—great men are often self-made. There are no great, self-made men lacking an unsavory component somewhere in their make-up. If you can make your way through life and say that the worst thing you did as a young man was bribe a fellow or two simply so you might have the opportunity to start your career and live your dream, then that's saying something. There are worse things you could do, Bel."

Stenstrom, feeling Lilly's weight on top of him, thought it over. "You'd not think ill of me?"

"No, Bel. Would you think ill of me, should I tell you some of things I've done?"

"What things?"

"Just things, Bel—so, will you do it?" She held onto him tightly.

Stenstrom fought with the thought for a bit more. "A bribe? What reputable gentleman would succumb to something as pedestrian and poorly thought out as a bribe?"

"Then I would avoid dealing with a reputable gentleman and confine your activities to the disreputable ones. And where are they? I would say in a place where anything goes if you have the coin to make things happen: Calvert."

Stenstrom lay there under the heat of Lilly's body and watched the posting swirl around the room.

A Fleet Paymaster …

19

—FLIGHT FROM BERN—

The following spring, Stenstrom graduated. At the Bones Club, he was hailed with raised glasses and fond, overflowing toasts. Several graduating members standing with him were, as usual, decked out in new Fleet uniforms.

This time, Stenstrom felt none of the sadness and envy he previously had when seeing the new recruits.

This time he had a plan.

He returned to his apartment to pack. When he got there, a message awaited him on his Com. He began getting his baggage ready and played the message, his back turned to it as he worked, glancing occasionally.

It was his mother and sisters Lyra and Virginia. Virginia was holding a large cake frosted in white icing. "Bel!" Mother said warmly. "We are so proud of you—a newly graduated alumnus of the University of Bern."

"Congratulations, Bel!" Lyra said, chiming in.

"I made you a cake, Bel," Virginia said.

Mother continued. "We are sending a coach for you tomorrow, to pick you up in grand style. You may expect the coach promptly at twelve bells. We have been laboring to restore your old room here at home and cannot wait for you to return. I'm also very excited to say that a Lord Fulmar of Bass shall be stopping by in a few days. Lord Bass is the proprietor of several successful firms here in Tyrol and he is eager to make your acquaintance. If you speak and present yourself well, Lord Bass might offer you a job."

He hastily filled his baggage. "Sorry, Mother, I've got other ideas for employment."

The Com continued. Virginia was sampling a little of the cake she had made, unable to resist. Mother spoke again. "It will be so nice to have you home again, where you belong. Don't forget, tomorrow at twelve bells. Do not be late—I would hate to have to come looking for you." The Com closed.

Stenstrom looked at the Com in horror.

... have you home again, where you belong.

Tomorrow, she's coming for him tomorrow? No doubt, the moment she gets him home, she'll ply him for information and update the Promise as needed.

It was imperative that he not be anywhere near Bern tomorrow.

He had to fly. He threw his clothes into the baggage without pausing to fold or arrange them.

There was a knock at his door. He nearly cried out in fright.

Who was it? It had to be his mother—or a Black Maiden.

Forgetting his baggage, he went to the window and started to climb out. He got his leg out into open air when the door swung open.

"Bel?" It was Lady Alitrix. She was peeking her head in through the door. "Hi, Bel—what are you doing out there?"

Stenstrom sighed in relief and pulled himself back into the apartment. "Hey, sorry, I thought you might be somebody else."

"May I come in?"

Stenstrom returned to his baggage. "Sure, sure, come in."

She opened the door and entered. She held a large straw basket. "I was hoping to share a small private celebration with you—to commemorate your graduation." She held out the basket. "I brought some nice food and cheeses from the Club, and some aged wine. I was …"

She saw his open baggage and clothes tossed in. "Are you… are you leaving so soon?"

"My mother is coming for me tomorrow, at twelve bells."

Alitrix approached him. She knew of his smothering mother—he spoke of her often. "Your mother? Are you worried?"

"I'm terrified as a matter of fact. If she manages to get me home, she'll wring out of me what I'm planning to do, then she'll put me to the knife and that shall be the end of it."

"Oh. What can I do to help?"

"If you really want to help me, help me pack. I have to flee the region as soon as possible. I'm not going home. I'm going where I've always wanted to go."

He grabbed another handful of clothes from the closet. "I really should have been more prepared. I should have ..."

Alitrix put her hand on his wrist and pulled herself into him. "Stop, for a moment. Take a break with me, please."

He resisted. He tried to pull away and continue packing.

"Please ..." she said.

They fell into each other's arms, Alitrix dropping her basket.

✶ ✶ ✶ ✶ ✶

Later that night, Stenstrom and Alitrix lay on his bed. He could see the squared-off landscape of open baggage beyond the foot of the bed and the partially empty closet. Alitrix smelled of perfume and fine soaps.

He thought she was asleep, but she wasn't. "Do you know where you're headed?" she asked.

"Southeast, to Calvert."

"Why Calvert?"

"There are some gentlemen I plan to call on in Calvert. I'm planning on plying my new trade in earnest."

"Oh?"

She was quiet for a minute or two, then: "You know, my father owns several banks in Inari. I've mentioned you to him—I'm certain he would be glad to offer you a position, and, who knows, with good work, you might quickly rise through the ranks."

Stenstrom looked at her in the dark: her thin, doll-like face, her hopeful eyes. "I appreciate that, I really do, but I've got other plans. I need to go to Calvert."

"Am I to never see you again?"

"Never's a long time. I'm certain our paths shall ..."

"Bel—I love you."

Stenstrom didn't know what to say.

"I know when we began this that it was simply two friends sharing the pleasure of each other's company, and that I promised I wouldn't expect anything beyond mere sex. I allowed the silly little girl in me too much sway, and I fell in love."

"Alitrix, you know I value you as one of my best friends. You helped me come out of my shell—taught me how to behave and interact as a friend. And the experiences we've shared over the past year and a half I'll always treasure. What can I say that will not break your heart? I love Lilly. You know that."

Tears fell down her face. "Yes, your Lilly, always Lilly. I didn't want to say anything earlier—and I know you'll think I'm just trying to make up a story to keep you from her, but I cannot remain silent any longer. Please, hear me out."

"All right."

"There is something odd about Lilly—I don't know what, but I just know. Haven't you thought it peculiar that she seems so in-tune with your thoughts and emotions? Always she's there to save the day just when you need her most. I would see you looking at the Club-members in their Fleet uniforms, and I knew you were feeling sad. Often, I wanted to come to your side, to try and comfort you, to make you smile. And always, there was Lilly, from out of nowhere walking up the steps, and I would sit there and wish that, for once, I could be the one to offer you comfort. I'm just a woman. Lilly is not a woman—she is something else. It's almost as if she's steering you to some predetermined destination. I don't know; I'm talking nonsense, but that's how I feel. I don't know what she is, but she's not a woman."

Stenstrom patiently listened and let her get it all out.

"I am a woman, and you have earned my love. That's all I have to give. That's all that I am. I'm nothing but a woman while Lilly is something else. How was I to ever compete with that?"

They lay there in silence, Alitrix sniffing slightly. "I'm, sorry," she said, "it's just the bitter little girl in me talking. I didn't mean to trouble you with this. Will you do me a favor?"

"Anything," Stenstrom said.

"Will you hold me tonight? I know you have to pack and are eager to leave before your mother's procession arrives, but I can help you in the morning. I shall meet the procession and stall for you, to give you added time to be clear. If I'm questioned, I'll tell them you're off to Barrow to seek adventure there."

He pulled her into him.

"Also, I would like you to write to me when you can—just so I know you're safe. And, one final thing. I will give you a year. Your Lilly gave you five years. I shall offer you one. One year, and if in that time you discover that I was correct about Lilly, then you may come to me and take my hand."

And they held each other all night long.

$$\ast \quad \ast \quad \ast \quad \ast \quad \ast$$

They had a busy morning. They rose with the sun and finished packing. Stenstrom had a lot of baggage. Alitrix promised to have the Club take care of his stuff until he called for it.

Alitrix showed remarkable toughness that morning. She must have been hurting inside, but didn't show it; she'd come a long way since he first met her. She was a big help.

Carrying a small overnight bag, he went out into the street with Alitrix and nearly ran into the procession of float cars Mother had promised to send—several hours early it seemed.

Pulling Alitrix aside, he gave her one last kiss and then made his way down the street toward the station. He caught a glimpse of Alitrix approaching the procession, his mother getting out and questioning her.

He had to act fast. He got to the station and booked a ticket for the first coach out—it didn't matter where. It was heading to Falz. Fine, that was fine. He bought a ticket and got in.

After getting to Falz, he then booked freight passage to the city of St. Edmunds, the so-called 'City of Lonely Hearts' in the heart of Calvert. Calvert was certainly the last place his mother would expect him to go, and it was also the best place for him to begin his career as a Paymaster.

20

—CALVERT—

Calvert—the veritable tossed-salad of Kana. There, among the know-nothings and ne'er-to-dos dotting the wharves and seedy streets, he set about his business.

Here was Calvert, a sliver of land against the sea, east of the Great Armenelos Forest, a collection of crowded cities and bad architecture, where showering and basic hygiene was, apparently, optional in some quarters. Still, walking the tight streets crowded with riff-raff and smelling the salt in the air, Stenstrom felt a sense of jubilation, of release. Not like the well-tended and stuffy city of Bern, this was real, full of Barbary-style buildings that have been lived in by real people.

He found he liked the place as it unfolded around him.

Moving about in the streets in the salty sunshine marred only by seabirds and the tall masts of sailing vessels, he noted a thriving cottage industry was at work everywhere—the Fiend of Calvert, that murderous madman who had terrorized the place for years was now like a second-son and grand celebrity. Stenstrom saw inns and taverns called "The Fiend's Hideout" and the "Madman's Pleasure." He saw vendors selling Fiend merchandise and, most prevalently, he saw people dressed in a variety of garbs offering Murder Tours, where the curious bystanders and amateur sleuths could visit the murder sites for themselves and try to figure out who the Fiend was.

As he made his way down the street near the docks, he became aware of a tall woman following him—a woman dressed in gray and wearing a broad gray hat.

It was her!! She had come again!

She closed the distance. From behind, she reached out for him.

Quickly he turned and seized her by the wrist, hauling her down and drawing a MARZABLE.

He put it to her throat.

"Oh!" the woman said as she fell, her hat falling away revealing a head of blonde hair.

"Who are you!" Stenstrom roared.

"I … I just wanted to see if you would be interested in joining us for a tour, sir … Please …"

Scattered at her feet was a stack of pamphlets. They read:

She looked up at him, wide-eyed. He checked his white Holy-stone—it was silent. No Astral Plane. She was just a woman dressed in gray.

"Good Creation, ma'am, I am so sorry!" he said picking her up. "Are you all right?"

She checked herself over. "I think so."

Stenstrom picked up her stack of pamphlets and her hat and gave them to her. "Please forgive me. Is there anything I can do to make this up to you?"

She put her hat on. "No, no, it was an accident. I shouldn't have sneaked up on you like I did. This is Calvert after all. I should know better."

Stenstrom felt miserable. "Please, I would like to purchase a tour."

He paid the lady his money, and she showed him to a large, fairly classy open-air hover float parked by the docks. Several people were already seated inside, awaiting the tour to begin. As Stenstrom took his seat, she handed him a rather thick packet of pamphlets detailing the layout of Calvert, the scenes of some of the Fiend's more gruesome crimes, and his escape route in the city of St. Edmund's. As Stenstrom looked it over, more people joined him in the hover float, lead by other ladies, also dressed in gray.

The lady he assaulted seated herself on an opposing bench and readied herself for the tour.

"What is your name, please, ma'am?" Stenstrom asked.

"I am Grand Dame Lady Miranda of Rosel."

Stenstrom looked at his pamphlet. "Ah, our hostess for the afternoon?"

"Yes."

"Again, I apologize for my behavior earlier. I have a rather sour history with ladies dressed in gray."

"Do you? May I ask what you've encountered? Obviously, as I make this subject my trade and chief point of interest, I am most keen to gather all information I can."

Stenstrom was puzzled. "Is a woman in gray a facet of the Fiend of Calvert lore?"

Lady Miranda became excited as she spoke, clearly a devotee of the subject. "Oh yes, sir, yes. As we shall discover on the tour, the Mad Lord of Walther, who engaged and pursued the Fiend across the rooftops of St. Edmund's, is the only person who ever saw the Fiend in person and lived to tell the story. He claims, and my colleagues dispute this, that he saw the Fiend of Calvert as a lady dressed in gray. That's why I and my assistants dress in gray, for I believe the Mad Lord's account. I believe there is evidence to support the notion that the Fiend of Calvert was indeed a woman."

She got out a roto-pad and took down Stenstrom's account, of the incident at the Fox Park when he was a boy, at Rustam Labyrinth, and again at the university, nodding as she took the dictation.

When he was done, she smiled at him. "Well, I think you've given me some remarkable information to think about. I shall perform research and …

are you staying in Calvert? You do not look like a local. Are you staying at the Empire Hotel, doing a little Native Watching as is the fad?"

"No, ma'am."

"I should be happy to call on you if I have further questions, and I know I shall. Oh, this is most exciting. I finally have mounting evidence to argue with Rodrick of Dee."

Stenstrom told her he was staying in town for a few days and would drop in on her in a day or two.

She was thrilled, and the tour began.

✳ ✳ ✳ ✳ ✳

He settled into Calvert the next day and began his task. He was armed with a ton of Belmont sesterces, which went a long way and opened a great many doors. He'd been stealthily deducting the money from his account and saving it over the past year—moving the loot from one unmarked account to another, his newly won skills at accounting helping him hide the deductions so that Mother would not get wise. Flush with cash and determination, he prowled the crooked streets and windblown allies, looking for scalawags and pinch-pricks, and not having a hard time finding them, much he mused as the Fiend of Calvert had thirty years prior. Soon, he discovered just the men he was looking for. He found the seediest Notary he could, a Lord Gissel of Wheeze, down on his luck and ready to deal. Stenstrom sat him down in the bars, filled his cups, and greased his pockets. Before long he had a whole stack of notarized endorsements, each more impressive-sounding and outlandish than the last. With Notary Gissel happily stamping anything put in front of him, Stenstrom could have proclaimed himself the governor of Planet Fall and gotten a notarized stamp to prove it. With this pile of bought paper, he could claim as much tenure as he wanted.

He bunked out in a fallen-down cricket shack near the wharf called "The Toothless Dame." Despite his lavish upbringing in Belmont Manor, he found something of an affinity with the peeling paint and the dirty flooring of his room, the air tepid with the smell of old stockings and people's dinners. Hiding out in Calvert, he felt like he was on one of the adventures he so longed for as a child, and he didn't want it to end. He decided to unpack and take his time. Nestled in his bag, he found a small card placed there by Alitrix as he unpacked. It read: "One Year" with the date and her holo-account information at the Bones Club. He set the card out on his desk, feeling close to her. He wrote her as he promised, using the seedy VX terminal in his room.

She wrote back stating his mother was not happy at all and looked the devil to pay.

So much the better.

She also wrote saying one year was provisional—that she would wait as long as he needed. She wrote she missed him terribly.

So far, Calvert had been fairly safe, his mother clearly not suspecting he was anywhere near the region. His most persistent caller was Lady Miranda of Rosel. He must have whetted her appetite for information, and he saw her prowling the streets, inquiring at every inn she could find, apparently looking for him. He was sitting in the tavern of the Toothless Dame having an ale when she happened to walk in. A casual fade into the shadows, and she walked right past him, marching up to the counter and persistently speaking to the innkeeper.

The innkeeper pointed at the table where Stenstrom was sitting.

She looked over. "Well, I don't see him," she said. She left her card with the innkeeper and departed, giving his table one last look as she walked past. He laughed and fetched the card.

He would be sure to meet up with her later once his task was finished and answer whatever questions she had. He still felt he owed her for knocking her down the other day.

On a more serious note, as the days passed, the net around him cast from distant Tyrol was finally beginning to tighten.

While walking back from Notary Gissel's office with yet another ream of bogus papers under arm, he was sure he saw the gossamer veils of a Black Maiden in the crowds, sniffing the air, heading in his direction.

Black Maidens, the airy watchdogs and nursemaids of his mother and bane of his wayward sisters—they were on the prowl, and were closing in on him. They honed in on his scent, and no hiding in the shadows could protect him. Sooner or later, they would have him right back at Belmont Manor with his mother ready to pounce.

He felt the hand of desperation. What was he going to do? Some of his sisters had been adept at evading the Black Maidens, at prolonging the chase. Constance was one, and his other sister Xantrope held the record for running from the Maidens, having successfully eluded them for two months. But, others were terrible at evading the Maidens: Calami the wayward was one, Nathalie, Elma and Lenta were others, rarely lasting more than a few hours.

Now it was his turn to run.

He tore down an alley, the reaching veils in slow but steady pursuit. He emerged on a crowded side street—the now familiar vendors and tour guides arranged in a row down toward the docks plying their "Fiend" trade in earnest. He saw Lady Miranda standing amid the crowd in her usual gray dress and hat looking for customers.

Thinking fast, he ran in her direction. "Lord Belmont!" she said seeing him. "Lord Belmont, there you are! I have been looking all over for you. You promised we could sit down and discuss matters in greater detail. I have a whole slew of new questions for you, sir!"

Breathless, he approached her. "Lady Miranda, I promise, you can ask me anything you want, but first I must ask a novel favor of you." He whispered in her ear, and she was shocked.

"What? You're not serious?"

"I'm deadly serious!"

"And, you'll answer my questions?"

"Yes, yes!"

"Well, all right, if you must."

Quickly, he got down on all fours and put his head up the folds of her petticoat as the Black Maiden passed.

Some people laughed. She stood there, clearly embarrassed, but determined to get her information. "Oh, do mind your own business, please," she said to some gawker.

After a minute or two, Stenstrom emerged, Lady Miranda red-faced, louts across the street clapping and hoping for a turn. "Will you kindly tell me what that was all about, please?" she asked.

"It's complicated. Suffice to say, I am pursued by unusual forces. Standing in your presence with my face obscured shielded me from being discovered. Your scent protected me."

"My scent—I see. I didn't notice anything just now."

"No, you wouldn't, unless you know specifically what to look for."

She got her rotopad out and added a few notations to it. "Well then, sir, I have delivered on my part of the bargain. I shall expect you to be at my disposal this evening, for I have many questions, and I expect a dinner to be provided by you at a place of my choosing."

Stenstrom just had his head up her dress; he couldn't refuse.

✶ ✶ ✶ ✶ ✶

That evening, he and Lady Miranda sat at dinner at the Empire Hotel, a giant, fortress-like walled structure in the heart of St. Edmunds, she with her roto-pad out, peppering him with questions.

"… And, going back to the Fox Park incident, you say there were many men there with the Woman in Gray?"

"Yes."

"What did they look like? How were they dressed?"

Stenstrom thought back. "I don't know … like sailors, I suppose."

"Like Calvert men? They looked like men from Calvert?"

"I suppose so, yes."

She added a few notations to her pad. She smiled. "Ah, see, this all ties together."

"What does?"

"I have long conjectured that many of the men suspected of being killed by the Fiend were actually abducted—there were no bodies found in many cases. The missing men were simply assumed to be murder victims, their bodies hidden and not found. The Fiend, however, took no pains to hide his work in most cases; therefore, I believe that those men were not murder victims after all, but abductees, somehow spirited away and kept hidden. See, many of my colleagues have failed to take the Mad Lord of Walther at his word—they considered him to be a drunken and unreliable source of information. Though he tended to freely embellish his exploits in his memoirs, there is a kernel of truth to everything he writes. The Mad Lord suspected that the mindless men he encountered in Woodward at the City of the Dead were somehow under the sway of the Fiend of Calvert, a theory that has been debunked by my colleagues as poppycock."

"I recall reading about the Mad Lord's exploits with my sister when I was a child. Something about zombies and lost men in a hidden place."

"Yes. I think those men you saw in Fox Park were more abductees from Calvert."

"That would mean that the Woman in Gray was in league with the Fiend."

Lady Miranda tapped the tablecloth with her fingers, her excitement clear. "No, no, the Woman in Gray you encountered at Fox Park *is* the Fiend of Calvert. The Mad Lord wrote that the Fiend of Calvert was, in fact, a woman in gray—it fits; it all fits."

People came and went as they ate, many wearing unusual clothes and speaking in odd dialects.

"Many come to this hotel to dress up and speak in a secret language. Right here, in this very place, the Fiend once sat, looking out the fancy windows, seeing all. Murders were committed here, though none made the posts—hushed up by the management. Oh, by Creation, how I wish I could have been there at Fox park with you."

They talked a bit further and concluded the meal, Stenstrom tired, unimpressed by the genteel clientele and ready to return to his rented room.

Lady Miranda, though, had other ideas. She bought a room for the night and bade him join her for a nightcap, and there she invited him to make love to her. Every bit of Stenstrom told him that this was a trap—that he was in mortal peril. However, Lady Miranda did not read as having been to the Astral Plane, and she did not smell of strong woman scent. No, this was simply a woman who desperately wanted to be close to someone who had stood in the presence of the Fiend of Calvert—her life's passion.

He obliged her, spending a steamy night in the tower of the hotel, listening to the laughter and strange languages spoken in nearby rooms, and then took his leave come morning.

21

—STENSTROM'S BAGGAGE—

Back in his rented room, he was again to his task, and the growing troubles that dogged him.

Mother. He saw five Black Maidens as he made his way back to the Toothless Dame—the lingering smell of Lady Miranda upon his body still offering him a bit of cover.

Mother was going to magic him back to Tyrol, and to fight fire with fire, he needed his books. He had them in a chest back in his room at the university in Bern; he had to leave them behind after his hasty flight from the city. He wrote Alitrix to send for his baggage, and he gave her the number of a locker at the air, sea and land port in St. Edmund's which was just up the coast.

In disguise, moving in the shadows, he staked out the place and waited for his baggage to arrive. He had to be careful. His mother had ways of finding people, both worldly and other worldly. Her vast network of friends was formidable. Any passing person could be on the look-out for him, hence his disguise. Additionally, any number of summoned entities could track him down if it got close enough, and he had no protection, other than his NTHs, which were overkill and sure to alert other entities should he use them. He needed a way to quietly detect the spirits and devise countermeasures.

He needed his baggage, and, specifically, his chest full of his books.

The Empire Hotel was problematic. It was centrally located, its massive tower commanded unobstructed views into the nooks and crannies of St. Edmunds—small wonder the Fiend used it as his base of operations. From the innumerable terraces and hidden nooks, he could see the wealthy, oddly dressed people looking out, many holding drinks and standing behind spyglasses, not pointing the lens upwards, but pointing down to the streets, honed in on the people, watching them intently.

Looking for him no doubt, on Mother's request. He would have to be

careful, use his Fade into the Shadows without question.

A few days later, the baggage arrived. Trying to be discreet, wary of the eyes looking down from the Empire, he carefully spied the surroundings and made his way to the port. There, he waited for a good moment to collect his baggage and be off.

Drat! Was that Lady Chatstra of Owens standing over there? What in Creation was she doing in Calvert? She was a friend of his mother's from Mercia, and she saw everything.

True to her name, she was chatting with friends near the counter where his chest was held, and she didn't seem to be in a hurry.

He waited in the shadows for her to depart.

Black Maidens! They were emerging from everywhere, and no hiding in the shadows would suffice against them—they were going to sniff him out sooner or later.

He could not linger—he had to flee the port and return to his lodgings, his mother having clearly won this round, and he seethed with frustration.

* * * * *

He waited in his small room, not daring to go out. Through his window, the Empire Hotel loomed, casting its shadow. He paced the floor, impatient.

There was a knock. He moved silently to the door and gave it a small rap with his knuckles. Three raps came in reply. He smiled and opened the door.

Lady Miranda stood there. "Lord Belmont, I have fetched your baggage from the port as you requested. I saw no one at the station. I felt no danger."

"Did you avoid the Empire Hotel as I requested? I see eyes there watching the streets at all hours."

She quickly walked in, pulling a float litter behind her. "They're not looking for you, sir. Patrons at the hotel enjoy people-watching the locals from their expensive, exclusive terraces. St. Edmunds, and its folk, is like a grand zoo for them to gawk at from a safe distance."

"Yes, well, we'll see."

There was his baggage—four large trunks emblazoned with a garish "B" and a slightly smaller wooden chest containing his books. They appeared innocent enough, but …

"Thank you, my lady. These trunks are trapped."

"Trapped?" Her attention turned to the baggage, and her interest began to pique. "I think you should explain in further detail, Lord Belmont."

"My mother … she is a Tyrol sorceress. And she has trapped my baggage with out-worldly snares. If I open these trunks, I'll be back to Belmont Manor in a flash."

Lady Miranda stared at the trunks, her eyes wide with interest. She then curtsied and lifted the front of her skirt. "Well then, let's see it. I'm not afraid. I offer you protection, as I did before."

Stenstrom knelt down and put his head up Lady Miranda's skirt. "The baggage, except for the chest, should be unlocked. Go ahead and open them— don't be afraid, it's me they want, not you."

"Will they not see you?"

"Not like this."

Stenstrom could hear Lady Miranda opening the trunks, her smooth legs flexing slightly as she worked. Her skin smelled of soaps and powders.

"I don't see anything," she said with a hint of disappointment.

However, there was no question they were there in the room with them at that moment, coming out of the baggage—he could feel it. "You're not looking correctly. Look to the shadows. Forget the obvious and mundane; see the

improbable and the half-formed around you and you will notice things few have ever seen."

"I don't understand," she said, rocking back and forth.

"Relax, close your eyes, and then open them—truly open them."

She stiffened up a little. Then: "Oh, what is this? I see them! I see them, sir! They appear rather ghastly. Are they evil?"

"No. No, they are not. They simply appear rather odd. Do you have all the trunks open?"

"Yes, all except for the wooden chest. It's locked."

"How many are there?"

Lady Miranda counted. "Twenty-six. They seem to be sniffing about."

"Let them sniff their fill. They will then present themselves to you. When they do, simply tell them to go away, and they will. It's me they want, not you, and they cannot detect me clothed in your scent."

Lady Miranda then did something he never would have expected. She suddenly crossed her legs, trapping his head between her thighs, her muscles cabling up in a taut manner. His ears muffled, he could vaguely hear her saying "Go away. Do go away, please."

She wrenched up the pressure, and then finally released him. He came rolling out of her skirt, face red gasping for air, the Black Maidens gone. Lady Miranda didn't say a word. Instead, she fell on him, tearing at his clothes, grabbing his hands and moving them to rather private places on her person. Apparently, her sexual desires and her intellectual curiosities were strongly linked together—as discovering new things deeply aroused her.

They had a rather torrid night, Stenstrom taking her several times, discovering that she had a rather sadistic side to her, as he found himself scratched and rather bloody as the night wore on. Her voice changed. She uttered obscenities as they had sex. She performed fellatio upon him and demanded he take her from the rear. She then demanded lengthy cunnilingus.

In the morning, she plied him with questions. She wanted to begin research on a new book uncovering the hidden truths of the world—Black Maidens and sorcery chief among them. She insisted he check out of the inn and come with her, to her home on the hill north of the city. She said she was alone, a widow, and would be glad to have him. "Think of the things we could do for each other ... and to each other ..." she said.

He promised he would consider it and sent her on her way, she first securing his various Com, holo-mon and holo-mail account information, and a flurry of promises that he visit her soon, for research ... and other things.

At last, he was alone with his baggage. The important one, though, his chest of books, was still locked—he'd forgotten all about that one. Lady Miranda couldn't open it.

He grabbed his NTHs and cocked them. He touched the surface of the chest, for he truly didn't want to hurt a Black Maiden. They were kind and benevolent, and though they were a tad gaunt, they were a glad presence. His sister Nylar knew how to tickle them and make them laugh. It wasn't their fault Mother had sent them after him. "I'm sorry, I'm sorry," he said as he pointed and fired. The throbbing mass of green energy passed through the wooden lid of the chest and didn't come out the other side. He took a deep breath and unlocked the chest, revealing the cache of books within.

There was no indication that anything had been in the chest waiting for him—perhaps it had been empty after all. He kept that thought with him as he unloaded his books. He vowed he would never point his NTHs at a Black Maiden ever again. He would run, he'd confound and divert them, but not kill. They didn't deserve that.

Finally, with his arcane library in hand, he set up a small apothecary in his room. He bought brass pots, tripods to hang them on, flame burners, mortars and pestles, an assortment of knives, tongs and other required utensils, and a laboratory's worth of salts, chemicals, flowers, herbs and metals. He also bought bags of plaster for Holystones.

The first thing he did was create a bolabung, which was a small bit of wormwood infused with a few chemicals. Bolabungs were normally used to shield one's mind from unwanted telepathy, but with a little modification, they could protect one from a variety of things—Black Maidens included. He infused the bolabung with a healthy amount of Lady Miranda's scent (he acquired a fair amount of it during their previous night together), strung it on a leather cord, and put it round his neck. The bolabung would require refreshing. Cooking down various oils and bees wax, he made a salve of her scent, strong and odorous, which he could smear on the bolabung every day.

Thus equipped, he began making Holystones.

Holystones were marvels of chemical design, and could be made to perform any number of useful, one-time functions. They took a skilled hand and a learned mind to properly make them—Mother had spent three years teaching their lore to him and his sisters. He prepared the plaster and cast them into hollow spheres, not too thin, not too thick, and readied them for filling.

Some of the more basic ones were quite easy to create:

Yellow: Creates a soft light equal to four or five candle power. Duration:

1 hour.

Ingredients: Tungsten, Salt (sodium chromate)

Red (rose): Creates a hot, energetic fire and shall burn until chemicals are used up.

Ingredients: Hydrogen-infused gel, kerosene, flint;

Green: Creates an expanding, sticky substance similar in appearance to a spider's web.

Ingredients: Titanium, Bromine, Mercury, Silk and Whisperwill (a flowering plant)

Blue: Creates a powerful Vitriolic acid

Ingredients: Sulfur, Pyrite, Manganese and water.

Those Holystones were nice to have and fairly easy to make. In one afternoon of crushing and stirring and heating over a fire, he had quite a few of them ready to go. Then he set to work to the more advanced ones—ones that could aid him in the detection and defeating of demons and invisible spirits. Those were the ones he needed most:

Purple: Oscillates or "Rumbles" in the presence of invisible creatures

Ingredients: Cadmium, iron, Henbane (a flowering plant), Yew

Black: Detects mystical objects or persons

Ingredients: Hornblende, antimony, zinc, Monks Hood (a flowering plant), beryl (crushed), natron, bismuth, Hardaway (a flowering plant), quartz, and obsidian

Pink: Renders those who touch it for too long unconscious

Ingredients: morganite, carbuncle (garnet), gypsum-weed, beeswax, rose oil, peyote, nightshade berry

White: Prevents the body from going into shock

Ingredients: granite (crushed), manganese, rhodium, and menthol.

The pink ones, or "Pinkies," were difficult to get used to, as in handling them he could just as easily be incapacitated as the person he was planning to use it on. During his training, he had gotten used to its effects to the point where he could hold one for an extended length of time and not be addled; it was part of his training. His sister Virginia, for all her various failings, was a champion Pinky holder, easily able to out-last both him and Lyra back-to-back.

He purchased several silver candlesticks and ground them down a little, ensuring they were perfectly level. He then placed a Purple and Black Holy-stone on the top of the stick where a candle would normally go. If the stones started rumbling, or if they jumped off the stick and began rolling on the floor, he would have immediate warning. Those, along with his Astral Plane detectors and his bolabung, should keep him reasonably safe.

Now he could relax a little and continue his business.

He now felt he had more than enough false papers and fake tenure to sustain him. The matter of officiating a public financial deal was a bit more challenging, as he needed witnesses.

A visit to one of the drop-down waterfront bars in Bezzel easily corrected that problem. He slid up to the bar one noisy evening, nursed a watered-down bottle of spirits, and kept a sharp ear. Before long, he eavesdropped on two filthy toughs in great need of arbitration.

"Garh, Morbagg, you Xaphan-spawn! I rolls sevens, sevens!" a painted-over merchant-man spat, pointing his crooked finger at a pair of grubby dice. "Ye' owes me the lot and more!"

The man sitting across the table begged to differ. "Ye' rolls sixes, Nosspin. See, three e' four equals six. Now hand over the till, lest I feels inclined to char-broil yer lungs!"

Stenstrom pulled a chair and sat down. Two pairs of blood-shot eyes turned to him. "Gentlemen," he said. "Well met. I am Stenstrom, Lord of Belmont-South Tyrol, and I couldn't help but overhear your small financial dispute. I would like to offer my services and assist you through this unsettling situation as a fair and impartial arbitrator. What do you say?"

"I says ye' best be moving' along, 'squire, les you be findin' these dice knockin' about inside yer body."

"Yeh'," Nosspin said, "an' you'll not have eaten them, either." The two men laughed in a phlegmy fashion.

Stenstrom was unfazed. "Yes, well, I think we can clear this up pretty fast, gentlemen. You see, Sir Morbagg, four plus three indeed equals seven, as currently displayed by these dice here. However, these dice appear to be rigged to unfairly land on seven a disproportionately high percentage of the time, and, therefore, the roll is invalid."

"Yo' sayin I'm rolling loaded dice, Slime-hauler!" Nosspin shouted.

"Yes, I am. My judgment in this matter, therefore, is swift. This roll is invalid, as are any previous rolls using said loaded dice, and you two shall receive all payouts back and let the matter be forgotten. The dice in question shall be impounded or replaced with fair set of dice with all speed. I additionally rule that you two shall be entitled to a small reimbursement equaling four thousand sesterces each for your inconvenience."

Stenstrom plopped two small moneybags down on the table.

He smiled. "There, that was easy. Now, I require that you two follow me down the street to the office of Notary Gissel, where you shall sign a sworn affidavit that I, Stenstrom, Lord of Belmont-South Tyrol, fairly and promptly arbitrated this matter in a public place."

The two grubby men gawked at him a moment. They suddenly drew a set of dirty blades. "Get out o' town, Wench-wanker!"

A massive brawl broke out in the bar. Courtesans screamed, things flew out the windows.

Sometime later, a rumpled Morbagg and bloodied Nosspin arrived at the office of Notary Gissel and signed, at gun-point, the sworn affidavit Stenstrom had asked for.

He was now all set.

22
—THE QUEST FOR IBBAANA—

His next task was to join the IBBAANA brotherhood. The problem was that there was not an IBBAANA office anywhere in St. Edmunds, or in the whole of Calvert for that matter. The nearest office was in the Remnath, city of Mercia, about fifteen hundred miles to the west. Apparently, one had to present oneself in person to join.

Armed with his dubious stack of notarized papers and phony affidavits, Stenstrom made his way to the station.

The purple Holystone hidden in his coat rumbled so hard in its pocket he thought he might go into palpitations. The station was blanketed with invisible entities, and he caught glimpses of gaunt maidens in black drifting about occasionally lifting their heads and sniffing the air.

If he went into the station, he would be overwhelmed—even his bolabung would not protect him from them all. Dragging his baggage, he headed north and wandered into St Edmund's small town square. He needed to think; he needed a plan. He thought about running to Lady Miranda, but quickly thought better of it. She was becoming obsessive and rather demanding as of late, and was starting to treat him like a lowly husband. She might not be inclined to let him go should he enlist her for help. He needed something else—something his mother wouldn't have expected and pre-saturated with Maidens.

An opportunity soon presented itself. He saw a modest caravan of ten weather-beaten float wagons covered with faded white tarpaulins lined up just off of the square. The tarpaulins were decorated with a series of red and green symbols and squiggles, highlighted in gold. Stenstrom easily recognized the designs—he'd seen them all his life adorning the old Merian ruins dotting his manor.

It was a caravan of Pilgrims of Merian. The Merians were sect of religious zealots preaching non-approved Elder lore. They roamed the country-side of Kana delivering good news, that the Elders were not gone and that all one had to do was look up into the sky to see them. They were tolerated at best, jeered and censured by the Sisters at worst.

They were sitting out in front of their caravan dressed in their usual: loose-fitting, white smock-like garments that went down to their knees. Over that, they wore longer green robes of fine brocade sleeved in gold cloth. They wore numerous thin necklaces of wooden red and green beads. The women all had their long hair held up in elaborate combs, while the men's long hair went down unkempt past their shoulders. They were all either shoeless or shod in simple sandals.

They'd set up several modest stands before their wagons and were attempting to sell hand-crafted trinkets and bolts of homespun cloth to the masses assembled in front to gawk at them.

As per usual wherever they went, the Merians were getting laughed at, and, worse, the uncouth of St. Edmunds were turning out in force to harass and torment them.

"You want to sell something, missy—I'll pay for something of yours all right …" a lout said.

"I'll buy the lot of you, and make you into fine street-walkers … You men too …"

The various people in the crowd who appeared to want to buy some of the Merian's wares were being overwhelmed by the hecklers and the uncouth gropers.

One burly man strode forward and seized one of the Merian females by the cheek. "Lemme' have a look at ya', Missy!"

She struggled. "Please … sir …" she stammered, trying to pull away.

"Hold still!" he yelled, knocking her little stand aside, scattering her trinkets.

None of the Merian men and nobody in the crowd seemed to want to help her as she struggled.

"Now, let's see yer' goods!" the man yelled as he began ripping her clothes.

Stenstrom had seen enough. He pushed through the crowd. "Take your hands off her!" he said with authority.

The crowd hushed. Spy glasses came down and centered on them from the tower of the Empire Hotel.

The man gave him a quick look, snorted, and returned to harassing the Merian woman. Stenstrom produced a pink Holystone in a blur and casually dropped it down his shirt. Immediately, the lout went limp and fell to the ground.

Everybody turned to Stenstrom.

"He killed Gasser!" someone yelled. "Get him!" A dirty fellow drew a Hertamer energy gun out of his coat.

Stenstrom drew his NTH and stuck the iron muzzle in the man's face. He cocked the hammer with a dramatic clank. "Care to join him?" he asked.

Another man raised his fists and rushed Stenstrom from behind. In a moment he was webbed up solid with a thrown green Holystone.

With that, the crowd backed up and gave Stenstrom space.

"But he killed Gasser!" the first man protested. "Where's the justice?" Most in the crowd appeared unsympathetic.

"He's not dead, just incapacitated," Stenstrom said. "Take him and clean him up, will you, and make sure he gets a shower with plenty of lye to defeat his choking stench."

The man began dragging the fallen Gasser and the webbed-up fellow away in stages, moving one for a time, and then the other. "We're going to be looking for you, mate—mark my words! You'll be seein' us again!"

"Grand, I'll be happy to serve you lot up the same a second time!"

Stenstrom turned and helped the Merian woman right her table and gather her scattered trinkets. "Are you all right, ma'am?"

"Yes, yes, I think so."

"Why did none of your group help out just now? That man could have hurt you."

She gazed at him, her eyes serene. "Our Star would not have allowed him to harm me."

"But, had I not been here, you might have been …"

"But, you were here. The Star sent you to me, and I was not harmed."

Stenstrom couldn't really argue with the logic and hope to get anywhere.

"May I ask—what are you doing in Calvert? Not a place I'd expect to see a band of Merians."

The rest of the Merians gathered around. "Several of our wagons are in urgent need of repairs," she said. "We stopped here to try and raise money to have them properly serviced."

"In Calvert? Nobody has money in Calvert."

"Our Star will provide. We must simply have faith. If we do that, then we shall be provided for."

He checked his coat—the Holystone within was quiet—so far he'd been unnoticed.

"How much do you need?"

"A thousand Calvert solaris. That's what we were told the price would be."

He had a thought as he looked at the unassuming Merians gathered around him. They appeared to want to thank him, that they were grateful for his help, but truly didn't know how to respond. Apparently, they weren't used to people being kind to them. He reached into his coat and pulled out several notes. "A thousand Calvert solaris … Here, this should be enough."

He handed the girl the money. She stood there holding it. "Our Star has indeed provided. If I may ask, why have you done this for us?"

"Because I wanted to. Because my home is on the grounds of an old Merian monastery and I've always felt a bit of a kinship with your order. Also, my sister can see the star you claim exists."

"Your sister? She can see our star?"

He had to be off. "Yes. She says it's in that direction," he said pointing to the northwest. "And, that it is a large yellow star with a red cloud swirling around it."

The girl smiled. "I see. Well, this is a wonderful day, as our Star intended. I am Nefia, and we are a humble band of traveler Merians from Westwood, seeking to offer good news to the people. May I ask your name, sir, so that I may properly thank you?"

"Stenstrom, Lord of Belmont-South Tyrol. I suppose I am in the market for a little good news."

"Lord Stenstrom, we are at your service for the unexpected kindness you have shown us."

"I was also hoping I might catch a ride with you. Are you heading west, by chance?"

"We head in no particular direction. The Star has sent you to us with purpose and speed. We will take you west, all the way to the sea if need be."

✶   ✶   ✶   ✶   ✶

With the money Stenstrom gave them, the Merians repaired their meager float wagons and gladly made their way out of Calvert. Safe with the Merians, an unlikely bunch, he was free of his out-worldly pursuers, his Holystones remaining quiet. He had out-foxed them and his mother to boot.

The caravan made its slow way west, up the coast, through St. Edmund's, around the bay, and into the wild lands of southern Zenon. To the south was the rocky, sea coast and to the north were the towering pillars of clouds covering the vast stretch of Lake Monama where the pale, black-eyed people lived.

Two days into the trip, he found the Merians had an old Maxim-style Com screen in one of the wagons. It had been over two weeks since his graduation and flight from Bern. He felt homesick and wanted to at least let his mother know he was all right. With this old Maxim Com unit, he could probably send word to her, and she wouldn't be able to trace him.

She appeared on the screen. She was in bed. Her face was haggard and spent. Her breakfast on a tray was sitting off to the side, barely touched.

"Bel, is that you?" she said trying to squint into the screen.

"Yes, Mother, it's me."

"I've been so worried about you. How could you do this to your mother?"

"I'm sorry. I didn't mean to worry you. As you can see, I'm fine."

She smiled a little. "Bel, why did you not come home after your graduation? Your sisters and I had had a lovely reception planned. Lyra and Virginia were so very disappointed. They had prepared a wonderful celebration for you." Her voice was tired and thin.

"I will apologize to them when I can. I have some business to attend to, Mother. I'm trying to accumulate my accreditations so that I might ply the trade you and father paid for me to learn."

His mother seemed so tired. "I'm glad you are embracing your schooling." She appeared pained for a moment. "You always talked of the Fleet and of the stars. I see you, even now in my dreams, as a boy wearing the little clothes your father sent home. I always see you as a little boy in my dreams. What have I done, Bel? Have I robbed you of what you wanted most?"

Stenstrom thought about his answer. "What's done is done, and I am no worse for it."

She smiled. "I'm glad. If I had it to do over again, I would have let you do whatever you wanted. Are you coming home soon?"

"When time allows; again, I am pursuing a lead."

Jubilee leaned back and sank into her pillows. "I … really think you should come home for a bit … to visit and catch up. It won't take long, I promise. Then you may pursue your matters in earnest."

"Why, is there anything the matter? Why do you look so tired?"

"No, Bel, no … nothing's the matter. I was worried, and I simply miss my son, and would like to see you."

"I'll be home when I can. I have some matters to attend, and then I'll be home."

Lady Jubilee gazed at her son through the Com. "All right then. But please, when you've concluded your business, will you promise to come home and see your old mother?"

"I promise Mother, yes."

It struck him as he concluded the Com that his mother was uncharacteristically timid and accommodating. He had expected her to be frothing with rage, full of recriminations and threats. He was used to speaking boldly to his mother; otherwise, she might have had him twisted in knots.

Perhaps she was mellowing, or possibly trying a different tactic.

As he rode the hovering wagon across the Zenon lowlands with the vast, cloud-shrouded plume of Lake Monama to the north, he began noticing something. In the far distance, he saw four thin figures in shroud-like robes following his procession.

The Black Maidens. They were slowly zeroing in on him. He'd almost forgotten about his mother's determination to forcibly bring him home.

Seeing them in the distance reminded him of the dire contest his mother insisted he play: *Resist. Be your own man.*

Very well—be it so. The game was on, Mother. She almost had him fooled.

Once in Mercia, the Merians dropped Stenstrom off at the local office of IBBAANA—the Inter-Stellar Brotherhood of Barrs, Attorneys, Actuaries, Notaries and Accountants, a modest red-brick structure in the center of town. He got out of the wagon with his chests. He bade the Merians a fond farewell and went inside the office.

He announced he wished to join the Brotherhood. Getting a stern eye, he was taken into a backroom, and his qualifications were reviewed.

As it turned out, it was his membership in the Bones Club that got him into the IBBAANA brotherhood, for the fellow reviewing his papers spotted them as fabricated at once. However, he, like Stenstrom, was a proud member of the Bones Club, so, after a bit of chit-chat and a healthy "entrance fee" was collected, Stenstrom was at last made an official member of the brotherhood, no further questions asked. Chosen Occupation: Fleet Paymaster, Status: Active.

So, he had come to Mercia and gotten what he came for—he was now an IBBAANA. As he exited the building, he saw four tall women in black standing at the end of the street waiting for him.

His mother—the Black Maidens. He had a quick thought that this game was becoming rather silly, that he was getting too old for such things. If he had had a more timid nature, he would simply go home and see his mother.

But, she herself had drilled into him: *Though I am your mother, consider me your enemy. I shall attempt to confound you and set you to my will. I want you to resist—to confound me in turn. Thus, using your wits, I shall make you strong. Nothing more than your best effort I expect of you.*

Not wanting to disappoint her, Stenstrom determined to get the better of this situation. Avoiding the front door, he found a convenient window out the back and bore away from the building through the craggy allies leading to the side-streets of Mercia.

With the Black Maidens dogging his heels, he waited in town, never allowing himself to stay stationary for more than a few hours at a time. He also avoided being alone as he bought one courtesan after another to stand with him. The Black Maidens couldn't get to him if he was in constant company. Female company was best. He would need to be careful. These Black Maidens appeared to be showing no sign of giving up.

Two days later he received a message from the Brotherhood. A Fleet vessel, the *Sandwich*, a small frigate making berth in Atalea, was in need of a replacement Paymaster at once, for theirs had died.

What was the reason for the man's death, Stenstrom wanted to know.

The official word was: food poisoning.

With the Maidens close at his heels, he accepted. Courtesan in hand, he immediately booked passage to Atalea and met up with his first charge, the Fleet Frigate *Sandwich*. If he could get on that ship, he would be victorious.

23

—The *Sandwich*—

He had to admit, he was a little disappointed when he first saw the *Sandwich* sitting in the water at Atalea dock. She was little more than a flying wreck. An ugly *Mermidon*-class frigate assigned the lowly role of hauling Fleet freight, refuse, and assorted goods back and forth across the League, the *Sandwich* was squat and saucer-shaped and in desperate need of both a painting and a fumigating. She was at one time white, but was now a patchy, unidentifiable red with the outer few millimeters of her thick, tough hull rusted. The capsule-like bridge sitting atop the saucer looked like a virus implanting its DNA into some unsuspecting bacteria cell.

Still, she was a Fleet ship and was going to the stars. After taking a moment to get used to her meager shape and rusty hull, she became like a magic carpet, ready to speed him away to adventure.

The Boatswain of the *Sandwich,* an untidy man named Pike, was waiting for him on the gangway. He was terse and unpleasant from the get go. "You shall confine yourself to the areas of the ship assigned to you, namely, your office, your quarters and the crew's mess. You are forbidden from entering the bridge, period. You shall not, under any circumstances, enter or dine in the officer's mess, nor shall you eat in the crew's mess during peak dining hours, unless you choose to take your chow to your office or your room. You shall be allowed on the boat deck for two hours a day at times so designated by myself or the captain. You shall be assigned one crewman as an aid when their duties allow. You shall not fraternize with the officers or the crew, and you shall not be permitted to sit in at the nightly film. Just remember, you are on this ship, but you are not a part of it in any way. Do your job, make sure we get paid, hide our expenses if you can, and be quiet about it."

And with that warm welcome, Stenstrom boarded the ship, walking up the bouncy gang plank. He could smell the heavy salt water in the air by the wharf, and he could almost hear the *Sandwich's* foot-thick duraplate hull rust-ing.

He looked back over his shoulder—the Black Maidens were just arriving on the dock, sniffing the air and swaying slightly.

Moving through the small, poorly lit corridors of the ship, Stenstrom found himself a bit appalled. The ship was a mess—dirty walls, peeling paint, marred floors, and the crew was little better, motley in the extreme: mis-matched uniforms in various stages of serviceable repair, filthy shoes, tar-nished buckles, paunched bellies, and unshaven faces. The crew, full of dirty looks and second glances, were also inked up in an assemblage of gaudy 4-D tattoos in the images of naked ladies, obscene gestures, grotesque body parts, and varied, profane verbiage spelled out (and occasionally misspelled) on arms, shoulders, faces and necks. As he descended further into the bowels of the ship, he was painfully reminded of the two times he'd been on his father's ship, the *Caroline*, and the difference between the two was night and day. His father's Warbird was a brightly-lit paradise of gleaming metal, spotless ap-pointments, ram-rod crew, shaved faces, and rigid discipline.

In comparison to his father's ship, the *Sandwich* was a veritable cave populated by a squad of unwashed, stinking cavemen. He found his tiny cab-in, which appeared to have been a bathroom at some point in the past, and he went inside and wondered if he really wanted to be here. He could de-ship, avoid the Black Maidens, and return to IBBAANA and announce his desire to wait for another more serviceable vessel.

The thought passed through his mind several times.

There was a knock at his door. A young lady stood there. "Hi!" she said in a cheery voice. "I'm Crewman Kaly! I've been assigned to help you!"

Stenstrom was pulled from his gloomy thoughts. He regarded her for a moment—again, as with most things on this ship, here was a lady stand-ing in the doorway, presumably a member of the crew, without an ounce of military bearing or protocol that he had assumed was a staple of the Fleet, no matter the ship. She could have been a lady walking down the street, a co-ed at school, a waitress from Onaris, or an urchin from Calvert, anything but an active crewman in the Stellar Fleet aboard a commissioned ship.

Still, unlike the dirty looks he got from the other members of the crew that he passed, this Crewman Kaly smiled in an inviting and genuine way.

What the heck, he thought. He stood and held out his hand. She shook it. "Wow, strong grip," she said. "I like that."

Kaly sat down on his small bed and began talking—she appeared to be a real yapper. "I man the forward sensing station on the bridge, day bell. Between ten and twelve bells after my shift, I'll be down to help you out."

Kaly studied him intently. "You're a lot taller than our last Paymaster, and a lot more handsome."

"Thanks," he said, not expecting the compliment.

"So, you're a Great Lord from Kana?"

"I am," Stenstrom replied.

"What House? Not that I'll know what you're talking about or anything, I'm just curious."

"Belmont. Officially, Belmont-South Tyrol, an off-shoot branch."

Kaly's eyes lit up—she had fascinating green eyes. "I have no idea what that means. We don't see many Great Lords on this ship. Our last Paymaster was just some guy—I didn't know much about him. I think he was an attorney—I don't like attorneys much. Oh … you're not an attorney, are you?"

"No."

Kaly was relieved. "That's great! So, what do I call you? I'm not well-versed on Kanan customs and such. Do I call you *Lord* or *Sir*, or *Great Lord*? I really don't have a clue."

"Call me Bel. All my friends do."

"Okay, Bel, I'll do that. You're sort of alone on this ship—no other Great Lords around, I mean other than Dunks. Do lords from Planet Fall count, in the social scheme, I mean? Planet Fall is where Dunks is from. We're pretty much all Browns here. I'm from Fig on Onaris."

"Who's Dunks?"

"Oh! He's our commander. Sorry."

"How long have you been in the Fleet?"

"Five years. I … didn't score too well in my exams and got stuck with ship duty on a frigate. When they don't know what to do with you, they put you on one of these ships. S'ok, it pays the bills, I guess, and we're pretty informal around here, if you haven't already guessed—that's a perk I imagine. I'm told every ship is in the image of its commander—Dunks is an informal guy, and so are we. I've got a big family to help support back home on Onaris, and a deadbeat ex-husband whom I have to pay for by court order—I guess that's why I don't like attorneys. Yeah, I think I'm going to like you; you're a heck of a lot better looking than the last guy. Did I already mention that?"

Stenstrom was mystified. "I believe you did. Um, will my superior pulchritude be a plus in your assisting me in the ship's financial matters?"

"Oh, yeah."

"I hear tell the previous Paymaster died of food poisoning. Is that correct?"

"Well, yeah, I guess so."

Stenstrom tried to make sense of that as Kaly chirped away. She seemed a happy-enough person, smiling; she had stunning eyes and a piled-up head of messy brown hair held in some bit of order with a pink hair band. Her skin was a pearly shade, and she had nice bone structure.

She saw his chests full of books.

"What are those?" she asked, looking at the old brown covers.

"Just old books."

The pipes overhead made a loud hissing sound, and Stenstrom could hear many doors clanging shut. His lights flickered for a moment.

"Oh," Kaly said, "looks like we're about to take off. You want to come to the boat deck and see?"

"The boatswain said I was forbidden to go to the boat deck except at designated hours."

"Don't worry about him; he's a knob. Come on. Taking off is always my favorite part."

She led him down the cramped corridor, up a gangway, and up two decks. There was the *Sandwich's* modest boat deck, just a long corridor lined on one side with windows. They went to the glass and looked down on the wharf. There was a jarring clank coming up from the bowels of the ship.

"Any moment now, the engineer is just building up pressure," Kaly said as people on the wharf began to back away from the ship.

Stenstrom looked around and felt weak. He remembered his father and the stars and the trips to Onaris, he and Lyra running through the manor halls playing with their models of the *Caroline.*

He remembered the knife in his chest, the clothes burning in the fountain. So, here he was at last, standing on a Fleet ship, ready to blast off.

The journey he'd taken to arrive on this rusty old vessel …

He leaned against the glass.

"Hey," Kaly said looking up at him. "You ok?"

He smiled. "I'm fine. I'm just fine. I've waited a long time for this."

"Yeah?" she said. "Well, welcome aboard, Bel, Lord of Belmont. I really think I'm going to like you. I'm glad you're here with us."

And the ship lifted away from the wharf and slowly soared into the heavens.

∗   ∗   ∗   ∗   ∗

Stenstrom stood there on the boat deck for hours. Kaly had left sometime back, and he stood alone, the occasional crewman passing by idly. He watched the sky turn to black and Kana fade away. He stared at nothing but little speckles of distant stars, barely able to take it all in.

Footsteps came clanking in approach.

A slender man in a Fleet coat was walking down the corridor holding a triangle hat under his arm. He saw Stenstrom and stopped.

"Are you our new Paymaster?" he asked.

Stenstrom turned. "I am."

The man smiled and held out his hand. "Well then, glad to know you. I'm the captain of the ship, though my official rank is lieutenant. Lt. Dunkster's my name. I'm from the House of Carew on Planet Fall. Just call me Dunks."

Stenstrom took his hand and shook it. "Stenstrom, Lord of Belmont-South Tyrol. Please call me Bel."

Lt. Dunkster thought a moment and tapped the felt of his hat with his fingertips. "Isn't there a Lord Belmont in the Fleet? Yeah, Captain Stenstrom, of the *Caroline*, right?"

"He's my father."

"A Warbird captain's your father, and here you are, a Paymaster? What's the story on that?"

"No story—I just never joined."

Lt. Dunkster looked a little dubious. "Hmmm, well, I'm certain we'll be fast friends in no time. It's a good ship here, good crew. Might not look like much, but we manage a decent service. Frigates—you know in ancient times a 'frigate' was a term that meant warship, a small warship, but a fighting vessel none the same. In our modern Fleet, however, a frigate is nothing more than a small ship relegated to small duties. But, somebody has to do this job, and I might say, we do it pretty well, and I pride myself on always managing to get my mates a little extra come payday—our Fleet earnings are a travesty. You'll see. Have you met Kaly? I assigned her to you."

"I have. Very nice lady."

"You … like her? I mean, I can get someone else for you if you want."

Stenstrom was puzzled. There was something fishy going on. "I like her just fine."

"Good, good. If you change your mind, let me know. Well, I've got to find the boatswain. Good meeting you."

"And you."

They shook hands again, and Lt. Dunkster continued on to the aft of the ship.

✳ ✳ ✳ ✳ ✳

As the first few days rolled by, Stenstrom began to get the hang of the ship. He could move around fairly well through the tight metal interior, and he'd met most of the crew. Most ignored him with a weathered scowl, while others looked at his nice clothes and seemed a bit jealous—he was obviously a man of wealth, a man beyond them socially and financially.

His duties as Paymaster were quite simple. Come payday, the money rolled in from the Fleet and dispersed to the crew—he just had to validate it and witness the computerized transactions. He was amazed how little they got paid. It didn't seem fair.

Every day, Kaly came down to his office after her watch ended and logged him into the ship's lists—he not having clearance to access them on his own. They then would go through all the ship's transactions, and he would validate them as OC: "Observed and Correct" and send them on.

His newly won knowledge of forged documents and his experience in hiding money from his Mother instantly told him the transactions he was looking at were faked: "cooked," "doctored"—call it whatever you will. Clearly Lt. Dunkster, the mate, and the boatswain were trying to hide money by moving it figuratively from one pocket or purse to another—it wasn't much, just a few coins here and there, but it added up and was fairly clear to see, if one knew what to look for. Once he validated them, the documents were sent on to Fleet, where they piled up in a dusty database somewhere and were probably never looked at again.

Kaly saw him puzzling over the documents. "Something wrong, Bel?" she asked.

He thought about it a moment. "No, no." He validated the documents and sent them on.

Perhaps it was simply an error.

As the days went on, the errors continued, always the neat little tricks, the missing coin or two here, and the extra money piled up there. It became obvious that there was more money floating around and exiting the ship than was coming in. Lt. Dunkster, the mate, and the boatswain were up to something shady. Some of the crew had to be in on it too—the dirty, mistrusting looks he got walking the corridors hadn't abated; in fact, they'd gotten worse. He wondered sometimes when he headed to the chow line or the showers if he was going to get jumped.

Let them try—they'd have a sore surprise coming. He could handle himself against this sorry lot any day.

Kaly seemed to be his only friend. She tried at first to be aloof and standoffish, but her friendly nature won out every time. She chattered about her home on Onaris and her friends, and she peppered him with questions about his home and his house—"Twenty-nine sisters, wow!" Her tendency to give tongue to her random thoughts made her appear to be a scatter-brain, a real ditz; in truth, such was not the case—she had a good head in there, somewhere, but simply didn't act like it. She appeared to be incapable of being anything other than herself, anything other than genuine. Her visits were the happiest parts of his day. He'd become genuinely fond of her.

After two weeks, he decided to level with her. "Kaly, tomorrow, I'm going to go speak to Dunks."

"About what?" she asked, a little alarmed.

"About whatever it is he's doing here on the side."

She turned a little pale and didn't try to deny it. Clearly she knew. "I don't think you want to do that, Bel," she said.

"I'm sorry, I must. I'm bonded to be honest, to report what I see. I want to know what he's doing—if he's running illegal goods and pushing things that harm folks, I'm not going to put up with it."

She sat there and looked sad. Stenstrom headed for the door. "Where are you going?" she asked.

"To the mess to get some dinner. I'll bring you something back."

He went down to the crew's mess and grabbed a tray, feeling eyes on him as he did so. He selected some chow and two cans of Gasol and headed back to his cabin.

He was in for quite a surprise when a got there.

Kaly was in his bed, the covers pulled up to her bare arms and shoulders—her clothes scattered on the floor. Her voice changed from her normal perky one, to a more seductive, low-pitched drawl. "Why don't you put down the tray, close the door, and come to bed."

"Kaly," he said holding his tray, "what is this?"

She smiled. "Just doing my job, and, like I said, you're a lot better looking than the last Paymaster—I actually want to have sex with you. I've been thinking about it a lot over the last few days. I was wondering when it would come to this."

She pulled the covers aside, and there she was, naked and steaming. A strong smell came out—she'd applied The Weed. It began to cloud his head.

"Kaly—we needn't do this. Please put your clothes on."

She looked a tad hurt. "Don't you like me?"

"I like you just fine."

"Then come to bed."

"I'm not going to come to bed, Kaly. I spoke to the captain the other day before we blasted off out of Minz. I got the distinct feeling that sexing me is part of your duties—am I correct?"

She sat up, staring at him hard with her lovely green eyes. "It is, though again, it is one duty I was looking forward to."

"Why are you to serve me in such a capacity? I'm certain such a thing isn't a standard Fleet practice."

Her smile faded. "You're on a frigate, Bel—we both are. We do what we have to do. And, I think I'm a little insulted. Sex is something we share on Onaris. To reject me is a huge slap. Do you think I'm beneath you, Lord Belmont? Is that what you think? Am I not good enough for a Great Lord like you?"

"Don't call me that, Kaly, and no, I don't think such a thing. I consider you my friend."

"Friends have sex on Onaris all the time—no big deal. You really must think I'm ugly."

He sat down on the bed. She sat up and put her arms on his back. "I think nothing of the sort. I just don't feel that having sex would be properly honoring you at this time."

"Bel," she said, a hint of desperation in her voice, "do you know what could happen to me if we don't do this—if you go to the captain?"

"No. What? What could happen? I don't understand."

She looked like she wanted to say something.

"Go on, Kaly, you can tell me. You have my word as a Great Lord, I won't tell or think ill of you, and the word of a Great Lord is something you can depend on."

He stood and got her the can of Gasol that he'd brought for her from the mess. She took the can and tossed it back. "I'm supposed to have sex with you," she said, swallowing. "We should have been having sex days ago—all the other fellows I've been assigned to took me right away. I was starting to think I'd lost my touch."

"Why?"

"To keep you occupied. To keep you from asking questions."

"Why?"

She finished her can and stifled a burp. "You've seen by now how little we make. To supplement our purses, we do a little extra on the side—it's no big deal; all frigates do it."

"What extra on the side?" he asked.

"I don't want to say. It's no big deal—but you're not supposed to know about it."

"Why not?"

"Because you're not part of the crew, because you are bound and no-tarized to be truthful when questioned. And, in your case, because you're a Great Lord. I don't want to say anymore. It's not a big deal, but if I can't keep you in here, if you start snooping around, I'm going to get in serious trouble. I could just disappear, you know?"

Stenstrom took her empty can and put it on the desk. "I certainly don't want to get you in trouble, Kaly, but I can't just let Dunks carry on. What if he's pushing something that's hurting people?"

"I would never party myself to something like that, Bel—honest! Please, it's nothing—nobody's getting hurt. If he was hurting people, if he was push-ing Maggs or Remax or something like that, I'd turn him in myself. Look, I know I talk a lot. I know I say out loud pretty much anything that rolls into my head, but usually everything I say is the truth, and what we're doing here is harmless, small potatoes. We're just trying to get by is all."

She stared at him. "And I was also hoping to share an open relationship with you. I'm not a whore—if that's what you're thinking."

"Of course not, though, the sex ploy seems to be lacking a tad in sophistication."

"Yeah?" she said, "it's always worked before—we stick with what works on this ship."

"So, you can assure me that none are being harmed by whatever Dunks is doing?"

"Yes, yes …"

Stenstrom gave her hair a toss. "Fine then—I trust your word. Don't worry about it. I won't go snooping about."

"Especially on Wednesday nights."

"Fine then. On Wednesday nights I'll just linger here, eat my dinner, and look at the Aire Net."

"Am I still invited to share your evenings on Wednesday nights?"

"Certainly—I was hoping you'd ask. We can talk, or hit the Net."

"Or, we can have sex. I really want to." She put her hands on his face.

"Perhaps another time. He stood up, got his tray, and began eating.

He froze. In the mirror opposite the bed, he thought he saw a shadowy figure standing there. It reached out for him with clawed hands.

He jumped back.

"Bel?" what is it?" Kaly asked. "What's wrong?"

He turned to the mirror again and the figure was gone. Even in the middle of open space, his mother's servants pursued. It was time to get out his gear.

"Nothing," he replied. "I need to unpack a few things. Would you like to help me?"

"Oh, Bel, come on … Well, okay. You promise we'll do it later, after I've helped you."

"Um, sure, sure."

Kaly sprang out of bed, and wrapped herself up in a sheet. Stenstrom pulled out his chest of books. She knelt down and looked at it.

"What's this one? It's got a funny lock."

Stenstrom considered his words. "You've shared a secret with me, Kaly.

Now I've got one to share with you."

"Yeah? A secret? Okay, what is it?"

"You promise not to tell?"

"I promise."

"I'm an … enthusiast in certain seldom-studied arts, Kaly. That chest is full of all my arcane learning and instrumentality."

Her eyes got wide. "You mean you're a magician, or something like that?"

"Yes, after a sort."

"Cooool!" she said. "Can I see?"

"The chest is locked tight right?"

She tried the lid. "Yep."

He reached out and put his hand against the lock and then pulled his hand back. "Try it now."

She did, and the lid opened easily. "How'd you do that? Is it a trick lock, or one of those neat palm-sprander locks on Bazz?"

"No, it's a real lock. No lock can deter me for long."

"Can you teach me that?"

"Maybe later. Can you bring me the wooden box within, please?"

Kaly, still wrapped up in the sheet, tentatively rummaged around in the chest. "You mean this one?" she said pulling out a brown wooden box.

"That's it. Bring it over here and open it, please."

Kaly brought it to the desk and carefully pulled the lid off. Inside was a silver device. It looked like a tall candlestick with a recessed pan at the top. She pulled it out of the box and stood it up on the desk. "What is it?"

Stenstrom reached up, waved his hand, and placed a black Holystone in the pan at the top.

Kaly gasped. "What's that? How did you do that?" she asked.

"It's a Holystone. It shall alert me if demons should come near. If you're going to be helping me, Kaly, you might as well know that creatures not of this world are after me, and might well tear my soul apart should they catch wind of where I am."

"Ok," she said staring at the black Holystone.

"Does that prospect disturb you?"

She thought for a moment. "They're coming for your soul, right?"

"That's right, yes."

"Just yours, not mine?"

"Just mine."

"Nope. I'm fine. I'm good."

24

—A Stain on His Soul—

Every three days, toward 18 bells, there'd be a knock on his door, and Kaly came in.

They had become very good friends. Sometimes they'd watch the Airnet, other times she'd bring a game or two. Sometimes they'd just sit and talk—Kaly going on and on for hours about her life, her dreams—whatever came into her head. He didn't mind; he liked listening to her stories. Eventually, Stenstrom's inhibitions fell to the point where they started having sex, Kaly being remarkably casual with it. She was also completely uninhibited, willing to do or try anything.

He lay there one night, Kaly wrapped around him. He began to wonder what was going on that he wasn't supposed to see. He took a pink Holystone and put it in Kaly's hand. She was already asleep, but the pinky would ensure she stayed out.

He rose from bed, dressed, and prepared to creep out. He looked back—there was Kaly, quiet and peaceful. He came back and gave her a quick kiss on the forehead and then sneaked out. Using his training, he was remarkably stealthy. He could silently slip from shadow to shadow, blending in with the dark. Several people passed by as he roamed about, not one realizing he was there.

He wasn't sure what he was looking for. Given what Kaly had said, he assumed there was some improper or possibly illegal enterprise in progress on the *Sandwich*. For decency's sake he could only hope it wasn't something too outrageous, though she had promised him it wasn't harmful. Moving silently, he eventually made his way to the hold. He had to be careful, as he could hear quite a few people talking within.

When he thought the moment was right, he drifted in.

Inside the hold, he saw Dunks, the boatswain Pike, and several other people tending a huge vat in the center of the hold. There was a heavy smell of chemicals and various herbs floating on the air. And, he saw a large apothecary full of all sorts of ingredients in shelved glass bottles and jars against the far wall. Normally, there was nothing but a blank wall in that area.

It looked like they were brewing some sort of potion. He silently made his way into the hold and crept up on the pot Dunks was stirring. Within was a clear bubbling liquid that reeked of chemicals.

"Keep stirrin'," the boatswain said. "It has to be just right."

Dunks agreed. "No worries, pops. This is going to be a fine batch of sun tan lotion. Now—everybody out 'cuz here's where I use my secret technique to polish it up. Come on—out!"

People set their things down and exited the hold.

The boatswain Pike lingered. "I think I'll hang about. You promised to give me your procedure, and I've waited long enough. I want it."

"You'll get it when I'm good and ready to give it to you, not a moment sooner," Dunks snapped. "Now, get out!"

The boatswain turned in a huff and nearly plowed into Stenstrom. Alone in the hold, Dunks donned a breather mask and began adding components into the vat. The fumes that poured out were enough to incapacitate Stenstrom. Clinging to the shadows, he staggered out into the corridor, the fumes soon mixing with all the other bad smells on the ship. That was a near thing, for the mixture was foul and nearly had him on the floor. He worked his way out of the hold unnoticed and back to his quarters. He undressed and climbed back into bed. Kaly, with the pinky in her hand, hadn't even moved.

✶　✶　✶　✶　✶

Two days later, Stenstrom still puzzled over what he'd seen in the hold. What exactly were they up to? He wasn't naïve enough to believe they were making "sun tan lotion," as Dunks called it. Perhaps it was a certain tincture, spirit or snake-oil remedy—though it smelled terrible, whatever it was.

Feeling himself a little flushed, he went to the basin to splash water on his face.

He looked into the mirror.

Behind his reflection was a demonic landscape. Strange objects festered under old cobwebs.

As he stared at the mirror, he saw four indistinct figures sitting in the distance.

He heard a voice *"Lone Rider... The Star that does not Fall. It man... You belong to us..."*

Hands reached for him.

And he felt a ripping in his chest, a sundering of soul from flesh.

His soul was being attacked. For the love of Creation—what had Mother set against him this time?

Wheezing, holding his chest, his staggered out of his cabin and blundered into the corridor where he fell to the metal floor.

A moment later, Kaly came by. "Bel!" she squeaked seeing him lying there.

She knelt down and tried to pull him up. "Bel! Bel, what's wrong?"

He struggled to catch his breath. "Kaly … I'm in trouble …"

She looked down at him. She seemed whole-heartedly disappointed. "You know, Bel—I've really come to look up to you. We were going at it hard having sex the other day and I thought—*you know, I respect the heck out of this guy.* And then I had a monster orgasm. I really thought you might be a different sort."

"Kaly … please …"

"I mean, I'm not one to talk. I had my fill yesterday, Creation knows. But you—I don't know, I had you up there. I thought you were above this sort of thing, you know?"

"Kaly … I'm dying …"

She put her hands on her hips. "You filthy drunk right now, Bel?"

"Help me …"

"You Balled-out? Kooked up?"

He wheezed for breath. "It's nothing like that …"

She leaned down and sniffed him. "I don't smell any booze. I do smell a little BO—no, wait, that's me. And your pupils aren't dilated so you're not 'Kooked' up either."

"It's my soul … it's sorcery …. I'm under—attack!"

She finally seemed convinced. "Sorcery, really? Oh, that's so cool! I'm so happy you're not strung out or drunk! What can I do?"

Stenstrom struggled to stay conscious. "Need … salts … chemicals… and a bit of tin or antimony …"

"Where—where am I going to get that stuff?"

"Cargo hold—I saw a hidden a—apothecary. Should have w-what I need."

"How do you know about that?" she demanded.

"I saw it …"

Kaly thought about it for a moment, then slung his arm around her shoulder and helped him down to the hold, stumbling often.

They passed several people on their way. They saw Stenstrom, apparently in bad shape, and they laughed and shook their heads. "Would you look at that—Paymaster Stenstrom, all Kooked up. Guess we're rubbin' off on *his lordship*…"

They got to the hold a few minutes later. Kaly sat him down against the wall. "Now, you think this is just an apothecary, right?" she asked. "Nothing more?"

Stenstrom felt his soul rip. He held his chest in agony. "I don't … don't care what it is, Kaly … help me."

She stood and went to the far wall. She pressed a hidden lever and a portion of the wall spun about revealing a vast cabinetry of shelves and drawers brimming with lined-up jars, beakers and bottles. "Ok," she said. "What do I need?"

"N-Natron …"

"What? What's that?"

"S-soda ash …"

Kaly looked around the shelves and browsed through the bottles, clinking them together. "Soda ash, soda ash … ah, here's some!" She pulled out a clear glass vial full of bluish salt. "What else?"

"Bismuth …"

"Bismuth, bismuth …" She looked around. "Ok—bismuth, this silvery metal here?" She showed him a clear glass vial with two bits of metal sliding about inside.

"Now, fox … fox glove …"

"What's that?"

"A purple ... flower, hooded, bell-shaped."

She looked around. "I don't think we're going to have that ... wait—what do you know? Fox glove—wow, Dunks has this thing stocked!" She pulled an earthen jar out of the shelving and removed a stalk of dried purple, hood-like flowers."

"Now ... I need either tin ... or ... anti—mony."

She looked around. "Ha—we have both!"

"A-Antimony ... It's better."

"What else?"

"Get a pot and start a small fire."

Kaly rummaged about and found a rough iron pot. She turned on a gas burner and put the pot on it.

"No ... no, Kaly, I need fire, not ... a gas flame."

She spun around. "Where am I going to make a fire, Bel?" She went to a stainless steel basin in the corner. "Here' I'll make one in here." She grabbed bits of paper and board and tossed them into the basin. She tried lighting bits of papers on the nearby gas burner and tossing them in, but she couldn't sustain a flame in the basin. "You got a lighter?"

"Kaly ... take this and be careful." He produced a red Holystone. She ran toward him and took it. "Throw it into the basin and step away."

Kaly threw the Holystone into the basin, and a hot yellow fire erupted, licking up the side of the metal wall. It subsided after a few moments and she put the iron pot into the basin, careful not to burn herself.

"Now, carefully put ... the natron into the fire. Be-be careful, it's going to jump up again."

Kaly unstoppered the natron and tossed it into the flames. The fire turned cobalt blue and leapt up. "Wow! Ok! What's next?" she asked.

"Put ... the rest of the ingredients in the pot and crush them—don't stir, crush ... them with something."

She threw all the ingredients in and, finding a large wrench, began crushing the ingredients. She sweated with the heat of the fire. "Ok. Everything's starting to melt together. Smells kind of good."

"Help me over there ... Kaly."

She put the wrench down and helped him up. She then led him to the basin.

"Now, find a cloth, a h-handkerchief or similar … sized rag."

She propped him up against the basin and went to find a cloth. Stenstrom readied himself, then reached into the pot and seized the contents in his fist.

Kaly returned with a length of course linen. "What are you doing?" she asked, looking at his hand. "You'll burn yourself!"

"That's the … price for … saving my … soul …" he said as the metals burned his palm.

He opened his hand. There were three small ingots of antimony, mixed with bismuth and foxglove, rapidly cooling though still hot in his blistered hand.

"Lay … the cloth out …"

Kaly cleared a spot and laid the linen out. Stenstrom then arranged it into a band with two triangular flaps coming down. He then rolled the three irregular ingots into the cloth and put the whole thing around his head. The flaps came down over his eyes. Sighing with relief, he tied the back.

"You ok?" Kaly asked.

"I am now. Thanks, Kaly, I really owe you." He put his arm around her and gave her a kiss on the cheek.

She gave him a large hug in return. "It's ok—I'm glad I could help. That was pretty neat, actually. What did we just do, by the way?"

"We made a set of hermelins. They are a sort of magical rock that protects your soul."

"Why don't you push the cloth back so you can see?"

"It has to go over my eyes—that way the spirits won't be able to find me as easily. Eyes are the route to the soul. Obscure them a little, and they'll have a harder time."

Kaly found a knife and they cut small holes into the cloth. "Oh," she said. "What sort of spirit is after you?"

"The worst kind. My mother summoned it."

25

—Calling on the Eryne—

"Hey, Bel! Over here!" Dunks yelled as Stenstrom entered the mess.

Dunks was a chatty fellow from Planet Fall. He was an able, if disinterested, officer, having long since resigned himself to the dregs of Fleet command. Stenstrom had heard he had a history of bad behavior and erratic manners, always the darting eye and the hand in the pocket. His Fleet uniform was rumpled and worn in places, his handsome face unshaved, and his blonde hair often uncombed.

And, without question, he was conducting some sort of illicit side-enterprise, all the stuff in the hold, the thinly veiled transactions, and the coin payouts to the crew that Stenstrom noticed. In several of their past conversations, he could tell that Dunks was trying to get information out of him, to determine if he knew anything. Stenstrom couldn't care less what he was doing—Kaly had promised him that the "Side Venture," whatever it was, wasn't harmful, and he trusted Kaly, so he took her at her word and left it alone.

By this point Stenstrom had seen a great deal of the League. He'd seen plenty of Onaris and Xandarr, they being frequent stops on the *Sandwich's* route. He'd also been to Hoban, Brindval, Poteete, and Goima.

The problem that dogged his heels was his mother and her Black Maidens. Every port the *Sandwich* arrived at, there they were, lurking in the background waiting for the first chance to get him. They seemed dark and sinister—as if Mother had something more terrifying than just Black Maidens set against him.

And, he had to wear his mask with its protective hermelins all the time now. If he took it off, even for a moment, he instantly felt the clawed hand tearing at his soul. The crew certainly thought it amusing seeing him walk around in his mask. "What—you think you're a pirate now—ahahahahar!" they'd say.

"We surrender, Captain Mask-face!" they chortled.

He refined the mask over time, replacing the original linen with fine black silk from Hoban. He also had redone and refined the mystical hermelins, adding a tiny bit of cadmium to the ingredients—the cad allowing him to sleep better.

He was now able to fold and situate the silk more skillfully, rolling the hermelins in with precision—now the mask was little more than a black headband with two modest diamond-shaped corners of cloth pulled down over his eyes and cutout so he could see.

Eventually, the crew stopped making fun of him—Kaly didn't even notice it anymore.

Lt. Dunkster sat there with him in the mess. Every so often he gave Stenstrom's mask a second look, but if Stenstrom's masked face puzzled him, he kept it to himself.

"Bel, I need you to do me a favor."

"Sure thing, Dunks, you name it."

"We're soon to anchor on Z-Encarr."

"Z-Encarr? Where is that, please?"

"It's a floating continent, one of three on Planet Fall. Being a gas giant, there's really no ground to walk around on except deep in the core where nothing can live, so we've built three massive platforms that float in the upper atmosphere—Z-Encarr's one of them. Marvels of modern engineering. I'm from Planet Fall. You know that, right?"

"Yes."

He placed a small money bag on the table. "I need you to off the ship once we anchor-up and take this moneybag to a lady I know. Can you do that for me?"

"A lady?"

"Her name's Christiana …"

"Just Christiana? No *Lady Christiana of...*"

Dunkster smiled. "No, Bel. She's an ex-dirty courtesan, and she's also my wife."

"I thought your wife was on Poteete?"

"She is on Poteete, and she's on Bazz too, and several places on Hoban, and here on Planet Fall as well. I have fourteen wives when last I counted, I think."

Dunks jangled the moneybag. "This one's important—this one knows certain things, and I need to keep her quiet. I need you to pretend you're me and take her this moneybag. It's for her and the kids. Upkeep and whatnot."

"Kids? I didn't know you have kids."

"I do—I've no idea how many, but it's a lot. Christiana has four, I think. She needs this money to help her survive, and I'm very late with this current payment."

"Why don't you put it into her account?"

"Christiana doesn't have a bank account—she's too stupid to know how a bank works. Come on Bel—can you be a pal? I can't make it out there, I've got too many meetings to attend. All you have to do is go to her address, hand her the money, and leave. That's it. You don't have to say two words to her if you don't want to."

Stenstrom looked at the bag. "I'm not nearly as good-looking as you, Dunks. I'm certain she recalls what her husband looks like."

"I got you covered on that one, Bel. She's nearly blind—got a dose of bad Weed some years back and lost a good deal of her eyesight. Of all my wives, she's probably the most broken down and threadbare—kind of embarrassing, you know. I'm used to something a little bit more polished up at my side." Dunks pulled his coat off and laid it on the table. "Just wear my coat and she'll never know the difference. She can sort of see shapes, I think."

Stenstrom stared at it. A Fleet Lt's coat. "Why? For feel or," as Stenstrom noted, "for the smell?"

"Both. Christiana knows the smell of her hubby sure enough."

Stenstrom thought it over. "Sure, Dunks, sure. Just give me her address."

Dunks wrote it down on a slip of paper. "… Appreciate this—you're saving me a lot of trouble. Oh, just between the two of us, you can bed her down if you want—I don't care. Maybe she'll have a heart attack right in the middle of it and save me a lot of further trouble and expense. I was hoping she would have keeled over a long time ago."

Stenstrom found Dunk's attitude toward his wife a little annoying—how bad could she be? He took Dunk's coat and went back to his room. Staring into the mirror, he put it on. It was a little dirty and somewhat threadbare in places, but he stared none the less.

A Fleet coat … Some of his lost little boy dreams returned to him, wearing the clothes his father had sent.

Looked good, fit him well. He was missing something, but he couldn't quite put his finger on it.

Ah, a hat! He needed a triangle hat, just like they wore in the Fleet. He went down the hall and knocked on the boatswain's cabin.

Nobody answered. The door was locked, but with a fast shake of his hand and nimble movement of his fingers, the door swung open. "Mr. Pike?" Stenstrom asked, peeking in.

The cabin was empty. He stepped in and borrowed one of the boatswain's hats, as they appeared to have a similar head-size.

He popped it on. Not used to triangle hats, it felt strange. Ah, well—he'd get used to it.

He locked the boatswain's cabin up, headed back to his room, and loaded up with MARZABLE, Holystones, and his trusty NTHs. He then left his room and exited the ship. Address in hand, Stenstrom walked off the plank of the *Sandwich*. He was wearing Dunk's coat and the boatswain's hat, and though it was dirty and rather seedy, the ensemble felt wonderful—even the hat. How he always longed to wear such a thing.

Kaly was walking out of the ship as well. "Hey, Bel!" she called. "I'm heading out to the bars with some of my friends. Want to come? Hey! Where'd you get that hat?"

"I borrowed it from the boatswain."

"Borrowed it, huh—looks like we're starting to rub off on you a little. Such a shame to mess up your handsome face with that hat."

She noted his coat. "Oh … Dunks has you on a mission, right? He wants you to go see one of his wives, doesn't he?"

"Something like that. Just a quick errand."

She looked a little concerned. "Well, you're a big fella'; you'll be just fine."

Stenstrom was apprehensive. "I detect a hint of concern in your voice."

She hesitated and pulled him aside off the gangplank. "Ok, look. Dunks has a thing for ex-Erynes. Do you know what those are? I mean, we're talking some pretty trashy stuff here, and I'm not sure a classy Great Lord like you divests himself much in that—I hope not anyway."

"Erynes? Those are courtesans if I'm not mistaken."

"They're more than just that. They're either the best or the worst, depending on how you look at it. The Erynes can do things to you unholy, Bel. You name it, secrets, thoughts, blind obedience … they can screw it right out of you, or into you as the case may be. You laugh, but they are nothing to trifle with. They use some sort of super-charged strain of The Weed and they know how to make the most of it. It gives them glowing red eyes. The Weed they use takes a toll on their bodies, wears them out, makes them old, and Dunks has a thing for those old, broken down Erynes. He marries them at a whim, and collects them like discarded bottle caps. Sometimes he uses them to find out things or to get into people's heads. Virtually every port we stop in, he's got an old Eryne wife stashed somewhere, and Planet Fall is no exception. And, just like an old attack dog that's all beaten up and tired, they still have teeth. They can still bite. Be careful, ok?"

"I will, Kaly, thanks."

She gave her lips a tap with her finger and Stenstrom shot her a kiss. She smiled at him and walked down the wharf. "If you change your mind, we'll be at one of the wharf-side bars!" she called out. She pointed at her neck. "I've got my Holo-mon, so just Holo me up if you need to find me, 'kay?"

He waved her goodbye. "I don't carry a Holo-mon, Kaly, but thanks."

Planet Fall was a turbid gas giant with several floating continents drifting through its upper atmosphere—it had no habitable surface. The vast metal continents floating on air were marvels of engineering, completely self-contained and featuring a sort of reverse-gravity, to counteract the crushing gravity of the planet below. Looking up, Stenstrom could see a banded lace-work of white, red and orange clouds swirling past at high, wind-driven speeds. Used to the soft blue sky of Kana, the perpetual clouds of the place with its wild orange tint made him feel a little uneasy. There was also Moedron, a small moon that was slowly being pulled into Planet Fall's interior. It orbited far below, hidden in the clouds, moving at a blistering pace, its passing pulling on his guts in a sickening manner.

He walked at a brisk pace into the interior of the massive, skyscraper-clogged city, his boots clacking on the metal street. Despite Kaly's rather ominous warning, he had a spring in his step. As he worked his way into the man-made canyons of Z-Encarr, many people stopped and tipped their hats.

"Evening, Lt."

"Nice day, Lt."

"Care for some company, Lt. …"

"Got a dime, Lt.?"

Only a few people stopped and noticed he was wearing a mask; it was hard to see under the boatswain's hat.

He felt true joy wearing Dunk's seedy coat and the boatswain's hat. The clothes made him feel … whole.

He had to be careful, though. He looked around, peering twice into the shadows and the distant reaches. He was certain he'd seen the hint of darting black robes and hooded faces looking at him in the far distance. His Holy-stone was rumbling steadily.

The Black Maidens. They were here. They had to be. He wore his mask and his bolabung, refreshed with Kaly's scent, and together they gave him protection as the Maidens couldn't see and smell him—but they could still sense him, feel his presence. And they appeared to not be giving up. He had to make this fast.

Moving on, Stenstrom found the address—it was a smallish, row house tenement on a seedy side street.

So, an Eryne lives here, he thought. *Like an old pet that still has teeth.* He wondered what sort of hellion raged within.

He walked up the steps and knocked on the door. After a moment, a red-headed woman with squinting brown eyes emerged. She was wearing a brown dress with an apron tied over the top.

He remembered Kaly's warning: *The Weed they use takes a toll on their bodies, wears them out, makes them old.* He was expecting a proverbial "old crone" to come out—bent and withered, like in his picture books he and Lyra thrilled over when he was a child—the ones Virginia was too scared to look at. Old crones were monsters from fairytales—nobody got old in the League, except for the sick and the badly bred.

Upon seeing her, he was a tad disappointed. Christiana certainly didn't look old and worn out. She was tall, nearly six feet, and stood with practiced posture. Her skin was a pleasing pearly shade. Her brassy red hair was thick and full, held back with unseen pins and clips. Her face was pretty, heart-shaped, with well-formed cheekbones and a large pair of striking brown eyes, lost in the confusion of blindness. Her waist was very thin—he imagined she'd probably spent years suffocating in a laced-up corset.

"Dunks, is that you?" she said tentatively, her voice accented in a brogue Planet Fall burr, opening the screen door.

Stenstrom didn't quite know what to do—Dunks hadn't briefed him on how to interface with his wife. He hadn't thought of that. The way Dunks described it, he figured he'd knock on the door, a gnarled hand would come out, accept the money, and go back in, shutting the door behind it with little or no interface.

But, there she was, standing in the door.

He tried to disguise his voice and sound like Dunks. "Uh, yeah, Christiana, it's me."

She smiled and reached out. "Let me look at you." Probing with her hands, she found his face and began feeling his chin with her fingers. Her hands found his hat.

Her hands—they were the hands of a hag: bony, withered, and the skin, dull and parchment-like. So that's what The Weed did to her.

"Have you lost weight, Dunks?" she asked.

"Umm, yeah, yeah. Stellar food, it's terrible."

Her bent fingers found the fabric of his mask. "What's this?" she asked.

"Oh, I got hurt—just a bandage. It's nothing."

Christiana pulled him forward and gave him a kiss on the cheek. "I've made lunch for us. Please come in and share it with me."

His Holystone gave a rumble. Stenstrom looked down the street and clearly saw four figures in black standing in the distance, teetering about, sniffing the air. Here, with Christiana nearby and his mask, he should be safe. "Sure, sure," he said, stepping in.

The interior of the apartment was small and modest. Childrens' toys lay scattered about. Piled up on the couch were sorted stacks of children's clothing. In a small closet, a primitive manual wash-basin full of soapy water and an old air-oven were crammed in. A scratchy program played on her battered Aire-net receptor in the sunken living room.

Christiana, holding his hand, led him to her tiny dinner table. Feeling her way about, she sat him down to a strange meal of meats and sauces he couldn't identify. He watched her carefully serve the food—her hands so terribly withered and gnarled from the degenerative effects of prolonged contact with The Weed. She held her ladle with the hands of a dead woman.

Standing there in her tiny, galley-style kitchen wearing an apron, he felt sorry for her as she put the finishing touches on the meal.

Dunks said she was stupid, but she didn't appear to be stupid; on the contrary, she seemed to be getting on and dealing with her blindness rather well.

Dunks said she was broken down—an embarrassment, yet, except for her hands, she was beautiful.

Dunks hoped she'd die, to spare him further expense.

"I've been practicing, Dunks—my cooking. I think I've gotten much better at it."

She served the food, and it was good. He had no trouble finishing it. Christiana sat next to him, eating with polished manners and grace, all of her very beautiful, except for her horrid hands. She held her knife and fork court-style, taking tiny bites, chatting happily with Stenstrom whom she thought was her husband. He could imagine her sitting in some lavish castle or manor—a prim and proper lady of the house.

And here she was, living in near squalor, married to a man that had collected her as a prize and probably didn't know their children's names.

She pointed out a small trophy sitting on the mantle.

"What's that?" Stenstrom asked.

"It's a merit award. Our son was at the top of his class again." She beamed with pride.

"That's wonderful. Um …which one?"

"Nathan."

"Nathan, he's the one who looks like his beautiful mother, yes?"

She blushed. Christiana was clearly attention-starved. As she ate she winced a tiny bit.

"Are you having trouble with your teeth, Christiana?" Stenstrom asked.

She shook her head. "It's nothing."

"Let me have a look." He leaned in, and she swallowed and wiped her mouth with her napkin. She opened her mouth. Several of her teeth were obviously rotten. "You need to see a Hospitaler for your teeth."

"I'm fine."

Stenstrom stood up. "Get dressed," he said.

She looked up at him. "What? Why?"

"I saw a Hospitaler sanctum a short walk away. We're going to walk there now, and you're going to have your teeth looked at, this very afternoon. And then, do you know what we're going to do?"

"What, Dunks?"

"We're going to walk the town, arm in arm, and when we've worked up a healthy appetite, we're going to eat at the finest restaurant we can find. I want to serve you, today, and show you off to the people, as a lady deserves. Go on, I'll take care of the dishes here. Where are the children?"

"I sent them away for the day. That sounds so expensive, Dunks," she said. "My teeth, a fine meal? We don't have the money for that."

"I … had a big score not long ago, and I've coin a-plenty. Come on— who better to spend it on than my beautiful wife?"

She smiled at the compliment. She got up and made her way into the bedroom. He began cleaning up their lunch, and he could hear her clinking around in the bedroom as he worked. A short time later she emerged. She changed into a slender black dress with a pearl heart charm about her neck. In her dress, her corset-created, hour-glass figure was clear. She had put her hair up and was wearing a curved straw hat with a ribbon hanging from the back. Thankfully, she'd put on a pair of black gloves.

She was still such a beautiful woman.

Stenstrom took her arm and led her outside. After a short walk they arrived at the Hospitaler sanctum, and they admitted Christiana. Their assessment—six teeth needed replacement, and they wanted to see the color of his money before they began. Stenstrom got his money bag out and paid them:

one hundred and four sesterces, equaling four hundred Planet Fall billets.

As they worked on her, his Holystone rumbled again, warning him of danger. He went outside. Sure enough, four black-robed Maidens wandered down the lane, their noses in the air.

He knew as long as Christiana was with him, her love, though misplaced, would protect him and mask his scent. It was a simple counter-charm he knew worked.

The Maidens appeared different from how he remembered them—more covered up, more sinister. He could simply shoot them with his NTHs and be rid of them for now, but he didn't want to shoot a Black Maiden; they were harmless and benign—and persistent and inconvenient as well. That, however, did not give him lease to kill them. He had made a promise to himself in Calvert not to harm the Black Maidens ever again.

A short time later, Christiana emerged from the sanctum. She had a brand new smile and didn't mind showing it off. What a face when she smiled—a classic beauty.

Stenstrom took her arm and led her outside. He watched the Maidens disappear into the distance, his scent masked. He strolled the streets with her, people tipping their hats as they passed. He walked her to a market and bought her a modern fabric cleaning unit, to replace the ridiculous wash basin she'd been using, and arranged to have it delivered to her apartment. He bought some toys for the children—again having them delivered.

He spent more money on her in one afternoon than Dunks probably had in their entire marriage. He wanted to do nice things for her because it felt good. He felt responsible for her somehow—that this afternoon she was his to care for, and he'd not spare a dime.

They passed a bank. "Christiana, do you have a bank account?"

"You know I don't, Dunks. I've never learned to use one."

Stenstrom pulled her toward the bank. "Well, come on. We're going to go inside, and I'm going to create an account for you, and I'm going to deposit money into it every month for you and the children. I'll show you how to access your account from home when we get back."

They finished at the bank and continued their stroll. He could see the rusty bulk of the *Sandwich* sitting at the wharf. He took her to an expensive-looking restaurant and let her have whatever she wanted. Through the meal, he told her about all the places they had recently been, she closing her eyes and listening.

As the gas-giant sky faded to a night-time brown, he walked her back to her apartment. There, using the Holo-net, he showed her how to access her new bank account. Using voice commands, she picked it up rather quickly. She wasn't stupid at all.

"That was a wonderful meal, what a delightful evening. And my teeth, to eat without pain. The children are gone, Dunks," she said trying to pull him into their bedroom, but he talked his way out of it. He then led her back to her small sitting room, put her feet up, and tucked her in with a blanket. He put the moneybag Dunks had given him in a drawer and told her where it was.

"Will you come back soon, Dunks?" she asked, looking at him with mostly blind eyes. "Please say you'll come back."

"You bet. I'll be back tomorrow. I promise."

He kissed her goodnight and took his leave, watching for the Black Maidens. He didn't see any, his Holystone quiet.

"Good night, Christiana," he said.

"I love you …" she returned.

As he began walking down the street, his Holystone suddenly went wild.

Four Black Maidens appeared all around him. They surrounded him, groping with their bony arms. They pawed at him, trying to see him.

He had no place to go. He felt his soul churn. They fell upon him. They reached out, grasping with their fingers, acting in an aggressive, belligerent manner that was unusual for Black Maidens.

They found his mask and tore it from his face along with his hat and his bolabung. They threw them aside.

Stenstrom put his hands up. "All right, all right—you got me. I guess it's time to go and see Mother."

"Mother … "

One of them tore away the veil covering her face. She had no face—only a large smiling mouth and chattering teeth. *"You are ours! We shall feast upon your soul …"*

Holy Creation!! What had his mother done? These weren't Black Maidens—these were Soul Devourers! Mother had put a stain on his soul!! He was doomed!

"YOUR SOUL!!"

He drew his NTHs and fired, getting one in the chest. She bent over and disappeared.

The rest pulled him down. He fired his other NTH and got another one. She disappeared too.

They closed in, giving him no space, no room to aim his guns. They pawed and tore at him. He dropped one of his NTHs and fell to the street.

A moment later the remaining two Soul Devourers seemed to recoil in pain and quickly retreated, covering their faces.

Stenstrom cocked his NTH. He fired, hitting one in the back where she vanished in a gristly spray. He picked up the NTH he'd dropped and then got the last with a longer range shot, the green blasts lighting up the street as he fired.

Something touched him from behind. He whirled around.

It was Christiana. She had emerged from the apartment. She was holding his mask in her hand. She reached out, searching. "What's going on? I thought I heard something. Did you drop your handkerchief? I can smell your cologne on it."

Her presence had driven them away, giving him a chance to be rid of them with his pistols.

"It's nothing," Stenstrom said, panting. He took his mask and put it back on. His thoughts spun in a panic.

Soul Devourers. What had his mother done? He was doomed. They'd be back. They'd get him sooner or later.

"It's nothing. Let me take you back inside and tuck you in again," he said, his voice shaking.

Stenstrom helped her inside while figuring out his next move. At least, now that he knew they were Soul Devourers, he would feel empowered to shoot and kill them—he hadn't wanted to treat a gentle Black Maiden in that fashion if he could help it.

Suddenly, there was Christiana.

She put her gloved hands on his face and kissed him with fire. "I was to question you today, to discover what you know," she whispered, kissing him. "My husband thinks you know something. He thinks you're a spy sent from the Fleet, and I was to uncover it. He wants to know who you're working for. And here you are, such a fine young man who knocked on my door today. You've done much for me: you entertained me, listened to my stories, and told a few in return. You asked the name of my son—something my husband has never done. You walked at my side and held my arm, as a Lord does for his Lady, and I was proud to stand there with you. I've not been admired as I walked down the street in some time. You took away my pain, and mostly, you've helped restore a shred of my dignity that I'd long lost. During our afternoon today, I indulged myself. I pretended that you actually are my husband and that the two of us share a love seldom seen. Wouldn't that be nice—to have a husband who actually loves me and our children? I am not a puppet, and I care not what my husband wants—you have earned my adoration. I invite you into my bedroom, not because of my husband, but because I want you. You've shared much with me today, and I want to share with you all I have to give."

He pulled away. "Please, Christiana."

"I'm blind, but I'm not dead, and I'm still a woman. You're not my husband—you're a good man, and I want to be with you."

She pulled him back into the apartment. He was feeling shaky from his encounter with the Soul Devourers. He didn't have the strength to resist.

And soon, he was in Christiana's bedroom, she all around him. She was still using a lesser strain of The Weed, and it belted him into places he'd never been before, stabbing him with frenzied jolts.

Making love to Lilly was a joy, a smooth scent of perfume.

Making love to Alitrix was fragile and private, she unsure and remarkably in need of assurance and tenderness.

Making love to Lady Miranda was weird and a little painful.

Making love to Kaly was fun and carefree.

But this? This was savagery. This was very nearly a fight to the death. This was top to bottom, skin and sweat, body against body. He could barely breathe, and he couldn't think. Christiana used The Weed relentlessly, prolonging the act, taking him to unbearable stages, flawlessly playing the notes of a complex tune on his body, whipping up small pieces of him into a lather of ecstasy and moving on when he could take it no more.

This was what it was like to experience an Eryne in action.

He thought he could hear her speaking to him. Not with her mouth; somewhere she was making a lot of noise with her mouth, but he was only partially aware of it—he was making a lot of noise too.

His heart pounded. He saw stars. He saw through time. He heard her voice.

"I was a queen once, a dame respected and feared—all my needs doted on and cared for. I've enslaved many—I've even killed and wrung out secrets. I had only to ask, anything I desired was mine. Then, I grew old, my body beginning to fail me, and I was a queen no more—cast out, used up, with no skills other than my lexicon of the night. You've nothing to fear, and I'm not going to harm you. Let me worship you."

Kaly's green eyes and pink hair band flashed into his thoughts. *"Dunks has a thing for old Erynes—he collects them like discarded bottle caps. I have no idea how many he's married to—but it's a lot. Watch out for the Erynes— even old, and used up, they can do things to you unholy. Man or woman, they can make you talk—no secret you have is beyond their reach. They can even kill you if they want—and that's old and rotten, using a crap Weed... just imagine a fit one on a mission, with that Red-eye stuff they use!"*

They can kill you if they want ...

Christiana was a master—she certainly could kill him if she wanted, or extract secrets. He was hers to do with as she would. Christiana, who walked with him in his arm, basking in the attention and eating her dinner with perfect grace, was now a fierce warrior using her body and The Weed as a terror weapon and execution tool.

She asked him no lengthy questions. The only secret she extracted from him: "What ...w-what is your n-name ...?"

"Sten—Stenstrom ..."

In psychedelic jolts, he saw techno-color splashes of Lilly. In psychotropic mush, he saw Alitrix, devastated, crying for attention and Kaly, smiling, ready to try anything.

And soon, when he thought he could endure no more, it was over, Christiana lying next to him, her lazy, gloved fingers dabbing away jewels of sweat from his chest, the both of them soon passing out.

✳ ✳ ✳ ✳ ✳

"And you banged her?" Kaly's green eyes were huge as she leaned over her lunch in the mess. They were back on the ship, both Planet Fall and Christiana far away.

"Must you be so crude? But, yes, I didn't have the strength to resist."

"You returned to her the next day, didn't you?"

"I did—but not for the sex. I returned for the company. I found her a lovely woman."

"But you still had sex again the second time, right?"

"Of course."

"See. Told you. They're tough. So, how was it?"

"Remarkable. It was remarkable."

"You ok, you look a little tired."

"I'm exhausted."

Kaly took a bite from her sandwich. "Well, you better buck up, 'cause I'm feeling it for tonight and I don't want to hear any excuses."

26
—THE HRN—

"Where in the name of Creation have you been?" Captain Stenstrom yelled through the Com. "Your mother is ready to die of worry." He was sitting in his large office on the *Caroline* and he looked positively livid. "This is very irresponsible of you, Bel!"

"I'm sorry, Father, I'm simply doing what Mother has told me to do—to be my own man. If she wouldn't continually harass me with Black Maidens and Soul Devourers, maybe I'd be in touch more often."

Captain Stenstrom squinted and tried to look past his face at his surroundings through the screen, noting the faded paint and streaks of rust. "Are you in a brig somewhere—and is that a mask you're wearing?"

"This is my office, it's not much, but it's mine, and I am wearing a mask to keep mother's demons from tearing my soul apart."

"Your mother has done no such thing. Your mother loves you." Captain Stenstrom's interest seemed to pique, his anger diminished. "So, where are you? Are you on a ship, a Fleet ship? You can tell me."

"I am on a frigate."

"A ... *frigate*?" he said with some distaste.

"Yes. It's a fine frigate, and I am its Paymaster."

"A Paymaster? You're the Paymaster of a frigate?"

"That is correct. Mother never thought of knifing a shipboard civilian out of me. I always wanted to join the Fleet, to soar the stars. I suppose this is as close as I am able to get."

"You never showed any interest in joining the Fleet."

"I always wanted to join the Fleet, Father—Lyra too. I wore the clothes you sent home to me, and I played with the toys you bought for us. Mother wouldn't have it. So, here I am, a Fleet Paymaster on a rusty old frigate. It's not much, and it's not how I expected it to be, but I am living my dream."

Captain Stenstrom, despite himself, beamed, smiling from ear to ear. "Well, what do you know? You are something, my son—you've got some wit. What ship are you on? Maybe I can swing by if I'm close. I'm very proud. Very proud indeed."

"I'm on the *Sandwich,* 15th Fleet, I think. Again, it's not much, but it's home. The places I've been to, the things I've seen—remarkable."

The captain noted the name down. "Is there anything you need? Just say the word, and I'll get you whatever you require."

"I'm fine, Father."

"Well, I must admit, this is a great surprise. The *Sandwich*, and my son is its Paymaster. Still, as to my previous point, when you're close, I do bade you come home and visit your mother. She …"

"She what?"

"Nothing. She would love to see you, is all. And your sisters too. You will be happy to learn that Virginia is betrothed."

"That's wonderful. To whom?"

"Lord Cobbleshem of Pole. She's very excited, and, as usual, your mother is home fussing over the details."

"How about Lyra?"

"She's actually planning on going to school. She managed to talk your mother into letting her go—can you believe that?"

Stenstrom was quite nearly open-mouthed with shock. "That's … amazing. What school, what is she studying?"

"University of Arden—she's studying stellar cartography. Your mother is mellowing, and Lyra attending school is the proof. I cannot believe she would conjure up demons to harass you. Come home, Bel. Tell her what you've become, and she will be as proud of you as I am."

✶ ✶ ✶ ✶ ✶

The *Sandwich* made berth in Mercia several days later to load up on supplies. Stenstrom and Kaly disembarked. He'd promised to take her out on the town.

As they walked down the gangplank, his felt his protective Holystones go off, jangling in his coat pocket. He stopped and scanned the area.

"What?" Kaly asked.

"Something's about …" He cleared his coat and put his hand on his NTH."

Kaly looked around. "Demons, you think?"

"Possibly."

He looked around and didn't see the usual black robed figures sniffing about. Instead, he saw a familiar shape standing on the dock.

He smiled. "Hey, Kaly, I'm going to have to take a rain-check. I promise I'll take you out tomorrow, okay?"

"What, what is it?" she asked. "Who are you ditching me for?"

"I see a friend down there. I promise I'll get you tomorrow."

"All right—tomorrow then. I wish you carried a Holo-mon so I can get a hold of you. Watch out for demons, okay?" Kaly gave him a wink and trotted down the gangplank and disappeared into the streets.

Stenstrom slowly walked down to the dock. A familiar person stood there waiting for him. "Hello, Lilly," he said.

"Hello, Bel," she replied, spinning her usual parasol. "I heard you would be in town here in Mercia, and I wanted to see you."

He took her hand and kissed it. "It's been quite a while, Lilly. Where have you been?"

"Here and there. Come on, Bel—take my hand and let's enjoy the afternoon."

Together, they strolled into the city.

✶   ✶   ✶   ✶   ✶

"I tell you, Lilly, it was wondrous, wearing Dunks' coat. I know, I know, it's just a coat, but it felt so good wearing it. I felt safe; I felt whole. I felt like I was a part of something."

They were sitting at a café on the water's edge. His Holystone was rumbling constantly, but he saw no demons and felt no particular danger. He could feel his NTHs at his side with fresh cinnabar strikers just in case he needed them—that was a comfort at least.

Lilly finished her lunch. "You young lords and your love of uniforms and pageantry." She gazed at him hard. "You look good in a mask. You have a face for it."

He closed his eyes. "The things I have to do to overcome my mother's efforts. I can't take it off, or else I feel my soul ripping apart. Even ashore I feel it—I'm not safe anywhere I go. Kaly suggested branding the hermelins within into my forehead, but I really didn't want to do that."

"And who is *Kaly*?"

"She's a friend."

"I see." Lilly appeared to flush for a moment. She grit her teeth, then moved on. "So, you enjoyed wearing a Fleet coat," she said, reverting to the previous subject.

"I did."

"And you enjoyed it because it made you feel like you were a part of something? You reveled in the comfort of wearing a uniform?"

"I suppose."

"Well, perhaps you might wear something similar—something that looks like a Fleet ensemble, but actually isn't. There's nothing to stop you from doing that, is there?"

Stenstrom finished his lunch. "No, but …"

"No buts," Lilly said dabbing her lips with her napkin. "Come with me. Let's go shopping."

"Shopping for what?"

"For your uniform, Bel."

Together, they plunged into the lovely city and prowled the many shops lining the streets. Lilly looked him over with a discriminating eye, not unlike his mother's. "I think you shall need a white shirt, a pair of black pants—knee britches if you must, and a new sash. Do you have any particular color in mind?"

"Green is the designated color of a Fleet Paymaster."

"All right, we'll get you a lovely green sash."

The pants and shirts were easy enough. His pants were simply black cotton pantaloons that they bought at a nice tailor shop along with several white shirts. Lilly insisted on a frilly shirt, though Stenstrom resisted at first. She also tried to get him to buy a different pair of boots, but he refused, having a love of his old Tyrol boots.

They moved on to a fine haberdashery. They looked at the assortment of men's hats, concentrating on Vith triangle hats, as they most resembled those worn in the Fleet. Lilly picked him out a large black one, inlaid with silver swirls.

Now, for his coat. That was the hard part. They looked all over, trying to find a coat that was similar to the long, tailed coat worn in the Fleet, but wasn't overly garish or mocking. That was a tall order. All of the tailors they went to had nothing like what he wanted. Too overblown. Too simple. Too dainty. Too modest. Too costume-like. Most of the coats they found that were cut in the Fleet style were for going to the opera, or a night at a ball.

Lilly finally had the answer. She pulled him down a side-street, the fine shops fading to run-down, rusted facilities and steamy, workman-like warehouses. Stenstrom looked around dubiously—what could they possibly find there?

At the end of the street was a large warehouse selling used and damaged goods at a discount to those encumbered with a more meager budget.

"Let's look in there," Lilly said, pulling on him.

Stenstrom didn't want to go in. "What could they possibly have in there, Lilly? It's a thrift store offering nothing but used sundries."

"Oh, come now, what could it hurt? We've had no success at the more prestigious establishments. Sometimes one can find lost or hidden treasures in second-hand stores."

Stenstrom stopped. "I really don't want to, Lilly."

"Please," she cooed, "for me ..."

He sighed and took her hand. Together they went in. The warehouse was vast, offering boxed and unboxed articles of clothing, shoes, stockings, undergarments, old pieces of furniture, and the like. None of it was displayed with any regard for presentation or aesthetics; everything was laid out no-frills and functional, nothing more.

They rolled around in the vast aisles, sorting through this and that. The other shoppers in the warehouse were dressed rather poorly, and gave the richly attired Stenstrom and Lilly reproachful looks: what did *they* need in an establishment like this?

Stenstrom half-heartedly looked at the used wares on display. "Shockingly, I'm not seeing anything I like."

"I don't think you're trying."

"May we go?"

Lilly pointed to a corner of the warehouse they hadn't checked yet. "Let's look over there, first. Then we can leave."

They walked to the far side of the warehouse. The items on display there were a bit more expensive than the goods laid out elsewhere and got little attention from the usual shoppers. The boxes laid out on the tables all were stamped: HOBAN. Stenstrom looked into the boxes—Hoban turned out some fine items, and he was mildly impressed by what he saw.

"Bel," Lilly said from behind. "What about this?" He turned around.

Lilly was holding up a long, dark green coat—it was so long it dragged on the floor in front of her. Stenstrom took it from her and held it up. It was a fairly heavy coat made of terlamane, a fine fabric made from the hair of a live-stock animal native to Hoban—the finished product mixing the feel of silk with the toughness of wool. The entire surface of the coat was embroidered with twisting ivy, highlighted in silver thread, mixing in lightning bolts and some sort of fruit-like objects. The stiff black collar and cuffs were heavily embroidered in silver and gold. It had silver buttons and silver clips. Centered on both sides of the collar, riveted in place, were the letters "HRN" in gothic, flawless silver.

He stood there holding the coat—it was the loveliest thing he'd ever seen.

"What do you think, Bel—I think it's a wonderful coat."

He continued to gaze at it.

"Try it on, see how it feels."

Stenstrom put the coat on, and it fit almost perfectly. The sleeves were just the right length and the tails were just an inch or two from dragging on the floor. It was almost like it was made just for him.

The terlamane fabric breathed well, so the coat wasn't too hot or too cold on him, and it had numerous pockets sewn into the interior—perfect places to put his Holystones, MARZABLE, his Astral Plane detectors, and other bits of arcane equipment. He imagined a coat like this could serve as a mobile office, housing everything he needed.

"Oh, yes, Bel—this looks wonderful on you—look how handsome. How does it feel?"

"Feels nice."

Lilly backed up a few steps. "Yes, it's elegant and Fleet-worthy, yet not too-overdone as to appear like a costume. From a step or two away, you almost look like an Admiral."

He was sold. He checked around and didn't see any other coats like this HRN one, and bought it as is.

As they left the warehouse, wearing his HRN coat, he felt like a new man. He felt like he was bursting with power.

It was getting late and the *Sandwich* was soon to blast off. Stenstrom and Lilly made their way back to the docks. As they did, Lilly's demeanor seemed to change a little. She looked lost, desperate even. Worse, she looked positively sad. He asked her what was wrong.

"Nothing, I suppose it's getting late and my job is done … for the day. I'm glad we found clothes to your liking."

They arrived at the docks, and Stenstrom gave her a kiss on the hand, as there were many people about.

Lilly's usual cool demeanor completely fell away. She wept bitterly, her mouth pulled back in anguish.

"Lilly, Lilly, what's wrong?"

She looked at him with her tear-streaked face. "I love you, Bel," she said putting her arms around him. "I love you so much. Don't ever let anyone tell you I don't love you. Don't let anyone tell you what I feel isn't genuine."

He was a bit shocked by this display of emotion—Lilly had been so standoffish as of late. "I love you too, Lilly. I've been around, I've experienced life, and I've not met your equal. I want you, Lilly. I want to make you my countess, the first of the Belmont-South Tyrol line. I want it now more than ever. I've learned a lot in these two years, I've learned there is no other but you."

Flushed, she managed a smile. She put her hands on his face. "Then, I've plans to make. I've steps to put into place. I don't know when you'll see me again, Bel, but I promise you will. As I have tried to impress upon you—there's always a way around a challenge if you want something badly enough."

"Lilly, your tone has a certain air of finality. It is frightening me."

She dried her tears and smiled. "Don't be scared, Bel. There's nothing to be scared of."

They kissed one last time and, slowly, Stenstrom mounted the gangplank and walked into the ship.

He turned as the door closed, expecting Lilly to be gone—Wafted away like she normally did, but, she was still standing there on the dock, her hands to her face, her parasol lying on the planks.

✳　✳　✳　✳　✳

Blasting off from Mercia was terribly emotional. Lilly was still standing there, crying as the ship lifted away. Hands on the boat deck glass, he watched Lilly's weeping form quickly fade into a speck and then gone.

He felt such a tide of loss.

Returning to his quarters, he fretted for awhile. Lilly was strange and rather odd toward the end of the day. He thought for a moment that she was going to break it off and cut ties with him for good. He was sure of it, but something had prevented her at the last moment.

He'd parted ways with Lilly many times, but this seemed different. It seemed like the end. He got her locket out and opened it, seeing her smiling, hand-painted face.

There was a knock at his door. "Come in."

The door creaked open and there was Kaly, carrying a few bags from her day in the city. "Hey, Bel, did you have fun today? I almost didn't make it back aboard. I had to run."

He didn't say anything. He stood, grabbed her, and kissed her hard. He spun her around, her bags went flying, and he threw her on the bed, her legs going up in the air as he closed the door.

"Ohhh," she said in a sultry voice as she popped off her shoes and began unbuttoning her pants, *"okay, okay...that's how you want it. Come and take it ..."*

He was sick of feeling out of control. His whole life—his mother, Lilly, the Sisters, Lady Miranda, even Alitrix, at every turn there was a woman in his way, tripping him up, confusing him, making him hurt. *Plunging knives into his chest.*

Tonight, just for one night, he was going to take out all his frustrations on a woman, and Kaly, ever eager to try new things, appeared to be more than willing to play along. With the locket open, Lilly watching, he tore into Kaly.

✶ ✶ ✶ ✶ ✶

They sat at breakfast the next morning. Stenstrom was wearing his new gear. "I'm really sorry about last night."

"Why?" Kaly said, smiling. "I thought it was fun—not a side I see of you often, though, we might have to sit out tonight—*I'm a little sore, you know?"*

He gave a short laugh and continued eating his breakfast.

"I like your new clothes," she said looking at him.

"I went shopping with Lilly. She was waiting for me on the docks as we departed the ship."

"I didn't see anybody on the docks with you yesterday."

"How do you mean?"

"I didn't see anybody. I looked around. I thought I saw you walking off with a mannequin or something, and I was thinking 'Hey, if he's going off to have fun with a sex mannequin or something, I want to join in', but I couldn't holo-mon you."

Stenstrom laughed. "That wasn't a mannequin; that was Lilly."

"If you say so." Kaly looked at his clothes. "You look like an Admiral, or something close to it. I've only seen a couple of Admirals—they make me sort of nervous."

"Yes, I found this coat in a second-hand store of all places. Can you believe that—a beautiful coat like this. I wonder what HRN stands for."

"Hoban Royal Navy, that's easy."

Stenstrom was surprised. "HRN? The Hoban Royal Navy? You know it?"

"Yeah—I might be stuck on this old tub, but I'm still a crewman in the Fleet. Everybody joining the Fleet has to pass a Fleet history course right off the bat, and there was a whole chapter on the Hoban Royal Navy. The Fleet *hated* the Hoban Royal Navy."

Stenstrom was curious. "Tell me."

"I think they were just a bunch of guys from Hoban, obviously—sort of like you, rich, highly placed. They tried to replace the Fleet around Hoban a few years back—said they could do a better job of protecting Hoban from the Xaphans than the Fleet could. According to the course, they were actually there to protect the Governor of Hoban, as he was an incognito pirate running contraband to the Xaphans and raiding passing ships. I guess they didn't last long. I think they lost the only battle they ever got into with the Xaphans and had to have the Fleet come and rescue them. A lot of them got killed, and some were thrown in jail for gross incompetence. But they wore coats just like that. I'm really not surprised you found that coat in a second-hand store as they're all washed up and outlawed now. Seeing it up-close, it is a really neat-looking coat."

The morning bell tolled.

"Well, there's my cue," Kaly said, standing. "Time to go to the bridge and stare into the little visor for awhile."

She put her tray into the trash and then leaned down and whispered into his ear.

"Hey—I know your lady must have troubled you yesterday somehow. I know you were hurting. I'm glad I could be there to help … to take your mind off things, you know? You're my friend, Bel—never forget that. If your lady broke your heart, or chose to discard you, she must be crazy. You are a wonderful man, in every way."

"Thanks, Kaly."

She gave him a quick peck on the cheek and headed off to the bridge.

He returned to his office and checked his mailings. There wasn't much—his duties were miniscule at best. He looked up the Hoban Royal Navy on his terminal. As he read, Kaly appeared to have summed up their history quite well: The Governor of Hoban, a Lord Crowe, had gotten into a tiff with the Fleet over a bit of contraband goods that had been seized. Apparently, the Governor had a little streak of pirate in him, and was enraged that the Fleet had busted up his ring. He then forbade the Fleet from approaching Hoban, instead forming a small navy of old Planet Fall *corvettes* and called it the Hoban Royal Navy. He was quite proud of it at first, and even thought that such a thing would become a trend, each local planet having its own small navy to protect against the Xaphans. Perhaps the Fleet was no longer needed.

The Navy proved to be a disaster. Sloppy standards, dubious morals and motivations, ships in worn out shape and barely space-worthy. The Fleet had to come and save them from breakdowns time and time again. The only battle they ever fought with the Xaphans at Two-Pitch Nebula was a complete rout. The great Xaphan hero, Princess Marilith of Xandarr, was, for once, victorious in battle driving the HRN *corvettes* before her until the Fleet came and covered their retreat.

Soon, red-faced, the Hoban Royal Navy was disbanded, and the Governor sought to hide all traces of their existence. He scrapped the ships, threw several officers into prison, and sent the uniforms off to be burned. All trace of the HRN was made to vanish almost overnight.

Not quite everything—this lovely coat, made with care and fine materials, still stood. Stenstrom would wear it with pride.

27

—An Incident at Terrabus—

Stenstrom's mask was feeling rather hot on his face today, and his skin beneath it was getting chaffed and red. He wished he could take it off, but he didn't dare remove it; the clawed hand searching for his soul found him almost instantly without it.

There was a knock on his door. He was sitting behind his desk trying to catch up on some paperwork, but his mask was bothering him too much to get anything done. "Come in," he said, hand on his face trying to adjust the mask into a comfortable position.

The door opened. There stood crewman Forest, one of the Sensing Station personnel from the bridge. "Bel, you got a moment?"

He looked up from his work. "Sure, Forest. What's up?"

Forest blushed a little. "Can you please come to the bridge with me?"

"Why?"

"It's better if you just come."

The Bridge? "I'm not allowed on or anywhere near the bridge—remember? The boatswain gave me the lecture."

"It's ok, really. Just for a second. You're not going to get in trouble or anything. The boatswain—he's a dork, you know that."

Stenstrom had no idea why he was being summoned to the bridge—maybe he was in trouble for something. Maybe Dunks wanted to let him in on their secret operation. "All right," he said, feeling a bit of mild excitement despite himself.

He stood up and put his HRN coat on, Forest waiting quietly as he did so. Stenstrom popped his hat on and then followed him through the seedy corridors, his Tyrol boots clunking on the thick, riveted metal flooring, to the *Sandwich's* tiny and rather primitive bridge at the top of the ship. Within, several crewmen sat at their stations. There was no holo-cone or viewing screen on the bridge—just an array of large, head's up infused windows all around, like a cathedral of glass lit up in occasional, computer-generated color. The far wall of the bridge was a solid pane of strong pyro glass, with small panes wrapping around either side trailing just past where the helm and the navigator sat. It was like being in a fishbowl.

The helmsman sat at his chair and looked nervous. So too did the navigator.

Through the windows, Stenstrom could see the ship was nestled in some sort of space-borne junkyard—the murky outsides lit up in some sort of blue filter through the windows. There were a number of old corroded relics floating about outside, nudging into each other in the solar tide. There were layers of wrecked ships above as well. It looked like an asteroid field of twisted and collided shipping.

"Where in Creation are we?" he asked.

"We're in the Kills, Terrabus Field—Xaphan armada ships. The site of an old battle a couple hundred years back," Kaly said, waving at him from her station.

Stenstrom thought a moment. "Terrabus field—isn't that near Xaphan space?"

"Yeah, Bel, it is."

"What are we doing near Xaphan space? That's not on our route, is it? What's going on here? Where's Dunks?"

"There, there's Dunks," Forest said, pointing.

Lying on the floor, on the far side of the command chair, was Lt. Dunkster, flat on his back, arms splayed out, the tips of his boots pointing toward the glass ceiling of the bridge. Kaly went to his side and took his limp hand. Stenstrom went to him and knelt down next to Kaly, Forest following. "What's this? What's wrong with him?"

Kaly cleared her throat. "Well, we're not sure, but we think he's in toxic shock. We think he got hold of a bad dirty courtesan on Bazz and is all tox'ed up with her."

"One of his wives?"

"eh …yeah …"

"It just hit him all of a sudden," Forest added. "Up one moment, down the next."

"He needs a Hospitaler," Stenstrom said.

"We don't have a Hospitaler aboard, Bel. You know that. We, umm, were hoping you could do something for him," Kaly said quietly.

"Me? What do you expect me to do?"

"Kaly tells us you're a sorcerer," Forest blurted out. "She was bragging on your powers the other day, says she's seen you do some remarkable things. We were hoping you could 'magic up' some sort of cure until we can get him to a Hospitaler sanctum. Cabril 17 is not too far. We just need to keep him alive until we get him there."

Stenstrom looked out the windows again and adjusted his mask. The *Sandwich* was not moving; it was stationary within the drifting masses of blasted Xaphan shipping.

"So, why are we just sitting here?"

"We have a slight issue at the moment and need to stay here for a time. Please, Bel—Kaly told us that you could help any who is in medical distress," Forest said.

Stenstrom shook his head. "Kaly is mistaken."

She looked a little desperate. "But, Bel, I saw you remedy yourself that one time—I helped you."

"You're confusing what addled me with this—this is a totally different thing. My soul was at stake. I hadn't tox'ed up on a dirty courtesan."

Dunks began to convulse. "Please, Bel. Is there anything you can do for him? Anything at all—it couldn't hurt in any case. I know you can do something for him. Please …" Kaly said.

Stenstrom reached out and felt his pulse—his heart was racing. He touched his forehead; it was burning up. "Forest, go get cool water and some towels." Forest got up and ran to the door of the bridge. "Kaly, I need merriander and a spring of rosemary from the hold, okay?"

"Merriander and rosemary," she repeated.

"Go now." Kaly ran out of the bridge.

With the crew watching, Stenstrom spread his fingers and shook his hand. A white Holystone appeared.

"What's that?" the helmsman asked. "What do you have there?"

"Holystone. This should slow his heart rate and stabilize his system a little. But, it's no cure—he needs a Hospitaler with all speed."

He placed the Holystone in Dunks' hand and checked his pulse again. It began to slow. The Holystone appeared to be working. "Okay, once Kaly returns with the stuff I asked for, he should be stabilized for now. Where's the mate or the boatswain? Come on—we need to get moving."

The helmsman swallowed. "Can't, Belmont … Dunks is just going to have to hope you know what you're doing for the time being, as we have a slight problem we're dealing with."

"Yeah? What problem is that?"

Stenstrom looked out the windows again—junked out hulks floating about everywhere in a filtered blue tint. He thought he saw something move in the distance.

A warning buzzer went off.

"We have a proximity alert! Vessel moving at 8:52 AM, mark 2:45PM," the navigator said to everybody and nobody at the same time.

"That's our problem, Belmont," the navigator said. "That ship out there. See him?"

"What? Why?"

The Com chattered. "We have an incoming message," Lt Varnay at the Com said. "What do we do?"

"Ignore it," the helm said.

"Play it," Stenstrom said.

The Com ignored the message.

"What is going on here?" Stenstrom asked as Kaly and Forest returned. Stenstrom took the sprigs of merriander and rosemary, bent them in two, and stuck them in Dunk's mouth. He then cooled his forehead with a wet towel.

"Will that stuff work, Bel?" Kaly asked, a little out of breath.

"For the time being, but not for long. Go, back to your station, okay?"

She got up and ran to her visor.

The Com went off. "It's him again," Varney said. "What do we do?"

"Elder's Balls, ignore him!" the helm barked.

Stenstrom spoke up. "Com, accept the message. Accept it."

The Com sighed and hit the button. A wheezy voice came on through the speakers. "Dunks, where are you?"

Everybody on the bridge looked at each other.

"Dunks, answer me!"

Stenstrom cleared his voice and spoke up. "My good sir, Lt. Dunkster is indisposed."

There was a pause. Then: "I see. Drink a little of that poison he tried to pass off on me, did he?"

"Poison? I don't understand."

"Yes, your mate and your boatswain, who are now in my lucrative employ, have come clean and told all to me. Tell Dunks he's going to be more than 'indisposed' in a moment once I get my crosshairs on ya'! Selling me ten years worth of cheap Zemuda tinted and scented to pass for Kanan grain spirits is a bad mistake, and a crime punishable by death. On second thought, I think I'll tell him… personally. Yes, this is about to get very personal …"

Stenstrom looked around—everybody on the bridge was wide-eyed with fear. "I'm … certain there has been a mistake. I'll inform Lt. Dunkster of your dissatisfaction at once and …"

There was a flash through the windows. Stenstrom saw a hulk in the distance go spinning off, a gassy chemical fire lighting up its dented hull. HUD displays and readouts followed it across the glass.

"That was a cassagrain attack beam," Kaly, manning her sensing station, whispered.

Stenstrom made a cutting motion across his neck, and Lt. Varnay muted the Com. "Look, I know Dunks is running some sort of enterprise here on the side and, if this Xaphan out there has something to do with it …"

The Helmsman spoke up. "Yeah, and just what do you know about it?"

"Only that most of the ship is involved in one form or another. Out of respect for Kaly, I didn't choose to pursue the matter further. But, I'm but not blind and I'm not stupid either."

"Could have fooled me," the helmsman said.

Stenstrom shot up. "How would you like to join Dunks on the floor? Huh? One more ill word out of you and that's where you'll be, got it?"

The helmsman started to reply, but then silenced himself.

The Navigator pitched in. "Look, Bel—you see our pay. You know we don't make a whole lot manning a wretched frigate, and none of us are society men like you are. I've a wife and four children to tend to. We all have families to support. Have you ever known a day when you didn't know where your next meal was going to come from for lack of money? Have you ever had to watch your little girls go shoeless—what sort of a father can't afford to properly shoe his children? We joined the bloody Fleet to make something of ourselves, and look where we are, stuck on this rusting tub going nowhere. The captain supplements our purses with the occasional sale of contraband to Xaphans. There's a big market for Kanan spirits in Xaphan space—that good Zenon whiskey they distill using water from the Great Blue Pierce—best water in the universe. That's some high-quality stuff, and the Xaphans have a real thirst for it. They buy up any that they can get for premium prices in unstamped silver."

Stenstrom stood there and listened. Kaly looked distressed and fidgety. "All frigates do it, Bel—just a little something to supplement our purses. We're just providing goods that the Xaphans really want and can't legally get, that's all," she said.

"Ok, that's fine—I don't have a problem with that," Stenstrom said. "So then what's this guy talking about—Zemuda?"

"Zemuda's a cheap, crappy liquor from Bazz. It's colorless and tasteless, and you can get it by the thousand gallon drum for next to nothing. With a little tending, Zemuda can be made to look and taste like most anything—Dunks is an artist with it. It's bad for your regularity, and it deals you a rocking hangover—not like the smooth, easy ride you get from the Kanan stuff, but normally, these Xaphan stiffs can't tell the difference."

"At least not until that Jo-Boy, Boatswain Pike, and the mate, decided to turn their coats and rat us out," the helmsman said. "Pike's been wanting in on Dunk's racket for a long time."

Stenstrom thought about it. "So, this fellow out there paid for a certain set of goods and Dunks cheated him? Is that right? So that's the reason for the hidden apothecary in the hold—to chemically alter the smell, tint and taste of your counterfeit spirits?"

Kaly wrung her hands. "Well, Bel, this is business—and when you're in business, that's what you do. Real Kanan grain spirits are too hard to get through League regulators, and just a few small casks are ruinously expensive. The fake stuff Dunks sells is pretty close to real and the Xaphans just love it."

"Except for the mind-wringing hangover and issues pooping afterwards," the helmsman said.

"Hope you're not too disappointed in us, Bel?" Kaly said.

"You don't have to ask for his approval, Kaly—who is he?" the helmsman said. "Just a cock-balled Paymaster, and a rich one at that."

"He's our mate, and he's my friend," she responded.

"Yeah, well he's not my mate. He's a rich, worthless Paymaster."

"Shut up!" Kaly screamed, anger cracking her voice.

The helmsman threw her an obscene gesture. "See that's how our last Paymaster bought it. He saw the money Dunks was making and tried to horn in on the racket. He even tried to come up with his own fake brew. Got tox'ed up pretty nasty taste-testing it and the old boy never woke up."

Stenstrom turned to Kaly. She nodded, verifying the story.

He stood there, looking at the people sitting in the bridge and the captain lying on the floor. "It's fine, Kaly. Don't worry about me," he said. "As was just pointed out, I've never been without or had to worry about money. Who am I to judge? Still, I believe that even a Xaphan deserves to be dealt with honestly and—"

There was another flash from outside. Another hulk, a bit closer this time, went spiraling. Alarms went off.

"Good Creation!" the navigator cried. "We're going to get blasted into small bits over a load of fake booze!"

The helmsman was a little frantic. "Dunks! Wake your Planet Fall-ass up and get us out of this!"

Stenstrom thought a moment. "Can we give the Xaphan trader what he wants?"

"We don't have any Kanan grain spirits!"

"Can we fight?"

"With what? We've got a pair of penny-toots in the fore-quarter, but that's it!" the navigator said.

"Penny-toots? Those are stationary guns, yes?"

"They're only good for clearing out unmoving targets like asteroids."

"Then let's call the Fleet for help."

"The Fleet?" the helmsman said, shocked. "Assuming we survive until they get here, we could all then expect a nice stay in Hagthorpe prison for running contraband to the Xaphans, Zemuda or not."

"Alive and incarcerated is preferable to a free corpse floating, is it not?" Another blast nearby.

Stenstrom sat down in Dunk's seat. "Com, call the Fleet—when they get here we can make up a story and talk our way out of trouble."

Lt. Varnay hesitated, and then began punching buttons to put the call out.

"What are you doing?" the helmsman barked.

"Saving my skin! I want to live, ok! I'm calling the Fleet. Bel will get us out of trouble."

The helmsman threw his hands up. "Well, we're good and stuffed now, aren't we?"

Stenstrom looked outside, at the maze of old hulks lit up in the blue filter. "Helm, can we run?"

"That's a Ghome 15 out there—got three times our speed."

"We're going to have to vacate this position and find suitable cover."

Stenstrom stood and walked to the windows and looked out. "I see a craggy mass of junked vessels over yonder and a rather large vessel of some sort behind them—might provide us a wealth of places to hide. I think our ship will fit into those spaces just barely. Helm, let's go there now."

The helmsman looked confused. Another blast. "Go where? What—what's our course?"

Stenstrom pointed. "That way, to my left."

"*To my left?* What the Frag does that mean? What orientation? What declination? What speed?"

"Can't we improvise here? This is an emergency!"

"No!" the helmsman cried. "We don't make things up on the bridge! Go back to bean counting in your toilet/office!"

There was a marked lack of coordination and initiative on the bridge just short of full-blown paralysis. Everybody appeared to know their jobs, but without Dunks screaming orders at them, they were quite powerless and unable to act. They were the proverbial body with its head cut off.

Stenstrom strode up to the helm. "That way!" he yelled pointing to his left. "Go that way!"

Baffled, the Helmsman pressed a few buttons, and the *Sandwich* lazily moved from its hiding spot. A mass of twisted metal moved into the windows, highlighted in HUDs. "There, there—tuck into that mass just there!"

"Where?"

"There! Go in there!"

The helmsman saw the space in the wreckage Stenstrom was talking about and slid the *Sandwich* in. Behind, a cassagrain shot blasted the hulk where the ship previously was. The helmsman skillfully backed the ship into the recess.

Through the glass Stenstrom could see the Xaphan ship drift into view. It was a white, somewhat potato-shaped vessel with a flat bottom. He could see the welded outer plates of the hull and its blinking running lights. It was decorated with long red streaks in the shape of lightning bolts painted on the sides of the ship. The engines were housed in cylindrical tubes attached low. It was about twice the size of the *Sandwich*. The Xaphan ship puttered about, rummaging through the ruined ships. Bluish searchlights panned. Stenstrom could see its gun ports were open.

Stenstrom stared at the Xaphan ship. "He doesn't seem to be able to detect us."

"There's too much metal in the vicinity; it's fouling his scanners, no doubt," Kaly said.

A pair of pulsing red beams burst out of the nose of the ship and several wrecks careened away. More alarms sounded.

"He's going to smoke us out sooner or later," the helmsman said.

Stenstrom went to the windows again. "What's behind us?"

Kaly looked into her sensor. "There's a burned out area, looks to be the remains of a large A-H freighter."

"Is there room for us to maneuver?"

"Yes."

"Let's go further in there. What do we have to lose?"

The helmsman was flustered. "Go in there? Elders Balls! I need orientation and declination, AM and PM. I'm sitting here blind. Every button press I make is recorded, and I'll get court-martialed if I damage this vessel! Besides, I'll probably tear the bottom out of the ship!"

Kaly turned to Stenstrom. "*Bel…*" she whispered. "*Come here.*"

He walked over to her sensing station. She put her arm around him, showing him various readouts in her sensor."

"Well, what's this over here?" he asked, pointing.

"That's the …" she said whispering in reply as they hashed things out.

"I have the coordinates!" Stenstrom said. "Can I send them to you, helm?"

"No!" he said.

"Why not?"

"The helm is isolated on frigates, Belmont. Xaphans in the past have been able to get through our encryption and take over frigates in battle, using our console to control the helm. So, the helm isn't connected. The captain has to tell me what coordinates to set."

Stenstrom gazed into the sensor. "Helm, turn to… 7:30…AM by 2:52PM."

The helmsman looked dubious, but then he slowly began turning switches. The ship spun around slowly, and a vast, dark space within the wreckage came into the windows.

"All right," he said. "7:30AM mark 2:52PM, moving at station keeping—hope you know what you're doing, 'cause I'm going to tell the court-martial that you hijacked the bridge and I was under your orders for fear of my life."

Stenstrom bent down over the sensor. "Now, turn to … 7:45AM by 6:12PM."

The helmsman slowly entered the settings. "Ok," he said.

Stenstrom moved away from the sensor. "Good. Now, stop the ship and turn us around.

The helmsman thought about it for a moment, glanced over at the fallen Lt. Dunkster, then slowly stopped the ship and turned it around. In the distance, the opening that they had just come through could be seen, lit up by occasional weapons flashes. The ship was within the cavernous hold of a

Xaphan A-H Cargoer. The *Sandwich* was swallowed up by it, like a goldfish in a large metal bowl.

"Let's wait here a moment," Stenstrom said.

The Com chattered. "Bel, the Fleet has answered our call. MFV *New Faith* is nearby and is proceeding to our location with all speed. She's broadcasting fair warning to all Xaphan vessels not to damage Fleet shipping on pain of retaliation."

"When will she arrive?"

"Advised fifteen minutes! We're lucky she was in the area."

Through the opening beyond, several spotlights shined in through the passages of metal.

"I don't think we've got fifteen minutes, Bel!" Kaly said. "And I don't think he cares about fair warning right now."

Stenstrom thought a moment. "What were those guns you said we had?"

"The what? The pennytoots?"

"Can we get them ready?"

"What for?"

"To buy us time."

The crew looked at each other just before the navigator opened a voice tube and called for the guns to be run out. A minute or two later a reply came. "The pennytoots are ready, Bel, for what that's worth."

Stenstrom went back to the windows and looked around. "Seems to me that, if we set two charges behind us, when they detonate, the Xaphan will believe that we are trying to blast our way out and go to the source of the explosion, thereby leaving the way ahead clear for us to make a fast exit through the wreckage field and out into open space. There, with luck, the *New Faith* should arrive and protect us at that time."

"That's a big gamble, Bel."

"Does anybody have a better idea, and didn't anybody think to do an honest, under-handed deal with this Xaphan in the first place?"

"But, Bel, we didn't know this guy was a—"

"Shh!" Stenstrom said. "All right. Let's plant two in the aft walls behind us, and, when they go off, let's exit the area in a hurry."

The navigator looked exasperated. "Fine. Don't expect a big explosion or anything." He spoke into the voice tube. "Fire the pennytoots to our aft, will you?"

Stenstrom waited a moment. "Did the weapons fire?"

"Yeah …"

"Fine, helm, move us back toward the opening and be ready to make a break for it."

The ship began moving. Through the windows, the opening approached. As they neared, there were two feeble explosions coming from the rear of the enclosure. "Were those the weapons?"

"Yeah … see!" the navigator said. "They stink!"

There was no time to wonder over it. The *Sandwich* came rocketing out of the enclosure through the hole of wreckage.

As they emerged, Stenstrom saw the rear-end of the Xaphan ship disappear around the side of the wrecked ships—his ruse worked, and the way was clear.

"Helm, get us out of this maze, best possible speed!"

"Aye!" the helm said, incredulous that the scheme worked.

Though hardly burning it up, the *Sandwich* clawed its way out of the field of wrecked ships, barely avoiding becoming a wreck themselves. Stenstrom bent down over Kaly's sensor. "Helm, steer 5:22AM by 1:15PM and make for clear space! Best possible speed."

"5:22AM by 1:15PM, Aye!" the helm said.

An explosion came from the Terrabus field and out charged the Xaphan ship. He turned after the *Sandwich*, and his starboard engine caught some wreckage and was fouled with it. He cleared it, squared himself, and came in a hurry, closing the ground with speed.

Stenstrom looked at Kaly's sensor. "Kaly, what does this bit of data here mean?"

"It means he's heating his weapons!"

"Helm, evasive to port!"

The helmsman moved his levers and the ship moved to port. A lance of red energy shot out, passing the ship. The beams panned into them and hit the *Sandwich* in the far starboard side, tremoring the ship."

The Com chattered. "It's him, Bel!" Varnay said. "It's the guy trying to kill us!”

After a moment the Xaphan’s voice filled the bridge. “Where do you plan on going, Dunks? You must know you can’t outrun me.”

“We’ve called the Fleet—they shall be here any moment!” Stenstrom replied.

“That’s a daring move considering you’re all a bunch of criminals. We detected your transmission, but thought it was a ruse. You wouldn’t dare bring the Fleet in on this. Who am I speaking to, please?”

“I am Stenstrom, Lord of Belmont.”

“Really … Lord Stenstrom of Belmont? Ah, Boatswain Pike tells me you are the son of Captain Stenstrom of the Warbird *Caroline*. Ha! The boatswain tells me he thinks you’re a spy sent from the Fleet to bear evidence again Dunks. Is that correct?”

“The reason for my presence here is none of your concern. And, be it known, should you damage or destroy this vessel, the Main Fleet captaincy shall know of it and be none too pleased. I shan’t think you’ll make it back to Xaphan space in one piece what with the armada of Warbirds—my father’s included—that shall descend upon this theatre, seeking your worthless hide. Ask Boatswain Pike the truth of that.”

The Com was silent for a moment. Then: “Lord Belmont, I have been cheated for years. Should this scandal become generally known, not only will my reputation be ruined, but I could lose my life as well. I simply wanted my spirits—I wanted what I paid for in good silver.”

Ahead came a clatter of light, as the huge bulk of the *New Faith* slid into the theatre. The *Sandwich* went to its side like a baby duck to its mother.

The *Sandwich*’s crew, all sixty of them, stood in the hold of the *New Faith*. The first officer, a tall woman with long, brownish hair, had them all lined up and was dressing them down loudly. In comparison with the dapper Marines and immaculate first officer, the crew from the *Sandwich* were an unshaven, slouching, spotty, and rather motley bunch.

Lt. Dunkster, still holding the Holystone in his limp fingers, was taken to the dispensary on a stretcher.

The *New Faith's* captain, a tall blued-haired Vith man, stood and watched as the first officer prowled through the ranks.

"I'm happy to say the fine Xaphan gentleman trying to kill you has quit the area after a bit of parlay. However, as he departed, he said he was here to purchase contraband liquor from you, and that you cheated him. Is that true?" she demanded to know.

Nobody said anything. Kaly wiped her nose and nervously adjusted her pink hair band. The helmsman held back a belch and scratched himself.

The first officer was irate. "The jig is up here, people!" she said. "We want to know who was running this contraband operation and we want to know now; otherwise, we'll have the lot of you in the brig!"

"Will all of us fit in your brig?" the helmsman said in a smarmy fashion.

"We'll excavate some brand new ones just for you, how about that?"

"I'll excavate something, all right," he said.

The captain strode forward. He was breathing fire. "I'm pleased you are enjoying yourself, sir," he said, towering over the helmsman, the point of his triangle hat bopping him in the forehead. "Yes, I'm told a pending stay at Hagthorpe prison is often cause for merriment. In the meanwhile, you are in my charge and I am permitted to deal you up to 100 lashes whilst you await trial and conviction. Don't think I won't go out of my way to make a career out of you, crewman. Therefore, open your mouth again at your peril—am I understood?"

The helmsman swallowed hard, looked at the wall, and said nothing.

The *Sandwich* crew was now thoroughly quaking in their shoes. The captain stepped back, and the first officer resumed.

"My question remains unanswered!" she yelled. "Who's ready to fess up?"

There was silence.

"I better hear somebody owning up real quick, or we're going to start flaying skin off people's backs!"

Stenstrom stepped forward. "It was me, Lieutenant."

She strode up to Stenstrom and looked him over, clearly baffled by his mask and his coat. She was a tall lady, but Stenstrom was a fair amount taller. She looked up at him, the point of her triangle hat nearly knocking into his. "I see. What is your name please, sir?"

"Stenstrom, Lord of Belmont."

The captain seemed to take a bit of exception. He stepped forward and addressed Stenstrom. "Belmont? As in Captain Stenstrom, Lord of Belmont? Of the *Caroline*?"

"My father, sir," Stenstrom replied.

The captain rubbed his chin. "Good man—great man. I've had the pleasure of sailing at his side many times. Is he aware that his son is conducting a criminal enterprise at sea?"

"I don't believe so, sir."

"Very well, and what is your role aboard the *Sandwich*, other than running contraband?"

"I'm the Paymaster, sir."

The captain was startled. "Really?"

"Yes, sir. In this criminal matter, I ran, planned, and financed the whole of the operation. It was my doing alone—the crew had nothing to do with it."

"Pure as the driven, huh, this lot?" the first officer said.

"Indeed. In fact I can say the crew vigorously voiced their objections; however, I forced them to accede to my whims."

"Yeah?" the first officer said. "How'd you manage that all by yourself?"

"With fist and NTH, I terrorized this lot and haunted the ship, though they remained unblemished."

The first officer laughed. "Wow—we normally don't see such sterling character coming from frigate crews. This is inspirational."

"It's the truth, Lt. This is all my doing and my fault."

The captain looked him over again. "I see." He turned to the rest of the crew. "Does anyone here have anything else to add? This man is about to go to the brig for the crime of running contraband goods to the enemy. He's about to face any number of charges that could lead to his lengthy internment at Hagthorpe Prison, and I am seriously considering putting him to the lash as well for imposing his malign will upon your stainless souls. So, with that in mind, does anyone have anything to say?"

The crew fidgeted about a little, but said nothing. "Very well," he said turning to a Marine. "Take this man to the brig."

The Marine came forward and clapped Stenstrom in irons. He reached out to pull Stenstrom's mask off.

"No!" Kaly shouted. "He needs his mask! Don't you touch it!"

The Marine looked back at the captain, who nodded and said, "Let him have his mask."

He then led him away.

As Stenstrom was marched out, he passed the bridge crew all lined up in a row. Kaly looked up, her face red and streaked with tears.

"... *thanks, Bel* ..." she choked out as he passed.

Though he had been manacled, he raised a shackle-free hand and wiped the tears off her cheek. "It's all right, Kaly. I'll be all right."

The Marine was shocked—clearly he couldn't understand how Stenstrom had gotten out of his irons. He refastened them and marched him through.

The other crewmen responded quietly as he passed. "Bel ... Bel ... Belmont... " they said.

"That's our mate!" somebody said.

"Better treat our mate right!" came another.

Though he was being lead away to the brig and a possible session with the lash, Stenstrom reflected on what had just happened. He had led his ship in battle and had gotten his mates out safe and sound. And he had the guts to stand for them. Now they sang his name, albeit quietly, as he passed.

"*Bel ... Belmont ...*"

The joy he felt as he passed by. So this is what it feels like ...

A day later, Stenstrom was fetched from the brig and led into the captain's office. What a difference from the *Sandwich*: clean carpeting, lush paneling, and shining brass. Waiting for him there was the captain, his first officer, and a smallish beautiful woman with red hair, wearing a blue gown. She had a strange mark around her right eye.

Stenstrom stood there as the Marine removed his irons.

The captain looked up at him. "Paymaster Stenstrom, I believe you've already met my first officer."

"The name's Kilos," she said sitting there, all arms and legs.

"And," the captain continued, "May I introduce my countess, Sygillis of Blanchefort."

"Great Countess," Stenstrom said, bowing to her, and she nodded in a courtly way.

"Finally, I am Captain Davage, Lord of Blanchefort."

"I believe I've heard my father mention your name, sir, as an esteemed colleague," Stenstrom replied.

Davage offered Stenstrom a chair, which he accepted.

"Sir," Stenstrom said, "before we begin, may I ask how is Lt. Dunkster?"

"He's fine. Just fine. My Hospitaler informs me he was tox'ed up rather severe, but he's in weather shape now. He had some plants in his mouth and an odd ball in his hand with unique chemical properties. My Hospitaler said those items helped calm his system and prolonged his chances of survival."

"I see," Stenstrom replied.

The first officer chimed in. "Yeah, a cautionary tale, right—mixing a potent strain of The Weed with a bellyful of Zemuda—not good for the body at all. It hits you all of a sudden—you're fine one minute and flat on your back the next."

"Which brings me to it, sir," Davage said. "I'm in quite the situation, aren't I? You claim to be the ringleader and unchallenged potentate of a contraband outfit aboard the frigate *Sandwich,* is that right? Am I correct?"

"Yes, sir."

"Such operations can be rather profitable. I'm certain you had to twist the crew's arms to get them to cooperate, yes?"

"Indeed, sir."

"Yet, according to our records, you have only been aboard the *Sandwich* for a year, while, at the same time, I have here a rather extensive dossier on the activities of the ship's captain, Lt. Dunkster." He thumbed through a thick file on his desk. "Let's see … originally from Planet Fall, a lord of the House of Carew. Long suspected of bootlegging, piracy, counterfeiting, and polygamy, with over thirty-four dirty courtesans in varying degrees of disrepair belonging to his harem—which, might I say, is an offense punishable by death on Planet Fall."

"He told me he only had fourteen wives."

"Yes, we'll add the inability to perform simple arithmetic to his list of crimes. He has thirty-four, not counting the ones who have passed away on him."

The countess spoke up in a regal voice. "And that is not all, sir. His various wives are suspected of being ex-members of the Erynes, a rather potent and feared band of dirty courtesans based on Planet Fall by way of Carina 7. Not a sedate bunch, they. Again, Lt. Dunkster appears to enjoy a dangerous lifestyle."

Stenstrom thought about Christiana on Planet Fall: a little weather-beaten, but unbroken, still beautiful, and a loving woman worthy of honor, with her son's merit trophy sitting on her mantle. Christiana was not a dangerous woman.

"Additionally," the captain added, "the fine Xaphan gentleman who was spoiling to cassagrain you into small bits says that he's been dealing in contraband with Lt. Dunkster for years. As we escorted him back to Xaphan space, he sang like a lark. Painted quite a lurid picture for us."

"Sir, I ..."

"Let's not mince words, shall we? We know all about Fleet frigates, and the little operations they often carry on. Of course, there are all sorts of rules and punishments regarding such a thing; however, let's be practical. We're out here in the Kills, far away from Fleet ballrooms and all the niceties that go along with that. We both know the crew of a frigate barely make enough to subsist—and that is truly a shame, for those are good people on those tiny ships, doing a rancid job that must be done. Other captains may feel differently, but I frankly do not care what side enterprises go on aboard frigates, as long as the merchandise being passed isn't harmful. Pushing dangerous things that have no good use, such as Remax and Magga-tabs is one thing, but selling a reputable product that is in demand is another. Xaphans might be conniving and evil, but they do enjoy a fine grain spirit as well as the next person."

Lt. Kilos objected. "Yeah, but Dav, they were trying to pass off Zemuda as Kanan grain spirits."

"Yes, and I imagine that's what got our fine Lt. Dunkster into trouble. He was probably taste-testing his batch of fake spirits after having had at one of his ex-Erynes wives, apparently while soaked in The Weed. A poor combination to be sure. Well, no harm done, I suppose."

"No harm done? Have you ever tried to survive a hangover from a night of Zemuda? And don't even try to go to the bathroom afterwards—you'll be in there all day," Kilos said.

The countess, who was sitting rather properly, laughed a little.

"Thank you, Ki, we get the picture."

Stenstrom stirred. "Sir, you mentioned that the lash might be in the offing for …"

"Paymaster, I've never lashed a soul aboard my ship, and I don't intend to start now. Sounds impressive though, doesn't it?"

Stenstrom was relieved.

The captain continued. "I am most interested in you, sir. Are you still purporting to be the sole mastermind behind this Zemuda-counterfeiting ring aboard the *Sandwich,* when I have reams of evidence to the contrary?"

"Yes, sir."

Davage held up a small report. "Such loyalty—I value that. I have here a signed confession from your fellow mates. Apparently, they had an attack of conscience over the night and claim that you had nothing to do with the operation. Additionally, they claim it was under your leadership that they survived the affair with the Xaphan scalawag in the first place, after the captain was incapacitated."

"Sir, what's to be done with my mates?"

"Nothing. I've dropped the charges, and they've already set sail—off to who knows where. They were hoping you would be joining them; a ... Crewman Kaly did not want to leave without you—made quite the fuss, I'm told, but I'm not quite done with you, am I?"

They sat there in silence for a bit. "I had a little talk with Lt. Dunkster as he convalesced in the dispensary. I informed him that, if he is purporting to sell Kanan grain spirits to the Xaphans, then that is exactly what he better be selling. I was most strenuous about it and I think he got the point. I can't fault the Xaphans for wanting Kanan grain spirits—it is a very lovely beverage."

"It's the best, Dav—come Saluting Day, that's all I drink," Lt. Kilos said.

Countess Sygillis smiled. "I must admit, I do enjoy a touch of it mixed together with …"

"No mixing, Syg," Kilos cried. "You'll ruin it with girly mixers and flavorings and little accessories that are meaningless. It's straight or nothing!"

Davage looked at Kilos. "Well, I suppose straight with a bit of ice …"

"No ice, Dav. Lukewarm, or, if you must, warm it up a little under your armpit, and then kill it."

"You are a bizarre person, Ki," Countess Sygillis said.

The first officer turned to Stenstrom. "So what's with the mask?" she asked. "What's the matter? You scarred under there or something?"

Stenstrom stirred, but didn't say anything.

"Yes, you were quite the picture, weren't you—standing there in the hold all shackled up," the captain said. "An apparently handsome fellow in a Hoban Royal Navy coat and a mask to boot. I haven't seen one of those coats in quite some time. And, I must say, you standing up for your mates under the threat of the lash was probably the bravest act ever performed while wearing a Hoban Royal Navy coat. That coat, that mask, like a vigilant right out of a penny-vid. I've not quite seen such a thing … ever, and I've certainly been around."

"I wear the coat because someone dear to me picked it out," Stenstrom said. "Because I once had hopes of joining the Fleet, and this is as close to wearing a uniform as I'll ever get."

"Yes, about that. Your father is Captain Stenstrom, an esteemed Warbird captain. With such a father, your place in the Fleet is assured, why didn't you simply join? The three of us were bandying that topic about yesterday at dinner, and couldn't come up with a suitable reason. Perhaps you'll care to explain."

"It's complicated, sir. I really do not wish to go into it."

"Well, perhaps someday you'll feel at ease to reveal your reasoning."

Countess Blanchefort spoke. "Your mother is the Lady Jubilee, formerly of Tyrol is that correct?"

"Yes, Great Countess."

"I know of her—a stern matriarch and, purportedly, a difficult personality to get along with."

"I have been told that on occasion, yes."

"I understand she is a member of the Ballwigs and has been under Wirguild for over a hundred years."

"Yes, though the Wirguild has been revoked."

"Yes, for violation of terms. We also understand that you have sorcerous abilities, is that true?" the countess asked.

"Yes, Great Countess, that is true. My mother taught me."

"May we see? We do not wish to gawk; however, we are truly fascinated."

Stenstrom leaned forward and showed them his empty hands.

He shook them. Six silver daggers appeared between his fingers.

The captain, the first officer, and the countess all gasped.

"These daggers are the MARZABLE, the LosCapricos weapon of my mother's house."

The captain was truly amazed. "You had those on you the whole time? We disarmed you prior to sending you to the brig."

"With the MARZABLE, one can never be disarmed."

"And these … MARZABLE are the LosCapricos weapons of House Tyrol, is that right?"

"Yes, sir."

The captain thought a moment. "I don't think we have a MARZABLE in our collection, Syg. Paymaster, we have a hall in our castle where we've collected what we thought was the complete family of LosCapricos weapons from all over the League and proudly display them. We do not have a MARZABLE."

"Yeah, you do, Dav," Kilos said. "It's by the …"

"No, Ki," he replied. "We don't. Paymaster, I would be greatly interested in purchasing one from you. It doesn't have to be a functioning example—it can be a mock-up. I would love to add a bit of your mother's heritage to a place of honor at our home where it may be properly appreciated."

Stenstrom shook his hand, and they disappeared. He shook it again, and one dagger appeared, shiny and silver. "Sir, for your fair-handed treatment of my mates, and for your understanding of the Xaphan trader's position …"

Stenstrom placed the dagger on the desk and slid it toward him. "I offer it to you as a gift."

Captain Davage took the dagger and looked at it with wonder. He then opened his desk drawer and pulled the NTHs out and placed them on the desktop. "I believe these belong to you. These I have on my wall. Remarkable weapons."

Stenstrom picked them up and returned them to his sash. "Thank you, sir. So, may I ask, what is to be done with me?"

"That is an interesting question. What shall we do with you? Have you ever been aboard a *Triumph-class* vessel?"

"No, sir."

"We have over a thousand souls aboard: officers, crewmen, a smattering of civilians, and a changeable number of Sisters; they come and go as they will. This is a big ship, a complex ship, and, in order for it to function, I have to know that I may count on every soul aboard to do their duty, to be their best. There are no unneeded souls aboard my ship. All have worth; all have value. All are people of quality, from top to bottom. You, sir, you were willing to give yourself up for your mates after I had promised prison and the lash. As an eye-opener and attention-getter, threat of the lash has no peer, and I saw how scared your mates were. You saw it too, and you took it upon yourself to bear the brunt of our wrath. I'm certain that you, with your family name and Belmont fortune, could have bought your way out of any troubles that might have been pending; however, such a thing is inconvenient, troubling, time-consuming, embarrassing— the list goes on. You jumped in front of your mates without fear or hesitation. Your actions say a lot about you, and, though I don't know you personally as of yet, I know your father, and I see him in you. I find favor with your character. You sit there in a mask and a Hoban Royal Navy coat, and odd sight to be sure. All the same, if those accessories empower you to be yourself, then they are well-served and most welcome."

"What are you trying to say, sir?"

"I'm saying that Paymaster Milke, my Paymaster of old, is soon to retire—my countess is planning his retirement gala. When he does, I would like you to replace him."

"Me?"

"We believe you would make a fine addition to our family aboard the *New Faith*—there is certainly no shortage of characters here," Countess Sygillis said.

"We mix it up a lot," Kilos said. "Get into it with the Xaphans all the time. Somehow, I think you'd like that."

They talked for a bit more, Stenstrom soon warming to these people.

28

—A Regretful Competition—

A few days later, the *New Faith* dropped Stenstrom off in Bern, where he took up residence in the IBBAANA apartments. There he caught up with Lady Alitrix, and she marveled at his attire and his stories. He was glad to hear she'd moved on, found a good man with whom she could be happy.

He also sent word to Kaly, who was frantic. She was certain he'd been lashed raw and thrown in prison. He told her what had happened, and she was overjoyed—though she was also very upset that he wasn't to be returning to the ship. He met up with her when the *Sandwich* arrived in Mercia again, and he was hailed as a hero by the crew. He and Kaly also shared each other's bed a few more times—"one for the road," as she said. He was going to miss Kaly—she was a good friend.

He also wrote to Lilly to share his good fortune. Lilly was silent. He received no reply.

As he waited in Bern, Stenstrom's Com chirped.

It was his sister Lyra. "Hello, Bel," she said.

"Lyra! This is a great surprise." It had been a long time since he'd last seen her. She wore a university pin on the shoulder of her gown.

She seemed sad. "Bel … you need to come home."

"Oh, Lyra, you're starting to sound like Mother. What is it this time?"

"Bel, Mother's dead."

He sat there and tried to comprehend. "What? How? It can't be …"

"Mother was old, Bel. It was just her time. I think she knew it was coming. She asked us all to come home. I think she wanted to see us all one last time."

He thought about that for a moment. He hadn't come home. He did what she asked. He resisted.

"We are all lingering here, to hold vigil with Father and celebrate her memory. You need to come home, Bel. We need you here—I need you."

"Yes, Lyra, yes. I'm coming at once."

✶ ✶ ✶ ✶ ✶

The four hour trip to Tyrol on the large liner was guilt-ridden and phantasm-filled. His mind was ablaze.

I knew something was wrong, I knew it. Why didn't I come home?

His mother's voice rang in his ear: *I told you to play the game, Bel. To the very end, I played the game. There're no give-backs.*

The Black Maidens, the Soul Devourers … creatures in the mirror and the stain on his soul—Mother was playing the game.

Why didn't she tell me?

As he waited for the liner to come in from Bern port, he wondered at the lack of Black Maidens—they were crawling after him previously, but now there were none; he even took off his bolabung. Nothing. Now that he wanted one to zap him home straight away, there were none.

He thought about finding a quiet spot and summoning a Black Maiden or two. The bad thing was he was terrible at it. The summoning was quite difficult despite the fact Mother made it look rather easy—even Lyra wasn't very skilled at it. Virginia was quite adept. Even if he could summon one, it wouldn't do any good. They weren't a taxi service—"take me here, take me there"—they would send him back to the place where they'd been summoned, period.

So he waited for the liner and felt the pounding throb of guilt seep into his mind.

He wondered about all the usual things. Did Mother know how much he loved her? Did Mother know how grateful he was for all she'd taught him? The recriminations could go on and on.

Surrounded by ghosts and pointed fingers, he drifted off to sleep as the liner lifted off and headed east.

SNAP!!

The old dream again. The sand pit, the afternoon sun, and the stars shining in broad daylight.

This time, the dream was different. This time, all twenty nine of his sisters and his father were there, watching him sailing through the air.

He landed in the sand. Something lurched out of it.

Everything went black, just like always.

"Open your eyes, Bel," he heard a voice say.

He opened them, and there was his mother, leaning over him, her swoop of Pewterlock hair shining in the sun.

"What's bothering you?" she asked.

"You died."

"What's so strange about that? I was two hundred and fifty years old. How old do you wish I get?"

"Why didn't you tell me?"

"Because I told you to resist me. Telling you I was dying would have been cheating."

"Mother, I wasn't there when you died."

"No, but you were there all the other times. You were in your crib every morning, snoring away—how I loved to watch you sleep. You were there in the manor, filling the halls with your laughter. You were there at the dining table, sitting right where I could see you. You were a good friend to your sisters, and a good son to your mother. I'm glad you weren't there, Bel. I'm glad your last memory of me wasn't one of weakness, of me on my deathbed. Remember me as I was, as a strong woman and a proud mother. Perhaps you'll tell my grandchildren someday of their old grandmother, and let them know she wasn't all bad."

The dream faded.

He heard one final thing. "I didn't send the Soul Devourers after you. Why would I do that to my beloved son? Farewell …"

✶　✶　✶　✶　✶

He stood there in the yard with his hat in hand. Mother's new tombstone was there, odd and big. He was wearing his HRN coat and his mask, which he still could not take off—Mother's spell holding even in death. Lyra stood next to him.

He'd been all through the manor. Mother's bed was fresh and made—Mother wasn't there. He'd been to the dining room where Mother held court for all those years, and the sitting rooms and the libraries she once haunted—no Mother.

Here she was, out in the yard under her gravestone. She would never again sleep in her bed and terrorize his sisters in the dining room, and she would tell no more gossip in the sitting rooms.

Mother was dead.

Crushed, unable to face the moment, he dropped his hat and fell to his knees in the new dirt of her grave.

He felt like he did when he was a child: he wanted his mother. He wanted to claw his way into the dirt and pull her out and shake her awake.

Lady Jubilee could not be dead. Death could be no match for her.

Mother, wake up! Wake up!

"Did you see her, Lyra, at the end?" he asked.

"Yes."

"Did she wonder where I was?"

"She wanted me to tell you it was all right. She understood. She wanted me to tell you that she was proud of you—of the man you've become."

He glanced down at his coat and felt the fabric of his mask, suddenly feeling very silly. "Yes. And just look at me … What am I?"

Lyra embraced her brother. "You are who you are, Bel. I think if Mother had given you every freedom, if she hadn't plunged the knife into your chest, you still would have ended up with a coat and a mask. Perhaps the fabric might have been a different shade, perhaps the mask less prominent, but they still would have been there all the same."

Lyra joined him in the dirt. "Look at me and the costume I wear—this gown ... Is my costume so different from yours? You followed your heart, didn't let your dreams die, and ended up in the stars like you always wanted. Coat and mask—you are what you wanted to be."

Stenstrom smiled and wiped his face. "Virginia's wedding. The planning is not finished, I'm told."

"I'm going to help her plan it, and so will Lucile. Though, a wedding at this time just seems…"

"It seems perfect to me," Stenstrom said. "Life goes on at our household—just as Mother would have wanted it. Her children's lives go on. I think I'm going to stay for awhile, until I ship out again. I'd like to help plan my sister's wedding."

"She'll be very glad to hear that. I'm glad too, Bel—maybe it will be like old times. Perhaps later, we can go to the sand pit and wrestle like we used to."

He laughed. "Sure—I'll beat you down now just like I did back then."

"That's not how I remember it, sandface."

He looked around: the hills, the manor, the Merian ruins—home, yet no longer familiar, no longer what it was without Mother's presence. He raised his hand and shook it, producing three MARZABLEs.

"Here's to our mother, and the richness she left to us," he said.

Lyra shook her hand, producing the same. "Here's to Lady Jubilee, the woman who watched over us. The woman who loved us," she said.

They embraced, the shadows of the afternoon growing long.

* * * * *

Three months later, he became the Paymaster of the *New Faith*.

Part 3
The Demon That Came For His Soul

1

—Missing—

The *Seeker* limped through open space, its progress painfully slow. They had managed, just barely, to get the *Seeker* going fast enough to break Kana's orbit, leaving the inviting blue ball with all its safety and comfort behind. They were flying the ship backwards, as the improvised engine of the *Westminster* was located in a forward-facing bay. Stenstrom, A-Ram, and Taara stayed mostly on the bridge. That's where they had lights and a bit of fresh portable air—the Macon setup, powered on, happily spewed condensed oxygen. In such a condition, the bridge was halfway livable.

They had completed several burns, using nothing but dead reckoning as their AM/PM compasses were off-line.

Taara's MOLLY'ed smarts were a godsend. If not for her and A-Ram's MOLLY, they would still be plummeting into Kana's atmosphere.

She was still at it, putting her soul more at risk with every use. "We'll keep Kana in the window for a few more hours, then, at the Mersy ice swarm, we'll bank to 2:30PM, do a long burn with the *Westminster,* and make a beeline for Onaris, riding Druries Belt the whole way. We'll course correct again once we're there, use its gravity to pick up some speed, and then it's on to Bazz for the final push."

Taara patted the golden chain at her neck, she gazed with wonder at the pages of calculations she'd made on scavenged paper, all fueled by the MOLLY. "This thing is great, A-Ram! You're going to have to fight me to get this back. I love this!"

"What about the hoard of demons you're going to have after you? You've generated quite a bill that your soul shall have to pay."

"Screw `em!"

Stenstrom was unsure. "Taara, you're positive you know where we're headed?"

"Well, come see for yourself."

They went in his office and looked out the windows. Taara had constructed a crude sextant-like device out of metal struts. She picked it up, aimed, and pointed to a large, whitish star hanging just starboard beyond the silhouette of the *Seeker*'s cranked wing. "That big whitish-blue star out there is Nu Torriander, *Ole Scrub*, as we call it—that's Onaris' and Bazz's star. Now, that smaller white star hanging off Ole Scrub's ear, that's *Lil Whiteface*, Nu Torriander's dwarf companion star—that's what freakin' gives us scorching hot summers on Bazz. Damn thing."

Stenstrom looked at Ole Scrub bright in the window. "Doesn't even look like it's moving, does it?"

"Nope," she said still staring through her sextant, "but it is, slowly but surely. Soon, we'll be seeing Druries Belt. It's just a big, long cloud of glowing gas they used to use as a navigational aid back in the day."

Taara laid the sextant down, stretched and gave a long yawn. "Wow, I'm bushed. It's been a busy two days."

"I'm feeling pretty used up myself. Here, you can have my office, Taara. Stretch out and get some sleep."

He went back out onto the bridge, Taara following him. "I'm fine. I don't need a separate room—I never had one in the Marines, so I really don't need one now." She went to her favorite spot at the Missive's panel and removed her coat and her boots. She balled her coat up into a pillow and plunked down into the chair, feet up. "Ahh, this isn't bad."

Feeling dead himself, Stenstrom flopped down into his chair. "A-Ram, why don't you lock the helm and get a little sleep as well. We're on-course, right?"

"According to the last dead reckoning Taara made, we're on course. We shouldn't need a course correction for another twenty hours. I've got the helm's alarm set. According to the charts, we're heading into the wastelands between the stars. The chart has a bunch of vague references to artifacts coming up."

"What are those?" Stenstrom asked.

Taara chimed in, her voice groggy. "Ice, dust, gas ... just 'stuff' floating around. Our next burn, that's an important one," she mumbled, settling into sleep. "Nice long five minute burn, we miss it, we'll go off into the Wildlands on the other side of Druries Belt. Bad things happen off in the Wildlands. That's what we say on Bazz."

"Oh please. We won't miss it," A-Ram replied. "I've got the alarm set in any case."

He locked the helm and stepped down into the bridge, finding a comfortable spot at he navigator's seat. A-Ram recited a short prayer and curled up on the chair. "Night, Bel," he said wiggling around.

Nearby, Taara was already out, her little chest rising and falling, accompanied by a bit of snoring.

"Good dreams," Stenstrom replied. As he watched the two of them sleep, he drew his NTHs and laid them on his lap. He felt like he'd known these two his entire life and he wasn't going to allow anything to happen to them, not now, not ever.

Taara snored a little more, and A-Ram twitched. The Macon blew fresh air, and every so often, a light blinked on the various consoles; other than that the ship was quiet. Stenstrom got out of his seat and set up his various bits of arcane protections: his silver candlesticks, pans, and various Holystones scattered about meant to warn him of danger. They were silent.

Silent was good.

After a time he allowed his mind to wander and his eyes to grow heavy. He was tired too. Soon, he slept.

✶ ✶ ✶ ✶ ✶

He was pulled out of his sleep by an alarm ticking steadily. He looked around, bleary-eyed. The alarm was coming from the helm.

"A-Ram, I think your alarm's going off," he said, trying to clear the sleep out of his eyes. He stretched and settled back into sleep.

The alarm dug a galling trench in his thoughts and woke him up.

"Didn't you say the alarm was set for twenty hours hence?" He opened his eyes. "There's no way we slept for that long. Right?"

No answer. The alarm continued to blare.

Stenstrom stood and stretched.

"A-Ram, kill that thing, would you please?"

A-Ram wasn't where he was when Stenstrom had fallen asleep. The Navigator's position was empty.

The Missive's chair was also empty. Taara was missing too. Her Marine coat and her boots were there—but no Taara.

He was alone on the bridge.

"A-Ram! Taara!" he shouted.

No answer.

He went into his office, seeing the motionless diorama of stars against the gigantic, blackened silhouette and cranked wings of the *Seeker*. It reminded him of the Tyrol coastline at night, long and black under a sea of stars.

Nobody was there.

He saw a light snap on far away in the rear section of the ship near the wings, glowing like a campfire, then it went out.

2

—Haunted—

Anger and frustration surged through him as he stood alone on the bridge. What had happened? Had A-Ram's "demon" come for Taara at last, and also taken A-Ram in the process, somewhere in the middle of twenty hours of sleep?

Blast! He was supposed to protect them. They trusted him and look what he'd done—fallen asleep, and not just for a few hours, but for nearly a day! And, furthermore, they needed to do a course correction and burn, change the angle of the ship; otherwise, they'd soar off course, rudderless into the Wildlands Taara had called it, an empty, lonely stretch of space.

Space? What a poor captain he was. Space was a term for scholars and astronomers. Fleet captains called the open stretches between the stars "The Deep Sea." As Captain Davage would have put it, the Wildlands was a patch of "bad sea," small, insignificant, passed over in the blink of an eye.

Of course, stuck in his dead ship flying backwards, this patch of "bad sea" was an unending ocean. He turned back and stared at the lonely helm wheel locked in place. Without A-Ram standing there, or without Captain Davage, the helm seemed to him an alien and incomprehensible thing.

The alarm rang.

It was time to alter course and burn the *Westminster*'s engines. He had no idea how to accomplish either task.

He checked the arcane detectors he'd set up. They were still in place. Whatever had entered the bridge and taken them had overcome several layers of arcane protection: his Holystones and bolabungs and his silver talismans.

He went to the lift and cranked open the doors. Darkness from the empty shaft filtered into the lit-up comfort of the bridge. As usual, he heard strange noises and a general feeling of dread bubble up from the bowels of the ship.

And, somewhere out there, in all of that, were Taara and A-Ram, his friends. He couldn't delay; he had to rescue them.

Forget the ship, forget the burn, their safe return was all that mattered.

He should have never brought them here.

He waved his hands and produced a small silver chest. Opening it, inside he found three oily Holystones with a shimmering, chromatic surface. These Chromatic Holystones were adept at locking onto specific people and zeroing in on them, the fun he and his sisters Lyra and Virginia used to have with them, hiding in the Manor grounds and then being discovered, the excitement, the laughter in the afternoon sun.

The Chromatics were difficult to make and expensive and they only worked for a short time, but they should help him locate Taara and A-Ram. He grabbed Taara's left boot and dropped one of the Chromatic Holystones down into it. The Holystone needed a few minutes, to "soak up" Taara's essence. He took advantage of the time. He checked his NTHs, replaced the cinnabar strikers, and gave them the general onceover. The strikers were locked into place and sound, the hammers oiled and smooth, they should be ready to fire. He cocked the hammers and put two shots through the near wall of the bridge. The shots were nice and bright, emerald green just like they should be. So beautiful to look at and so dangerous as well. They passed through the wall without damaging it and continued on unseen until they dissipated.

He sashed them. He checked his HRN:

MARZABLES: ready.

Holystones: fully kitted out, greens, reds, blues, the works. He was ready to go.

He shook his hands and there, gleaming, was his locket with Lilly's face hiding within; the demure smile, the hopeful blue eyes. He'd fantasized about bringing her aboard someday, giving her the grand tour of his amazing ship, arm-in-arm.

He'd give anything to see her again, to give him courage.

He placed the locket back in his HRN and moved Taara's boot around, hearing the Chromatic Holystone rattle around inside like a marble. Enough time should have passed, and he dumped it out onto the floor. The oily surface of the Chromatic had dried up turning into a dirty-looking brown. Now, the Chromatic should point the way toward Taara for the next hour or so.

It lay there on the floor next to her boot doing nothing. It had to work. It just had to. He leaned down over it. "Don't mess this up," he said and gave it a slight tap. The Holystone began rolling, picking up speed. It headed toward the lift at a quickening pace. He picked it up and allowed it to settle into his palm.

Time to go.

He steeled himself and plunged into the low-grav dark beginning the perilous climb down the groaning, sound-filled lift shaft.

The shaft was rotten and noisy; groans, creaks, unidentifiable titterings and, other, softer sounds lurking behind the louder noises.

So far, the *Seeker* had been, except for the bridge, a groaning mess haunted with shadows and twisting movements of the night that they'd rather avoid if they could. Stenstrom had tried to ignore it at first, but the sounds he heard coming from the bowels of the ship couldn't be explained as simply the aches and pains of an old, silent ship torquing through space. His old ship, the *Sandwich,* was also a noisy, groaning vessel ready to sink in open space at any time, but it never made eerie sounds like what the *Seeker* was doing. The *Sandwich* never formed words and made dire sentences.

The Astral Plane? Could it be at work in the bowels of the ship, clouding his mind? His Holystones meant to detect the Astral Plane were silent. It did not seem to be present. Something else was at work in the dark.

As he made the climb down the shaft, Stenstrom tried not to listen, but he could hear, plain as day: "….beeeeeeellllllmontttt…. wheeeeere's yoo-ourrrrrrmooooooothherrrrrr beeeeeeeellmmontttttt…."

He looked up at the open door to the bridge with its yellow cone of light pooling out into the shaft—it was a comforting sight.

He had to concentrate; he had a job to do. He checked the Holystone. He felt it tugging. A few more levels down.

He continued on, trying to ignore the sounds.

"… *Belmont!* … *Your mother died alone* …" a voice whispered in his ear with startling clarity.

The things haunting the ship were getting personal. He closed his eyes. "My mother died surrounded by her husband and her children, all except one."

His mother's death, and his not being at her side, haunted him to the present. It was a place in his thoughts he tried to avoid—the guilt and recriminations. The voices brought her loss back to him fully, and the evil lurking in the shaft seemed to know that.

"Where was her son?"

"Doing what she asked me to do. My mother is at peace."

"Is she? Are you sure?"

He had to say it to himself several times.

"My mother is at peace. My mother is at peace."

The insufferable noises dogged him all the way down to Deck 7. The Holystone "knocked," indicating he was approximately level with Taara's position. He pried the door open, and plunged into the dark. The shadows and noises were even more pronounced in the corridor than they had been in the lift shaft. The air was cold and stale.

The thought of Lilly, bright and pink and full of light, flashed across his mind. This dark abyss was certainly no place she belonged.

He shook open a yellow Holystone for light and instantly dropped it in shock.

Four towering figures lit up in the Holystone's glow. They stood not three feet away. Four pairs of dark eyes boring into him. He dropped the Holystone and drew his NTHs.

When he looked back up, the four figures were gone; just the great darkened cavern of the deck lay ahead stretching out into the gloom. He panned around with his NTHs at the ready. He thought for a moment that he just imagined seeing the figures, but no—they had been right there. He had seen them standing there thin and tall wearing white course-spun robes stained yellow in the Holystone's light. He didn't recall seeing their faces, for there hadn't been time: only their eyes, which had been dark and mirthless. Shaken from the phantom encounter, Stenstrom set the Chromatic on the metal floor. He gave it a shove, and it started rolling, slowly at first and then quickening down the corridor. He followed, NTHs ready.

The corridor was like a witch's dance, echoing with disturbing sounds and hidden noise. The previous captain, Captain Gona of St. Paris, had retired, it was said, because he thought the *Seeker* was haunted, and with a cacophony like this, who could blame him? Stenstrom concentrated on his friends: on Captain Davage, on dear Lt. Kilos, and the beautiful Countess Sygillis. This was once their ship; they walked these very corridors. They are still here in the dark somewhere; he tried to remember their goodness and their light.

The Holystone continued on into the dank reaches of the ship, rolling fast with a fuss.

He was moving through the long neck of the vessel. It was quite a walk to the rear section. Wait! Ahead, he saw a figure moving in the dark.

"Who's there? Answer me, who's there?"

A chiding laugh came back in return.

He lifted his NTH and cocked the hammer.

"Where is Lord A-Ram? Where is Taara?" he asked, not expecting an answer.

One came: *"We have her. We have your little girl."*

"Return her!"

Laughter in response.

"Return her to me at once!"

"HHHAHAAHAHAAHHAHAAA!!"

There was a momentary respite of silence, then: *"She belongs to us, as do you."*

"Who are you?"

"You know us ... " a voice whispered.

"Show yourself!" He whirled around, dropping the yellow Holystone and drawing his second NTH.

"You want her back? " the voice asked.

"Show yourself!"

"Very well ... " In the dark a figure emerged, thin and tall, leering and dreadful.

Stenstrom covered it with his pistols.

"If you've come for Taara's soul, you cannot have it," he said.

The figure giggled. *"We are here for a soul, but it's not hers or that little man's either."* It paused. *"We're here for yours!!"*

It revealed its face: a huge, smiling mouth all over the disk of its face. A great tongue sticking out.

Soul Devourer!!

It cringed and wrung its hands. He raised his NTHs, ready to fire.

"No, no, wait ..." it said. *"We've your friends. I'll let my companions kill them, eat their souls, consigning them to oblivion."*

"Where are they?"

"Not far."

"Show me."

The Soul Devourer led Stenstrom down the corridor. It danced around him, savoring his smell, wringing its clawed hands. It was just barely containing itself.

"Why didn't you just take me on the bridge while I slept and been done with it?"

"Safe on the bridge, couldn't get to you ... But your friends ... ahh ..."

"How do I know they're still alive?"

"Their souls are tiny and bland, hardly worth the trouble, but yours ... ah, yours shall make fine eating."

It tittered and reached with its hands, opening and closing its fists. *"Took us on a merry run, did you? Think you could get away from us forever?"*

"My mother is gone, and her spells are finished. You ought to go back from whence you came and leave me in peace. You may have my soul once I'm done with it."

"We'll have your soul now! Understand? We'll have it now!!" The Soul Devourer pushed him up against a bulkhead and put its clawed hands at his throat. It lost whatever patience it had and pawed at him. *"They promised us your soul; it belongs to us! Give me your soul!! Give it to me!! GIVE IT TO ME NOW!!"*

Stenstrom pushed his NTHs into its chest and fired. Green light emerged from the Soul Devourer's groaning mouth, and it fell, collapsing into smoking ash.

Panting, feeling the familiar tug in his chest caused by the infernal grasp of the Soul Devourer, he took a moment to compose himself.

Footsteps came running down the corridor!! A tooth-filled, smiling face and reaching hands. *"YOUR SOUL!!"*

He aimed and fired. Its body fell in the dark.

Behind him!

Fire! Two green globes surged out. Did he hit? He wasn't sure. He cocked his hammers and waited.

Laughter came from down the corridor. *"We have your friends. You cannot kill us all. We are ready for you. Keep us waiting and we'll savor their souls in your place."*

"Leave my friends out of this!" he shouted. "My soul for theirs!"

"Then come, come to us ..."

Mother's demons had finally caught up to him, and now they had his friends. He searched for the Chromatic Holystone, finding it down the corridor, still rolling slowly. Steeling himself and, determined to save Taara and A-Ram, he continued on.

3
—THE DEMON??—

Down the corridor was the Sisters' Priory, a cloistered set of small rooms where the Sisterhood of Light stayed when aboard a Fleet vessel. They often came and went from the Priory and often times disappeared into it, vanishing even when the ship was out far away in the deep sea. Many times, new and unfamiliar faces emerged from the Priory only to vanish back into it just as quickly. Stenstrom thought it was a mystical gateway of some sort. His sorcerous training told him such things could exist.

The Chromatic veered in the direction of the Priory entrance and stopped.

Taara was somewhere inside, A-Ram as well probably, along with who knows how many Soul Devourers.

Within was a small abandoned anti-chamber with an innocent door leading into the interior. All that lay beyond the door was forbidden to any but the Sisters—even the captain of the ship was not allowed past it. Stenstrom himself certainly had never set foot in one. NTHs at the ready, he opened the door; it swung open with a mild squeak.

Musty darkness lay ahead. He entered.

Inside were a confusion of modest rooms and chambers littered with overturned chairs, beds, dressers, and other forgotten bits of furniture once used by the Sisters, all rather sparse and unassuming, now dark and abandoned.

His arcane protections and warning devices were all sounding off at a steady rate, the interior of his HRN vibrated and squirmed as though it were infested with mice. There was danger all around.

"YOUR SOUL!!" came a Soul Devourer out of the dark at a run. He shot it down.

Another came, and then another, his NTH shots sending them away one trigger pull at a time. They came at him with no fear, faster than he could cock and fire his NTHs.

One reached out of the dark for his throat. He aimed and fired.

Pfft!

Misfire! His cinnabar striker cracked and the NTH didn't fire. He was tackled in the mid-riff by the tittering Soul Devourer. They struggled for a moment as the monster wrangled to get at his soul. He plunged one MARZ-ABLE after the next into its wiry body, burying the silver daggers up to the hilt, doing nothing. The monster wore a headdress of his daggers as it got its hands to his throat. He felt the tepid beginnings of his soul being siphoned away.

A fast, whirling cone of gritty wind, like a sudden dust storm, plowed into the both of them. The Soul Devourer was lifted up and pulled away in a roar into the dark where it disappeared.

Stenstrom stood and readied himself for the next wave of them to attack.

Silence. It became very quiet in the corridor of the Priory. No groans, no moans or other hidden sounds, just blessed silence.

His waiting NTHs shook. He sashed the one with the bad striker and waved up three MARZABLES ready to go.

"Bel!" he heard from ahead. He saw a point of light emerge, strong and clear, threatening to blind him. He didn't wait. He fired his NTH and let fly with his MARZABLE. The corridor lit up in emerald green as the deadly globe shot out into the dark. He cocked his hammer and conjured up more daggers.

"Bel, how could you?" he heard a hurt-sounding voice reply. He squinted to see.

The point of light grew to a blinding beam. Someone approached in the dark. *"Bel, it's me."*

"Who are you?" he asked shielding his eyes, his NTH leveled.

"It's Lilly."

"Liar," Stenstrom said, trying to keep his head. He took aim.

All around him came the hissing of grit rubbing together, like coarse sand whipped up into a whirling storm. He blinked and covered his eyes with his sleeve.

The wind abated. A lilting form emerged from the gloom ahead holding a lantern. Tall and regal, inviting pink gown, and blonde hair done up in pins and curls, a little parasol resting on her shoulder. It looked for all the world like Lilly, his love.

Lillian of Gamboa.

He stepped back, NTH at the ready.

"Bel ... it's me. It's Lilly," she said smiling. His danger detectors rattled. His heart pounded.

He struggled to maintain his bearing. "You are not Lilly," he said. "You cannot be Lilly."

"But why?" Her eyes glittered in the lantern light.

"Why? Because I am in the middle of open space on a dead, abandoned ship. Lilly is thousands of Stellar miles away, home on Kana in Esther."

She blushed a bit and raised the lantern. Her blue eyes sparkled. "But, Bel, don't I always arrive when you need me most? Am I not always there to help you?"

She took a step forward. "Stay back!" he cried, NTH cocked and ready to fire.

She set the lantern down, reached out, and placed her delicate hands on the barrel of his NTH. "Perhaps you should fire your gun then. Perhaps you should just kill me."

He struggled. This apparition was a Soul Devourer—it had to be.

"Remember our first meeting in the Chalk House? Remember me drawing my MARTIN on you?" She laughed. "Seems so long ago, doesn't it?"

"You are a Soul Devourer come to deceive me."

"How could I know about the Chalk House if I were a Soul Devourer?"

"You could have read my thoughts, peered into my memories, and regurgitated them back to me."

Lilly puzzled a moment. "I don't think Soul Devourers can do such things, always so hungry and driven, they are. They really aren't much into planning things, are they; they just eat."

"How do you know about such creatures? They are spirits of the arcane and not generally known outside of Tyrol."

Lilly spun her parasol. "I know lots of things, Bel. Remember me giving you the idea to become a Fleet Paymaster? Remember me talking you into bribing people and doing questionable things in Calvert? Remember shopping for your coat with me? How happy I was ... how happy. I remember all those things, because I was there with you. Do you remember the afternoon I gave you the locket with my portrait? How hard I worked on it, it had to be perfect. Remember me offering you five years to explore you heart? Remember that? I sat there and had to watch you fall into the arms of one woman after the next; your 'puppy dogs' I called them. How jealous I was."

"You wanted the five years, Lilly."

"Did I? Did I really, or did someone else make me say that?"

"Who? Who made you?"

Lilly smiled and held her hand out for him to take. "I'll show you."

Mesmerized by her beauty and used to submitting to Lilly's wishes as a matter of habit, he nearly took it. He shook his head, remembered where he was, and stepped back. "I have to save Taara and A-Ram."

"Your friends? No harm shall come to them. I promise."

"How can you make such a promise?"

Lilly came in close; he could feel her heat and smell her perfume—the same scent she always favored wearing. The Soul Devourer wearing her image certainly left nothing to chance.

"Come now, Bel, when have you ever known me not to keep a promise?"

She held her hand out, lit up in the yellowish light of the lantern, impatient for him to take it. He sashed his pistol and shook his hands, producing his various kit of protective Holystones, prisms, and his Astral Plane detector. "Will you submit to a few tests?" he asked showing them to her.

"You wish to inspect me with your arcane instrumentality?"

"I do. Do you mind?"

"Of course not." She gestured to a nearby side room. "May I sit?"

"Of course."

Lilly picked up the lantern and walked into the room. She waited for Stenstrom to offer her a chair. He picked one up, dusted it off, and set it down. She then placed the lantern on the table and properly seated herself, sitting with the same grace and shape Lilly always sat with. She looked up at him, waiting for him to begin the examination.

He hoisted his prism to his right eye and carefully looked her over. If Lilly was a Soul Devourer wearing a disguise, she should appear fuzzy and indistinct, possibly tinged with red. He saw none of that. He switched prisms; again she appeared normal.

He set the prisms down and picked up his silver pyramid, moving it up her arm past the wrist. "What is this one?" she asked.

"Astral Plane detector. If you've been to the Astral Plane, it will react."

"I see. Are you expecting such a thing?"

"Possibly. I've encountered it before. The Astral Plane is …"

"I know all about it," she replied.

His detector remained inert. He put it away and ran his crimson Holystone down her arm, rolling it along her skin. "This one should detect the presence of Soul Devourers."

"Oh my. This is a key test, then. Is it reacting?"

Stenstrom took the crimson Holystone and held it close to his face, examining it for damage. "No. It's not."

"Well then," Lilly said happily, tapping her fingers on the table. "It's settled, per your instrumentality. I'm no Soul Devourer."

He held the crimson Holystone to the lantern lens, dousing it in the strong yellow light, further inspecting it. This apparition had to be a Soul Devourer; she had to be.

He noticed the lantern. It wasn't just an ordinary lantern one might see anywhere, it was exquisite. It was made of beaten copper, molded and inlaid with lapis, gold, silver and garnets. Its lens was some sort of flawless crystal, and the light coming from it wasn't produced by a conventional power source, like a battery pack and a filament or nano tech; nor was it a candle and mere flame; it was some sort of arcane glow.

"What is this?" he asked in wonder.

Lilly stood and put her arms around him. "I borrowed the lantern from home. I'll need to have it back soon—it'll be quickly missed. I think it's called *Paramel*. It illuminates much."

He moved his olive Holystone along the lantern's copper face. It rattled steadily.

"What is that?" Lilly asked.

"This Holystone detects the presence of the arcane. See …" the Holystone created steady noise next to the lantern. He took it and moved the olive stone along Lilly's arm.

It continued to rattle.

"Ah," he said, "look here!"

"It seems to be making quite a bit of noise," Lilly remarked.

"Yes, it does. That means you are of the arcane as well."

He expected her to protest or make some plausible argument against her being of the arcane.

"But of course I'm of the arcane, Bel," she replied, smiling.

"Lilly, *my Lilly*, is not of the arcane. She is a sweet, wholesome girl of Esther. She is rooted in the mundane."

She laughed. "Oh Bel, can it be you have never put things in the proper perspective all this time? It's really rather shocking considering your training. I should think you'd have an eye for such things." She rolled her eyes back in fond remembrance. "I remember seeing you as a little boy as you walked down Tyrol Lane, running away from home. Remember that? I fell in love with you right there and then, I think."

Stenstrom froze. He remembered that event from his childhood. The Fox Park, the Woman in Gray. The terror it still inspired in him, how alone he felt. "That ... was just a dream."

"No, no it wasn't, Bel, and you know it."

"Then that means you're the Lady in Gray, the woman in the hat who tried to kill me."

"I've never worn gray in my life, Bel. And I would never try to kill you. If I would have stayed and witnessed what transpired that night in the park, I would have helped you. There would be no Lady in Gray today, for I'd have killed her."

"Are you a killer, Lilly?"

She seemed stung a bit. "No! No ... but ..." Lilly took a moment and composed herself. She moved onto another topic. "And then ... and then there was that time during your training in the culvert under your manor grounds when you walked away from your mother ... I was there with you, Bel."

"I didn't know you then."

"But I knew you. And then there was that time at the university ..."

He stood there staring at her. "What are you, Lilly?"

She held out her hand. "Come, let me show you. Come see."

He went to take her hand, and then stopped himself. "But, Taara, A-Ram?"

"They're safe, I swear it."

He stood there, wondering if he could actually trust her or not.

"Bel, I swear your friends are safe."

Finally, Stenstrom took Lilly's hand. With her free hand, she picked up the lantern, and they went deep into the Priory following the penetrating yellow beam of the lantern. Very quickly, he no longer felt like he was on the *Seeker*. He felt the temperature change from the cold staleness of the ship to the cool humid of early night. Leaves crunched under his boots; overhead, he saw familiar evening stars in a clear azure sky.

"Is this Kana?" he asked.

"Where else?"

"How can we be on Kana?"

Lilly didn't answer. She skipped along and hummed, swinging the lantern with its eternal beam panning back and forth. They seemed to be moving through a dense needle tree forest. The lantern cut a clear path through the murky trees. Lilly was invigorated and child-like. The Lilly he knew was reserved and composed.

"Ah, home. Home!" she cried. "It feels so good!"

"This landscape doesn't look like Gamboa," Stenstrom said.

"I'm not from Gamboa, Bel. I went there once out of curiosity and didn't like it much. So swampy and closed-in. Too overcast." Lilly twirled around, enjoying the cool, damp air, the lantern rattling in her hand. "This is where I'm from."

She beamed. "Oh … you must have so many questions for me, and, at long last, I'm going to answer. I'm going to introduce myself to you, Bel, properly this time, and nothing will be left to chance."

They crossed a shallow creek flowing with cold water and came into a clearing. Far off to the north was a tumbled barricade of massive gray mountains frosted in snow. Only one place possessed a mountain range like that on Kana: Vithland, the lands of his friend and mentor, Captain Davage.

"Are we in Vithland, Lilly?"

She laughed. "Come on, just a bit farther."

Continuing through the clearing, Lilly became more and more excited. She giggled and bounced on the balls of her feet. "You don't know how long

I've wanted to share this with you!"

"Why didn't you?"

"Because they make me tell you lies. I don't like lying. It doesn't seem right."

"Who? Who makes you tell lies?"

Again, Lilly didn't respond. They entered into a small glade. The ruins of some ancient Vith structure sat in the center of it. It was mostly down to the foundations, sunken into the ground and mirror-like with a coating of cold shallow water. The ruins continued on to the west and were apparently quite extensive.

"This is an old Chapter House where the people used to meet. There's still a little left of them here in this water. This is where I come to find things out. This is where I've watched you from."

Watched him? Lilly's been watching him from afar? The thought gave him a rather uncomfortable feeling. He was square with the notion of looking in on other people, but not being looked in on himself.

"I do not like the idea of you spying on me, Lilly," he said.

"I'm sorry," she replied, rather perfunctorily.

Lilly approached a protruding buttress and placed the lantern on top of it. She then pulled off her shoes and waded into the shallow water, savoring the feeling. "Come on in, Bel. The water feels so good."

"Lilly, I've not the time."

She wouldn't give in. "Come in, Bel. There are things I want to show you."

He sighed and removed his HRN, folding it up and placing it next to the chapter house foundation. Without removing his boots, he waded in. The water was shallow, barely covering his shins. Lilly giggled.

"All right, Lilly. I'm in the water with you. What did you want to show me?"

She splashed to the lantern and pointed the lens at him, engulfing him in the yellow beam. "Does the light hurt your eyes?" she asked.

"Of course not."

"Good, that means you're not evil then," she said with a wink. Lilly opened a small door near the lens. Inside there was a yellowish, facetted crystal mounted on its points so that it could rotate on its axis, and she gave it a fast spin. Globes of multi-colored light came drifting out of the lantern, racing through the water in rapid, circular pools.

"I wanted to show you what I've seen, Bel. I can help you. I want to help you."

A blue circle of light moved through the water. In it, an image formed. It was that of a small Fleet vessel, white with a central saucer and three curved tubes arranged around the saucer. It looked like a Fleet scouting ship. The ship was studded with the barrels of run-out guns.

"I've seen this ship quite a bit lately. I think the lady captaining it is hoping to bring you in so she can gloat."

In the pool of blue light, the stern, unsmiling face of Captain Gwendolyn came into focus: tall, her brown hair pulled back into her hat, given a wide berth by her crew.

Her rapier was drawn and held fast in a strong hand.

"She's a Zenon woman," Lilly added. "I think Zenon women are very snobby, don't you? Not your type at all. She's coming to kill you, Bel. Look at her sword, look at the guns ready to fire. Her ship is small, compared to yours, but it functions, and she has a crew and she's armed. I can ... I can take care of her for you, if you like, Bel. Would you like that?"

"Take care of her? How so? There's no Priory on a scouting ship, so you have no way to get aboard."

Lilly blushed. "I have my ways."

Stenstrom watched the image of the scouting ship as it glided through space, hot on his trail and studded with guns and a captain with a drawn sword. "No, Lilly. I'll deal with it myself when the times comes."

"Are you certain?"

"Of course."

Lilly splashed up to him and stood on the tops of his submerged boots. "Oh, you are so quaint, Bel; that's why I love you so. You have such resources available to you, and you choose to forego them and accomplish things the hard way. What if this Zenon woman aboard the scouting ship shoots her way aboard your ship? You'll lose your chair, will certainly be sent back to the Fleet, and possibly Barred into trial. You could face censure or worse."

"Let me deal with her. I've a good ship, even unpowered, unarmed and unlit, and my crew is the best."

"All two of them?"

"They are all I require."

Lilly laughed. "All right, Bel, have it your way. When I'm rescuing you from prison as I'm certain I shall soon be doing, don't ever forget that I offered to spare you such an inconvenience."

He struggled to make sense of all this. Though Lilly was speaking plainly, she was never more cryptic. How was she doing this? How was she doing any of it?

Lilly adjusted the lantern. "Let me show you a few more things." As the blue pool of light containing the image of Captain Gwendolyn went out, it was replaced by a green one, moving across the water. In the light, Stenstrom saw an odd lumpy shape, green in color, like a great bean sprout. He looked closer, there were two heads sticking out of the sprout. One had blonde hair.

A-Ram?

Yes, it was A-Ram, and Stenstrom thought, at first, that A-Ram had been devoured by a gigantic plant with only his head sticking out. On second glance, he saw that A-Ram was actually sitting on the ground huddled up next to a second person whom Stenstrom didn't know. It was a female with pinned-up black hair. She was wearing a vast green cloak and had it draped around A-Ram, sharing it with him. It looked like a comfortable place to be.

"Do you know who that woman is? I recognize Lord A-Ram."

"No, I don't."

"I am quite fond of Lord A-Ram."

Stenstrom was confused. "You are? Have you met him before?"

"In a fashion, enough to know his heart. He set me free."

He had no idea what to make of that. The green circle of light faded and was replaced by a red one. "Look at this one, Bel. I've also been seeing this ..."

In the red light, he saw a mass of chaotic movement, like looking into a beehive. The bits of movement seemed to be a multitude of tiny machinery, squared-off, finely crafted and etched, moving in an orderly confusion. There were four distinct colors to the tiny machines: yellow, blue, green and red.

Stenstrom and Lilly watched as the tiny machines separated themselves into their respective colors and then began forming roughly man-shaped masses.

"Do you know what these are?" Lilly asked.

"No. Looks like robotistry or nano tech. That's not my area."

Lilly gazed at the tiny machines buzzing with movement. "Whatever they are, they mean you no good, Bel, of that I'm certain. Look …"

In the red light, a man was on his knees, surrounded, hacked to pieces, moments away from death.

"I'm worried for you, Bel."

"I can handle myself."

"Did you not see that? I think that man on his knees was you."

Lilly gazed at the circle of light. "I've been searching for these men or machines or whatever they are. So far they've eluded me, but when I find them, I am going to finish them for no one will put my Bel on his knees. No one." There was a hard edge to Lilly's voice.

The image faded. The last thing Stenstrom saw was a great yellow circle swirling in the water.

"I see this circle a lot when I look in on you. Circles and circles."

Stenstrom observed the circle. He could see faces locked within its boundaries. He saw himself and Taara and A-Ram. Odd, he saw the squared-off yet pretty face of his pursuer, Lt. Gwendolyn. He also saw four tall figures swaying in the background. Surrounding the circle was a fifth figure clad in gray rapidly approaching.

Clad in gray? The woman from his Fox Park nightmare. The Astral Traveler? He looked away. When he looked back the images in the circle were gone.

Lilly rose up and kissed him, and for a moment he forgot about his situation and his crew and that this creature, with apparently vast arcane capabilities, couldn't possibly be Lilly.

The kiss felt like Lilly. It had her warmth and feeling.

What could she be? What was she? He should be impassive and calculating as his mother taught him when faced with the arcane, collecting data, demanding answers, sorting out truth from conjecture. But, come to think of it, Mother had hand-picked Lilly herself. She picked her not merely for her grace and beauty, but for her normalcy, her seemingly entrenched hold on the mundane and the well-trodden. Mother hadn't wanted a sorceress for her son, another Tyrol graduate of the black schools, a brewer of poisons and caster of spells. She wanted a quiet, unremarkable woman, someone stately and of society to sit in the parlor and love her son as a proper lady should, balancing his forays into the dark woods of sorcery with the more well-lit paths of the mundane world.

And, she'd picked Lilly. Nothing odd about Lilly, nothing supernatural about Lilly.

But look: here's Lilly appearing from nowhere, Lilly possessing some sort of vast power with access to arcane devices like the Paramel, Lilly triggering his arcane detectors, Lilly fooling his mother into thinking she was from unremarkable Gamboa, when she was, in fact, from the wilds of Vithland in an area simply crawling with the arcane.

Lilly was some sort of monster.

But, all that mattered little at the moment. Her embrace was comforting, her kiss sweet and familiar, bringing back all those memories of the woman he loved.

She leaned against him. He could feel the ovular shape of the locket in his breast pocket pressing against his heart.

He put his arms around her, savoring her feel.

"I take back my false words, Bel," she said between kisses, "I don't want five years, I never did. I want you now, with me forever. Make me yours."

"I've always been yours, Lilly. As before, I extend you my hand."

"And I accept. I accept, I accept!" She leaned back and shouted into the cool air: "I ACCEPT!" She screamed it, as if to make her voice heard to those listening from afar. "And now, it's time that I told you exactly what I am, so that you'll understand. I ..."

A horn sounded in the distance, filling the clearing and chapter house ruins with a melancholy note. Lilly's demeanor instantly changed. She cut herself off in mid-sentence, cringed and scowled. She stomped through the shallow water and kicked "No!" she screamed. "It's not fair! Not fair! I'm not ready!"

"What?" Stenstrom asked.

"They're calling me! I thought I'd have more time!"

"Who are?"

"Them!" Lilly pointed.

Through the trees, Stenstrom thought he could see a domed structure made of gray stone. A door slid open. Sitting inside were four indistinct figures.

The horn sounded again, and the wooded setting became cloudy. Stenstrom felt himself being pulled back into the dank confines of the *Seeker,* leaving Vithland and Lilly behind.

"They did it, Bel!" Lilly shouted as he was pulled away. "They did it all ..."

The next moment, Stenstrom was back aboard the *Seeker*, the yellow light of the lantern fading.

"Remember, Bel ... " came the ghost of Lilly's voice. *"You just extended me your hand, and I'm not giving it back."*

He was standing in the darkened rooms of the Priory. What had he just seen? Was that apparition really Lilly? He hadn't felt threatened. It seemed like Lilly, smelled like Lilly ... felt like her.

The olive Holystone had determined Lilly was of an arcane nature. Lilly had always seemed so grounded to him, so steady and sure, painting her pictures in Gamboa. She was a rock of sanity and sure footing in an occasional turbid shoreline of mysticism and fog-shrouded places his mother took him to.

And now it was proved she is of the arcane.

"I'm not from Gamboa, Bel."

She might not even be human.

He pressed on into the depths of the Priory, finding nothing but overturned chairs and unmade beds, the Sisters long gone and all the magic sucked out of the place.

"A-Ram!" he cried. "Taara!"

No answer.

His mind spun. Lilly not from Gamboa. Lilly something other than just a beautiful woman. He reached a locked door. He took a moment to replace the bad striker in his NTH, discarding the cracked one.

Lilly couldn't have been a Soul Devourer in disguise, or she would have attacked. Soul Devourers were driven by their lust and hunger for souls; even the one that was supposed to lead him to Taara and A-Ram couldn't resist and attacked him en route.

Lilly didn't attack him. Gods, what did Lady Alitrix say?

"I don't know what she is, but she's not a woman."

And Kaly that time at the dock:

"I saw you walking down the street with a mannequin."

He pulled on the door harder and it wouldn't budge.

Locked tight.

What did Kaly see? What was Alitrix sensing?

What was Lilly? She had been on the verge of telling him but had been summoned by her masters. Whatever she was, he had just offered her his hand. That, given the circumstances, probably wasn't wise. He had just committed himself to some sort of monster.

He sashed his NTHs and had his lock picks ready with a wave of the hand. He stuck his probe in and tested the lock. Though the door appeared old and simple, its lock was complex, very sophisticated and trapped—he could feel a coiled needle hidden in the lock's workings, ready to spring.

"They did it. They did it all!" Lilly said.

Who was *"they?"* Stenstrom shuddered to find out.

He selected his picks and skillfully worked the lock, disarming the needle in the process. Soon, the lock was picked clean. He put his picks back into his HRN and drew his NTHs.

He pulled the door open, and something behind it fell out to the floor with a limp thud. A thin, sinewy arm lay there. It was a slender arm, like a lady's, smooth and delicate, only the hand at the end of the arm gave it away that it was something more sinister: the fingers curled, gnarled, and studded with claws. Stenstrom swung the door open wide and aimed down, ready to fire.

A Soul Devourer lay there, its gigantic mouth and elongated tongue lolled on the floor. It appeared to be dead. It smoked slightly. He knelt down into the grit and inspected the body. Its neck appeared to be broken, and only recently so. It was still warm. Taking no chances, he put two NTH shots into its chest. It collapsed into ash.

Beyond the door was a long corridor. Continuing on, he found another Soul Devourer smashed up on the floor, and then another, both dead.

More bodies waited for him further down. Look at them: piled up in heaps, hanging from the ceiling, curled up on the ground, a vast number of them, more than he cared to count; all dead. Some were arranged in fanciful, post-mortem positions. Some were lying there holding hands, and some were propped up against each other chest to chest, fingers inter-laced like they were dancing. Several were seated at a small table as if they were having a tea party. All dead, dead bodies pushed into seated positions around the table in the illusion of merriment, their tongues all tied together in the center, knotted.

What had happened here? Could Lilly have done all this, killed all these supernatural creatures by herself.

How?

The corridor ended in a transparent dome that jutted out the underbelly of the ship, lit up in stars and some sort of bright yellowish cloud that seethed with energy. He wondered what it was for a moment—oh, it's Druries Belt. He remembered.

The Sisters' dome was some sort of meeting place lined with consoles that rolled and sputtered with hazy life. Wooden benches lined the dome, like a courtroom. This must be the heart of the Priory, a place only the Sisters had previously seen.

More Soul Devourers, everywhere. Dead, mangled, pushed against the dome, slumped over the railing, one dangling by its tongue from a light fixture.

In the center of the dome was a wooden dais. Two figures were slumped atop it.

Taara and A-Ram!

He made his way to the top of the dais. Taara and A-Ram appeared to both be submerged in a deep sleep. They were warm, and their pulses were good. Taara was sitting there in her white untucked shirt and woolen socks. A-Ram's MOLLY gleamed around her neck. As before, she snored slightly.

A pink slip of paper was stuffed into A-Ram's coat pocket. It read:

I told you they would be fine
—Lilly

"Taara!" he said, trying to wake her up. "Taara!" He tapped her twice on the cheek. She didn't awake. It was the same with A-Ram, deep in sleep.

He hoisted the two of them over his shoulder and carried them out. They were both so light, like carrying children.

He went down the long corridor, passing all the carnage along the way. He was glad they weren't awake to see any of it.

All the bodies. The charnel house of Soul Devourers, all killed and posed by Lilly.

Recent events sorted themselves out in his mind.

Lilly, no longer a stately girl from Gamboa.

Lilly, an arcane being of great strength.

"I accept."

Lilly, a killer.

"I accept..."

Lilly, his betrothed.

"I ACCEPT!!"

He made his way out of the Priory and back down the long corridor to the bridge, the ship serenading them with haunted chants the entire way. Up the lift shaft and back into the bridge they went, like nothing ever happened, save for the troubling thoughts rolling through Stenstrom's head.

Soul Devourers ...

Lilly in the dark ...

"I ACCEPT!"

4

—DRURIES BELT—

Stenstrom laid them out on the floor of the bridge. "Taara! Taara, wake up!"

She stirred. "Hey, Bel ... how about a few more minutes? I was having a nice dream. Ok?"

"Taara, you've been asleep for twenty hours; we all have. We're missing our burn!"

That news opened her eyes. She sat up. "What? Twenty hours? Bel, we can't miss that burn, or we'll be headed out into the Wildlands." She wobbled to her feet and grabbed her boots.

They turned to A-Ram and shook him awake. Eventually he stirred and awoke, holding his head. "Gods, I feel like I've slept for days," he said.

"You have."

"I seem to recall dreaming of ... monsters."

Quite appropriate, Stenstrom thought.

A-Ram made his way to the helm and was shocked. "For the love of Creation, we've slept through our burn!"

Taara pulled on her boots and ran into his office. She checked her sextant, pointing it toward the window. The great yellowish rope of Druries Belt stretched off into the distance like a golden lasso.

She cursed as she worked.

"Taara, what's our bearing?" A-Ram asked.

She stared out the window, gazing through the sextant.

"Taara!"

"Give me a minute, will you! Gods, we are well off course!"

Stenstrom watched her work. "What's that going to do to us, Taara? Can we get back on course?"

"We're way out of the shipping lanes, that's for sure." She ran back into the bridge and flopped into the Missive's chair. She brought up a screen and punched in a series of numbers.

Feeling drained, Stenstrom plunged into his chair and closed his eyes.

His leaden thoughts spun.

Captain Gwendolyn: coming in her scout ship to board and possible kill him.

Lilly: killed over a hundred Soul Devourers. He, with just his two pistols, would probably have been overwhelmed by such a number.

"A-Ram, hard to port three turns, Z minus 15 degrees," Taara said.

He heard the helm groan as A-Ram turned the pegs.

"They did it!" Lilly said.

Who are *"they?"*

Taara again, her little voice confident and full of authority. "I'm burning the *Westminster* for five minutes, in three, two, one ..."

The ship shuddered.

"I accept," Lilly said again in his mind. *"I accept."*

✳ ✳ ✳ ✳ ✳

"Bel, Bel, wake up."

He opened his eyes. Taara and A-Ram stood over him. "Did I sleep?"

"Sure did. Just a few minutes."

He stood up, seeing the now familiar environs of the bridge laid out with the clunky machinery of their threadbare existence on the ship: the stolen generators and dangling wires, the hiss of the Macon, and the bundle of insta-meals.

"Are we back on course?"

"Yep!" Taara said. "All fixed."

"A-Ram, how's the helm?"

"Locked and marked. We shouldn't need another burn until we get to Onaris, about four days hence."

Stenstrom thought about it. Taara and A-Ram could have been killed. Look at all of this: the dead ship, the jury-rigged parts, the vast gulf between here and their destination, a ship full of demons and a possible confrontation looming with Captain Gwendolyn. Had he the right to endanger Taara and A-Ram any further?

"I'm thinking ..."

"Thinking what, Bel?" Taara asked.

"I think we should turn around and head back to Kana, and I should give myself up. I can't endanger you two any further. Creation knows if this scuttled tub is up to making the journey to Bazz. It'll probably break down right in the middle of nowhere. And then there's Captain Gwendolyn and her scouting ship. You two don't need that sort of trouble."

"What's brought this on, Bel?" A-Ram asked. "Did something happen while we were asleep?"

Stenstrom considered his answer. "You, and Taara were abducted and taken into the rear section of the ship, Deck 7, deep in the Sister's Priory."

"Who abducted us?"

"Demons, and, no, they weren't after Taara's soul, they were after mine. They abducted you to get to me."

A-Ram turned a slight shade of white. "And, what happened? You rescued us?"

Stenstrom shook his head. "No. No I didn't."

"Then who did?"

"The apparition of the woman I love; Lillian of Gamboa."

Taara was stumped. "You mean the blonde-headed lady in your locket?"

"The very one."

"What was she doing here?"

Stenstrom sighed. "Apparently, she's a monster too. She was waiting for me down there in the dark, dressed in pink. Pink is such a lovely color on her. And she killed every one of the demons holding you two. She stacked their bodies up and arranged them in fanciful poses—always the artist, Lilly. And then she demanded I offer her my hand, and I gave it to her. I really couldn't help myself."

Taara and A-Ram stood there listening.

"And so, I want to come about, head back to Kana as best we can and pray the ship holds together. There's some deviltry here. I don't think you two will get into trouble. They just want me."

He closed his eyes and thought about all that awaited him. When he opened them, Taara was leaning over him.

"Well heck Bel, if you're worried about your lady, I'll date you."

He chuckled, despite himself. "I'll keep that in mind, Taara. Come on, let's get this ship turned around."

"Now look, Bel," Taara said. "If you think you're doing us some sort of favor by returning to Kana, you're wrong. I don't want to go back, and I don't need you to fret over me like I'm some stupid kid. I want to be here. I want to go to Bazz, and when we get there we can say we did it all on our own, just the three of us. Look what we accomplished. Sending me back to Kana so I can guard the statue again and be despised by my entire company because I'm a screw-up isn't doing me any particular favors." She turned to A-Ram. "What about you?"

A-Ram held onto the pegs of the helm. "Well, I certainly don't want to see any monsters, that's for certain, and I also don't want to get into a shoot-out with a Fleet vessel. Bel, you don't strike me as an unreasonable fellow, I'm certain things won't come to that. Piloting a Fleet ship at sea is what I've always dreamed of doing, and, after this experience, after laying my hands on the wheel, I don't think I could go back to the Admiral's office again. I ..." He gave a sheepish laugh. "This has been exhilarating, quite frankly, and everything I'd hoped it might be. I have faith in you and in Taara that we'll all be just fine."

Taara beamed. "This is a great ship, Bel, don't let her current condition fool you. The Admiralty has taken away almost everything, but not her heart. And she, through us, is going to prove to them back there at the Fleet that she is not done, even if she has to go to Bazz crawling, on her knees. If she breaks along the way, she breaks. So what? We'll fix her. We've already done the hard part, the rest is easy. So, enough talk of quitting, Bel. We've got a job to do, so let's get to it. We've got some crazy brandy to deliver. What do you say?"

"Lilly's apparition also shared with me a few visions of the future, and some of the items I saw appeared rather disturbing."

"Oh, no, no," Taara said. "The future sucks, that's what we say on Bazz. All those damn prophet-types, don't listen to any of them. They'll scare you to death if you let them. The future always looks a lot scarier than it actually is. You'll give yourself an ulcer, trust me."

Stenstrom peered into his office and saw the carpet of stars bisected by the glowing line of Druries Belt with Ole' Scrub, their destination, hanging in the distance. Taara's homemade sextant lay on his desk.

"All right," he said with new vigor. "If you two are game, let's do this. Taara, man your post."

She cheered and plopped back down into the Missive's chair. "Ready Bel!"

"A-Ram, how's the helm?" he asked.

"A little heavy, but otherwise wonderful."

"Well then. We've a slow few days ahead of us. Things will probably be quite dull until they're not, then we'll deal with 'whatever' accordingly."

They settled into their positions and listened to the Macon clank.

On to Bazz.

What more could possibly happen?

Camalopardis, the Sisters' Constellation

BOOK II
AGAINST THE DRURIES

PART 1
THE SISTERS' FIST

1

—THE DEEP SEA—

Three souls huddled in the dark of the great, airless ship flying backwards through the deep sea to Bazz.

A fabled ship with a proud history, the *Seeker* had seen better days. She was designed decades prior to be fast and strong, to be agile, to inflict damage upon the enemy, and to comfortably house several hundred souls deep into the empty cradle of space, the "Deep Sea" as the Fleet sailors called it. The MFV *Seeker* had done that and more. A veteran of such classic battles as Sorrander-quo, Mirendra I and II, Two-pitch Nebula, Hardee and Xandarr, the *Seeker* had survived them all, had sunk many enemy ships, and was feared among them.

But, as in all things, time passes, the new becomes old and the state-of-the-art becomes obsolete. The glory days of the past become footnotes on withered pages in a forgotten history book and the *Seeker*, old and worn, in need of costly repairs and refits, ought to be barge-towed to the Kana-Jana bone yard, smelted, and remade into something fresh and useful. Many great ships had taken that sorry trip.

But, the right people favored the *Seeker*. The Sisterhood of Light, beloved of the Fleet Admiralty and of the League in general, was fond of the old Warbird. "How is the *Seeker*?" they often asked during their visits, and those casual asides, frequently posed, helped save her. The Admiralty could not simply smelt the Sisters' favorite ship, that would not do. So, they decided to raise the *Seeker's* chair for debate one last time, and appoint a captain with vast sums of money to donate for her repairs and demonstrate to the Sisters, once and for all, that the *Seeker* was simply too old and unsafe to continue flying. Why, they could melt her down, sell the refined metals to the Sisters, and they could build a new convent from it if they wished. That would be a bold irony.

So, they put the *Seeker's* command chair on the blocks one last time, and they appointed a captain, an odd man from Tyrol wearing a hated HRN coat and, of all things, a mask: Lord Stenstrom the Younger of Belmont-South Tyrol, a self-styled eccentric and a Paymaster to boot. He had been the only person to make a serious offer for the chair, and he had privilege, he had Programmability, and best of all, he had money. Lots of it.

Giving the chair to a Paymaster, a civilian clerk, was unheard of, and, not only that, he was a clown as well in an HRN coat and mask. Such an appointment would make the Admiralty a laughing stock—if such a man could take a Fleet Warbird's chair, why not anybody? Soon every peg-legged Diddy from Calvert would be storming the Admirals' Hall demanding a chair. What would become of the Fleet?

So, they kept the appointment quiet, out of the Posts and usual gossip mills and intended Paymaster Stenstrom to not sit on the *Seeker's* chair for long. Admiral Derlith of the 3rd Fleet devised a wonderfully devious plan to ensure just that.

They went in and gutted the *Seeker*, had her huge SM coils ripped out, her thermoplant dismantled, her Battleshot batteries and canisters hauled away, and her bridge partially disassembled. They took everything: carpeting, tables, chairs, beds, and they even took food from the pantries, stationary from the drawers, and toilets from the heads, leaving bare, knurled metal and gaping holes where toilets once resided. As for the crew, they were allowed to conscript onto other vessels and were encouraged to do so.

As per tradition, a newly appointed captain was obliged to perform a mission at the pleasure of the Admiralty. Normally, this mandatory mission was something simple and easily accomplished, however, if Lord Belmont was to fail in this mission, then his chair would be lost and his money forfeited.

Lord Stenstrom's mission for Admiral Derlith: Deliver brandy to a ball being thrown at the Fleet HQ annex Teflegar-Martin II on Bazz in twelve days hence by Kanan counting. It was more of an errand than a mission. Bazz was barely a full day's hard sail away, unworthy of a once great Warbird.

But, with the *Seeker* disemboweled in a steadily decaying polar orbit, with no crew to man her, and with his orders specifying that the *Seeker* herself be the one to deliver the brandy to Bazz, Admiral Derlith and the rest of the Admiralty couldn't conceive of any way that Paymaster Stenstrom could possibly succeed.

In one devious stroke, Admiral Derlith would take Lord Stenstrom's money, humiliate him in the process, and prove to the Sisters that the *Seeker* was done as a Main Fleet Warbird—why, it couldn't even make an easy trip to Bazz; the fact that she was scuttled and without propulsion was irrelevant.

In sporting terms, the plan was the Cinco Pass. It couldn't fail.

✳ ✳ ✳ ✳ ✳

One small thing Admiral Derlith didn't plan for or anticipate: great ships are said to have a soul and a will of their own. Like a champion race horse that refuses to lose though its competition might be stronger and faster, the *Seeker* had never before failed a task it had been assigned, not in decades and after hundreds of engagements. Its current task: deliver brandy to Bazz, a demeaning, worthless task, but, regardless, that's what was set before it, and if it had to make the trip to Bazz on its knees, gasping, crawling every inch of the way with stolen parts and a misfit crew, then so be it.

Great ships found a way.

And events were set into motion. Lord Stenstrom needed help, and somehow, someway, he managed to secure the assistance of two unlikely people, one a worthless Marine private known for her sloth and lack of discipline. The other was shocking: Lt. Josephus, Lord of the tiny House of A-Ram, Admiral Derlith's own personal adjutant. A modest, rather milquetoast young man thought to be of limited skill outside of the office, and rather grounded in his aspirations; a man who feared his own shadow. The Admiral always felt he was doing Lt. Josephus a grand favor keeping him safe and secure in his office at the 3rd Fleet.

But look! Josephus turned out to be a rather accomplished pilot, and flew the three of them aboard the *Seeker* in a Suborbital of all things—a very bold and dangerous thing to attempt.

Tiny Josephus, Lord of A-Ram had done that?

Furthermore, Paymaster Stenstrom and his crew of two mismatched and unskilled personages somehow managed to correct the *Seeker's* decaying orbit and, by means of a stolen scouting ship, the *Westminster*, blasted out of orbit using her engines and were on their way to Bazz at slow speed with the brandy.

Great ships have a soul and find a way.

Annoyed by this turn of events and careful to keep things under control, Admiral Derlith saw to it the "*Seeker* Situation" was kept under tight wraps. Paymaster Stenstrom, though a buffoon and eccentric, had powerful friends in the Fleet Captaincy and beyond—namely his venerable and well-liked father, Stenstrom the Older of the Warbird *Caroline*, and his mentor and sponsor, the famed Captain Davage of the *New Faith*. Fleet captains loved to stick it to the Admiralty whenever possible, and this situation was tailor-made for such an intervention. They just might swoop in from all over, tend to the Paymaster's scuttled ship in flight and give him a grand escort to Bazz, all the while laughing in the Admiralty's face. Such a spectacle would be unacceptable and never lived down. Paymaster Stenstrom also had an impressively high Programmability with the Sisterhood of Light, and, should they become involved and dissent in his favor, this exercise would end ... immediately. But, until that time, the game was afoot.

Admiral Derlith used his influence and kept things nice and quiet. He ordered standard communications in the shipping lanes between Kana and Onaris/Bazz blacked out for "maintenance purposes". He then summoned his niece, Lt. Gwendolyn, Lady of Prentiss, to intercept the *Seeker* in space with her scouting ship, the *Demophalon John*, board her, clap Paymaster Stenstrom and Private Taara in irons, and return Lt. Josephus to the Fleet. He gave her carte blanche in her assignment to do whatever she needed to get the job done. Period.

Ever dutiful, Lt. Gwendolyn agreed and, even now, was nearing the *Seeker's* position, her small guns run out and ready to fire on the unarmed, unpowered Warbird should they be needed. And, if she had to kill Paymaster Stenstrom in the process, then so be it.

So be it.

2

—The Lantern—

"Goddammit! This piece of goddamn shit!" came an echoing voice.

A-Ram covered his ears and Stenstrom shook his head. Such language, truly shameful.

✳ ✳ ✳ ✳ ✳

All things considered, they weren't doing too bad on the *Seeker*. They'd been through quite a bit since boarding the tumbling, silent hulk of the ship several days earlier, crashing through a large window in their gasping Suborbital, praying to Creation that the ship's emergency shutters would close and seal the hole they'd made.

Fortunately for them, it did.

They'd gotten used to the stale air and slightly stuffy interior of the ship due to the excellent insulation of the *Seeker's* armor. They were amazed how quickly they could learn to do without such essentials as running water, hot meals, clean clothes and a warm bed. The lack of a comfortable place to sleep was rather trying. Taara did fairly well curled up at the padded Missive's station's chair, while Stenstrom, and A-Ram had to make do with uncomfortable chairs and, sometimes, the unyielding floor.

There was one thing, however, they couldn't live without.

They were in Stenstrom's office just off the main bridge, the place glittering with fresh starlight and steady lighting. The bridge and the office were their home base using all the improvised bits they'd collected from the dry-dock, the only thing they lacked was running water and a working toilet. As answering the call of nature was a long inconvenient process walking through the unlit, noisy bowels of the ship, which none of them really wanted to do, getting the bathroom in Stenstrom's office working was a top priority, and they'd been hard at it all afternoon since the last *Westminster* engine burn.

The pristine commode that once resided in the captain's bathroom had been removed by the Admiralty leaving a bare, surprisingly large hole and unappealing smells.

The three of them, under Taara's direction, had managed to get the water lines to the bathroom working by sacrificing a bit of generator power and connecting up a condenser on Deck Six. Of course Taara had no knowledge of engineering or shipboard plumbing. She was wearing A-Ram's MOLLY, a mystical charm that allowed one to know things one shouldn't know and to do things one shouldn't be able to do. A-Ram was too bashful to use it himself, as the Sisterhood of Light required registration before using it, so Taara, unafraid, was game to try, and the knowledge it gave her was invaluable. The price for using it unabashed and unregistered, A-Ram said, would be a demon hungry for her soul.

It had been a great deal of tight, grungy work, crawling through the maintenance shafts, hooking up lines and hoses and turning valves. The plumbing system on a starship was a complicated tangle of positive and negative piping, relief hoses, valves, nitrogen tanks to aid in maintaining pressure, and so on. Taara sometimes got a little cross and impatient as Stenstrom and A-Ram fumbled around and started yelling. People from

Bazz had a reputation across the League for coarse language and raised voices, and Taara was proving the notion to be true. She yelled at A-Ram when he mis-connected a hose, calling him some choice Bazz names and hurt his feelings.

"Hey, hey," she said. "I didn't mean anything, that's how we talk on Bazz. We do a lot of yelling. I didn't mean anything by it. You know I love you guys. If I make you mad, just yell back, that's all." She hugged him and the matter was forgotten.

Later, they crowded into the bathroom, the three of them staring at the fine pewter faucet like it was some sort of pagan altar ready to spew fire.

"Well, come on, let's do this," Taara said and Stenstrom opened the faucet, they listened to the network of pressurized pipes groan and then marveled as clean water gurgled into the basin. It was cause for a celebration, lots of hugging and splashing of water.

Now, for the star of the show: the commode. The Admiralty had done a smashing job of removing every toilet, head and potty trench they could find from bow to stern. Taara, with her MOLLY'ed up smarts, had worked up plans for connecting a sink to the head and supplying it with a trickle of water to flush it out, but then Stenstrom had a mind wave.

He remembered Lt. Kilos, the former First Officer of the ship, once talking about a secret head near the main mess, installed for the captain's private use during important functions when excusing one's self for protracted periods might not be possible. It didn't appear on the blueprints for the ship and was a custom addition built specifically for Captain Davage, as Lord Milos of Probert, the ship's designer, was a close personal friend of his. Ki used to say she'd hide out in the "Secret Potty" from time to time when she wanted to be alone, sneaking in when nobody was looking and she'd have a long, relaxing constitutional free of people bugging her.

Such a prize, if it was still there, was worth a plunge into the dark, and they made the long, disturbing trek through to the unlit back section of the ship to the mess, the place of their initial entry days ago. The trip was like walking through a haunted wood at midnight, the inky black of the ship was squalid with ghosts and noises.

Stenstrom remembered the last time he'd plunged into the darkened reaches of the ship.

Taara and A-Ram missing. The corridors over-run with Soul Devourers.

Their horrid touch … Their tittering ... Starving for his soul which his Mother had promised them.

And then Lilly appeared from the dark. Lilly, his Lilly, a talented but mundane girl from Gamboa his Mother had selected for him years earlier. His Mother had wanted a distinctly non-arcane girl to balance his forays into the mystical realms, and Lilly fit the bill perfectly. She seemed as "normal" as a girl could get.

But then there was Lilly, emerging from the dark in the bowels of the ship carrying an arcane lantern, smiling as if there was nothing odd or unusual about appearing from nowhere when she should be thousands of stellar miles away back on Kana.

"Bel, don't I always arrive when you need me most?" she had said.

Once they arrived in the mess, they found the remains of their destroyed Suborbital mangled in the corner, along with the all-important case of brandy bottled at the home of Admiral Derlith himself.

The brandy was his "cargo", he had to deliver it to a ball at Teflegar-Martin II on Bazz in twelve days, otherwise, his appointment to the chair of the *Seeker* would be lost. Given the barely habitable condition of the ship, the brandy had been largely forgotten in the last few days. They had left it where it sat.

A disturbing display awaited them as they arrived. There were fresh footprints dotting the mess area, clearly visible as clean spots in the thin layer of grime covering the floor. They scampered along creating a crazy trail, going this way and that along the floor, in and out of the remains of the Suborbital and even up the walls.

"What are these?" A-Ram asked with trepidation.

Stenstrom inspected the footprints: bare feet with hints of claws. "Soul Devourers," he announced. They had been all over the ship, conniving in the dark, starving for his soul.

... YOUR SOUL!! they had screamed.

"Do you think there are more of them hiding about?" A-Ram asked, somewhat panicked.

"I doubt it. Not much for hiding and stratagem, Soul Devourers. If they were here, they would attack. We would know it by now."

"What happened to them?" Taara asked.

Lilly, she had killed every one of them and pushed their bodies into fanciful positions. Always the artist, Lilly. Hundreds of their corpses turning to ash ...

"Don't know," Stenstrom lied.

Taara quickly discovered the secret head off in a corner, and there it was through the hidden door: a pristine commode the Admiralty had missed, a wondrous prize worth its weight in gold. Wringing her little hands, Taara fell on the commode and had it disconnected in minutes, scooting it out along the floor leaving a trail in dust. Heavy, the three of them hoisted it up and lugged it back to the bridge, so intent they were with their prize they barely noticed the voices from the dark cajoling them along the way.

"What happened to Lilly? Where did she go?" A-Ram asked.

Where had she gone?

Standing on what appeared to be Kana, Lilly was about to reveal all to him when a horn sounded and Lilly shrieked in frustration, tearing at her golden hair. And then Stenstrom had been returned to the airless dark of the *Seeker.*

"No, no! It's not fair!" Lilly had cried. *"I thought I'd have more time! Remember, you just extended me your hand, and I'm not giving it back!"*

"She was called home," Stenstrom said.

"Hey Lilly!" Taara cried out. "We could use a hand, right! This thing's awkward and heavy!"

A-Ram was alarmed. "Don't call out for her, Taara. She's a demon."

Stenstrom took momentary exception to A-Ram calling Lilly a demon, but then, after all that had happened and been done, what else could she be?

"Why, Bel, of course I'm of the arcane ..." she had said.

Lilly ... a demon.

They hauled the commode up the low gravity of the lift shaft and into Stenstrom's office. Taara double-checked all the connections before they seated the toilet in place. She quickly got flustered.

"What's wrong?" Stenstrom asked.

"Damn thing. I can't get pressure. I don't get it. This should be ready to go."

A-Ram leaned over and placed his hand near the mouth of the hole. "I don't feel anything."

"Well, that's just it, there should be negative pressure. You should be feeling a slight breeze sucking everything down the hole to the pipe junction below. All right you two, out of the way!"

Taara set back to it and soon was swearing up and down, making both Stenstrom and A-Ram blush.

"Why don't we take a break?" Stenstrom suggested.

"No way, Bel—no damn way! This thing isn't kicking my butt! I want this commode working, and then I'm going to celebrate by having a nice, long poop!"

Minutes later, Taara stared at the hole in disgust and pushed her black hair and dangling sideburns from her face. "It's like there's something stuck in there. There's got to be a blockage or something gumming everything up." She removed her Marine coat and boots.

"What are you doing?" Stenstrom asked.

"I'm going in. I'm going to fix it."

A-Ram gazed down the tight hole. "Down there?"

"Yep. See what things I do for you guys, huh?"

She smiled up at Stenstrom and he gave her trademark Mollock sideburns, a mark of being unmarried on Bazz, a yank for luck—it was a ritual they had begun. Without a hint of fear, Taara shimmied into the hole and squirmed down, reaching a T-bend about two feet below. She moved her legs into one end of the T-bend and carefully stretched out on her stomach into the other side. Stenstrom watched, fearing she might get stuck.

She squirmed around for a minute or two, and then she reacted violently, her body tensing up. They heard the muffled sound of a scream.

Stenstrom reached down and grabbed her by her shirt. "Taara!" he yelled. He pulled back, revealing her head and shoulders and she clambered out, shaken. She hung onto him.

"Taara, what happened? What did you see?"

She sat there a moment and collected herself. Stenstrom drew his NTH pistols and gazed down into the hole, seeing nothing but the pipe leading down and the T-bend.

"Let me get you some water," A-Ram said running out of the office.

"Taara, what did you see?" Stenstrom asked again.

Taara composed herself. "I saw somebody down there, stuffed into the pipe."

"Down there? You mean a body?"

"It was alive, a lady, I think, with blonde hair and blue eyes—I remember the eyes." She regained her composure and laughed. "Wow—that ... that was a rush!"

Blonde hair, blue eyes, sounded like Lilly.

"She looked really, really pissed, like she wanted to get at me or something. She reached out and that's when I freaked."

A-Ram returned with a bottle of water and gave it to Taara and she accepted it with trembling hands. As Taara drank, Stenstrom leaned down and listened for sounds coming from the hole.

He heard a tiny noise issuing from the pipes: *"... teehee ..."*

"Lilly?" he asked.

No answer.

"Lilly!"

No reply.

Her final words to him before she disappeared rang through his mind. *"I ACCEPT!!"*

"A-Ram, I'm going to give you one of my NTHs. I want you to go down there and have a look."

A-Ram swallowed hard. "Me? You want me to go down there?"

"I do. I won't fit, and you'll have my NTH's. The NTH's can slay anything."

A-Ram didn't want to go. "Well, perhaps Taara can ..."

"Taara's a girl, she can't use the NTH's. They only work for men." He tried to lighten the mood with a bit of levity. "You are a girl, right, Taara?"

Lilly? What was Lilly? Not a woman.

"V-very funny," she replied. "You wanna' find out first-hand?"

With great uncertainty, A-Ram took off his coat and gingerly lowered himself into the hole, taking Stenstrom's pistol in his little hands. Stenstrom also gave him a yellow Holystone to see. He shook it and was bathed in warm yellow light.

"Cock the hammer, A-Ram," Stenstrom said. "And, don't worry about damaging anything—the NTH's don't affect inanimate objects. Oh, make sure you don't shoot upwards in our direction, the NTH-shot will go through the floorboards."

A-Ram gulped and worked his way into the T-bend.

"See anything?" Taara called down.

He wiggled around a bit and then came back out, his head emerging from the hole. "There's nobody down here, not that I can see," he said with relief. He waved the Holystone around.

"You don't see anybody?" Taara called down.

"I don't, and thank Creation for that. I do think I see something wedged in the pipe a fair distance away."

"Can you get it out?" Taara asked.

"Must I?"

"Yeah, if you wanna' poop anytime soon."

"I'll try."

He plunged back into the pipe and worked his way in. A minute or two later he re-emerged, backing out inch-by-inch and holding the end of a glittering golden chain. Stenstrom and Taara helped him out and pulled on the chain. Whatever was on the end of it moved easily.

"Look at this thing," Taara remarked. "Is this real gold? It is! What's it doing stuffed up in the plumbing? And look how clean it is, it ought to be crusted with filth."

They continued pulling on the gold chain until something large and prickly like a pinecone emerged from the T-bend.

"What is that?" A-Ram asked, moving the Holystone around.

They hauled it up. Dangling at the end of the surprisingly lengthy chain was a brass lantern, about a foot long sporting four ovular lenses, one on each side, and a steepled top. The lenses were dark and full of mystery.

"Bel, is this the thing you were talking about?" Taara asked, pointing at the lantern.

Stenstrom stared at it. "Looks like it, sure enough. This is the lantern Lilly was carrying."

"Lilly? You mean the angry lady in the pipes?" Taara said.

"I saw no one," A-Ram said.

"Oh, she was there all right, and she brought her lantern with her."

Taara took the lantern out of the office and set it on the Missive panel. Its flawless lenses were dark and inscrutable.

A-Ram approached and leaned in, adjusting his glasses to get a good look at it. "Seems rather sinister to me. And you say, Bel, your lady was carrying this contrivance?"

Stenstrom agreed. "She was. Lilly called it the *'Paramel'*. It's an arcane object of some sort. I'm not certain how it works. It seems to function when it wishes."

"So what's it doing stuffed up our pipes?" Taara asked.

"I've no idea."

A-Ram was nervous and backed away. "We shouldn't have this, Bel. The Sisters keep a tight hold on such arcane things. They might have something to say about it."

"The Sisters have something to say about everything."

"We should put it back where we found it."

"Back in the pipes? No way, I want my toilet working!" Taara cried. She inspected it, messing with the lenses and tugging on the fittings. She knocked on its steepled cap.

"What are you doing?" A-Ram cried.

"I'm just tinkering," she said. "The MOLLY's not telling me much about it."

"That confirms it's an arcane device. Don't dally with it, Taara, for Creation's sake."

"Relax, will you?"

"Taara!"

Taara turned from the lantern sitting innocently on the Missive's panel. "Ok, ok! Whatever! Now, let's get back to that damn toilet. If What's-Her-Name wants to hang out in the plumbing, then I've got a nice little gift coming her way real soon."

They went back into the office and installed the commode, muscling it into place, inflating the ring, attaching the lines, and screwing it down. It only took a minute or two. Taara turned the valves and it filled with water. They flushed it with grand celebration, both Stenstrom and A-Ram patting Taara on the back. "Well done," Stenstrom said. "This working commode will serve us well and save a lot of steps."

She couldn't help but bask in their praise.

As they stood there admiring the commode, Stenstrom noticed something out the windows of his office.

They turned to the windows. Outside was a dramatic view of the aft of the ship, the long neck and the swan-like rear section with its cranked wings far away. Had the ship been fully functioning, the *Seeker* would have been lit up in a cityscape of sparkling lights: random windows burning in a yellowy glow, blinking white-light runners mounted dorsal and ventral, and cones of scanner light moving like spotlights along the length of the ship looking for imperfections in the hull, including the massive main sensor throwing out a great funnel of light ahead of the ship into the night of space. With the ship dead, the lights were all out, the bulk of the *Seeker* was like a blackened piece of driftwood in a midnight sea dappled with stars.

At that moment, however, the ship was blinking and flashing at an insane rate, like a wild carnival: window lights snapped on and off, spotlights panned and went out and runners came on and went out in a random, grid-like pattern.

"What's going on out there?" Stenstrom asked, taking it all in. "Taara?"

She wandered to the window sill and watched the ship as it lit-off like a rolling thunderstorm. "It's like power has been restored but isn't being properly controlled. I don't get it."

A-Ram peeked out onto the bridge and pointed. "Taara, Bel—look at this!"

They stepped out of the office onto the bridge. The Missive's Panel was lighting up like a sky full of fireworks. Taara seated herself at the panel and punched buttons.

"What's wrong?" Stenstrom asked.

Taara's eyes moved up and down the panel, her face lit up in a mosaic of reds, blues and yellows. "It's ... got full power. The Missive's Panel is now fully operational. It's a little messed up without the Com Panel to control everything. The Com Panel is sort of like the 'spinal cord' of the ship while the Missive's Panel is like the right side of the brain—it can control much of the higher functions of the ship such as turning on and turning off lights, but without the Com Panel, it's not very coordinated."

"So it's is turning on and turning off lights all by itself?"

Taara punched buttons in a flurry, the MOLLY in her head working overtime. "Yep. I'm trying to see if I can get it under control here."

A-Ram watched Taara work. "How is the Missive's Panel fully-powered? We don't have the energy to do that, do we?"

"Nope," Taara replied. "With the *Westminster*, we have just enough spare power to turn on a few sub-systems."

"So, where's the power coming from?"

Stenstrom turned to the lantern. It quietly sat on the Missive's Panel, its four lenses dark and mysterious. "What about Lilly's lantern here?" he asked.

"What about it?" Taara replied.

"Could it be somehow imparting power to the ship? I've witnessed this lantern do some amazing things," Stenstrom reached out and tentatively lifted it from the panel. It felt cold and bare metal in his hands.

The Missive's Panel immediately went dead. "Hey!" Taara cried lifting her hands. "I had this baby accepting data!"

Stenstrom put the lantern back down and the panel sprang to life again. "Sorry," he said. "So, that confirms it—Lilly's Lantern is an arcane device of immense power."

"Yes," A-Ram agreed. "Which is why we should not be making use of it in any way. The Sisters will find ill-favor with this."

Taara clacked away. "The Sisters can bill me, A-Ram. This thing's acting like a super-charger, and with it, we've got power to spare. I don't see the harm of making use of a tool that's been given to us."

"Who gave it to us?" A-Ram asked.

"Bel's lady, I guess, the lady in the pipes. She stuffed it up our plumbing."

A-Ram crossed his arms. "Lilly clearly has nothing to do with the Sisters and her having it must be illegal. Bel, we need to get rid of this lantern immediately. We risk the Sisters' wrath."

"Oh, screw the Sisters, A-Ram! You touch that thing and we're fightin'."

He turned to Stenstrom. "Bel!" he pleaded.

Stenstrom thought about it. He rubbed his chin. "Taara, what can you do with the Missive's Panel powered up? What is there to be gained?"

"All kinds of things! I can route power from the *Westminster* and get the lights turned on, I can get the ship's intercom system running and the security monitors as well. I can also get sensor data going. It'll just take me a little time to get all the kinks worked out of it. I can make this trip a lot easier for all of us, Bel, trust me."

He thought it over some more. "Well, I think there's no harm in making temporary use of this device. If it belongs to the Sisters then we'll give it back to them once we arrive at Bazz, no harm done."

A-Ram wanted to protest, but Stenstrom cut him off. "I'm certain the Sisters will be pleased to learn their lantern, assuming it is theirs, helped safeguard the lives of League citizens while in peril at sea."

"All right!" Taara cried. "That's what I want to hear! Give me a few hours and I'll have this baby humming."

The matter settled, they sat down for some lunch, eating cold insta-meals that they'd stolen from Dry Dock 275. Taara took her meal and returned to the Missive's Panel, engrossed in what she was doing. She called up several screens and punched buttons in between bites of food.

"Making any progress?" Stenstrom asked from his chair.

"Yep, slowly but surely. I'll have this ship flying right in no time."

"When's our next burn due?"

"Couple hours." She turned to Stenstrom and gave him a wink, her face framed by her sideburns. "I love this, you know, being up here with two handsome guys all to myself and doing all this crazy stuff with the ship. I hope it never ends."

A-Ram cracked into his lunch. "You won't be liking it so much when the demon comes for your soul. You can't just use the MOLLY all you want without expecting severe consequences."

"Yeah? I'm not worried."

They finished their lunch and, with full bellies, got sleepy, except for Taara who was deep into it at the Missive's Panel. She wiggled out of her Marine coat and pulled her boots off and sat cross-legged in the seat in her socks, playing the controls like a grand organ. A-Ram collected their empty insta-meal boxes and took them away. He wandered into Stenstrom's office, and, a few minutes later, out came the merry sounds of the commode flushing. He returned to the Navigator's position, folded his hands over his chest and was lightly snoring minutes later. Stenstrom sat back in his chair and wanted nothing more than to have a nice long nap. He hadn't had a regular sleep since being aboard the ship.

"I'm feeling tired, Taara. Stop for a while and rest," he said.

"I'm fine. I want to get this done. Go ahead and sleep, Bel. I'll yell or something if I need you."

He resisted the urge to sleep. The last time he'd fallen asleep Taara and A-Ram were abducted by Soul Devourers. He laid his NTH pistols out on his lap and struggled to keep his eyes from closing. Taara padded out of her seat and came to him in her socks. She balled up her coat and put it behind his head as a pillow. She lovingly adjusted the silk mask over his eyes and situated the folds of his coat.

"I've been waiting my whole life to get here," she whispered. "This ship is a long way from digging for clams on a Bazz delinquent farm. No time to sleep now."

She went over to A-Ram and removed his hat and adjusted his coat, doting on him in a motherly fashion. Sitting in his chair on the verge of sleep, Stenstrom felt very close to Taara and A-Ram. She returned to her seat, got comfortable and continued manipulating the Missive Panel, Stenstrom could only guess what she was doing.

It didn't take long for sleep to take him. The last thing he saw was Taara leaning over the panel, lit up in color, her sickle-like sideburns hanging down near her collar.

3

—Three Letters …—

"Bel! Bel, wake up!"

Stenstrom opened his eyes. Taara was leaning over him, her sideburns tickling his chin.

"Did I sleep?" he asked, rather groggy. He sat up and rubbed his eyes.

"Bel, I need to show you something," she said.

Still in her socks, Taara led him over to the Missive's Panel. Before he'd nodded off, the panel had been a confusion of random lights and strobe-like flashes lighting up the bridge like a gaudy dance hall, now it was tamed and orderly, lighting up with calculated precision with Lilly's Lantern sitting innocently in the center giving life to it all. "Did you get the system under control?" he asked.

"Sure did. I had to re-master it from scratch and get it away from the Com Panel, but I did it."

"Great work, Taara. You deserve an 'E' degree in engineering."

"Thanks. I managed to get the lights working on key decks on the ship—not many, but we can turn them on and turn them off from here now. I also got the cameras and ship's archive going."

"That's great news, well done."

Taara wasn't happy. "I was going over the ship's old records, they're still in the archives. They go back a pretty long way. Look here …" Taara manipulated the controls. On the screen, many people appeared, mostly crewmen, all apparently vacating the ship, many dragging luggage and other assorted personal items with them.

"What we're seeing is the final service day of the previous crew a couple of months back. This is Deck Six, Central Section. Everybody's heading to the Ripcar bays to fly on down to the surface. The captain had given up his chair, the engineer and boatswain were gone by this point and the ship's

Priory was closed. The crew was vacating in favor of other vessels. Look at all the hugs and thumps on the chest."

Taara pointed at the screen. "Look! Look there! See that?"

On the screen, mixed into the throng of departing people, was a blond-headed woman, a civilian, wearing a festive pink gown carrying a small handbag.

Stenstrom was astonished. "Is that … Lilly?"

"Looks like her to me, and I got a nice long gander at her in the plumbing."

The image of Lilly waded through the passing crewmen until the crowd thinned out to a trickle. Finally, as they watched, Lilly was alone in the now deserted corridor. She reached into her bag and pulled out a tiny white envelope, which she placed on the floor in the center of the corridor. She looked up at the camera for a moment, smiled and slowly walked away.

"Look at that—what's she doing?" Taara asked.

"Seems to be an envelope of some sort. Yes of course! Remember when we first came aboard and we found that odd letter lying in the central corridor?"

Taara rolled her eyes up, thinking back. "Seems like a long time ago. Right! I remember. It was sitting there on the floor in the central section of the ship just after we boarded. Wait! Wasn't it addressed to me?"

"That's what you thought and A-Ram thought it was addressed to him. We had a lot of work to get done, so I put it in my little case here to prevent it from distracting us. I had assumed we were all a little oxygen deprivated due to our upload and were seeing things."

"And, your lady Lilly left it there for us. Why?"

"One way to find out." Stenstrom waved his hands and produced the case. He opened it. Inside was an innocuous white envelope lying face down. His picked it out and tossed the case aside. He held the envelope and flipped it around, reading the heading to himself. He held it out and showed it to Taara. "What's this say?" he asked.

She squinted and looked at it. "It is made out to me. It says: 'TO: PRIVATE TAARA DE LA ANDERSON, 110 MARINES'. Pretty handwriting."

"You're certain that's what it says?"

"Yes, Bel, I'm from Bazz but I can still read LC, you know." She puzzled at the envelope and fiddled with the golden charm of a fish hanging at her neck. "The MOLLY's not telling me much. The thing's giving me the creeps."

Stenstrom produced several Holystones, a prism and a polyhedron. "What are you doing?" Taara asked.

"I'm checking the envelope for the arcane. This Holystone here shall determine if this is actually a letter or some sort of arcane object disguised as a letter."

"Is that possible?" Taara asked, fascinated.

"Anything's possible."

He moved the Holystone along the face of the letter. The Holystone did nothing as it touched the surface of the paper. "Well, the letter is not Astral."

"What's that mean?" Taara asked.

"The Astral Plane is a sort of pocket dimension that is all around us, the Xaphans sometimes make use of it to travel great distances very quickly, though that's a dangerous proposition. The thing about the Astral Plane is that it plays havoc on your perceptions, you can't trust any of your senses. You say the envelope is addressed to you, but when I look at it I see it as being addressed to me, and, if A-Ram were to look at it, he'd see it as being addressed to him—that's what the Astral Plane does."

"Were you expecting such a thing?"

"I had a notion. When we arrived on the ship, the bridge was contaminated with the Astral Plane."

"It was?" Taara asked. "You didn't say anything."

"I didn't want to alarm you, and, while incursions of the Astral Plane can be intentionally created, they can also happen on their own and are more common than you might realize."

The bridge studded with steel-jaw traps, waiting to bite ...

"So, you were hoping the Astral Plane just happened to be here on the bridge by itself and not put here by somebody on purpose?"

"I suppose so, yes."

"You're more of an optimist than I would have been. How did you get rid of it?" Taara asked.

"How? Blue Holystones. They're full of certain metals and solutions that block out the Astral Plane. They are fairly effective at short range and I used them to clear the bridge. I have a few more here. So, I think this is probably the safest place to trigger the letter and deal with whatever happens afterwards. Then, it'll be done."

He waved his hand and produced an olive Holystone. He rolled it across the face of the envelope. It rattled with a fuss. "Arcane. The letter detects as arcane."

The same Holystone detected Lilly as being arcane as well. She had quietly sat and allowed him to roll the Holystone down the length of her arm, rattling the whole time.

"Why Bel ... of course I'm of the arcane ..."

"I guess that's bad," Taara said as she pulled her boots on and wiggled into her coat. "What do we do?"

Stenstrom put the Holystone back into his coat. "We open the letter and face whatever is inside." He shook A-Ram, who was still sound asleep at the Navigator's position. "A-Ram, wake up."

He muttered and opened his eyes. "What? What is it?"

"We're opening that creepy letter we found the other day. It's all hexed-out. Bel's lady left it for us."

"So, why in the Name of Creation are we opening it?"

"We're going to discover its intent and be done with it. Taara, go ahead and open it."

Without fear or trepidation, Taara seized the letter and tore it open. "So far, so good," she cheerfully said. She pulled out three slips of scented paper. "Looks like a couple pieces of paper to me."

Taara laid them out on the panel. "Now what?"

While A-Ram held a few steps back, Stenstrom examined the slips. Continuing his bizarre examination, he rolled his Holystones over top of the paper, taking note of the results. He ran his finger across one of the slips. "I'm looking for grit, for minute scents and hidden writing on the paper, all of those things can be significant."

Taara sniffed the slips. "Smells like nice flowers to me."

"Lavender—that is Lilly's favorite scent, and lavender can be an ingredient in arcane tinctures."

"Perhaps that should have been a clue that your love wasn't all she seemed," A-Ram said, disconcerted by all of this. "There shall be nothing odd about my love, whoever she might be. Are you finding anything?"

"No," he stated flatly. "I'm not. The envelope reads as arcane, but the slips within seem to be just that: paper."

"Well, that's a relief."

Taara leaned in. "Looks like there's one for each of us. Here's one for me, the one in the middle is yours, A-Ram, and that one on the right is yours, Bel."

"How can there be one for me and you, Taara? We just met Bel a few days ago, and neither one of us know Lady Lilly from Lacerta."

"Who's Lacerta?" Taara asked. "Never mind, probably some crazy Kanan lady. Well, 'Rammy', I don't know. Apparently, Lilly isn't quite right, is she? She was all nice and snug up in our plumbing not long ago." She turned to Stenstrom. "Bel, what the heck is Lilly? Is she a demon?"

"The word 'demon' can be applied to most any creature or entity not of a standard classification, so, in that reckoning, yes, she is a demon. As to the exact nature of her arcane status, I have no idea. She was about to tell me and got 'summoned' by her masters, whomever they are before she could finish. I'll say she had me and my mother completely fooled all these years. Mother thought, and I did as well, that Lilly was a highly talented, intelligent, but otherwise mundane woman from Gamboa. She even revealed to me that she's not from Gamboa, so all of the things I thought I knew about her were incorrect. In any case, she walked the planes between our little ship here and Kana and was powerful enough to kill literally dozens of Soul Devourers all by herself without so much as breaking a sweat."

"Dang!" Taara exclaimed. "Now, that's a girlfriend. You should suit her up and put her in the arena or something. The most I've ever done was fight two corporals, a slut, and an MP in a bar once."

Stenstrom picked up the paper made out to him.

"Read it, Bel—even the mushy stuff. I actually sort of like that," Taara chirped as she settled down to listen.

He cleared his throat and read. "It says: *To my dearest Stenstrom. As it is no doubt obvious at this point, I have not been entirely honest with you these past years, about myself and other things as well. For various reasons, I have been compelled to lie to you, to not be forthright as to my true nature and purpose, though it pained me to have to do so. I have dreamt of the moment when I can reveal all to you, to allow you to see me as I truly am. I'm certain you have many questions, however, all I can do at this time is to state that my love for you has never been greater or more complete. Please know that, as you read this note, I am taking steps to ensure we are never parted again.*

'I've watched you for most of your life, from afar, and long before our 'introduction' a few years ago. I've protected you too. I will inform you that your ship was heavily contaminated with the Astral Plane purposely placed there by parties unfriendly to you. I have cleaned the ship out as best I can, though pockets of Astral material might remain, and I do bade you to be careful. I have sought to locate these parties and deal with them, however, they have eluded me to this point. Once matters at hand have been squared away, you may rest assured that I shall discover and dispense with them. ''

They all looked at each other. Stenstrom continued.

"'And now I see you sailing alone into peril. Given my current situation I might not be able to help you directly, therefore, I have left you the Paramel, an Elder device that illuminates many things. It has agreed to help you and I have secured it at great risk to myself. I beg you use it well. I have determined that, on your present course and given the diminished condition of your ship, you shall soon sail into great danger. The old mariner tales that abound in this lonely region of space, whispered stories of the devil and missing people and of bad dreams, seem, at least in part, to be true and I have seen your death in a dark place hidden from sight. I do not have time to fully explain myself, I will say only to beware Druries' Belt and, most importantly, the leeward side of it. I have plotted you a safe course through the deep sea where you will not be detected. Please trust in me, follow Paramel's beam and you shall be safe, I promise.

'Please allow your companions to read their notes, and, when they are finished, place this paper into Paramel and let it guide you to safe shores where I hope to be waiting.

'How I long to stand at your side.
'Follow Paramel's light and 'ware Druries' Belt.
'Your Betrothed.
'Lilly"

Stenstrom put the note back down on the Missive's panel. "And, that is all," he said.

A-Ram stood there, contemplating what was said. "Beware Druries' Belt? I don't understand, it's just a cloud of gas. I've heard of old pirate stories and rumors of raider activity and the like near the Belt, but, in our modern League, the Fleet ensures safe passage for all. There are no more pirates or raiders, we're in the heart of the League, after all."

"That's not what we say on Bazz," Taara said, picking up her note. "Old timers used to call the route to Kana 'Nightmare Way'. Lots of nasty dreams and a whole lot of bad out there."

"But, the Fleet, the Marines ..."

"What about them? How can you stop a bad dream?"

Stenstrom sighed. "What does your note say, Taara?"

4

—A Curse ... —

Taara scooped her note up with vigor. "Let's see here. Mine says: *'To Private Taara de la Anderson, 110th Marines, Armenelos. Private: It is indeed fortunate my Lord is such a charitable and goodly man, otherwise you would still be ...*" Taara paused a moment as she read the note. *"... rotting at your post at Fleet Headquarters, merely a few swills away from total inebriation, both literally and figuratively. Had I a say in the matter, that's where you would indeed still be.'"*

Taara looked up. "Wow! Ok, Lills', let's hear how you really feel, babe. Don't hold back or nothin'."

"Continue on please, Taara," A-Ram said.

Highly annoyed, Taara continued. "She says: *'Please note that I have allowed you into my Lord's presence ...'*" Taara was aghast. "Allowed me?" she cried. "Who does this dame think she is?"

"Lilly has demonstrated a jealous and rather uncharitable side at times," Stenstrom agreed.

"I wouldn't antagonize her, Taara," A-Ram warned. "She killed a hundred monsters via arcane methods."

"So?" she stated, unimpressed. Taara read on. "And then she says: *'I have observed that you are cursed ...'*" Taara did a double-take. "I'm what?" She was getting more flustered by the moment. *"'You have carried this curse with you for over thirty years and it seems to have somehow infected Lord A-Ram and my Stenstrom as well. I do not fully understand barbaric Bazz medicine at this time, however, I shall thank you to do whatever is necessary to break this curse as soon as possible. Please remember, your presence at my Lord's side is by my leave, and should you anger me, should you attempt to impose your unclean Bazz self upon my Lord, the consequences shall be swift and severe. Place this note into Paramel's cavity and you shall see the curse*

I am referring to.'"

Taara was red in the face. "By her leave? Impose myself? I'll show her 'by her leave'!" She thundered forward and gave Stenstrom a good swift kick to the shins, her Marine boot clanging off of his metal Tyrol boots. "How about that, huh?"

"What in the Name of Creation was that for?" Stenstrom asked, astonished.

"Shin kicking!" Taara replied, having regained her usual humor. "It means a girl likes you on Bazz. I love you Bel, I love both of you, and I don't give a Flying Toot what Lilly says!"

A-Ram shook his head and laughed. "A girl likes you and then kicks you in the shins? Creation you have some novel customs on Bazz."

"Gets your attention, doesn't it?" she replied. "Girls where I come from don't like to be ignored. And, I'll bet you two have had your shins kicked a lot." She turned to A-Ram to give him a kick too and he hopped away.

"Don't you dare! I don't have metal boots to protect my shins!"

Taara read through the note again. "So, I guess I'm supposed to put this inside the lantern or something?" She looked around, the MOLLY failing her in this case. She fumbled with the lantern, trying to get it open.

"Now, just a moment," A-Ram scolded. "This is an arcane Elder device, and you really shouldn't manhandle it. There could be repercussions." The two of them probed the surface, having no luck getting it open.

Stenstrom came in. "I recall seeing Lilly open it here, I think ..." He located a hidden switch and one of the lenses swung outward, revealing a hollow interior with a curious trapezoidal prism mounted in the center in such a fashion that it could spin freely if rotated. They placed Taara's slip of paper into the cavity and closed the lens.

"So, now what's supposed to happen?" Taara asked.

After a minute or so, the three of them heard the sound of movement within the lantern, followed by the crinkling of paper.

"I hear the prism moving," A-Ram said.

Slowly, the lantern came to light, the lens awash in a soft yellow glow that focused into a great, meaty beam. The beam of light issued from the lantern and played out on the far wall of the bridge.

Images formed, uncoiling in 3-D tableau.

In the beam of light four figures emerged standing back-to-back in a rough circle all bound at the waist by a common golden band like a group of shackled prisoners awaiting execution. There was Stenstrom in his green HRN and hat, A-Ram in his blue coat, Taara in her vivid red Marine jacket and a fourth person—female, tall, brown-hair pulled tightly into a bun under a small hat and wearing a ladies Fleet *Tremblar* uniform. A handsome rapier-like weapon hung at her side. All four figures were completely lifelike and motionless, as if frozen in time.

"So what's all this?" A-Ram asked.

"Appears to be the three of us, and a tall Fleet lieutenant," Stenstrom said. "All bound together."

"It's Captain Gwendolyn. I've served her coffee many times in the Admiral's office. This sword here at her side is a FEDULA, her family's LosCapricos weapon."

Stenstrom rubbed his chin. "So, this is the woman who wants to knock my block off? You were right, Taara, she is pretty tall, and ... Taara?"

Taara stood there silent and ashen. "Taara, what's wrong?" Stenstrom asked.

She said nothing.

"Taara!"

She shook her head and blinked. "What? What …"

"What's wrong?"

"Bel, don't you see it?"

"What?"

"The circle! Look at the circle around us. We don't like circles on Bazz. We're afraid of them!" Seeing the circle sent Taara into near hysterics.

"Why?"

"Vendetta. Vendetta Circle."

"What's that?" Stenstrom asked.

"It's something we believe in on Bazz. It's a weird curse that starts with one person and tends to spread out and suck people in. You know you're in a Vendetta Circle when you see yourself or your name in a circle. You never see circles at eye level or placed near a mirror or window that you might possibly see yourself in—it's a big taboo on Bazz. Want to start a fight, write down somebody's name and draw a circle around it and see what happens."

A-Ram inspected the image of himself in the lantern light, running his hand through their immobile bodies like a hologram. "What does this curse imply, from a Bazz perspective?"

"It implies that we're all going to die. That's what it implies."

"Die?"

"That's what the Vendetta Circle Curse does, it pulls you in, messes with your freakin' life, and then kills you all at once."

Stenstrom joined A-Ram and closely examined the figures in the Lantern's beam—the two of them figuring this to be some sort of Bazz nonsense and unconcerned with Taara's discomfort. He looked over Lt. Gwendolyn in particular. "She's a handsome lady: strong face, square jaw, thoughtful eyes. So tall, very un-Zenon-like. Most Zenon-girls I'm acquainted with are rather petite."

Taara hugged herself and fearfully observed the circle, taking in every detail. "Then she can be fitted for a nice big coffin once she's dead."

"Taara, it's going to be ok," Stenstrom said.

"No, no ..." she moaned.

"Listen, we all have our regional beliefs and they mean a great deal to us, don't they? If I told you some of my personal beliefs you'd probably laugh. And, one thing I do know is this: your belief in a thing can fuel it, give it power, can make it real. I know the arcane, and I can tell you there is nothing that cannot be undone or unmade. Nothing—that is a constant. You said you're cursed, if that's the case then there must be a way to break it—Lilly even said so. How do we do it? You're the expert here."

"I don't know. There's these ladies back home, Ganaadas they're called, they prowl the streets waving their Cred Sticks around demanding money and claim they can either curse you with the Circle if you piss them off, or they can cure you."

"All for a fee, of course," A-Ram said.

"Yeah, yeah, their Cred Sticks are never far from empty. Too much Zemuda drinking. They certainly don't use the money they collect for bathing."

Stenstrom was cheerful. "Well then, when we get to Bazz, we'll simply hire one of these Ganaadas, you'll submit yourself to whatever rituals are required, endure their foul smells, and that will be that. Price is no object. Will that make you feel better?"

"What? No—the Ganaadas? I wouldn't trust those dirty cows to do anything but take your Creds and run to the nearest bar. And, Bel, it's not just me stuck in the Circle—look at it, *we're all in it.*" She pointed at them and then at herself. "You, you and me are cursed!"

"And Lt. Gwendolyn as well?" A-Ram asked.

"Yep—her too. We probably won't even make it to Bazz. Maybe I'll get to watch her beat the hell out of you before we croak."

"Please ..."

"And," Taara cried. "You know what? This means we're all related to each other, all three of us."

"Umm, Taara, you're from Bazz and we're from Kana, Lt. Gwendolyn as well. We're not related," A-Ram said.

"I don't mean by birth, Ignaz!" she snapped, calling him some obscure Bazz name. "I mean we're related by something, by events, by circumstance, by random encounters that seem innocent at first but have monumental effects later on. My aunt on my mom's side, she was stuck in a Vendetta Circle. She was hopping into the sack just about every guy in town, and one of the dudes had a jealous wife. She got really mad, and that's what triggers a Vendetta Circle—strong emotion from one person, and it just grows and grows from there."

"I don't understand," A-Ram said. "It's clear how a messy love triangle can generate ill will, but what's that have to do with us? We just met a few days ago and had no contact prior to that. I certainly didn't sleep with your aunt. How did we get pulled into a Bazz curse?"

"But remember what Bel's crazy demon girlfriend said—that this Vendetta Circle has been running for thirty years. Thirty years! That's a long time for all sorts of things to happen."

"Are you over thirty, Taara?" Stenstrom asked, noting her youthful appearance. It was always difficult to determine just how old an Elder person was as they remained youthful throughout their lives no matter how old they got, and it was a topic generally left undiscussed. In Taara's case, her jittery demeanor implied tweener youth.

She blushed. "Yeah, I am. And don't ask, because I'm not telling you how old I am."

"I'm not over thirty," Stenstrom said. "I'm only twenty-seven."

A-Ram was adamant. "I myself am over thirty as well, but, again, we just met. The three of us have no connection—zero—prior to our meeting at Fleet a few days ago."

Taara shook her head. "No, A-Ram, no, no. This curse walks around, it's subtle and it's sneaky to boot. This curse isn't stuck on Bazz—whoever started it could easily have taken a transport to Kana or anywhere else and brought you two into it. The Vendetta Circle curse tends to throw people stuck in it together, it plays with them, taking years to develop making you think you're safe, giving the people involved a subtle glimpse of each other every now and again, and then WHAMO!! It constricts and brings everyone together where they die! My aunt—she and all the people stuck in her Circle all died together in a bloody restaurant by the Endax Sea."

"How?" A-Ram asked.

"How? They were having a reunion dinner and a big freakin' wave thirty feet high took them out—restaurant, pier, beach, diners and all. And, you want to know what caused the killer wave?? The Endax Sea is just a big crater full of water, right? The angry lady who began the Vendetta Circle finally had had enough of her cheating husband, so she poisoned his breakfast. He didn't die until he got to work. He worked at an antimony mine on the other side of the Endax. When he finally died, he somehow set off a massive explosion, which caused a landslide into the sea which triggered the killer wave which took out the restaurant and everybody inside it. See, that's how Vendetta Circle curse works."

A-Ram considered that for a moment. "Poppycock," he finally said.

"Oh yeah? The more I think about it, the more I'm convinced we're all stuck in a Vendetta Circle, Lt. Gwendolyn as well. It makes sense, look at how we ended up here, look how circumstances seemed to push us toward each other. You needed a helmsman, Bel, and look who turns up in a virtually empty Fleet HQ building: A-Ram. You needed an engineer, and A-Ram's got his MOLLY that he's too scared to use, but here I am, and I couldn't care less, so I use it and get us out of our terminal orbit. We need an engine to break Kana, well there's the *Westminster* just waiting to be stolen and converted into a drive engine."

"And Lt. Gwendolyn?" Stenstrom asked.

"I don't know, but she fits into this too, somehow. She's only out there in her scouting ship coming to get you right now."

"So, if I'm following your aunt's analogy correctly, since we're all together now on the ship, with the exception of Lt. Gwendolyn who is en route, that the Circle is near to running its course and we are soon to die?" Stenstrom said.

She nodded and mumbled into Stenstrom's coat for a bit, trying to sort herself out.

"And, you're also saying that this Vendetta Circle we find ourselves in is caused by one person who has ties to all of us across two worlds?"

She nodded again. "I mean this is probably my fault. I got into a big fight with a Ganaada once. She was running around spouting off about my uncle who ran the local pharmacy, and I told her to shut up. She wrote my uncle's name down and drew a circle around it and then we were going at it. Maybe that's where it started?"

"How does that involve us, then?" A-Ram asked. "You're most certainly the only person from Bazz I know."

Taara sobbed. Stenstrom took her gently by the sideburns and she looked up at him in rapt attention, cheeks shiny. "All right, Taara. Obviously this is a belief you take a great deal of stock in, and we appreciate that. You say that this curse is something that's probably been brewing for some time now, yes?"

She nodded.

"Fine. Once we get to Bazz and deliver the Admiral's brandy, we will stay on until we get this sorted out. Our first priority will be to get out of this death curse, our second will be the refitting of the ship. We'll perform research, we'll prowl every library and sage's sanctum, we'll consult with the learned and the local shamans, we'll purchase whatever goods need to be bought, and together we'll determine a way out of this. Time and money is no object."

Hope filled Taara's eyes. "You promise. The three of us will do all that?"

"I promise. Right A-Ram?"

"Oh yes, absolutely," he replied.

"I've never been much in a library," she said.

"No time like the present to catch up." Taara gave Stenstrom a grand hug. She broke away and went to A-Ram, embracing him in the same fashion. "Hey, A-Ram, I'm sorry I called you 'Ignaz', ok? I didn't mean it."

"It's quite all right, Taara. I don't believe I know what it means."

"Good, that's good." Taara then pulled back and gave him a swift kick to the shins, just like she had Stenstrom, only A-Ram didn't have metal Tyrol boots to ward it off. He hobbled about in pain on one foot.

"Gods that hurt!"

Taara recovered from her funk. "So, what I think we need to do is figure out who started this Vendetta Circle, confront them, and ..."

"And what?' A-Ram asked rubbing his shin. "Kill them? Murder them?"

"Well yeah, I guess. We have to deal with this person and change this Vendetta Circle Curse up."

Stenstrom spoke up. "I don't like the idea of murdering someone, Taara."

"It's them or us, right? We have to change the circumstances of this curse, I think that's how we can get out of it."

"Like I said, when we get to Bazz, we'll sit down and puzzle this out. I'm certain we'll not need to resort to something as crass as cold-blooded murder. And, I suppose, as you mentioned, our primary task will be to determine who this 'central person' to all three of us is. At this stage I have no idea who that might be. I also suppose that keeping Lt. Gwendolyn off the ship is more important than even, to prevent the circle from closing."

"Ok, now you're thinking! Right now our primary task is to survive until we get to Bazz in the first place. Your demon lady said there's great danger out there, and we better listen to her," Taara said.

"We'll follow her advice and stay well clear of the leeward side of Druries Belt as dictated by the solar winds."

"That'll add some time to our trip," Taara said. "Staying windward of the Belt is the long way around."

"Will it cause us to miss our deadline for the brandy on Bazz?" Stenstrom asked, still fascinated by the images in the lantern's beam.

Taara thought a moment. "Nah."

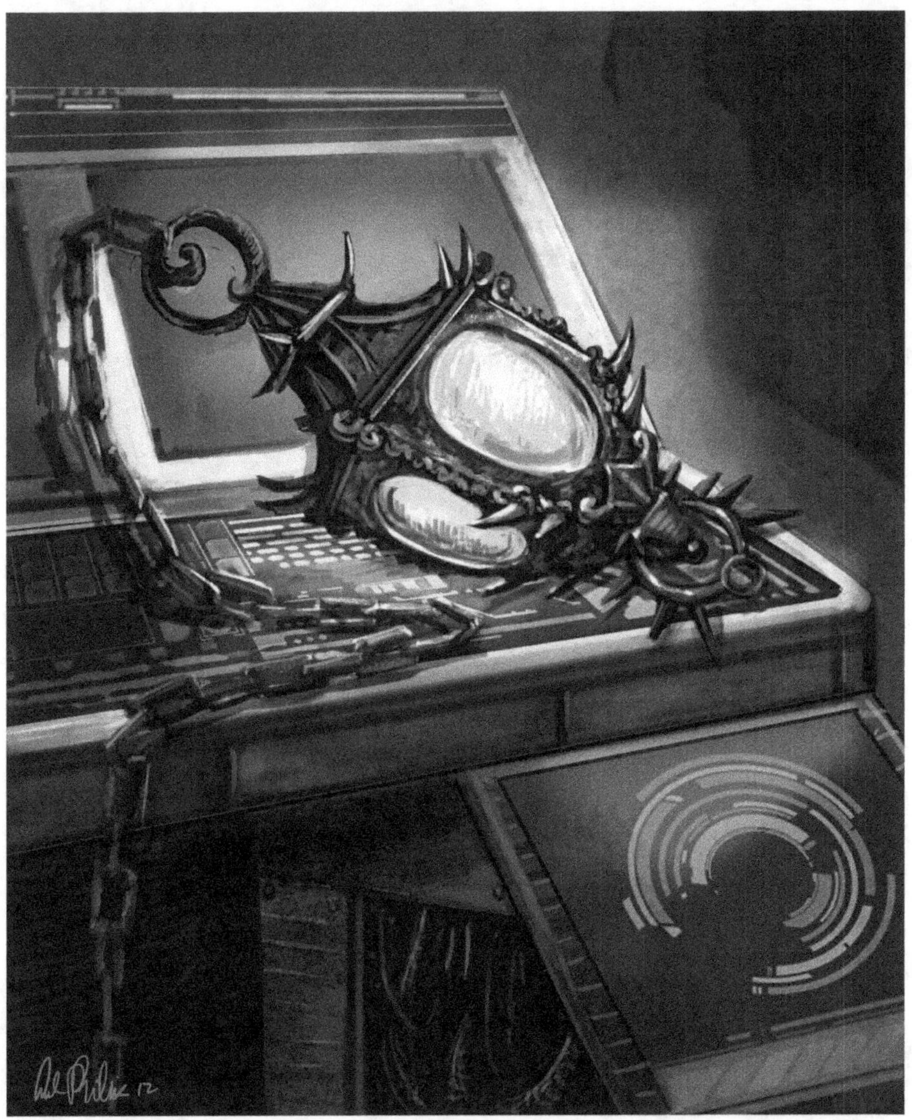

The Lantern

5

—... And an Apparition—

One note remained unread on the Missive's Panel: A-Ram's note. Taara scooped it up and held it out. "Here's yours, A-Ram. Go on, read it. I've got some course correcting to do, but first I want to hear what Bel's lady said to you. Make it snappy!"

Tentatively, A-Ram accepted the note. He glanced at it and cleared his throat. "Ahem, it says: *'To: Josephus, Seventh Lord of A-Ram, St. Edmunds. My Lord: Though I do not approve of my Lord Stenstrom's current situation, I am pleased he has made your acquaintance and calls you his friend.'*"

Taara interrupted. "How come she's all nicey-nicey with you? I got the 'by my leave' bit."

A-Ram continued on. "*'I must say, though we have never met, I feel a kinship with you. I feel I understand your heart. You are like a beloved brother to me, and I look forward to the occasion when my Lord may properly introduce us. Steer the ship well and bring to me my Lord. You have my favor and I wish to offer you a gift. Place this note within Paramel and it shall reveal to you your future love—such power it has. You have often felt lonely, and unworthy, spurned by the Sisters and by members of your own family. I felt for you, and I wish to assure you that a fine love awaits. I have seen her. Behold, please, and know, with my compliments, that great things are in the offing.*

'I leave you with a warning, and pray you heed it,'" A-Ram swallowed and continued reading with dread. "*'Your love is in danger and could easily fall to a terrible fate. She lives at the mouth of Edam and tempts death every day. She is very brave, and you would be most proud of her.'*" A-Ram paused. "What's Edam?"

Taara replied. "It's the Vith word for hell."

A-Ram pondered that for a moment. "*'Follow the course I have set and you need not fear, your love will be safe, though a chance meeting with her will be lost. You would otherwise never meet her. When I am rejoined with my Lord on Bazz, I shall lead you to her side.*

'Remember, beware Druries Belt.

'Your sister in spirit

'Lilly.'"

A-Ram puzzled over the note. "Well, gee, A-Ram," Taara said. "Looks like Lilly just loves you, doesn't she?"

"She seems like such a kind person, I feel enchanted ...""

"Yeah, yeah, you got the muzzle, I got the horns."

"My love?" A-Ram asked holding his note. "I've never really had a love before. I was always too awkward and shy for such things. What should I do, Bel? Should I do as directed, or should I leave my fate to the unknown?"

"Must you ask such a question? Don't you know?" Stenstrom asked.

"Well, I ... I mean, who wouldn't want to know such a thing, but then there's always the joy of chance and circumstance."

"Whatever you choose, A-Ram, hurry it up. I've got to get the course corrections laid in," Taara said.

He considered the matter a moment further, and then fumbled with the lantern. "Lilly said my love's in danger, she might need me. Bel, can you get this open for me, please?" Stenstrom touched the lantern to open the lens. The images displayed in its beam reacted to his touching the lantern. The golden band trapping the figures together disappeared and, freed, they capered about in a demented fashion.

"Wow!" Taara cried as she watched.

The A-Ram image staggered to a far wall and placed his hands on the bulkhead. He pounded on the wall and reared back in apparent anguish before vanishing.

The image of Taara transformed before their eyes. The MOLLY hanging at her neck dug itself into her flesh and she grew, blossoming into a goddess-like woman with luminous violet eyes.

"Hey—look at that!" Taara cried as the image faded away. "What was that?"

The Stenstrom image collapsed to the floor on all fours, his body seem-

ingly broken under his HRN coat. His left hand fell away from his arm leaving a stump, as if chopped off. "What happened there?" Taara asked as the sad image vanished.

The Gwendolyn image lingered. She looked around with crazed, lamplike eyes, her face sunken-in and pocked with insane suffering. She stumbled forward toward Stenstrom, drawing her FEDULA.

"Captain?" he asked. "Can you hear me?"

She reacted a little, her head turning, darting eyes trying to make sense of her surroundings. She dropped her FEDULA and raised her arms in a teetering zombie-like manner. A clean, straight cut formed on her left cheek, as if from a sabre strike. A curtain of fast flowing blood raced down her face and dripped off her chin.

"Captain, you're bleeding," Stenstrom said, trying to assist her.

She opened her mouth, not to speak, but to scream. She fell back and was gone as Stenstrom tried to catch her.

"What in the Name of Creation was all that?" A-Ram asked still holding his note. "Was that the future we were seeing? It was terrifying."

"I'm not certain, but I'll agree it was disquieting," Stenstrom said. He took A-Ram's note and placed it within the lantern's cavity, closing the lens back up. Inside, the prism turned and the paper crinkled.

"You sure you want to see this?" Taara asked. He didn't answer.

The lantern came to life again. Appearing before them in a whirling column of rising fog, like a clay pot taking shape on a wheel, was a solitary figure bathed in greenish lantern light. A-Ram gritted his teeth and watched.

The figure appeared to be a small female clad in an emerald hooded cloak made of shimmering brocade lined and sleeved with gold fabric. Under the cloak was a white linen smock made of coarse thread. She wore a number of red and green beaded necklaces around her delicate neck and, around her waist, a loose belt made of red and green shells. She was quite attractive with a pearly sort of smooth complexion and delicate features, slender hands and a pretty face. Her hair was thick and black held back in a loose bun with several sticks and combs. She didn't appear to be wearing any shoes, though her feet were wreathed in fog.

"Wow, pretty cute," Taara chirped. "What do you think, A-Ram? She's a looker."

A-Ram stood there and stared at the figure, taking in her features. He seemed quite speechless.

"Well, say something, A-Ram," Taara said.

"Hello?" he stammered. "Dearest madam?"

The figure didn't speak. She looked back over her shoulder. Her features were etched with concern.

"This woman looks like a Pilgrim of Merian, the white smock, the red and green beads, the green cloak. That's what they wear, all homemade stuff," Stenstrom said.

"What's a Pilgrim of Merian?" Taara asked, A-Ram too stunned to speak.

"It's a religious order on Kana and elsewhere preaching an alternate view of the Elders. They're very benign, simple people. My family manor is a former Merian monastery and I used to play with my sisters in their old hermitage near Merian's Hill. They are good, honest people."

"Hmmm, I've never seen this woman before, nor do I recall ever seeing one of her order," A-Ram said. He approached the woman. "What is your name, ma'am?"

She reacted and turned in his direction. When she saw A-Ram, her face lit up in delight—how pretty she was when she smiled, full lips and straight, well-tended teeth. Her blue eyes sparkled. She said something, though her voice could not be heard.

"What did she say?" Taara asked.

She said it again. Stenstrom read her lips. "It looks like she said 'Whammy' or something like it."

"No, no, she didn't say 'Whammy', she said 'Rammy'," A-Ram said. "She's saying my name." He took another step forward. "Ma'am, do I know you? What's your name? Please tell me."

The apparition appeared concerned. She pointed to Stenstrom's office. "Do you want us to go in there? What are you trying to tell us?"

A-Ram went into Stenstrom's office, followed by the silent apparition of the Pilgrim of Merian. She pointed at the windows. Outside was the usual carpet of quiet stars, the darkened bulk of the ship, and the long yellowish band of Druries Belt drifting off toward the Onaris/Bazz system imperceptibly fluttering in the solar wind.

"She's pointing at Druries Belt!" A-Ram said. "Remember the warning! 'Ware the Belt!"

Alarmed, Taara flew back into her chair at the Missive's panel. "I think I can get some of the ship's sensors working. I'll bet we've got a visitor out there!"

"A-Ram, get to your post!" Stenstrom said. He ran out of the office with the apparition slowly following.

Stenstrom opened the lantern and placed his note, the one Lilly said would guide the ship, into the cavity.

"Don't jostle the lantern!" Taara cried. "It's what's powering the panel right now."

For a third time, the lantern lit up, this time in a tight, bluish beam. The beam went out into Stenstrom's office toward the aft of the ship, floating like the needle of a compass moving steadily in a clock-wise motion.

"I think it's giving us a heading," Taara said. She burst out of her seat and followed the beam into the office. She picked up her sextant and, using the beam as a point of reference, took a reading. "A-Ram, give me five pegs hard a starboard, Z plus 260 degrees. Hurry!"

A-Ram kicked the floor levers and strained as he turned the wheel, the female apparition in green silently watching him. Outside, the thrusters ticked and the ship banked. The lantern skittered to the right as the ship's bank deepened, threatening to slide off the panel. Stenstrom held it fast, preventing it from moving further.

Taara thundered back into her seat and continued with the panel, furiously manipulating the screens.

"Five pegs starboard, Z plus 260 degrees, aye!" A-Ram said from behind the wheel.

"Ok, ok, hold that," Taara said staring at her screens and watching the lantern's beam change direction centering in Stenstrom's office. She stared at her screens. "Whoah!"

"What, what is it?" Stenstrom asked.

Taara rechecked her screens. "For a minute we were reading something big out there."

"Big like a passing ship?"

"No, I mean big like a planet. I'm serious. It filled up the screens, but it's gone now." She crunched more data. "I don't see it anymore—must have been a glitch. Ok, A-Ram, now, go three pegs hard a larboard, Z to level and hold."

The helm groaned as A-Ram turned the wheel. The lantern's beam moved slightly.

"Got it—three pegs hard a larboard and Z to level, aye!"

"Are you seeing anything out there, Taara?" Stenstrom asked.

She was engrossed, crunching data fast.

"Taara? Talk to me."

"A moment ..." She pulled up another screen, her eyes moving up and down the data. "Contact!" she announced.

"What is it? What are we reading?"

"Something small this time, moving fast. It's a vessel."

"Is it a Fleet ship?"

"Unknown, reading motion only. Our sensing capabilities are for shit. Not seeing any hoisted flags or other forms of identification. But it's out there, dead away at 9:45AM."

"No flag?"

Stenstrom went into his office and gazed out the windows, seeing nothing but stars and the glowing yellowish band of Druries Belt—Lilly's warning fresh in his mind.

Beware Druries Belt ...

"Should we burn the *Westminster,* Bel?" Taara asked. "We're going to have to do it sooner or later."

"No, let's wait. Let's keep the ship quiet for now and stand fast."

The apparition gave A-Ram a warm smile and slowly faded away. "Wait!" he cried holding the wheel. "Don't go! Please!"

A moment later, she was gone.

"I wonder what—"

"Shh!" Stenstrom commanded from the office. "Stand your post."

"You see something, Bel," Taara asked.

Through the windows he squinted out at the vast glowing ribbon of Druries Belt. For a moment, a distant black silhouette, like a speck of dust appeared, back-lit by the Belt, and then was gone.

6

—A FRIEND FROM PRENTISS—

Working the wounded *Seeker* kept the three of them busy for the remainder of the afternoon, putting gloomy thoughts of arcane Vendetta Circles aside in favor of more immediate issues such as the *Seeker's* tendency to drift and roll. Eventually, the unknown contact they had just managed to avoid drifted off the scopes and Taara was permitted to perform a long burn of the *Westminster's* engines, following the meandering course laid out by the lantern's blue beam. She announced they would have to burn-correct every seven hours. For now, they were safely windward of Druries Belt.

It was good to be busy.

A-Ram was dour and sad behind the helm. His thoughts were riveted on that woman in green.

"I wonder who she was?" he asked. "Wasn't she pretty?"

"She certainly was," Stenstrom said. "You've never seen her before?"

"No, no, I'd remember a lady like that. What would she want with the likes of me? That's what my brother would say."

"You brother's a jerk," Taara replied.

The lantern sat on the panel near Taara, its lens issuing the long, tight beam which had become a comfort for them. They had lashed it down to the panel with disused optical cabling, keeping it from sliding off.

"I ... I hope she'll like me."

Taara laughed. "You know, 'Rammy', I don't think now's a good time to be fixing yourself up a date. She didn't even have Mollocks or nothing."

"Well then, Taara, I suppose she's not from Bazz." A-Ram held the helm wheel, his eyes distant.

As far as they could tell, they were on their way to Onaris following the lantern beam. Once there, they would use the planet as a sling-shot to pick up speed and continue on to their final destination, Bazz.

A-Ram stood there, the helm in his hands. "I feel a lot better now that we're underway. It'll be nice to get to Bazz. Where on Bazz are you from again, Taara?"

Taara was sitting in the Missive's chair, her favorite place to sit, eating another insta-meal. "Dyson Clampton, in the western continent. I'll show you around when we get there—you'll love it. You guys like spicy food?"

"No," A-Ram said flatly.

"Oh, come on, A-Ram, you Master Helmsman you. Stick with me, I'll have you loving it. You and your lady can try it. That's the one thing I really wish I had right now was a little hot sauce to give this insta-meal some life."

A-Ram let go of the helm and walked to the box of meals. He rummaged around. "I thought there was a chicken meal in here."

"There was, A-Ram, I just ate it," Taara replied.

He sighed and selected a beef concoction.

Stenstrom thought a moment. "Taara, you say everything on Bazz has two names, right?"

"Yep."

"Then how come the name of the place is just Bazz? Shouldn't the name of the planet have two names also?"

Taara gazed back at him from the Missive's chair—for a second he thought she looked a lot like Crewman Kaly, only with sideburns. "I wasn't around when they came up with all that stuff, Bel. When I become the Queen of Bazz, I'll fix that problem. We'll call it Bazz Bazz, how about that?"

Stenstrom laughed. "Taara, how long before we get to Bazz Bazz?"

"About ten days—depends on this lantern here, and on how much speed we pick up around Onaris."

"Ten days—that's really going to be cutting it close."

"That's the best we can do. What are we going to do once we get there?"

"I'm hoping, once we fulfill the Admiral's mission, we can get our various legal issues sorted out in earnest, and then we can look to the ship."

"Don't forget the Vendetta Curse," Taara said.

"Right, right. Once we get our 'Curse' issues corrected we'll refit the *Seeker* and press in a fresh crew. We'll first need an engineer and a boatswain—those shouldn't be hard to get, I'm hoping, if we make enough noise."

"Can we prowl the docks, Bel, scope out people, beat them up, and bring them aboard?" She popped her small fist into her palm.

"I'm certain we'll have no trouble finding a willing group to fill our needs, Taara. No need for the hook or for rough stuff."

"It'll be nice to sleep in a real bed once we get to Bazz Bazz," A-Ram said. "Oh Creation—now you two have got me calling it that too."

"Addictive, isn't it?" Taara said.

"Bel?" A-Ram asked, "those Pilgrims of Merian? Can you tell me about them? I'd like to hear more."

"Well, they're ..."

The Com chattered, interrupting him. "Incoming message, Bel, you want it?" Taara asked from her lit-up Missive's panel.

"Who's it from?"

Taara looked into the viewer. "It's your friend, Captain Gwendolyn."

Stenstrom sighed. "Are we certain it's her this time? No more mirages?"

"Looks like a real Com to me."

"Sure. She probably wants to yell at me again. Put her on. Go ahead."

The bridge's central Holo-cone jumped to life, though the image

was still poor at best. There was Lt. Gwendolyn, standing tall in 3-D. This time her eyes were not sunken and crazed, no gushing blood on her cheek.

"It appears I'm not where I'm supposed to be, Captain," Stenstrom said from his chair. "Is this your declaration of war between us?"

She stood there a moment in the cone. "Paymaster, I would appreciate a word with you in private if possible." She spoke in a calm, dignified manner.

"Whatever threats you wish to make to me, you may say in front of my crew."

"I would be more at ease speaking to you in private, sir."

Stenstrom stood. "Taara, please send the Com to my office."

She casually pressed a few buttons. "Hey, Bel! Don't lock the door, I might want to use the toilet in a bit."

"Fine."

He walked across the bridge and went through the door. There was his office, small, full of windows. In it was the old oak desk where Captain Davage used to sit and a fully functional bathroom. Taara's strut-metal sextant sat on the ledge. He opened the Com, which, thanks to one of the stolen generators, had power. Captain Gwendolyn appeared on the screen.

"Paymaster, thank you for giving me this opportunity to speak with you in private," she said in her cultured Zenon accent as he sat down.

He regarded her—a sturdy-looking lady, as before. On the tallish side as with her mirage, dense, but not unattractive in the least, her long brown hair tucked into her hat. Rather like Private Taara, she was deceptively good-looking. "Of course, Captain," he said. "You scared several days and nights worth out of me earlier."

Lt. Gwendolyn was puzzled. "Sorry? I what?"

Stenstrom laughed. "Never mind. So, Captain, still wanting to beat my brains in, are you?"

She smiled. "No, Paymaster. I want to apologize for my outburst earlier. It was unprofessional, and rather rude of me. I suppose I've been known for having a hot temper, and perhaps I justly deserve such a reputation. Please forgive my previous lack of manners, and if you wish to file a formal complaint against me, I encourage you to do so."

Stenstrom laughed. "Oh, please. My first officer doesn't seem to think that I would have stood stand much of a chance against you, should we have come to blows."

Gwendolyn lifted her eyes and looked at him through the Com. "Well, sir, if I am to base my response on your appearance, I should say that I think you would have fared quite well."

"Thank you. So then, Captain, what's on your mind?"

She continued. "I want to clear the air between us. I want to make it plain that I, like you, have been forced into this situation and I find it rather uncomfortable. I have no desire to cost you your chair—though the essence of my mission is to do just that. Rather, I must say that I have been most impressed with what you have accomplished to date. I simply want to say that I have my orders and I must carry them out, but that doesn't mean that I have to like them, or to agree with them for that matter. Furthermore, I want to say that it is my hope that, after all this is over and matters have been sorted out, we could sit down, like two civilized people, have lunch, and shake hands."

"Are you trying to say, Captain, that you want to be friends?"

"I would like that, sir, yes. I just want to assure you that what happens over the next few days is not of my making. I'm just following my orders, such as they are."

Stenstrom glanced out the windows. The stars appeared to be frozen in place. Far away was Druries Belt, glowing and ominous. "Are you still intending to arrest Private Taara and forcibly return Lord A-Ram to his slow death at the Fleet?"

Lt. Gwendolyn shook her head. "No, Paymaster. I have done as you previously suggested. I have sent word to the Fleet of your conscription of Lord A-Ram as helmsman and your appointment of Private Taara as your first officer. The movements have been logged at Fleet and duly noted. There are no further penalties awaiting Private Taara. Her unit appeared to be rather glad to be rid of her, truth be told, however, the Fleet office and Admiral Derlith demand payment for Lord A-Ram—it is their right to request compensation."

"Fine, whatever they want, I will pay it. I'll let Taara and A-Ram know. It will be a load off their minds."

Gwendolyn looked at the floor for a moment. "Now, Paymaster, I wish to know what your feelings are on this matter. As I have said, I have no desire to cost you your chair, yet I must do my duty."

"My feelings, Captain?"

"Yes, as you touched upon, I was hoping we could be friends, and that is not simply idle talk, that is my genuine position. I must say I admire your tenacity."

"How about this, Captain? If you bag me fair and square, you may rest assured that I will sit and lunch with you. You may do your job in the knowledge that I harbor no ill will toward you or any of your crew. If you get me, you get me, and that's that. However, I am not going to make it easy for you. I intend to fulfill my mission and deliver Admiral Derlith's gasp-inducing brandy to Bazz Bazz."

"Sorry?" Gwendolyn replied. "To where?"

"Oh, forgive me, it's a habit I've acquired. I am going to deliver my cargo to Bazz. You will not step on my ship until I have fulfilled my mission, and that is the simple truth."

Gwendolyn lit up. "So it's settled. I can't tell you how much better I feel having had this conversation with you, Paymaster—now that we understand and appreciate each other properly. I am certain that you will give me all I can handle and then some—I had better be on my top game. Paymaster, do you enjoy playing cards?"

"I'm afraid I don't know any games. And please, Captain, you may call me Bel, short for Belmont. All my friends call me that."

She looked at the floor and smiled. "Thank you, and you may call me Gwendolyn, or simply Gwen if you prefer—my family calls me that. I would like to teach you a game or two. Playing cards is a passion of mine that I wish to share."

"I thought boxing was."

"I like to box as well. If you want to box instead of playing cards, we can do that. I have a famous right hook." She seemed to be enjoying the conversation as it advanced from business to more personal matters. "Bel, I have heard that you can make items appear from thin air. Is that simply a story, or can you actually do such things?"

"Who told you that?"

"Oh, various people. My uncle, for one."

Stenstrom raised his hands and showed her his palms. "Watch carefully." In a blur he waved his hands and produced a MARZABLE between his fingers. Another wave and it was gone again.

Gwendolyn clapped. "Oh, well done, Bel. Now, to prove my good faith, I'll inform you that I expect to arrive at your position, after our course correction, in four hours. I have a fully functioning *Tekel*-class scouting ship at my disposal, and I have been authorized to use whatever means necessary to board your vessel, including disabling it. You have my word, I'll not do such a thing."

"Thank you Captain … I mean, Gwendolyn. But, you needn't hold back because of me—do what you feel you need to do, and I shall do the same."

Gwendolyn looked at him over the Com screen. "So, Bel, can you assure me that your life support and other critical systems are functioning well enough to sustain you and your people? Both myself, and my Hospitaler, are genuinely concerned about you."

"I can. The items we borrowed from Dry Dock 275 are working rather well. We have fresh air and a fair amount of power. We even have a fully functioning bathroom."

Gwendolyn seemed surprised. "Shipboard plumbing requires extensive training and experience. I am amazed by your industry."

"Necessity begets industry."

"How did you manage that?"

"We shunted power in from the *Westminster.*"

"Really?" Gwendolyn said. "Do you have any engineering skills, Bel—that's a fairly complicated procedure."

"I don't. Private Taara did it."

"She did? That's very impressive—she must have some experience in that area. I have a degree in engineering from the University of Arden and I'd hoped to sit on the Engineer's chair of a larger Fleet ship some day. See, my pin here?" Over the screen she pointed to a tiny pin on her lapel—it was the same kind of pin his sister Lyra now wears on her gown.

He recalled the circle Taara had mentioned. He'd seen Gwendolyn's face there in Lilly's lantern light. She was in the Circle too. He recalled her mirage on the bridge: eyes sunken and crazed, face hollow, blood gushing, full of delirium.

"That's a very difficult degree to achieve, so I'm told. You've cause to be most proud. I believe my sister is currently matriculating at the University of Arden as well, though not in engineering."

She sat down and appeared to relax a little, she even took off her hat. "Belmont is a Zenon House, yes? I think, geographically speaking, that we are neighbors. I am from Prentiss, just a ways north from you I think."

"I grew up in Tyrol near my mother's holdings—my cousins still live in the Zenon region, however."

"Tyrols are of the Esther line, correct?"

"Officially, but Tyrols consider themselves a tribe apart."

"They have gray hair if I'm not mistaken."

"It's called Pewterlock, and it's more a silver color. My mother had a proud head of Pewterlock hair and many of my sisters have it. I have more of a Belmont look with black hair. If I may say, Gwen, you appear to be rather taller than a typical Zenon Girl."

Gwendolyn laughed. "Not all Zenon Girls are petite. Prentiss girls are fairly tall. I am just a shade under six feet, which is normal in my family. May I ask how tall you are, sir? It's an odd thing to ask, but I am most curious."

"I'm six-seven. I'm a lot taller than both my mother and my father, and all of my sisters. I'm not quite sure where it came from."

The Vendetta Circle ...

"Captain ..."

"Gwen, please."

"Gwen, may I ask an odd question of you?"

"Certainly."

"Thank you. Have you sustained an injury to your right cheek lately, as if from a sword cut?"

Gwendolyn appeared puzzled. She reached up and touched her cheek. "My cheek? No, not that I'm aware of? Why do you ask?"

"I ... had a dream recently where your cheek was injured and bleeding."

She laughed. "You're dreaming of me, are you, Paymaster?"

"Yes, apparently so."

Gwendolyn's panel lit up and she glanced at it. She pressed a few buttons and then resumed the conversation. "Well, I look forward to putting this business behind us, and I am certain that we'll laugh over it someday soon. I have to return to my duties. As we are now friends, will you promise me that you will contact us immediately should your life-support situation change?"

"Sure, I promise."

"Good. So, Bel, until we meet again—and we shall meet again, make no mistake—I bid you good luck and fly safe."

"And to you, good luck, Gwendolyn, Lady of Prentiss, for you shall need it."

"Oh, Bel, one more thing?"

"Yes?"

"You posed an odd question, and now I have one for you. I … I must know. That mask you wear … Why, why do you wear a mask?"

"It's a long story. I say, after this is over, and I've delivered my cargo on Bazz Bazz—I mean Bazz, we'll sit down, have a nice dinner, and I'll tell you all about it—the whole sorry story. How does that sound?"

Gwendolyn lit up in a smile and put her hands together. "I look forward to it."

"You should do that more often."

"Do what, Bel?"

"Smile. How your face fills up when you do so."

7

—STANDOFF—

It was the slowest chase in League history, the huge, but limping Warbird *Seeker* against the fully functional but much smaller *Demophalon John*. The *Seeker* was big and swan-like, graceful and menacing, but she was darkened and mostly dead. She was flying backwards, her lone motive power being supplied by the *Westminster,* strapped down in forward facing Ripcar Bay 5.

Stenstrom could see the scout ship on the holo-cone, a jumpy, blurry image. "Right on time," he said. He went into his office and gazed out the windows, to get a clearer look. "Taara, get in here!" Taara joined him on the run.

There she was, swooping in from 12:45pm: the *Demophalon John*. She was a standard *Tekel*-class scout ship, about three hundred feet long. Its structure consisted of an elliptical disk five decks high, buttressed by three evenly-spaced convex cylinders roughly shaped like bananas—hence the *Tekel's* long standing nick-name: the Banana-Boat. The upper conning run was shorter than the lower two and buttressed with a tail assembly.

She was nimbly orbiting around the length of the *Seeker*, looking it over. She was lit up with service lights, scanning cones, and glowing windows. Stenstrom thought he could see occasional movement in the windows, people passing by—and he wondered if Lt. Gwendolyn was looking out of one of them even now.

She, stuck in Taara's closed Vendetta Circle, just like he was … maybe.

"Taara," he said. "What are we looking at here?"

"It's just a run of the mill *Tekel*-class scout ship. It's a fairly fast boat, got four J-400 Stellar Mach coils, but those are pretty small. If we were normal, they couldn't keep up with us at full sail—but we're not normal right now, are we?"

"What's its armament?"

"It has six X-MaSS rim-fired armored tip, caseless chain guns mounted forward."

"Those are 'Christmas Guns', right? I remember hearing about those."

"Yep. Just a fast-firing light gun. Got punch, but we're pretty heavily armored."

"How badly can that type of gun hurt us?"

"They can do a fair amount of topical damage, but that's all. A Christmas Gun's not going to put a Warbird out of commission. Why, are you afraid Captain Gwendolyn's going to shoot us up?"

"She might. I'm thinking she's going to do the following: I'm thinking she's going to try and land several Ripcars first, then she's going to try and dock, then she's going to go for the *Westminster*, light it up and shut us down. That's what I'd do."

He looked over his shoulder. "A-Ram! Do you have a good reading on your Helm displays?"

"I do. I see her orbiting around, trying to casually lock on and dock using automated signaling. Won't work, as we don't have power to those automated systems. It'll be like making love to a dead man."

"Don't knock it 'till you've tried it, A-Ram," Taara replied.

"Keep her at bay," Stenstrom said, "and feel free to give her a little love tap if she comes in too close."

He gazed at the *Demophalon John* floating around outside. "You once said there was somebody aboard that ship that I care deeply over, Taara."

"I don't recall saying that."

"You did, back when you first put the MOLLY on."

"Hmmmm. No clue."

They shook on it and returned to the bridge. "How're we looking, Bel?" A-Ram asked.

"Slow. How are we doing for maneuverability?"

"We're fine—we can maneuver with a scout ship any day, we just can't outrun her."

The Com crackled on the bridge. "Paymaster Stenstrom," came Gwendolyn's voice. "So, here we are, sir. Are you feeling thirsty? The sooner I board, the sooner I'm buying you an ale back at Fleet," she said in a good-natured manner.

"Nah, Captain, I'm good, I think," he replied.

"Well then, fair hunting," she said. The Com clicked off.

"A-Ram, the only two places she's going to be able to dock is dead forward and to the starboard off the neck, right?"

"Right!" Taara answered for him.

"Very well, keep the nose and the starboard side away from her—you are free to maneuver however you see fit."

"Gotcha,' Bel," A-Ram said, tugging on the wheel.

"Just remember, keep clear of the damn Belt. No need to test fate."

"Agreed."

"She didn't sound mad or anything, Bel," Taara said with a hint of disappointment. "Not like before."

"We smoothed things out. She doesn't seem like a half-bad person really, but I'm still not letting her on the bloody ship."

"So, you're not going to fight?"

"I rather doubt it."

"I was hoping to watch a good fight, and I think she would have beaten the daylights out of you, if you really want my thoughts."

"Thanks, Taara."

A-Ram looked into his screen. "Reading four small vessels exiting the ship. Ripcars, Bel, and they're coming in fast."

Stenstrom saw the flickering images on the holo-cone. "Which one is she in, Taara? Can you tell?"

"The one that's heading for Ripcar Bay 7."

"Right. A-Ram, don't worry about the rest of them. Track that one heading for Number 7, and keep her from docking. The other ones are just decoys."

A-Ram, spun the wheel.

The Ripcars from *Demophalon John* chased the *Seeker* around for a while. Though the small ships were relatively fast and maneuverable, they weren't as fast as the *Seeker* with its *Westminster* drive engine. Even though the *Seeker* had no Stellar speed available to her to fare the deep stars and was flying backwards, she was faster at maneuvering speeds than the *Demopha-*

lon John's Ripcars, it was like a pigeon being chased by a slightly slower swarm of bees. A-Ram kicked the bar, and the *Seeker* outpaced them. After a time, the Ripcars gave up and returned to the *Demophalon John.*

"That had to be humbling for her," Stenstrom said. "Now that her Ripcar gambit has failed miserably, I think she's now going to try and hard dock the ship."

Sure enough, the *Demophalon John* tried to slide in, first to the front of the ship, and then to the starboard. But, even in a diminished state, the *Seeker* was fairly light on the helm and A-Ram, with a bit of doing, kept the scouting ship at bay, matching it turn for turn. The two ships performed a swirling dance, the scouting ship moving one way and the *Seeker* matching.

"You didn't think I'd let you just up and knock on the front door, did you, Captain?" Stenstrom asked.

Gwendolyn's voice came back on the Com. "You can twist away all you want, Bel, where are you going to go? I can out-run you with one coil in lock. At this speed, you've got a ten day trip to Bazz ahead of you, and you have to sleep sometime—me, I've got the night bell to take over when I get tired. You might just wake up and find me smiling down at you. You said you liked my smile—why not see it in person?"

"A-ha!" Taara said. "See."

Stenstrom laughed as A-Ram pulled on the wheel. "Ah, but haven't you heard, Captain?—I've got Tyrol sorcery. I don't need to sleep. I can brew up a potion to defeat the need for sleep."

"Tyrol sorcery isn't real."

"Oh, yeah—think so?"

There was a silence over the Com. Then: "Bel, is everybody on the bridge?"

"Yes, why do you ask?"

"Because I'm thinking about running out a Christmas Gun and shooting out your engine. I just wanted to make sure everybody is safe and whole on the bridge before I do it."

"Thought you said you weren't going to do that."

"I thought you said you wouldn't mind if I did."

"You might want to think twice about shooting my engine. My engine is the tach-scout ship *Westminster*. If you shoot her out, you'll be willfully destroying a Fleet vessel."

"Ah, just a couple of rounds, just a hole or two—she'll be fine after I board and patch her up."

Stenstrom laughed. "But, Captain, you're not giving me enough credit for having a devious mind. I figured you'd try such a thing, so I rigged the *Westminster* with a shaped charge of Shaddout. You run out a Christmas Gun and light her up, she'll blow hard."

"I see, and where did you get a shaped charge of Shaddout? That's not usually to be found in any quantity on a half scuttled ship."

"I borrowed it from Dry Dock 275—a virtual grocery store, that one."

On the Holo-Cone, Gwendolyn put her hand to her chin and thought. "Hmmm."

The two ships continued spiraling around each other, the *Demophalon John* darting in, and the *Seeker* matching the move.

After an hour or two, Gwendolyn Commed back in. "So, what are we going to do here, Bel? You can't get away from me, and I can't dock. I don't want you to exhaust yourselves needlessly. May I please make a suggestion?"

"Shoot."

"Why don't we dock, and you come aboard my ship—I promise I won't try to board. Then, you and I can, between ourselves, see if we can come up with a fair way to settle this."

"How do you propose we do that?"

"We'll have a contest of some sort. We'll play cards."

"I don't know how to play cards."

"I'll teach you a game. Something simple. I'm certain you'd be a natural, and I should think you'd have beginner's luck on your side. You win, you get to go to Bazz., I'll even help pull your ship, allow it to pick up a little speed. And, if I win, then you let me come aboard and we head back to Fleet."

Taara shook her head and butted in. "No, no, no … you don't settle something important with a game of cards. Got an issue to settle, you fight it out, and let me watch. Come on, Captain, you can take Bel here."

Gwendolyn looked at Taara, somewhat incredulous. She seemed for a moment like she was going to get mad, then she composed herself and smiled. "Quite the little thing, aren't you, Private?"

"I am. So, are you two going to fight or not?"

One of her crewmen handed Gwendolyn a report. She looked at it and appeared concerned. "Bel, in all seriousness, we've drifted off the shipping lanes. I ask that we bear to 9:45PM and get back into the patrolled regions. There's a whole lot of nothing out here, moving this slow and all, and drifting off the lanes is dangerous. That's how ships and people end up missing."

"Sorry I'm cramping your style, Captain."

Taara muted the Com and pointed at the lantern. "Fun and games aside, Bel, she's right. We're drifting awfully close to the Belt."

Gwendolyn continued. "It's all right. Come on, follow me back into the lanes—and for Creation's sake, stop calling me Captain—we're past that already. Once we're back in the lanes, we can continue this.—and I really think we should dock, and you come aboard my ship. If you don't want to play cards, we can box, as your first officer suggested. Then I'll knock you out fair and square and this will be over. If you don't board, I'm still thinking about using a Christmas Gun on you, so keep that in mind. In the meantime, follow me!"

Taara looked into her sensing visor. "The *Demophalon John* is turning away to 9:45PM, Bel."

"Very well, A-Ram, go ahead and follow her—just make sure she doesn't try anything funny along the way."

A-Ram adjusted his stance and made to turn the wheel. "Hey, Bel,—something's resisting me. I'm having trouble."

"Are we breaking down?" Stenstrom asked.

"I don't know, I don't think so. It just doesn't want to turn."

Taara looked at her visor. "Bel, I'm reading a large gravity well forming to our ventral. It's pulling us down."

Gwendolyn's voice filtered back over the Com. "What are you doing, Bel? Quit loitering back there. I'm not going to try anything until we get back into the shipping lanes."

"I'm not certain where's it's coming from, Gwen, but we're falling into a gravity well forming at our 6:00am."

The Com Holo flickered. Gwendolyn sounded alarmed. "I'm reading it too. I don't see anything on our charts indicating the presence of such a thing in this region of space. Look, Bel,—you need to let me dock and take you out of there. It might not be safe."

The lights on the bridge flickered and went out for a moment except for the lantern which burned steady and true.

They all heard a cold voice. *"Taara…"* it said.

"Oh, not now, for Creation's sake!" Stenstrom yelled.

There was a clank and the lights flickered. "Bel, the *Westminster* has just shut down!" Taara said.

"The Helm has gone dead right along with it!" A-Ram added.

"Bel!" Gwendolyn cried, her voice crackling over the flickering cone. "Your ship is fading from my screens. Enough of this, Bel, we're boarding to get you three out of there! We've played this game long enough! I want you out of there, now!"

Something enveloped them.

"Bel!!"

And the *Seeker* vanished.

8

—The Woman of Sand—

Stenstrom shot out of his chair. "Taara, what happened to the *Demophalon John*?"

"I don't know. According to this half-working viewer, we are on the other side of the League now." The lantern light spun about like a crazy top.

"What's our exact position?"

"Near 0, the Camalopardus area. Uninhabited space."

He turned to A-Ram. "Do we have helm control?"

"Yes, it's back, Bel. And I agree with Taara. According to my helm screens, we're way over on the other side of the League, near Xaphan space.

The Holo-cone suddenly came to life.

Something moved. A voice spoke. *"Paymaster Stenstrom, Lord of Belmont. Welcome, we have been expecting you."*

Stenstrom stood up. "Identify yourself!"

"Please come to the ship's Priory as soon as you are able. We will be waiting."

"Who is this?" he said. "Lilly? Is that you?"

No answer.

"I am not going anywhere until you have properly identified yourself."

"We have known you all your life. We held you aloft when you were a baby, barely a few moments old. We watched over you, and we protected you. We returned you to your mother's arms. And, we have known you … intimately, many times."

"Sisters?" Stenstrom asked.

"The Priory. We are waiting for you, Lord Belmont."

The lantern moved of its own accord. It wrenched itself free from the Missive's Panel and floated in mid air, its golden chain moving like a silk ribbon. Its guiding blue light went out, replaced by a purplish one.

"Hey!" Taara cried. "What's happening to our lantern? All my shit's dead now!"

The voice spoke again. *The Paramel is our property. We forgive you its unauthorized use. We await you in the Priory.*

"Umm, we sort of need that?" Taara piped. The voice did not reply. The Holo-cone then went out and died.

"Taara, what do we have left?"

"Nothing right now. The panel's shot without the lantern."

A-Ram held the wheel. "I don't like the sound of that, Bel."

"Me neither," Taara said. "The Sisters give me the horrors and they're stealing our bloody lantern."

"I told you we'd get into trouble using it," A-Ram said.

Stenstrom stood and checked his NTHs. "Well then, let's go, what are we waiting for?"

Following the floating lantern they slowly made their way out of the lit up bridge once again into the dark, stuffy interior of the ship.

They climbed down the Lift shaft and into the lower reaches of the "neck" of the ship. The dark halls of Deck 6 seemed even darker than before as they made their way down the corridor; the metal walls and looming shadows were alive with noises, rattles, and half-seen movement.

"Taara..."

"Belmont..."

"A-Ram..."

"HAHAHAHAHAHA!"

Shadow figures darted about in the lantern's purple light. Stenstrom drew his pistols, ready to fire.

They reached the Priory area and the lantern drifted in, its beam throwing all the tossed furniture and fallen pieces of art into bloody, jagged relief. Taara drew her huge SK and cocked it. They made their way through the antechamber to the forbidden rooms beyond.

"Lilly was in there," Stenstrom said, pointing to a side room.

A-Ram poked his head in. "There's nobody in there now."

Stenstrom looked around. "Lilly?" he called out, not expecting to hear a reply.

Wait …

"… Bel …" came a soft voice from the depths of the Priory.

"Did you hear that?" Taara asked. "Is that Lilly?"

"Sounds like her." Stenstrom quickened his pace. "Lilly!" he called out again. They reached a great oaken door and an adjacent open archway leading out into what looked like a dense wooded space that was slightly lit up in soft purple, joining the lantern's beam. "Through this door is a passage leading to the bottom of the ship. That's where you two were being held."

"That's where all the bodies were, right?" Taara asked, holding her SK.

"Yes." He pointed at the open archway. "And this … was filled-in when I was here before, it was just a blank wall. The lantern must be opening a gateway, just like Lilly had done."

"Gateway to where?" Taara asked.

Through the archway, Lilly's voice drifted out again, only this time it was anguished and sorrowful. *" …Bel …"*

"Lilly!" Stenstrom cried. "We're coming!" He turned to A-Ram and Taara. "Come on, let's go!" They continued through the arch and down the path. Trees and low brush were everywhere. An obvious path led away to a bend through the trees. Grass and dry leaves crunched under their boots, and the temperature changed. Looking up, there was sky, purplish and dusted with starlight.

"Where are we?" A-Ram asked. "Is this the Astral Plane?"

Stenstrom checked his gear. "No, no it's not. Lilly said that the Sisters' Priories are connected to some sort of pocket plane or dimension that they have free access to. That's how the Sisters always seem to escape a doomed starship," he said. "Lilly led me through here to Kana, just like we're doing now, only this time it's not Kana. The sky's the wrong color and I don't recognize the stars."

"The damn Sisters can't have the lantern back, we need it, Bel!" Taara said. She reached for its chain, but it moved away, floating on air light as a filament, easily avoiding her grasp.

They continued down the path until they came to a clearing. In the center of the clearing were two structures. One was a large gray building made of stone, squat and dome-like rising up about a hundred feet. The other was a narrow, cylindrical tower composed of lacy, purplish-blue metal. A-Ram craned his neck—the tower went up and up until it broke the clouds and faded from view—a rather dizzying sight to behold.

"What's that?" A-Ram asked.

"That tower looks high enough to enter orbit. I'm going to puke," Taara said.

"Oh, come on, where's the pluck I've come to expect from you?" Stenstrom said. He took a good look at the gray stone building ahead and stopped. "I've seen this building. Lilly showed it to me. Come on. Let's get to the bottom of this."

A-Ram was apprehensive. "I know the Sisters' protocols, Bel—entering the Priory is forbidden unless you've been invited. You were invited, not either of us—not me certainly as I'm a bloody Untouchable. The Sisters might get angry."

"I'm certain the Sisters won't mind your presence."

"The Sisters have belittled me and my family for as long as I can remember," he said with a distinct touch of bitterness. "For those of us here who have not had the pleasure of their repeated attention, I find it most galling."

A door opened in the center of the dome-like building with a gritty slide. The darkened doorway invited them to enter.

"Lilly?" Stenstrom called out.

No answer. The lantern cast its beam on the open doorway.

Slowly, they approached and went inside. They rubbed their eyes and struggled to see in the dark, the lantern's light lost in the vastness. Within was a modestly furnished open space, with the heights of the dome hovering and rustling overhead with over-grown ivy and nesting birds. Dead leaves littered the floor.

Four figures sat in the center of the dome. Stenstrom remembered seeing them also.

"They did it all, Bel," Lilly had said.

"Who are you?" Stenstrom called out. The figures didn't answer.

Four Sisters sat on small couches in the center of the dome. They had no Marines with them, which was an odd sight for Stenstrom who honestly couldn't recall a time in the past when he saw a Sister without one in attendance, even when he was participating in their Program. As usual, they sat with perfect posture and grace, their hands placed properly in their laps.

"They did it all ..."

"Sisters?" he asked.

In addition to the missing Marines, the Sisters seemed a bit odd in other small ways as well. Though they were sitting, they appeared abnormally elongated, and Stenstrom guessed they might very well be freakishly tall if they stood up. As per usual for the Sisters, they were quite pretty—in a motherly sort of way, though one of them had a rather ovoid, somewhat reptilian face; Stenstrom imagined that, if she were to open her mouth, she might have a forked tongue and possibly snake's fangs. Also, their complexions, though perfect, appeared distinctly green, though that was probably a trick of the dim lighting of the dome.

Their dress was also a little off from most of the Sisters Stenstrom had ever seen. They had the usual white robes, wrapped-up arms to the wrists, and large, cornette-like headdresses, but instead of the usual sky blue traveling cloaks the Sisters always wore—a very comforting color—these wore either dark blue or black cloaks over their white robes.

Under the heights of the dome, the two opposing sides stared at each other for an agonizingly long stretch of time. Leaves crunched underfoot, as birds overhead rustled about and chirped.

Finally, Stenstrom spoke. "Great Sisters, it is with profound relief that we find you here today. Your presence is comforting, as always."

The Sisters smiled and then looked at Private Taara. She gulped and took a few steps forward. "I am honored that the Sisterhood of Light would grace me as the vessel of their thoughts," she said in a quiet, practiced manner.

She spoke again, this time words not of her own making. The Sisters barged into her head and took her over.

"Lord Belmont," Taara said, suddenly carrying herself in an alien demeanor. "It pleases us truly to see you safe and unharmed. You have caused quite a stir in the Fleet Admiralty, so we have been told."

Another Sister barged into Taara's head. Again she spoke. "We are pleased at your progress, Lord Belmont. You have shown great ingenuity and tenacity in this matter. We are most impressed."

Again, there was a bout of silence as the two groups stared at each other, Taara trying to clear her head.

The lantern floating high overhead came to life, throwing a strong yellow beam down on the Sisters. Bathed in its living light, they suddenly no longer seemed green or reptilian or overly tall. They appeared as fair, flawless ladies. "Yes," Taara said, "we ought to be more careful with our things. The wonders the Paramel shows true."

There was another bout of silence, then Taara spoke again. "Lord A-Ram," one of them said through her mouth. "We are curious—why did you choose to join Lord Belmont in space? Certainly, you knew there might be consequences. We had you decided as a hopeless wretch, a spineless coward and progeny of bad chefs and bad Brandtball players not worth another look. You and your family."

A-Ram slightly reacted.

"Why not just Stare him and find out for yourself?" Taara said, momentarily regaining control of her mouth. Just as quickly, the Sisters wrenched it back.

"Because that is so uncivilized, Private," she said responding to herself.

A-Ram looked at the floor and answered. "I thought what the Admiral was doing to Lord Belmont was unjust, and most cruel. I thought the Admiral was cheating Lord Belmont out of his coin, and for no good reason. And I thought he was a decent fellow who deserved help. I wanted to help him. I wanted to be his friend."

"And, you've no regrets?"

"None, Great Sister."

"Ah, true friendship. You shall be rewarded, Lord A-Ram, for your unexpected display of courage. We appreciate and newly admire you, sir. Perhaps we, like everyone else, were wrong about you, and failed to see the heart beating within your frail chest."

The Sisters turned to Taara. It was odd hearing her speak about herself in the third person. "And you, Private Taara. Always the little rebel, are you not? So lonely and starving for attention, and, like Lord A-Ram, not near the hopeless wretch your people thought you to be, are you? You too shall be rewarded for your bravery. And yes, you are correct, Private—we are dangerous. We are savage and brutal, truth be told, which is why we have asked you three to come to us. We have work for you all, you in particular, Lord Belmont. And, you shall be suitably rewarded."

"Work?" he said. "I don't understand."

The Sisters were silent.

"I heard Lilly's voice," he asked. "Lillian of Gamboa. Is she here?"

Taara approached him, fully under the Sister's control. "Of course she's here."

"May I see her? She needs me."

"Does she? Ah, young love. Yes, you will see her, but first, allow us to ask a question. That mask, Lord Belmont. Tell us, why do you wear it?"

Stenstrom struggled for words. "I … admired the exploits of Lord Terrance of Walther."

Taara gazed up at him, her eyes alien and unfamiliar. "Ah, we understand. The Mad Lord of Walther. How interesting. Certainly you know our official policy regarding the Mad Lord of Walther was public dismissal, seizure of lands, censure, banishment, and, his eventual execution. And, is that the only reason?"

Stenstrom stood there.

"You feel shy," Taara said. "You needn't feel shy with us—of all people, after all we've shared together." Her hand, controlled by the Sisters, wandered to his chest and moved down past his sash in a provocative manner. "Allow us to answer for you. Could it also be that you wear a mask because you believe that your late mother once cast a spell that will tear your soul apart should you choose to engage in dangerous activities, and that the mask, and the magical items you have hidden within it, protects you? That, in trying to save you, your mother poised a knife at your throat—just like she always had? In your chest, perhaps? Ah, the price of love. And now, being deceased, there is no way to remove the spell—that you have an everlasting stain on your soul, is that correct?"

Stenstrom answered: "Yes, Great Sisters." What was the point in lying?

"Clearly, we know all about your mother's former activities, and could have acted should we have had a mind to do so. We did not, for your sake. Tell us, how do you feel about your mother?"

"I love my mother, to this day. I would have her no other way than what she was. I failed her. I didn't come home when she asked."

"Spoken like a true son. It will interest you to know that your mother *did not* cast the spell that has imperiled your soul. Your mother, throughout your life, loved you very much—to the point of madness. She set no demons against you. She put no stain on your soul."

Stenstrom considered that for a moment. "Then where did the Soul Devourers come from?"

Taara's eyes grew wide. "We did it, Lord Belmont," she said. "It was not your mother who put the curse on your soul … it was us, in this very spot."

Lilly, and the scene at the pool came flooding back to him.

"They did it!" she said. *"They did it all!"*

The Sisters did it.

Stenstrom stood there. "I don't—I don't understand …"

"Do you not remember seeing us in the mirror aboard your old ship? Do you not recall feeling our hands claw at your chest? Yes, we have been lending our influence into your life for some time now, since you were a child. It was through our efforts that you survived your birth, for you nearly perished. We have been always near, guiding you with a firm but loving hand."

Stenstrom didn't know how to take any of this. "Sisters, I do not understand your continued interest in me. Who am I but a Lord of Belmont?"

They looked at each other and smiled. "Who indeed? Across the League there are whispered tales of solitary men who are of exceptional quality. On Kana there are tales of the Star that does not Fall. On Onaris, the Lone Rider. On Bazz, there is the 'It' man—the man who comes and goes. You, Lord Belmont, are the 'It' man, the Lone Rider. You are the Star that does not Fall."

The Sisters paused for a moment. Stenstrom didn't know what to do or what to say. A-Ram shuffled uncomfortably. "Sisters," A-Ram said quietly, looking at the floor, unable to meet their gaze. "Those are children's stories."

The Sisters ignored him. Taara continued in their voice. "These special men have the genetic ability to receive and utilize our power. They are no child's story, Lord A-Ram. There have been others like you through the centuries: Homma of Telmus Falls, Atrajak of Want, Billus the Knave, Darius Jones of Bazz, and, most recently, Terrance, the Mad Lord of Walther. Normally, the birth of these 'It' men, using the Bazz reference, are rare—perhaps once in the passing of centuries," another Sister said. "We had our Lord Terrance of Walther and did not expect, per our calculations, to see another 'It' man for three hundred years—and he was to be born in the Barrow region according to our charts. We do manipulate things a bit with our Celebrants. And then, there was you, out of the clear blue sky, the 'It' Man we never saw coming."

Taara held her hand where it was at his crotch, her eyes burning. "We checked our calculations—certainly we'd made a mistake." Her fingers tightened. "No, no … we made no mistake, there was to be no 'It' Man from Esther for another thousand years, yet there you were. How could this be? How, how?" Taara spoke in a dreamy, breathy sort of fashion. "We were quite determined to find out, so much so that a Grand Abbess gave your case her personal attention. And, eventually we had the answer: you are a manufactured 'It' Man. You came to be via chemical methods, not genetics. Your departed mother used chemical tinctures to enhance her body for years to prevent the creation of a male child, to blackmail your father into quitting the Fleet and staying home with her. Her internal chemistry, we found, had changed because of the prolonged exposure to these chemicals, creating a unique situation in her womb. And then your father, craving a son after twenty-nine daughters, took the so-called God-Sperm potion from Bazz. These two tinctures collided in your mother's womb, creating quite the spectacle.

"And there was yet a third element to this odd puzzle. We found, in our analysis, that the potion your father took on Bazz was tainted with an unknown substance of caustic properties. We believe the potion he drank on Bazz was poisoned. The exact nature of this poison remains a mystery—clearly, an extraordinary set of circumstances conspired together to create you, Lord Belmont,—the 'It' Man who nearly slipped through our attention."

Stenstrom opened his mouth to pose several questions, and Taara, under the Sisters' control, cut him off.

"We are fortunate to have you, Lord Belmont, for there is work to be done. Please attend. The recent Kestral Affair revealed to us that we are arrogant, and possibly out of touch with the happenings of the League. It is our responsibility; all the people who died—they are on our hearts. We are here to protect the people, and we failed. In light of this, we feel it is time to resurrect an old custom—for the good and safety of the League. Your hero, the Mad Lord of Walther, was our Fist—he performed our bidding. Homma, Atrajak, Billus, Darius Jones—they were all our Fists too."

Another Sister barged into Taara's head. "You are our Fist as well. We of the Sisterhood are in an unusual situation, Lord Belmont. We have power—it is largely understood that we have power, yet, if we openly display too much of it, the people begin to fear. The people fret for their freedom, and we suppose there is validity to such a feeling. Therefore, we cannot allow the League to see us unchained, unfettered. We must smile and bow and be suitably demure for the people. We, in times past, have granted some of our power to select male individuals—the 'It' Men with extraordinary qualities—the Lone Riders. A heroic male figure doing extraordinary things seems much less threatening to the masses at large than we of the Sisterhood doing it—appearances are everything, are they not? You, Lord Belmont, possess those exceptional qualities, and we thanked the Elders for your birth. We have steered you to this moment throughout your life. You, like those select men before you, are our Fist."

A-Ram found his voice and spoke up. "But, Great Sisters, all the men you mention—Homma of Telmus Falls, Atrajak of Want, Billus the Knave, Darius Jones, and even the Mad Lord of Walther—they were all lunatics. Homma was a cannibal, the Telmus area of Vithland still reeks with the ghosts of the devoured he made. Atrajak was a Slayer of Sisters and has been erased from the history books, Billus the Knave nearly committed genocide on Hoban, Darius Jones was a raving madman running nude through the streets, and the Sisterhood burned Lord Terrance of Walther's holdings to the ground, publically called him out and executed him."

All four Sisters were suddenly pained—heartbroken. They wiped away tears.

"In the case of Lord Walther, that was a carefully crafted public ruse. As his name implied, Lord Walther truly went mad toward the end of his life. We took too much from him. We cherished Lord Walther—he honored us, he did his service to the League well, though at great cost to himself. Behold …"

Floating high overhead, the lantern cast a beam of strong yellow light to the far end of the dome.

A crypt appeared. Standing over the crypt was the large statue of a man. Hat, billowy pantaloons, spurred boots, the handsome face behind a jeweled mask—Stenstrom had seen this man before when he was a child—it was the Mad Lord.

"We keep his remains here, close to us, for we loved him so. As he inspired the hearts and minds of the League, so too he did for us as well. To keep our secrets safe, we had to destroy him, to take everything he had, though the penance we pay in grief continues to this day. You, Lord Belmont, can only hope to be half the man he was."

The Sisters let Taara go for a moment. They all turned to the crypt and looked at it with longing and reverence.

They then turned back and continued. "To properly honor that man, we are not going to repeat our past mistakes with you. We of the Sisterhood are not perfect. We have failed several times with the 'It' men of old. Homma had access to our power all the time, and it tore through his soul—he went mad with the power we gave him. Atrajak too, showed the same degeneration. We hit upon the idea of limiting the 'It' man's access to our power, and Billus seemed to thrive much better than Homma or Atrajak, but he too eventually fell into madness. Darius Jones was simply unhinged from the start. With the Mad Lord, we used Sisters who were genetically compatible with him to fill the tower, and he thrived for years and years. His madness came upon him suddenly."

Another Sister spoke. "And hence, our coming to you, Lord Belmont, as often as we did. Many of the Sisters slumbering in the Great Tower outside are of your blood—are of your seed."

And another. "It wasn't our power that drove Lord Terrance truly mad. It was something else. Someone introduced a poison into his system, and that's what drove him mad. Additionally, Lord Terrance, as was Homma and Atrajak and Billus before him, was alone. Alone with the weight of the League on their shoulders, alone with our power. We have made mistakes with the 'It' men of the past. We shall not repeat our mistakes with you. At last, the Lone Rider shall be alone no more. Those who have chosen to stand at your side, shall guard your soul, your sanity, and keep you well. You shall be surrounded by people who love you. Look, Lord Belmont, look what we have given you."

Stenstrom found himself rather mesmerized by all of this. He struggled to speak. "What … what have you given me?"

"We've given you everything. We gave you the desire to long for the stars, to want to be a part of something larger than yourself. We gave you your thirst for knowledge and adventure. We gave you your membership to the Bones Club, and the IBBAANA, and we gave you the *Seeker*."

"The *Seeker*?" You gave it to me?"

"Yes, we wanted you to have it. Captain Gona, hearing those troubling noises—thinking his ship was haunted, went fleeing into retirement. The Admiralty wanted to decommission the ship, and we pressured them not to. We kept our thoughts plain to the Admiralty regarding the *Seeker,* leaving the way open, for you."

"Captain Gona is correct regarding the haunting, Sisters. This ship is infested with demons, as we heard them as well," A-Ram said, finding his voice after some time.

The Sisters smiled. "Is it?"

From behind Stenstrom came a chilling voice: *"… Taara …"* He turned and, of course, nobody was there.

Another voice came. *"… Where is your Mother, Lord Belmont …"*

He turned, but again, nothing was there.

"We are the demons besetting this ship, Lord Belmont. It is we who haunt it," Taara said. "We needed certain things of you. Your training as a sorcerer, we assisted with that. The Soul Devourers who pursued you across the face of the League, we did that as well, to drive you in the direction we wanted you to go. We could not allow you to simply join the Fleet and become another officer. We had to make you something else—something novel. The HRN coat you wear, your mask—we wanted to self-style you as an eccentric, as with the Mad Lord before you. Great men are always eccentric, are they not? We had to turn you into the fool, into a cad, so that we could publically dismiss and laugh you off as a mere oddity not worth a second thought.

Who would suspect that the masked fool actually wields the Sisters' power? And then, to top things off, we gave you this ship."

Stenstrom took exception. "No, no, Great Sisters. I am sorry, you did none of that. My coat, my schooling, my admission to the Bones Club, my occupation as Fleet Paymaster, that was all Lilly's doing."

The Sisters smiled. "And we gave you your Lilly as well."

"Come again?"

"You refer to Lady Lillian of Gamboa, of course. Lillian of Gamboa does not exist, Lord Belmont."

They paused a moment to allow Stenstrom to drink in the information. Then, they continued: "Oh, there actually is a Lillian of the House of Gamboa, a small, insignificant woman your mother once fancied, and she did come to your home on two occasions to meet you, but not a third time, for she developed a powerful dislike of you. The woman you met and came to know is not her."

Stenstrom, from his previous meeting with Lilly in the bowels of the ship, knew all that, but it was still odd to hear out loud. "I don't understand. You must be mistaken."

The Sisters smiled. "Are we? Look, Lord Belmont," one of them said pointing to the far end of the dome near the Mad Lord's crypt. "See your Lilly …"

Stenstrom turned. There, in the far distance, he saw a blonde-headed woman in a pink Gamboa gown emerge from the shadows. He saw her holding a parasol.

"Lilly?" he said. "Lilly!"

"Stand fast, please, Lord Belmont," the Sisters said.

Not hearing them, he sprang over the Sisters' couches and ran toward her, his HRN coattails flapping. "Lilly, Lilly!" he cried.

The possibilities registered through his mind as he sprinted toward her. The question that had been festering in his mind, "What is Lilly" was about to be revealed.

Was she an enchantress?

Was she a Sister?

????

As he approached, she glanced at him and backed up into the darkness near the crypt. After a few more steps, he was there, the statue of the Mad Lord towering over him.

In a corner next to the crypt, Lilly stood. She was pressed into the wall, the back of her hand demurely covering her face. Her expression was that of sorrow and anguish.

"Lilly?"

No answer. She didn't move.

The radiant beam from the lantern floating high overhead panned down and shined on Lilly.

Lillian of Gamboa transformed in the light—in her place was a perfectly formed pillar of sand in her image; pink gown gone, blue eyes gone.

Just sculpted sand in human shape.

He gazed at it in horror. "… Lilly…" he managed to stammer.

The sand glistened back at him. The molded face in sand looked sad, like she had just lost something dear to her.

"You have loved a woman of sand, Lord Belmont, all these years," the Sisters said from far away. "She was our gift to you—your protector, your tutor … your lover, arming you for battle, sending you in the direction we wanted you to go. That was her purpose and it has come to an end, as has she."

Everything spun—he felt his brain short-circuiting. All the truths of the world were suddenly gone—now there was chaos.

Lilly emerged from the darkness, Lilly slayed hundreds of Soul Devourers.

"I accept!" Lilly had said, taking his hand.

Everything he had done, he had done for her, for Lilly. She suggested he go to school, and so he went to school. She suggested he join the Bones Club, so he did it. She gave him the idea of becoming a Fleet Paymaster, she selected his HRN uniform for him.

She wound him up and set him to it …

She did it …

She did it all!

How could this be? How could he have not known? Even his mother had been fooled.

Rooted in normalcy. Talented, but mundane.

Sand … All this time.

Alitrix. Lady Alitrix knew. *"I don't know what she is, but she's not a woman … It's as if she is steering you to some pre-determined destination."*

And Kaly. What had Kaly seen? *"Who was that you ditched me for?"*

"How do you mean?"

"I don't know, she seemed kind of strange … like a mannequin …"

And here was Lilly, and she was naught but a woman of sand. There was a word scraped into the sand above her breast:

"I ACCEPT"

He reached out to her, his mask becoming damp. "It's … it's all right, Lilly, I'm going to take you home …"

He touched her face and she fell apart. He watched the sand slip through his fingers and fall to the floor in an uncaring hiss. There was something hidden in the mound of sand as it fell away, many thin, squarish objects stacked together in the center. He probed the mound with his hands.

The square objects were letters, dozens of them. All the letters he'd written Lilly over the years, here they were, unopened, unread—intercepted, discolored in sand. His love's discourse stacked up and hidden near the heart of an artificial woman.

"LILLY!!" he choked. The letters slipped out of his hands and drifted to the top of the Mad Lord's crypt.

He fell to his knees. The loss, the feeling of total loss. He openly wept.

The Sisters were unimpressed. "Come now, Lord Belmont, do get a hold of yourself. You are making a scene. Please, attend to us at once."

His eyes flashed in anger.

The Sisters!

How could they?

HOW DARE THEY?

This was all their fault! They murdered his Lilly!

"They did it all …"

He drew his NTH's, ready to slay the four of them here and now.

Before another moment passed, he was TK'ed off the ground, his pistols pointing toward the dome above, and was carried back in attendance to the Sisters. They spun him around and forced him to face them.

"What is the point of this, Lord Belmont?" Taara asked for them in a stern voice. "It is done. Cry over your phantom love another time, and face reality. We tried to give you love, albeit temporarily. We tried to guide you, to do you a favor."

He hung there in their TK and wept, uncontrollably.

One of the Sisters appeared perturbed. "Really, Lord Belmont, this display is most unbecoming. You should …"

A-Ram stirred. He spoke up. "And so, this is the Sisterhood of Light, is it? I spent my youth believing there was something wrong with me and my family: 'See the A-Rams,' they said in Calvert. 'Look at how the Sisters regard them not. Look at them—they are fools.' And we were humbled and shamed, not worthy of the Sisters' attention. Now, here you are revealed before us: tormentors, manipulators and inflictors of pain … little more than Black Hats without the masks. Look what you've done to him, and all on a whim!"

One of the Sisters turned to face A-Ram, but another one seated nearby raised a hand, and the first sank back into her seat.

The Sister in the center couch watched Stenstrom weep and her expression changed. She pulled him close to her, reached out, and wiped away one of his tears.

She appeared sad. "We meant to give you love, safety and guidance. We did not mean for you to become devoted to her—we expected your long departures to prevent that. What do you want, Lord Belmont?" Taara said in a kind voice.

"I want Lilly! I want to kill you!"

Taara walked up to Stenstrom, reached up, and took his sobbing face into her hands. "Perhaps we have underestimated the effect our woman of sand would have on you. Perhaps we underestimated you as well. We have used similar tactics before, and our fellows did never respond in quite this fashion. I wonder if all those who came before you were men at all—even our beloved Lord Walther. Perhaps we underestimated the capacity of your heart to love—to cherish the woman of sand, to truly love Lillian of Gamboa. Perhaps our hearts are so old, that we have forgotten what that is like. If that is the case, then we repent what we have inflicted upon you. We do not mean to be cruel."

The Sister lifted her hand, and his hat and mask were gently TK'ed off his head and face. "We wish to offer you a gift." She took the hovering mask and unwound it with TK. The three silver hermelins he had fashioned to protect himself from the Soul Devourers came out of the fabric and floated on air. Taara spoke. "Were we truly cruel and uncaring, we would simply give you back the woman of sand, the phantom of Lillian of Gamboa that we made all too well."

His golden locket with Lilly's portrait in it came floating out of his coat pocket. It hovered near his face and opened.

There was Lilly's beautiful face. He wondered if she had actually painted it herself, or if a Sister somewhere in one of their strongholds had done it. He was racked with anguish.

"But, you would be living an illusion—a lie," Taara said. "She is not real, her love for you fabricated, pre-programmed. A heart such as yours deserves a heart in kind. She was simply a tool we used—a touch of jasmine, a hint of rose, and a pile of virgin sand is all she ever was. We would not have you trapped in such a fantasy. Your fine heart is broken, and it is our fault— fear not, for we shall repair your broken heart, yea, we shall strengthen it. You deserve a real love, one that is earned and cultivated with time. You, It Man, will not be alone as was our beloved Mad Lord. You will be surrounded by your friends and those who love you, your soul kept safe. You shall love another and forget all about Lillian of Gamboa."

With a flick of her wrist, the three hermelins and his golden locket clattered away and fell to the floor. "You won't be needing those anymore—we take back the curse on your soul," Taara said. In a flash of blue light, a new hermelin formed, spinning in mid-air. It formed into the shape of a man in a long coat holding his hands to his heart. "We replace the old magic with a new hermelin, one that shall tend to your broken heart and shield you from all the torments that go with it."

The hermelin floated into the loose folds of the mask. It returned to him and settled back over his eyes, the cloth damp from his tears. "Wear this and be protected, until your true love comes to steal your heart afresh. Your true love shall unmask you, Lord Belmont, our It Man and Lone Rider. Through you, we shall atone for our mistakes of the past."

Stenstrom stopped weeping and the Sisters released him from their TK. His hat floated back down onto his head. He stood up, wiping his face, catching his breath. A-Ram put his hand on his shoulder.

"You all right, Bel?" he asked.

He tried to speak. "I'm all right, A-Ram." He turned to the Sisters. "Why, why have you done this to me?" he asked wiping his eyes.

"To groom you to serve the League, as all the It Men before you have done. You have work that is bigger than us all. Dedication to the League is the hallmark of the Sisterhood. Everything we do is for the good and safety of the League. That tower you were admiring on your way here. It contains over a thousand Sisters, many of which are of your blood, all of whom have dedicated themselves to this task. They sleep within it, adding their power to the service of the League. You shall have occasional access to this power. We shall allow you to borrow it when we see fit."

Another Sister grabbed into Taara's mind. "Likewise, to protect you from the prolonged exposure that damned Homma and Atrajak, we shall take the power back when we see fit. As long as you can see Camalopardus in the sky, the constellation of the candle flame that is the center of the Solar Empire—the Elder's universe, you will have access to the League's power. All under its light is the domain of the Solar Empire the Elders founded long ago, that which we keep in trust from ages past. You will be our Fist. You will follow our commands, searching the League in your *Seeker*, looking for signs of the Kestral, and where you find them, you will destroy them. That is your ongoing task."

9

—KNIFE—

"Protect us from evil, Lord Belmont. The Kestrals are intertwined in the fabric of the League, and you shall save us from them. We have prepared you to protect us. There are others serving this cause as well. Your new friends—they are at your side. There is this great ship, which we have given to you. And look, there is another as well …"

From out of nowhere, a slim female appeared before Stenstrom. She was about 5'7 in height, slender and silent. She wore a loose-fitting scarlet robe that ended just above her knees. Her legs were covered in black wrappings, and her arms and hands were also covered in black. She wore a nimble pair of black shoes. On her head was a featureless black sash, completely covering her face.

"Who is this? A Black Hat?" Stenstrom asked.

"Allow us to introduce Knife, a Shadow tech female who is in the service of the Sisterhood. Not a Painter, not a Hammer, she is of Knife-class, mobile, solitary and deadly. It is through her that we shall command you. Where she goes, you will follow. She is your enemy. You will pursue her, dog her every step, and flush her out time and time again, and it is there you will find signs of the Kestral and destroy them. Our Lord Walther had his Sedgwick of Kold, his constant enemy; you shall have your Knife, your ready Knife."

"I will not do this," Stenstrom said.

"It is done, Lord Belmont. And, you will notice that we have not asked you—we are telling you. We have not labored this long to be denied. You are our Fist, square with it or not. Your flesh belongs to the League, as do we all."

"You cannot compel me to do something that I do not choose to do."

"Oh, can we not? We are dedicated to the preservation of the League, and in that task we are prepared to do what needs to be done, even if that includes sacrificing ourselves, Knife, and you in the process. Consider the scores of Sisters asleep in the tower outside—your flesh and blood. Consider Knife. She has given her life in this effort as well—look what she has sacrificed, no hearth, no home, no loving Lord at her side—she would have made you a fine wife. But, instead, she is alone and she is your Knife, and all out of love for the League. She is a hero, though none but you three will ever know that. She shall be a dark spirit, despised, feared, her name reviled in the posts, forever your enemy. Where she goes, you will follow, else she will create chaos and shed blood, all on your hands should you choose not to follow and stop her."

Knife stepped forward. She pulled her mask off. Underneath, there was the face of a pretty young woman, blue-eyed, sandy haired. She looked at Stenstrom hard.

"I wanted you to see me," she said quietly. "You will never see my face again, nor hear me speak. My service to the League begins now, and there shall be no mercy—for neither you nor me. My service shall end with my death."

She put her mask back on, turned and vanished.

"Sisters, this is barbaric," A-Ram said.

They turned to him. "We are barbaric, Lord A-Ram. We are passionate, savage, ruthless, brutal, and determined. We are the dark arm of the Sisterhood, seldom seen in public. We are not the smiling Sisters who walk the streets. We are not the Sisters who drink tea in the Houses of the Great Lords. We are the ones kept in the shadows, scorching the earth, punishing those needing punishing. We are the slayers and the death-dealers. That does not mean we do not love the League any less, or feel not for a man whose heart we broke. We do what must be done out of love, and so shall Knife, and so shall you."

"I shall not," Stenstrom said.

The Sisters smiled. "Ah, how nice—suitably outraged and demure. You play your part well. Now, to your reward. And we do not simply offer a single reward—our rewards are ongoing. We can offer you most anything you desire."

"I told you, I want no part of this."

They ignored him. "Do you want this little girl here? We will give her to you if you wish, in place of your Lillian of Gamboa. You may do what you will with her—love her, cherish her, abuse her … kill her; it's your choice."

"Taara is my friend."

"Yes, indeed …" One of the Sisters waved her hand and, before Stenstrom, an image appeared. In it, he could see Lt. Gwendolyn walking around on her bridge. She seemed concerned as she prowled the floor.

"How about this one," the Sisters asked. "This Zenon woman? Is she your friend too? She's looking for you, and she is frantic, though she'll not find you, not here. She's a firm, strapping girl—will provide you with many fine children."

"I've never even met Captain Gwendolyn in person."

"Well then, look …"

On the bridge of the *Demophalon John*, Stenstrom could see Gwendolyn and the crew busily moving about.

And there was Knife, red-robed and black-masked. Apparently Cloaked in some fashion, she walked up behind Gwendolyn and raised her hands, clenching them into claws.

"It begins Paymaster," the Sisters said through Taara. "Knife is on the prowl."

"What is she doing?"

"She is doing her duty—she is forcing you to act, to follow her, just as Sedgwick of Kold forced the Mad Lord to follow him. No telling what she might do on that ship. Might find the Captain in pieces—might find them all in pieces, the ship that became a ghost ship, its crew mysteriously slaughtered. No telling how many people she will be willing to sacrifice to compel you to do your duty. Do you wish that on your soul, Lord Belmont, that you could have stopped her and did nothing?"

"The Zenon woman is moments from death, Lord Belmont," another Sister said through Taara.

Stenstrom stared at the image in horror. He saw Knife move her gloved fingers and a small cut appeared on Gwendolyn's right cheek. It began gushing blood—the Captain apparently not aware she'd been cut, continued doing what she was doing. Somebody pointed at her and she reached up and touched her face, horrified.

Knife's hands went to Gwendolyn's throat.

Stenstrom couldn't take it anymore. "Sisters, you said I was to have a reward … then I wish Captain Gwendolyn as my reward. Safe and unharmed, along with her crew."

"And why, Paymaster? This woman, as you say, means nothing to you. And, if we are not mistaken, she threatened to physically assault you earlier."

"We got off to a rough start. It was my fault—I insulted her. She had a job to do, like it or not. Do not harm her, Sisters, I am warning you."

The Sisters eyes widened. Then they smiled. "Very well, be it so."

On the *Demophalon John's* bridge, Knife disappeared and Lt. Gwendolyn turned away, her face bleeding, unaware of the death she had just avoided.

"A fine choice, sir," the Sisters said. "She will bear that cut upon her face as a scar for the rest of her life. Again, she is a fine, strong woman—your match in many ways. She is yours, now and forever."

Stenstrom shook his head. "I simply did not want Gwendolyn or her crew harmed."

"You love her, Lord Belmont," the Sisters said.

"I do not know Captain Gwendolyn. I love Lilly, though your sorcery has currently drained it from me," he replied.

"As we said, Lillian of Gamboa, as you know her, does not exist. Your fate is with Gwendolyn, Lady of Prentiss—Gwendolyn the Scarred. She will remove the mask and its protective hermelin from your face."

Stenstrom made to object, but Taara cut him off. "And you, Private Taara, what do you want?"

The Sisters released Taara and she staggered to the floor. Stenstrom knelt over her and took her hand. She wheezed for a moment. "Taara," he said. "Say nothing—you needn't be a part of this."

She spoke, this time with her own voice. "I … want to keep doing what I've been doing. I like knowing things that I shouldn't know and doing things I shouldn't be able to do. I want to continue."

The Sisters took her back over. "Ah," she said. "Most practical. Look, you shall have your wish."

As Stenstrom watched, the MOLLY around her neck somehow began to melt into her flesh. After a moment, it was gone. "There, now you may continue as you have been."

"But, demons will come for her soul," A-Ram said.

"As we have established, Lord A-Ram—*we* are the demons. We take exception when mystical objects such as the MOLLY are used too much, and we punish the practitioner, sometimes with death. As Private Taara is in the service of our Fist, we will waive that punishment. As long as she serves our Fist, she need not fear."

A-Ram stepped forward. "Sisters," he said quietly. "You said I too was to have a reward?"

Taara, fully possessed by the Sisters, smiled and sauntered up to him. "Indeed we did, Lord A-Ram. You showed great spirit in assisting Lord Belmont—we've not seen that from you before. Therefore, you will have a reward—the first of many. What is it to be?"

A-Ram stood there. "I—I would like you to Stare me for the answer. I'll not say it out loud."

The Sisters, sitting on their couches, tittered. One of them leaned forward, eyes-wide and Stared him.

Stenstrom watched. The Sister's eyes were big and fixed on A-Ram. They were the eyes of a beast, a wild animal. He noticed A-Ram twitching under her Stare. He was in pain.

After a few more moments, the Sister leaned back and gave him an open-lipped smile. *"Oh, really ... "* Taara said under her influence. She snorted. "You feel ignored? You feel slighted, do you? You showed us nothing, Lord A-Ram. You were a cowardly simpleton not worth our time, as was your whole family. Bad chefs, bad Brandtball players, conceited liars for brothers and you, using your MOLLY to win a pie-eating contest. Again, perhaps we misjudged you—underestimated you, just like Admiral Derlith and everybody else, seeing nothing but the frail little man with morbid hobbies. You hide your admirable qualities well, but they are there, nevertheless, and, on your tiny shoulders rests the soul of our Fist. Very well, Lord A-Ram, make your choice."

The light from the lantern panned away. The fair guise the Sisters had been wearing passed with it. There they were again: strange, elongated, somewhat sinister.

A-Ram stood there a moment, and then he walked a step or two and took his place in front of the Sister who had just Stared him. Slowly, her wild-animal eyes fixed on his, she stood up. Sitting there on her couch it was hard to tell just how tall she was, but, as Stenstrom had suspected, she, standing erect, had to be at least eight feet tall.

Towering over A-Ram, she pulled off her headdress and tossed it aside.

Cinder black hair came spilling out of her wrappings. She opened and closed her fists, knuckles popping, her fingers moving in a spidery fashion. She appeared to want to eat A-Ram. To his credit, he stood there and didn't flinch.

Taara hovered next to A-Ram. "Oh, we are going to enjoy this, Lord A-Ram. You have made an interesting and exotic choice. Again, you have impressed us with your unexpected bravery today, and we shall make it worth your while. Again, this shall be but the first of many rewards you shall enjoy."

Taara leaned into him—fully possessed. She started speaking in the first person—Sisters rarely did that, and the things she said gave Stenstrom considerable pause. Her voice was laced with savagery.

"I am going to take you places seldom seen! And I am not going to be gentle—I am going to burn you, A-Ram. Burn you!" The Sister reached out and grabbed him by the nape of his shirt. She lifted him off the ground and pulled him close ... and she licked him slowly, passionately.

Stenstrom, shocked, couldn't look any further, he turned away.

Taara spoke. "The meeting is over, you two may leave. Lord A-Ram shall be returned to you tomorrow."

As commanded, Stenstrom began walking away, not really of his own accord. Soon Taara, released from the Sisters, joined him. "Bel!" she piped, out of breath. "What is A-Ram doing? That Sister, she's not just a Sister, she's one of the Grand Abbesses I think ... and she's going to ..."

"He's a grown man, Taara, and the Sisters aren't going to hurt him. If that's what he wants, then let him experience it himself."

"But Bel ..."

Taara stumbled and fell to the floor, her sideburns touching the stone. Stenstrom helped her stand. One more time, Taara seized up and was possessed by the Sisters. *"You will follow Knife and you will look for signs of the Kestral, and where you find them, you will destroy them! Your first assignment is at hand! Do not fail!"*

As they exited the building, they heard the Sister speak in her own voice. It was harsh, tinny, like the voice of a demonic child. *"Come along, A-Ram ... I'm ready for you ..."*

10

—Parting Gifts—

Like two scolded children, Stenstrom and Taara returned to the bridge without A-Ram. The place was a darkened, flickering mess.

"Well," Taara said, "I guess I better start getting this place back in order. It was nice having the lantern while it lasted. I guess the Sisters don't want nothing to be easy on this trip, do they?"

"I suppose not. Better get a fix on our position." He felt dizzy and seated himself in his chair.

Lilly . . .

Where was his heart?

Where was his love? He searched for it. Not there to be found, just a confused empty spot.

His feelings ripped from him by the Sisters.

Taara went into the office and picked up her sextant. She looked the horizon over, full of stars.

"Well, we're still over *Camalopardus*. The good news is we're really, really far from Druries Belt. You can't even see it with the naked eye from here. The bad news is we're also really, really far from Bazz too. We'll never make our brandy deadline now. We'd be lucky to get to Bazz in under a year."

She popped back out onto the bridge still holding her sextant. "I suppose we'll need to set sail and get moving. We'll run into League traffic eventually and perhaps we can get a lift home." She passed Stenstrom and went to the helm, mumbling to herself. *"A couple of pegs larboard and a + 250 Z and that should get us pointed at Corvus . . ."* Taara kicked at the foot levers and struggled with the pegs.

"Creation, where's A-Ram when I need him? Messing with the helm is more art than science. I think we should be good. I hope he comes back soon."

"Me too."

She suddenly dropped her sextant and doubled over. Stenstrom flew out of his chair and went to her. "Taara, what's wrong?"

"Sick, I feel sick. The Sisters do that to me every time."

"Sit down and rest."

She shook her head. "No, no . . . Let me get some systems going first, then we'll adjust our orientation and take off." Taara stumbled to the darkened Missive's Panel and began making her calculations. "We're going to have to start . . . from scratch without the Lantern."

Stenstrom picked up her sextant. "Did you notice how quiet it was out in the ship as we returned? I recall no groans, no oppressive noises or feelings of dread and cold breezes. No half-heard screams. I suppose what they said is true—they were the demons haunting this vessel, and now that they've announced their intentions they've cleared the ship of their influence."

Taara finished her calculations. "Told you, the Sisters are way creepy. Get ready for a jolt, I'm firing the *Westminster's* mains."

Stenstrom returned to his chair and felt the tug of the *Westminster's* engines pushing the ship ahead.

"How long's this burn, Taara?"

"Five minutes. That'll get us off and running at least."

Taara slumped over, holding her stomach, her sideburns dangling.

"Still not feeling well?" he asked. "What's hurting, your stomach?"

"My stomach, my head, everything."

"Well, as soon as this burn's over with, turn in and get some sleep."

"But, the bridge . . ."

"We can worry about the bridge later. I want you to rest, agreed? In the meantime, I think I can whip up something to help make you feel better."

"Thanks, Bel."

He stood and went into his office and produced a red, blue and yellow Holystone. Conjuring up a MARZABLE dagger, he scored them open and sorted through the dried ingredients to calm Taara's system. Through the window, he could see the distant, bluish glow of the *Westminster's* engines as it burned. As he mixed the selected ingredients together, he noticed something. A large leather bound book sat on the sill.

The ship shuddered and the *Westminster* went out, the burn complete.

He threw the book onto his desk, scraped the ingredients into an emptied Holystone shell, shook it up, and took it out to Taara.

She looked miserable slumped in the chair. "Burn's done, Bel," she mumbled.

"Here, hold this, it should make you feel a little better."

She took it. "What is it?"

"Just a little something to quiet your system. Go on, stretch out and get some sleep. When's our next burn due?"

"Ten hours. You think A-Ram will be back soon?"

"He should be."

Taara's voice was groggy. "I want him back. You, me and A-Ram, we're family."

She pulled her coat and boots off and situated herself on the padded Missive's chair. He took off his HRN and draped it over her; the large coat was easily big enough to serve as a blanket covering Taara's small body.

"So, I guess I don't need to worry about demons coming to get me no more," she mumbled, her words slurred.

"I suppose not."

"I didn't mind. I liked you watching over me. Made me feel safe . . ."

Moments later, still holding the Holystone, Taara was out.

Stenstrom returned to his office and got the book he'd seen. It was a book about monsters, summoned creatures and other fanciful beings. It was elaborate and hand painted. It looked like a book belonging to the Sisters. A navy blue, silk bookmark was placed a quarter of the way through the thick pages. He turned to the bookmarked page.

NARGAL

Nargals are any of a number of summoned, invoked, or otherwise artificially created creatures made for purposes of servitude and/or task fulfillment.

If this was a book belonging to the Sisters, what was it doing here? Did they leave it for him to find to emphasize the point that Lilly was not a real woman, perhaps attempting to appeal to his sense of logic? As Stenstrom read on, he discovered that Nargals could be made of gold, silver, or bronze. They could be fibrous, made of wood, rock or gemstones. They could be elemental, of earth, fire, water or air. They could also be made of dead flesh, offal, bones, and ashes. He then came to an interesting sub-heading:

SAND NARGAL

Sand Nargals are generally of least construction and least potency compared with other, more advanced types of Nargals. They are comparatively easy to assemble with common materials. They have a rudimentary intelligence and can be programmed to perform simple tasks with great reliability. They, unlike most Nargals, have multiple forms, the first being a free-formed rotating column of sand indistinguishable from a cyclone or dust storm, and secondly, their desired programmed form which can be plant, animal or human. Such versatility makes them highly desirable as guards, spies, and warriors; however, there is a great danger regarding the prolonged use of Sand Nargals as they tend to dream that they are alive instead of being a mere construct. At such times they can become spiteful and rebellious of their masters. They are also easily taintable and turned from their original task or intent. (See: BLACK SAND).

So, there it was. Lilly was a semi-intelligent, conjured woman of sand, who possibly dreamed she was alive but was not.

"Don't ever let anyone tell you what I feel isn't real . . ." she once said.

Despite the Sisters' hermelin suppressing his feelings for Lilly, he felt sad and somewhat lost. He fetched some paper and a marker from his coat and scribbled down a few notes. He put the book away and went back out to the bridge. He sat down next to the sleeping Taara and leaned against the chair. Before long, Taara's little hand came sneaking out from under the HRN and made its way to his shoulder.

Something small and golden rested in her hand.

Taara's voice was groggy. "I took your locket, Bel. I lifted it. I thought you might want it later. So I lifted it . . ." She faded back into sleep.

There was Lilly's locket, a gift he'd kept with him for years. He opened it. Inside was Lilly's smiling face painted with meticulous skill. There were also three small shards of metal rattling within—the hermelins from his mask. Taara must have lifted them too. Comforted, he closed the locket, leaned against Taara, and slept.

11

—The Lady in Gray—

Strange dreams. Voices.

I've escaped!!

He felt himself being shaken awake. "Bel?"

A-Ram was leaning over him. Stenstrom rubbed his eyes and awoke, his dreams quickly fading to oblivion. "A-Ram, you're back."

"I am, Bel," he said in a rather dreamy way. He walked up to the helm, and surveyed the area. He adjusted the foot levers a little. "You don't have this set correctly." He moved in a light, boneless sort of way.

"Are you all right?"

"I'm excellent," he said calmly.

"You certain?"

"Yes." He checked his helm screens. "Everything's dead."

"The Sisters took the Lantern back," Taara said. "It sucks!"

"Ah. Are we still in the middle of nowhere?"

"Yep, though we've set sail for Corvus."

Stenstrom was burning for information. Taara awoke, stretched and yawned. "Hey, Buddy, you're back!" She quickly asked the questions Stenstrom was too shy to ask. "So, how was it?"

A-Ram stood there a moment, his hands on the helm's pegs, and then he smiled. "It was worth the wait. I've never experienced such a thing. Re-markable. I—I feel like a new man."

"She didn't … hurt you?"

"Of course she didn't hurt me—quite the opposite in fact."

"She said she was going to burn you!" Taara said.

"Burn me, in a metaphorical sort of way. I think it was rather enjoyable for the both of us."

"Weren't you nervous?" she asked.

"No … no. It's remarkable really considering how long I've waited for Programmability." He held the helm and thought back. "You know, I found my thoughts returning to that beautiful woman we saw here on the bridge."

"The Merian woman?" Stenstrom asked.

"That's the one. I recall she looked rather sad. I was wondering why she was so sad?"

Taara put on her Marine coat and bounced over to A-Ram's side. She pinched his cheek. "Because she probably misses her 'Rammy'. You did all this fancy thinking while you were muff-mashing and carpet-banging with the Sister?" Taara asked.

A-Ram blushed. "Well, yes, if you must put it like that. I had a few moments of amazing clarity, especially as we came close to ..."

"To busting a nut?" Taara added.

A-Ram, and, to a lesser extent, Stenstrom, was shocked. Such frank language. He spun the helm a turn or two and thought a moment. "I recall reflecting on quite a number of things as we came together—my thoughts gained an unprecedented speed. I could even hear the Sister's thoughts. It was incredible."

He paused a moment. "I believe that Taara is correct," he stated.

"About what?"

"About us, about how we are linked together. Whether the linkage is due to a Bazz curse or not I don't know, but I saw how tightly we're interwoven—*how we have influenced each other's lives long prior to what we thought was out first encounter at Fleet a few days ago.* It's all so clear. The closed Vendetta Circle that you mentioned, Taara, it really does appear to exist."

"See, I told you so," Taara said with a bit of triumph.

"I also believe I know who the common person that links us together is."

Stenstrom was curious. "That's remarkable. All right, so what did you discover on your introspective journey with the Sister?"

He began. "We are three separate people, four if you count Lt. Gwendolyn, and I believe that we must. We are all disjointed in not only geography, but in class and age as well. Bel is from a Tyrol Great House, Lt. Gwendolyn from a Zenon. I am a Calvert from a House Minor and Taara is a commoner from Bazz. We have minimal ties, no previous meetings, no familial connections, no nothing. But, search your thoughts, and be honest with yourself, I'm going to ask an odd question and just respond with the first thing that pops into your head."

"All right," Taara said. "Hit us with it."

"Who do you fear most?"

Stenstrom and Taara exchanged glances. "Pardon?" Stenstrom asked.

"Who do you fear most of all?" he repeated.

Stenstrom was stumped. "I don't think I really know. I can't pinpoint anything, and ..."

"How about a woman dressed in gray?" A-Ram said jumping in. "How about that?"

Stenstrom thought a moment. "I ... um, had a nightmare once about a lady dressed in gray who came to kill me. I was just a boy, and I'm certain she is simply a manifestation of my fears. I've actually seen her many times throughout my life, usually during times of great stress or uncertainty. She's just in my head."

"And you, Taara?" A-Ram asked turning to her.

"I'm afraid of fire."

"Why?"

"Because my uncle's pharmacy burned down with him in it. I haven't liked fire much since then."

"Could it be that the fire you mention was most likely set by a foreign woman dressed in gray about thirty years ago?"

The three sat there silent.

"How do you know that?" she finally asked.

"I'll explain. I'm certain you all know I am most afraid of the Fiend of Calvert, that mad man who terrorized us in St. Edmund's years ago. He was like a ghost, prowling the alleys and wharves, leaving dead men behind. My brother used to try to make me believe he was the Fiend and that he was going to kill me. I spent a lot of terrified nights hiding under my covers, and then there was the evening I actually heard the sound of the Fiend's footsteps as he fled from the Mad Lord of Walther across our rooftop ... bump, bump,

bump! Bel, remember discussing the Fiend with me when we first boarded the ship? You said that a colleague of yours suspected that the Fiend was a woman dressed in gray, contrary to the popular opinion that he was a man in a gas mask? I recall I scoffed at the notion."

"Yes. A friend of mine, Grand Dame Miranda of Rossel, believes that to be the case, and she also believes that the woman I encountered as a boy, the one who tried to kill me, was herself the Fiend of Calvert. But, that cannot be, as I said she is ..."

"Your colleague is correct. I was wrong. The Fiend of Calvert was a woman who dressed in gray. My encounter with the Sister has allowed me to remember everything for as long as I have served Admiral Derlith—every meeting, every idle word that was exchanged that I was there to hear as I served him coffee and buttered his bread. Years of disconnected comments and unexamined detail all came together, and from that, a new and somewhat sinister picture emerges. Much of what I previously assumed to be true, is not true after all. I now understand that Admiral Derlith's older sister, Lady Vendra of Cone, has had a long and varied life. I never gave her much thought, she's such a frail, unassuming person, and she visits the Admiral often. Her health is quite fragile. I have served her coffee and tea four-hundred and fifty-seven times in the Admiral's office."

"That's a lot of cream and sugar," Taara remarked.

Stenstrom interrupted. "Admiral Derlith's sister? Does she wear gray all the time?"

"Yes and no—I thought she always wore the colorful gowns of Cone—very vibrant colors of red, blue and yellow, and she usually wore a shawl to keep her warm—her health always an issue."

"Sounds like a parrot," Taara remarked.

"Yes, the colors are rather like a parrot," A-Ram agreed. "She never married, and that is because she gave her heart to a man who was stolen from her. That man was your father, Bel, and the stealer was your mother—and that's what started everything. That's what made her so angry. Maybe that's what prompted her to start killing all those men in Calvert, for revenge. Lady Vendra of Cone is the Fiend of Calvert."

"My mother stole my father away from Lady Vendra of Cone? Where did you get that idea from?"

"From her own lips, and from the Admiral's. Oh, not at once. I heard it in bits and fragments over a long period of time, whispered comments and the ends of sentences that I walked in on and didn't piece together."

"You said she gets herself-up in parrot colors," Taara said. "Where's the gray?"

"That is what she wants you to think she's wearing. However, she actually wears nothing but gray; a hat, a conservative Remnath dress, and button-up boots. That's all she ever wears."

Stenstrom shrugged. "Ok, A-Ram, let's hear your logic."

"She appears to be adept at disguise, whether it be by Cloak or some other means, I don't know. I don't think she's using a Cloak—it has to be something else. She appears to have some sort of mastery over the senses—the sense of smell being particularly potent. I recall her leaning over my desk discussing, of all things, the Fiend of Calvert one day. I remember seeing her reflection in the Admiral's tea service that I had to keep so brightly polished,—and her reflection was all in gray, though to my eyes she appeared to be wearing a bright Cone gown."

Stenstrom threw his hands up. "All right, A-Ram, let's say for the sake of argument that Lady Vendra of Cone is a woman who dresses in gray. You say all of this started because she thinks my mother stole my father away from her? That would have been, let's see, almost a hundred years ago. I would think she would have gotten over it at some point."

"The Cones are stubborn people. The Admiral is in love with a girl he met in passing during his young manhood and never forgot. Once they give their hearts, they do not take them back easily. I don't know the gross details, and, of course, all I know of the matter is from her perspective—she feels your mother willfully stole your father after she had declared her love for him. She was an influential member of the Ballwigs, and much of her hatred and anger bled into the group, souring them ever after."

"Who are the Ballwigs?" Taara asked.

"A sect of ladies who enjoy breaking people's hearts at balls and parties and all that nonsense." Stenstrom said. "My mother always warned me to avoid them."

"Oh, that's rotten," Taara said. "Matters of the heart are prime for kicking off a real shitty Vendetta Circle, ask my aunt."

A-Ram continued. "Apparently so—Lady Vendra never allowed herself to forget the matter. She then declared Wirguild against your mother."

"She's the one who Wirguilded my mother?"

"She is."

Taara jumped in. "So, lemmie' get this straight. According to the MOLLY, a Wirguild is a formal declaration of revenge. So, if you have it in for somebody, you can go to the Sisters and declare your desire for revenge. If granted, then anything that person does to the other is perfectly legal. Is that right?"

"It is."

"Gods," Taara exclaimed. "You Kanans make a big deal out of everything, don'tcha?"

A-Ram continued. "Moving on, events then become fuzzy for a short time. The next significant thing that happened was that Lady Vendra received a short apologetic letter from your father, trying to make amends to some extent. The letter didn't work, and she tried to kill herself. She survived the incident and was declared insane by the Hospitalers and shipped off to a distant convent to prevent her diminished condition from scandalizing the family.

Several years later, she returned from the convent apparently fully recovered—that was when she started wearing gray, and has worn that color ever since, though, again, she disguises that fact."

"What convent did she go to?" Stenstrom asked.

"I don't know—it was never spoken of; again, her madness was a family secret and hidden shame. Clearly though, the convent is the key—whatever happened to her there has influenced everything since. The Admiral recalls through quiet conversations and mournful correspondence that she returned from the convent a very different person—that the loving sister he remembered was gone, replaced by an outwardly smiling woman, but who inwardly was bizarre and remorseless and seething with rage. He recalls she often vanished for days at a time without telling anyone where she went. He also remarked upon the strange assortment of gentleman callers she often had—dirty, unshaven, and seemingly in a trance of some sort. That was right around the time when the Fiend of Calvert was holding sway in the south."

"Are we assuming that she was somehow controlling these men?" Stenstrom asked.

"We are."

"How?"

"The Admiral never made a definite connection as to how she was doing it, but he was certain she was. He made a curious note, one that I think is significant. He once found a mysterious box in her room. He looked into the box and discovered a number of vials full of unusual chemicals. There was also some sort of device in the box, one with a long stinger or barb attached to it. The general shape of the device reminded the Admiral of an internal, female contraceptive appliance."

"With a stinger on it?" Taara said, shocked.

"Yes, and with that discovery, he became very afraid of his sister and left home to get some space from her, joining the Fleet and eventually becoming an Admiral. His sister often visited him in his office at Fleet—I saw her there many times. I had always thought they were simply close, brother and sister; however, I now see that she was constantly chiding the Admiral, pushing him to do this and that, and her frequent visits weren't something he enjoyed. The Admiral believed that his sister somehow had a method of controlling men, of turning them into zombie-like slaves. He also thought she was trying to control him as well, but was having a measure of mercy on him as he's her kin. They also had a long disagreement regarding the Admiral's niece ... Lady Gwendolyn."

"Gwen? This Vendra of Cone, the Fiend of Calvert, is Gwen's aunt?" Stenstrom asked, somewhat astonished.

"Yes indeed. See how things are coming together, but I've only just started. The Admiral believed Lady Vendra was attempting to corrupt Lady Gwendolyn, to make her more like herself, into an angry, hateful woman, and he was determined for that not to happen, as he loves his niece very much. He got her into contact sports, such as wrestling and boxing and managed to channel her aggression in a positive fashion. There's also Lady Vendra's involvement with your lady, Lilly."

"Lilly? This woman somehow influenced Lilly?"

"She did."

"How so?"

"The Admiral once sent me on a strange set of errands. These errands sent me all over the countryside, the purpose of which was unknown to me at the time. I am now convinced those errands were specifically to gather the materials necessary to attack Lilly, to taint her, to turn her into one of her slaves."

"You're certain of this?"

"I am."

"Then go on."

"The Admiral had me collect five parcels and deliver them to an undisclosed location in the city of Dee. I remember feeling all day long that I was being followed, that I was seeing glimpses of a figure in gray following me. The figure in gray was Lady Vendra, confirmed by her own words in the Admiral's office. Then, that evening after I'd completed my task and returned to Fleet HQ, the figure in gray came upon me and pulled me into a bathroom. I think she was going to kill me right there and then. In the bathroom was a Marine girl sitting on the veranda drinking from a bottle. The figure in gray was startled and I managed to escape. Taara, that Marine girl was you—I recall seeing your sideburns and thought at the time that you had a dirty face.

You saved my life."

Taara thought back. "Oh yeah! Right! I remember that! I was having a nip of home brew when a crazy woman in gray smelling of bunny scent came in. I recognized her and got scared. I thought she was there for me I tore out of there fast."

"You recognized her?" Stenstrom asked.

"Yeah, she was dating my uncle ..." Taara's eyes grew distant and she went pale. "The same one who got burned up in the fire."

"Yes," A-Ram said. "See how this Lady in Gray touched us all? Taara saved my life, and as I continue to give tongue to my thoughts, we shall see that Taara not only saved me from the Lady in Gray, she saved you too, Bel."

"Me?"

"Indeed. To continue, Lady Vendra suffered a few setbacks about thirty years ago. There was a sensational story that hit the wires about a city of the dead under the old ruins of Woodward in Remnath—a place populated by zombies. The Mad Lord of Walther, who was being paid by Lord Catherbaum to investigate the Fiend, uncovered it, and, shortly thereafter, defeated the Fiend of Calvert. I think, the Mad Lord uncovered Lady Vendra's hidden place where she kept her men, within easy telepathic reach of her home in Jacarta, discovered the Calvert connection, and engaged her. Beaten, and pursued by the Mad Lord across Calvert, she left Kana for a time, heading for Bazz of all places, giving herself an opportunity to recover and lay low. To a stuffy, upright Kanan woman, Bazz no doubt seemed like a wooly, uncivilized place to hide in plain sight. I'm certain that's where the Vendetta Circle began, when she went to Bazz, and that's where you fall in, Taara."

Taara swallowed and listened.

"You've mentioned that you're a kid fairly often, however, I'm going to wager that you are much older than both Bel and me. I'm forty-three. How old are you, Bel?"

"I'm only twenty-seven."

"And you, Taara?"

She blushed a little. "Ok, I'm sixty-eight. So, I'm the granny of the group here, what difference does it make? You guys better not tell nobody."

"Nobody here is old, Taara. I'm just making the point that you were around when Lady Vendra was hiding out on Bazz. From what I gather, while she laid low on Bazz, she attempted to lure your father to her, Bel, and snare him."

"How so?"

"I'll get to that. Taara, you mentioned seeing a lady in gray about your uncle's pharmacy, correct?"

"She was sleeping with my uncle, throwing money around, and renting those crazy guys who make air for a living."

"Atmospherics, you mean," Stenstrom added.

"Yeah, whatever. She bought one of those Atmospheric guys to keep her cool like most well-heeled Kanans do when they visit Bazz. I remember she used to sit at a cafe near his shop basking in the cool air. The Ganaadas pestered her all the time because they thought she had money, and then my uncle's shop burned down and she vanished. We didn't see her again after that. My family figured since I was there that day the shop burned, I must have had done something, so I got sent to youth camp on the Endax, digging for nasty clams in the stinking mud."

"The fire. Think back. What exactly happened?" A-Ram asked.

Taara rolled her eyes back and thought, "What happened? Things didn't start off well. The day before, I got into a big fight with this crazy Ganaada. You're not supposed to fight Ganaadas because they'll put a curse on you, but she drew my uncle's name in a circle and was waving it around, running her mouth about my uncle and I told her to shut up, and the next thing you know we were rolling around all over the place. She just about pulled my shirt off, and I lost my shoes; it was a big mess. It was one of those fights where everybody's watching and hollering and betting Cred Sticks—sort of embarrassing, you know."

"So, who won?" Stenstrom asked.

"I'd say I did, and she'd probably say she did. I busted her lip and scratched the hell out of her, and she blackened my eye and tore my clothes to shreds. So, the next day, there I was wearing rags. I needed some Creds to buy some new clothes, so I decided to steal the Lady in Gray's bag. I was a thief back then, well, I'm still a thief, sort of. I saw her sitting there at the cafe, this time without her Atmospheric and she was sweating it out. I thought she might be easy pickings, Kanan ladies never have a clue what's going on, so I gave it a go. She caught me, though, and bent my arm back. I thought she might have broken it or something. It really hurt, and so I wanted to get at some Lytol from my uncle's shop to ease the pain. My uncle caught me and we struggled, making a fairly big mess of spilled bottles and such. Once everything calmed down, he made me spend all morning helping him clean the place up. I didn't know what went where, so I just started putting things wherever."

"See, I think that's the key," A-Ram said. "I'm fairly well certain Lady Vendra sent your father an unsigned note informing him of the legendary God Sperm potion Taara's uncle sold in his store. The potion is supposed to ensure the birth of an exceptional boy, right?"

"Yeah," Taara said. "It's a swirling gold color and it smells like sweat."

"She knew of his lack of an heir and played upon his fears of losing everything to the Lords of the City. So, she lured him to Bazz with a carefully crafted note. Her intention was to slip him a Bazz Love Potion, also sold in Taara's uncle's shop, and enslave him to her. On a side note, she also mentioned that, when she saw your father in the square, she decided to take him right there and then using whatever means she had available to her. Taara's little wrestling match with the Ganaada sorceress thwarted her attempt to get to him, so, she waited until the next day to slip him the Love Potion. Taara, I think your messing around with the bottles that day played a critically important role in what was to come—perhaps Bel's father, Lord Stenstrom the Older, didn't get the bottle Lady Vendra intended he get, the Love Potion. Perhaps the bottles got mixed together somehow, or perhaps he got something else entirely—we shall never know. In any event, you Taara—in fighting the Ganaada, in creating chaos in the pharmacy—are wholly responsible for Bel's existence as is and his status as an artificially created It Man; so, that's your connection."

"I did have his stuff all scattered around. You really think I helped bring Bel into existence?"

"I do."

She pondered it a little more and then looked a little teary-eyed. "Then, I guess I did something right as a kid after all." She gave Stenstrom a friendly pop on the shoulder.

A-Ram continued. "So, that's it. See how all things connect with the Lady in Gray at the center? Also, Bel, as a side note, I caught a few glimpses into the Sister's mind as we came together. I saw some things. I'm pretty sure the Sisters let Lady Vendra try to kill you as a lad to see if you actually had the It Man capabilities. They knew she was exceeding the limitations of her Wirguild. They knew she was coming at you, Bel, as a baby. The Sisters can be remarkably analytical, and instead of revoking her Wirguild, they allowed her to proceed. They watched her men place a rather horrid-looking steel trap in the sand pit behind your manor where you and your sisters played and cover it up."

Stenstrom twitched.

Snap ...

"That was just a dream," Stenstrom said, shuddering. "That's my old dream I have from time to time."

"It wasn't a dream. It happened. The Sisters were watching and saw you spring that trap and survive unharmed, then, they knew for certain."

Stenstrom felt the walls closing in on him. "Well then, here we are in a place where our deepest nightmares are actually real and the truths we've clung to are nothing but dreams."

"Are you referring to Lilly?" A-Ram asked.

"Of course. Of all the women in my life, other than my mother and my sisters, she was the most real, the most grounded. And now, look ..."

Lilly, a fallen piece of enchanted sand.

"Well, I guess I'm a little creeped out by all this, but it's actually great news," Taara said. "Now we know who we need to hunt down and kill—the Lady in Gray, and it's not like she doesn't deserve it."

Stenstrom sat there in his chair and pondered the notion. The Lady in Gray, the person he'd feared since childhood and had rationalized away as a mere phantom, was real.

She came at him in Fox Park, ready to kill ...

He remembered the knife she carried. "I'm sorry," she had said as she raised it up.

She tried to abduct him at the reunion dinner years later in Rustam ...

The Mad Lord had recognized him as a fellow "It" Man.

She came at him through the Astral Plane at the University of Bern ...

A cyclone had burst through the clouds and distracted her. A Cyclone? Lilly in her true Sand Nargal form, protecting him as she claimed she did?

The Lady in Gray deserved to die, Taara had said.

His mother had stolen his father away from her years ago. A broken heart turned to murderous rage.

He wondered what he would do now should he come face-to-face with her.

He wondered ...

"I'm sorry for your Lady," A-Ram said. "I had hoped to meet her."

"She's a Nargal, a Sand Nargal to be specific, some sort of conjured creature," Stenstrom said. "The Sisters left us a nice book on the subject."

"And, are you all right, Bel? Are you in pain for your Lady?"

Pain? After all he'd discovered, shouldn't he be in pain?

"No. The Sisters took it from me. I feel nothing. Remarkable, isn't it, how they can empty one's heart when they see fit?"

"I'm truly sorry, Bel. What they did to you is unthinkable, and even in making amends I'm horrified for you. To strip a man of his feelings, I think I'd rather be heartbroken."

Stenstrom remembered the stabbing anguish, the heart-stopping total loss. Now, just hollow and devoid of emotion.

The woman of sand standing before him.

"No, A-Ram, no you don't."

Taara tried to lighten the subject. "Hey, Bel, you still got me. I love ya'!" She threw her arms around him and gave him a big kiss on the cheek.

"Thanks, Taara."

"That book the Sisters gave you," A-Ram asked. "May I see it, please? I'm curious."

Stenstrom got out of his chair and fetched the book from his office. He brought it out to A-Ram. A-Ram took it and opened it to the bookmark, admiring the detail and craftsmanship of it. He paused a moment to admire the unfamiliar constellations. Four bluish stars nearby shone bright through his office window.

"Taara," Stenstrom called out. "What are those four bright stars to our starboard?"

She immediately answered: "Alcalla, Ecar, Savel and Penta, all big ole' magnitude 1 stars making up the constellation *Camalopardus. Camalopardus* is the brightest constellation as seen from Kana and is visible throughout the League. Xaphan space too. It's the Sisters' constellation."

A-Ram got out the paper with the notes Stenstrom had written earlier. "Hey, Bel, what's this?"

"What?"

"This paper?"

"Just some notes I took down while you were gone."

A-Ram showed him the paper: hard scrawl, circles mashed in blunt violent strokes from a demented hand. Unreadable names nested within.

"What's that?" A-Ram asked.

"I don't recall doing any of that?" Stenstrom said.

Taara saw the scrawl and gasped. "It's the Circle—I knew it!"

As if by design, a blinding light flooded the bridge, and there before them was the Lantern, star-like in its brightness and floating like an angel, this time guided by the Sisters' hand.

"Hey, it's back!" Taara cried. "Come here, you, and get back on the panel where you belong."

The Lantern went to supernova in intensity. They covered their eyes and a voice filled their heads

"Lo to thee, It Man, Lone Rider . . . It is not for you to walk the pathways of others. Your road is the road to perilhood, to damnation. We shall return you to where you are needed, and, ever after, you shall follow Knife wherever she goes.

"Find the Kestrals and Destroy the Kestrals and remember our light."

The Lantern increased in intensity until it became overwhelming.

12

—The Heade-on-the-Hearth—

When the light subsided, the Lantern had gone. They rubbed their eyes. "Hey!" Taara cried. "I've got a little power on the panel here—must have bled some energy from the Lantern. Probably won't last." She manipulated screens.

Through the windows in Stenstrom's office, he could see more familiar stars laid out around them, along with the shimmering yellow band of Druries Belt. "Looks like we're back where we started from," he said. "The Sisters are always full of surprises, aren't they?"

Taara stared at the panel. "Bel, A-Ram …" she said. "Remember what Lilly said in her notes, about making sure to avoid the leeward side of Druries Belt? Well, guess where we are? Guess where the Sisters put us!!"

Stenstrom stared at the stars, and at Druries Belt in particular, in horror. Before their encounter with the Sisters, the Belt had been roughly to the left of the ship, following the safe path Lilly had laid out for them. Now, it was far to their right. The Sisters had dropped them right in the very place Lilly said they needed to avoid.

Your road leads to perilhood, they said.

"A-Ram, hard a-starboard! Taara, get us out of here, best possible speed!" A-Ram tugged on the wheel and the ship pitched around until Druries Belt was dead ahead.

"A-Ram, wait!" she cried. "I need to plot a vector and set our course, otherwise, we'll head off in the wrong bloody direction and we'll never get to Bazz."

"Hurry, Taara!"

She slammed the panel, moving screens around. "Hang on, hang on … Give me a minute!" She stood up. "I need my sextant!"

A light went off on the panel. She stared at it wide-eyed.

"What's that?" Stenstrom asked. "What's blinking?"

"Contact …" she replied, somewhat breathless.

"What is it?" Stenstrom asked.

"Unknown, but it's coming in, and fast."

"Could it be Captain Gwendolyn?"

"I don't know—we're reading motion-only. But it's on us. It's coming in due port, 5:00AM and climbing. We should be able to visually see it through your office windows."

"Keep an eye on it! Hold Fast, A-Ram, and keep it at station should it try and get too friendly."

"Aye, Bel."

"Keep our thruster ticks to a minimum. Perhaps they won't notice us."

Stenstrom and Taara exited the bridge and entered his office. "Which way?" he asked.

"That way," Taara said pointing down past the wing to the right.

Through the windows Stenstrom saw a distant patch of black moving in, blotting out the stars. Lilly's warning rang through his head.

'Ware Druries Belt.

The patch of black came in, getting bigger and bigger.

Distant spotlights came on and honed-in on the ship.

"They got us made. They're scanning us," Taara said.

As they watched, the unknown vessel came into clear view. Through the windows they could see the latticed, partial hulk of an old *Webber* ship lit up in dash-like running lights, its superstructure loaded-out with capsules and decrepit add-ons.

"A *Webber*?" Taara snorted. "I got my knickers all up in a bind over a stupid *Webber* ship? What's an old beater like that still doing flying?"

It approached swiftly and then slowed, a node of strong spotlights eyeballing the *Seeker*. It moved in a deliberate fashion across the length of the *Seeker's* neck, the spotlights making round, lit-up circles on the hull, caressing it in light. The vessel looked hodge-podge and pieced together in comparison to the sleek *Seeker*, rather like a hermit crab under a tin-can shell.

Stenstrom knew about the old *Webber*-class ships from his father. The old *Amazing* was a *Webber.* It was the precursor of the *Straylight*-class of

Main Fleet Vessels. They were crude vessels in comparison, about half the size of a *Straylight,* composed of a number of crew and maintenance capsules connected by an unwieldy set of gantries and networks of naked metal scaffolding. A *Webber*, seen from a distance, looked rather like a capital H. Once, they made up the bulk of the Fleet and were associated in a romantic light with the Golden Age of the League/Xaphan conflict, as the Xaphans matched up much better against the *Webbers* than they did against the *Straylights* and *Triumphs* that came later on.

This *Webber* was missing much of its starboard side, its classic 'H' silhouette looking more like a toppled-over 'T'. Its starboard engine was gone, and the port engine was bolstered with a series of smaller, capsule-shaped rockets that were strapped on with welded metal bands. It seemed to have a number of odd accessories attached to various quarters along its length. The whole ship seemed to have a vacant, rather decrepit feel to it.

"Who is that out there?" A-Ram asked.

"Dunno," Taara said. "Pirates, Raiders? It's got to be pirates, rocking an old beater like this one."

"In the middle of League space?"

The *Webber* spun around and focused its attention on the frontal section of the ship, the roving spot-lights greedily panning about, casting the silhouette of the *Seeker* in a passing whitish glow. It reached the forward main hatch just aft of the *Seeker's* frontal section. A flexible, tubular docking assembly snaked out of the ventral of the *Webber* and made its way to the *Seeker's* main docking ring. It moved in a sinuous fashion—it reminded Stenstrom of the sex organ of a male bird.

"What is that?" Taara asked. "Doesn't look like a standard piece of equipment a *Webber* would mount."

"She's trying to dock, A-Ram. Move us away."

He turned the wheel. As A-Ram rolled the *Seeker* away, several flexible arms, like the vast tentacles of a cuttlefish, shot out of the *Webber's* forward sections and wrapped around the neck section of the ship, holding it fast. The whole mass of the *Webber* seemed flexible and articulated in an advanced way; it was balling up and unballing, like the movements of a pillbug in a manner well beyond that of any ordinary *Webber*, which was a notoriously rigid class of ship.

Clinging fast, the odd ship latched on with a clank that they could hear all the way in the bridge as its advanced docking assembly coupled with the *Seeker's*.

Taara stared at it through the window. "Look, the name plate reads … *Heade-on-the-Hearth*. That particular ship was listed as lost at sea decades ago," she said.

"We better get down there!" Stenstrom said heading to the lift. "Taara, can you route a little power from the bridge to that section of the ship. I want lights."

Taara stopped at the missive's panel and pressed a few buttons. "Ok," she said as the lighting in the bridge dimmed.

"Come on, A-Ram, let's go. We need all hands down below."

"Me?" he squeaked.

"Yes, you, let's go!"

Taara appeared uncharacteristically nervous. "This part of space is not liked by us on Bazz, Bel. In the old days, lots of ships turned up missing in these parts—lots of souls never seen again."

"Those are just old wives tales," A-Ram said from behind the helm.

"Yeah, old wives tales—but look, there's the *Heade-on-the-Hearth* out there—an honest-to-god ghost ship."

"Taara, any thoughts on who's on that vessel?" Stenstrom asked.

She looked at it. "Four guys."

"Four, that's all?"

"That's one more than what we've got," A-Ram said lowering himself into the lift shaft.

"Not true—we've got Taara. She counts for at least three people," Stenstrom said. "Who are they?"

"I don't know," she said moving down.

They climbed down to Deck 4, which was dimly lit in unsteady light from the bridge, and made their way to the docking ring. They arrived and waited. Taara drew her SK and cocked it.

They waited a few minutes more. The docking ring clanked, and they could hear droll male voices chattering on the other side of the hatch.

`Ware Druries Belt, Lilly had warned.

Stenstrom wondered what sort of monstrosity awaited.

Through the slim windows, they could see hints of movement flickering by.

Finally, the docking hatch swung open.

Four men came in. They were smallish and skinny, though, in a side-by-side comparison, they were a bit bigger than the very small A-Ram. They wore a mish-mash of faded and out-of-fashion clothing, rather in the old Fleet style: washed out coats with dirty frills, seedy shirts that were clearly once white but now an unidentifiable gray, filthy knee britches with tarnished brass buttons, and worn black shoes. Their hair was straw-like and unkempt. They also smelled—not like body odor or dirt, but like innards, raw and stinking.

They appeared to be rootless scalawags in dire need of a shower and a nourishing meal, nothing more. He breathed a sigh of relief.

"Halt and identify yourselves!" Stenstrom said in a commanding tone, trying to sound authoritative. Taara hefted her SK and made sure they could see its gigantic barrel pointing at them.

Stenstrom found himself struggling a bit—he wasn't sure how to handle a situation like this—to be boarded in the Deep Sea. He recalled his father once mentioning that to board a vessel at sea without due sounding and invitation was the most provocative act one could commit, short of opening fire. His father said something about *"should he ever be boarded"* he would have to respond with deadly force.

Should he ever be boarded... That implied that, in his long career sailing the heavens, his father had never been boarded to that point.

And now here he was, on his maiden flight, and he was boarded. And

he had been warned as well.

And, of course, Stenstrom had no security detail, no Sisters, no Marines, no ship hands to hoist weapons and back him up, not to mention the fact that he had no able-bodied ship, no guns and no engines—he couldn't even tuck tail and run should it come to that. It was just he, Taara, and A-Ram, and there were four boarders, so he was down a man.

The boarders were surprised, standing there big-eyed and open mouthed.

"Great tap-dancin' gods!" the first man said in a gruff accent.

"Indeed," Stenstrom replied. "You know of course that boarding a flagged Stellar Fleet vessel is a capital offense. I am well within my rights to put the lot of you to the sword here and now, gentlemen."

The second man raised his knobby hands. "Hold up there, Gov—this didn't look to us to be no flagged Fleet vessel. We didn't detect no flag flyin'. We thought she was a derelict, adrift and towed out."

"Yeah, performin' a safety service we was," the third man said. "She's out the shipping lanes. This here's the backwater, mate, the open country."

The fourth man saddled out of the dark. The smallest of the bunch, he had a shifty look, his goggle-eyes panning about, seeing everything. He wore a modest merchant's hat on top of his nest of messy hair. *"Oh, merde!* Who, pray, are you?" he asked.

"I am Paymaster Stenstrom, Lord of Belmont-South Tyrol, captain of the Main Fleet Vessel, *Seeker.* To my right here is Lord A-Ram, ship's Master Helmsman, and to my left is Private Taara de la Anderson of the 110th Stellar Marines, my first officer."

The fourth man looked about and then carefully studied Stenstrom. He had a groping, invasive sort of stare. *"¿Y qué tenemos nosotros aquí?* You have a Fleet adjutant for a Master Helmsman, and a Marine private as first officer? A novel bit of selection there, a-heheh. And you sir, that is not a standard uniform you are wearing, is it? What is your rank, Lord Belmont, pray tell?"

"You'll pardon us if we ask the questions for the time being," Taara said, jumping in giving her SK a shake.

The smallest man turned to her. *"Ah, ce qu'une petite fille délicieuse ..."*

"What?" Taara replied.

The man chuckled. "Your pardon, I have a love of irrelevant and obsolete languages of old. A hobby of mine, a-heheh. I merely said what a handsome young lady stands before us." He waved his arms in an inviting manner. "Please, allow me to introduce myself. I am Chance Venable, and these are my brothers, Clem Venable, Innocent Venable, and Lemmuel Venable. We are simple traders scraping by as best we can."

"Yeah?" Taara said. "What do you trade in?"

"None o' yer business!" Lemmuel snapped.

Chance quieted him with a wave of his hand. *"Замолчите, сейчас же!"* he said to him. "Pardon my uncouth brother, Private. Out here in the wilds we have seldom occasion to practice our good manners. We trade in sundries—barley, tobacco, spirits when we can, fine finished goods, and scrap metal when we happen upon it. You must pardon our attention. Surely an apparently abandoned ship such as this would be a rare find for the likes of us—*un cadeau rare*. We beg your leave."

Stenstrom thought it over. He remembered Lilly's warning, however these four didn't seem to be any great threat, and, what they said made a bit of sense, they might have indeed thought the *Seeker* to be an abandoned hulk and were hoping to cash in on their good fortune. He couldn't fault them for that. "Well, I'm not one to hold a grudge. We shall overlook this matter. However, do not try my patience any further. You are free to go."

Clem looked around. "Where's yer' security detail, Gov?"

"En route, sir," he responded. "Now, I suggest you turn around and walk out the way you came. I'll not ask again. My first officer has an eager trigger finger and a full fifty caliber mag."

"Yeah?" Clem said, puffing himself up a bit to match Stenstrom's size.

Chance Drury laughed. "A-heheh. Now, now. We have a unique situation here, Lord Belmont. Please attend from our perspective: you fly no flag, you have no apparent crew besides that what stands before us, and no motive power—we scanned you quite thoroughly. There is also no bonded captain of this ship at present as the MVF *Seeker's* current status at Fleet is determined to be: half-scuttled. Given all that, by Fleet rule, this ship is deemed rudderless and we have every right to board her as fair salvage. Additionally, are you, by chance, the same Paymaster Stenstrom of Belmont-South Tyrol who currently has twenty-two minor and four major queries posted for your detainment at Fleet headquarters, hmmm?"

Clem stepped forward. "Sounds like we got us a hardened criminal on our hands, a real scalawag."

Innocent balled his fist and clapped it in his open palm. "Looks clear we'd be doin' the League a favor bringing you in fer' justice. Mebe' there's a reward."

Lemmuel grinned in anticipation. "An', it looks to me like all the crew you got backin' you up is that twerp standin' over there and this little girl holdin' the big gun."

"This little girl could kick your ass up and down the corridor," Taara replied.

"Ah … well then, let's go, babe!"

Stenstrom drew his NTHs. "Enough! Now, you lot need to turn around and march back to your *Webber* out there, and I'll forget this matter ever happened. If you choose to tarry a moment longer, I shall have to put you to the sword right here and now."

The Venables looked at each other and slowly raised their hands. *"Hay que aguita…* Dear me, looks like you have the drop on us, a-heheh," Chance said. "We wish no troubles here, Paymaster. Come on, boys, let us retire. We are clearly overmatched by this galactic scalawag and his fearsome crew."

They slowly began moving back toward the hatch. Stenstrom moved into an advantageous position where he was close enough to cover the Venables, yet remain far enough away that they couldn't rush him and hope to be successful. Taara skirted to his right, SK at the ready.

"Oh," Chance said stopping and turning around, "Paymaster, before I depart I must know, that coat you wear, are you always in the habit of wearing a garment once used by the Hoban Royal Navy—a Grand Plantain's coat if I'm not mistaken, and a mask to boot? You are quite the cad."

"It's my good luck charm."

Chance tittered. "I see …" he said in a sinister voice. "How quaint."

Things unfolded quickly. In a sudden movement, Chance Venable reached out and snatched both NTHs from Stenstrom's grasp. It was a lightning strike, faster than any person should be able to move; it happened so fast Stenstrom didn't really know what to think. How did he reach him in the first place? There was no possible way! It seemed for a split second that Chance Venable's arms expanded to two or three times their normal length, stretching out past the seedy frills and the rotten sleeves, reaching out and seizing his NTHs.

Whatever had happened, the end result was undeniable—Chance Venable was now pointing his NTH's right at him. Stenstrom was flabbergasted.

In a similar blink-of-an-eye move, Clem pulled Taara's SK out of her hand. In a matter of half a second, they were both disarmed and menaced with their own weapons.

"Hmmm," Chance said. *"Meine Schätzchen, es scheint, als habe die Feier begonnen.* A-heheheh!!" Chance looked at the pistols. *"Ich glaube, mein Schwein pfeift!* NTH's if I'm not mistaken, very nice. LosCapricos weapons of House Belmont. Can kill anything, I hear tell, living or dead, real, unreal, man or machine. *C'est juste?"*

"Not sure what you're talking about," Stenstrom said. "They're just old pistols."

"Oh, please, I do have my sources, truth be told. These are death-dealing NTH's, no doubt about it."

Chance stood there beaming, like a vulture eyeballing a dying bit of prey. "Lemmuel, Innocent, shackle this lot please."

The two grubby fellows produced three sets of manacles and roughly bound their arms behind their backs. Lemmuel pulled Taara's Monica from her belt, admired it a moment, and tucked it into his sash. They then pushed them into a kneeling position, the four Venables standing triumphant in the flickering light of the corridor.

"A-heheh, a shocking turn of events, indeed. Now then," Chance said casually pointing the NTHs at Stenstrom. "Oh, and by the by, our family name is not Venable—I believe that was the name of the most recent family of unfortunate wayfarers we waylaid and killed in space. My name is Chance Drury and we are the Drury Brothers."

"The Drury Brothers are dead!" A-Ram cried from his knees.

Chance Drury smiled with glee. "Are we? I don't feel dead. The Venables, now they're dead, I agree. Now, what to do with the three of you?"

Lemmuel approached and gave the kneeling Taara a rough kick in the stomach. "Lemme' have this Marine bitch! I wanna' show her a good time!" He seized her by the sideburns and yanked her head up. Lemmuel looked like he was aching to mess Taara up—a sadistic little man.

Clem shook his head and gave a toothy grin. "Nah … Let's feed `em to the Cronyns nice as ya' please. That's wha' I says."

Taara, looking up the barrel of her own gun, scoffed. "Cronyns? Cronyns don't exist, shinepole," she said, adding a dirty name from Bazz.

"Ya? Think so? Oh, they'd like ta' chaw down on your little carcass, Missie," Clem said.

Lemmuel took exception. "Little slut called you ah 'shinepole'! I want her! I wanna' hear her scream! I love making jumped-up little whores like her scream!"

"Shaddap an' do as yer' told!" Clem barked. "She's for the Cronyn's an' thas' the end of it, les you want me shoved up yer' works right in front of her so's she can watch!"

Lemmuel stewed and was visibly raging.

Chance stood there with Stenstrom's NTHs and lorded over the situation, enjoying every moment. "No, no. *Der Chorstuhl füllt sich mit Arschgesichtern!* I hear tell there's a ship coming to rescue this lot. Not a Warbird, but a scout-ship under full sail. The *Demophalon John*—only a short distance away too. Да имаш да вземаш! That is a *Tekel*-class ship, I'd say minimum compliment of eighty-eight souls aboard. We shall give the scout ship and her miserable crew to the Cronyns, and then, when they're done having their fun, we'll salvage the hulk. By the Belt, this haul is made to order!"

Creation, Stenstrom thought, how is he knowing this stuff?

"Eighty-eight souls," Innocent said. "That'll keep `em happy for a spell, won't it?"

"My very thought, though I always detest taking Fleet vessels—somebody is sure to come looking for them, *oh bien,*" Chance said. "Still, we'll guide them in nice as you please, then ride out the aftermath, as we always do, nice and sweet."

"They'll not fall for such a thing, whatever it is you're planning," Stenstrom said.

"Oh?" Chance replied. He paused a moment, then: "*Seeker* to *Demophalon John*," he said, his voice taking on an echoing, broadband-type sound to it. Chance Drury was speaking in Stenstrom's voice—a perfect match.

After a moment, Stenstrom heard a response. "Go ahead, Bel, did you get your Com fixed? You sound a lot better than before, though we don't have a picture. What in Creation happened to you? We've been worried sick." It was Captain Gwendolyn's voice.

"We managed to cobble something together, Captain, and our ship is a mess. It looks like we've reached our wits end with this old beater; everything's shot. We'll send you our coordinates straightaway. Can you come and get us with all speed?"

There was a delay, then: "Well, I must say I'm a bit surprised after the fuss you made, but sure, I'm glad you've come to your senses, Bel. We have your coordinates and are only about a half hour from your position. Sit tight and we'll be right there."

Stenstrom couldn't let this continue. He had to warn her. "Gwen!" he yelled from his kneeling position. Chance cocked the NTH and pointed it at A-Ram's head, furrowing the muzzle into his hair.

"Yes, Bel?" she replied.

Stenstrom winced and lowered his head.

"Nothing, Captain—sorry," Chance said in his voice. "I'm just eager to get off of this wreck is all. We shall stay on station and await your arrival."

"And Bel?" Gwen said.

"Yes?" Chance responded.

"When we get back to Fleet, don't forget we're having lunch. Whatever you're having, ale, beer, spirits, it's on me, okay, and while we eat, I'll teach you a card game or two. There's a game I love called canasta. You'll be a natural."

"I'll hold you to it, Captain," Chance replied rolling his eyes.

"Call me Gwen, all right? How many times do I have to tell you?"

"Of course, Gwen. *Seeker* out."

Chance giggled. "*A-heheh. Je suis impressionné.* Canasta, how droll. She sounds like a Zenon—too bad for her she won't be making that lovely lunch date at Fleet, and nor shall you. There," he said, his voice back to its normal, wheezy sound, "that wasn't hard, now was it? Little does your friend know what's in store for her. I almost feel sorry for the lady—what the Cronyns are going to do to her and her crew—really is quite a mess. Now, where was I— *no me puedo recordar.* Ah yes, what to do with you three?"

"Kill 'em, Chance, and be done with it," Clem said looking around. "I'm thinking this Warbird will do us up nice. We can use her to get those golden braggarts in the Tank off our backs once an' for all."

"Nah," Lemmuel said. "She's stripped. Got no engines, jus' like this little girl here." He kicked Taara again. She whuffed.

"Kick me again … and I'm going to ghost you, Shinepole!" she replied in a surprisingly icy voice.

"Not if I ghost you first, darlin'!" He kicked her a third time and she wheezed in pain.

Chance looked around. "Lemmuel please— Для любви к Богу. I realize you enjoy showing the ladies a capital time, however, there's really no need to knock her about. These three are a pack of cretins and rogues just like we are, so let's show a modicum of respect to our peers, shall we? And, yes, I agree with you, Clem, this ship, with a bit of touching up, shall do us nicely. I am invigorated—*revigoré.*"

He stared down at A-Ram. "You, sir, you shall have the distinction of going first, a-heheh." He pointed the smooth-bore, iron barrel of the NTH at his skull and smiled, exposing his picket-fence of yellowy teeth. "Then let's get on with it. This is nothing personal, and, at least we're not giving you over to the Cronyns like we are that Zenon woman—be thankful for that. *Auf Wiedersehen.*"

Stenstrom looked up. "You might want to forget about him and worry instead about me."

Chance glanced at him. "And why is that?"

Stenstrom rose up, free of the manacles, the lock picked clean. He waved his hands. In a flash, he had six MARZABLE daggers nested between his fingers. He swept out with his left hand, and the daggers buried themselves in Chance's arm and hand. Chance, greatly surprised, dropped the NTH.

"Heilige Scheiße!"

"You huntin' dog!" Clem yelled.

Stenstrom cast the three daggers from his right hand and hit Clem in the neck and face. He cringed and bent over. "You huntin' dog!" Clem yelled.

Chance recovered from his shock of getting stabbed and fired at Taara. Still shackled, she nimbly rolled out of the way, the flashing green globe just missing to her right, clipping her coattails. With a roar of delight, Lemmuel dove onto Taara. "Now we's gonna' dance, bitch!" and they rolled about on the floor.

Clem, daggers protruding, kicked A-Ram over and pointed Taara's huge SK at his head. He pulled the trigger.

Nothing happened. Puzzled, he examined the gun. "Oh, jeep-doggy, she's palm-spranded it!"

Stenstrom thanked Creation for A-Ram's good luck and shook his hands again. Six lime green Holystones appeared between his fingers. He quickly threw them at Chance and Clem, where they exploded into a stout tangle of spider webs. Chance completely disappeared in the mass, Clem too. Innocent was partially captured, as was the struggling A-Ram.

Stenstrom dragged A-Ram free of the webbing.

"Zavallı köpek! Think you're smart, do you?" came Chance's muffled voice from within the webbing. "Innocent, get me out of this!" He tore at the webbing.

A few feet away, Lemmuel and the shackled Taara tumbled about, she using her legs fairly effectively while he toyed with her—apparently enjoying attacking a lady. He glanced up and saw Stenstrom quickly undoing A-Ram's shackles. He lined A-Ram up and threw Taara's Monica. The large knife spiraled through the air and got A-Ram in the brim of his hat, pinning it to the wall. Taara, taking advantage of the moment, reared back and head-butted him in the jaw.

"Ow!" she cried, nearly knocking herself out.

From within the mass of webbing, Stenstrom heard a familiar clicking sound. He dove for A-Ram and pushed him out of the way as a lit-up, green mass came shooting out of the webs.

"NTH—shot!" Stenstrom yelled.

Growling, Taara peppered Lemmuel with bites and kicks as Stenstrom created several more daggers and pumped them into his scrawny chest. He was seemingly unfazed. He easily pulled the hissing Taara off of him by her shackles and seized Stenstrom by his HRN coat. He then conked them together once or twice with a sickening series of crunches, and threw Taara down the hallway, right into A-Ram, sending him sprawling.

Stenstrom recovered and, hauling back, socked Lemmuel square in the jaw.

It was like hitting a block of iron. Lemmuel spat and gave him a ruinous head-butt in return.

Everything spun. He picked Stenstrom up by the collar of his HRN and threw him, stunned, into the airlock, where he landed upside down with a thud.

"Now I'm gonna' git ya, Missie!" Stenstrom heard him yell. "Come here!"

The hatch shut and sealed with a hermetic "hiss!"

Inside the airlock, Stenstrom recovered, stood, and banged on the hatch, but he couldn't open it—it was locked from the other side. Through the narrow window he could see hints of movement in the dark corridor beyond, covered up mostly by the sticky tangle of spider webs created by his Holystone throw. He thought he saw a flash of green light traveling down the hall—another NTH shot.

Someone ran by—was that Taara? No, it was A-Ram, Lemmuel hot on his heels.

Another green flash.

Creation! His friends could be dying on the other side of the hatch.

13

—THE SISTERS' FIST—

Stenstrom thought to pick the lock and open the hatch, but there was nothing to pick, no exposed locking mechanism to get his hands on.

He desperately pounded on the hatch in fear of what was happening to his friends on the other side. His friends were possibly dying, and Captain Gwendolyn was sailing into a trap of some sort.

The Cronyns? What are those? Didn't sound good, whatever they are.

There was a shot and a strobe-flash of green light through the window.

Stenstrom struggled with the hatch.

A voice entered his head, a chiding, laughing voice.

You are our Fist. Camalopardus is out. We lend you our power.

He felt something filling him up.

He looked at his hands. For a moment they no longer looked like flesh and blood, they looked metallic and machined, like the hands of a thoughtfully crafted robot made of silver and gold.

He pushed on the hatch door and, surprisingly, it opened this time.

No, it didn't open—it was twisted and wrecked. He had pushed through it, past the stout metal and hermetic seals, and bent the armored hatch like it was made of spun sugar.

No time to consider what he'd just done. He ran into the hallway to save his friends.

Down the corridor, A-Ram and Taara were hunkered down in a service nook. Lemmuel was fiddling around with Taara's SK, trying to get the palm sprander off (apparently Clem, partially stuck in the web, had tossed it to him). Chance had escaped the web and was pressing them with green shots from the NTH pistols. Clem was still stuck in the web and was swearing to beat the band. Innocent was tearing at the web, trying to free him.

Although Chance appeared to know quite a lot of things, he didn't seem to know that the NTH shots could pass through obstructions, such as walls. He could shoot through the wall straight at them and that would be it. That was the Rumalore working—false information about the capabilities of the NTH. That flaw in his knowledge was saving Taara and A-Ram at the moment, for he kept trying to shoot around the wall.

Stenstrom fell on Innocent and Clem from behind.

"What the—!" Innocent choked as Stenstrom hauled back and cuffed him in the face, knocking him into the wall some distance away.

Chance turned to shoot Stenstrom with his own pistols and was shocked.

"Mein Gott! What are you?" he asked, staring at him. "You're like us? You're like us!" He leveled the NTHs at him.

Stenstrom quickly seized the barrels of the pistols and got them out of Chance's hands before he could fire.

No, he didn't pull them out of Chance's grasp—he pulled his NTHs away with Chance's hands still clinging to them—they hung there like two grim decorations, trailing streamers of flesh and gore. Chance, handless, roared and drew away. Clem freed himself from the remains of the web and attacked.

Stenstrom turned the pistols, cocked and fired, getting Clem in the chest. He groaned and fell over, clunking hard to the floor.

Chance started to say something, but Stenstrom was on him. He picked him up and roughly head butted him.

"!Hay chingado!" Chance piped, and Stenstrom head butted him again with bone-crushing force.

A strange sound filled the corridor at that moment—a rapid, hitching guttural sound, like a machine gasping in its death throes: "EEEE..uuuuu… GGGGHHHHHHHH... EEEEE!!" The noise seemed to be coming from Clem. Taara gritted her teeth and A-Ram covered his ears. Stenstrom blocked out the noise and threw Chance, head over heels through the smashed air lock into the hold.

"產生泡沫！" came from beyond the hatch.

Picking up the fallen Clem, Stenstrom also threw him into the air lock.

He then turned to attend to Lemmuel. Taara and A-Ram had exited their hiding place and were engaging him, though they didn't appear to be having much luck. Lemmuel spun and threw Taara aside. He aimed the SK at her and pulled the trigger, but it didn't go off—again it was palm spranded. A-Ram worked his way behind him, while Taara engaged afresh from the front, charging him with her lowered shoulder—a spitting little ball of fur she was, even shackled. A-Ram fell to his knees and, with Taara pressing him backwards, Lemmuel tripped over him, shoulders back, filthy shoes in the air.

The SK flew out of his grip as he fell.

A-Ram sprang and grabbed it. He struggled with the heavy weapon, aimed and pulled—again nothing happened—the palm sprander defeated him too.

"I'm gonna poke ya, Missie!" Lemmuel roared, trying to stand. Taara hauled back and kicked him square across the face with her hard, Marine Brussard boot. His face seemed to fall apart and go shapeless for a moment, like a sack full of broken glass.

Stenstrom picked Lemmuel's scrawny body up with one arm and tossed him into the air lock along with Chance and Clem. There was a commotion of bodies colliding within.

"Get these damn things off me!" Taara hissed, leaning over and presenting her shackled hands. Stenstrom quickly removed them from her wrists. "Gimme' this!" she yelled, snatching her SK from A-Ram and clearing the palm sprand. She saw Chance peeking out of the air lock door and laid a roaring burst on it—he backed away into the interior as the blast riddled and blackened the hatchway.

With another wave of his hand, Stenstrom produced three red Holy-stones and three more lime green ones. He cast two reds into the smashed hatchway and they burst into hot flames—Chance screamed from within. He then cast the greens and thoroughly covered up the smashed inner hatch of the docking ring air lock with webbing, preventing them from exiting.

A-Ram ran to the controls and hit the purge. The outer doors opened and Chance, Clem, and Lemmuel Drury were swept out into the vacuum of space, Stenstrom's webbing sucking in with the change in pressure, but holding. The venting pushed on the *Heade-on-the-Hearth*, and she lightly bounced into the neck of the *Seeker*, still grappled on by her metal tentacles.

Taara's eyes grew wide. "Hey!" she managed to say. She pointed.

Behind A-Ram, Innocent Drury rose up.

Stenstrom let fly with three more MARZABLE daggers, getting him in the face and chest. With his other hand, he threw a red Holystone which he had saved—Innocent burst into a tower of green and red flames.

Taara got a bead on him and loosed a burst. There was a throaty blast of gunfire and a spray of blood. Innocent fell forward, riddled to the chest by fifty caliber fire from Taara's SK, the corridor filling with the smell of cooking flesh and gun smoke.

"Good Creation!" Taara exclaimed, running her hands through her hair, her SK smoking. "What in the name of Hell was that? It's a damn good thing I was too lazy to remove my palm sprander from my gun, or it would have been curtains!"

"Are you two all right?" Stenstrom cried.

A-Ram nodded and looked at the webbed up hatch of the air lock as he shut the outer doors. He noted the twisted wreckage. "You did this, Bel?"

"I suppose so."

"When you first came out of the air lock, you looked a little strange," he said.

"How so?"

"I didn't have time to take it all in, but you looked like a robot. Just for a moment."

Stenstrom shook his head. "Must be the Sisters' doing somehow."

Taara pulled her Monica from the wall and approached the fallen, mangled form of Innocent Drury. She and gave him a kick, stirring up tails of dark smoke. "Did you see how fast those guys moved? These are eaten-up looking shinepoles—they shouldn't be able to move that fast."

"What is a 'shinepole', Taara?" Stenstrom asked. "Enlighten me."

"It's not a nice name to call somebody on Bazz."

A-Ram was quite shaken. "How were they doing all that stuff, Bel? How did they know the things they knew, and how did they contact the *Demophalon John?*"

Stenstrom slid his NTHs back into his sash. "I have no idea. They must have had some sort of Com device or long-range holo-mon hidden on their person. Speaking of which, let's get to the bridge at once and raise Captain

Gwendolyn. We've got to tell her she's heading into a trap."

A-Ram pointed at Innocent's dead, smoking body. "What should we do with him?"

"Leave him for the moment, we've not the time. We'll dispose of him later."

They moved down the hall at a run. "Chance Drury mentioned something called the Cronyns. What are those, Taara?" asked Stenstrom.

She cleared the chamber of her SK and cocked it. "Bad dreams, Bel, and I don't need the MOLLY to tell me that," she replied, trotting at his side. "They're supposed to be evil spirits who eat your dreams and lead you astray, trying to cause you harm. On Bazz, in the old days just after the fall equinox, there was a two week period that we called the 'Time of the Cronyn'. During that time, we'd start having bad dreams; we'd begin hearing things, seeing things, too. As the stories go, you couldn't trust your eyes or your ears. People sometimes would walk right off a cliff and have no idea they were falling. Sometimes people would gravely wound themselves and have no idea they were hurt—that sort of thing. People stayed home during the Time of the Cronyn and hid, doing as little as possible and hoping to ride it out, but, every year, lots of people got hurt or killed. Your boy, Darius Jones, rose to prominence during the Time of the Cronyn—he didn't seem to be affected by it. That was a long time ago though, and now it's just an excuse to drink and not work. I never believed in them myself."

They climbed the lift shaft and arrived on the bridge. "A-Ram, get us some space from that pirate ship out there, and then, once we've room, we'll pick up some speed, Slap her hard amidships and sink her!"

A-Ram took the helm and Taara flew into her seat at the Missive's Panel. "Standing too, Bel," he said.

"Very well, A-Ram, pull us away and swing up, Z minus 4:45pm. Taara, raise the *Demophalon John* if you can."

A-Ram spun the wheel and the *Seeker* banked away, as usual, moving backwards. "She's grappled on out there, Bel. I can't shake us loose."

"I've got the Captain, Bel," Taara said. "Audio only—the Com's messed up."

Stenstrom was relieved. Static came down from the Com.

"Gwen, is that you?"

"Paymaster, I'm right here," came a reply over the Com. "What is your situation?"

"Gwen, that previous transmission you received from us was bogus. We ran afoul of a group of pirates calling themselves the Drury Brothers. They told us that they were attempting to lead your ship into a trap of some sort—I don't know the exact nature of what they had planned, but it didn't sound good."

"I see," she said. "Sobering news."

"Gwen, I suggest you return at once to Kana and report the situation to the Fleet. Tell them that they should send an armada to sweep this area and keep a weather eye for something called the Cronyns. I don't know what they are, but the Druries were planning on feeding you to them."

"Yes, excellent, Paymaster. I shall make sail for Kana at once and advise them there."

Stenstrom stood and looked up at the ceiling. He sensed something was wrong.

"Gwen, you seem awfully compliant. What about your mission?"

"My mission is important, but secondary at this time. You advised me of danger in this sector and I see the good sense in it."

Stenstrom rubbed his chin. "When we spoke initially, Gwen—what did you say you were going to do to me?"

Her voice came back over the Com a moment later. "As I recall, I invited you to play cards."

Taara looked into the visor. She muted the Com. "Bel—we're not sending out any signal. It's being jammed and we don't have the power to overcome it."

Stenstrom turned to A-Ram. "Are we free from the *Heade- on- the -Hearth*?"

"No."

"Taara, un-mute the Com."

She did. Stenstrom continued. "You didn't mention wanting to play cards, Gwen. As I recall, you mentioned wanting to knock my teeth out. So, to whom am I currently speaking, please?"

There was a crackling pause. Then: "A-heheheh. I fancy your ship, Paymaster," came Gwendolyn's voice. "It's a little weedy, but nothing a few acquired parts won't fix. You're going to die, sir, you know that, don't you?"

"Identify yourself, please."

There was another pause. "Come into your office and see for yourself. *Je vous ose à a*-heheheh."

Stenstrom drew his NTHs and headed toward his office door, Taara following.

He took a deep breath and went in.

Outside, through the windows of the office, he could see the girdered bulk of the *Heade* still latched onto the neck of the *Seeker*. Two figures floated near the window—bobbing in naked space.

It was Chance and Lemmuel Drury. And, though they had no pressure suits, they both appeared to be very much alive. Lemmuel was, with one hand, holding into the outer skin of the ship, and with the other he was holding onto Chance, who had no hands and was badly charred, his hair and clothes mostly burned away.

Eyes glittering, Chance's mouth started moving, and the Com came back on. "You've no idea what you're dealing with here, Paymaster. We inhabit the spaces in-between the mundane and the well-traveled. The small stretch between Kana, Onaris, and Bazz isn't so small, and that is where we prey on the unwary, in the heart of the League, yet right under its nose. You, and your friends on the scout ship are our prey, our latest victims. You are simply among those unfortunate souls lost at sea and hailed in memoriam. Your empty chair shall be saluted with raised glasses and thumps on the chest."

Taara lost her bearing a little. "What in the Name of Creation are you?"

"*Je suis le diable.* The devil …a-heheh…"

Stenstrom aimed his NTHs at the window. Chance drew back and gave a hideous grin, his burned face nearly splitting open.

"What are you going to do with that, Paymaster, shoot us? You'll out your window and space yourself. NTH's do quite a lot of damage, so I'm told. *Le c'est une vraiment grande explosion,* eh?"

"Don't believe everything you hear."

Stenstrom pulled the trigger. The hammer swung and a green ball of energy lanced out, passing harmlessly through the window and out the other side, hitting Lemmuel in the chest. He thrashed in surprise for a moment then was still. Stenstrom cocked the other NTH and fired at Chance. He partially hid behind the bulk of his dead brother and the green shot hit Lemmuel in the shoulder, sending both of them spiraling away toward the aft of the ship.

He watched them flail into the distance. "A-Ram!" he yelled, "I want a 360 degree wing roll on my mark!"

At the helm, A-Ram kicked a lever on the floor. "Ready!" he said.

Stenstrom waited a few seconds more, then: "Now, A-Ram, roll!"

A-Ram spun the wheel and the *Seeker* barrel-rolled fast, the *Heade* moving with it through about ninety degrees of the roll, then it let go, its gangly bulk spiraling away, tentacles flailing like a tick that had been pried loose of its host.

"Oh, look!" Taara cried with glee. "The *Heade* got one of them, did you see?"

Through the window, Stenstrom could see that the bulk of the *Heade* had plowed into one of the Druries before it let go. The second Drury, and they couldn't make out which one, managed to avoid getting hit by the *Heade,* but instead got clipped by the rolling wing of the *Seeker*—his body rocketing off in a random direction like a ping pong ball smacked by a fast-moving paddle.

"Serves 'em right, the buggers!" Taara said. "Creation, Bel—what are we dealing with here?"

"I truly have no idea. Is the MOLLY telling you anything?"

"Nope. The MOLLY seems to be a whizz with technical stuff, but a little less so with the weird, and those shinepoles were way weird."

They left the office. "What happened?" A-Ram asked at the helm. "What was that?"

"Our friends were back."

"Those guys? The pirates? Outside?" A-Ram was a bit panicked.

"Yes."

Stenstrom thought a moment. "Which gives me a bad thought. The one we left in the corridor, Taara, you hit him with an SK burst, right?"

"Yep, got him right in the chest, full auto. Probably put ten fifty-cal slugs into him. No man could survive that."

"And no man could survive naked in space without a pressure suit, yet the two of them didn't appear inconvenienced in the least. I recall hitting Clem Drury previously in the chest with my NTH, and we did not see him out the window just now, so I'm assuming he's dead somewhere." Stenstrom started for the lift.

"Where are you going?" Taara asked.

"Back to the docking ring to make sure our friend is still where we left him, good and dead. And, if so, I'm going to Space him out."

"You're not going alone."

"Yes, I am. You two stay here. A-Ram, get us into position to finish the *Heade- on- the- Hearth.* I want you to create some distance, lay on two, and sink it. Taara, keep trying to raise the *Demophalon John.*" He handed A-Ram one of his NTHs and went out into the dark of the lift shaft. "If anything comes through that lift door and it's not me—use it."

Stenstrom made his way down the dark lift shaft and out to the waiting corridor beyond.

14

Her face was killing her.

Captain Gwendolyn snatched the report out of her crewman's hand. She looked at it, her green eyes flashing. "Allistar, I told you I wanted this status report three hours ago!" she yelled, her voice ugly.

Her cut face had been completely sealed, but it hurt like hell. She felt mad and short. To top things off, she was quite worried about Paymaster Stenstrom—what had happened, where did he go? Her worry and pain, all those things mixed together in her soul and let the Grizzly Bear come out in full force.

"Yes, Captain, I'm sorry." He stood there looking at the floor.

Gwendolyn felt a wave of anger pass over her and was on the verge of giving him a good lashing, but, for her new friend, the Paymaster, she was trying to turn a new leaf and better herself. She sighed and took a deep breath, allowing her anger to diminish. Her face was stinging, creating pain that was just bearable. "It's all right. Just try and be a bit more punctual next time," she said lightly touching the wound.

"Aye, ma'am."

She paced the small bridge. Crewmen bustled about. "Sensing," she said turning to a crewman near the front of the bridge, "do you have anything yet?"

"No, ma'am, the sector is clear."

"A dead Warbird cannot simply vanish. The *Seeker* has to be here somewhere. These are the correct coordinates they gave us, yes?"

"Yes, ma'am."

"Very well. Keep looking."

The navigator checked his settings. "Ma'am, I must inform you that we are currently well out the shipping lanes on the leeside of Druries Belt. I highly advise we return to the lanes and call for an organized search party."

"Noted. Keep looking. The sooner we find the *Seeker,* the sooner we're windward of Druries Belt and back in the lanes."

She turned her attention to the Com officer. "Com, send to Fleet—advise them of our situation, current position and heading."

"Ay, ma'am. Message sent."

"Thank you. Now, raise the boatswain. Tell him as soon as we make contact with the *Seeker* I want him to run out a Christmas gun. He shall then carefully—and I emphasize *'carefully'*— shoot out their improvised drive engine, and we will board. I want to ensure Paymaster Stenstrom doesn't suffer a change of mind. I want him and his crew brought safely out of there as soon as possible. No more games—this is getting too dangerous."

"Aye, ma'am."

"Once aboard, he and his crew shall be treated with the utmost respect and courtesy, understood? I expect all present to go out of our way to make them feel welcome, so let's look lively."

The holographic displays moving about the Navigator's head spun. Something blinked. "Ma'am, new contact bearing 7:45AM of 11:16PM."

"Is it the *Seeker?*"

"Looks to be. It is a large metallic object, offering a Mag-reflection that is typical for a *Straylight*-class vessel. It is not flying its standard colors."

"They must be shutdown. Plot intercept solution. Com, send to *Seeker* and raise Paymaster Stenstrom immediately."

The helmsman, pressing buttons at his small chair, banked the ship and soon the dark mass of the *Seeker* jogged into view in the display.

The *Demophalon John* had a small view screen and several large, holo-infused, blue-filtered windows that were lit up with various displays and readouts. Gwendolyn often didn't look at the screen. She looked out a window and saw, far off, a small form holo'ed with a red circle. The ship was still quite a ways off in the distance and Gwendolyn glanced at the screen to see enhanced detail.

It was the *Seeker* sure enough.

The *Seeker* was dark, all running lights off and the roving eye of the main sensor dead. She was flipped over in relationship to their orientation, and was slowly spinning to port.

"Com," Gwendolyn said. "Any luck raising the *Seeker?*"

"No, ma'am."

"They must have blown their engine. Keep trying. Are we detecting any venting?"

"No, ma'am, the *Seeker* reads as whole with a sufficient pressure of breathable gasses within to support life."

The doors to the bridge opened and in walked Morgan-Jeterix, decked out in her black uniform with an array of silver tools peeking out of her pockets and a winged helmet sitting on her head. She was a Hospitaler of Samaritan class. Scout ships normally didn't have Samaritans aboard, but, being favored with Admiral Derlith, he had managed to get one for her regardless.

✶ ✶ ✶ ✶ ✶

Morgan was a lean but solid lady with dark blonde hair, braided in many, thin, beaded twists under her silver helmet. Most Hospitalers were Browns, but Morgan was not a Brown—she was a lady of Thompson, an old family from the Hala region of Kana. She became a Hospitaler, Gwendolyn had heard, because she wanted to, because she felt a personal calling. Her smooth skin had that "tanned-hide" look that many Halas had. She wore a large ring on her right hand emblazoned with a proud "E" for the Ephysians, an esoteric order within the Hospitalers

that Gwendolyn didn't know too much about.

She and Lt. Gwendolyn didn't get along most of the time. Sometimes they did, and sometimes they were just on the cusp of becoming friends, but that was more the exception than the norm—their personalities appeared to be too similar in certain regards and, therefore, they clashed at inconvenient but predictable moments. Being a Hospitaler, Morgan wasn't under Captain Gwendolyn's direct command, a fact she enjoyed pointing out often. The two frequently fought openly and were occasionally not on speaking terms, but Morgan was a good Hospitaler and was a handy asset to have around. Morgan had engaged in several brief but very public and rather messy affairs with some of Gwendolyn's crew (both male and female), which she did not approve of at all. She'd also heard whispers that Morgan had a thing for her as well, though she tried to not think about it much.

Morgan also was a registered empath and supposedly bore a body-length tattoo that only the Sisters could detect, branding her as such. The Thompsons had a reputation for being highly empathetic, to involuntarily know the feelings and surface thoughts of another without overtly being tele-pathic. Being empathic, Morgan also had the annoying habit of tapping into Gwendolyn's thoughts and saying out loud what she was thinking. It was not only frustrating for Gwendolyn, but embarrassing as well, to have a running tap from the well-spring of her mind to the open, wagging mouth of Morgan. She hadn't heard of Morgan doing that to anybody else—just her. It was mor-tifying—anything coming out of Morgan's mouth could be hot, right off her brain.

Morgan adjusted her helmet, as it always seemed to sit askew on her head on top of all those tightly run braids, and she walked up to Gwendolyn.

"I recommended that you sit a spell," she said in her Hala-inspired, Thompson twang. "You actually lost a fair amount of blood from that cut before I could get it stopped."

"I've work to attend to," Gwendolyn replied curtly. "Do you need something?"

"Yeah, I'm worried about him out there too. Tough to be all prim and proper when you're worried, isn't it? I could give you a sedative."

There she goes again. "I really don't know what you're talking about, Morgan."

"I've heard he's really handsome."

"Who is?"

"Paymaster Stenstrom."

Gwendolyn flushed up. "What do you want, Morgan? I'm really rather busy."

"Reeling in the Paymaster, I know. I wanted to share my findings with you. That cut you received, I know how it was made."

"All right, let's hear it."

Morgan looked around, seeing the crew moving about the bridge. "In private, Captain."

"I've no time for dramatics, Morgan. Helm, match PM base with *Seeker*, and lock." She gave Morgan a hard look. "Out with it."

Morgan huffed. "Fine then. Your cut was made with Shadow tech, no doubt about it. A micro-point beam of it to be precise. The presence of Shadow tech prevented your blood from clotting—you would have bled out in short order, had I not sealed it."

Gwendolyn stopped what she was doing. "How in the name of Creation did I get cut with Shadow tech?"

"You tell me, and ..."

Morgan suddenly looked around. "What's that noise?"

"What noise?"

"That!" she said impatiently. "That loud beeping sound. It sounds like an alarm of some sort to me."

The crew looked at Morgan, clearly thinking her mad. "I don't hear an alarm, Morgan," Gwen said, impatient.

She spun around. "You're telling me you cannot hear that? Creation, my eardrums are going to burst. Beep! Beep! Beep!"

She turned to the Com officer and pointed at him. "You! What are you doing?"

The Com was confused. "Pardon, ma'am?" he said.

"You're standing there with your arms held out in mid air, touching nothing."

He looked down. "I'm manning my position at the Com."

Morgan pointed to his left. "The Com's over there—you're standing over nothing right now." Morgan glanced at the windows. "And what, may I ask, is that?" she said pointing at the window.

By this point, the crew stopped what they were doing and became a bit apprehensive. Hospitalers often did strange things—but this display was too much.

"We are currently involved in a rescue and recovery operation, Morgan. Thank you for the update. Please allow us to continue—I believe you are upsetting my crew."

Morgan pushed her helmet back. "What are we rescuing?"

"Paymaster Stenstrom and his crew off the Warbird *Seeker*. Is that not obvious?"

"What's that outside?" Morgan pointed to the windows again. "Oh, dear Creation! We nearly got creamed by an asteroid just now!"

Gwendolyn looked to the screen. There she saw the approaching form of the *Seeker* floating alone in a clear field.

"An asteroid? As I said, there's nothing out there but the *Seeker*, whom we are endeavoring to rescue. Have you gone blind?"

Morgan marched up to one of the windows. "Doesn't look like any Warbird I've ever seen. It looks to me that we are heading straight for a small cluster of planetoids."

Gwendolyn turned back to the screen. There was the *Seeker*, slowly approaching, its orientation now in synch with theirs after the helm corrected for it. "Morgan, I think you need to take one of your potions and rest up a tad." She thought back to Paymaster Stenstrom, and one of the insults he once used on her. "Perhaps your braids are a bit too tight and your skull requires circulation!" There—that was a good one. See, he was already having a good influence on her.

Morgan didn't appreciate the joke. "Captain, you know as well as I that my House can see through Cloaked illusions."

"So you enjoy saying."

"I think we're flying right into one!"

Morgan's eye grew wide. "Grab onto something! Everybody! Brace for impact!"

And before Gwendolyn could say anything in reply, the ship was rocked by a massive collision.

Everything went dark on the *Demophalon John.*

Lady Alesta of Dare

15

—A Falling Star—

Lady Alesta prayed by the great tree, hoping for a bit of inspiration. It was odd—she usually found divine guidance coming to her at the strangest of times; while sleeping, eating dinner, doing her chores—just not when she was praying like she was supposed to do. It was getting cold and she wanted her bed. She had stoked the fire in her small room before coming out so that it should be nice and warm by now. Her room would be snug and toasty for her upon returning. A large bell mounted on a post near the tree was showing signs of frosting over.

She was wearing the standard clothing of her order: a white woolen smock that went down to her knees, lined with home-spun frills, a belt of red and green shells stitched together and tasseled with gold thread that she had loomed herself, several necklaces made of smooth, painted wood beads and the same red and green shells as her belt, and a long, green brocade robe lined with embroidered gold fabric.

Most everything she wore she had made herself, and her belt and her necklaces were infused with the love of her Star—they protected her mind and shielded her from sight.

Her thick black hair was held up with several wooden sticks stuck in near the nape of her neck, creating a large, onion-shaped bun. Without the sticks, her hair would have gone down to her ankles. She hadn't cut it in years, She sometimes wondered if she had a "special someone", a person to whom she'd given her heart, what he would think of her appearance; the clothes, her thick hair, her unshod feet. The road she had chosen for herself was indeed a lonely one.

Her feet were getting cold—she wished she was allowed to wear shoes when praying, but they were forbidden. Cold, tired of kneeling, she stood up and bushed herself off. No inspiration was coming to her. She rubbed her hands and blew on them, her breath steaming through her stinging fingers. She turned to make her way across the green back to her room.

She looked up at the close sky one last time.

She could see the star shining there to the west, the star that only she and her brothers and sisters could see.

The Star of Merian, lighting up the sky in a yellow veil.

✶ ✶ ✶ ✶ ✶

She had been a Pilgrim of Merian since she was very young—for over a hundred years now. Growing up with her family in Dare on the windswept isle of Barrow, she had always been able to see a star that nobody else could. She was a lady of the Dare line, 10th order—there were a lot of Dares in Dare, and her order was placed somewhere in the middle. They weren't the richest, but nor were they impoverished outlanders either.

The star she saw was a bright, yellowish globe, easily the biggest star in the sky. On clear nights, and sometimes during the day, she even thought she could see a red cloud moving around the star in a slow spiral.

She asked her father what the star was called—it was so pretty.

"What star?" her father asked.

"That one, just there."

"Where?"

It became clear to her in time that she, of all her brothers and sisters and friends, was the only one who could see that star with the red cloud. Sometimes that made her happy as she had something so beautiful all to herself, but other times it made her sad. Such a pretty thing should be shared, should be available for all to see.

When she was twenty-three, she went into Dare market with her parents to gather items for the Fall Feast. The Fall Feast was a big event in the Barrow region, celebrated proudly in the cities of Dare, Saga, Rhoda and Tuk, and there was much planning to be done.

When they got to market, there was quite a commotion going on beyond the usual comings and goings of the shoppers and traders. Many were gathered around the square and were hooting and hollering at a small group of people wearing green robes and white smocks. The people were laughing at them.

Alesta went to her mother. "Mother, who are those people, and why are they being laughed at?"

Her mother tried not to look in their direction. "Those people are Pilgrims of Merian—just a cult of harmless zealots from the mainland."

"Why are they being laughed at?"

"Because they have silly ideas. Just ignore them."

Alesta was curious. She pulled away from her family and approached the crowd gathered around the Pilgrims. There were five of them standing in the town square. They were trying to pass out literature, which nobody seemed to want to take, and they had a collection basket, which had a fair amount of money in it. "Here—for real clothes and breath mints! Brush your teeth next time, Pilgrim!" people derided as they tossed in money. Nobody was harming the Pilgrims or roughing them about, but those in the crowd were sharp and vulgar with their jabs and quips.

Through the heckling, she listened to what they said.

"It is our sworn mission to bring you good news," they said, shouting above the noise. "We bring you news of the Elders. They are not gone. They are with us still."

"I don't see them!"

"Where are they?"

"Hiding in the clouds surely, full of tuck and play!"

"Hahahahaha!"

The Pilgrims took the ribbing with serene patience. "The Elders are there for you to see; all one need do is look."

"All I see is you with your muddy feet and outrageous skirt, quite out of line and well off the hook!"

"Hahahahahahah!"

"Put some pants on, Pilgrim—your legs are a fright."

"With wickets like those, the ladies surely take flight!"

"Haaaaaaaaaaaahahahahaha!"

The Pilgrims took it in stride. "The Star of Merian is plain. Lift you your eyes and revel in its light."

"Again, your legs are blinding all else from sight!" a jokester mused.

"I see nothing but pale skin and patches of hair."

"He's either a very ugly troll, or possibly a half-shaven bear!"

"Hahahahahahaha!"

Alesta spoke up. "I see it," she said in a tiny voice.

Everybody quieted down and turned to her. The Pilgrims were shocked. "You? My dear, you see the star?"

"Yes."

The Pilgrims made their way through the crowd and approached her. The people in the crowd rubbed their chins. "What star? Where is it?"

"It's over there," she said pointing to the west.

The Pilgrims were open-mouthed. "You can see it! You can see the star!"

"It's a big yellow star that's always out, and it has a funny red cloud floating around it."

Before a year had passed, Lady Alesta herself stood with the Pilgrims of Merian wearing homemade clothes and green robes, her fine gowns of Dare and delicate shoes cast aside. She held literature and got laughed at in the town squares of Kana and beyond. She had given up everything she had to join them. Her mother had gone into mourning over her decision, grieving for her daughter as if she were dead.

"Don't cry, mother," she had said. "I hear a voice that will not yield."

"No lord or goodly man will have you. You will be alone forever wearing rags," her mother said.

"I believe this is my calling. This is what I am here to do."

The Star called to her and she became a Pilgrim of Merian.

As she settled into her life with the Pilgrims, she found that their order was much more pervasive and committed than she first thought. There was more to the Pilgrims of Merian than harmless oddities good for a laugh in the town squares. They served the Star of Merian, and it asked much of them.

In the modest dens of the Merians, she learned to speak their secret language. There they spoke of the star. She discovered that it watched over them, and that most could not see it—not even the Sisters. They told her that the Elders were there, orbiting the star, waiting for them to be rejoined with their children. She went to the place of Westwood and marveled at its beauty.

And, there was much work to do. The Star demanded it.

In Westwood, they sent Alesta out into the night when they thought she was ready, to pray, to seek enlightenment. Whatever the Star's judgment for her would dictate the rest of her life, no matter what.

On her knees in the snow, she prayed for hours, her skin freezing, her feet numb, her fingers close to frostbite.

None of it mattered.

Her efforts were rewarded. In delirium she heard the star speak to her.

It said: *Save all those who fall astray.*

Such was her command, and she would follow it without fear or question. She walked the Merian's Road with her brethren for decades, and was taken into the stars with her brothers and sisters, to a secret place where she could pray and do as she was commanded.

Her road was to be the most dangerous, the Star commanded it.

✶ ✶ ✶ ✶ ✶

As she readied to return to her room and modest bed, she saw a star fall. It traced a gentle line across the sky and disappeared behind the nearby planetoid.

Edam, the Star called it.

Hell, a hideous, haunted place.

Alesta often saw stars falling into Edam, and she knew what it meant.

She watched the star fall, and a tear came to her eye.

"Lost souls! Lost souls!"

Her prayers had been answered, though not quite in the way she had expected. Gathering her robes, she ran to the nearby bell and began ringing it, the small shards of frost vibrating off it as it rang. Beyond, lights in her small village came on in response to her ringing of the bell. She could see outlines of people moving about in their rooms through their frosty windows, getting dressed.

The Pilgrims of Merian, impoverished, laughed at, disregarded, never failed to answer the call of the bell no matter what the hour.

Save all those who fall astray.

In Edam there shall be many who need saving.

Stenstrom, Lord of Belmont-South Tyrol

16

—THE DRURIES—

NTH at the ready, Stenstrom made has way toward the docking ring. Though the corridor was now quiet of the preternatural groans and shrieks that had earlier plagued it, the silence that now pervaded was ominous and nearly as bad. The dim lighting, routed via the generators by Taara on the bridge, flickered a little bit.

He reached a crossroad. He was now familiar enough with the layout of the ship to know that around the corner to his left was the docking ring. If everything was as it should be, then the dead body of Innocent Drury, stabbed, burned, and devastated with fifty caliber slugs, should be right there where he'd fallen.

But, and this was a big "but"—seeing Innocent's two brothers floating about in space alive and well made all bets void. Stenstrom was certain he'd leap around the corner and Innocent Drury would be gone, lurking loose somewhere on the ship, creating all manner of chaos.

That's how things seemed to go on this ship—the improbable would probably happen.

Stenstrom stood there, propped up against the wall, grappling with his courage. He could smell the burnt flesh and explosive shells of Taara's gun lingering in the corridor from the battle that took place earlier. He cocked the NTH's hammer, checked the cinnabar wedge to make sure it was in good and tight and wasn't cracked, took a deep breath, and jumped out, barrel leveled.

Lying in a pool of drying blood was the body of Innocent Drury, face down, his arms tucked up beneath him like he was praying. His body still smoked a little.

Stenstrom breathed a sigh of relief and swallowed. "Com," he said.

Taara's voice, a shower of worry, came down in reply. "That you, Bel? What's your status?"

"I've arrived at the docking ring—Innocent's still here, right where you shot him down."

Taara's voice over the Com sounded relieved. "See—he took a full SK burst to the gut—that's tough to spring back from."

Stenstrom aimed his NTH. "Yes, well, I'm going to put one into his dead body just to be sure—the NTH never fails."

The hammer swung in its fussy manner and he fired a green globe of energy that pierced Innocent right above his shoulder. His body didn't move as the globe struck it, just lay there—nothing unusual with an NTH shot, as its globes of energy did little visible damage. A victim of the NTH simply dropped dead, oftentimes not knowing what hit them. Knowing the infallible killing nature of an NTH shot and feeling much better, Stenstrom slid the pistol back into its sash.

"A-Ram, what's the status of the *Heade-on-the-Hearth*?" he asked.

"We're just swinging into position now," came his reply over the Com. "Another few minutes and we'll ram her into bits."

"Very well. Just say when, and I'll give the order."

As Stenstrom stood there, he thought he heard a distant clank. The lights overhead surged, and then went out, wrapping him in inky darkness.

"Taara, what's happening?"

The Com sputtered and quickly faded. "Bel, we've lost the *Westminster*, this very moment."

The Com buzzed. "Taara?"

"Bel—we..." And the Com went out.

Struggling in the dark, Stenstrom produced a Holystone and shook it, creating a soft yellow glow. He suspected deviltry. Taara's handiwork so far had proven reliable, and the *Westminster* didn't just now go quiet by itself. Holding the Holystone up, he strode over to the fallen body of Innocent Drury, the wounds and ripples of his body thrown into grotesque relief, and gave him a kick, flipping him over.

He looked down.

Laying there was a pile of clothes with a ruddy skin inside that looked like a fallen, scorched cocoon. His filthy shirt was slit open. His chest was burst open and hollow—no innards, no skeleton, just a shot-out, burned husk.

"Taara!" Stenstrom yelled. "A-Ram!!"

Nothing.

The lights in the corridor surged back to life for a hopeful moment, and then went out—for good this time, it seemed.

He flushed up against one of the walls and drew his NTH again.

For a moment, he had no idea what to do. He stood there in the dark, terrified.

Come on, Dav, Dunks, give me an order! Father, tell me what I'm supposed to do!

Mother—Mother, what am I supposed to do?

Lilly, tell me what to do ...

Stenstrom stood there and struggled, trying to regain his composure.

He had to square up with the fact there was no Captain Davage or his father or mother, or Lilly, or even Lt. Dunkster around to prop him up. He was the captain. This mess was his to solve. Taara and A-Ram: those were his people to keep safe.

This is what he wanted, dreaming as a boy by the fountain, in his rusty office aboard the *Sandwich,* and on the red velvet crush of the Admiralty floor—now here it was.

Enjoy.

He took a minute or two and wallowed in the dark, allowing himself to be weak, to be scared. Then he stood and set to it.

First thing's first: The *Westminster.*

He tried to remember where the *Westminster* was currently kept. It amazed him how much he already depended on Taara and A-Ram. With them he felt quite at ease—without them it was a different story; the interior of the *Seeker* became barren and alien.

So, where was the *Westminster?* If Innocent Drury was out to cause mischief, then that's where it would be easiest to do so. Of course, Innocent Drury wouldn't know that the *Westminster* was their sole source of locomotion, nor would he know where it was berthed.

Yet, Innocent's horrid brother, Chance, appeared to have command of a vast cache of up-to-date information, and he couldn't rule out the possibility that Innocent had access to it too.

He had to head to the *Westminster,* secure it, and get it going again, then he could deal with whatever sort of grotesque creature Innocent Drury was under his stinking hide.

So where was it? If his memory served him, the *Westminster* was bolted down in the big Ripcar bay, number 5.

Yes, that's the one. Where is it—it's in the tower, in a forward compartment.

He recalled seeing it burn from his office windows: 5 dots of blue fire far away in the rear section of the ship.

NTH in hand, hammer cocked, he made his way through the dark, his Holystone lighting the way. He could feel the slightly sickening tug of the ship banking hard to the starboard. A-Ram must be lining up the *Heade* for a ramming shot.

Or, maybe, the pirate ship out there is attacking. Maybe A-Ram was maneuvering for their lives up there.

He had to hurry.

After a bit of blundering about, he felt his eyes getting used to the dark. What at first looked to him like pitch black, even with the lit-up Holystone, was now half-way passable. He could see the floor, as well as see the ceiling and the girders and panels lining the walls. He waved his hand in front of his face and could see it just fine, he could even see the silver embroidery on his coat sleeve. He let the Holystone drop and continued on without it.

He got to the lift shaft. He'd have to go down two levels and bear down the neck of the ship toward the rear section, and then go up three levels into the tower; always with the *Seeker,* there was a lot of walking to do, unlike the *New Faith,* on which one could take a lift to just about anywhere: up, down, sideways, it didn't matter. Lifts on the *Seeker* were just up and down. He knew the tower layout pretty well, and shouldn't have too much trouble finding his way around once he got there. He opened the door to the lift and waved his NTH around, half expecting Innocent Drury to pop out of any convenient shadow at any moment.

Nothing—the shaft was deserted. He imagined the old days, lights, people in uniform walking this way and that: the *Seeker* full of life.

Now, just depressing, lifeless darkness.

Stop! He sensed danger.

Squinting, he could see hints of something fibrous and stringy stretched out across the opening of the lift shaft. He could see it was a sort of viscous wire strung from the port side of the shaft to the starboard. It appeared taut, but sloppy and irregular, like a thick gauge wire that had been pulled tight but wasn't quite straight. At intervals, he could see things jutting up from the wire—barbs or pointed razors that stuck up in a predatory manner.

Now he could see that one strand wasn't the only one stretched across the shaft—there were many. The shaft was clogged with them, like a messy spider web of barbed wire.

Innocent Drury has been busy, left him quite a grisly present, he thought. Such a spectacle only made the whole mystery of the Druries all the more delectable. He had to admit his curiosity was piquing at what he would encounter when he met Innocent Drury again. Were they demons? Were they Nargals, creatures like Lilly?

He'd have to come up with another way down. Too bad his NTH didn't damage inanimate objects, otherwise, he'd just shoot them out. Taara's SK would do wonders about now. One or two blasts would probably clear out the bulk of it.

Stenstrom was about to head back out of the shaft and find an alternate route, when the ship was rocked with a massive, pounding blow dead astern.

BOOM!

Caught unaware, Stenstrom was rocked from his perch out into open space—into the lift shaft and the stringy carpet of waiting razor-wire below.

17

—The Dream Begins—

When Captain Gwendolyn, Lady of Prentiss, opened her eyes, she saw her ship in great disarray. Most of the bridge crew were down, some obviously badly wounded. Crewman Allistar, the fellow she'd just yelled at for giving her a late report, was near the navigator's position, face-down on the floor. She struggled to get to him, but her FEDULA, a rapier-like weapon of her House, was tangled up in her coat. Could have been worse—it could have been tangled up in her flesh. Carefully, she freed it and stood.

Pain, great pain in her leg. She disregarded it and got to Allistar, rolled him over, and saw his face covered in blood from a deep wound. His blood made a large red stain on the floor.

There were groaning sounds and signs of distress all around her. The bridge was a charnel house. The Navigator, Lt. Merce, was out, though he showed no outward signs of injury. The Helmsman, Crewman Protherow, appeared to be dead; he just seemed dead. The Com officer, Lt. Sai, was sitting up against the wall, holding his groggy head. Gwendolyn made her way to the helm. Unlike Warbirds, with their elaborate wheeled set-ups, the helm on the *Demophalon John* was nothing more than a small panel with a number of levers and gauges that controlled the movement of the ship. Not nearly as precise and maneuverable as a *Straylight*, it, nevertheless, sufficed on a small scouting ship. The levers all appeared to be floating, out of joint. She tried to re-adjust them as best she could, but helmsmanship really wasn't her area. She guessed at the positions. She then checked the helmsman—as she thought, he was dead.

Ahead, crumpled up near the rail, was Morgan-Jeterix. Her silver helmet lay some distance away, upside down. Some of her Hospitaler tools had emptied out of her pockets and lay on the floor all around her.

"Morgan!" Gwen managed to say as she stumbled toward her. "Morgan, wake up. We're sure to have wounded all over."

Morgan appeared to be out. Gwendolyn shook her. "Morgan, wake up!"

She groaned and slowly her eyes opened. "Oh, Creation, it's you … What happened?"

"I don't know. We appear to have crashed."

Morgan closed her eyes again. "Did I not tell you we were about to crash?"

"We can discuss that further later, Morgan, for now we've wounded needing tending, casualties to sort out, and …"

"Yes, casualties! This is all your fault. Never listen to me, do you? You arrogant cow …"

Gwendolyn roughly pulled her up by the scruff of her black Hospitaler uniform. "Morgan! Yes, yes, you're right—I'm an arrogant cow! This is my fault! You can call me all the names you wish, as you start tending to my crew! There's Allistar—help him!"

Morgan shook her head, trying to clear it, and unsteadily went to crewman Allistar. As Morgan began working on him, Gwendolyn went to the main Sensing station and peered into it.

The sensor was ruined, full of static, and random streaks of color that bled across the screen. No good—no readable data.

She could hear the ship "gassing" all over—trying to equalize pressure. Clearly, the hull was breached somewhere. At least some of the automated systems of the ship were functioning.

Gwendolyn spun around, not quite sure what to do. This was a calamity—situation unknown, location unknown, personnel still on-duty unknown. They needed rescuing. "Com," she said after a moment to Lt. Sai. "Com, get me Engineering. Right away, please."

Sai blinked at her in a vacant manner and slowly began to stand.

Nothing, silence from the Com. "Com functional but unanswered, Captain," he said, still groggy. "We have internal, we can … receive, but our outgoing range is very limited. I think … we lost our mast."

"Keep trying. See if you can raise anyone, yes?"

She turned to a dazed crewman who was just now picking herself up. "Crewman, I need you to find the boatswain. Tell him I want an accurate injury report, and then I want all wounded organized into a large area—the mess, Cargos one and two—any place that can hold them. Morgan and I will then be down to begin treating them. Go now!" The crewman left the bridge.

Gwendolyn returned to Morgan. She was closing the wound on Allistar's forehead. "How is he?"

"He has a fractured skull and a deep laceration of the forehead," she said continuing her work. "I suppose he's lucky to be alive."

Gwendolyn stood and went to a window. Outside was a solid, inky black. "Where are we?" she said, almost to herself.

"I told you, Captain, we were heading straight for a cluster of planetoids. We're probably crash-landed on one."

"And, Morgan, you were aware of this how?"

Morgan threw down her instruments and got into Gwendolyn's face. "I have told you my family can see through illusions! You have never properly appreciated my candor and clarity of vision! We just flew into a minefield of illusion. If I were not such a lady, I think I would …"

"You'd what—hit me? I don't see anything stopping you! Go ahead, let's get this out of the way, so that we can—"

Morgan was gawking wide-eyed at the windows.

Gwendolyn turned.

Outside, in the darkness, a round pair of red, unblinking eyes gazed in through the windows.

"You see that?" Morgan cried.

Gwendolyn was transfixed. She just stood there and stared at the eyes.

Then, after a long stretch of time, the red eyes turned and vanished.

"Did you see that?" Morgan said again, walking to Gwendolyn's side.

"Yes, yes, I saw it."

"What was it?"

"An animal of some sort. I'm not a zoologist."

Feeling disoriented, suspecting she was heavily concussed, Gwendolyn assisted Morgan as she tended to the remaining bridge crew.

She looked back to where Allistar had been lying in a pool of his own blood.

The blood was gone.

"I feel it coming," Morgan said.

"What?" Gwendolyn asked.

"Illusion, forming all around us."

Gwendolyn vaguely felt herself falling into a strange dream. She must be delirious.

The Com beeped—an incoming message. "What's that message, Com?" she asked, hopeful.

Lt. Sai was not there.

She made her way to the Com to answer it herself.

"What are you doing? There's no message," Morgan asked as she worked on another crew member, her voice unsteady.

Gwendolyn hit the button. "Yes this is the Fleet scouting ship *Demophalon John*. We are in immediate need of—"

"*Gwendolyn!*" came a sharp, unpleasant voice over the Com followed by a lurid pause.

"Hello?" Gwendolyn asked. "Is anybody there? We require assistance."

"Who are you talking to?" Morgan asked.

"*Gwendolyn!*" came a hideous shriek. "*This is your aunt! Your loving, loving aunt. What a silly, weak little girl you are! He's out there close by, and I want you to kill him, do you understand?*" Her voice became a demonic howl. "*I want you to kill him, Gwendolyn! Kill! KILL HIM!*"

She put her hands to her face and backed away. She felt herself plummeting into a dream.

18

—LORD A-RAM—

"We should never have let him go alone," Taara said, holding the NTH. She cocked it and fired—nothing happened.

Girls couldn't fire an NTH, Bel had said. Guess he was right.

Everything had been working wonderfully. Using the remaining charge on the Missive's Panel, Taara had managed to get a few shipboard systems hammered out. The ship was moving reasonably well under power from the *Westminster.* A-Ram had gotten a fair amount of distance between themselves and the pirate ship. He was going to line it up, build up some speed, and Slap it into bits. That grungy *Webber* out there would never stand against an armored behemoth like the *Seeker.*

Stenstrom called up from the docking ring—the body of Innocent Drury was still there, which was good news.

And then, the *Westminster* vanished off the grid—pop!—like it had never been there at all. It was like somebody pulled the plug, and the ship went dark again.

The bridge was still lit up—the stolen generators providing power.

A-Ram stood behind the helm—it barely turned. Taara fiddled around with the Com, trying to get it started again. All of the sensing and scanning equipment was dead.

A-Ram cursed. "Taara, I need you to go into Bel's office and shout out the position of the *Heade-on-the-Hearth.* I have no idea where it is. My screen is dead here."

Taara ran into the office. "I don't see it!"

"It's got to be out there—it can't have gone far. I had it all lined up."

"I think it might be to our left. Go that way."

A-Ram pulled on the wheel and the *Seeker* banked steeply to the left.

"Hey—there it is—to our 10pm. It's turning! A-Ram, it's firing!"

A series of hard shocks rocked the *Seeker.*

A-Ram hung onto the helm. "What in Creation was that?"

"It was an energy beam of some sort—looks like a hot cassagrain."

"On a *Webber?*"

"They've got a moveable, long-barrel cannon mounted under the ship's nose, and that's what they're hitting us with!" Taara's voice was panicked. "A-Ram, they're coming around again for another pass!"

"Where?"

"7:30pm!"

A-Ram tugged on the helm with all his might, feeling the ship protest. "Do we have any weapons at all?"

"Take a guess, A-Ram!"

The *Seeker* was rocked again. "A-Ram, the dorsal quarter, rear section, is starting to glow!"

Her voice became a shriek. "Watch the tentacles! Watch the tentacles—it's trying to grab us!"

"Taara, all we've got is partial maneuvering thrusters! What am I supposed to do?"

He pulled the on the helm and tried to present the other side of the ship to the *Heade,* to give the heated-up quarter of the hull time to cool and to create some space. The helm fought him. He pulled harder. Of all the great men who had once turned this wheel, in its time of greatest need, a tiny man from Calvert would turn its pegs. He would not be meek, he would not be denied. A-Ram bent the helm to his will.

Taara watched the *Heade's* movements. "A-Ram, I think he's going for the *Westminster.* He's heading for a shot in that direction. High noon!"

A-Ram cursed, kicked the bars, and pulled on the wheel with all his might, forcing it to turn, forcing the ship to respond. He spun the nose around trying to get the *Westminster* as far away from the *Heade* as possible.

Another rumble from outside. Hit again. "Where'd he get us, Taara?" A-Ram shouted.

"Rear-quarter ventral!"

Good, A-Ram thought—armor's thickest there.

The *Seeker* shuddered.

"They're hitting us long, A-Ram!" Taara cried. "They're pouring it on!"

"Fine—let them! Taara, do we have any locomotion at all?"

She thought a moment. "No! Without the *Westminster,* no!"

A-Ram spun the helm as the *Heade* came about and blasted them again, its cassagrain lighting up cherry red.

"A-Ram, watch out! A-Ram!!"

... *A-Ram!!*

* * * * *

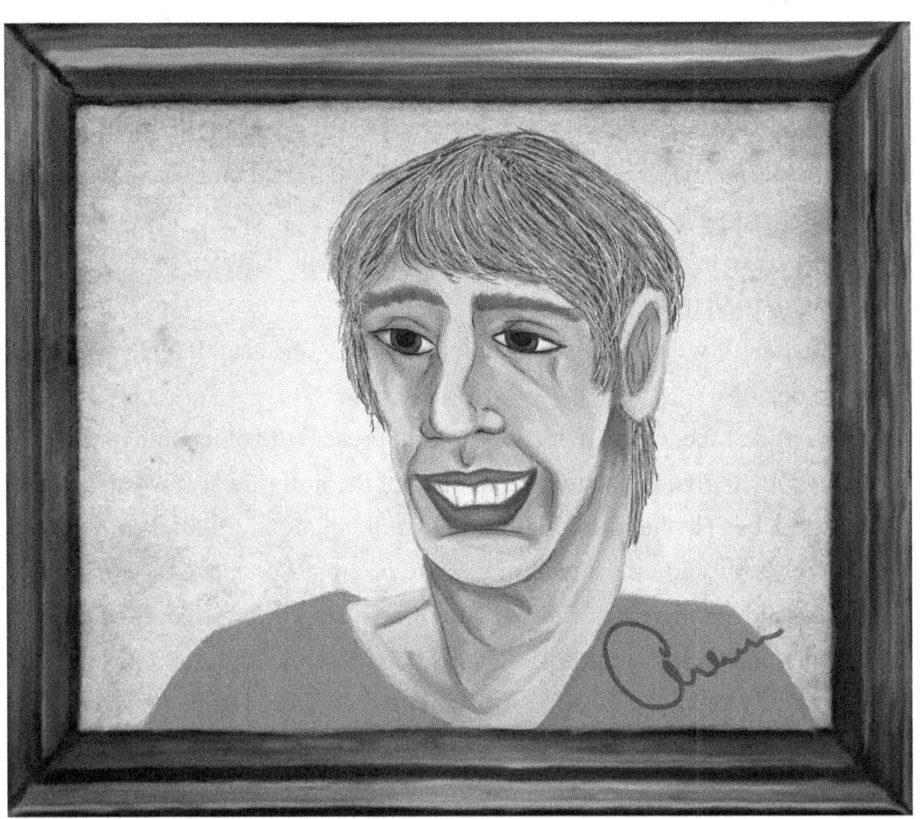

Self portait of Josephus, Lord of A-Ram

Adjutant Lt. Josephus, Lord of A-Ram, lived in the flower-potted, balconied Fleet apartments south of the main complex yard just a block or two from the weedy growth of the Great Armenelos Forest. The forest surrounded the city and was constantly threatening to engulf it. His apartment was small, but well-appointed and decorated in a sunny fashion—he'd done it himself, Lord A-Ram having a love of bright color and texture. He had tried his hand at various artistic pursuits: painting, sculpting, and so forth, but his skill was limited. Some of the paintings he had finished were colorful enough, but all were rather formless and abstract in nature.

He was well-liked and had his fair-share of friends, but they were mostly working peers, other adjutants, and folks from the mailroom he knew from his doings at the Fleet. None of them were people he roamed about with when not at work. He was considered 'cute,' that adorable, tiny fellow working for the unsmiling and dreaded Admiral Derlith, his faithful little shadow.

He came from a House Minor in Calvert. His father was Joshuah, and his mother, Dame Rihan. He was the youngest and the smallest of all his brothers and sisters. Coming from a Calvert House, the A-Rams didn't live in a huge manor or stately villa, instead, they lived in a serviceable townhouse in the heart of St. Edmunds a few blocks from the docks on St. James Road with a smashing view of Lonely Hearts Point. A-Ram had no complaints—he had had a good life.

His father was a fisherman, owning a few boats berthed in the St. Edmunds dock that normally brought in enough money to keep the family living fairly well. The House of A-Ram was originally a House from the eastern city of Dee hailing from the old House of Aramtwillinger, but when the Sisters announced that they were going to destroy the city of Dee for decadence and vice, the House broke apart—the Houses of Twill and Atlinger moving north to the new city of Dee, while the House of A-Ram went southwest and resettled in St. Edmunds. The A-Rams thought it best to get back into the Sisters' good graces as soon as possible, and avoiding Dee altogether would be wise. They took the name 'Aram,' but when they submitted their patent to the Sisters at Valenhelm, they miscopied it, coming up with the legal name "A-Ram," which the Sisters refused to correct afterwards.

Such would be their usual treatment from the Sisters: miscopied, mishandled, and unsatisfied.

The A-Rams would have an occasional and rather sordid history with the Sisters through the years, with each event lessening them ever more in esteemed sect's eyes. All Houses wanted the Sisters to approve of them, and the A-Rams were no different. Clovis of A-Ram had become a noted chef at the Empire Hotel in St. Edmunds, however, when a Sister came to sample his latest dish, a bad piece of halibut made her dreadfully sick, bending her over to full-blown food poisoning complete with carpet kneeling and projectile vomiting right there in the hotel dining room. That incident, however, paled in comparison to the Brandtball Affair years later, where Lord Arlie of A-Ram, the Charger of Beasley Canning Brandtball team, put a Sister from Saga Convent into the wall, and, subsequently, into traction while attempting to make a rough play.

Such things the Sisters tend not to forget, and so the House of A-Ram fell off the Sisters' Programmability schedule entirely and became UNTOUCH-ABLE. When one poisons a Sister, when one injures her playing Brandtball, one can bet they won't want to have Programmability anytime soon.

Untouchable. Venti Nomi.

A-Ram.

Everybody helped out with the family trade—his mother and his siblings included. His brothers went out with father every day to harvest the catch. His mother and sisters waited to help unload and process the fish when they returned. When Josephus grew old enough to accompany his father out to sea, he was miserable. Not only was his eyesight appalling, he was a grand klutz as well, making messes on the boat, tangling nets, and losing catches. He was also chronically seasick, and that was something he never got over. Eventually, father, shaking his head, relegated him back to the shore where he helped out with the women—his older brother Ephelrood tormented him relentlessly on the matter. Helping mother was no small chore—she kept everything regimented and precise—possibly that's where he learned to keep a clear, uncluttered head and work in a logical manner, from his mother's teachings.

As he grew, he learned that salt-sprayed and sunny Calvert was considered a lowly place, the least of places on Kana, unlike the stately lands to the north and the west, and the mountainous regions far to the north where he heard the god-like people with blue hair lived.

What was wrong with Calvert? The weather was warm and the people were good; not overly rich or fashionable, but cheery and neighborly none the less. People helped each other in Calvert, would go out of their way for each other. As Josephus developed into a small, slope-shouldered boy with ridiculous glasses and bright blonde hair, he and some of his brothers and sisters often walked home from school, moving through the alleys and crooked streets among strangers but having no fear. They didn't think twice about it.

Calvert was a good place.

Then, there came word of strange doings—of murders, people turning up dead. The wharves and seasides began buzzing of a 'Fiend' who was committing the murders—the Fiend of Calvert. People began looking at each other twice, strangers became untrusting—the Fiend not only killed men in the streets, he killed a little bit of the spirit of Calvert too.

Josephus was terrified of the Fiend; who was doing this? Who could do such a thing? His brother loved to torment him. *"It's me, Joe, you little fish monger ... I'm the Fiend ... and you're next."*

In an attempt to protect him and his school-age brothers and sisters, A-Ram was sent off to day school in Dee, where the Fiend so far hadn't showed, coming home only on the weekends.

Josephus was a fine student and was generally at or near the top of his classes on a consistent basis. The top students of the school were often invited to have lunch with a faction of important ladies known as the Sisterhood of Light—it was an honor, he was told—the Sisters were wise and influential and currying their favor was the key to success in the League. Sitting at the large table, he was in awe of these tall, skinny ladies dressed all in white, each with huge, cranked headdresses shaped like the wing of an airship. The Sisters never spoke, but their presence spoke volumes, and their gaze could stop you in your tracks. Many of the students sitting at lunch were selected to read essays and poems they had written to the Sisters. Josephus wanted to read something to them as well, and he was determined to sharpen his writing skills so that he too might one day have the honor.

He wrote a short poem about summer that delighted his teachers, and, he got his wish. He was selected to stand, approach, and read to the Sisters at lunch. He stood with his paper and stepped forward, his ugly black glasses trembling on his face. The Sisters' presence was piercing. They sat with perfect posture, their arms wrapped up in thin strips of white cloth like bandages beneath their loose robes, their delicate hands holding their soup spoons. They sat there looking at him with inscrutable eyes, the wings of their headdresses bobbing slightly.

Josephus choked up, he couldn't summon the courage to read his poem. After a while, humiliated before his snickering classmates, he returned to his seat, devastated.

When school let out for the summer, he returned home. The Fiend was still on the prowl and his parents kept a close eye on him. He told his mother of his shame before the Sisters. His mother told him it was probably just as well; the Sisters didn't favor Calverts much—they preferred the Remnaths and the Zenons, and their favorites, the Vith, with their god-like abilities and their blue hair. She also mentioned something about the Sisters' Program— and that they rarely considered the House of A-Ram worthy. His brother, Ephelrood, liked to tell his friends he'd had Programmability with a Sister, and that she'd fallen in love with him in the process. He received occasional notices from the Sisters; Ephelrood said it was correspondence from his 'Sister Admirer.' Josephus managed to get a quick glimpse of one of the notices once. It was a warning from the Sisters and a fine for lying to the people regarding Programmability. Josephus didn't understand what his mother meant, about the Sisters' Program and all, and his brother often told lies, so that wasn't a surprise; he simply knew that he'd lost something special when he couldn't read his poem to the Sisters. How he wished he had had the courage to read it to them. Maybe they would have liked it.

That summer, his mother kept him close to the docks so she could watch him, what with the Fiend running amok as never before. He found himself bored, waiting there on the docks for his father's boats to return. One day, while poking about the shed his family owned, he found something hidden under a tarp. Pulling the tarp aside, he discovered a small, open-aired vehicle of some kind, barely big enough to seat four people. It reminded him of a mechanical dolphin. It was a faded blue, with seats and a dash full of control mechanisms. He ran out onto the dock, found his mother, and demanded to know what it was.

She told him it was an old Suborbital—an airship that hadn't worked in years. Apparently his older brother had messed it up somehow and nobody ever bothered fixing it. The A-Rams weren't air people, they were sea people.

But, Josephus was fascinated. He spent the rest of the summer working with it every day before the boats came in. He studied up—discovered the ship was a Merc22 Suborbital built by a now defunct manufacturer in Zenon. In the greater scheme of Suborbital classification, the Merc22 was a Class 4, just a toy, small and under-powered. It was a starter vehicle not rated to go very high or fast.

Taking apart much of the rusty internals, he soon had a pile of parts laying about the shed and no idea where he'd gotten them from or how to put them back into place. His brother Ephelrood made a big deal about it, saying he had been planning to fix the craft "next week," but now Josephus had ruined it beyond hope of repair.

"Great going … *dweeb*!"

For his sixteenth birthday, his parents gave A-Ram a powerful gift: the MOLLY, the LosCapricos weapon of his family, delivered in a plain box complete with a certificate from the Sisterhood of Light. They told him that the MOLLY could do wondrous things. It could allow one to do things one might not ordinarily be able to do, and know things one shouldn't know. His father apparently used the MOLLY to help him steer his boats to where the fish were, and his mother admitted she used it to know exactly what sorts of fish he had caught and how best to prepare for his return. His brother swore the fabled powers of the MOLLY were nothing but a hoax, for he'd tried to use it for all sorts of grand things and never got anywhere with it.

Josephus didn't listen to his brother, as he was in awe—here it was, the MOLLY—it looked like a golden charm in the shape of a fish and, apparently, despite his brother's protests, it could work minor miracles. The MOLLY was rumored to have come from a captured chest of cursed Xaphan treasure won from a sunken ship during the Battle of Sorrander-Quo. The Sisters took the chest and, not certain what to make of it, smelted the pieces into various trinkets and distributed them to a number of House Minors of low repute for 'Testing Purposes', the A-Rams being one of them. His parents, though, were full of warnings. They said the MOLLY came with a cost—you couldn't use it without first registering with the Sisters, and its overuse could imperil his soul.

Being a remarkably empirical boy, Josephus decided to test the MOL-LY, to see what it could do. There was an eating contest that was held every year in Calvert Square, a messy affair with blueberry pies. He decided to enter it and use the MOLLY, to see what might happen. There was a pre-generated form his parents had for using the MOLLY. He filled it out and sent it along to the Sisters, wondering what their response would be and how long it would take.

He didn't have long to wait. He got back a quick response. The Sisters weren't kind in their assessment. In every column they responded with the words NEGLIGABLE and INSIGNIFICANT and OF NO CONSEQUENCE. Their final assessment: APPROVED: LEAST CONCERN.

Though Josephus was just a little boy—he began to understand full well that the Sisters, those skinny ladies in headdresses he so wanted to impress with his poem about the wonders of summer, didn't think much about him and his family. He'd heard of his uncle the cook and his other uncle the Brandtball player and their embarrassing misadventures with the Sisters, but those stories meant little to him. Here, in his response from the Sisters, was proof of his family's lowly situation with them, and that was galling for him.

He went out, MOLLYed up, and won the eating contest—all the big-bellied older kids scratching their heads, wondering how such a small, skinny lad could have put so much pie away. The MOLLY really did appear to work if used properly. With it, he could probably have the Merc22 fixed in no time. But, as the Lords of the Contest pinned his ribbon on his chest in the sunshine of Calvert Square, the Sisters' comments rang through in his mind:

NEGLIGABLE …

INSIGNIFICANT …

LEAST CONCERN …

He made a momentous decision at that point, especially for a child. He decided he was going to fix the Merc22 all on his own, and, what's more, once he fixed it, he was going to teach himself how to fly it; again, all by himself, no assistance from the MOLLY. If he could do such a thing, perhaps the Sisters would approve.

Working all summer, he gathered as much information as he could from the Holo-net, from the libraries, and from the handymen down the lane—

even though the Fiend had everybody worked up, there still remained a good measure of neighborly decency floating around Calvert. The handymen got used to seeing him every day, always with fresh questions. Soon, he had a basic understanding of the simple systems making up the Merc22: there were the Collective systems and the Cyclic systems, the superchargers and the gyroscopy governing it all. He learned about unified thrust, the disk of anti-gravity the ship created, and harmony of control. Pouring over his materials, reverse-engineering the craft, he discovered what had happened to put the vehicle out of commission: his brother had damaged the mechanical linkages controlling the canards and flight surfaces, and the two bottle motors mounted in the rear were blown out—apparently from improper use. Ephelrood had, as the handymen put it, flown the Merc22 "out of the envelope" and the result was a dogged-out ship.

He figured all this out on his own—no help from the MOLLY.

Josephus saved his money and scoured the nearby junkyards, looking for the correct replacement parts. As a birthday gift, his parents bought him the two replacement bottle motors. Finally, with everything re-installed and fitted, the Merc22 was ready to go.

A complication occurred when his brother appeared.

He discovered all the work Josephus had been doing and laughed at him—no way, no way could that old wreck be fixed, for he had tried himself and couldn't do it.

When he found out that the Merc22 had in fact been fixed, he was elated and Commed his friends that he had fixed the old Merc and was coming to take them out for a spin over the rooftops. A-Ram was terrified; his brother had been the one who wrecked it in the first place, and would probably do it again.

All that work was about to be shot to the moons.

He ran to the shed just as an unsightly gaggle noisily stepped onto the dock. It was his brother, one of his meathead friends and a bouncing pair of painted trollops from the cemeteries arriving, fueled by smoking menthols and clinking bottles of cheap spirits.

"Oi, Joe! Get away from my ship, you little bug! You'll mess up all my hard work!" his brother cried.

"Let's get him!" his friend yelled with glee. "Let's pull his pants down and throw him in the water!"

Straining with all his might, A-Ram pushed the Merc out onto the dock and jumped into the cockpit. He could hear his brother and his friends running up fast across the planks of the dock.

bump ... bump ... bump ... bump ...

"Joe, I'm going to pull your little wings out, you fly! You worthless bug!" his brother called on the run, throwing an empty bottle of wine at him.

He set the controls and took off down the dock just as his brother and his crew got there, dodging a hail of thrown bottles and shoes as he climbed into the air.

"I'm going to get you, Joe!" his brother yelled.

Flailing about in mid-air, he struggled with the Suborbital, like an unruly bronco. He knew from his reading how the controls worked. He knew pulling back on the yoke made it go up, and pushing forward caused it to descend. He knew the side stick controlled the collective attitude of the vehicle and the foot pedals made it yaw, or slide. After a few minutes and a few close calls—he'd almost hit the patinaed roof of the Empire Hotel and caused a group of strollers in Calvert Square to scatter—he got the hang of it. After an hour of playing in the clouds, he had mastery of it, soaring over the colorful seaside of Calvert, waving at the people below as he passed.

Thus began his love of flying and the sky, moving in the direction of the sun far away from roving Fiends, from the ocean that made him sick, from brothers who mocked him, and the Sisters who disregarded him.

✵ ✵ ✵ ✵ ✵

When he was twenty-nine, A-Ram made an appointment to see Lord Catherbaum, the local House Major lord in St. Edmunds. Though he was a Great Lord, Catherbaum was a man about the neighborhood, often seen strolling the docks with his bags of purchases or sitting in the lobby of the Empire Hotel laughing and smoking with the comers and goers. He was on a first name basis with Josephus' mother and father, and he often bought his father's catches at premium prices. A-Ram's goal was to join the Stellar Fleet. He wanted to become a helmsman, he wanted to fly a great ship and, for that, he needed a Letter of Recommendation. He had high hopes—he could fly, he could soar. All he needed was the chance to prove it.

In reviewing Lord A-Ram's petition, Lord Catherbaum didn't have good news. He sat there behind his desk, hands folded, and quietly laid it out for him. "Josephus, you know I think you a fine young lad, and I would happily draft you a Letter of Recommendation, but let's be reasonable. You wish to be a Fleet helmsman—your eyesight is so poor, and, not only that—it's uncorrectable via surgery. You have your opticals there, but I know the Lords of the Fleet—they would not look kindly upon that. Even the Marines, I ..." He cleared his throat. "Additionally, and I don't know if you're aware of this, but the Sisterhood of Light has long placed a *Venta-Nomi*, upon your House's patent."

A-Ram didn't know what that meant.

Lord Catherbaum was pained. "It means, my boy, that they think your House is flawed, imperfect, not worth their Program. You are, in their eyes, untouchable and the Lords of the Fleet would see that, and disqualify you because of it. A lot of nonsense really, but the Fleet values the Sisters' assessments."

Josephus sat there and felt ashamed. "I'm sorry," Catherbaum said.

Venta-Nomi. Flawed, imperfect?

Untouchable. Unwanted.

He was devastated. He looked at his hands through his glasses, quietly stood and left the office.

"Josephus, wait!" Lord Catherbaum said catching up to him. He put his hands on A-Ram's tiny shoulders. "Wait. Please attend, for I do not wish you to walk out of here thinking that this is any of your fault. I've seen you flying that little ship around, and I'll wager your skill against anybody's. The Sisters and their damned *Venta-Nomi*! Who are they to place summary judgment on you ... on us? They've never given the people of Calvert our due—never! We are good people, thought low by the rest of Kana. Even when there's a mad killer in our midst, slaying us at his whim, we can get no help—just another dead man in Calvert—who's to bother? Who's to care? Well, I care, and I'm bringing in someone of my own, some fellow from the north who wears a mask, paid out of my own coin. I heard he gets results. And tomorrow, I march with our people to Calvert Square, and we shall demand justice, and there will be justice for you as well, Josephus. There is a contest that I know of—oh, it's just nonsense, but if you win, you shall have an honorary admittance to the Fleet. It's not much, but, if you win, you shall be in the Fleet, and once there you can make your own way, and make them see you for who you are."

Having no idea what to make of that, Josephus left Lord Catherbaum's office and went home.

✳ ✳ ✳ ✳ ✳

Josephus lay in his bed. In the morning he would go to Dee and participate in an essay-writing contest that Lord Catherbaum had signed him up for. To the winner went a low-level administrative position in the Stellar Fleet. It wasn't much, but, assuming he could win the contest, it might lead to better things.

It might ...

He was excited.

As he tried to settle his thoughts and get some rest, he heard some sort of commotion outside. His room was on the top level of the family townhouse and sounds carried up there. It sounded like a struggle, a distant crashing getting steadily nearer, then he heard a loud toppling sound coming from the roof overhead, followed by: *bump, bump, bump, bump...*

Footsteps, somebody running across his rooftop, and then the sounds were gone. He would come to know that the footsteps belonged to the Fiend of Calvert, running for his life from the Mad Lord of Walther—the man brought to Calvert by Lord Catherbaum.

That was the last time the Fiend was heard of in Calvert.

That was also the last night of Josephus' old life at home. A new day was soon to dawn, and a new life as well.

19

—An Unusual Errand—

There was a rather thick envelope sitting on his desk as he came into the office that morning, the envelope simply reading: JOSEPHUS.

✳ ✳ ✳ ✳ ✳

A-Ram had been at work in Admiral Derlith's office for ten years. He had worked his way up after winning his essay-writing contest in Dee, starting in the Fleet's cavernous mailroom—a thankless job by any measure. He was liked well enough, and often praised for his uncluttered mind and his admirable work ethic, but, his glasses and his ever-present 'Sister Problem' kept him from advancing—quite unfair. Most of the people who started in the mailroom at the same time he did were promoted years ago, or kicked out for not passing muster.

Eventually, he received a great promotion, by default. Admiral Derlith of the 3rd Fleet, Lord of Cone, was in immediate need of a new adjutant, for his old one had quit in a froth. The post of assisting an Admiral was normally a highly sought after job, but this was the dreaded Admiral Derlith and the paucity of applicants to join his office was notable. Admiral Derlith was a known crab-head, a hard and often humiliating man to work for, and not only was he a yeller and a screamer, there was something strange about him, something haunting and unsettling hanging over him that was palpable enough to be noticed by all. In any event, Josephus was game, and for lack of anyone else seeking the job, he was posted to the Admiral's office.

Admiral Derlith, gray-haired, big-toothed, was indeed a difficult man to serve—short-tempered, critically inclined and fickle in his caprices, he often called him out and reproached Josephus in public in a brusque, loud manner. But, Josephus endured, patiently serving the Admiral in a steady, competent manner. Despite his unflattering treatment of him, the Admiral was a kind benefactor, paying him rather well and personally seeing to his needs. His biggest problem was his glasses, as the Admiral refused to allow him to wear them when guests were present in the office. Too ugly.

✳   ✳   ✳   ✳   ✳

JOSEPHUS, the envelope read.

It was just a touch after four bells, and the office was quiet and dark on that hushed edge waiting for the day to begin. He set his armful of things down and opened the envelope. Inside was a rather thick letter from the Admiral.

It read:

Josephus

As you might well be aware, today is Tuesday. It is possible you might also be aware that on Tuesdays you are normally expected to retrieve my uniforms from the bags, shine up the office tea set, and type my usual correspondence.

Today, however, I have a novel set of errands for you to accomplish that supersedes all else. As follows shall be a detailed set of instructions. You are to follow the instructions TO THE LETTER, there will be no need for you to deviate from the instructions, question or embellish them in any way. Follow your instructions to a point, complete your task, and tomorrow we shall resume our routine as usual.

OVERVIEW: You shall retrieve five small parcels currently located in places listed hereafter. The parcels are small, each not weighing more than five pounds. You have been provided with a compartmented carrying satchel to accomplish this task (please see below).

CARRYING CONTRIVANCE: You have been provided with a custom carrying satchel that you will need to complete this errand. The satchel is located in the bottom drawer of my credenza. You will note the interior of the satchel is compartmented into five sections. Each section of the satchel currently contains a key—you shall need these keys to complete your errand (see below). The parcels you collect shall be placed into each compartmented section. I would appreciate you placing the parcels in order of acquisition in the satchel from left to right.

KEYS: *As stated above, there are five keys contained in the satchel. The keys, from left to right, shall be situated in order of their required use (i.e., the first key on the left shall be the first key you will require, the key immediately to the right of that shall be the next one required, and so on).*

PARCELS: *As above, the parcels you shall collect are fairly small, will weigh no more than five pounds each, and will be packaged in a standard paper delivery wrapping. The contents of the parcels are rather delicate, and I will advise you not to handle them any more than is necessary to secure and place them into your carrying satchel. Once placed within the satchel, do not remove them from their compartment for any reason. WARNING—Do not mingle the parcels, again, keep them in their separate compartments, and, for Creation's Sake, do not open them—that goes without saying.*

CARRYING WEIGHT: *I do not anticipate your carrying weight to exceed twenty pounds. If you feel this weight is excessive, you may, under my authority, requisition a pull float from billeting for your use. Authorization code: A11B946621*

MEAL ALLOWANCE: *As this errand shall consume the better part of your morning and afternoon, I have set aside a money bag containing fifty Fleet solaris for your use to be spent for breakfast and lunch at your discretion. Given the current rate of exchange, the money should be sufficient to purchase you a respectable breakfast and lunch. You may use all of the money left to you; however, if your costs exceed the sum in the money bag, you will have to pay the difference from your personal funds. I pray you use the money wisely. You shall find the money bag inside your custom carrying satchel.*

DETAILED ITINERARY:

6 Bells: *A Fleet coach shall be waiting for you at the Billson Avenue dock—he will await you under the name: Lord A-Ram. You will have until 6 bells and one quarter to board the coach. Do not be late.*

Instructions to Driver: *You shall inform the driver to take you at speed to the Grayson Memorial Land, Air and Stellar Port at 1 West Munson Street, King's Way, Armenelos.*

7 Bells: *You shall arrive at the Port. Instruct the driver to wait and enter the West Portico. Once inside, proceed to the locker yard and locate locker A1501. Using the first key in your satchel, open the locker, secure the* *parcel within and place it in the open compartment. You will no longer need the first key and will discard it.*

Proceed now to the East Portico of the port and locate locker W884. As before, using the next key in your satchel, open the locker, secure the parcel, and place it in its compartment. Discard the key at that time.

9 Bells: *You shall then re-board your coach and head west to the incorporated hamlet of Mystery.*

Instructions to Driver: *You shall inform the driver to take you without delay to the Mystery Land and Air Port located at 5234 Borgelund Way, Pitcairn, Mystery.*

11 Bells: *You shall arrive at the Port. Again instruct the driver to wait. Inside, proceed to the locker yard and locate locker 155673. Using the third key from the left, open the locker, retrieve the parcel within and place the parcel in its compartmented section. Discard the key.*

Once you have secured the parcel, your task is done at the Mystery port. Your next destination shall be a great distance from Mystery. I recommend you take the time to have breakfast, however, I advise you not tarry past 12 bells.

12 Bells: *You shall then re-board your coach and head east to the city of Conwell.*

Instructions to Driver: *You shall inform the driver to transport you at speed to the Gates-of-Esther Land, Air and Stellar Port located at 77 Withelwell Road, Monforton, Conwell.*

16 Bells: *You shall arrive at the port. Instruct the driver to wait. Inside, proceed to the locker yard and locate locker Blue 888 and use the key located in the compartment second from the right. Use the key, secure the parcel, place it in its compartment, and discard the key.*

Once you have secured the parcel, your task is done at the Gates-of-Esther Land Port.

17 Bells: *You shall then re-board your coach and head south-east to the city of Dee.*

Instructions to Driver: *You shall inform the driver to take you to the City of Dee Land, Air and Sea Port located at 1622 Monmouth, Seaquay, Dee. Once arrived, you will instruct the driver to carry on and return to the*

Fleet. You shall receive additional instructions at the Port as to your return arrangements back to the Fleet Complex.

***19 Bells:** You shall arrive at the port. Dismiss the driver and proceed inside. Make your way into the private locker area and locate locker BN77789A. Use the final key, secure the parcel and place it in the compartment. Once secured, you will have successfully retrieved all required parcels.*

***FINAL INSTRUCTIONS:** You shall receive a final set of instructions at the port. These instructions shall contain the address where you are to deliver the satchel and the details for your return arrangements to the Fleet.*

I cannot accurately describe to you what you shall encounter in Dee, however, I pray you use your best judgment in the matter.

I will thank you to accurately, and safely, follow these instructions and be returned to Fleet no later than 25 Bells. I shall have no further need of your services for the remainder of the day, but will expect you to be at your desk promptly at 5 bells the following morning for work as usual.

Signed

Derlith, Lord of Cone, Admiral of the 3rd Fleet.

The letter was a typical Admiral Derlith creation—full of detail, leaving nothing to chance. He went into the Admiral's office, dark and quiet in the early morning, and pulled open the drawer to the credenza.

Sitting inside was a black carrying case, rather on the largish size with an ugly but functional set of handles. He pulled it out and set it on the Admiral's desk. It was a clamshell-style case, opening from the top like a carpetbag. Inside, as promised in the letter, were five neatly laid out compartments running the length of the bag, each section about two inches wide. Lying within each compartment was a key. The keys were of a simple style—clearly keys that would fit into a lowly, disused locker at a public port. Also sitting inside was the money bag the Admiral had promised.

The lining of the case was an odd, flexible latex covered with a gritty and unevenly sprayed-on layer of gray paint that had a very metallic quality to it.

He closed the case, got his hat and readied himself to leave the office. First, though, he watered the Admiral's plants and prepared the coffee set—

all the Admiral would have to do when he got in is turn it on and he would have his coffee. He then locked up and headed in the direction of the Bilson Avenue dock to await the coach. He expected a long day ahead of him.

The hover coach sped across the Kana Avenue toward Conwell—a broad green highway cutting through the Great Armenelos forest. There was no roadway or macadam or concrete making up the highway, only a winding passage of compacted earth that hindered the growth of trees, where only tough short grasses could take hold. Lining the avenue were grand estates and fine Zenon manors mixed into the dense, vine-filled tangle of the forest.

Josephus had already collected three of the parcels—the whole exercise had gone just as the Admiral had laid it out. He arrived at the ports and asked the driver to wait. He then walked in, found the lockers (which was probably the most difficult part of the procedure), opened them and got the parcel out. The parcels, again as advertised, were small, square packages of a soft nature. He thought he could hear sand or some other gritty material hissing about within the carefully wrapped paper. He slid them into their compartments.

It could be said that Josephus, always a bright, big-headed fellow with a flighty imagination, often embellished his daily doings, transforming the mundane into the suspenseful and the extraordinary—imagining, as he watered the Admiral's plants, that he was tending to some infirm alien species, or that, when he fetched the Admiral's mail, he was retrieving some piece of covert intelligence crucial to the safety of the League.

All sorts of rubbish like that.

But today, he couldn't help but feel his fanciful embellishments were hitting a little too close to home.

He was certain he was being followed.

The feeling began rather early on, as he was searching for the lockers in Armenelos Port. He had the quick notion that his footsteps were being retraced and his actions scrutinized from afar.

He'd look back, checking over his shoulder, and, of course, there were people there, moving randomly, going about their business, betraying nothing that would prompt him into believing that somebody was actively following him.

He tried to shrug the feeling off. When he got to the port in Mystery, the feeling returned, if anything a bit more forcefully this time. He decided to sit down to some breakfast, as there was a lovely café nearby that he was partial to. As he ate, he caught glimpses of something behind the usual traffic of people—just a hint of somber cloth, a brief silhouette that added up to nothing concrete. His imagination was on the verge of going on a full rampage. He hurried, finished his breakfast, and departed, getting on the coach and moving off eastward into the heart of the forest.

As the lovely green highway floated past at a comforting speed, he began to relax, settle back, the partially full satchel sitting on the seat next to him. He thought to shut his eyes for a bit.

As his eyelids closed, he saw something.

He sat up and stared out the window.

Standing at the side of the avenue was a tall figure wearing a gray cloak and a broad gray hat. The figure stood before a stand of dense growth hold-ing its hands out in front of it in a rather threatening manner. The cloak and hat that the figure was wearing obscured most of its body and made trying to determine its features or its gender pointless.

It looked to him like he imagined the Fiend of Calvert might appear. There were no clear descriptions of the Fiend, and even scholars and tradesmen seeking to profit from the Fiend-lore varied widely in their personal interpretations of how the Fiend should look. Some envisioned him as a scruffy, tattooed sailor, coming ashore for murder and mayhem, and then slipping safely back to sea. Others saw the Fiend as a proper gentleman from the Empire Hotel, dressed for a night on the town wearing a gasmask, as the Fiend left no Genetics behind for the Evidencers to collect.

A-Ram had always imagined the Fiend as a tall figure clad in gray, thin and agile, his clothes covering up most of his body, except for his grinning mouth and teeth.

… and that was, for the most part, what he was seeing standing by the road.

As the coach passed by, the figure stood there, motionless. A-Ram put his face to the window glass and gawked at it—it was simply a person standing by the road-side, but its intent seemed odd. Its presence felt malicious.

As he passed, it glanced up, ever so slightly. Its hat covered the upper portion of its face, he could see hints of a chin, and a mouth pulled back into a mirthless grin.

The figure fell into the distance in just a moment as the coach continued on its rapid way. Straining to see, he thought he saw the figure step out onto the avenue green and watch as the coach moved east.

✶   ✶   ✶   ✶   ✶

He was relieved when he got to Conwell. He'd been fretting a bit, over this gray figure standing on the side of the road. He bounced down out of the coach with his satchel, trying to convince himself he'd dreamed the whole thing.

As he made his way into the port, he again had the feeling he was being followed. Turning as he had before in Armenelos and Mystery, he looked back, expecting to see nothing. Across the street, standing in the sunshine, was a tall figure in gray—the same one he'd seen standing on the Kana Avenue in the forest. The bustling people moving around it as if it were invisible.

But, this was not possible. How could a person standing on the side of the road miles away in the Great Armenelos Forest travel so fast and get here ahead of him?

He dismissed the idea as hogwash, chided himself for being foolish and hurried inside.

After he secured the parcel, feeling oddly invigorated, he decided to have lunch. He took his time and enjoyed his meal, sitting in a nice café in the center of Conwell. He was impressed by this lovely city, and thought it truly a place he should return and explore in greater detail. With his nearly full satchel sitting next to him, he relaxed and even thought to order a spot of dessert.

As he looked over the menu, his heart leapt into his throat. Sitting at the far end of the café was the now familiar figure in gray—closer this time. Much Closer.

Blaring eyes fixed on him in a side-glance.

A-Ram left the money bag on the table, grabbed his satchel, and fled back to the waiting coach.

✳ ✳ ✳ ✳ ✳

So far, with the exception of his phantom pursuer, the day had gone according to the Admiral's plan. He arrived in Dee—a Calvert city he was much more familiar with and got out of the coach. As instructed in his letter, he dismissed the coach and watched as it floated down the lane, joining the flow of traffic.

Holding his satchel, which was getting a little heavy (he wished he'd opted to get the float lift), he marched up the steps toward the grand entrance to the port. A helmeted guildsman in blue wearing a cloak and holding a Ma-san pulse rifle stopped him.

"Afternoon, citizen," the guildsman said.

"Good afternoon, sir," Josephus replied.

"Do you have business in the port today?"

"I do."

"I'm afraid I cannot allow you entrance to the port."

"Why not?"

"Your bag is reading as slightly radioactive. It's not harmful, please have no fear, but our regulations are clear—your bag will have to be inspected and properly shielded.”

A-Ram looked at his satchel. Radioactive?

“I’m not embarking on a trip, I simply need to go in and retrieve a bit of property that is stored there for me.”

“That’s fine. Please, attend across the street.” The guildsman pointed to a small building.

“If you have temporary business in the Port, you may, at no cost, check your bag there and retrieve it once your business is concluded. A momentary inconvenience I assure you, however, it must be done. Otherwise, I cannot allow you to enter.”

A-Ram thought a moment. “I’m from Calvert—I recall no such regulations.”

“It’s new—there was an incident where a group of Xaphan scalawags attempted to blow up City Dock. The Magistrate of Dee has enacted a standing order to visually inspect all bags prior to entering the port until further notice. A bit of paranoia perhaps, but there it is.”

He considered his options and looked across the street. His instructions were clear—handle the parcels as briefly as possible. He opened his satchel and pulled out the final key. “You say my bag is radioactive, sir?” he asked.

“Yes—not much, but it triggers my goggles here. You might be surprised how many mildly radioactive items are rolling around out there—I’m seeing things everywhere. Again, it’s nothing harmful and just a formality until things blow over around here.”

He considered his situation. He assumed that the checking of his bag would add no more than a few minutes to his process. It shouldn’t be a problem. He took the final key from his satchel, marched across the street, waited in queue for a few minutes and checked his bag. He received a baggage ticket.

Armed with his key and his letter and his ticket, he entered the port and waded into the locker area. After a bit of fruitless searching, for these lockers were not setup as orderly as they were in the other ports—again Calvert lagged a little behind everybody else, doing things not quite as well as is done elsewhere. Eventually he came to the correct one and opened it.

Inside was the usual square parcel wrapped in brown paper and an envelope.

He opened it:

To: Josephus, Lord of A-Ram

You are to be congratulated. You have done well in executing this important assignment, and you shall be justly rewarded.

Bring your satchel to: 1144 Dunwoodwell West, Fehklar, Dee and go to apartment 212. There you will deposit the satchel and you shall receive your reward and your ticket for your return journey to Armenelos.

Signed: Unsigned.

He read the letter. It was vague and a little unsettling, clearly written in a hand other than the Admiral's. This was very irregular—to deliver a satchel to a civilian address when, for the whole time, he'd been operating under the notion that he was performing Fleet business.

And why was the letter unsigned.

And why were the contents he had picked up radioactive, albeit slightly so?

He bent down and picked up the parcel. Unlike the other parcels, this one didn't rattle, instead, it had a clay-like, moldable quality. If he squeezed with his fingers, he could feel the contents changing shape slightly.

He recalled the Admiral's warning to not handle the parcels too much. He tucked the parcel under his arm and headed back out toward the street. It was best to finish up and get back home. He'd ask the Admiral in the morning what this was all about.

As he neared the street to get his satchel, he heard someone clearing their throat.

Standing a few feet away was a Sister, on the smallish side in her white robes and headdress. She was looking over her shoulder at him. She stood there for a while.

"Great Sister, is there something I can do for you?" he finally asked.

She glanced down. There was a small puddle on the street in front of where she wanted to cross.

He was a little dumbfounded. A Sister—a woman who could probably boil away the puddle with TK or wish it away, or do any of a number miraculous things to make it vanish, was content to wait for Josephus to do the chivalrous thing and lay his coat down for her.

Venta-Nomi

Flawed ...

Imperfect ...

He set the parcel aside, and took his Fleet coat off. He laid it out over the small puddle and the Sister lightly stepped over it. His coat barely got wet, the puddle was so small.

She then looked back at him, lifted her hand and touched his face. The white wrappings of her thin arm went up past the loose folds of her robes.

Her small hand was so warm. She smiled at him, curtsied and went on her way.

Josephus took his coat and thought about what had just happened.

Did that Sister know he was *Venta-Nomi*? Would she have cared?

Holding his coat, he sat down by the curb and picked his parcel back up. He was filled with a sudden longing. He forgot about his task.

Venta-Nomi

Flawed.

Imperfect.

... Unwanted.

Those words kept flashing through his mind.

Her smile.

Her warm hand on his face.

Those thoughts flashed too.

Without realizing it, he was crying, holding the parcel to his chest. He didn't want to be *Venta-Nomi*. He wanted the Sisters to like him, to accept him—everybody wanted that, and perhaps he wanted it a little bit more. He wanted to do great things and be a great man, so that the Sisters might look at him and be impressed, to look past the bad halibut and bad Brandtball, to look past his lying-assed brother and see him for his own merits.

He was filled with ambition and desire, to be something more than what he was—a flawed, imperfect Calvert.

As he sat there lost in thought holding the parcel, he noticed it became strangely warm and also became much more freely bendable than it had been.

Creation! How long had he been sitting there, weeping like a school boy?

Don't handle the parcels any more than is necessary ...

Thoughts of radioactivity entered his head. He got up and found a Guildsman and had him scan the parcel for radiation. The Guildsman looked at it and reported he saw nothing—no radiation, which was a big relief.

He retrieved his satchel from across the street with his ticket and placed the warm parcel into its slot. His task was done and he wanted to go home.

1144 Dunwoodwell West. The fairly happy streets of Dee gave way a bit to a more fallen down area. Hidden by the facade of a respectable street-front, the interior was crowded with crooked buildings, strange smells and unpainted, termite-infested wood. Even being a Calvert man, A-Ram found himself a bit appalled. This area was a dreadful slum at its worst.

Eventually he found the correct address. The building was a tenement, an uneven three stories in height, the shape of an elongated 'L', and tiled half-heartedly in lime and white with a fair amount of the tiles fallen and piled up around the base of the building. The whole structure of the building appeared rotten and ready to come down; even the yard it sat in was barren of grass and strewn with unhealthy rocks and discarded refuse.

He stood there for a moment and wondered if he really wanted to go in. His instructions were clear, but it didn't seem safe, structurally or socially—who knows what sorts were waiting inside.

Desperate to get this over with, he opened the creaking door and went in. Inside was a seedy corridor lined with sullen doors of old, mirthless wood. The place reeked, not smell-wise or anything tangible like that, rather, it had a terrible *feel* to it. He felt overwhelmed, felt something pressing down, waiting to get at him.

At the end of the corridor was a dusty stair leading up. Carefully, he made his way up, the steps groaning and teetering a little with each step.

At the end of the corridor was his destination: 212. The oppressive feeling he had struggled with on the first floor was doubled here on the second.

212.

It seemed an unhealthy, unholy place—why, he didn't know. He felt for certain that whatever was waiting for him on the other side of the door was the end of his life, the last thing he would ever see.

His death was on the other side of that door.

He was no match for his fear—he turned and fled, moving back down the steps in a clumsy racket, out the door and into the street, shuffling as fast as he could go until he spilled back out into the more reputable sections of Dee.

He purchased a ticket back to Armenelos out of his own money and took a rumbling, slow pub-trans across the forest. He didn't arrive back at the Fleet until 28 bells—he was exhausted after a long day. He brought the satchel and placed it in the Admiral's office. He'd apologize to him when he came in and say, in his judgment, he didn't believe the final drop-off point was safe.

He decided to head back to his apartment to grab an hour or two of shut-eye.

Moving slowly, he made his way down the sparsely populated complex.

✶ ✶ ✶ ✶ ✶

He wasn't overly surprised when the figure in gray came upon him; he expected it, rather. It seemed inevitable. He was certain the figure in gray had been waiting for him behind door 212 in Dee. It hadn't been able to settle with him then, so it would do so now. It made perfect sense to him.

It reached out and seized him by the arm. A-Ram was too bewildered to put up much of a fight. He was filled with a complacent, rather peaceful sort of utter terror, where he was a mere spectator on a hell ride into madness and death. He wouldn't be inconvenienced long, it would all be over soon. The figure dragged him into a nearby, out-of-the way place—a bathroom and pulled him in.

Inside, a small Marine was sitting cross-legged on the vanity top, tossing back a flask of something, boots removed and set aside, streaks of dirt running down the sides of her face.

The Marine, a tiny black-haired girl, looked at them and blushed. "Oh, you guys want to be alone or something?"

The figure in gray appeared startled and released him. He quickly stumbled away, reaching for the bathroom door that seemed an eternity away. He bolted out, followed shortly by the Marine girl. She also seemed quite scared. She hadn't even collected her boots—she ran out in her wooly socks.

He went to security and reported the matter. They searched the complex, but found no mysterious figure in gray. He saw the Marine from the bathroom, a little intoxicated and on-duty as well, bootless, getting berated by her superiors. A-Ram watched with a bit of discomfort as she was taken away to be disciplined.

That little Marine probably saved his life.

Later, he sat down and explained what had happened to the Admiral. He thought the Admiral might be angry at him for not fulfilling his instructions to the letter; and he was angry—he was furious in fact, but not at him.

Speaking in his kindest voice, the Admiral thanked him again for fetching the parcels, and for his vigilance, and told him he would be compensated for his pub-trans fare back to Armenelos. He also bade him to not worry about the figure in gray.

The Admiral said he would take care of the situation, and that he was sorry he'd been inconvenienced.

True to his word, A-Ram never saw the figure in gray at the Fleet again and what became of the satchel and the parcels he'd collected was out of his concern.

20

—Innocent Drury—

Stenstrom climbed up out of the lift shaft. He had been badly tangled in the razor-wire gift that Innocent had left for him. He should have been hopelessly impaled.

But, as he was quickly discovering, the Sisters weren't kidding. Something filled him up as he fell into the deadly razor-wire. He bounced off the bedding of wire and found himself barely inconvenienced. Once he got over the shock of his situation and acknowledged the fact that he wasn't hurt, he casually pulled the wire away, the odd strands easily breaking and being tossed aside. Somehow, even his HRN coat wasn't torn or ripped—apparently the Sisters wanted his carefully crafted "costume" to not be inconvenienced and imparted their protection on it as well.

He emerged into the dark of Deck Five and quickly made his way down the hall. The hallway was plunged in pitch blackness, but he could see just fine.

For just a moment, you looked like a robot, A-Ram had said.

The It Man, the Sisters said.

We will lend you our power ...

He pondered that as he continued down the corridor. A robot. He recalled seeing the Mad Lord of Walther up close as a boy at Rustam, and he clearly recalled thinking he looked like a silver and gold robot. He too was the Sisters' Fist—whatever that was.

He pulled the final bit of razor wire off his clothes and examined it. It was odd and sinuous, a little slimy, almost organic in composition. The barbs looked hard and sharp, of a bony sort of composition.

The ship gave another shudder, long and protracted this time. He heard a muffled, distant rumbling from outside.

He needed to hurry.

He moved out of the 'neck' region of the ship and into the winged rear section. Now, all he had to do was go up three levels, put on a pressure suit, on, go into Ripcar Bay 5, as its doors were open to naked space, and somehow fix the *Westminster*.

That's all.

Ahead was a lift shaft that he could climb up. Situated in front of the shaft was a tangle of more razor-wire. Clearly, Innocent had been here.

He pulled the wire down, not being hurt by it, but still mindful. He hacked his way to the lift shaft and entered, finding the interior of the shaft also clogged with strands of razor-wire. He climbed up as quickly as he could, clearing the stuff away with swipes of his hand.

Several minutes later he emerged on the correct deck. The corridor was clear, and he saw the various boxes of items they had stolen from the Dry Dock 275. He recalled Taara chirping happily as they sorted through their assortment of stolen booty. *"Just like a grocery store,"* she'd said.

He heard something: a sort of quizzical, machine-like groan.

He looked around, NTH at the ready. He didn't see anybody.

Quickly, he put on one of the pressure suits, steamed it up, the helmet lighting in colorful displays and readouts, and entered the sub-lock to Ripcar Bay 5 with a momentary rush of air, as the bay was currently open to space.

The bay was completely clogged with crazy runs of razor wire, like a spider's lair overgrown with webs. It was stretched out everywhere running this way and that, making the whole bay look liked a badly cobwebbed barn. In the middle of all this confusion was the *Westminster*. Its condition was impossible to discern—he had to get closer.

Clunking ahead, he pulled aside the strands, making a slow path to the ship. He arrived and looked it over. It was powered off and darkened. The bullet-shaped, white hull didn't appear to be damaged at all—the plates (what he could see) were intact, the front glass was fine, and he could see the quiet, unoccupied crew seats within.

So, what was wrong with it?

He moved back along the length of the ship, clearing the razor wire as he went. There was the open panel that Taara had set up. She had strung up a thick cable and connected it to the *Seeker's* mainframe—she did a great job, her MOLLYed-up smarts proving to be quite effective.

The cable was missing. Looks like Innocent simply popped it out of its socket. It didn't look like he ripped it out or damaged it in any way—as, apparently, he wanted to still make good use of the *Westminster* later once he and A-Ram, and Taara were eliminated. So, all Stenstrom had to do was find the cable, hook it back up, and re-fire the *Westminster.*

The ship gave a long, protracted shudder. Looking back through the open doors of the bay, he thought he could see movement: a spiraling of stars and flashes of cherry-red light.

He made his way in that direction, again, clearing himself a path as he went. When he got to the bay opening, he could see the *Seeker* was in a slow, rolling battle with the *Heade-on-the-Hearth.*

The *Heade*, although in the general shape of an old *Webber*, was clearly not simply a derelict spacecraft decades old—it was articulated like a gigantic insect, studded with robotic armatures and other odd technologies, and crawling with small and large guns. It was reaching out for the *Seeker* with tentacles tipped with claws, surveying it with clusters of robotic eyes, and firing with a cassagrain-style main weapon mounted on a long armature that reminded Stenstrom of the proboscis of an assassin bug.

The stars slowly churned about as A-Ram, far away on the bridge, struggled to match turns with the *Heade,* using nothing but maneuvering thrusters. A nearby thruster every so often spat out a torrent of compressed propellant as A-Ram moved the wheel.

The *Heade* moved rather nimbly. It darted in, reaching out with its tentacles, trying to snare the *Seeker.* The thruster again roared as A-Ram matched its maneuver, and the *Heade* fired, a long, burning arc of cassagrain weaponry from its main gun, hitting the *Seeker* somewhere in the tower section above.

The *Heade* came about, and A-Ram banked hard, forcing Stenstrom to hold on, and then the enemy fired again, hitting the *Seeker* in the rear quarter this time. Though he had no propulsion, no hermetics, and no weapons, A-Ram was doing a masterful job of giving the *Heade* different angles to hit. The *Seeker* was heavily armored with dura-plate, and the only way to really damage her was to keep hitting the same section with cassagrains over and over again, heating the armor up to the point of failure. A-Ram wasn't allowing them to do that, he was forcing them to strike different areas of the ship, thus prolonging this one-sided struggle. And, he was clearly successful in keeping the *Heade* from latching on with its tentacles—that was key.

The thrusters blasted a torrent again and the *Seeker* did a slow roll. The *Heade* came in again. Seeing it up-close, Stenstrom could clearly see the different sorts of techs strapped to the ship that didn't belong there. He was no expert—where was Taara when he needed her—but he could clearly make out various Xaphan techs, mixed in with miscellaneous scavenged League stuff and other completely alien techs mounted all over the ship that baffled Stenstrom. There were those tentacle-like grapplers that he'd never seen before, probably some sort of Xaphan tech, and there was the vastly improved docking umbilical and a smattering of other things that he couldn't identify.

He could see that their cassagrain main weapon was mounted on flexible, robotic pods and could articulate about, giving them a vast field of fire.

He wondered. His NTH was fully able to kill robots and robotic machines. Maybe he could hit the robotic pod and put the cassagrain main gun out of commission. It might just work.

He waited a moment or two for the ship to swoop in, which it did, tentacles waving, casually displaying its underbelly, knowing full well that the *Seeker* couldn't shoot back.

A-Ram rolled away and matched the turn, the *Heade* appeared to momentarily come to a stop as he did so.

There was the robotic pod, moving the cassagrain cannon about in a smooth arc.

Stenstrom lined up his shot and fired. His green blast shot out, travelled across space, and hit the pod. Without any great fanfare it stopped moving and froze in place.

The *Heade* twisted away, its cannon silent.

Something approached through the tangle of wire behind Stenstrom, something that rattled the floor with pounding steps.

Stenstrom turned.

There, emerging through the tangle, was Innocent Drury.

He didn't look at all like he remembered Innocent Drury looking, but it had to be him. He was nine feet tall—obviously quite a bit larger and bulkier than he had appeared previously when he looked like just a thin, scabrous man.

He was a robot. His metal body was vaguely man-shaped (he had arms, legs, and something that passed for a head) but he was bulky and mechanical. His hands were big and blocky, nipper-shaped, with at least twenty variously sized fingers on each hand. His feet were squared-off and robotic.

He appeared to have a rigid central framework at his center, like a metal skeleton of some kind. On top of the framework was an abundance of movement. His body was composed of a multitude of metal squares, each about half the size of a fist and all colored a deep hunter green—similar to Stenstrom's coat. The squares were adorned with blinking lights, and they were made, on some sides, with recessed tracks, while other sides had obtuse rail-like ridges sticking out—Stenstrom was reminded of a tongue-and-groove system of joining pieces of wood together. These green squares moved, they traveled about on top of each other, the ridges jutting out of the square's sides fitting into the grooves of other squares seamlessly—like the pieces of a gigantic, interlocking puzzle. The green, blinking squares on Innocent's body were constantly travelling about, changing his shape in a bee-like cloud of movement—it was as if he were composed of many tiny robots piled up on top of each other to create a huge, blocky one.

Such technology. He'd seen robots before on Planet Fall and Bustoke, where they were most common, but he'd not seen any quite like this.

On the area of Innocent's body where a stomach might be placed, the green squares had joined together to form a spinning pan. Organic, flesh-like tendrils of stuff kept dripping out of the rotating pan and slopping to the floor. It reminded him of a grotesque sno-cone machine, spinning, spewing molten flesh instead of flavored, shaved ice.

That must be where the fleshy razor-wire came from.

At his shoulders was an array of variously sized antennae, some rather short, while others were long and flexible. He was broadcasting and receiving data through the antennae—Stenstrom could feel the strength of the incoming and outgoing signals vibrating his teeth.

Innocent didn't have a head, per se, instead, he had a large, hinged monitor screen that could fold up and descend into the cavity of his chest. A straight line of light that oscillated in the center was all that was displayed on his head-screen.

Although Stenstrom couldn't hear it in the vacuum, he could imagine Innocent making a skittering sort of sound.

They stood there, regarding each other for a moment.

Stenstrom quickly raised his NTH, cocked hammer, and fired. The blast hit Innocent in the chest—about a dozen little green squares fell off and clattered to the floor of the bay, dead.

Apparently, in this blocky, robotic form, Innocent was too decentralized to kill with a single shot—he was like a colony of little robots working together, each one alive all by itself.

Innocent raised his fist. In a surge, the green squares migrated en masse to his fist, where it grew huge, like a massive hammer.

Stenstrom tried to fade into the shadows, but he couldn't—there was too much razor wire about—he had no space to move.

Innocent swung with terrific force, flattening Stenstrom into the bulkhead wall, where the metal deformed around his body, making a sort of form-fitting imprint with him in the center.

As he got punched, Stenstrom dropped his NTH, and it spiraled away from his hand and was caught up on several strands of razor wire.

Innocent turned to it and, spewing fleshy material from his chest, covered the weapon in a thick, tumor-like ball wreathed in razor wire blossoms.

A moment later Stenstrom's partially flattened helmet cracked and depressurized in a cloud of rapid condensation.

He felt all the air rush out of his lungs.

This was it!

Stenstrom sat there, buried in the bulkhead, his pressure suit no longer holding pressure. He considered his situation—he should be dead, squashed flat, helmet cracked and sputtering. His pressure suit was making air, but it got pulled out of the crack in his helmet just as fast as it did so.

He should be dead—flattened, broken, suffocated in his pressure suit.

But, as far as he could tell, he was fine.

He felt fine.

He considered what he had done up to this point. He had smashed his way through the docking ring, passing through the hatch effortlessly. He pulled Chance Drury's hands off without a thought—and certainly, Chance had to be a robotic creature similar to Innocent. He was able to see clearly in the pitch black corridor

A-Ram said, that, just for a moment, he looked like a robot.

The Mad Lord had looked to him like a robot as well.

And, apparently, he was a man just like the Mad Lord …

✶ ✶ ✶ ✶ ✶

Innocent Drury didn't pay Stenstrom, stuck in the wall, venting gasses, any mind—clearly assuming he was dead.

He gave his cracked helmet a slight pat with his nipper-like hands—rushing air vapor answered in response.

With that, his head screen folded up and disappeared within his body cavity as did the cluster of antennae on his shoulders.

The multitude of green squares traveling about his body began rearranging themselves in a flurry, locking into place, compacting down smaller and smaller. A collection of squares twisted about, creating a perfectly formed head.

Soon, the huge, blocky robot that had punched Stenstrom into the wall, appeared like a smallish, green man made of metal, he even had a toothy, weather-beaten head and a phallus of locked-in green squares. A funnel of flesh-material came twisting out of his stomach and coated him completely. After a moment, Innocent Drury stood there, naked, but otherwise perfectly man-like. He pulled cancerous-looking stalks of mal-formed flesh away from his body and cast them aside. He teased the flesh at his scalp, creating an unruly nest of frizzy hair.

He seemed to be arguing with someone unseen—probably with his brother over on the *Heade*. Silently cursing, he turned and marched toward Stenstrom and began pulling what he thought was his dead, flattened body out of the indentation in the wall.

Stenstrom's fist shot out and clobbered Innocent in the face, knocking him back into the tangle of razor-wire. He then pulled himself fully free of the wall.

His brand new flesh lacerated, Innocent clambered out of the tangle and stared at Stenstrom with a mangled face, clearly astonished.

His mouth moved, but was silent in the vacuum. The Com housed in Stenstrom's pressure suit came to life—Innocent's voice filtered in, partially masked in whine.

"What in Creation are ya'?" he said.

Stenstrom responded in kind. "What are you and your folk?"

"We's eternal, we are. We serves our masters and they's given us eternal life for our trouble."

Outside, the *Heade* screamed by. Guns mounted to her broadsides sparkled and the bay was carpeted in contained explosive shells. Stenstrom was hit at least a dozen times, his pressure suit shredded.

Innocent raised his scrawny arms and charged. Stenstrom, unharmed by the straffing run, stood his ground, hauled back, and landed a hard shot to Innocent's ribs, doubling him over. He then balled his fists up and swung, getting him in the jaw. Arms and legs flailing, Innocent rocketed into the far wall of the bay. He bounced into the bulkhead. Just at that moment, A-Ram hauled the ship around in a sudden movement, and Innocent went out through the open doors of the bay into space, his naked, meaty body looking like a huge mandrake root as he spiraled out.

Certain he'd not seen the last of Innocent, Stenstrom turned to his NTH, which was balled up in an ugly, fleshy cocoon. He tore at the cocoon with his fingers—the fleshy material being remarkably resilient and durable. Finally, it gave way and Stenstrom pulled his pistol free,

He ran to the edge of the Bay.

Outside, there was Innocent moving about. He wasn't flailing or out of control, instead he was moving with precision. The flesh-spewing hole in his stomach was now protruding and directed down toward his legs, like a nozzle. Streamers of flesh were squirting out in a rapid dash-dash-dash succession and he was apparently using it like a jet.

He hovered in front of the bay, about a hundred yards distant. He fumbled with something in his hands, hiding what he was doing from view. As he worked, the long shaft of a green lance or missile appeared, getting longer by the moment—apparently, Innocent was shedding some of his green squares and using them to create a weapon of some sort.

Stenstrom wasn't going to give Innocent a chance to finish whatever he was doing. He cocked and fired, aiming for his head.

He darted away from Stenstrom's shot, where it missed over his shoulder.

Stenstrom cocked the hammer to fire again, but Innocent had finished his work. He had created a ten-foot long, missile-like lance that was lit up with blinking lights. He hauled back and threw it like a javelin heading directly for Stenstrom.

Stenstrom aimed and fired, hitting the lance in the nose. Its blinking lights went out and it careened off target. But it was too late.

The dead lance hit Stenstrom across the chest, knocking him backward into the tangle of razor wire with incredible force.

And then there was Innocent flying in on his jet stream of flesh like a ghoul.

He flew into Stenstrom, pounding the base of his neck with devastating blows. His left hand changed shape and expanded into a hideous claw, stretching and tearing through his artificial flesh. Before Innocent could use the claw, Stenstrom punched at it with a back fist. The claw lost its shape and fell apart with the force of the blow, many green squares scattering about.

Innocent reached up, trying to rip Stenstrom's helmet off. He seized Innocent's arm and wrenched it out of the socket, the arm quickly changing shape and roiling with movement, like a dead bird full of bugs. He tossed it aside.

"Ye' can't beats us. We's eternal," Innocent said over Stenstrom's crackling Com.

Stenstrom picked him up by the chin. "Where is Captain Gwendolyn?"

"In a place ye' can't get to her. She's going to be eaten by th' Cronyns, she is."

"Where? Where are these Cronyns you keep talking about?"

Innocent didn't answer him. Stenstrom squeezed and his chin collapsed.

"I'll be rememberin' this score, les' ye' forgets," Innocent said. "Now, this is personal betwixt us."

He rolled his eyes back and opened his mouth. A moment later, Stenstrom could hear a boiling, frenetic cacophony of noise being broadcast by Innocent through his helmet.

Stenstrom reached down and ripped his head off, where his body went limp.

He went to the open bay and searched for the *Heade*—there it was, coming in fast and angry, its array of many small guns coming to bear on him, ready to apply a devastating blast to the Ripcar bay.

The thrusters ticked, A-Ram steered into the *Heade*, forcing it to veer away or collide, an encounter the sturdy, much larger *Seeker* would surely win.

The *Heade* twisted away and moved out of his field of view.

Given respite, Stenstrom checked the *Westminster,* certain shells from the *Heade* had riddled her into wreckage. To his surprise, the *Westminster* seemed sound. The shells had bounced off. He smiled as he looked her over. She was armored plated. Apparently that's what she had been doing in Dry Dock 275, having a brand new carapace of armor plating installed for Admiral Pax, turning her into a bullet-proof chariot. Why the Admiral needed such a thing Stenstrom had no idea.

Stenstrom looked around, found the power cable and hooked it back up to the *Westminster.* All by itself the ship powered back up and fired its engines.

✳ ✳ ✳ ✳ ✳

He exited the bay through the sub-lock. "Taara!" he shouted into the air.

The Com opened, given new life by the *Westminster.* "Bel, that you?"

"It's me. What's our status?"

"How do I know it's you? You could be one of those creepy idiots out there."

"Because I bought you your lunch while you were guarding Admiral Pax's bust the other day."

Taara gasped. "Bel! We were so worried!"

"I'm fine. What's our status?"

"The *Heade* was having its way with us—A-Ram did a great job keeping us in the fight."

"I saw that—incredible flying, A-Ram!"

Taara continued. "After awhile, she just stopped firing and cleared the field in a hurry though she tried to hit us with an induction mine that A-Ram had to roll away from. Where's Innocent?"

"He's here, he's dead. I got him."

21

—The Search for the Demophalon John—

"Bel!" Taara cried.

Stenstrom climbed up to the bridge.

"Welcome back! It's great to see you! A-Ram flew like an old pro, Bel. You should have seen him."

"I did see. Well done, A-Ram."

"What happened with Innocent Drury?"

"I got him, he's here." Stenstrom hauled Innocent's body out of the lift shaft and threw it to the floor where it fell with a surprisingly heavy thud. He tossed in his severed head and his arm as well.

He's a robot," Stenstrom said brushing himself off. "I guess all of his brothers are robots as well."

Taara knelt down and looked at him. "Pretty complex robot. Got some sweet hardware."

A-Ram had a thought. "They're Flesh Replicas. I remember now, the old stories of the Druries. According to mariner legends, they were a bunch of worthless pirates from Onaris a few centuries back—problem was nobody could get rid of them. Sink them, kill them, and they came right back to rob and pillage again. Druries Belt right outside the window there was named after them. Annoying lot. Always preying on the weak and helpless, always appearing when things were most favorable to them and then vanishing when things got hot. They operated out of a place called The Swarm."

Stenstrom pulled Innocent's flesh apart, revealing the tightly packed, green metallic innards. He reached in and pried several of the green squares away from the core—they were dug in surprisingly snug.

"He's mostly made up of these things—like a bunch of little robots working together to form a large robot. They sort of move about in a chaotic fashion, one riding atop the other—I was reminded of a bee hive, an organized cluster of many individuals working together under a collective mind."

Taara took several of the green robots and gazed at them. "That would actually be a Mecon—'Mechanical Construct', a bunch of little robots working together to form a big one. This is an elegant little design."

Stenstrom pulled the covering of flesh away, revealing his circular stomach cavity.

Taara covered her nose. "Wow, that stinks! Oh, it's like smelling a bucket full of guts."

Holding her nose, she took a few more squares out and examined them. Two squares in her hand suddenly formed together and started moving on their own. Perplexed, she watched the squares struggle, adding on two more squares until the mass began undulating undulated like a metallic worm.

Tara pulled the squares apart and they went dead. "That was weird," she said. "These squares suddenly linked up and appeared to form a rudimentary colonial consciousness. Kind of cool."

A-Ram was concerned. "If we refer again to the legend of the Druries, then, we can expect to have not seen the last of any of them. The Druries always came back—that was the hallmark of their legend."

"Innocent Drury did mention that he was eternal before he signed off. I also recall he made a furtive sound before he died—as if he were broadcasting a blizzard of data."

"I'll wager he was off-loading all of his up-to-date thoughts and memories and transporting them to a remote location where a new body shall await him, and be fully briefed on all his prior activities once made whole," A-Ram said.

Taara shuddered. "At least that explains how his brothers were floating around out there in space, right as rain. I have to tell you that really gave me the creeps, flat out."

Stenstrom stood and started pacing around. "So, what about Captain Gwendolyn, have we been able to reach her?"

Taara shook her head. "No, Bel, we haven't. And she's not on the scopes either."

"She said she was only half an hour from our position. Even in our diminished sensing state, we should be reading her plain as you please. She should be right on top of us."

"Unless the Cronyns got her," Taara said, fiddling around with one of the green robotic squares from Innocent's body.

Stenstrom plunged back into his chair. "A-Ram, make sail. I want the captain and her ship found immediately. Forget our previous mission to Bazz—our new mission is locate the *Demophalon John* and ensure the safe rescue of all souls aboard. All else is secondary."

A-Ram took the helm. "Shall we head back to Kana and inform them there of our findings?"

"No, it's taken us days to get this far, and just as long to get back to Kana or be in Com range. I don't know if the Captain and her crew have that time—we have to assume they are in dire peril and in need of immediate rescue."

"Heading?"

"A-Ram, you said the Druries operated out of a place called 'The Swarm', what is that?"

"Not certain. Asteroid field I suppose."

"Remember when Taara caught that brief glimpse of a large body on the sensors? I'll bet that was The Swarm lit up in the lantern's beam. Let's navigate there now."

"But, Bel, how are we going to detect it? Before we were using the Lantern."

"Use your best recollection."

Taara began the calculations.

He turned to her. "So, these Cronyns, tell me about them, Taara."

"There's not much to say, Bel. They are some sort of beings that used to terrorize my people with illusions for two weeks every couple of years. Evil spirits that could make you hear and see things."

"What do they look like?"

"Well, nobody knows what they look like—nobody's ever seen a Cronyn, as far as I know. The thing with them, as I said, they could make you see and hear things that weren't real. Some folks, I think, could overcome it by meditating. In the 'Time of the Cronyn', you just could walk off a cliff or stab yourself in the face with a knife and never know that you were all Painted up in an illusion. To my people, the Cronyns were no joke. They could kill you dead."

Stenstrom thought a moment. "As the Druries referenced them by name, we must assume they are real entities and somewhere in the near vicinity. It's also reasonable to assume that we could, even now, be under the sway of their illusions, yes?"

"I guess so. Yeah, I guess so." Taara looked around.

"That body we scoped in the Lantern light has got to be it: this Swarm, this Cronyn World, the Lantern saw through the illusion. Even though we can't see it now we know it's there. It's also safe to assume that they have been using illusions to hide their presence from the Fleet to this point," A-Ram said.

"Agreed. Chance Drury said something about toying with Captain Gwendolyn and her crew before eating them. Perhaps these creatures somehow derive sustenance from the fear and confusion their illusions create. They may, even now, be feeding on Captain Gwendolyn and her crew by locking them into some sort of squalid diorama and allowing it to play out. Though it might sound morbid, such a situation may buy us a bit of time to sort this out and affect a rescue."

"True," A-Ram said. "Taara, you said this 'Time of the Cronyn' used to happen a lot but is no longer an issue?"

"Yeah, it's just a holiday now. Just an excuse to drink Zemuda and stay home, which is always popular on Bazz."

"Taara, hasn't the League, or the Sisters, investigated this phenomena to any degree?"

"I don't know. They think we're crazy on Bazz all the time."

Taara was ready with her calculations. "A-Ram, go nine pegs hard a larboard, Z plus 22. That'll send us right where I saw the contact. You know, if I think on it, there's an old story about Darius Jones—the Sisters 'It Guy' from Bazz. According to the story, he took a long journey across Bazz, following a guiding star to a place of shallow seas and many moons. There, as the story goes, he fought the Cronyns and that was that. Haven't heard much from them since. It's: Jones 1, Cronyns 0."

"Hmmm," Stenstrom said. "I wonder if we can interpret Jones' journey as not one across the seas of Bazz, but across the heavens, and maybe where he ended up was a world of shallow seas."

"How do you make that leap?" Taara asked.

"Well, it stands to reason that if Bazz was terrorized by some sort of entity that once manifested itself at a regular interval, then it follows that the entity in question could be celestial in origin, as Bazz's orbital positioning might be critical in dictating when such an entity would have sway over the planet."

A-Ram spoke up. "I tend to agree. As there are no significant celestial bodies between Kana, Onaris and Bazz, it would follow that these Cronyns could be located on something small with a highly irregular orbit, such as a comet or asteroid. Such an irregular orbit would account for how the Cronyns once could affect the people of Bazz and now cannot."

"But, one thing. We don't have the Lantern anymore," Taara said. "How are we going to detect it? We could fly right past it and not know a thing."

Stenstrom sat there and had a thought. "Innocent Drury …"

"What about him?" Taara asked.

"He and his brothers seemed to be in cahoots with the Cronyns, that they feed them, provide them with prey."

"Ok …"

"So, as these characters are robots—highly advanced, but robots just the same—they must have some sort of technological method for detecting them, of seeing through their illusions."

Stenstrom went to Innocent's body and began pulling him part, his body crumbling into a huge amount of green squares. "He was packing all sorts of antennae and sensory equipment."

Taara joined Stenstrom, and before long, with little green squares littering the bridge, he pulled all of his sundry antennae and his head screen out of his body cavity. "What do you make of this, Taara?"

She examined the hardware. "Give me a little bit," she said, flopping down onto the floor and crossing her legs.

With Taara sitting amid the scattered wreckage of Innocent's body,

Stenstrom went into his office. There, standing in the darkened room, he gazed out the windows, seeing the stationary stars and the glowing curtain of Druries Belt.

Out there somewhere, was Captain Gwendolyn and her missing ship.

PART 2
THE WOMAN IN GRAY

Vendra, Lady of Cone

1

—The Twilight of Carina—

Her life ended that night at the grand Nether Day ball, looking around on the floor for the man whom she given her heart to and not finding him.

Where did he go?

Where indeed.

Stolen—she stole him from me!!

Lady Vendra of Cone had longed to meet Lord Stenstrom, the eighth son of the Zenon House of Belmont, in person for months. She was newly of age and wished to seek a dashing husband in the Stellar Fleet. She joined a sect of similarly-minded ladies called the Ballwigs. She sent out many queries along with her Ballwig friends to young officers in the Fleet, hoping to strike up a rapport.

She soon received an exciting reply, from a Lord Stenstrom of Belmont, a promising Lt manning the navigator's position aboard the Fleet ship *Amazing*. They shared a steady correspondence, his letters were full of tales of excitement and grand adventure as he sailed the stars. His letters to her were things she came to cherish, and she waited anxiously each day to see if one might arrive. Thinking him something special, she followed the old Remnath tradition of no vids or live coms—if he wanted to see her, it must be in person; if he wanted to speak to her, it must be longhand with pen and paper. How happy she was when she convinced him to come to the grand Nether Day ball in Jacarta held at the fabulous St. Gala's Veil ballroom. Most of her Ballwig friends would be there with their respective catches. Oh how it would be an enchanting affair, and she promised a night they would both remember for the whole of their lives.

It certainly was that, as she stood there alone on the ballroom floor looking for her man whom the silver-haired strumpet and Ballwig renegade, Lady Jubilee of Tyrol, had just stolen off the floor.

She lived in a mental cloud of her own making for years after that. She went to the Sisters, enraged.

"I declare Wirguild! I want revenge!"

The Sisters reviewed her petition. Their Marines: "We see you have set Wirguild upon the entire House of Belmont South-Tyrol. We cannot allow that. You may have Wirguild upon Lady Jubilee of Belmont South-Tyrol, and that is all."

"I want to kill them all!"

"You may not."

And she left Valenhelm, her tail between her legs. She was frightened of the Sisters. She could not go against the Sisters.

*　*　*　*　*

St. Gala's Veil—anger and hurt bubbled over to violence.

She tensed up in her rainbow colored gown, pulling the long hairpins from her head—they glistened in her hands. Her heart pounded, matching the music coming from the nearby ballroom.

Her enemy, Lady Jubilee, stood there a few feet away. She shook her hands and conjured from nowhere six silver daggers between her fingers like claws.

They circled. Vendra had longed for this moment, to come to grips with Lady Jubilee—to kill her, and right in the very place where she had stolen her love. She reared back and struck out, ready to plunge the hairpins into the bitch's hated chest.

Lady Jubilee disappeared and her strike missed.

"Ha! What a sight," came her smug voice. *"I could kill you at any moment I wish."*

Vendra turned, where was she? "Fight me fairly!" she cried, brandishing her hairpins.

"Fair, there is nothing fair about this, is there?" She felt a foot roughly kick her in the rear, and she fell, dropping her hairpins.

"This is ridiculous," Jubilee said, again from the shadows. *"This isn't a fight, this isn't Wirguild—this is murder. I suggest you pick yourself up, move on, and find a man in some other pasture; otherwise, the next time we meet,*

I will kill you."

Her hands, skinned after the fall, stung. She slowly stood.

Jubilee's voice was taunting and chiding. *"To think that you could hurt me with your little Wirguild and your hair pins. How pathetic."*

How pathetic…

✳ ✳ ✳ ✳ ✳

The open letter sat on the bed. She'd read it many times.

He had written this letter, he had touched it.

Stenstrom …

She wanted to hate him, like she hated Lady Jubilee. But she couldn't. She savored the words on the paper, touched them with the pads of her fingers. She tried to find hidden meaning in the words, some encrypted message, but there appeared to be none.

In the letter, he apologized for what happened at the ball, that it was all his fault. He said he was sorry, that he wished her feel no pain, no harm, but that his heart was lost to Lady Jubilee. He said it was quite beyond his control.

It's not your fault, my love… she did it. She put a spell on you.

Lady Vendra stood, gazing at herself in the mirror, nude, her closet full of colorful Cone gowns all thrown aside.

She looked at her thin body, at her unskilled hands. She looked at her gaunt face, unable to smile.

How pathetic… came Jubilee's voice time and time again.

She turned to her clothing and threw the beautiful gowns out the window. She saved one garment—an ugly gray dress that she'd never worn before, put it on, and then threw herself out the window too, falling several stories to the grounds below, her gowns spread out like colorful, fluttering tissue paper all around her.

✳ ✳ ✳ ✳ ✳

Lady Vendra survived her suicide attempt, the Hospitalers mending her broken bones and lacerated tissues. In examining her, they declared her insane.

"She is mad. Her soul is lost," they said.

"She fell in love with a man and lost her mind," her mother said in the darkness.

"Such things happen," the Hospitalers said.

Not knowing what to do, her House of Cone sent her off to dark, remote Carina 7 to live out her days in a convent of stone for troubled women—the madness festering within her was a scandal and needed to be kept quiet. A remote, seldom travelled world out of the social eye was an ideal place to keep her.

Carina 7 was far off and rather disassociated with League society. It was perfect. There, she could spend her days in quiet, undiscussed comfort in a convent surrounded by other troubled women.

She arrived at the convent and was given a small room. The pale Grand Dames of the convent assured Lady Vendra's family that she would be well taken care of, and that they had brought her to the right place.

The Cones were worried as they took in the dark skies and mirthless environs, listening to the perpetual thunder rumbling. Her mother, Countess Jessathiela, had a change of heart. She could not leave her daughter in such a maudlin place.

The Grand Dames assured her mother Carina 7 was just the place for her daughter. The climate was ideal for Lady Vendra's care, the expertise without peer. Why, with a bit of luck, they might even see her make a full recovery; such miracles happened often on Carina.

Comforted, the Cones boarded their transport and left, confident that she would receive the kind of care that she needed in a discreet setting.

No sooner did they break orbit did the Dames of the convent convene in Vendra's small room, she sitting there, mouth open and flaccid, only mildly aware of what was going on around her.

"Yes," they said slamming the door shut behind them. "Your House has done you a great service. We have seen your like many times. You are neither mad nor insane—you are downtrodden—you are beaten. You are lost to your rage."

Lady Vendra mumbled something.

"What's that?" The Grand Dames asked. "Speak up!"

" The ... sorrow, the regret ..."

"Oh," they sneered. "Such things have no proper place. You shall see. We have schools here where we can teach you to harness your madness— your scorn. We can teach you things here that are unheard of. We can teach you the art of hatred and revenge and your quaint feelings of 'sorrow' and 're-gret' will be naught but distant memories. Simply stand, and be one with us."

Drooling, Lady Vendra sighed and stood.

*   *   *   *   *

Though a chartered League world, Carina 7, or simply Carina as the locals called it, was an odd, poorly understood place. Far from its parent star, its brightest days were nothing more than a dim twilight, the surface of the planet warmed mostly by prolific geo-thermal energy that radiated out from the planet's core with great efficiency. Laced with giant calderas and super-volcanoes, much of the surface was pocked with bare, scalded rock and tow-ering geysers. In the north was a fair amount of habitable land, grown green with imported low-light plants and studded with gothic, fortress-like castles. The original inhabitants of Carina were members of a vast harem serving the mysterious Emperor-King of Ming Moorland, a non-League world several clicks away past the great nebula. Forgotten on the dark world of geysers and imported plants, the harem grew and was left lonely. When they were called upon by the Emperor-King, he abused them, sometimes torturing and killing them in droves, making them fight to the death for his amusement. He also used Carina as a place of reward for warriors in his service who pleased him. The warriors could go to Carina and do there anything they wanted ... anything.

The women of Carina, abused, tormented, kept in the dark, raped and murdered, developed a powerful hatred of men—of all men. They kept their numbers replenished via ovarian fusion, the generations of females becoming oddly mutated in the harsh climate.

When the lords of the League came, they found themselves terminally unimpressed with the gaudy men in their odd clothing—at least the Emperor-King was a man who knew what he wanted, whereas these League types were powdered fools. Standing side-by-side with the League men were the Sister-hood of Light, a powerful matriarchal organization whom the Carinan women found themselves greatly admiring. As they listened to the lords and envied the Sisters, they found the League had a fair amount to offer, and they craved the protection and technology the League promised. They became a chartered League world in 000271EX with one seat on the League Ex-Commons, though the odd climate, dark days, and frosty nature of the female inhabitants discouraged most who thought to migrate there. They participated very little in general League doings and were, most often, left alone.

✶   ✶   ✶   ✶   ✶

Over the next few years, Lady Vendra learned many things. In dark classrooms of stone and perpetual twilight, she learned the arts of seduction and deception. She was taught how to fight, using methods designed to hurt and maim men. She learned that men could easily be manipulated by scent of body and tone of voice. Occasionally, bands of snatched rogues and other disreputables unlikely to be missed, were brought to her, and Vendra was free to practice her newly learned skills upon these doomed men.

She felt something of a grim rush of pleasure as the men easily died before her.

She learned that men could just as easily be enslaved. She was taught the esoteric doctrines of *gynology*—the science of controlling and killing men through sex, scent and substance. Through *gynology*, she learned that the female pheromone was a very versatile tool, and she mastered the art of increasing her pheromones as needed. She was also taught that the male psyche, when stimulated into the heights of ecstasy, could be permanently and drastically altered by way of chemical and hormonal means introduced through the tip of the phallus. She was trained in the use of 'The Barb,' a studded, diaphragm-like device that was inserted into the womb. The Barb was smeared in chemical substances, and would repeatedly prick the phallus of a male sexual partner while at the height of bliss. Once pricked, the man could be paralyzed, made blind, made dead, or, best of all, made a hopeless slave of her scent.

She was warned:"The Barb is illegal—Sisters will kill you should you be discovered in its use, though the Sisters themselves make practice of it," her school masters told her.

That was a recurring theme she came to learn—the Sisters publically decrying a thing while secretly making heavy use of it.

The Sisters were a long point of study. Though greatly admiring their undeniable power, the Dames of Carina found the Sisterhood of Light a significant threat. The Sisters were too enamored with the men of the League, were too ready to give ear to them, to placate them. The Sisters should put the men to heel, to subjugate them and kill them if need be—and as they were unwilling to do so, they were, therefore, a threat. Vendra spent several months learning to best the Sisters, to evade their vigilance. The Sisters could read minds even from a great distance, and thus trained, her true thoughts were quite hidden from the Sisters, giving them only a sham core of simple thoughts to read.

Her training continued, and the men brought to her to practice upon continued. She was a model student, a master *Gynologist* in the making.

2

—The Tenets of Revenge—

The last thing she learned was possibly the most important. She learned how to hate and how to wage revenge.

In the stone classrooms of Carina, she learned the Six Carinan Tenets of Revenge:

1: A Master revenge is decades in the making.

2: Revenge should strike at the Heart many times and at the Flesh only once.

3: Failure to Act when the time is ripe is the poison one drinks.

4: Patience is the key attribute in conducting Revenge.

5: Uncertainty is Revenge's deadliest weapon.

6: There are no Innocent Bystanders in Revenge.

Revenge on Carina was an all or nothing proposition, utterly vicious and invariably fatal one way or the other.

Armed with this new education, Lady Vendra's family was summoned. They were told that, under their care, she was restored to sanity. Elated, the House of Cone came for Lady Vendra and the Woman in Gray went home.

She took her time as she settled back into her manor, her family over-joyed she was well and returned to them, seemingly recovered. Externally, she appeared fine, and she said all the things they expected her to say. Her father bought her a whole wardrobe full of new Cone gowns of vibrant colors—how she used to love them.

Little did her family suspect that she never once wore any of those lovely gowns. She never wore anything but gray again and a pair of button-up boots in the Carina style, however, to her family's eyes, to her friends eyes, they saw her wearing Cone gowns. Her skills with deception and disguise learned during her dark days on Carina were near perfect.

At a leisurely pace, she put her plans for revenge against Lady Jubilee into motion. She followed the tenets, she took her time. She resumed her place in Remnath Society. She attended social functions and drank tea with her circle of friends, returned to them whole and much wiser. Under her steady but imperceptible influence, the Ballwigs, once a cheerful gathering

Revised Sigil of the Ballwigs

of ladies hoping to win the hearts of Stellar Fleet officers, became dreadful and notorious, rejoicing in gossip and lies and, above all else, hoping to inflict misery and pain upon any foolish enough to fall for their tricks.

She began her work.

She told her friends that she had been on sabbatical on Carina 7. She spoke about how harrowing the trip there and back had been, how space travel was not nearly as safe as the public had been told. She knew Lord Stenstrom of Belmont was in the Fleet and was soon to be made captain of a ship. She also knew that the lurid stories she told of mutiny, mishaps, sodomy, and botulism and other perils of space travel would take wing and travel all the way to Esther to the eventual ears of Lady Jubilee.

Uncertainty was indeed a powerful tool. Lady Jubilee, fearless for herself, was no doubt hand-wringing in fear for her handsome husband doing such a dangerous job. The seeds were planted, vile fruit was soon to grow.

Next, she needed a network of slaves to do her bidding without question. She went to Calvert, a place no one would ever expect a fine Lady of

Cone to go, and stayed in an exclusive room at the Empire Hotel. She wore the odd clothes and spoke the hidden tongues reserved for the wealthy, and watched the people below come and go as was the fad for the elite—to watch Calvert from high above like a great anthill on full display. When she was ready, she ventured out. There, in the dark twisting streets, she preyed upon the dirty urchins and filthy men that were there in quantity.

Pretending to be an innocent, bewildered woman, she had no trouble luring the men in, ending up flat on her back in seedy rooms and crooked inns near the docks, playing service to drunken, stinking men who, with every thrust, made themselves more her slave, for waiting deep within her womb was The Barb, doing its job with terrible effectiveness. Sometimes she didn't enslave them, sometimes, behind closed doors and stark naked, she fought and killed them, just for the fun of it, their screams and dying pleas like sweet music soothing her. There were no shortage of victims in Calvert, and no shortage of suspects to take the blame for the killings that had cropped up in earnest. She carried with her chemicals from Carina that removed all trace of her passing, leaving no material for Evidencers to find. Eventually, as years passed by, she developed a thirst to kill more and more men—sometimes she would go to Calvert not to collect slaves, but simply to kill. 'The Fiend of Calvert' as the mysterious killer was soon to be called, was loosed upon the region. She loved seeing articles about 'him' in the posts and the pictures of the Fiend as a man in a gas mask made her laugh, none suspecting a skinny woman in gray was responsible for it all. From her room at the Empire, she collected slaves and made dead bodies, snickering into her tea and acting shocked as she sat in the hotel dining room and lobby, watching the Evidencers and Gifted Inspectors sift through non-existent genetic evidence and Stare for the guilty, not knowing her Carina-trained mind was unpierceable and shut.

Soon, she had a whole gallery of filthy men who would do anything she asked, and a pile of dead men that she had made, killed by her hand. There was an old, underground vault near the ruins of Woodward where she kept her men, within easy reach whenever she needed them, and they roamed the ruins alive, but in a daze, a hopeless trance. Far away in Calvert, the simple folk were burning with fear. From high above at the Empire Hotel, she gazed through the spyglass at the terrified people and laughed.

One of the first things she did was order one of her slaves, who had access to an old Xaphan *Merci* freighter, to load it full of shaddout and encounter the Fleet Vessel *Amazing*—where Lord Stenstrom served as the navigator.

"Encounter the *Amazing*, and then detonate the shaddout," she told the man, and he did it without question, killing himself in the process.

Returning to Remnath and lying low, she listened to the winds of gossip. Her slow-burn efforts were working—Lady Jubilee in distant Tyrol was said to be beside herself with fear, desperate for her husband to quit the Fleet.

Splendid! Additionally, she learned that Lady Jubilee had told her husband that he would have no sons until he met her wishes.

And Lady Jubilee was true to her word, punching out one daughter after another with regularity every two or three years.

The obvious thing to do was strike at her children. The frustrating thing was Lady Jubilee was a tight-fisted, controlling mother and getting to her children was difficult. She sent her remaining Calvert Men-Slaves out to scout the Belmont South-Tyrol manor and grounds. They reported the grounds encompassed five square miles of old Merian lands south of the city of Tyrol. There were no obvious technological protections about, yet *something* appeared to be protecting the grounds, for several men who got too close disappeared without trace and were not seen again.

Her army of slaves was utterly disposable, and she continued, sending them off on one-way missions. She succeeded in poisoning one daughter with tainted candy placed on the grounds, but nothing happened except that her hair turned blonde instead of the usual black or that odd silver color.

These Belmonts were damnably tough.

So, Lady Vendra sat back and waited. Something would present itself. She needed to be patient.

✶ ✶ ✶ ✶ ✶

Lady Jubilee was up to her fifteenth daughter, over forty years had passed, and even Vendra's remarkable patience was beginning to wear thin. She decided to change her tactics a bit and went after Lord Stenstrom directly. She had generally avoided attacking him—perhaps it was because she still loved him, even the dark school mistresses of Carina couldn't beat that out of her. Her love for him was a tiny ember in the dark she labored to keep alive and warm. In any event, it was time to make something happen. She began making herself available at Fleet—her brother, Derlith, was a newly minted Admiral and with his connections, she had the run of the place. She had dinner with Captain Stenstrom many times, her appearance disguised— yet another skill she'd learned on Carina. However, unlike the Calvert men whom she easily had her way with, Captain Stenstrom showed no interest in her beyond what the demands of social civility called for. The other men at the table were near fainting with the amount of pheromones she was pouring out, but Captain Stenstrom did not react—apparently he was protected by a natural addiction to his wife's scent.

She sighed, she collected new slaves, but could never enslave the one man she truly wanted.

So, her attempts to 'get' Lord Stenstrom failed—however, the effort was not a complete loss. At one of the dinners she attended, she overhead Captain Stenstrom talking to another captain about inheritances. Apparently the captain Lord Stenstrom was talking to was going through a nasty rite of succession with his two sons, as they both claimed to be the next lord of his House—it was quite a scandal. Lord Stenstrom admitted that he himself had no sons, and the captain he was talking to laughed. "Well, I thought I had problems," he piped.

Lady Vendra listened, and the wheels started turning. The House of Belmont South-Tyrol had no sons, no succession of line, as spelled out in the rigid rules of Kanan society.

That's how her revenge would proceed.

3

—A Love Potion—

Lady Vendra sat in her Remnath manor and considered the situation.

Fifteen daughters. Lady Jubilee had to be doing something to prevent the creation of a boy-child. Lady Vendra knew from her Carina training that it was possible to pre-select the sex of one's child without using external methods, such as the Hospitalers used. The Black Hats could do it with Shadow tech, Carina adepts could do it with concentration, and there were any number of herbal methods that would work as well. That must be how Jubilee was doing it—via herbal methods.

Vendra began a fresh attack. She circulated information that the House of Belmont South-Tyrol could not have males—that Lord Stenstrom was not virile in that manner. As with everything, the attack took time to put into place and grow. The years rolled by, daughter after daughter were added to the Belmont household, and Lady Vendra continued the pressure. She ventured into the Zenon region and frequented areas where she knew the distant relatives of the Belmont South-Tyrol House would be. And she filled their ears full of tales of the South-Tyrol's soon to be lost House, and all their wealthy holdings and lands to be redistributed to the lords of the city of Tyrol. She even added the tidbit that the lords of the city had already drawn up plans reapportioning the South-Tyrol manor grounds.

That really got the people talking. Weeks later, she began hearing how the cousins and distant relatives of the Belmont South-Tyrols were actually going there in person to present themselves and make their various cases for the favorable distributing of lands and properties after the passing of the lord and lady.

The very real problem of succession began to tell on Lord Belmont, and Lady Vendra caught wind of him making his concerns known to Lady Jubilee. By this point, they had twenty-nine daughters, and Lord Belmont knew that they would be left with nothing should there be no male heir.

Lady Vendra's revenge had been in progress for over eighty years, and her Wirguild had been running for nearly ninety. Now, it was time to really apply the screws to the House of Belmont South-Tyrol. Revenge was at hand.

Unfortunately, she ran square into a series of troubling setbacks. Her stockpile of slaves in the Woodward vault was raided and decimated by a paid vigilant from the north known as the Mad Lord of Walther. One man, by himself, got through all her defenses and killed most of her Calvert men, rendering the stronghold useless.

She tried returning to Calvert and snaring more men, but again, the Mad Lord presented himself, challenging her in direct combat.

Piecing together information taken from the Woodward vault, the Mad Lord had discovered the Fiend of Calvert connection—and personally investigated her doings in the region. Showing remarkable skill, he tracked her down, rousted her out of her Calvert lair, killed many of her remaining slaves, and engaged her across the rooftops as she tried to flee from an adversary whom she, even with her Carina-taught skills, was no match against. She had become jaded and careless, giving the Mad Lord no regard, however, she quickly found he was no ordinary man—he was strong beyond compare, impervious to harm, and seemingly immune to the female tricks she threw at him as they battled. With no recourse left, she was forced into full flight before the Mad Lord, running for her life over the rooftops of St. Edmunds.

She was lucky to escape. Licking her wounds, she added the Mad Lord's name to her list of people to hate.

Rightly fearing the Mad Lord and his continued investigations in Calvert, she decided to go off-world for a time, which, as it happened, served her needs nicely.

Bazz was a fine world to get lost in, as there she could bide her time and hide in plain sight. While Carina was most certainly a female-oriented world, Bazz was a more male-dominated place. The men there were arrogant and sweaty. Their heroes were all men. The women of Bazz were noisy and pugnacious but clearly subservient. They even wore their hair in a certain way (those long strands of hair they called "Mollocks") to announce their marital status to the grotesque men. She considered going on a murder spree, but thought better of it.

As she sweated it out in the tawdry villages, she became aware of a virility potion the Bazzers called the so-called 'God Sperm' tincture, a chemical extract that ensured the creation of a boy-child, and not just any boy-child, an exceptional boy child—Lord Sixtus of Grenville was said to be a product of the God Sperm tincture. This tincture was some sort of Bazz tradition, once again heralding the men over the women.

Finding the heat and humidity intolerable, she allowed herself the luxury of renting an Atmospheric to create her a pocket of dry, cool air. Settling in, she found a reputable pharmacy that sold the tincture in the city of Dyson-Clampton by the banks of the Dan River. It didn't take her long to enslave both her Atmospheric, creating the pocket of cool air around her, and the pharmacist himself, the two of them making sweaty love on the balcony under the hot, Bazz summer sky as the Atmospheric stood nearby. Her new slave told her that he had, in addition to the God Sperm tincture, a foolproof love potion that worked on pheromones. He would simply take some of her scent, create the love potion, and any who drank it would be lost to her.

He, however, advised against mixing the two—random and unexpected things might happen.

Excellent—this appeared to be working out better than she had hoped for. Sitting at a café, basking in the cool air created by her Atmospheric slave, she quickly penned an unsigned letter to Lord Belmont, informing him of the existence of the God Sperm tincture and what it could do for his heirless household. She hoped to put a powerful seed into his head.

4
—The Ganaada's Curse—

The plan was working. Several weeks later, sitting in a Bazz café with her Atmospheric slave, doing her best to avoid the terribly hot local cuisine, she caught wind from the Ballwigs that Lord Stenstrom was on his way to Bazz personally to fetch the God Sperm potion, which she was going to make certain that he did not receive. Instead, he would get the Bazz Love Potion, and that would be that. All she had to do was wait until he arrived and monitor the transaction to ensure he took the potion she wanted him to take. She sat at a nearby cafe and watched. Trying to blend in, she dismissed her Atmospheric, and fanned herself at her table, trying to keep cool without much success.

And, it couldn't happen fast enough. She'd had her fill of Bazz and Bazzers in general and was ready to return to civilized Kana as soon as possible. The locals, a pesky, sweaty people leaching spices from their pores and growing hair in places where hair ought not to grow, she couldn't walk down the street or take a meal without vendors and self-styled mystics harassing her the entire way. She had come to Bazz to blend in and hide, however, her fair complexion and her use of an Atmospheric fingered her as a Kanan lady of means and the Bazzers gave her no peace. The worst of the lot were these strange, loud women prowling the cafes and wharfs wearing gypsy garments. They called themselves 'Ganaadas' and claimed to possess mystical powers. With no shame and little tact, the Ganaadas would approach and demand she secure their services, waving their depleted Cred Sticks in her face.

"You got a bad flow around you," the Ganaada would say. "I can fix, just cost you 1500 creds."

Though Lady Vendra tried to be respectful of women and promote their success as she was taught on Carina, these Bazz females were intolerable. They were noisy, hairy, they stank and they seemed to gravitate to her, peering through crystals and other totems and babbling about the 'bad flow' around her.

A lot of Bazz nonsense. And, as the Ganaadas were female, she had nothing in her bag of tricks to combat or control them as she could with males. She simply had to sit there and endure them.

* * * * *

She watched Lord Stenstrom, sweating in his Fleet uniform; he had arrived in the square a bit early. She hadn't been expecting him until the morrow, and the pharmacy was closed, He made his way to a small inn on the other side of the square and stood at the counter, hoping to rent an air-conditioned room and pass the time. This was the moment to strike. There he was, alone, unsuspecting and vulnerable, and she was running out of patience. In her jaded observations of Bazz, she learned that Bazzers were always assaulting each other and having minor scuffles in the street. Nobody paid any attention. If she were to walk over there and assault him in plain sight, nobody would pay it any mind or come to his aid.

She pushed out her chair and made her way across the square. Time to take Lord Belmont one way or the other. Why wait? Why linger on this barbaric hellhole any longer than necessary? By sundown, she would be returning to blessed Kana, arm-in-arm with Lord Stenstrom at last.

As she neared the center of the square, a heated scuffle broke out in front of her. A grotesque Ganaada and some little, black-haired girl urchin were going at it, clawing at each other, ripping clothing and throwing each other about, their two heads of black hair and tassels bobbing around and whirling in concentric circles. Unseemly fights were always breaking out on the streets on Bazz she noted, but this particular fight was inconvenient. The two were going at it hard and literally ripping each other's clothing off. Shoes flew. Nobody paid them much mind until somebody started waving a Cred Stick around hoping to take wagers on the fight. Interest quickly piqued. A circle of people formed to bet money and watch as the girl and the Ganaada rolled around with unskilled fury. People cheered as blows were landed and as one combatant got the upper hand only to lose it moments later. Vendra had to push her way through the crush of noisy people, and it was slow going.

When she got through to the inn, Lord Stenstrom was gone, her opportunity lost. She felt hot and tired and returned to her seat at the cafe and ordered a drink. Frustrated, she would wait for her scheme to unfold as planned.

What was another steaming day on Bazz?

* * * * *

The Problem with Bazz, aside from the heat, was Bazzers.

The next day she was back in her seat at the cafe as she waited for Lord Stenstrom to arrive at the pharmacy. Soon, a Ganaada came up to her table and became particularly forceful and rude, giving her no peace, demanding money. She noted the Ganaada's face was marked up and bruised. She recognized her hideous clothing; this was the Ganaada whose ill-timed fight had foiled her attempt to get at Lord Stenstrom the day before. She wanted her to hurt, to feel real pain. Vendra was hot and irritable and had had enough. She stood up and dragged the foul woman out of the cafe and into the alley where she proceeded to beat her. The Ganaada fought back with surprising tenacity and Lady Vendra found herself in a heated and rather desperate brawl. Her skills were too much. She punished the foul woman and laid her out, hitting her where it hurt most. Leaving her in a pile of rubbish, she brushed herself off and headed back to the cafe.

The Ganaada stirred. "I curse you," she mumbled from behind, half insensate in the trash. "I curse you to the Circle!"

Fine. Whatever. Savage from Bazz, lay there in the trash and lick your wounds, and be thankful you're not dead.

She returned to her seat at the cafe and ordered a refreshment. As she waited for it to arrive, she felt a sly hand slide into her pocket. Whirling around, she caught a small, black-haired girl, whom she recognized as one of the pharmacist's worthless nieces, trying to steal her purse. She was in a filthy state, torn clothes with a black eye. Vendra thought at first to break her arm and send her off crying, such was the state of her mood, but instead, she smiled and opened her purse, giving her a few coins. She patted her on the head. "Off you go," she said and the girl with her ridiculous "Mollocks" scurried away.

Hopeless urchin, she thought—what good would she ever be?

* * * * *

It should be any time now. The afternoon seemed odd, the frequent Ganaadas roaming the street gave her a wide berth; they must have heard how she gave a beating to one of their own and wanted nothing further to do with her, giving her only sideways glances. One of them made an odd sort of gesture toward her, joining her thumb and forefinger together forming a crude circle, and then she scampered away.

At last her patience finally bore fruit.

There was Lord Stenstrom emerging from the inn, no doubt miserable in his hot Fleet coat. She watched as he crossed the square, approached the pharmacy, and entered.

Stenstrom ... All of this is for you ...

Inside, she had marked a bottle of tincture the pharmacist was to sell to Lord Stenstrom, one that was full of love potion laced with her pheromones. She wasn't going to take a chance. Lord Stenstrom thought he was purchasing the God Sperm tincture—instead he would be getting nothing but the love potion. Smiling, Lord Stenstrom left with his purchase and took his leave.

Whatever happened to the love potion after that, she did not know, for Lord Stenstrom never came calling for her, as the pharmacist promised he would. Something happened—somehow Lord Stenstrom didn't get the love potion, or it got mixed into the God Sperm tincture by mistake. How could this be? She'd labored for this opportunity. She stormed into the pharmacy and grilled the pharmacist for information. He told her the day Lord Stenstrom came to buy the tincture one of his nieces had tried to steal something from the store before he arrived, and, in catching her, they made a mess, spilling and knocking over bottles all over the place.

That must have been what happened—the bottles were fouled, and, therefore, who knows what Lord Stenstrom took.

Good Creation—these Bazz savages—if only she could kill them all! In frustration, she murdered him in a slow, humiliating session, making him suffer for hours, and then burned his pharmacy to the ground.

She then murdered her Atmospheric slave and departed Bazz, vowing that if she ever returned, it would be to face the devil himself.

✳　✳　✳　✳　✳

Two years later, Lord Stenstrom the Younger of Belmont was born, after a difficult pregnancy that was nearly the end of his mother.

Though the love potion had been a failure, the tincture he took had been a raging success—as shown by the end result. Finally, after eighty-plus years, the House of Belmont South-Tyrol had its heir.

And now Lady Vendra had her prime target—this brand new baby boy. Her revenge would take full flight against Lady Jubilee's son.

She decided to thoroughly terrify Lady Jubilee with several harassing attempts on his life. Using an array of hastily acquired and disposable slaves, she sent them out to the Belmont South-Tyrol grounds, and many times they never returned.

She did the obvious things, placing a deadly wasp into his nursery, attempting a few intentionally ham-fisted abductions, just to make Jubilee sweat. On a lark, she tried a ploy where she had her slaves place a steel animal trap from Bazz in his play area, which, apparently, failed miserably for nothing came of it.

4

—IMPRISONED—

Lady Vendra lost a bit of her mind as time went on. She became rather curious about this baby boy born to the House of Belmont. For reasons she couldn't understand, he dominated her thoughts.

She wanted to see him, to look him in the eye, though she wasn't sure why. Disguising herself, she went to Tyrol and waited, biding her time as always.

There was Lady Jubilee one day, pushing a stroller with two of her daughters. One of the daughters, a slightly chubby one, wanted something from a stand, and Lady Jubilee turned for a moment to get it for her.

Lady Vendra struck. In a flash, she had the boy and was off. Quickly she took him to the waterfront, thinking to drop him into the sea—after all, there were no innocent bystanders in revenge.

Right?

It would be perfect—perfect. Lady Jubilee could have no more children after his difficult birth, so she had heard. Not only would she be killing the boy and putting a knife into Jubilee's heart, she would be putting an end to the Belmont-South Tyrol line as well.

She had only to drop him in—her revenge was finally at hand. Now was the time.

This was the moment.

The decades of waiting ...

She looked at him.

That perfect little face, bright eyes, a tiny baby's smile.

How he looked like Lord Stenstrom ...

She forgot all about the last century of revenge. She forgot about Lady Jubilee, and Carina and the sordid entanglements of revenge. She forgot about her rage, and all the souls who had died at her hands. She forgot about the Third Tenet: Failure to Act. She knew that not doing what needed to be done at this perfect moment, after so much time and planning, could be the death of her.

For a fleeting moment, she sat by the water with the infant, just like a new mother would with her son, and she held him, humming slightly.

Just for a few minutes, she discovered what it was like to live the life of a simple mother, to feel the joy that went along with it.

What happened after that was a blur, a clouded rupture of movement. Something came at her and hit her full in the face.

Everything went black and she had no idea what was happening.

✳ ✳ ✳ ✳ ✳

There was a storm raging all around.

She heard voices around her, could feel eyes staring. Then it became clear.

The Sisters. They had her.

The vise around her was tormenting—unendurable. She fell back into her Carina training—pretend to submit in the face of an insurmountable enemy, feign weakness and show fear. Let them think you are beaten. Let them think they are in control.

"Please, please, stop! I die! What do you want?" she cried.

You attempted to kill the son of Belmont South-Tyrol and are in violation of your long-standing Wirguild. Thus, you are our prisoner and out of the League's eye. We have questions for you ...

"I'll answer anything—anything!"

You recently attempted to poison your enemy, Lady Jubilee of Belmont South-Tyrol. We care not why you wished her dead, that is your concern. We want to know what additive you used in the poisoning. We demand it.

Lady Jubilee?? Poison??

She hadn't tried to poison Lady Jubilee. There was the fiasco with the God Sperm tincture and the love potion on Bazz, but that was all.

Why were the Sisters so interested in that?

The vice tightened. She felt her life and her sanity ripping apart.

Simply tell us what you used, and all this can end. You shall be sent home, free and goodly. We shall even kill Lady Jubilee of Belmont South-Tyrol for you, if you wish. We shall take care of everything. Simply tell us what you used.

Kill Lady Jubilee? No … NO! This is between me and her!

She is mine! Mine!!

She babbled in torment. "I don't want her dead—I want her on her knees, wailing for death. I want her kneeling at the gravesite of her son!"

You are in a position to demand nothing! Tell us what we want to know!

Somewhere deep within, her resolve formed again, bubbled up, and built a wall around her. Despite her training, she was defiant. She would not be meek. "Lady Jubilee is mine! I will tell you nothing."

Tell us!!

And her torment began, for years, her hatred sustaining her through the ordeal.

✳ ✳ ✳ ✳ ✳

After an unknown length of time, her tormentors became unsure, their arrogance faltering

Has she revealed her secret?

—She has not.

Time is of the essence. We cannot hold her forever. She must be returned unmarked and whole.

—She will not reveal unto us her secret. We must know what she used.

The Ex-Commons has heard the arguments of her kin, and desire her release.

—Let them be damned!

We cannot go against the ruling of the Ex-Commons. We will extract her secret, and then release her, whole and unmarked!

And they came at her again, doling out pain, shouting threats. She, however, rode the torrent out. Let them prod and scratch. Let them wail.

She laughed.

✳ ✳ ✳ ✳ ✳

She clutched her cloak about her now frail body as she rode in the coach, her family all around her, concerned, supportive. The hills rolled by. It had been years since she'd seen these hills, but she knew every one of them. Soon, the Cone manor appeared in the distance.

She was home. Her health was shattered, and her body somewhat bent. Yet, she had won.

Pampered and caressed in riches, she recovered from her ordeal quickly in the familiar confines of her home.

The Sisters.

She hated the Sisters, for their cruel embrace, for stripping her bare, for hollowing her mind into a cesspool of vapor, and applying agony to her flesh.

She was now going to return them the favor. She was going to apply the brand to their flesh, as they had done to hers. There was room in her soul for all the things she hated—there was room aplenty.

She had learned much during her pained captivity. Her tormentors, aloof in their arrogance, allowed their thoughts to be heard.

A name kept popping up: the 'It Man'. The It Man had returned. And he was everything to them.

The It Man? What is that? Who is that?

Everybody, it seemed, had a hero, everybody had someone whom they looked up to, and for the Sisters, the It Man was that somebody.

It took her a while to piece it together, but, eventually, a picture formed. There was not one, but two It Men running around—one was mature and in service for the Sisterhood, the second was new, a work in progress—a happy surprise that almost slipped through their fingers.

She wasn't clear on who the second It Man was; his identity was a secret the Sisters kept well. The first It Man, however, she discovered fairly quickly—Terrance, the Mad Lord of Walther.

The Mad Lord of Walther? The man who destroyed her lair under Woodward? The man who nearly "got" her in Calvert years before? Coming from her social circles, she knew the Sisters publically disdained Lord Terrance of Walther, for his bravado, for his vigilance. They mocked and belittled his exploits.

But look, behind the scenes it was quite a different story. Terrance, Terrance, their beloved Terrance. How they secretly worshipped him, drew strength from him. Again, as with the Barb and with other things, the Sisters had a tendency to disdain a thing in public while embracing it in private.

Yes, of course, of course! Outwardly mocking him, yet, secretly controlling his actions, it was a classic ploy worthy of the Dames of Carina themselves. So, the Mad Lord is their beloved It Man, is he? It made perfect sense to her—if she could inflict great pain on the It Man, then she would inflict great pain on the Sisterhood, and, even better, she could have revenge for being bested by him in Calvert.

Yes, yes …

Therefore, the It Man, the Mad Lord of Walther, was doomed.

But, how to go about it? As she knew firsthand, the Mad Lord demonstrated great strength, speed, endurance and resistance to damage, and he easily defeated her even when she was at her fighting best in Calvert. Looking at her now, she was a wrecked, frail woman huddled up under a blanket in the warm Remnath climate, a distant shadow of what she once was.

Nevertheless, he was doomed.

5

—The Taking of Sedgwick of Kold—

She had indeed learned much as the Sisters' captive. She had discovered ways to spy on the Sisters, to hear their hidden ethereal conversations from far away; the League, as she learned, was rife with their infernal chatter. Safe in her Remnath home, she could sit out on the manor terrace with her blanket and a cup of tea and tune right in on them, hearing everything.

The covert spying sessions revealed much to her. She learned, among other things, that there were Sisters and there were Sisters. There were all sorts of little groups, splinter sects and sub-casts within the Sisterhood. There was a large sect that walked the streets and sat in the parlors of the Great Houses. There was the sect that extended their minds and grappled with the Black Hats. There were the sects that experimented with the Gifts. And there were the darker, hidden sects tasked with doing rather unsavory things—doling out punishment, secretly 'correcting' those needing correcting, and hoarding knowledge. Those shadow sects were never seen on the streets or in the Houses—the League would gasp in shock otherwise.

Near the vernal equinox, she listened to a solemn gathering of one of these hidden sects taking place somewhere far to the north, as they summoned someone to their presence whom she thought was the It Man.

Terrance of Walther did not appear.

Instead it was Lord Sedgwick of Kold, the notorious Pirate of Remnath, a scalawag and arch enemy of the Mad Lord of Walther. Was he in their service too? He had to be.

Yes, of course—how deceptively simple. The Sisters commanded Kold, making him go here and go there, and where he went, the Mad Lord would follow. It was through Kold that the Sisters commanded Walther, using their alleged public animosity toward each other as a cover.

Kold was always an enigma. He was a known criminal, yet he and his men had never killed anyone, only rarely resorting to 'roughing people up.' He and his band stole things, of course, but their thefts were never anything big—and the Mad Lord was always there to foil them and return the booty. And their battles were always a cavalcade of swashbuckling swordplay, fisticuffs, and daring do—very romantic, and, now that she understood the truth, were clearly staged. She fancied Kold and the Mad Lord were actually friends, simply fulfilling their roles for their masters: the Sisters.

Hmmmm … very interesting.

She knew that Lord Kold and his band of pirates made berth on the shores southwest of the city of Champion. She went there alone, attired in her usual, a simple gray dress with button-up boots and her hat. She didn't even bother to disguise herself.

The pirates were remarkably easy to find. They laughed and cajoled the frail woman as she was dragged into his presence. Lord Kold sat in his gaudy chair, a fat, round man with an unhealthy-looking beard. He was loud and threatening, but she knew it was mostly an act.

She went to the offensive. She insulted him, challenged his manhood and boasted that she, a frail woman, could service not only he, but all of his men as well, and be ready for more once it was over.

Kold and his men took the bait. He ravished her joyously, laughing and chiding, his men encouraging him on. He flopped her onto the table as his men feasted around them and demonstrated his prowess. He pricked himself over and over again on the poisoned barb hidden deep within her womb, and then passed her off to the next man down the table, and on and on as if she were a basket full of hot rolls being shared by all. She took control of them by the shores of the sea one by one, though the strain of bedding so many men and the splintery surface of the wooden table nearly killed her. Before the night was over, Lord Sedgwick of Kold, the garish man, the fop, was hopelessly poisoned and addicted to her scent. He and his lot now belonged wholly to Lady Vendra of Cone.

She then started slowly so as not to alert the Sisters, neither they nor the Lord of Kold having any idea she had her hooks in him. She joined him on his paltry raids and was amazed by some of the exotic devices he possessed. One especially intrigued her—a Xaphan pendant he called a 'Planar Bridge' that he used to rob the outlying Xaphan worlds, and with it she walked the Astral Plane, moving great distances in mere moments. She was pleased with it, and incorporated it into her plans.

Under her control, Kold and his men became actual villains, stealing, killing, and creating small bits of chaos.

She then set out to take the Mad Lord, her old enemy.

Oh, the Mad Lord—the Mad Lord! He was very difficult to snare. He was a known hedonist with an eye for great pulchritude and found the frail Lady Vendra not to his liking, and she could not trick him into bed and give him The Barb as easily as she had Lord Kold. None of her Carina-taught charms or disguises worked and she was wholly frustrated. She certainly couldn't challenge him directly with a physical confrontation, as she was no match for him …

Or wasn't she? She tormented Lord Sedgwick of Kold for information—the Mad Lord, he had to have a weakness. What was it? What was it?

Kold didn't know of any. She pushed him—find out! The Sisters will certainly know. Find out!

As she awaited news, it was time to turn her attention to Young Stenstrom of Belmont South-Tyrol again—and this time, there would be no weakness, no mercy.

Hearing that the Belmont children had a predilection to run away from home, she set several men to watch the roads near their manor in case Lord Stenstrom the Younger happened to come walking down one of them.

Again, her patience was rewarded, for one evening she received a report that the little boy was indeed walking up the road toward Tyrol, carrying a sack of possessions—apparently running away from home. Moving swiftly, using the Planar Bridge to travel quickly between Remnath and Tyrol, she waited for him in a small fox park along with a number of Kold's men—the effects of the bridge causing the area surrounding the park to fade into the Astral Plane for a time.

There he was, wandering into the park—he was growing so fast. As she stood to put a dagger into his heart, he backed away into a tree, terrified. There was no place for him to go.

He then did something unexpected. He ran to her, putting his tiny arms around her waist.

Clever boy.

She had another moment of weakness again as she briefly held him, but this time she cast it aside.

As she reared back to plunge in the knife, he was somehow whisked away, right through her grasp. Something black and veiled had appeared and taken him. Additionally, in retrospect, that was the first time she saw the Nargal—a creature she would one day become quite familiar with. It appeared as a small tornado of sand and grit, roaring into the park shortly after Lord Stenstrom vanished, causing her and her men to flee back into the Planar Bridge.

After the fox park incident, she ramped up her efforts to take and slay the boy. Using Lord Kold and his band of louts, she tried to abduct Lord Belmont from a family gathering in Rustam, hoping to cause a stir. The plot was foiled when the Mad Lord interceded, and quite a few henchmen were lost in the process.

* * * * *

The Mad Lord was proving to be a frustrating bore. She had to either get him out of the way or utterly enslave him and take him from the Sisters.

She plied Kold for information. She began to gather interesting tidbits from Kold as he ravished her bony body—about how the Sisters were obsessed with the second It Man. She'd heard of that man before while incarcerated, but could never glean his identity. If she could get to him *and* deal with the Mad Lord, the Sisters would be utterly devastated.

Finally, Kold had a breakthrough. He learned that the Mad Lord somehow received his power directly from the Sisters, that it came from a certain, far-reaching type of starlight. It was possible that, if she could lure the Mad Lord deep underground, he might be deprived of that power and she could take him.

She decided to entice the Mad Lord into battle. She resumed her guise as the Fiend of Calvert. She penned several sinister open letters in which she promised to continue terrorizing the Calvert wharfs if he didn't agree to meet her. She called him out in the letters, calling him 'coward' and 'fraud,' insults certain to bring him out in the open.

Sure enough, the Mad Lord came, and, in a carefully prepared venue, she lured him into a deep mine shaft. There, deep underground, the Mad Lord lost most, if not all, of his power, and Lady Vendra's henchmen were able to subdue him.

There, tied down, she got on top of him, took him into herself and barbed him over and over again.

The Mad Lord now belonged to her just as Sedgwick of Kold did.

The Mad Lord pursues the Fiend of Calvert

6

—The Mad Lord on his Knees—

Taking the Mad Lord paid instant dividends. As her slave, he told her what he knew about the mysterious second It Man. He said he knew who the second It Man was—that he saw him with his own eyes.

The second It Man whom the Sisters had discovered was none other than Lord Stenstrom the Younger of Belmont-South Tyrol, the little boy of Lady Jubilee whom she had repeatedly tried to kill.

Elder's Balls … What fate!

That explained much. Was that how the little nipper survived the kill-trap placed in his play pit—with his latent It Man abilities?

Could that also be why the Sisters were so keen on discovering what additive she had put into the God Sperm potion that Lord Stenstrom the Older bought on Bazz? They must be convinced whatever she had spiked the potion with helped artificially create the It Man and they wanted the secret, desperately.

So … young Lord Belmont was the Sister's It Man, was he? Oh, how things relate—how the circle closes—the Vendetta Circle that she heard of while on Bazz but didn't believe in. Maybe there was something to it after all.

She would make him submit before her, just like the Mad Lord had.

Something completely unexpected happened at that time. When she released the Mad Lord back into the light of day, he appeared to go utterly mad as the Sisters' power jostled about with the poisons she had introduced into his system—now truly living up to his name. He became a raving lunatic.

The Mad Lord went wandering across the face of Kana, babbling the Sisters' secrets, and babbling her secrets too.

Fearing her activities would be discovered, she set Lord Kold against him in open battle.

And it was truly terrible, a much more brutal battle then she would have anticipated. They fought in Rustam, doing a significant amount of damage to the city where, eventually, the Mad Lord prevailed. Torn and ragged, he continued his wandering and babbling.

She couldn't have him spouting her secrets, but there wasn't much she could do to him out in the starlight.

Fortunately, the Sisters took care of him for her. In a public display of outrage, they burned his holdings, stripped him bare, and bore him away, killing him behind their walls, silencing him once and for all.

She savored their thoughts after his killing—wailing, in grief, bemoaning their lost Mad Lord whom they secretly cherished and had to slay like a rabid pet.

It was perfect and, it was well worth the wait. Every tear the Sisters shed was a drop of gold. And the Sisters shed many tears for him, their grief was succulent.

In a panic, the Sisters began to rally toward the second It Man, Lord Stenstrom the Younger of Belmont South-Tyrol, though he was still only a child.

Now, she could fully turn her attention to him.

7

─The Nargal─

Over the next few years, she and Lady Jubilee played a puerile game of ruse and deception. Lady Jubilee was sending 'things' after her—veiled creatures, invisible to all but the most rational of mindsets, sniffing the air and seeking her out. Apparently there was something to Tyrol Sorcery after all. The first few were rather troubling, however, she quickly discovered their weaknesses and was able to divert them reliably by using her slaves, rubbed with her scent.

Attacks came and went; sometimes years went by with nothing. Vendra also kept Jubilee confused with reports of infirmity, near death, and other such rumors.

In the meantime, she learned that the Sisters, ever hiding behind layers of ruse and deception, were planning on controlling Lord Belmont's development from child to young man via external means. They had created some sort of creature they infrequently referred to as a 'Nargal.' They called it his 'Tutor' and 'Protector.' As he aged, another word entered their vocabulary: 'Lover.' The Sisters had painstakingly created this Nargal, this Tutor and Lover using rare elements gathered from far-reaching places. She also knew that this creature was kept in a pen in a Vith ruin near their mountainous stronghold of Westron.

She went to places of great learning in Ferenz and Arden, researching more about Nargals and what they were.

The texts she read were fanciful and unclear. A Nargal was some sort of elemental creature given partial life—a 'monster' out of a fairytale and that their summoning was illegal in League space. Again, as before, the Sisters freely went against their own establishment when it suited them to do so.

Seeing great potential to cause mayhem, she researched further, and she listened, ever the fly on the wall, to the Sisters' chatter. Some of the details became clear. The Sisters had created a Nargal of Sand, a useful servant of supposedly limited intellect, easy to program, easy to control. She realized that she had seen this Nargal with her own eyes, at a fox park, south of Tyrol, years before, when it was new and small. It had looked like a pint-sized tornado of sand.

Ah, but look here. She found old texts in Arden that discussed the perils of Nargals—that, should the proper precautions not be taken, and should certain forbidden ingredients be introduced, a Nargal of Sand could be infused with Elder-like feelings and 'think' it was alive.

Sand Nargals, easy to create, easy to control, were also confoundedly easy to taint. Such a tainted Nargal could become unpredictable. Such a tainted Nargal could easily turn on its masters.

More research, more reading. Not much to go on—the Sisters apparently kept a tight lid on such arcane learning. A trip back to Bazz, however, was illuminating.

She discovered on Bazz in a filthy library run by The Jones, a branch of the Hospitalers, what was needed to taint a Sand Nargal: something called Black Sand. There were five major components:

BLACK SAND

1: Zerterite: a certain type of mildly radioactive volcanic sand containing copious amounts of obsidian, feldspar, magnetite, and a touch of garnet.

2: Morningwell: a type of flowering plant native to Casiarchus, an obscure world located in the Great Xaphan Nebula.

3: Podantium: an alkaloid (that ingredient was fairly easy to obtain).

4: Magdalyte: a purple salt compound illegal in League space for its ability to simulate life in dead bodies (and addle the minds of the living at the same time).

5: Rumbob: a Shadow tech 'tar' that was highly emotive—that is, one could infuse it with one's feelings and desires—again, highly illegal.

Such a mixture of Black Sand would certainly wake the Sisters' sandy beast up a little.

Who knows what might happen then.

In her reading, she discovered that it was critical to be careful with the Black Sand components—once combined, the sand took on the aura of the person near it—it became *like* that person, it became infused with that person's feelings, thus adding that element to the Sand Nargal. She was going to create a batch of Black Sand and put a powerful hatred of Stenstrom, Lord of Belmont into the creature, and also a hatred of all he loved. Additionally, and best of all, she was going to add a blind obedience toward her into the sand, making the Nargal her slave instead of the Sisters' slave—perhaps she could use it as a tool or a foil. It might prove useful.

She went to her sisters on Carina and had little success gathering the required ingredients there. Vendra then went to her brother, Admiral Derlith, and mentioned what she needed. He replied that such ingredients were deemed contraband by the Sisterhood of Light and therefore illegal—particularly the Magdalyte, the Rumbob, and the sand itself.

She was unfazed. She pushed him, insulted him, and cajoled him; she even considered putting him, her own brother, to The Barb, but reconsidered. She, however, continued to pressure him until he gave in.

"All right, enough!" Derlith said, exasperated. Putting his career and his freedom on the line, Derlith procured a quantity of the five components through illegal, back channel means. They arrived shortly thereafter in five separate parcels delivered to anonymous lockers in the cities of Dee (the Rumbob), Conwell (the Magdalyte), Armenelos (the Morningwell and the Podantium), and Mystery (Zerterite)—it was important to keep the ingredients in the parcels separated, and it was important to deliver them discreetly to different cities, as the importation of many of these ingredients was an offense punishable by imprisonment, or—put together—execution. Also, great care had to be taken in the transportation of these ingredients, as once combined, the assimilation process would begin and there would be no turning back. The process would have to be started all over again should that happen—and that would be unacceptable given the difficulty of acquiring the components in the first place.

She required a mule to gather the items and deliver them to her personally in Dee, for she had a hideout there that she once used during her heady Slave-collection days. There, she would accept the parcels and kill the mule. She had a thought as she exited the Admiral's office—she saw his worthless secretary, that silly little man with the blonde hair, sitting at his desk researching the Fiend of Calvert. She wondered how many shades of white he would turn if he knew that *she,* standing by his desk listening to him go on and on about murders, was the murderer herself?

She was eager to find out.

She would be waiting for him in her dingy murder room in Dee, and when he came into the room, she would reveal herself as the murderer, the Fiend he was so afraid of, and watch him swoon in fear. She might offer him a sporting chance, provide him a weapon, or perhaps a head start to run. Though she was nothing of the fighter she once was, this puny little man would be no match for her. She looked forward to killing him.

✴ ✴ ✴ ✴ ✴

The gathering of the items was going well—the little man in his outrageous hat, hideous optical glasses, and buckle shoes, was following the precise instructions left to him rather well. She followed from afar, using the Astral Plane to shadow his movements. He started the last day of his life in the Grand Port of Armenelos, pushing his way through the crowds, gathering the two items hidden there in two separate lockers and enjoyed a small breakfast after he'd collected them. He then moved on via Fleet coach to Mystery where he secured the parcel of Black Sand itself from the station. She watched, making sure he correctly handled the parcels—should he become careless, should he even come close to mixing them together, then she would strike and kill him.

So far, his careful attention to detail was prolonging his life.

He then took the Fleet coach northeast to Conwell, the trip taking an hour or two. The collection of the components was going well, and she felt a little playful. She gave him tantalizing little glimpses of her, using her Planar Bridge to keep ahead of his coach. She allowed herself to appear tall, in gray, covered in her billowy cloak, her hands kept at mid-riff in a threatening manner. She laughed—she saw his bug-eyed, open-mouthed little face in the window as the coach passed by, the large brim of his hat pushed up against the glass, clearly startled by what he was seeing.

What must be going through his mind?

Arriving at Conwell, she saw him come out of the coach slowly, looking around to see if anybody was out there. He was tarrying about too much for her liking, so she gave him another peek to get him moving—his leggings and buckle shoes churning in flight when he saw her. He went to the station and secured the Magdalyte. Well done. One more to go, then his life would come to an end in her dreary room straight from a nightmare.

He boarded the coach again, and headed southeast to Dee, perhaps the nicest of the Calvert cities. He sat down to lunch by the seaside, eating alone, looking at the people passing by. She allowed him to have his lunch, but when he called for dessert, she had enough and gave him another glimpse of her to once again get him moving.

Again, he left his table and hurried on, hoping the crowds of people might offer him safety. He mounted the steps to Dee's small station to gather the last of the items, the Rumbob.

Now, she went to her room on the second floor of a crooked tenement to prepare and await his arrival. As she once did in Calvert, she undressed and sat back. When he opened the door, she would allow him to savor the horror of the moment seeing her nude body seated in a charnel room of tortured dead, then, using nothing but her two hands, crack every bone in his body. She imagined taking him by the hands and whirling about with him as if they were doing a grim waltz, with him dying a little bit more with every turn.

Should be any minute now.

Time passed. Something was wrong. The little man never arrived.

What had happened?

She dressed and went out looking for him. He was gone—she had lost his trail. For some reason, he hadn't followed the last of his instructions and diverted from the plan. Perhaps the seedy nature of the tenement had put him off. Perhaps he sensed danger.

Very perceptive. Surprising.

She figured that he would go to the Fleet and leave the bag full of parcels in the Admiral's office. Using the Astral Plane, she went as far as she could—Fleet Headquarters was sealed against Astral Plane incursions by the Sisters. She went the rest of the way in a fast coach she flagged down and hired. When she got to the Fleet, it was dark and mostly empty. Going into her brother's office, she found the bag there by his desk. All five parcels were present in their compartmented packaging, just as instructed. She had her components, and they appeared whole. Still, the little man was going to die. She went out after him, determined to wring his neck.

She quickly caught up to him—he must have just left the office. She followed him through the vast complex, and, when the time was right, struck, clouding his senses with pheromones. She seized him by the wrist and pulled him into a nearby bathroom where she could murder him in peace.

Unfortunately, the bathroom was not empty. There was some pathetic Marine girl sitting in there on the vanity drinking from a flask. She was temporarily taken aback; that Marine girl—she seemed oddly familiar, though she couldn't quite place her. She wore her hair with those annoying little dangling sickles of hair like they did on Bazz. She must be from Bazz, perhaps she'd seen her there.

While she was pondering that, the little man recovered, pulled away from her grip and fled from the bathroom. She thought to first kill the Bazz girl and take off after the mule, but she had a Marine communicator chattering somewhere in her coat. One cry for help and the complex would be put on alert. She might have to flee, there might be a spectacle. She decided not to chance it.

No matter, she would settle with Lord A-Ram later.

✶ ✶ ✶ ✶ ✶

Her brother, Admiral Derlith, was surprisingly angry and forceful the next day. He surmised from A-Ram's account of the day's events that she had planned to do something sinister with him.

She told the Admiral to mind his own business, if he knew what was good for him.

Surprising. He shot back that he suspected her of committing all sort of crimes, and that only the memory of her, as she was long ago, before the

Nether Day Ball and the convent on Carina 7, prevented him from going to the authorities. He also told her that he had a dossier stashed somewhere containing what he thought was evidence pertaining to her supposed activities. He said that, should he go missing or become addled, the dossier would circulate and she would become a wanted fugitive.

She was impressed—he had never shown her any backbone before. Among his many conditions for keeping quiet was her to promise to leave Lord A-Ram alone. He was an innocent man, and knew nothing.

Fine—what difference did he make?

Installing the "hated up" package into the Nargal was quite troubling—almost as difficult as gathering the components. The first few slaves she sent to Westron were never heard from again. The next were transformed into mindless idiots by some sort of trap the Sisters' had set up protecting the compound. She decided to try using Lord Kold's Planar Bridge, which was a risky gamble as the Sisters might be ready for such a thing. And, indeed, the Planar landscape surrounding Westron was studded with deadly traps. On one trip, she caught a glimpse of a vast sunken basin in the center of a fallen Vith temple with a view of majestic mountains rising high into the north. Spinning in the center of the basin was a towering geyser of yellowish sand rising up for several hundred feet, the grains spinning in a counter-clockwise direction. And that was all, the way was blocked.

So, there was the creature, there was the Nargal. She'd had her first fleeting glimpse of it. Now, to get to it.

She travelled north using conventional means as the Sisters' holdings were all blocked from Astral incursions using the Planar Bridge. She skulked about the hills and pine forests of mid Vithland, looking for a way to pierce the Sisters' defenses.

As it happened, the creature came to her.

She saw it as a massive tornado of wind and sand, just as it looked in fox park years before, only now it had gotten much bigger. It reached up high into the sky, nearly touching the clouds.

And then it changed, it collapsed down and disappeared into the pine trees. Moments later the small, unassuming form of a blonde-headed girl wandered out of the woods. She seated herself by the bank of the river, bathing her feet in the water. She absently toyed with the mud lining the bank with a stick.

Vendra approached, startling her.

"You frightened me," the Nargal said.

Vendra smiled. "I'm sorry, and no need to be frightened of me. I am merely a lady enjoying the afternoon."

"I've never seen anybody out here in the woods, except my mothers."

Vendra looked around, taking in the wooded scenery. "Then people in this area don't realize what they're missing. So lovely. What is your name?"

"Lilly."

"Ah, very pretty name."

The Nargal had been apparently scratching something into the mud with a stick.

"What are you doing?" Vendra asked.

The Nargal flushed up a bit. "Nothing."

Vendra leaned over. The Nargal had been writing the word 'Bel' in the mud with her stick.

"What is 'Bel'?" Vendra asked.

"'Bel is my love. I love Bel."

"Bel is a fortunate fellow. Does he live near here?"

"No, he lives far away. I'm only allowed to see him every so often, though I miss him so."

"Who prevents you from seeing him?"

"My mothers. They only allow me to see him infrequently."

Vendra was sly and full of cunning. "One should not be kept from one's love. Can you draw me a picture of him so that I may see what he looks like?"

The Nargal puzzled for a moment. It moved the stick about in an uncertain fashion. "I ... he's ... rather like ..." The Nargal put the stick down, flustered. "I can't draw."

"Can't draw?"

The Nargal was concerned. "Is that bad?"

"Proper ladies are expected to paint pictures of their men, it's the custom."

"And, if the lady can't paint?"

Vendra smiled. "Then, unfortunately, she stays alone. How sad."

The Nargal sat there, confused, in a growing panic. She processed this troubling information in her Nargal brain. Her blonde hair puffed up and she seemed to grow in size a bit as if she were about to transform into her whirling tornado form. "What can I do? What will Bel think of me?" Her voice had the edge of desperation in it. "Can you help me?"

Vendra reached into the folds of her dress and produced the package full of tainted sand. "Of course I can. Take this," she said. "It will help you. It will lead you to your love. With this, you can be with him whenever you want. With this, you can be whatever you want to be."

She looked at the package. "What is it?"

"Magic sand. Here, take it."

The Nargal thought about it, and then happily took the package full of 'magic sand' that she thought would lead her to her love. Sand hissed within the paper wrapping.

"This will help me learn to paint?" the Nargal asked hopefully.

"Most certainly," Vendra replied.

The Nargal smiled and thanked her. She walked away with the package tucked under her arm.

Vendra watched her depart, her eyes narrowing.

Magic sand that will lead one to one's love … If only such a thing existed.

Weeks passed, leading into months. Vendra was burning to know what the results of her tainting the Nargal were. Surely now, befouled with her black sand, it was filled with utter hatred for both Lord Stenstrom and the Sisters. She tried calling out to it, as she did for the men in her thrall, but it didn't respond.

Risking much, Vendra again ventured out to the wooded hills of Vithland, hoping to encounter the Nargal she now owned. She had to have information.

She reached the shallow river where she'd seen the creature before, and there it was, once again sitting by the water. Its hair seemed longer and even more golden than last time. It seemed to be carrying itself in a more mature, more regal fashion. The Nargal had out a small palette of watercolors, some cloth, and a selection of fine two and three-haired brushes. It was sitting by the stream painting into a tiny golden locket, very fine and meticulous work requiring a sharp eye and steady hand. With regularity, the Nargal stopped what it was doing, peered into the stream, beheld its own reflection, and set back to work in the locket.

"Hello again!" Vendra said, approaching.

The Nargal looked up and smiled. "I knew you were there."

"Ah, I pride myself on my stealthy passage. How is it you knew I was there?"

"I sensed you. It is good that you have returned. I was hoping to see you again."

"Oh?"

"I wanted to thank you. The Gift you gave me was truly wondrous."

Vendra was elated and cautious at the same time. If the Nargal now hated Lord Belmont, she showed no outward signs of it. "I'm glad it helped."

Confound it, what had come of the Black Sand??

You, Nargal, belong to me! Bow before your master!

Vendra glanced at her palette and brushes. "What are you doing?" she asked.

"I'm painting. I'm making a gift to present to my love."

"A self-portrait?"

"Yes."

"Ah, such a warm and heartfelt gift, may I see?"

"Of course." The Nargal put her brushes down and held up the locket. Inside was a tiny, partially completed portrait of herself, blonde-haired and blue-eyed, done dot by dot in watercolors. Even only partially finished, Vendra could see that the painting was exquisite and full of skill.

"And this is for your love? That 'Bel' fellow from afar?"

"Yes, it's for no other."

"And you still love this man?"

The Nargal closed its eyes. "Oh, yes, more than ever. I've worked so hard on this painting. I want it to be perfect for him."

Vendra was stumped. What happened to the tainted sand? Clearly it had had an effect. The Nargal now could paint with rare talent whereas before it had none, but what about the hatred and malice she poured into it? If anything, the Nargal was even now more enthralled with the Sisters' It Man than it had been.

Oh, this was a dismal failure.

The Nargal put her things away and stood. "You need to go back home, or wherever you're from, it won't be safe here in a few minutes and I bid you fair warning."

"It won't. Why not?"

"Because I'm going to go see Bel. He needs me."

"Have your mothers authorized your seeing Bel?"

The Nargal paused. "I don't really care what my mothers want. I'm going regardless. So please, I bid you safe passage and good afternoon."

Vendra's ears pricked up. *Ah, the taint is having an effect after all. Rebellion is forming within the Nargal. Independence as well.*

Good, very good. That was something she could work with, manipulate.

Vendra took her leave, but, instead of departing, she waited behind a tree. She wanted to watch what was going to transpire. After several minutes waiting, however, she wished she'd taken the advice and fled.

The Nargal transformed into a savage tornado, churning the earth and ripping through the trees, climbing into the sky, parting the clouds, terrifying to behold, deafening to hear. Vendra had to hang onto the tree for dear life in the tempest.

✳ ✳ ✳ ✳ ✳

The Sisters' thoughts in the next few weeks were telling.

—The creature is exhibiting unusual traits.

The creature was not in its enclosure yesterday ... it escaped.

—Was it found? Was it found?

Yes, in Esther

—We detect a taint in it—it has been poisoned.

How?

—No matter. Its task is nigh complete. When it is of no more use... kill it. Be done with it.

Oh, but this was priceless.

8

—INVITATION TO DINNER—

A year passed and nothing significant happened. The Sisters' thoughts gave away nothing too much out of the ordinary. The taint she had applied to the Nargal had not immediately taken great hold or manifested itself to any extent. She'd hoped it would rip him limb from limb, but so far it hadn't. Curious and needing information, she set out to test Lord Belmont directly, to see what he was made of. He was an It Man like the Mad Lord, so he must have similar power, which was daunting—however, he was young and inexperienced, and, possibly, unaware of his status. She thought to test him, to prod him, to see what sort of a man he was. If he was a weakling, she might just barb and take him right there and then.

She heard that he was newly attending school at the University of Bern—and for a young man whom she knew to have been isolated and sheltered his whole life by his bitch mother, a bustling environment like a university must certainly have him on edge. He might be confused and lonely ... and extra vulnerable.

Disguising herself as a charming student, she travelled to the school via Planar Bridge and couldn't find him about the grounds mingling with the other students—apparently he wasn't coming out much, which, she supposed was to be expected. She stationed a few of her remaining men about the campus, with orders to keep an eye out for him.

Eventually, they spied him, walking alone on the green in his Tyrol clothes. She Bridged in and quickly found him wandering amongst the buildings.

He looked so much like his father. He had grown into such a handsome young man ... again, as when he was a child, that creeping weakness came up. When face to face with him, she had a hard time doing what needed done.

She stammered, losing her cool, and invited him to share dinner with her. It was a lie, of course, and hastily made up, but, now that matters were at hand, she truly did want to simply sit with him and share a meal. Maybe she, over a hundred years his elder, could somehow inspire his heart—no barbs, no tricks. If she couldn't have Lord Stenstrom the Older, perhaps the Younger—the It Man—would do.

Perhaps that might be the ultimate revenge after all—to be welcomed at Belmont Manor as a houseguest, sharing the bed of the son of her hated enemy.

Lord Belmont, however, resisted and refused her invitation. Spurned again, she left his presence and thought of another plan. She decided to give it to him full bore. She stoked up her scent to maximum levels and went after him. She would take him by force, barb him by guile, and have him in turn.

But he was gone. Surely he couldn't have quit the area so soon? She looked around and couldn't find him. Just like his mother had done decades earlier at St. Gala's Veil, he had simply vanished into the shadows. She was determined to follow him and pounce while he was weak. She pulled a bottle full of Man detector from Carina out of her bag, rubbed it on a steel ball and placed it on the ground. The ball rolled into the nearby greenery.

He was there, he had to be, hiding somehow. Just like his mother had once faded into the shadows, so too could he. She reached into her bag and slipped on a pair of barbed knuckles. If he was there, she was going to physically overcome him, pull him away and take him.

The sirens went off; bad weather was wafting up. A funnel cloud formed over the school; people all around were scrambling for cover. She saw it in the sky.

It wasn't a funnel cloud—it was the Nargal, she could recognize it by its brownish color. It was huge, even bigger than the last time she'd seen it. What was it doing? What incredible timing. Or was it merely bad timing? It must be protecting him, watching over him.

Gods!!

Completely frustrated, she opened her bridge and went back to Jacarta, determining once and for all that coming into Belmont's presence personally was not a good idea. She couldn't control herself, and his pet Nargal was a deadly nuisance.

She had to regroup.

*   *   *   *   *

The Nargal gambit finally appeared to be paying off.

The Sisters' thoughts grew frantic two years later:

—It killed a Sister yesterday. It is out of control.

Enough, be done with it. Our It Man needs it to guide him no longer. He has gone where we wanted him to go. We have shown it to him—he now knows what it is. Its purpose is done.

—No, no, it has fled.

Where could it have gone?

—Find it! Kill it!

Where indeed … Where indeed …

10

—WRITING AN OVERDUE LETTER—

So, there she sat on her familiar terrace, looking out on her familiar hills.

What had ninety years of hate and revenge bought her?

Lady Jubilee was dead at last, though of natural causes. The Sisters' It Man was dead. And now the second It Man, Lord Stenstrom of Belmont, was at roam in a stripped-bare ship. She had persuaded Admiral Derlith to place several beacons aboard the ship so that she could hone in on it with her Planar Bridge and torment him with her men. When she discovered that the Admiral's adjutant had joined in with Lord Belmont, she sent a few of her slaves to leave him several calling cards, knowing Lord A-Ram's fear and preoccupation with the Fiend of Calvert.

Good fun, but the Sisters' appeared to have taken note and blocked the vessel from further incursions. Something killed her men and destroyed her beacons. Possibly the Sisters had done it; more probably, it was the Nargal, protecting her 'Bel' to the last. Small matter. Lord Belmont was soon to be humiliated and knocked off his chair, and possibly killed by her niece, whom Admiral Derlith had sent after him.

While her personal control was certainly questionable in Lord Belmont's presence, surely her niece, Lady Gwendolyn of Prentiss, an undeniably cold woman worthy of Carina itself, would not be so swayed. Vendra had made a minor project out of her, hoping to fill her with all the rage she had felt over the years.

The closed Vendetta Circle, the Ganaada on Bazz had said everybody's in it with her.

She sighed.

Ninety years of revenge and hatred. Lots of dust and an empty bed.

Empty soul.

Her sisters on Carina had taught her much: patience, skill and resolve.

The only thing they hadn't taught her was how to live with an empty life full of old bones and cold shadows.

What of the sorrow, my sisters, what of that? You promised to rid me of it, yet it remains. What am I to do?

Years ago, when she sat there by the sea holding the tiny Lord Stenstrom—the man she was even now scheming to humiliate, then kill—that was the only time in the past ninety years she'd been truly happy. How wondrous it had been to hold a child in her arms and be a mother if only for a few moments. Her sisters on Carina had taught her nothing of that.

Circles on a page. A landscape full of curses and voices from the past.

With Lady Jubilee passed away, the dark, murderous person she'd become on Carina was dying as well, becoming less and less with each passing day, joining Jubilee in the grave at long last. The Dames of Carina had taught her that Revenge, Scheming, Getting Even with those who wronged you is all that matters.

Look at me in your final moments, you bastard, and know who bested you!

What were paltry things like Hope and Love compared to the majestic finality of Revenge, the Dames would certainly argue.

What indeed?

She wondered as she looked upon herself in the mirror, no longer a dark, frightful presence, just a bent, mirthless form life had passed by.

Can this be me?

She'd watched life evolve at the Belmont Household despite her continued efforts to derail it. She'd watched the comings and goings, the little triumphs and the tearful tragedies all part of daily life. And there she was, still angry, still stuck in the past, alone on the ballroom floor at St. Gala's Veil. She'd watched Jubilee's son, the 'It Man' survive all the murder attempts and roadblocks she could hurl at him, overcome an overbearing mother, a tainted Nargal, and a stripped-dead ship, and keep trying, keep plowing ahead no matter what, giving chase to his dreams. She remembered his eyes as she raised the knife to kill him; so full of dreams. Perhaps there was much to be learned from that. Hope and Perseverance were things the Dames of Carina never put much stock in, and perhaps they were wrong.

Perhaps they were blind, as she had been blind.

Could it be that Revenge, despite all its fearful trappings, was nothing more than a fitful cry for attention from a desperate, empty person?

Look at me!!

She did something ninety years overdue, something she had wanted to do for a long time but hadn't the courage. She got out a piece of paper, not gray, but soft pink. The paper was old, from the long-ago Ballwig days before they, under her influence, became callous heartbreakers and petty vixens; this paper was from the days when they wrote smiling letters together in the hope of finding love. She steadied her hand and picked up a marker. The old curse was closing in on her. Anymore, whenever she tried to write, her hand did of its own will and drew an endless number of scrawled names inside an ugly circle. The names of faceless dead men and her name mixed in there as well, a murdered victim just like the rest. Damn Bazzers and their magic, they had gotten to her after all.

Paper after wasted paper came and went: scrawl, circles and names shouting out from the grave. She concentrated, forced her hand to obey. She wrote with all the strength she still possessed:

To my Dearest Stenstrom the Older, Lord of Belmont South-Tyrol. I have been seeking the words to write this letter for far too long ...

Ninety years of hatred and scheming, fading into nostalgia and regret. Revenge was fleeting, it was deceiving. What was strong? What endured: the tiny ember of love she'd managed to nurture and keep glowing all that time. As she wrote, she prayed for his son, for the man she'd tried to kill, prayed he might somehow endure just a bit more, complete his mission and get to Bazz. If he could do that, then perhaps there was absolution to be had for them both.

"Look at me, sir," she fantasized herself saying to him. "I have done these terrible things, and I beg you to forgive me."

She finished the letter, sealed it, and called for an attendant to send it on its way. It sat there on the silver plate ninety years in the writing, the long-awaited triumph of Hope and Love over Anger and Revenge.

PART 3
THE PILGRIMS OF MERIAN

1

—Nightmare—

Beep... beep... boop, boop, boop...

Captain Gwendolyn kept hearing that noise as she stood on the bridge. It was a vaguely familiar sound, and she was sure she knew it from some-where, but couldn't quite place it.

It was just out of reach. It was troubling, maddening. It was a sound she knew she should know. She tried to put it out of her mind.

Even on a tiny scouting ship, the bridge was a bustling nerve center of activity. The navigator sat there surrounded by holos and grids, the red and blue faces of the AM/PM wheels slowly rotating and readjusting as the helmsman, sitting nearby, occasionally corrected the ship's course.

On the other side of the bridge, the Com stood behind his panel, moni-toring all inbound and outbound communication traffic. The vast majority of the messages were automated, one of the ship's myriad of systems trying to talk to others and needing command approval to do so. It was a rather stodgy system, but it effectively kept the ship from being taken over by outside or hostile forces.

Through the windows, Gwendolyn could see the stars moving by in a tide of white, yellow and bluish dots of bigger or lesser size.

Their current mission had come down from the Admiralty: transport a visiting dignitary to Tantan on Brindval for an important summit meeting. She had to shake her head—scouting ships, always taking this person here and that person there, each one a priority. Basically, they were an overly large taxi.

The lift doors opened. Someone came through.

It was the dignitary. There he was wearing his usual long black coat and hat.

"Evening, sir," Gwendolyn said. "It is evening back home you know.

Rather late, actually."

Beep... beep... boop, boop, boop...

There's that noise again. Gwendolyn looked around.

"Captain," the dignitary said, "she is at it again. Your crew is beginning to panic. I think you need to take action."

She nodded. "Yes, you're right. I'm sorry you have been made a party to such a thing."

"It's all right. Please, shall we?"

Gwendolyn stood and straightened her coat. "Thank you. You needn't come. This is ship's business. You should return to your cabin and rest."

She excused herself and walked into the lift. The dignitary joined her. Nervously, she selected her floor.

Beep... beep... boop, boop, boop ...

"Pardon me," she said as the lift began moving, "do you hear those sounds?"

"What sounds?" the dignitary asked. "I hear many sounds. Can you be more specific?"

"Never mind."

Several moments later, the lift arrived at the proper deck. Captain Gwendolyn and the dignitary stepped out.

Beep... beep... boop, boop, boop...

She cursed to herself. "That noise is driving me crazy. I'm sorry, sir, I should be more mindful."

"Again, I hear nothing out of the ordinary."

They walked down the hall, passing the occasional crewman as they went. Gwendolyn looked up at the dignitary. He was so tall. "If I may, sir, you promised you'd tell me why you wear that mask. You haven't forgotten your promise, have you?"

The dignitary looked down, his gem-like blue eyes sparkled through the holes of his lace mask, the HRN at his collar glinting in cursive gold lettering. "No, I haven't. Please, let us attend to this sorry matter, then I'll keep my promise."

Gwendolyn walked at his side, struggling to keep up, the man had such long legs.

"Then what, then what are you going to do?" she asked.

He smiled. "Then we'll to your quarters, we'll have at a game of cards, and then who knows. That's what you want, isn't it?"

Gwendolyn, shy, fumbled with her FEDULA for a moment. "I …"

"Isn't it?"

Beep… beep… boop, boop, boop …

That noise was driving her mad. "Yes … yes …"

They rounded a shallow bend and arrived at a door.

"Here we are," the dignitary said.

Gwendolyn stood there, her thoughts still wrapped around what was to come like a giddy school girl awaiting a promised treat.

The dignitary knocked on the door. "Morgan …" he said. "Morgan, darling, we're here …"

There was a troubled bumping about from behind the door.

"Go away!" came a panicked reply. *"All of you, go away! Leave me alone! I'll kill anybody who comes too close! I've already killed all the ones you set against me. I can! I'm a Hospitaler, a trained killer! I can fight! I will fight again if I must!"*

The dignitary laughed. "Come now, Morgan, you don't wish to create a scene, do you? You're just making this harder than it must. It needn't be so …"

The dignitary opened the door. It was dark on the other side. He motioned for Gwendolyn to go in. "Go on, Captain, through there."

She hesitated. He approached, his hands finding places decency demanded they did not.

"Remember what awaits," he whispered into her ear.

Gwendolyn felt her body react. She drew her MiMs from its small holster. "All right …" She stepped through the doorway. "All right …" she repeated.

On the other side of the door was a nightmare version of the bridge: dark, in disarray, huddled bodies pushed in the corners, pools of drying blood on the floor, the place tinged with howls and gibbering shrieks.

Through the windows a skittering, wavy sort of light funneled in, illuminating the place up in a kaleidoscope of shimmering lighter and darker spots. It was like being at the bottom of a deep aquarium, standing by the glass, watching the fish swim—just like the ones in Fazo that her uncle used to take her to see.

"Morgan?" she said.

Somebody rustled in the distance. *"I said keep away!"* The voice she heard was ragged and flecked with panic.

Gwendolyn stepped further into the bridge. "Morgan, I'm not going to hurt you." Feeling her MiMs in her palm, she tightened her grip on the handle.

I'm just going to shoot you in the head, and then I can have him ...

Beep... beep... boop, boop, boop...

That noise—it was deafening.

Just then, Gwendolyn saw Morgan Jeterix, Lady of Thompson. She was standing there near the wall holding her Jet staff out.

"Come to kill me, Captain? Is that what they sent you here to do?"

"Nobody sent me here to do anything, Morgan. I just want to have a talk. Your behavior is frightening my crew." Her knuckles went white as she squeezed the MiMs in her palm.

I'm just going to aim at your head, pull the trigger, and that's that. Then you can have peace, and I ...

Such thoughts she indulged in.

Morgan shifted positions and set her Jet Staff to the ready. Gwendolyn would need to be careful—Hospitalers were nothing to trifle with.

"I've been watching you, Captain, wandering aimlessly around the bridge, lost in your little dream, acting it out in mid-air, talking to nobody. They've got you! It's just an illusion!"

Gwendolyn stood in front of her. She readied to raise her MiMs and shoot. She wanted to look her in the eye when she pulled the trigger. If Morgan managed to survive the MiMs shot, then she'd draw her FEDULA and they'd fight to the death. Gwendolyn was as deadly with it as Morgan was with her Jet Staff.

Morgan's image vanished. Gwendolyn spun around, trying to see in the dark. "Where are you, Morgan?"

"Illusions are a funny thing, aren't they, Captain. I can Cloak and Paint illusions, I inherited these skills from my grandmother ... she was a Vith, had

blue hair and everything. And I can Cloak too, but nothing like what They can do."

Gwendolyn stood her ground and looked about. "I'm trying to help you."

Morgan's voice came again. *"My grandmother... do you know what happened to her? Have I ever told you? My grandfather was killed in a battle with the Xaphans. Halas had no business going to the stars, she said, and look what happened to him. Dead. She ... couldn't bear the thought of going on without him. She recreated him, in illusion, and she spent the rest of her life interacting with a person that only she could see. She grew gaunt and famished, she stopped eating, washing, and she completely withdrew into her own mind."*

Gwendolyn looked down at her gun. "What's the point of this, Morgan?"

"Illusions, Gwendolyn! My mother used to make me go up and feed her—she roamed around on the fourth floor of our manor. It was so hard, to get her to sit still, to open her mouth and eat. Usually she said nothing—just stared off into space. One time, though, one time I got her talking and she sounded almost like a sane person. She said that everything, beyond the limits of her head, was a nightmare. The real world was a place of uncertainty, and sadness, and dead husbands and lost memories. She said she'd rather stay where she was and be happy. And that was that ... I never heard her speak again. She just continued on, soiled and starving, walking hand-in-hand with the illusion of my grandfather until she died in the fire that consumed our manor."

The door to the bridge opened, admitting a shaft of gold light from beyond. He was standing in the doorway.

"We're waiting for you, Captain," he said. "She's over there." He pointed.

Something appeared in the dark. There was Morgan Jeterix. She was lying supine on the floor at the base of the Com panel, her expanded Jet Staff resting at her side. She was reaching up, trying to get at the Com panel's control board.

Around her, six crewman lay dead, twisted up, staved to death. A variety of improvised weapons were scattered about.

"Captain Gwendolyn," she said. *"So, here I am. I'm dying ... they want me dead because I can see. I can see everything. I'm hurt, been attacked. They set the crew against me. I had to kill them., I didn't want to but I had to. One of them injured me before they died—it wasn't their fault. They didn't know what they were doing. Can't reach my wounds, in my back. I'm bleeding out ... can't stop it. Going into shock. Gwendolyn, help me ... please! Fight it! See what there is to see. The windows! Look to the windows and see!"*

Gwendolyn glanced at the windows. Just that same watery darkness.

Wait.

Something big moved past the windows and then was gone.

"Morgan," Gwendolyn said, "I'm going to help you."

"You are? What are you going to do with that gun you're holding?"

"I'm going to help you, Morgan," she said, cocking the MiMs. "And then he and I ..."

Morgan struggled a little and tried to pick up her jet staff. *"Him, you mean Lord Belmont? That's not him, Gwendolyn ... and you know it."*

Beep... beep... boop, boop, boop...

Morgan weakly pointed at the Com. *"Hear that? That's him, Gwendo-lyn! He's out there, looking for us. He's trying to help us. For Creation's sake, answer the Com, and save us all!"*

She slumped to the floor.

Gwendolyn smiled and shook her head. "No, Morgan. He's right out-side, and he's promised me things. I'm going to do this, quick and painless, and then you'll have peace, and I'll have peace. I've wanted this for a long time."

"You've ... only just become acquainted with him."

Again, Gwendolyn shook her head. "No... no, I used to hear my aunt talking about him all the time in the parlor with my mother when I was a girl. I would hide and they didn't know I was nearby listening. My aunt would talk about Lord Belmont, and how she hated him and his mother. And my mother, she would speak up and say how my aunt was trapped in a closed circle that could have no good end. My aunt didn't care—she was caught up ... Now, he's just outside the door, waiting for me. I want to go to him, Morgan."

"But, you first have to kill me, is that right?"

"Yes."

"There is nothing but an illusion on the other side of that door. You and I—we're both ladies of Great Houses. We could have been such friends—we should have been. We wasted the opportunity that we had. We're both too similar in many regards, and we are both at fault. I understand how you feel...and They understand that too. They've given you what they think is the perfect illusion. The man standing outside that door is everything you want him to be. He'll say everything you want him to say, do everything you want him to do ..."

BEEP... BEEP... BOOP, BOOP, BOOP...

So loud! Gwendolyn bent over and covered her ears.

"That is him, Gwendolyn, the real thing, the man you say you want. I'm too weak to fight you, I haven't much time left. You need to make a choice. Kill me and go to the illusion and have everything you want for as long as it lasts, or ..."

BEEP... BEEP... BOOP, BOOP, BOOP...

"... answer the Com and face the uncertainty of the real, imperfect person;, venture out into the nightmare that is the real world. On the other end of that Com is the man that you really want, whose heart you could truly stir, whose love you could genuinely earn ..."

Gwendolyn stood over Morgan Jeterix, Lady of Thompson, blood slowly throbbing out of a deep wound in her back where she couldn't reach. Her tightly braided blonde hair was scattered about her head as if pre-arranged. Her Hospitaler helmet was missing. Absentmindedly, Gwendolyn looked around for it.

Morgan swallowed. *"So, what's it going to be, Gwen?"* She closed her eyes and didn't say anything else.

Gwendolyn thought about Lord Belmont standing on the other side of the door in his black coat.

Wait, was his coat black, or green? She didn't know. She thought it was black, but maybe it's supposed to be green—HRN coats were always green in her courses at the Fleet.

Was Morgan right? Was the man standing out there just an illusion provided to her by Them, the things moving around in the dark?

BEEP... BEEP... BOOP, BOOP, BOOP ...

Was she to become a lost soul, like Morgan's grandmother?

She safed the hammer, holstered her MiMs, and went to the Com panel, stepping around Morgan to do so.

"Gwen ...what are you doing?" came a voice.

She pressed a few buttons on the Com. "I'm saying hello."

A form stood there by the door. *"But, I've promised you ..."*

She looked at him. "I know you have. And I really wish you would."

The Com snapped open. "Gwen? Gwen, is that you?" came a worried male voice behind a load of static.

"Bel?"

"Yes, it's me. We've been worried sick about you and your crew. What's your status?"

"I don't … I don't know … My Hospitaler is in bad shape. I think she's dying."

"Do you have any knowledge in the medical arts?"

"No…"

A spry female voice came on. "What's wrong with your Hospitaler?"

Gwendolyn squinted in the dark. "I think she's been stabbed in the back. She's … bleeding, in shock I think."

"Oh, that's easy. Tell us what you've got, and we'll talk you through patching her up. Do you have any medical instruments?"

She looked around. "Morgan … she has all her tools in her pockets I think."

"Fine, lovely, we'll use those."

By the door of the nightmare bridge, she could see the shape of Lord Belmont standing there.

"Bel, are you out there?"

"I'm right here, Gwen ..."

"I'm right here, Gwen. Taara and I are going to talk you through patching up your Hospitaler, and then we're going to get you out of there."

She smiled a little. Once and for all, she chose the voice on the Com over the image in the black coat. "Don't forget, Bel, you promised …"

There was a pause. "Oh, oh yes … I certainly did promise. You're absolutely right," he said in a quizzical voice. "But first, you've got to help us get your Hospitaler on her feet. Agreed?"

"Ok, what do I do?"

*　*　*　*　*

Sometime later, Gwendolyn finished sealing the large wound on Morgan's back. She had a number of Morgan's instruments scattered out in front of her. Her hands were red with blood.

Several times during the procedure, she saw things: her hands weren't where they were supposed to be, and she thought she had one of Morgan's knives when she was really carrying nothing at all. One time she saw Morgan as a corpse, withered and dry. Another time, she saw Morgan as a terrifying green monster that could not be killed.

She concentrated on Stenstrom's voice over the Com, clinging to it like a drowning person holding onto a piece of wood. She made them repeat their instructions over and over, and they patiently did so. In a sea of illusions, she treaded water, just barely, at the surface.

"That should do it," Taara said over the Com. "Great job, Captain. How is she?"

Gwendolyn knelt down. She could hear Morgan breathing. She felt her neck. There was a steady pulse. "Ok. I think she's ok."

Stenstrom spoke. "Smart work, Gwen. Now, can you give us your position?"

She looked around at the darkened bridge. "I … I don't know where we are …"

"It's all right, Gwen. Find a safe spot, and stay there, try not to move around too much. These creatures are supposed to be able to make you hear and see anything they want. If you stay stationary they'll have a harder time of it. Meanwhile, we're searching for you. You can't be far. We're going to get you out of there."

He paused a moment. "We're going to lose signal in a moment here. Sit tight and try not to move around too much, promise?"

"All right …"

The com went to static. Gwendolyn straightened her coat and sat down next to Morgan, who was out cold.

As the darkness closed in laced with hidden bumps and cries, she took Morgan's limp hand and held it. "Sorry I was going to shoot you."

Without the Paymaster's comforting voice, she was led away, falling off a cliff of sanity and feeling herself plummet.

She fell and fell ...

2

—The Merian's Road—

The Merians assembled in their simple hall and shared a meager breakfast of bread and savory sauce. Lady Alesta sat on one of the benches, quietly eating, her thick black hair held up with her combs.

A man stood in his robes and addressed the group. "Brothers, sisters … friends, again, souls have gone astray into the mouth of Edam. Again, we hear the Star's call, and again, we shall not fear. We shall walk our Road and perform the duty for which we have been commanded. I look among you, see your pure faces, and am proud to call myself a Merian. Who, besides we, is brave enough to walk our road? Eat well, friends, for this meal, as always, may be our last. Trust in our Star to deliver us from evil."

Alesta finished her breakfast and was led out with the others onto the green. It was a chilly morning and she held her green robe to her. Her shoeless feet were freezing. She looked around, the huddle of modest buildings, the small sparse line of trees, and the outlying cluster of fields where they grew their food. After that, there was nothing—bare, lifeless rock.

The Star gave them this little place, on a tiny ball of wayward rock that had no business supporting life. Here is where the Star needed them. Here, it maintained them, for nearby was Edam, the world of terror, the world of evil they were tasked to keep watch over. She looked up and it filled the sky, a gray, oblong world; outwardly, a peaceful-looking place. Here, they watched the skies, waiting for the lost souls to arrive—which happened with remarkable frequency.

These simple, defenseless people stood as sentinels at the gates of Hell hoping to lead the unwary away to safer pastures. That was their mission.

In the center of the green ahead was a large, flat-bottomed boat, pointed at both ends, made of stout timbers and bearing a Merian sail. The boat was tarred black for floatation, and generously decorated with red and green symbols. The boat sat solidly on the green—an odd sight as there was no appreciable water anywhere near. Stairs were placed at the boat's center on either side. Alesta really didn't like the boat, its tarred surface always got her clothes and feet dirty.

Noisily, the Merians clambered up the steps and into the boat's large, open deck. Lady Alesta shivered as she awaited her turn to board.

Finally, a man took her hand and helped her aboard. She found a spot on one of the benches toward the rear of the boat and sat. She reveled in the warmth as others piled in tightly in next to her. The larger men all sat toward the rails and unshipped the long oars that were positioned there, lowering the decorated paddles down to rest on the frosty grass.

As always, the boat appeared just big enough to accommodate the people who were piling into it. It was always just big enough, no matter how many or how few people climbed aboard. Such were the Merians, awash in poverty and simple things that weren't so simple. The boat that got bigger and smaller as needed was the Star's boat. And that wasn't all. There was the simple belt at her waist made of red and green shells, a modest, homemade item. Yet, that simple belt shielded her from evil sight; time and time again it worked. All she had to do was have faith in the Star, and she would be protected. And there were the thin beaded necklaces she and her people wore to allow them to see through the nightmare creature's illusions. Again, the key was faith.

The Tools of the Merians, which they took to battle, were: simple, homemade and quite effective. The only tradeoff—they had to be primitive—no modern contrivances, no power. In the presence of power, most of their Tools failed, and so, to accomplish their mission, they allowed themselves to exist in apparent squalor.

The boat on the green was mostly filled, Lady Alesta waited. There was an eerie quiet as everybody settled in.

One of the brothers mounted the platform at the back of the boat and took the tiller.

"The Road comes. Be ready!"

She looked around, the faces of some sitting nearby were lowered, hung to toward the floor boards of the boat, their mouths moving in silent prayer, and others were blankly looking up, resigned to what was to come—they acknowledged her with a slow nod.

She contemplated her fate as the familiar wall of fog drifted in and formed around the boat. Here she was, a Lady of Dare of the 10th Order, wearing homemade clothing and homemade items of mystical properties, shoeless in the freezing cold, once again plunging into the heart of darkness, ready to give her life for those who were often hardly grateful.

Still, this was her calling, to face the denizens of Hell unarmed with her adopted brothers and sisters. She would change nothing. The Star's words to her were a comfort and re-affirmation: *Save all those who fall astray.*

All around the boat was a tunnel of fog and an unearthly stillness. Ahead was the yellow beacon—the Star, the same one that demanded much of them. The Star that demanded that they have nothing, and allow themselves to be laughed at and be scorned. It was the same Star that also demanded that they offer their lives time after time before a merciless enemy.

"Ready ..." the brother at the tiller said. The men at the oars readied and braced themselves.

CRACK!!

And then came Edam, the raging sea and the gray sky over a relentless pelting rain. The boat plummeted, was rocked in the sudden surf and was battered at its sides. Alesta held on as the men fought the waves.

"Brothers, we must row!" yelled the man at the tiller.

Their longboat was suddenly in the middle of a storm-tossed sea, the prow rising and falling in the steep waves. Lightning stroked overhead. Rain and sea-spray soaked them.

Alesta closed her eyes and huddled up against the driving rain.

Up and down, the prow of the boat rose and fell, Alesta's stomach being jammed up into her throat as the boat went to near vertical in the waves.

"Hay-Two, row!" the man grappling with the tiller cried, trying to synch the rowing. "Hay-Two, row!"

This storm on the water was worse than normal, more savage, more pounding. She glanced out at the angry sea and saw a frighteningly tall wave quickly coming in to her right.

The brother at the tiller saw it too, and he pulled with all his might to turn the prow into the killer wave.

They would be swamped!

The boat rode up the side of the wave, nearly going past vertical as they crested the top.

After the passing of the mammoth wave, the Merian's boat found calmer waters, and they picked up speed as the men's rowing became more effective.

"Hay-Two, row!" the man at the tiller continued to count.

There was a loud whine overhead.

Alesta looked up.

A gangly vessel appeared through the belching clouds and soared away to the north, making a noisy fuss as it went. Lady Alesta had seen that ugly vessel many times, flying over the water, scanning with searchlights and other means. It flew low enough that she could read the name plate on the ship's blackened nose, though she knew it by heart: *Heade-on-the-Hearth.*

Lights rained down, panning over the rolling water as it passed overhead.

The lights caught the Merian's boat square, lighting it up for a good second or more in white light.

The ship paid them no mind and continued north. Alesta knew they were cradled in the Star's grace. She knew the vessel overhead could not see them. The Star, though hard and demanding, did not leave them completely defenseless. As the Star could not be seen by most, nor could they in their primitive boat.

They were invisible, all they had to have was faith.

The vessel flew ahead several more miles and became interested in something in the water. It hovered and shined its sundry beams of light down.

Something stuck up out of the water.

Suddenly, the tillerman! "A-lo!" he cried, and wrenched the prow to the west, the stable boat coming close to tipping as a result of the violent maneuver.

As the boat bore west, Alesta caught a glimpse of something breaking the water for a moment, something long and black, something swimming with a large heaviness, making a bulging wake as it passed.

When the tillerman thought it safe, he steered the ship again in the direction of the distant mass sticking up out of the water.

Alesta looked at it—a collection of large metal tubes arranged around a central disk, once painted white, was now a patchy, scorched black, lit up in the round circles of the *Heade's* spotlights.

The drowning vessel had a name: *Demophalon John.*

"Make ready!" he cried.

The *Heade* quit its lights after a minute or two and veered away to the north where it disappeared over the horizon.

With every oar-stroke, the Merians in their tiny boat got closer to the lost souls their Star had sent them to save.

3

—Lost in the Briars—

"That was bang up work with Gwendolyn," Stenstrom said as Taara, her sleeves rolled up, blushed. She enjoyed receiving compliments.

"It's nice being able to do this without having to worry about getting attacked by a bunch of demons," she replied. "Now I can really do work."

The *Seeker's* bridge was literally knee-deep in little green squares that once made up the body of Innocent Drury, some piled up in neat stacks, other scattered about.

After a good bit of tinkering, Taara had figured them out enough to be able to string them together into a long chain ending in the antennae they'd mounted atop the Missive's panel.

"These are all individual robots, each self- contained and fully functional—sort of like cells in your body. The only thing is they don't appear to have a brain, so, without a central consciousness to control them, they go limp, though there's nothing wrong with them individually, per se," she said.

They had mounted several antennae from Innocent's innards to the Missive's station and, behind it, strung together over a hundred green squares to both power and interpret information picked up by the antennae. The last piece she added was Innocent's head screen.

The screen didn't display any images at first, just sounds and disembodied voices that were rather terrifying to listen to over rigged up speakers:

"They's feedin' aplenty from that ghost ship ... "

"As soon as they's dead, we'll put the ship in the hopper. We's gettin' low a metal."

"We needs the Seeker, they're gettin' impatient to go home, they is. They're startin' to make noise about takin' the Heade unless we can offer up something suitable."

"I's ready to rejoin you, and I've a score to settle ... That man in the

coat is mine ..."

"Do yer' job and tends to the House. You can have's yer' revenge later. They's not goin' nowhere ..."

"I wants his body trussed up on the front of the ship!"

A-Ram swallowed hard. "I take it our friends are out there afresh."

Stenstrom agreed. "Seems to be. Taara, the Druries appear to be a persistent and unique foe, however, I dispute the fact that they are eternal. Yet, they do appear to be able to re-manufacture themselves with great efficiency."

"They've obviously got a plant here somewhere with new robotic bodies standing by ready to go. All they have to do is download their current memories and the new ones won't miss a beat."

"And," A-Ram added, "I'll wager they need a steady supply of shipping to provide them with the raw materials to continue producing these flesh replicas."

Stenstrom stood. "Well then, first thing's first. We locate and save Captain Gwendolyn, then we shut these cretins down, cold."

Working hard, Taara eventually refined the jury-rigged setup to the point that they were able to lock onto the weak signal of the *Demophalon John* and contact a ragged-sounding Captain Gwendolyn.

And then, they helped save the life of Gwendolyn's Hospitaler, Morgan-Jeterix.

As they talked Gwendolyn through the procedure, Taara took several of the other antennae pulled from Innocent Drury's body and slowly panned them around, trying to get a fix on their position.

As Stenstrom spoke to her, Gwendolyn seemed to fade into madness. She gave strange orders, responding to people who weren't there. She reverted in time, speaking like a child.

Taara cut the sound. "She's losing it, Bel. The Cronyns must be hitting her hard."

"What about her position?"

"I don't have it."

"We need them out of there, Taara."

"I'm trying!"

As Taara moved the antennae around, a picture formed on Innocent's head screen. In it, Stenstrom could see the battered interior of the *Demophalon John,* patched into the bridge's Tele-corder. Their bridge was smashed, and debris was everywhere. There, sitting next to the Com, was Gwendolyn, in a ball, holding the hand of a fallen Hospitaler. Must be Morgan-Jeterix.

"That's them! See if you can get a readout on that position. Gwen! Gwen, can you hear me?"

She slowly looked up. "Bel?"

Stenstrom could see the flickering image of Gwendolyn on the screen, rolling, grainy. Her face resembled the mirage of her from the Lantern: face sunken, eyes darting.

"Gwen, I can see you on my screen. I think we're getting close."

She looked around, wide-eyed. "You can? I can't … I can't see you?" She smiled. "Oh, there you are …"

"Just relax and try not to move too much. Tell me what your status is, Gwen."

She strained to concentrate. Stenstrom could hear the occasional wailing and guttural cries of people going mad on her ship. The sounds reminded him of the howling carnival sounds the *Seeker* was making not long ago, only this was worse. Much worse.

"I think … I think we're submerged—the instrumentation is unreliable, but I'm pretty sure. I look through the windows, and I see water, bits of debris and a little light high above. I don't know how deep we are. We … seem to be at an acute, nose down angle … but our shipboard gravity is still working, for now …"

She clutched at her forehead. "Something's out there. I see them … moving past the windows." She mumbled, lips trembling: "My crew, my crew …"

"Gwen, your duty to your crew is to stay strong and be a leader. Remember, just a few days ago you were wanting to beat my brains in? Remember that?"

She gave a short laugh and ran her hands through her hair. "Seems like a long time ago."

"Sure does. You need to be that strong lady again. You need to stand tall. Do it for your crew."

Gwendolyn looked as if she were on the verge of tears or delirium. She seemed to be fading away.

"Talk to her, Bel," Taara warned.

"Gwen, how's your Hospitaler?"

She looked around, her eyes blank. "No … no, I don't want any more …"

"Gwen," Stenstrom repeated.

"I can hear you, Bel … Is that you over there?"

"Gwen, how is your Hospitaler?"

Gwendolyn looked down. "All right. I think she's all right."

"What's her name again?"

"M-Morgan-Jeterix, Lady of Thompson."

"Jeterix? What's that—part of her first name or something?"

"I don't know, I've … never asked her."

"Well, when she wakes up, be sure to …"

There was a clanking in the background. Gwendolyn's eyes grew large with fright. "What was that?" she said, her gaze lost in delirium. "I heard a noise."

"I heard it too, Gwen. It was just the ship."

Gwendolyn was frantic. "No—no it wasn't. There's somebody outside, trying to get in. It's them! They're coming for us!"

"Gwen, don't panic!"

She tried to stand. She drew her FEDULA. "Stay back! Stay back, I'm warning you!"

"Gwen!"

Something passed in front of the Com—something indistinct. Gwen gave a cry and swung her weapon wildly.

Weakly she was taken down, out of sight.

"Taara, what's going on? Do you have them?"

She was working the antennae. "Wait, one more moment!"

A-Ram spoke up from behind the helm. "I'm reading a lock, Bel!"

As Stenstrom stared into the screen, he thought he saw a pair of blue eyes look up at him for a moment, and then was gone.

The screen went dead.

"I got them, Bel. I have a lock on their position!" Taara cried.

"Where?"

"7:47AM mark 6:58PM."

Stenstrom turned. "A-Ram, make sail, 7:47AM mark 6:58PM, best possible speed! Let's get the *Westminster* fired up and ready to burn!" He thought about it for a moment. "Good Creation, I have no idea what we're going to face or how we're going to fight when we get there—it's just the three of us and this wounded, toothless bird. But, we're getting them out one way or another. You two, A-Ram and Taara—I've got one hell of a crew around me."

A-Ram held out his hand. "I'm with you, Bel. I've dreamed of this my whole life. To stand at your side in this great Warbird, whatever the outcome, I'm a happy man."

Stenstrom took it. Taara's small hand joined theirs. "Don't forget me. Whatever awaits, let 'em be damned! After this is over, they'll know where I came from, that I wasn't such a little freak after all!"

4

—The Road Forsaken—

Gwendolyn could barely understand what was happening. In her clouded mind, she saw grappling hands reaching for her throat. She tried fighting back with her family FEDULA, but it didn't do any good. She fell back, waiting for it all to end.

Sometime later, she felt soft hands pulling her up. She felt herself walking, an arm around her shoulder.

Boneless, she moved, meekly stumbling toward whatever awaited. She felt herself stepping out into space, the maudlin dark of the ship replaced by sudden gray light. Distantly, she heard her boots thumping unsteadily on hollow wood.

A few moments later, she felt herself being seated on a hard, flat bench. She noticed, with eyes heavy-lidded with delirium, that a beaded red and green necklace had been placed around her neck.

Slowly, things came into focus. She concentrated on the necklace, on the small, polished beads—the red ones appeared to be tumbled stones of some kind while the green seemed to be dyed wood, she could see the grain of the wood through the dye. Gwendolyn looked up.

Standing over her was a small, smiling face, like that of a porcelain doll. A tiny lady looked down on her. She was wearing loose robes, a larger green and gold one over a white one that went down to her knees, tied together at her waist with a green and red belt. She appeared to have thick, dark brown or black hair that was pulled back out of her face, long tendrils of hair hung down to her shoulders. Around her neck were a number of necklaces similar to the one around her own.

She had remarkable blue eyes and rosy cheeks. Behind her smiling face was a turbid gray sky overcast with thick clouds.

"Who are you?" Gwendolyn asked, shivering.

"A friend," she replied. "My name is Lady Alesta, and we are a humble band of Pilgrims of Merian. We're here to take you home. You needn't fear, everything will be all right."

The girl leaned down and kissed Gwendolyn on the cheek.

"What … are you doing here?" Gwen asked.

"We are here to save all lost souls gone astray. It is our life's work."

As she slowly regained her senses, she could see she was sitting in a long, wooden boat with sloped sides and a fairly flat bottom. All around her were similarly dressed people in robes, each one attending a member of her crew. They were Merians, the people she often saw in the square of Prentiss spouting their odd religion—people she never looked twice at.

All of her crew appeared out of their heads. Each wore a red and green necklace.

In a bumpy fuss, people were disembarking the *Demophalon John* via one of the forward docking rings, which was open. Gwendolyn could see that a good part of the aft section of the ship was sticking out of the water at a shallow angle. Conning cylinder Number 1 looked to be fairly intact, while what she could see of Number 2 looked badly damaged.

Nearby, she could see a huddled up Morgan-Jeterix under a blanket, again wearing a Merian necklace.

"Morgan?" she said quietly.

She responded. "Yeah?"

"Is this another illusion?"

"No …"

More and more people filtered out of the ship—certainly this wooden boat couldn't carry many more—however, it seemed just big enough to seat everyone, no matter how many streamed out of the ship.

Soon, the last of the crew came out and the robed men picked up oars and rowed away from the wreck of the *Demophalon John* as it bobbed in the water.

Mouth open, drooling slightly, Gwendolyn took a count of her crew.

Fifty-eight.

Wait, she had over eighty crew under her command. "My people, still on the ship … There's more, many more."

Lady Alesta was sad. "We cannot take the dead, my lady. We prayed for their souls and bid them peace."

Gwendolyn's addled mind pondered that. She'd lost nearly half her crew.

As the boat slowly picked up speed, Gwendolyn thought she heard the roaring of rocketry coming from somewhere behind them.

Lady Alesta was sitting next to her and didn't appear concerned by the noise.

"Where, where are we going?" Gwendolyn asked.

"Someplace safe. We shall have a large, wholesome meal waiting for you. Are you hungry?"

"Yes … I'm starving …"

A tunnel of fog slowly formed from nowhere around the ship obscuring the sea and the sky. There was an unnatural quiet.

"The Road comes. Soon, you shall be safe."

Something happened. The fog abruptly vanished from sight. Lady Alesta, who, up to this point, had appeared quite calm, suddenly stood up in apparent surprise. She looked around.

"The Road?" the Merians muttered. "What has happened to The Road?"

A small black vehicle, just barely large enough to house a single person, appeared from nowhere at the prow of the boat. A slender figure wearing red and black robes was seated within. The vessel's power plant thrummed.

The figure looked like a Black Hat to Gwen.

The robed Pilgrims of Merian, who had helped her crew onto the boat, reacted with surprise. They chattered in confusion.

"What's going on?" she asked.

Lady Alesta shook her head and looked seemed genuinely frightened. "I—I don't know. Our Road has been fouled by a power field. We cannot be carried to safety in the presence of power."

The person seated in the vessel looked at the Merians and the distressed Fleet crew. Morgan lifted her head and locked eyes with the person seated in the vessel. She started speaking.

"Knife, Knife, Knife ... I am Knife ..."

"Morgan?" Gwen asked. She'd seen this from Morgan before, her empathic tendencies were at work.

Morgan continued. "This is … so much more difficult than I anticipated. The Kestrals have been at work here and the It Man must come to cleanse this place. Behold all these people … all about to die. Where I go, the It Man will follow. He will come. He must come… I'm sorry. I'm sorry you are about to die."

Morgan screamed. "Where I go, the It Man will follow! He will come to save the scant survivors!

"He must come …

"I'm sorry!

"I'm sorry you are about to die!"

The black vessel, quickly as it had come, lifted away and vanished. The Merians' boat sat there in the water.

A light shined in the distance, illuminating the ship. Alesta appeared relieved.

"Ah, see, there is the light. Any moment now, and we shall be safe. All is well, all is well."

The light got brighter, and then there was a loud whine.

Something was wrong, and Alesta appeared to know it.

A gangly vessel overflew the boat at about a thousand feet, making a terrible racket as it did so. Gwendolyn strained to get a look at it.

Strange—it looked like part of an old *Webber*-class ship to her. She could read its name plate: *Heade-on-the-Hearth*.

The name sounded familiar to her.

Spotlights rained down, and panned about the water and the aft of the *Demophalon John*.

The Merians murmured in confusion.

"No, no," the tillerman said. "Brothers, sisters, have faith!"

"Forsaken, we are forsaken!" someone shouted.

"We must have faith! Our faith is our shield!"

The Merians chattered in fear.

The *Heade* spun about, and its searchlights found their boat and settled on it, lighting it up in blinding cones of white.

There were three heavy splashes into the water. Several moments later, three scrawny men hauled themselves into the Merian's boat, their seedy clothes dripping with water. They looked at the huddled Merians and *Demophalon John* crew with a wicked gleam. "Well now," one of them said in a thick voice. "Lookie what have we here ..."

One of the Merian men stood to protect his folk. A scrawny man, with apparent strength beyond measure, seized the Merian by the neck. "Aww, what's the matter, Gov? We're not gonna' hurt ya."

He threw the man down to the deck. One of the other men quickly picked the Merian up by his ankle and dangled him over the side, dunking his head and shoulders into the sea.

The Merian waved his arms and struggled. "Seems you lot's the ones what been stealin' our pet's prey. Caused us a lot `o aggravation, ya' have."

The drowning Merian man screamed underwater. His robes fell up over his waist, revealing his britches.

With a laugh, the man lifted him up. "What ya' say?" he said and dunked him again, this time holding him down until the man thrashed no more. Laughing, the scrawny man let him go and his dead body slipped into the water.

The vessel overhead came down and settled onto the water. It approached the prow. A hatch opened. "All right, git aboard! We's goin' to take you's someplace nice ..."

They then herded the Merians and the dazed Fleet crew into the ship. Lady Alesta was terrified.

A Fleet crewman, dazed, in shock, fell to the deck. One of the three evil men came to his side and savagely kicked him. "Get up, ya' Momma's lad!" He kicked him again. "Get up!"

A Merian female knelt down and tried to help the poor crewman.

"Oh looks, she wants ta' help the miserable wank, does she?" The scrawny man hauled her up and tied them together using a length of rope. The Merian woman wailed at the tightness of her bonds.

The evil man struck her across the face. "Shaddap!" From their ship, the evil men fetched some ballast and tied the loose end of the rope to it. They then kicked the ballast over the side, the rope rapidly uncoiling. A few seconds later, the Merian and the Fleet crewman were yanked over the side and down under the waves, never to be seen again. The Merians collectively moaned in misery.

The evil men selected twenty of the strongest-looking Merians and crew and made them stay aboard as the others were roughly shuffled into the ship. They stood there on the boat, huddled in a mass. One of the Merians dumbly picked up an oar, as if to row away. Gwendolyn saw her boatswain standing there among the men, and Lt. Sai from the Com.

She tried to pull away. She tried to stand with her men. One of the fellows grabbed her by the shoulder and squeezed with crushing strength. "Quit yer' fussin', Missy, an' git on the ship!" He then picked her up and bodily tossed her through the hatch.

The port door closed, and the *Heade-on-the-Hearth* soared away. Inside, the foul men lined the Merians and crew up and forced them to look out the windows.

"Look!" they said. "See how we treats 'em."

Gwendolyn's face was shoved into the window, as was Lady Alesta's, her eyes filling with tears.

"Take ah' good hard look!"

Down below, Gwendolyn could see the long, flat shape of the Merian boat with the peppering of men standing on the deck.

"Waits for it!" one of the men said.

Lady Alesta couldn't look. She tried to turn away.

One of the men seized her roughly by the chin. "Look out there, Missy! Look I say! See every bit of it!" He made her watch.

Beneath the boat, something black rocketed out of the water, splintering it into planks and launching its pieces high into the air. Gwendolyn could see the green specks of the Merian men's robes and the white specks of the Fleet crew's uniforms being thrown up into the air and splashing back down.

She heard the splashes. She heard the cries of dying men.

The vessel orbited around, lowering a bit. Gwendolyn could see shapes struggling in the water; men thrashing. Men struggling for life.

More black shapes shot out of the water, long, black, worm-like—taking the men whole in a wide open, tooth-filled maw and then plunging back down in a spray of white water.

"Oh yeah, lookie that! Look at `em go!" the man said.

Again and again, the black shapes launched out of the water, taking the men, eating them whole.

It reminded Gwendolyn of feeding the catfish in the pond near her manor home—she throwing the food in and watching as the fish leapt out of the water to get at it. For the first time in her life, she felt utterly helpless as she watched her men and the Merians, who had tried to save them, die.

I am the captain. I should be down there, defending my men ...

Nearby, Lady Alesta wept uncontrollably. "My brothers ... my brothers ... what has become of us? Where is our Star?"

But wait—look. Gwendolyn saw a pocket of three Merians and two Fleet crewmen swimming away from the killing fields, the Merians helping the still dazed crewmen as best they could. They made their way to a large bit of wreckage from the ship and seem to be unnoticed as the creatures continued devouring some distance away. They got on the wreckage and tried to paddle with their hands and bits of flotsam.

Maybe they could get away and be saved—please, let them be saved.

The man holding her chin laughed. "Ah, would ya' look at that? Some of our ducks trying ta' swim away." He let go of Gwendolyn. "Jus' a moment."

The ship banked a little.

Please, she prayed. *Please ...*

The *Heade* banked and a wall of gunfire opened up. She saw the men convulse in the hail of shot, dropping their makeshift paddles. Their raft splintered into twigs. Geysers of white water shot into the air. They fell into the water and floated, facedown, the fabric of their robes spreading out around them.

"A-har, har, har!" the man bellowed. "Potted `em like a bunch o' bunny rabbits. Did ya' see that, Clem?"

Gwendolyn could take no more.

Her men, and those brave Merians ... dead. She huddled to the floor, holding her stomach, and wept bitterly.

A soft hand touched her on the back. It was Morgan-Jeterix, bleary-eyed, but coming around. She embraced her.

"My fault, all my fault," Gwendolyn said.

"It's not your fault, Gwen. None of this is your fault."

One of the men leaned down. "Awww, feel rotten for yer' boys down there, do ya?" he said. His eyes lit up in an evil gleam. "Feel bad for your-selves, Missies—at least they gots' it quick. No such luck for you lot … No, no, we's got somethin' much worse in store fer' you all."

As the people wept, the *Heade* bore away from the terrible scene below and disappeared into the waters.

Paymaster Stenstrom, Lord of Belmont-South Tyrol

5

—The Swarm—

A-Ram navigated the ship deep into the wildlands, the poorly charted, supposedly empty space between Kana and Onaris.

According to the charts, there was not much out here—just a brief mention of methane ice chunks left over from some primordial comet and a few pockets of noble gasses and the long, charged line of Druries Belt.

A-Ram's helm sensors concurred—there was little if anything interesting out here.

The head screen of Innocent Drury, however, begged to differ.

With Taara carefully aiming the antennae mounted on the Missive's panel and fine tuning the connection, they could see a massive asteroid field developing all around them. "Looks like the remains of a primordial planet or large moon," she said squinting into the screen. "I guess this is the Swarm A-Ram was talking about."

"Planets clear out the debris in their vicinity," Stenstrom said, "I'll wager that this was some unfortunate planetoid that got pulled apart by the competing gravity of Kana's sun and Onaris' sun."

They continued on, the *Seeker*, wading backwards by the stern through the unfolding fields of smaller and larger rock.

"Taara, where is the lock on *Demophalon John?*"

"Right in the middle of all this stuff, Bell," she replied.

With minor course corrections, A-Ram brought the *Seeker* through the rocky field. Ahead was the apparent core.

"Bel, we've got several larger masses on dead approach. I'm reading the *Demophalon John's* signal on the largest one. It's an irregular dwarf planet, reading approximately four-thousand miles in diameter. It appears to be made of ferrous rock that does not look to be native to this solar system, and it's covered with a surprisingly thick atmosphere for such a small body that reads as breathable, and I'm also detecting a warm, liquid sea covering the surface."

"How is that possible? Any water on such a distant body should be frozen solid," A-Ram said.

"I'm reading a great deal of heat being generated internally. I'm also reading signs of life on a small moon orbiting the dwarf planet. There's no heat being generated internally, so I have no idea what's supporting that life—but it's there. It's reading fairly clear."

Taara stared at the watery dwarf planet coming closer and closer. "Is that Cronyn World, Bel?"

"Looks to be."

She did some quick calculations. "It does appear to be moving in a highly irregular orbit—I calculate it coming close to Bazz again in another three hundred, seventy years."

Stenstrom wondered as he looked at the grayish world. "How are we going to do this? What are our possibilities?"

Taara returned to the screen. "Let's see, again, I'm reading it as Type I—a breathable atmosphere, a surprising amount of gravity for such a small body, and a brackish, shallow sea covering the planet. I read it as no deeper than two hundred feet at any point. Also getting indications of life down there—plenty of it."

"A-Ram, can we fly in?"

"We can't, Bel—no power to the gas-compression engines."

"All right, we'll need to be creative, then. I'd say we should tuck into one of these outlying bodies and take the *Westminster* down."

"We're not going to be able to land on the water with the *Westminster*. Tach scout ships are not designed for water operations. Additionally, tach ships are noisy—our friends out there will have no problems detecting us. We'll be defenseless and out maneuvered."

Stenstrom stood. "We're going to have to risk it. We cannot just sit here while the Captain and her crew die."

He suddenly felt an overwhelming fatigue. "A-Ram, just get us into position somewhere close, and we'll figure it out from there."

"The *Heade* can fly rings around the *Westminster*. We'll be in a shooting gallery."

He headed for his office—suddenly, all he wanted to do was sleep. He couldn't fight it off.

"Where are you headed?" Taara asked.

"My office, just for a moment."

He walked in and closed the door. Outside, he saw nothing but empty space.

Barely able to stand, he tried to make it to his desk. He reached his chair and passed out in it.

6

—THE STAR WEEPS—

Sleeping in his chair, Stenstrom dreamed.

He dreamt of his home by the churning sea south of Tyrol, of Belmont Manor in the fall, the meadow burning with rustic reds and yellows.

Off in the near distance was one of the many Merian ruins that dotted the manor grounds, the old, bumpy stone coated with moss and a windy covering of fallen leaves. The ruin was awash in a yellowish glow. A twisting column of red smoke drifted upward.

He took a step or two nearer and the light faded.

Someone was sitting there in the ruins.

It was his sister Virginia, her face covered by her hands, her Half-Pewterlock hair, a marbling of black and silver, messy as normal.

She was weeping.

"Sis?" Stenstrom said. "Sis, why are you crying?" he asked, his heart going out to her.

"My children," she said in a voice that didn't belong to Virginia. "I couldn't help them. I couldn't shield them. I couldn't bear them away."

"Sis," he replied, "you don't have any children."

She stood and paced about, moving in a manner alien to Virginia. "I am not your sister, but she knows me. She has seen me. So many dead. Died … for me, doing what I've asked them to do."

"Sis, what are you talking about? You don't have any children."

She turned to him, desperate. She grew to giant size, her head splitting the clouds. "You'll help them, won't you? You're a good man, Lord Belmont. The Sisters have given you their power—you don't need it. You're a good man. I will send you my Road and I beg you take it."

Virginia faded away, fog quickly filling the ruin. Stenstrom blundered about.

"Sis?" he said.

Ahead he thought he saw a hazy yellowish globe wreathed in a twisting, red cloud.

"You're a good man ... Power down your ship ... My Road comes... Save my children ..."

Stenstrom emerged from his office.

"Feel better, Bel?" Taara asked. "What happened?"

"What's our status?"

A-Ram spoke up. "We're on station near a large asteroid. Cronyn World isn't far to our 1:00AM. It's the best I could think of."

Something beeped. Taara turned to the screen. "We've got a contact—incoming object at 1:00am, coming fast straight out of Cronyn World. Guess who it is."

Must be the *Heade on the Hearth.*

He thought a moment. He remembered his dream. "A-Ram, Taara, let's get everything powered off."

"What?" Taara cried. "What about the contact? It's probably the Druries coming to get us."

"You heard me—power off everything—the porta-gens, the *Westminster,* even the rigged up screen here. Everything."

"You know how long it took me to get this rig tuned?" Taara protested, her Bazz accent sputtering out as she got more and more flustered.

"Trust me," Stenstrom said.

She looked like she wanted to argue, then, began turning everything off.

"Let me lock the wheel real fast," A-Ram said as he readied the helm.

Soon, the lights went out and they were in near total darkness with only the starlight from Stenstrom's office to see by. "So, we're standing here in the dark with the Druries coming in fast," Taara said. "Are we waiting for something, Bel?"

He looked around. "I'm not really for certain. Come on, let's gather around."

The three gathered in the center of the bridge and waited in the dark.

"It's really peaceful," Taara said.

"What's that?" A-Ram said, pointing.

Ahead, a corridor of fog formed, quickly enveloping them. Stenstrom drew his NTH's. "Everybody, back-to-back! Taara, skin your piece!"

They backed into each other, Taara drawing her SK. She handed her Monica to A-Ram.

"What is happening?" A-Ram cried, as they stood in the thick fog. He held the Monica with both hands.

There was a light in the distance.

"It's the Road," Stenstrom said. "The Merian's Road. It actually exists."

They could feel the humidity of it, the change in temperature.

"Where's it taking us?" Taara asked.

"Someplace we need to be."

The fog closed in on them.

7

—Lady Alesta—

In an instant, they emerged from the fog.

They were no longer on the *Seeker*. They were standing in a small, irregularly-shaped corridor of sweaty black metal with barely enough room for the three of them and almost no light.

A fierce wind roared past them—Stenstrom and A-Ram had to hold onto their hats. Taara's sideburns took flight. They looked around—they appeared to be alone, so they put their weapons away.

"Where are we?" Taara said, having to shout to be heard above the roaring wind.

"Looks to be an air shaft of some sort," A-Ram replied.

"What?"

"An air duct!"

Stenstrom produced three yellow Holystones and passed them out and the corridor lit up in soft light.

"How'd we get here!" A-Ram yelled.

"The Merian's Road—don't ask me how because I don't know! I had a dream and I was told the Road would come for us," Stenstrom replied.

"How are we going to get back?"

"The same way we got in, I suppose."

Getting their bearings, they found themselves in a long shaft that went on for as far as they could determine. Above them was a cut-stone ceiling. Below was a metal grating that led down to darkness. Only about six feet high, Stenstrom had to stoop, but Taara and A-Ram could stand erect. They made their way down the shaft, trying to find a way out, A-Ram concentrated on the grating, waving his Holystone over it, trying to see within.

"I think these grates service the chambers below us with fresh air!"

"Doesn't smell all that fresh to me!" Taara called out, noting the slightly briny smell to the rushing air.

A-Ram knelt down low and inspected the grates, holding his light close.

He stopped. "Hey, hey—I think I hear something coming from this one!"

Stenstrom and Taara made their way to his side. They leaned down and strained to hear—sure enough, there was the faint sound of many people rustling about, barely audible over the fast-moving air.

Stenstrom and Taara tried to create a wind brake with their bodies as A-Ram struggled to listen.

"What do you hear?" Taara demanded.

"Shhh!"

He put his ear against the grating. "I hear many people—they sound frightened. It must be Captain Gwendolyn and her crew." He tapped on the grate with Taara's Monica, making a sharp "tick, tick, tick."

A-Ram took his hat off and leaned down against the grate as far as he could. "Hello?" he said. "Is anyone down there?"

There was movement from below. A pale face emerged through a grate at the end of a short shaft. It was a small woman, the hole just big enough for her head and one shoulder. There were hints of hands behind her neck and shoulder, as if she were being hoisted up.

"Who's there?" she whispered.

"Are you a part of Captain Gwendolyn's crew?"

The woman squinted to see. "No, but I think she is here … there are so many."

"What is your name, my lady?" A-Ram asked.

"Alesta. My name is Alesta."

A-Ram reached through the grate and stretched, taking her warm hand. "My name is Josephus, Lord of A-Ram. Call me A-Ram."

"Can you help us, A-Ram? Can you please help us?"

"We're trying."

The woman squirmed into the vent. A-Ram got a better look at her: pale skin, thick black hair, blue eyes, hints of a green robe.

A-Ram gasped. "You! It's you!" he cried.

She looked up at him "Pardon?"

"I've seen you, standing on our ship through the Lantern," A-Ram said with excitement.

"Pardon?" she said again. "I don't understand."

Stenstrom and Taara moved down the shaft looking for a larger opening.

"I've been looking for you," A-Ram said. "Alesta, Alesta, what a beautiful name."

Despite the situation, Alesta smiled. "Well, sir, here I am."

There was a clank from below. "A-right, you scum, come here!" came a surly voice through the grate.

Alesta appeared panicked. "A-Ram, A-Ram they're here! They're here!"

She was pulled back down through the hole. She tried to hold on to A-Ram's hand but lost her grip and vanished.

"Bel!" A-Ram cried. "Did you see? It's her, from the Lantern. She's here! She needs us, immediately!"

They checked the grate—it was too small for them to go through it.

"There must be another way down!" Stenstrom said. "Keep looking."

Taara wandered down the corridor a little. She knelt down and became interested in a small chute. "I think we can go this way."

A-Ram handed her Monica back and she used it to pry open the grate.

Before anyone could stop her, Taara climbed in and quickly disappeared. A-Ram hauled himself into the chute and followed. Stenstrom trailed.

It was a three foot by three foot tube that led off at a sharp downward angle and then bent away out of sight. Stenstrom slid down and struggled into the bend. Ahead, he could see two pools of light from Taara's and A-Ram's Holystones.

Stenstrom caught up. They were huddled around a small grate—a brindle light came up strongly from it.

"I think we should go down there," Taara said. "Looks like a long drop, though."

They pried the grate up and out of the way and Stenstrom stuck his head down to get a better look.

Upside down, Stenstrom saw empty, glasslike coffins lined up against the stony wall, stretching off for as far as he could see, like a line of transparent teeth.

"Is there anybody out there?" Taara asked.

"Not that I see."

"How far down is it?"

"About fifteen feet."

Stenstrom lowered himself out of the grate and dropped down. He landed on his heels and the fall hurt him a lot more than he would have figured. He stood there, smarting. Odd, Innocent Drury could punch him into a metal wall and he didn't feel a thing, but, take a fifteen foot fall and he nearly broke his ankle and fell on his duff.

Everything stung.

"Come down, you two. I'll catch you," he said a little unsteady.

A-Ram carefully lowered himself out, his small legs and buckle shoes flailing. He let go and Stenstrom caught him without too much trouble.

Taara then launched herself out of the grate and slammed into Stenstrom, knocking him down.

"That was cool," she said picking herself up.

"Yep," he replied, feeling his aching ribs.

Taara was flush with excitement. She punched him in the arm, getting him in the nerve cluster between the muscles. "Oww!" Stenstrom cried.

She was perplexed. "What's wrong with you? Why did that hurt?"

"I don't know—I don't seem to have it right now. I'm just flesh and blood at the moment."

"The Sisters' power?"

"It's gone."

"Fine timing."

A-Ram looked around. "What, in the Name of Creation, is this?"

"This is, according to League conjecture, is where the Kestrals created *Killanjo*. I recall Captain Davage and Countess Sygillis describing it in detail. Looks just like how they described it. They called it a 'Tank'."

Taara shuddered. "*Killanjo?* Those creepy people with no skin I heard about?"

"Yes. They're placed into these glass containers and soaked in some sort of corrosive fluid until they go mad."

A-Ram was anxious. "Then, we've no time to lose. We must locate the crew at once. And Lady Alesta, she's out here somewhere. Did you see her, Bel? It's her!" he repeated with excitement.

They moved down the corridor, passing coffin after coffin. "Taara, do you have any impressions?"

She thought a moment. "I want to say we need to go in that direction," she said pointing to her right. "We need to wait, though."

"We've no time, Taara!" A-Ram protested. "Alesta!"

"No, no, we need to wait. If we don't, we'll have a lot of trouble. I feel it. If we're assuming the Druries are stuffing the crew into these coffins down there somewhere, then we need to let them finish and retire—the very size of this place will work against them. We're going to have a lot of scared and hurt people on our hands, and we need to remain undetected for as long as possible. I don't see the Druries moving around in this area much. Then, we'll have time to free the crew and come up with a plan. How in the Name of Creation are we going to get out of here, anyway?"

"We'll figure that out when we get to it, I suppose," Stenstrom replied.

They moved to the side of the corridor near the coffins and hid themselves as best they could. They seemed to wait for a long time.

"How much longer?" A-Ram cried, impatient.

Taara looked around, "Ok, let's go. That way. Make sure we stay quiet."

Silently, they moved down the corridor, all three of them amazed how long the corridor was. Eventually, they heard something in the near distance. They heard a muffled moaning.

A-Ram shot forward, Stenstrom and Taara following.

Ahead, the line of coffins in this area appeared to be full. Indistinct bodies stood inside, pounding on the glass, muffled cries barely heard.

Stenstrom knew from the recollections of Captain Davage what was going to happen. He could see the coffins were partially full of brown fluid, soaking the occupants.

The pain! Captain Davage described the agony the occupants felt.

"We've got to get these people out of there, now!" he said.

Taara and A-Ram selected an occupied coffin and tried to open it. "The door's locked!" Taara cried. She drew her SK, silenced the muzzle, and tried to carefully shoot the lock off.

PHOOT!

Her slug bounced off and ricocheted about, A-Ram having to duck.

Stenstrom strode up to the door and tried to pull it open. He expected it to easily open—he should be able to smash this enclosure to bits.

Nothing happened. The surface of the door wouldn't budge. It didn't even bend.

He tried again—still nothing happened. The lid of the coffin looked like nothing more than frosted glass, but it was diamond-like in its hardness. Still—he'd been able to smash through duraplate like spun sugar and break Innocent Drury's robotic neck like a rotten egg.

He recalled hurting himself jumping out of the grate. He suddenly had a thought. "Taara, how far down are we right now?"

"Over a mile, I'm sure of it. Probably a lot more than that."

Over a mile? Could it be that, entombed in this Kestral Tank, the Sisters' light from Camalopardus could not reach?

"Bel, this coffin's starting to fill with something."

The person within began a muffled scream. Small fists pounded on the interior.

Taara backed away. "There's got to be a central control panel or something around here." She turned and ran down the hall, past the coffins, her coattails flying and boots churning.

Stenstrom strained again to pull the lid open—nothing. He was no stronger than he ordinarily would be. So here, deep in the Kestral's horrid Tank, he was no Fist, no It Man, no Lone Rider. Here he was just a man with naught available to him but his wits and his skills.

He couldn't help but be disappointed.

"Bel, what are we going to do?" A-Ram asked, frantic.

The person's muffled screams become slightly louder. "A…rrrm! A…rrram. A-Raaam!!"

A-Ram was horrified. "Alesta? Alesta!!" He pounded on the door.

Stenstrom looked at the sophisticated lock for a moment. "I think, it's a composite lock of some kind." He shook his hand and produced a Grimtooth pick. With a skittery click, he began working the lock.

"Bel, Hurry!" A-Ram looked down the corridor. "Taara, get back here!"

"I'm trying to figure out how to open these things!" she shouted back. "Hello? What's this?" She shuttled into an alcove.

Stenstrom drowned all the noise out. He put his mind elsewhere, back into the hidden culvert with his mother and two sisters years ago. He recalled the years of hard training, his mother's harsh evaluations and critical eye always present.

He could hear her words in his head. *"No lock shall hold you or keep you out …"*

Then, he could feel it.

He didn't hear anything, as this lock had a magnetic mechanism, but he imagined the sound in his head: *click!*

The lid came free and they pulled it open. Lady Alesta fell out, her feet and the front of her clothes covered in a noisome brown fluid.

Stenstrom noted her garb, white and green robes, beads, shoeless. Lots of hair. A-Ram was correct; she was the same Pilgrim of Merian they'd seen on the ship. The apparition was now real. Here she was.

"Get her cleaned off, A-Ram—that's important, that fluid is highly caustic! I'm moving on to the next one!"

A-Ram produced a number of small handkerchiefs from his inner coat pocket, Stenstrom took several.

As Stenstrom ran to the next coffin, he caught glimpse of A-Ram holding the crying Alesta to him out of the corner of his eye, whispering into her ear.

Not a good time for that, A-Ram, he thought. *Not a good time at all.*

He worked the lock of the coffin, becoming familiar with its complex mechanisms. He had another open, and then another: a Merian female and a male crewman from the *Demophalon John* came spilling out. He put his curiosity out of his mind—what are Pilgrims of Merian doing here in a bloody Kestral Tank? As he moved to the next coffin, he was about to yell at A-Ram to get to the fallen and start cleaning them off, but he was already doing so, and so was Alesta, apparently recovered somewhat, helping as best she could.

"Hey!" Taara's voice echoed from down the hall, "I think I've got it knocked!"

Before another moment had passed, all the coffins down the line opened, spilling out their living and caustic contents. As quickly as he could, Stenstrom pulled the people out—some Merians, others Fleet crewmen, and there were also a few civilians thrown into the mix here and there. Merchants, by the look of them, with horrid, blackened skin.

There were so many to assist.

8

—THE KESTRAL TANK—

Down the line he came across a tanned, sturdy-looking female Hospitaler with long blonde hair sectioned off into dozens of thin, tightly-wound braids.

Very attractive—sort of reminded him of Lilly in a tanned, husky sort of way. Her eyes were open, though she seemed especially incapacitated. "Are you Morgan-Jeterix, of the Grand Order of Hospitalers?"

She weakly nodded, her eyes cloudy.

"Are you all right?"

"…sure …"

"I'm very glad to meet you at last," he said cleaning her off as best he could. "Can you tell me, where is Captain Gwendolyn?"

"Down there, I think," Morgan said, indicating down the far end of the hall.

"Thank you. A-Ram and Lady Alesta are coming. We're all getting out of here."

"Don't think I can walk," Morgan said, her voice barely a whisper.

"Then we'll carry you."

Several coffins away, he saw a tall woman in a lieutenant's uniform slowly trying to stand, her long brown hair in a tangle. A rapier hung at her side.

Despite himself, Stenstrom smiled as he pulled yet another Merian free from a coffin. "Are you Captain Gwendolyn?" he asked as he cleaned the Merian off.

She seemed startled at the sound of her own name. She stood tall, with excellent posture. She appeared to be out on her feet, her mind locked in a loop.

"Captain?" he asked.

She gave a start. She turned. "Lieutenant Gwendolyn, commanding officer, Fleet scouting ship *Demophalon John*." She looked at him without seeing. "What's our status?"

"Status is: getting better."

Gwendolyn shook her head. "That is not a proper response, crewman."

Her green eyes were glassy and far away.

The mirage. Stenstrom remembered the mirage, her crazed face. Here it was.

"I'm not a proper fellow," he said moving on to the next coffin.

Gwendolyn looked like she was going to get mad for a moment. She stared at Stenstrom hard and didn't appear to have any recollection of him— she was confused, lost, on the precipice of utter raving madness. "Who are you? What sort of uniform is that? I shall have to demerit you for being out of dress," she said.

"I'm a friend, remember?" He noted she was wearing a Merian beaded necklace—all of the Fleet crew were.

She blinked as things sorted themselves out in her muddled mind. She exhaled. "Are … are you perhaps … Paymaster Stenstrom?"

He smiled at her. "In the flesh, at last. You are a tall thing after all, aren't you?"

She strode up to him, her boots pounding on the shiny floor, wet with the fluid from the coffin. She stood there in a proud, formal way. "Then I would like to properly introduce myself. I am Lt. Gwendolyn, Lady of Prentiss, commander of the Fleet scouting ship *Demophalon John*, 3rd Wing. I, as of this moment, formally relieve you of your unbonded command now that I have boarded. Please, do not take that as an indictment of any kind. I wish to entertain you aboard my ship as a welcome visiting dignitary."

She went silent, apparently expecting Stenstrom to offer a formal greeting in kind.

She obviously had no idea where she was, had blanked the last day or two out of her head. He looked up at her as he cleaned a Merian's face.

"Hi," he said in return. Gwendolyn was covered in the brown fluid from the coffin, as were her boots, her coat, and her hands, which were turning an irritated shade of red.

Stenstrom stood. "Captain, you are covered in Kestral fluid. It is very bad for you."

As if awaking from a daydream, she looked at her hands, pulled a hand-kerchief from her coat pocket and began dabbing her fingers. "Oh … oh. I am sorry for being a bit out-of-sorts." Her whole body was trembling. "Your pardon."

Her handkerchief was equally soaked in fluid. He gently took it from her and tossed it aside, cleaning her hands with his cloth.

She stared at her hands as he worked, as if afraid to meet his gaze. "I am sorry I have had to cost you your chair today. I wish to make it up to you."

Taara linked up with them. "I think that's all of them, Bel," she said, a little out-of-breath.

"What's the count, Taara?"

"Looks like we got thirty-four Pilgrims of Merian, forty-two Fleet per-sonnel, and ten civilians—appear to be from Mallets, if their dress is any in-dication. The civilians appear to be in the worst shape. Who knows how long they've been trapped in these coffins."

Gwendolyn reacted a little. "No, no," she said. "There are eighty-two souls under my command. They are still on my ship at their posts. I was not aware you had civilians aboard your vessel, Paymaster. Private, I wish a complete accounting of these civilians—their names, points of origin, and business aboard a Fleet ship. Report back to me on the hour. Understood? I'll expect a more accurate count next time."

Taara looked at Gwendolyn, puzzled for a moment. "Oh, are you Cap-tain Gwendolyn? She reached up and felt Gwendolyn's bicep through her coat. "Oh, yeah, Bel, I really think she would have beaten the daylights out of you," she said, trying to lighten things up.

"That's really not appropriate, private," Gwendolyn said.

Stenstrom interceded. "Taara, get everybody rounded up—I think there's a sizable alcove down that way," he said pointing behind him. "It's defensible and I think we can use it to recover a bit and get things sorted out. Move them along as best you can—get A-Ram to help."

"Ok, Bel." She trotted away and started pulling people to their feet.

"Captain," Stenstrom said. "May I have a word with you?"

"I don't think now is a convenient time. There's much to do and …"

"I sincerely think we need to have a momentary word alone."

She appeared hesitant. "Well, I … all right. For a moment only."

They walked down the corridor a bit and found another alcove. Moving deep into it, they stopped. "Yes, Paymaster, what can I do for you? As you can see, I've …"

"It's all right, Gwen," he said, interrupting her.

"Pardon?"

"It's all right. It's just you and me here. No crew watching, nobody to see."

"I … I don't understand."

"We are not on the *Seeker*—I have no real idea as to where we are, but it's not the ship."

Gwendolyn looked around, trying to sort things out.

"Where is your ship, Gwen? Can you tell me?"

She became frantic. She gulped in fitful grabs of air. "My ship? It … it's crashed—end of mission. No … No, that can't be. Where's my ship?"

She righted herself, eyes darting, hysteria moving over her.

"My ship! The water! I must … I must …"

"Gwen, I know you've been through a lot, and I know you must be in pain. We have a few moments to ourselves, so take it. Sort it out—ride it out. We're friends, remember? Let me help you."

She looked down and put a reddened hand to her hair, then her face collapsed into utter anguish.

She fell into his arms and wept in wracking stages. "My … crew … dead. Ship … lost. They were in my head, sifting my mind. I couldn't get them out."

"Who was? Who was in your mind, Gwen?"

"I don't know—the things in the water. Couldn't think, couldn't see reason … Morgan, I think I almost killed Morgan. And then—and then those people came, they killed my men on that boat ... And then they … they strafed the survivors, all those bodies in the water … I couldn't save my men …"

"The Merians, Gwen, where did the Merians come from?"

"I don't know where they came from. They … they were trying to help us. They got us off the ship …"

Stenstrom let her get it out for a minute more. She dried her tears and gazed at him, a fair amount of the confusion melted away.

"Thanks, Bel," she said, her previous formal bearing gone. "I think I was just a hard shove away from falling into utter madness. I really needed that. I feel much better—thank you. I've been looking forward to meeting you for some time—just, not under these circumstances."

"How are the cobwebs?"

"Clearing. Thank you. I wish I could be more presentable."

"You're most presentable, Gwen. How's your skin feel?"

Gwendolyn held her reddened hands out and wiggled her fingers. "It hurts. I'll be fine. I'll be fine."

Stenstrom checked her hands. Her skin was red and inflamed, but the Kestral fluid was gone. It was fortunate that she had spent so little time in the coffin.

He checked her clothes—they were damp, but appeared to be quickly drying—at least that was something.

"Where are we, Bel? I think we were taken underwater. How did you get here?"

"I'm not for certain. I think I got here the same way the Merians got here. I'm just not sure how we're going to get back out."

Drying the last of her tears, they made their way back to the group, moving past the open coffins and spilt fluid.

Gwendolyn was highly conflicted as they walked. "I really don't feel up to fighting with you over who's in command, Bel—you or me. I truly don't want it. I don't feel up to it right now, but, for my crew, I have to …"

"I wish to conscript you, Gwen."

"What?"

"Your vessel is End-of-Mission, her bell lost. I wish to temporarily conscript you to the crew of the *Seeker*, assignment: Ship's Engineer. I recall you mentioning that you had training in engineering. I think that will …"

"Done," she said quickly, approving of his suggestion, the idea apparently taking flight in her head. "I accept. I submit to the conscription and am honored. Good thinking, Bel."

"Gwen, I don't want you to feel that I'm usurping your authority."

"Not at all. In fact, I would argue that going from the captain's chair of a scouting ship to the engineer of a Main Fleet Warbird is quite a promotion. I'm honored."

"It's just temporary."

"Absolutely." She brightened a little, having settled the command issue which, apparently, had been troubling her.

They continued down the corridor. Taara had moved the group a good distance from where they had been confined, which was a good thought. She had gotten them all into a large alcove, where they were all huddled up tightly. Tucked inside, most of the Merians and crew were scattered about on the floor, asleep. Taara was sitting near the mouth keeping guard, humming a song from Bazz, her SK laid out on her lap. She looked dreadfully tired. Morgan-Jeterix was next to Taara, either asleep or unconscious, her Marine coat draped over her. A-Ram was asleep nearby. Lady Alesta was tucked up next to him, also quietly asleep, her head resting on his chest. She had shared her green robe with him, the both of them bundled up within it.

The whole alcove was full of the sounds of people sleeping—a rather peaceful sound.

He looked down either end of the corridor, seeing nothing but coffins and tubes stretching off into infinity. No Druries in sight. He listened—he heard the steady pounding throb of machinery. Seemed safe for the moment.

He carefully stepped into the interior. The Fleet crew was suffering from overwhelming fatigue. Those who were still awake seemed as addled as Gwendolyn had been, their mental state delicate at best. Stenstrom knelt and introduced himself, the crew listening with mouths lolled open. As with Gwendolyn, after a little talking, they began to sort themselves out and make sense of what had happened to them. Elsewhere, he saw the Merians soothing other crewmen, holding them, singing in their ears. They acknowledged him with a simple nod as he passed.

The Merians showed a remarkable toughness that greatly impressed him. Without wanting to wish this situation upon anyone, he was glad they were here, nevertheless.

He returned to the mouth of the alcove. "See anything, Taara?" he asked quietly.

"Nope. Just a whole lot of nothing."

"I suppose it a good thing—these people are exhausted."

"I'm not doing too well myself. A situation like this just makes you tired. I'd almost rather the Druries show and get it over with."

Gwendolyn looked wearily down the corridor. "Any thoughts on who those men might be? They're monsters."

Taara shrugged and closed her eyes. "They're called the Drury Brothers."

Gwendolyn seated herself. "The Drury Brothers? Aren't those pirates from antiquity?" she said. "I recall my uncle telling stories about them when I was a child. Silly tales, like the Boogie Man, the Druries would fall upon lone travelers when they were at their weakest and take flight the moment help arrived."

"Sounds like them," Stenstrom said.

"But that would make them at least 400 years old."

Taara gave a wry smile. "Boogie Man never dies, that's what we say on Bazz."

Gwendolyn's state of mind appeared fragile. Though she tried to mask it, her eyes betrayed her—she was utterly terrified.

"Taara, let's not ascribe any supernatural powers to these cretins, for they don't deserve it," Stenstrom said. "The Druries are robots, Gwen, nothing more."

"Robots?"

"Yes, Flesh-replica robots, well-crafted, highly complex, but robots none-the-less. I took one down myself on the *Seeker* and discovered the truth."

Gwendolyn wasn't convinced. "They didn't act like any robot I've ever seen."

"Ghosts in the machine," Taara said. "Their spirits override their circuitry and haunt the logic. We hear tell on Bazz the Druries were so rotten even Hell won't have anything to do with them, so they walk the wastelands, giving life to the lifeless." She craned her neck and looked down the corridor. "I get the creeping feeling there's a lot more than just four of them running around here somewhere, and the sad thing is they could hit us any moment and we're just sitting ducks."

A-Ram awoke and shifted his position, Lady Alesta moving with him. "Looks like you've made a friend," Stenstrom said quietly.

"She's quite the thing, isn't she?" He gently adjusted the ends of her thick, black hair.

"Sure is."

Stenstrom saw Morgan asleep under Taara's coat. "How's Morgan-Jeterix?" he asked.

Taara looked at her. "She fine, but she's in no fit state to go on a long hike. She's going to have to be carried out of here, and so are all these civilians we just picked up. I did manage to salvage most of her Hospitaler instruments and scanners—those might come in handy."

"Are you trained in the medical arts?" Gwendolyn asked.

"Nope."

She paused, seemed confused for a moment. "Have I asked you this before?"

"Yep," Taara replied.

Stenstrom gazed down the corridor: deserted, except for the long line of clean glass coffins. He kept waiting to hear the sounds of the Druries charging down the corridor—but so far he heard nothing but the steady rumble of machinery.

He turned to all the people huddled in the alcove, both Fleet crew and Merians. "Gwen, how long has it been since you and your crew have eaten or had anything to drink?"

"I can't recall—it's been awhile." She toyed with the Merian necklace around her neck, rubbing the beads back and forth with her fingers.

"And you don't know where these Merians came from?"

"I really don't. As I said, they got us out of the ship. They were trying to help us. They put these necklaces on us, and the dream began to fade," Gwendolyn said.

He shrugged and spoke quietly. "Tell me about it in more detail later. We can't stay here for long. Taara, how deep are we?"

"At least three miles. And, I don't think there's an accessible entrance or exit to this place that we can use. I'm pretty sure we're under the sea."

"There's got to be a way out."

Stenstrom stood. "I'm going to scout around and get a feel for the lay-out of the place. Perhaps there's a more defensible area to hide in, or an obvious way out. We can formulate a plan when I get back." He pulled one of his NTH's and gave it to A-Ram.

Gwendolyn stood and brushed herself off. "I'm coming with you. It's not safe."

"No, you stay here Gwen, and keep everybody quiet. I won't be long."

Taara smiled. "He'll be all right. He's really sneaky—they'll never know he's there."

Gwendolyn was determined. "No, no, he'll need my help." She adjusted the scabbard of her FEDULA and cocked her MiMs.

Stenstrom did his usual fade into the shadows.

"Bel?" Gwendolyn said, looking around, still holding her MiMs. "Bel?"

"See, I told you," Taara said. "I have no idea how he does that—but he promised he'd show me. Isn't it cool?"

"Bel?" Gwen said wandering out into the corridor, trying to keep her voice down.

Stenstrom laughed a bit as he proceeded down the corridor, certain that, of all the skills his mother taught him, the ability to move unseen was the most useful.

Now he must get to it.

As before, he was in a long corridor lined on one side with glass coffins, about seven feet tall and three and a half feet wide. He called them "glass," for he had nothing else to call them—they looked and felt like glass, though, as he now knew, they were much, much stronger than glass. Above him was a metal ceiling thoroughly packed with tubing and wires, marked at intervals by grates admitting air. Below was a clean stone or concrete floor polished to a mirror-like shine.

On the other side of the corridor, to his right, was a maze of machinery and piping—very complex and very well-crafted, eventually giving way to a large alcove exactly like the one his people were hiding in down the way. A simple railing, painted olive green, ran along the length of the piping. Apparently, the alcove was some sort of expanded maintenance area. As he moved, keeping to the shadows, he began to see a pattern to the machinery, piping and alcoves: they repeated every hundred and fifty feet—apparently, they serviced a set number of coffins in brown fluid and oxygen and then began again. Each coffin, he saw upon close examination, was serviced with two thick hoses and a web-work of delicate wiring.

He was struck by how clean and orderly the whole place was, everything from the shiny floor to the painted pipes and railing were squeaky clean and well-maintained—not a speck of dirt or dust to be found.

And, another thing: not another soul for as far as he could see. The place seemed to be quite deserted.

He continued on, wondering how far he'd come. How big could this place possibly be?

After a bit more walking, he came across a narrow side corridor. Plunging in, he saw several holding cells guarded by a single metal door, each cell empty. Must have been where the crew and Merians were held before being put into the tanks. The corridor ended after a hundred feet. He thought to bring the group into this area, but decided against it—this area was really no better than their current hideout. No place in this Tank was safe or secure— the best thing was to get out as quickly as possible. He returned to the main corridor and continued.

After he'd walked a good mile or so, the machinery and piping to his right gave way and opened up into a gigantic space. He went to the railing and looked over the side. He saw a huge artificial chasm. On the other side of the chasm, about a thousand feet away, was a similar corridor to the one he was standing in. Below, he could see more corridors dropping down into the distance until they faded into darkness. The same for above, floor after floor of long corridors strewn with glass coffins going up and up.

He leaned over the side and looked up. That certainly must be the way they had to go.

He continued on—part of his thoughts quickly becoming convinced that this place was truly endless. He wondered about the Kestrals. Clearly, they once used this mammoth facility to create *Killanjo* at their leisure— soaking the unfortunate victims in the coffins for an unknown length of time to sufficiently drive them mad and bend them to their will.

But, the Kestrals were gone.

He had been at the conference with Captain Davage and the Sisters at Armenelos following the Kestral Affair. Though he didn't understand all of what was said, apparently the Kestrals came from very far away, well past the outer reaches of Xaphan space, and had access to Kana and the League at large by means of some sort of temporal device that was determined to be located in the Halalands of Kana. He'd stood in it himself: the Temple of the Exploding Head. This demented temple allowed the Kestrals access to the distant past and allowed them to step out of thin air without the need for starships or vehicles of any kind. The Kestrals were not human, they were some sort of alien shape-shifting species and were immune to the effects of temporal gravity. And, he recalled that the Sisters fell upon the Kestral's temporal device and laid it waste—in theory denying the Kestrals its further use from their fastness in the distant future.

So, if that was the case, and the Sisters' assessment that the Kestrals were no longer able to reach the League at will was correct, then this facility is most likely abandoned, or populated only by those who were present at the time of the Temple's destruction—the Druries and possibly a few now shipwrecked Kestrals. The Kestral's horrid facility was marooned in League space.

Escape. Just how were they going to do this? They were, as a group, exhausted from fear and their ordeal, hungry, near-psychotic, and in pain from the coffins and the Cronyns' mental attacks (Gwendolyn had seemed at the brink of insanity not long ago). And, they had to think about the wounded—Morgan-Jeterix and the civilians they'd found—those would have to be carried, a grueling task considering the distances involved. And what about the Merians? He thought about the Merian's Road—the mystical wall of fog that transported him, Taara, and A-Ram to this place in a flash. He didn't expect such a Road would be available to spirit them back out again. It could not be so easy.

No matter—they were all getting out of here. No one was to be left behind.

He continued on, but he felt far away from his people and he wanted to return to them. The sheer size of the place and the loneliness began to get to him. He felt spooked.

Ghosts in the machines, Taara said. The Druries, not even Hell wanted them. He began seeing leering faces and reaching hands coming out at him from the nooks and crannies, and behind the drone of machinery, he heard his people screaming.

After another half mile, the corridor ended in a solid stone wall with a down turn of pipes, hoses, and cabling. He looked around—there simply had to be a way up, though no apparent way presented itself. The Kestrals' habit of simply teleporting where they wanted to go was proving inconvenient. Assuming nobody in the group had the Vith Gift of Waft, (He didn't have it, and he didn't think Taara, a Bazzer, or A-Ram, a Calvert, did either; it was possible Gwendolyn could and perhaps some of her crew—the Merians certainly couldn't do it), they needed a physical way to ascend to the surface and climb out. He supposed that they could try climbing up the open face of the chasm to the next level above and so on—he could do it, Gwendolyn no doubt could, as well as Taara—but what about the rest? Could they, even assisted, make the climb, and then to have to do it over and over again? Not possible. They would be terrified, and some might even refuse such a route. There had to be another way.

Investigating the compaction of pipes and tubing overhead, he discovered a fairly wide hole leading up to the next level—apparently some sort of raceway allowing for the connection of piping from floor to floor. He checked the floor of his current level and found the same thing—a large hole about eight feet wide full of tubes. If all floors had a similar hole, then they could climb up and out. He dug into the cables leading up, and they were a tight mess, the hole seemingly packed solid. He produced a MARZABLE and poked around, finding a number of ties that he could cut and discard. After several minutes of work, he found he had cut enough ties that the solid mess of tubes and cable began to give way. Soon, squeezing through the mass, he emerged on the level above. Just to make sure the feat wasn't a fluke, he tried it again, and soon made it to the next level after several minutes. He did two more floors, and found that the ascent, though tight, was perfectly possible and much safer than climbing up the open face of the chasm.

Good—good. So, unless something else presented itself, this was how it had to be.

Moving quickly, he made the long walk back to the others to relate his findings.

$$\ast \quad \ast \quad \ast \quad \ast \quad \ast$$

When he got back, he was greeted with a terrible commotion. One of the civilians they'd rescued was on a rampage. He stumped about with blackened skin. His eyes were alight in madness. He drooled and gnashed his teeth.

He was holding Taara's SK, waving it around.

"Now look," she said holding her hands out. "I know you don't want to hurt anybody. Give me my gun, and we'll try to get you relief."

The civilian stood there holding the gun in a shaking grip. "Gotta' get out … gotta' get out of this … it hurts! Ah … ah … Creation, it hurts!"

He waved the gun around in his shaking grip. He put the gun to his temple. "It hurts …"

He pulled the trigger, but nothing happened—the palm sprander prevented the gun from firing.

Stenstrom got behind him and pulled the SK from his grasp. The two struggled for a moment. He slipped a Pink Holystone into his palm. He put his arms around him and together they slumped to the floor.

"Gotta'… get out …"

"You're fine," Stenstrom said. "You're fine. Just relax. Hold on tight to the Holystone and relax."

The civilian, though still in pain, calmed and relaxed a little in Stenstrom's grip. Taara fetched her gun. "I was just sitting there when he jumped me—and I wasn't sure if I'd set the palm sprander on my SK—good thing I did, or his brains would be all over the place. The poor fellow's in a lot of pain, Bel. He's out of his head."

Stenstrom picked him up. "The Holystone should keep him quiet until we can get him help." He carried him back into the alcove and gave a pink Holystone to the rest of the civilians—all of them writhing and blackened, the Merians trying to help them. The pinkies seemed to be helping a little.

They sat back down at the mouth of the alcove and Stenstrom described his findings.

"And you think taking this route is our best option?" a very tired-looking Gwendolyn asked. "And, by the by, I can't Waft, in case you were wondering. A few of my crew can, I believe."

"That makes two of us. Climbing through the tubing is the only option I saw. It's a little cramped, and doubtless many shall need assistance, but that shouldn't be an issue. We will assist all those needing it."

Taara was skeptical. "I don't know, Bel—I just don't get the feeling going up is our best bet."

"What are your thoughts?"

"It's confusing—but I'm pretty sure if we go all the way to the top, we're going to find nothing but stone once we get there." She paused. "I really think going that way is the way to go." She pointed down and to her right a little.

Gwendolyn rubbed her eyes, heavy with bags. She had a straight, clean scar on her right cheek.

"Gwen, how's your skin?"

She nodded. "It's all right."

"Why don't you get some sleep, we all need to rest up before we get started anyway," Stenstrom said.

Gwendolyn didn't argue. She laid her FEDULA down in its sheath and was about to lay her head on Stenstrom's shoulder, but saw Taara watching and instead tucked up onto the cold floor next to him. Moments later, she was asleep.

"See, told you she likes you," Taara said.

A few moments later, A-Ram, carefully stepping over sleeping people, joined them. "Oh, how I wish we had some coffee," he lamented, stretching.

"Welcome awake, A-Ram. We were just discussing our plan for getting out of here. I thought to lead the group up, but Taara thinks we should bear down and to the east—if that way is east."

He nodded. "I'd agree with that."

"What are your thoughts?"

"I was thinking about what Lady Alesta was telling me."

"You mean your girlfriend over there?" Taara said, smiling.

A-Ram thought about it. "Yes—why yes, my 'girlfriend'. I rather think so. She was saying that she and her Merian cadre have been coming to this watery place for years, freeing those lured in by the Cronyns. They call this place Edam. Apparently ships crash into this planet with a fair amount of regularity—not Fleet ships normally, but smaller, solitary vessels: merchantmen, yachts and the like. Alesta and her group watch for the arrival of fallen shipping and come to this place in an effort to save them. They don't use starships to arrive here, they use something Alesta calls 'The Road'."

Stenstrom smiled. "The Merian's Road. It's some sort of arcane portal leading from one place to the next. The wall of fog we saw aboard the *Seeker*—that was the Merian's Road, I'm certain."

"Alesta says, in this case, their Road was dispelled, and has led to this situation. A small vessel appeared on their boat just as they were about to make good their escape— the arrival of that vessel fouled the Road and threw off their cloak of invisibility as their faith waivered. She says the vessel with its power field dispelled the Road."

"I suppose these events prove there truly is something to the Star of Merian that they claim exists. In my office I had a dream. I saw my sister, Virginia, and she was sitting in one of the Merian ruins scattered about our manor. She was crying—she said her children were dead, and that she couldn't save them."

A-Ram took interest. "I've always been fascinated by dreams. What do you interpret the image of your sister to mean?"

"My sister Virginia has always claimed that she can see the Star of Merian—that it's plain as day to her. I think that this Star of Merian was talking to me through the image of my sister. The Star was pained by what had happened to the Merians and the Fleet crew. She told me to depower the *Seeker* and a Road would come for us. And, here we are."

"Apparently, power fields disrupt this metaphysical road that is created—that appears to be proved. Alesta also says that there was someone in a red and black robe sitting inside the vehicle that foiled their escape," A-Ram said.

"Knife. It sounds like that Knife person we saw in the Sisters' presence. She is supposed to lead me in the direction the Sisters want me to go. Obviously they wanted me here, in this Kestral dungeon, and they want me to destroy it."

"Yes. I thought much the same thing, and, apparently, they don't care who suffers in the meantime." A-Ram looked back at the sleeping Alesta. "Look at all these innocent people."

Taara took exception. "Yeah, but, things tend to work out. Things happen for a reason. People die. Maybe they would have died regardless, no matter what happened—your number's up, it's up. At least in this case, maybe some good will come out of it."

Gwendolyn awoke and looked at the floor in uncomfortable misery. She took off her coat and wadded it up into a ball to use as a pillow.

"Gwen," Stenstrom said, "it's all right. Come here, please, and sit next to me." Bleary-eyed, she looked glanced at Taara.

"Don't worry about Taara. Come on, Gwen, make yourself comfortable and get some sleep. You're going to need it."

She scooted up to him and laid her head on his chest. Stenstrom draped his HRN coat around her. She took a deep breath and sighed.

"Take your boots off, you'll feel better," Taara said, her boots long since removed. Gwendolyn didn't respond. Instead she closed her eyes and she slept.

Taara smiled. "Stubborn. Ah well, what'd I tell you?"

"So, let's organize our thoughts. Clearly, this facility is a Kestral Tank where they create *Killanjo*. As the Kestrals are now denied access to the League, this facility is cut adrift and abandoned. Now, what is the Cronyn connection to this puzzle, and, in turn, what is the Drury connection?"

Taara spoke up. "The Cronyns are probably here to protect the facility, to prevent it from being detected by the League. I mean—look where we are—just a crotch-shot away from both Kana and Onaris, the bloody heart of the League, on a dwarf planet that does not appear on any charts. They're using their skills with illusion to cover everything up."

A-Ram agreed with that line of thought. "And, I'll wager the Druries are here, in turn, to feed and maintain the Cronyns and possibly maintain this tank. You say that, at one time the Cronyns actively attacked Bazz—they must have been here on this water-logged rock the whole time, starving, and sought to satiate themselves by feeding on the people of Bazz. Four hundred years ago—that's when the legend of the Druries sprang up on Onaris. I imagine the Kestrals captured them, found them to be of suitable disreputable ilk and imprinted their minds, recreating them as powerful robots, here to oversee this facility and stealthily seek out discreet prey and feed it to the Cronyns."

Quietly, so as do not disturb Gwendolyn, Stenstrom responded. "That might also account for the Druries' apparent need for metal—recall, Chance Drury mentioned wanting to take the *Seeker*, I assume, for salvage. If that's the case, they probably need to keep themselves stocked in refined metals for the construction of their replacement robotic bodies and the upkeep of their ship. I got a good look at the *Heade* as I battled Innocent Drury, and though it's in the basic configuration of a *Webber*-class vessel, it's packing a host of add-ons. That's the key—the Druries must have a large dock here somewhere—large enough to house a starship or two. And, I'll wager the *Demophalon John* is currently in it—and I'll further wager that the *Seeker* is there too. We did see an incoming blip just as we powered off."

A-Ram was distressed. "Pardon me," he said. He stood and made his way out of the alcove and, choosing a direction, went down the corridor.

A minute later, Alesta quietly appeared. She stepped to the mouth of the alcove and looked around. She held her green robe shut.

"He went to the bathroom," Taara said.

She blushed and sat down, waiting for him to return.

"Lady Alesta," Stenstrom said. "I wanted to thank you for doing what you could for Lt. Gwendolyn and her crew. You and your folk are very brave. I have always admired the Merians, and I do so now more than ever."

She smiled. "Thank you, sir. And thank you, for coming to our aid. We are very blessed."

"Just returning the favor," Taara said.

Alesta was perplexed. "Pardon?"

"Never mind," Stenstrom said. "I believe your Star came to me and asked us to help you. We arrived here in a wall of fog," Stenstrom said.

"That is our Road," she said.

"May we expect that 'The Road' will return and spirit us back out?"

She shook her head. "No, my Lord. There is too much power here. In the presence of power, the Road will not form. We may be deposited into a place brimming with power, as this place is, however, we cannot be retrieved unless the power is cut or otherwise dispelled."

"So, unless we turn off the lights, we're stuck here?" Taara said. Alesta looked sad.

"May I ask, Lord A-Ram says he saw me standing in the corridor of your ship? Is that true?"

"Yep," Taara answered, "and he hasn't stayed quiet about it since."

Alesta was confused, she turned to Stenstrom. "My Lord?"

"He did, and we saw you too. We saw you in the light of an arcane lantern. A-Ram was very taken with you. He has been most anxious to make your acquaintance."

Alesta smiled and blushed a bit. "He is in your service?" she asked.

"He's my Master Helmsman," Stenstrom replied. "And, I'm proud to say, he's my friend as well."

"Mine too," Taara said. "He's a great guy."

Alesta nodded. "Helmsman, he steers your vessel?"

"Yes, a very important posting."

"Where is your ship? I shall inform you that the people are sick, and hungry, and need tending as soon as possible."

Stenstrom looked back, saw the lumpy huddles of sleeping people jungled up in the alcove. "Our ship is far away. We're on our own down here."

A-Ram returned. Alesta looked up at him and burst into a smile. She opened her green robe and invited A-Ram to sit next to her. He did and she snuggled into his side, closing the robe.

Stenstrom put his arm around Gwendolyn and she settled into him a little further, gripping him tightly. "Taara, A-Ram, I think I'll let Gwen sleep for a bit, then I'm heading out again."

"Where you off to this time?"

"I'm going the way you suggested—east and down a little. I'm going to see if the *Seeker* is nearby. If so, I'm going to board her and get us food and drink, and then we're getting out of here."

Alesta took off several of her beaded necklaces. "Sir, may I offer you and Lady Taara one of my necklaces—it shall protect you from the unreal."

Taara took one and put it on. "Thanks," she said.

Alesta put one around A-Ram's neck and straightened it for him. She gazed at him with big blue eyes. "For you," she said softly. She then offered one to Stenstrom. "Please, good sir."

Stenstrom reached out and took it. "With great thanks," he said.

He started to put it on, and felt a warm hand stop him. It was Gwendolyn, partially awake. "Wear mine, Bel." She took off the necklace she was wearing and put it around Stenstrom's head. "I want you to wear mine."

Unused back cover concept, by Carol Phillips

9

—The Dock—

Stenstrom made his way down the corridor, this time in the opposite direction from the way he'd come. Again, the going was long, with the unbroken line of coffins on his right this time, pipes, hoses and wiring on his left. As before, he came to an open space to his left and he stopped to get his bearings.

He was surprised by what he saw. In the near distance was a wall of rough hewn stone. He could see several bulbous spheroids of glass and metal sticking out of the rock face, lit up in effulgent, yellowish light like several transparent zeppelins sticking out of the rock. Housed within the spheroids he could see a black latticework of machinery, gantries and walkways. He could see what looked like a highly advanced dock and hints of calm water.

And he could see the battered nose of the *Demophalon John* looming over the dock, he was sure of it.

There she was, Gwendolyn's ship. There was a tiny, ant-like cloud of mechanized movement all around her, like the corpse of a bird being dismantled in a slow, methodical fashion by a colony of ants.

So, their theory had been correct. The *Demophalon John* was being taken apart, bit by bit.

Looking further, he found he could access the spheroid by way of a gantry several levels down. He quickened his pace.

Shortly, he got to the end of the corridor. It was a relief, to finally reach the end. He guessed he'd gone about a mile and two-thirds. Given the length of the other side of the corridor, he guessed the corridor was nearly four miles long in total.

As on the other side, there was a hole cut in the floor for the plunging descent of wires and tubing. He cut their ties and moved them aside. He squeezed in.

He went down three levels. Ahead, a gantry snaked along the rock-face wall and entered the glass spheroid. Moving in the shadows as only he could, he worked his way across, unseen.

There! Look there! From his new vantage point, he could see the *Seeker* floating at the dock next to the *Demophalon John* through the spheroid's glass. The *Seeker* towered over her. It was a stirring sight seeing the old War-bird in one piece, and he took heart. The Druries must have intercepted the depowered ship shortly after they departed, found it abandoned, and grappled it down to the planetoid's surface using the advanced tech mounted on the *Heade.*

Moving quickly, he entered the spheroid. At once the atmosphere changed. The lengthy, coffin-lined corridors beyond were clearly deserted and out-of-use; here, however, near the dock, such was not the case.

He instantly heard the sounds of intelligent movement, metal clanking and muffled conversations.

Druries. There was Clem, over just beyond the threshold, and also In-nocent, both were stumping about, fully clothed in their dingy wares, looking like nothing more than two scrawny men who'd seen a hard, unhealthy life.

They shambled into the interior of the spheroid. Stenstrom followed.

He needed information—he needed to know what their capabilities were and were not. It was a terrible gamble, but he had to take it, his people were depending on him.

He made a deliberate noise.

"Whass' that?" Innocent said turning around and walking right past Stenstrom.

"It's nothin'," Clem said. "You been jumpy lately."

Innocent looked around. "Ya? You'd be too, huh—that guy in the coat we fought gives me the creeps—an, we ain't caught him yet—he was no-where to be found on his ship when we hauled it down."

"The life ring was gone. Mebbe' he an' his lot abandoned ship. Mebbe' the Cronyn's done eaten him by now."

"Mebbe', mebbe'—but I doubts it," Innocent said. "He could be squea-lin'. He could be bringin' th' Fleet."

Stenstrom moved right past them.

"The Fleet won't find us—the Cronyns'll see to that."

Stenstrom listened to this exchange. They couldn't detect him. It seemed when the Druries were compressed down into their man-like state, their vast sensory abilities were no greater than any ordinary man's would be. All this—their foul, accented language, their distressed clothing—their pretending to be scrawny men when they were in fact huge, vaguely man-shaped robots indicated that all of their frailties, fears, and mortal limitations were imprinted into their computerized brains right along with their despicable nature, reducing them in their scope and the manifestation of their power.

They were robots playing at being foul, unrepentant, cowardly men, armed with boundless cruelty and limited intellect. They didn't need to be overly smart to fulfill their role—just had to be mean and unprincipled. Any potential these great machines had was lost on this lot.

An excellent bit of information, Stenstrom had learned all he needed. He looked around, and there was nobody other than the three of them at the moment. He decided to try and take them out—two less to have to deal with.

He crept up behind Clem, aimed his NTH, and got him square in the back. Instantly, without saying a word, Clem crumpled to his knees, then fell over, face-first.

Innocent looked. "What are ya' doin'?"

Stenstrom got Innocent too. In this compressed form, their robotic bodies were fully subject to being killed by his NTH pistols—when spread out and expanded, their decentralized bodies were much more resistant.

He hoped they didn't figure that out as this situation progressed.

Stenstrom then tried to drag them off into the shadows and stash their wretched bodies. Creation—he could hardly move them—they were so heavy. Grunting, straining, he managed to slide them out of the way, but the effort of it was monumental and completely exhausting. His It Man abilities would do well at this moment, but, of course, he was denied them. He had to rest up a bit after his ungainly chore was complete, as he'd had so little sleep and he was near exhausted.

Good to know, good to know—some more useful information gained. He would have to pick his targets more carefully should the opportunity arise to slay a few more Druries. Despite it all, he felt slightly gratified slaying these two. He wished he had more to kill.

He returned to the shadows and continued.

Ahead was a vast chamber cut of solid rock. The *Seeker* and the *Demophalon John* were floating side-by-side in shallow water by a highly mechanized dock—the *Seeker* dwarfing the much smaller scouting ship. There were a number of robotic arms mounted all about the *Demophalon John*, cutting off orderly pieces of hull plating with huge torches, swinging over and dropping them onto a vast conveyor belt, which ferried the hull plates off to a large hopper. The *Demophalon John*, its hull cut away in sections, looked like a skinned and partially dissected animal, the mechanical innards of the ship on gory display.

Above Stenstrom were several levels of walkways connecting offices, mezzanines, and other support structures all made of gangly black metal.

There were a number of robotic arms mounted near the *Seeker* as well, but they weren't at work cutting it up, quite the opposite, they seemed to be at work adding parts to her hull. The arms were busy welding some sort of brace to either side of the rear of the ship. Additionally, two cylindrical tubes, each about a hundred feet long and twenty feet high, were being constructed nearby by other robotic arms, some arms at work welding, others machining complex parts out of solid blocks of metal; other arms delicately adding circuitry to the interior of the tubes.

The tubes looked, to Stenstrom, like Xaphan-style stellar engines.

What were the Druries up to?

More movement caught his eye.

Overseeing the work on the dock was Chance Drury, holding an open chart of some kind. At his side stood two bizarre creatures. One of the creatures looked like a giant-sized circular ball of frizzy black hair, supported by four jointless, prehensile legs, also covered in black hair. The other looked like some type of prehistoric bird with a sharp beak and long, flapping wings.

The creatures intently watched the progress on the ship as Chance, showing them the chart he was holding, pointed various things out.

These creatures must be shape-shifting Kestrals, possibly stuck here in this facility after the Temple of the Exploding Head was destroyed.

Ah, it came to him—he knew what was going on. Marooned here, far from their home and no longer able to simply Blink back using their temporal anchor point, the Kestrals were planning on hijacking the *Seeker* and using her to return home, possibly via an alternate temporal anchor point located elsewhere in the cosmos. The Druries probably found the *Seeker* a sturdy, worthy craft capable of making a long voyage through trackless space, simply needing engines—and, hence, the two new engines being constructed for it nearby. Therefore, the *Demophalon John,* damaged beyond easy repair, was to be scrapped, melted down, and turned into parts for the *Seeker,* which would then be sailed a great distance back to their destination, wherever that might be. He could not imagine that the Druries would want to part with their modified *Heade-on-the-Hearth,* so the addition of the *Seeker* was a godsend for them, no doubt.

Good to know. Good to know.

He moved away to his right, toward the hopper—he wanted to see where it went. Along the way, he passed three Clems, two Innocents, and five Lemmuels, all moving about, cursing in their fashion, doing this and that. The Kestrals appeared to have them all quite agitated.

He saw a clear hierarchy forming. Chance, as their leader, was the queen bee—with only one of him running around at any given time, while the rest were workers and present in quantity. There were a few Clems moving about, a greater number of Innocents, and a whole lot of Lemmuels performing the manual labor and drudgery.

Following the hopper as it led away from the dock, he found it went into a vast adjacent room, thousands of feet in diameter and several stories high. The room was set up like a massive assembly line: automated machinery was bolted to the floor everywhere, moving in well-timed unison. The collected metal was received from the hopper and went into a small, but highly effective furnace, where super-heated slugs of metal were then extruded into various dyes and molds and worked with precision. In the distance, Stenstrom saw four bands of color reaching up into the heights; he saw bands in green, red, blue, and yellow. The bands, stacked neatly into tall, individual chutes, were composed of tiny robotic squares—obviously, the green squares were for Innocent, and the other colors must be for his brothers.

As A-Ram surmised, the once proud *Demophalon John* was getting picked apart bit by bit to be melted down into replacement parts for the *Seeker* and the Druries, complete with their bad hair, bad grammar, and bad intentions—an inglorious end to be sure.

He looked at the whole set-up and took it in. Taara liked to ascribe supernatural attributes to the Druries, saying that they were in fact manifestations of the Boogie Man; but here it was, nothing but a product of automation, technology, organization, and a twisted conception.

Lined up beneath the chutes on hooks, were man-shaped robotic frameworks hanging from a silent assembly line that snaked off into another section of the room. The robotic frameworks were preloaded with a number of antennae and a folded up head-screen. The frameworks seemed peaceful as they hung there—asleep almost.

Something was coming at him from his left!

He quickly aimed and fired. The NTH shot hit what looked like a seated person several feet away. Investigating, it was a primitive robot seated in a stuffed chair. It was a 'soup can' robot with a cylindrical torso and basic, articulated arms and legs, its feet nothing more than a simple set of casters. It had a pair of cone-shape metal funnels bolted to its chest area, almost like a pair of breasts. It had a primitive servo-motor head and sported a wig of blonde hair and full latex lips. Scrawled across the torso was the word: DUNCE.

Stenstrom could only wonder what the thing was used for.

As he puzzled over it, a long bank of computerized machinery came to life in lights and sounds. Screens printed high-speed readouts and hydraulic pressure built up with a hissy fuss. The line of hanging bodies gave a clank—the bodies nudging into each other, and they began moving in assembly-line fashion.

The first body in the line stopped underneath the chute populated with green squares. Like ice cream being extruded from a tap, the green squares filtered down onto the body. Knocking about in a cloud of movement, the squares covered it from bottom to top—Stenstrom was amazed how many green squares it took to cover the frame—the green chute above was now almost empty.

Covered with squares, the green, blocky body moved on to a finishing station where specialized squares for his head, stomach section, and phallus were added. These squares were not green, but a shiny silver color.

The next body in the line stopped under the red chute and soon was similarly covered.

Two robots, Innocent in green and Clem Drury in red, were newly created—possibly to replace the ones he'd just dispatched.

In front of a flickering screen, a massive amount of information was then downloaded to them—their rotten souls and their demented memories converted to computerized patterns. Their large head screens came out and unfurled. A huge amount of data was printed off on the screens as they received the information.

An automated piston slowly came forward. Behind the piston was a rack of seedy Drury clothing, just waiting to be put on.

The two blocky robots, one red, one green, finished receiving their downloads. They then clunked away in ponderous steps and began changing, their head screens retracting, the squares moving about their bodies in a symphony of coordinated movement, locking into place, shrinking, and becoming dense.

Flesh shot out of their stomachs, and soon there stood a naked Innocent and a naked Clem.

"What in th' Name o' Creation jus happened?" Innocent asked as they walked up to the rack and selected clothing.

"I dunno'," Clem replied. "We was standin' in th' anti-chamber when all of a sudden, here we are."

"Betcha them Kestrals did us again. Them fools be crazed. Be glad when they's gone."

The two began dressing.

"Wha' we gonna' do with our new guests marinadin' in the Tank out there?" Innocent asked, pulling a white shirt on.

"Who cares. Let `em rot. This place is shut down. Once we gets rid `o those two golden Sad-Sackers, we'll need to start thinkin' bout our future. Mebbe' we's can use the Tank for ourselves. Create an army of slaves and have at Kana."

Stenstrom watched. Beneath the rack of clothing was a track carrying refuse back to some unknown point—Innocent and Clem pulled off lumpy bits of mal-formed flesh and tossed them onto the refuse track—like a tailor pulling off loose strings from a new coat.

He didn't wait. Stenstrom slotted up behind Innocent and shot him in the back. He instantly fell into the refuse track. Clem shortly followed him, the two of them balled up with the rest of the trash.

That's what happened to you, babes ... again, Stenstrom thought, taking devilish pleasure in killing the Druries.

He watched their dead, naked bodies, Innocent wearing a partially buttoned shirt, rumbling back to the refuse center, arms and legs akimbo.

Stenstrom had a thought. He went to the rack of hanging robotic bodies. The rack was delicately calibrated, with each body hanging on a hook separated by removable spacers. He pulled several spacers out, dividing the first few bodies. Not spaced out correctly, there should probably be quite a mess when the system starts back up again.

Oops, he thought. *So sorry about that.*

He then had at the various consoles and stations involved in the complex creation of these monstrosities. He fired his NTHs, "killing" the various bits of equipment and circuitry. He felt greatly satisfied by all of this.

He then stole back out of the automated room onto the dock.

He encountered a group of Clems walking by. One of them was yelling. "Get that shite a-workin', or I'll have my wank up ya! Now move!"

"Yeah, yeah, shut it!" came a reply. Near the wreck of the *Demophalon John*, he saw a single Lemmuel working on one of the robots cutting up the hull plates high above. He had a panel open and was waist deep into it, performing some sort of maintenance. As Stenstrom previously guessed, in the hierarchy of the Druries, Chance was at the top, Clem and Innocent were somewhere in the middle, and Lemmuel, the most common of all he'd seen, was at the bottom, doing the 'crap' work whenever it needed doing.

"Camon', you bitch!" Lemmuel cursed, having issues with whatever it was he was working on. He rose up and threw his tool aside, where it clattered to the dock near the water.

Cursing and lamenting, he reached out to pick it back up and start at it again, his arm doubling in length.

Stenstrom sprang, shooting him in the neck. Without a word, Lemmuel's body balled up and did a cartwheel into the water with a proud "kersplunk!" He sank quickly and did not reappear, a few bubbles danced to the surface marking his sinking.

Stenstrom returned to the shadows and quivered. *Ohhhh, but wasn't that fun ...*

He resumed his mission and approached the *Seeker*.

Chance and the two Kestral monsters were still standing there, observing the work. Chance then motioned for them to follow him. He walked toward the cylindrical engines being constructed nearby.

"And here, the engines are well under construction, as you can clearly see," Chance said. "With the refined metals derived from the Fleet wreckage, we shall have just enough materials to complete construction in a hundred hours, and all the necessary metallurgy may be assumed as the Fleet uses high-grade materials. *C'est le bon truc.*"

The Kestrals gazed at the engines with interest. The one in the guise of a reptilian bird changed shape, transforming into a tall, toga-clad, golden woman. She stepped into the circular intake and looked close-up at its workings.

Chance responded to some question he was being asked. "Oh, yes, we have salvaged the coils from the scout ship, however, they are far too small for such a heavy vessel—they would not last you long enough into the deep sea before they burned out—*hou la!* These stellar engines we are constructing shall work nice as you please. I have personally leant to their engineering and vouch for their construction."

The Kestral woman stepped out of the engine intake and opened her mouth to an impossible diameter, like a snake readying to devour a large prey item. She vomited in a projectile spray on the engines, coating the front ends in glistening fluid. She then closed her mouth and turned to Chance.

He rolled up his chart and clapped. "Ah, well done, my mistress! *Que bonita!* Our endeavor is now properly anointed and blessed!"

More questioning.

"Once the engines are complete, we shall then stock the ship with provisions for a several month-long voyage," Chance said. "We shall set out and abduct a passing ship, a freighter, merchantman, or other lone vessel.

We shall then process the crew and ready them as quality foodstuffs for your consumption during the voyage. Fear not, masters, for you shall eat hearty— *avoir un bon dîner,* a-heheheh."

The Kestrals appeared to be pummeling him with questions.

"Oh, yes, yes. This is a *Straylight*—a classic ship, as tough as they come. I am rather envious—I should like to plant my personal flag on such a craft. With this vessel, you may rest assured your trip shall be swift and uneventful."

As the group inspected the engines now dripping with Kestral vomit, Stenstrom saw an opening into the frontal section of the *Seeker.* Quickly, he started to go inside.

"What is that?" Chance said.

Stenstrom froze. Chance took a few steps forward and looked around.

The Kestrals came to his side. "I thought I saw something," he said to them.

He took another step forward—he was just feet away from Stenstrom, who was hiding near a dock baffle.

He clapped the rolled up charts he was holding into his palm several times. "Clem," he said calmly.

"Aye?" came a radio-like response.

"You have stowed the most recent batch of 'Trogs' in the tanks, yes?"

"We have."

"Did you have any issues? Did any try to escape?"

"Nah, they was all zapped out, like usual."

"How are they reading?"

"We're not reading nothing, Chance. None o' the stuff out there's properly functionin' since we got cutoff."

"I see. We shall have to design custom telemetry units of our own to compensate. When time allows, I wish a manual inspection be made of their tanks and an exact head-count delivered. I shall not tolerate this continued inefficiency— *entiendo?"*

"You an' that fancy talkin' you like to do. Ok. It'll be awhile, as we's a deadline to keep. We're tryin' to crack into the bowels o' this scout ship an' get at the good metals there. Fleet ships are a' whole lot tougher than the usual rustpots we's snag. The dock cutters are having a hard time with it, and some are goin' down with the effort."

"Please inform Lemmuel that he may work the problem day and night until engine construction for the *Seeker* is complete, or I shall have him reconstituted in the female DUNCE body and compel him to inhabit it for a year or so, understand?"

"Aye."

"I would rather we not dance with the Fleet, however, the situation calls for remarkable action—our mas-

ters demand immediate return to their home … *ezek vezetői nekem nehéz.* Proceed as best you can. Be advised, we shall shortly have a need to set out and intercept a passing craft. The captured crews shall be prepared as foodstuffs to feed our masters for their long voyage. They must be alive, that is a must—ensure the *Heade* is serviced and ready for launch."

"Why can't we jus' prepare those fools we got in th' tanks right now?"

"Because, they are to serve as *Killanjo* deckhands for our masters' voyage home—they are to crew the *Seeker*. Inform Innocent he shall accelerate the Trog's soak to speed the process. They must be fully ready in one hundred hours. *Comprenez?*"

"Yeah … yeah."

Chance appeared inspired. "Ah—look at what fate brings us. In twenty hours, I am reading that a scheduled flight of school children from the Kanan city of Champion are to be bouncing down the lanes on their way to Onaris for a field outing at a lovely museum in Innari. How sweet. I want the *Heade* made ready to sail, I want their ship lured off the lanes, and I want the children taken and processed. A-heheh, they shall make for tender eating. Inform Lemmuel, I want no breakdowns with the cassagrain weaponry this time, or, again, it's to the DUNCE with him."

"Aye, twenty hours, the *Head'll* be ready."

"Fine. *Vamos! Andale!* Chance out!" He looked around one more time and then stumped back to what he was doing.

Stenstrom had a clear shot of the back of his head—no way he could miss. He burned to get this started, to settle with this miscreant, and then go marching into the assembly area and await his re-construction, only to kill him again and again as a kind of recurring purgatory that he so justly deserved, with himself cast as the punishing angel. Perhaps, with the damage he created on the assembly line earlier, Chance might come out mal-created or only half-made as some sort of deformed midget—wouldn't that be grand? Or, better yet, he could make Chance get programmed into the dreaded DUNCE body and dance around in it.

But, such a spectacle would be selfishness in the extreme. He had his people to think of, and he had to attend to their needs before indulging his own. He could not endanger them by alerting the Druries before he was ready to do so.

He aimed his NTH and pulled the trigger without cocking the hammer.

Another time, Chance Drury, another time …

Stenstrom then carefully made his way into the *Seeker.*

The interior of the ship was lit up, the Druries having tapped it into a central power grid. He saw a Lemmuel wandering around with some tools, but that was it—the ship was, at this point, deserted.

He went to the bridge, taking a lift, which was working. Ha!—This was the first time he'd ridden in a lift since he took command of the *Seeker*—rather ironic, he thought. Once there, he saw that Innocent's remains had been cleared away. At the Missive's panel, the Druries had installed a computerized node of some sort with a flat, ovular view screen. A sinuous, acid-like line of color traced across the display.

The Druries had been busy getting the *Seeker* ready to take the Kestrals to wherever they needed to go, and they were planning on using the Fleet crew and the Merians as *Killanjo* ship hands in the process.

The good thing was, given the information he'd just received, the Druries couldn't monitor the tanks beyond—this facility must have been at least partially controlled and monitored by the Kestral home world, and the far-flung link had been severed—that was something working in their favor. The Druries, therefore, could not know that they had been freed from the tanks.

They were also heavily occupied trying to get the *Seeker* ready for its voyage, the Kestrals understandably impatient, and they had their hands full—that bought Stenstrom and his people additional time.

But, as Chance said, the Druries would soon be setting out, this time to acquire live provisions for the Kestral's voyage—children, kids on their way to Onaris to visit a museum in just twenty hours. He couldn't allow them to fall victim to the Druries.

Looking around, he saw the box of insta-meals that they stole from Dry Dock 275. He counted—eleven meals for over fifty people. That would have to do for now.

He took the box, and hunted around for the bottled water they'd stolen. It wasn't anywhere he could quickly find, so he settled for a mesh sack full of warm cans of Gasol that A-Ram had previously scrounged, and left the bridge.

Outside, Chance and the two Kestrals were gone. Beyond, he could see the *Demophalon John* steadily being taken apart. He saw the Druries had stacked up several of the ship's Stellar Mach coils—the twenty-foot tall rings of tightly wound wire were being assembled to be taken somewhere via a massive treaded craft—probably to the furnace for smelting as the coils were too large to fit on the conveyor belt.

Stenstrom put down the box of insta-meals and the sack of Gasol he was carrying.

He was going to misbehave a bit before leaving.

He reached the craft. It was a squat, treaded design, meant to haul large, heavy items. It had a round, robotic node at its front packed with blinking sensory equipment. He gave the craft several shots with his NTH and the node went dead. The weight of the coils, no longer being actively supported by the workings of the craft, began to lean noticeably.

Moving on, he went to several of the robotic arms that were currently busy cutting apart the *Demophalon John*. They were bolted to the dock by means of a large cylindrical base. The base had a door for maintenance. Stenstrom tried the door and found it locked.

After a shake of his hand and a quick action, he had the door open with a magnetic lock pick; all manner of cables and circuit boards were fitted inside. He reached in and shot the circuitry several times. Far overhead, he could see the robotic arm go dead, swaying slightly.

Satisfied, he mounted a red Holystone inside, and he tricked the lock of the door as he closed it, knowing it would not reopen without a savage struggle. When a Lemmuel did manage to get the door open, a tongue of fire from the Holystone would belch out.

He then repeated the procedure on several more arms, killing the circuit boards and breaking the locks on each one as he went.

Have fun with those, Lemmuel old boy.

Felling rather happy with himself, Stenstrom retrieved his box of insta-meals and the sack of drinks and stole off—completely undetected. He returned to his people far away in the Tank.

✶ ✶ ✶ ✶ ✶

"Who's there?" Taara said, poking her head out of the alcove. Gwendolyn's head soon followed.

"It's me," Stenstrom said emerging from the shadows. He set down the box of insta-meals and the sack of Gasol. "I've been to the *Seeker.*"

"It's here?" Taara cried.

"Yep, and I've brought food and drink. I think we've got about ten or eleven insta-meals and about a dozen cans of warm Gasol. I couldn't find the bottled water."

"Yeah, I used the bottled water to take a shower," Taara confessed. "Sorry."

He reached into the box and pulled the meals out as people gathered around.

"Lady Alesta," he asked, "can you go through these meals and equally portion them out seeing that everybody gets a share?"

She smiled and took them. "Praise be to you, sir. I will, thank you."

Half an hour later, Alesta and A-Ram gave everybody a third of a helping of insta-meal and a quarter can of Gasol. It wasn't much, but the food was a life saver, it had been so long since the crew from the *Demophalon John* had eaten a proper meal.

As before, Stenstrom, Taara, Gwendolyn, and A-Ram sat at the mouth of the alcove eating their food. Between them, they had two cans of red and green Gasol, which they shared. Morgan-Jeterix was nearby, eating her meal with lady-like precision. Though still quite weak, she was becoming more alert by the moment. Lady Alesta, A-Ram's new shadow, was in the back helping to feed the civilians, who were in bad shape. Their skin, ravaged by the Kestral tanks, was in severe distress, and they cried out in agony. Helping them as best he could, Stenstrom produced several, fresh pink Holystones and put them in their hands, partially re-sedating them. It appeared that only Stenstrom's pink Holystones were keeping them moderately comfortable.

As the group ate, Stenstrom saw A-Ram and Alesta exchange frequent glances.

He laughed—*Making love to a Sister one day, winning the pure heart of a Pilgrim of Merian the next, you've certainly come a long way for the better, A-Ram. Well done.*

"So, here's what I discovered. The *Seeker* and the *Demophalon John* are in a large bay about two miles from here, three levels down," Stenstrom said as he ate. "The *Demophalon John* is partially taken apart and melted down. The Druries have several robotic arms mounted to the wharf, cutting and slicing off squares of the hull and feeding them into a hopper. They also have many of her SM coils stacked up on the dock. For the *Seeker*, they've got other plans. As we speculated, there are two Kestrals marooned in this facility. The Druries are in the process of retro-fitting a pair of alien engines to the *Seeker*, which they plan to give to the Kestrals so that they may voyage far into the deep sea, destination unknown. They probably have another temporal anchor point out there somewhere that they wish to utilize to return to their home world. They are also planning on using the Fleet crew and Merians to man the ship for the voyage as mindless *Killanjo* deckhands."

"Are they currently aware we are no longer imprisoned in the coffins?"

Gwen asked, concerned.

"No. I heard Chance and Clem Drury discussing that very topic. It seems a fair portion of the monitoring of this facility was accomplished remotely, so, with the link to Kestral space broken, the Druries currently have no way of monitoring the goings-on out here. And, in that lies a bit of concern. Clem Drury has been ordered to personally inspect the coffins and count up all those present. He, however, has more pressing issues at the moment, as I sabotaged a good number of the robotic arms disassembling the *Demophalon John*. From Chance's tone, readying the *Seeker* for their Kestral masters is their top priority at the moment. And, they are planning on setting out and capturing a ship full of children to use as live food for the Kestrals on their trip back."

"Kids?" Taara cried.

"Yes, in twenty hours. Obviously we cannot allow that to happen in any case."

Gwendolyn was finishing her portion—a bit of chicken with rice. "What about the Druries themselves?"

"I counted at least a dozen—the four of them being repeated quite often, except for Chance Drury, of whom I only saw one. This area of the facility, where we are now, is mostly deserted. They seem to be concentrating their activities on the docks near the ships." He turned to Taara. "Taara, what's our capability right now with the *Seeker?*"

"None—she has no coils and, therefore, no way to power her gas-compression engines. She is, for the most part, a dead ship. Did the Druries say how long it would be until they completed the retro-fit?"

"One hundred hours."

"Well shoot, why don't we just wait until they're done with the engines, storm the ship and take it. Creation—they're getting it ready for us," Taara said.

"That's an interesting thought, but you're forgetting about the children, Taara. Also, the bad thing is the Druries are going to come looking for their 'crew' well before then and shall be, no doubt, put off when they find those coffins empty. We can't wait for that to happen—we can't place them on the offensive. I think what we'll need to do is pile up into the *Westminster* and high-tail it out of here—let them have the *Seeker*. Do you think we'll all fit?"

Gwendolyn spoke up. "The problem with that is an old tach-scout ship like the *Westminster* will not be able to fly through water, as we're assuming that the entrance to the cargo bay is deep underwater. It just can't do it, its engines aren't designed for such a thing."

"And, she's too heavy to float up to the surface, regardless," Taara added.

They sat and thought for a moment. Farther back in the alcove, Lady Alesta was carefully feeding one of the civilians, who was struggling a little bit, quietly begging for relief.

"I think, Bel, what we should do is occupy the *Seeker*," Gwendolyn said.

"To what end? She's useless."

"I think as far as being a place to easily gain entrance, hide and defend, the *Seeker* is ideal—she's like a fortress. Also, I think there's a way to get her powered up prior to the Kestrals stealing her."

"I'm listening."

"We can take the J400 SM coils from the *Demophalon John* and mount them on the *Seeker*."

Taara disagreed. "J400 coils are too small for a *Straylight* Warbird."

"Yes, that is true, but, they provide up to thirty-five percent power of the *Seeker*'s maximum—more than enough to run the gas-compression engines, get us up through the water and into orbit. We can run them at over-boost—that'll burn them up in a hurry, but, all we need to do is get to either Kana or Onaris—just a few hours journey at speed, and we'll have power for communications."

"Assuming that the J400 coils haven't hit the Druries shit-can yet," Taara said.

"Yes. Bel, you said the coils from the *Demophalon John* have already been unmounted?"

"Three or four of them, though some appeared to be damaged."

"Well then, the Druries have done the hard part for us. The coils on a scouting ship are very difficult to remove without a proper dry-dock and tooling due to the smaller size and tight internal tolerances of the vessel. All we'd need do then is pop them into the *Seeker.*"

"It's that easy?" Stenstrom asked. "Just pop them in?"

"Well," Taara said jumping in, "a *Straylight* is designed to be able to change its coils in a battle-situation, so they're fairly easy to mount. A standard Fleet armada always had several V-7 *Antilles* barge-lifters along to do just that."

"Quite correct," Gwendolyn said, licking the sauce off her plate, obviously famished.

Stenstrom offered the rest of his portion of beef and noodles to Gwendolyn. "Here, Gwen, have the rest of mine. No, the hard part will be getting everyone past the Druries. They're everywhere down there, and there's the Kestrals as well. So, here's our task—We shall need a detail of qualified people to get the coils mounted on the *Seeker*. We shall also need someone to lead the rest of the crew and the Merians and civilians to safety aboard the *Seeker.*"

Gwendolyn put her plate aside. "I'll lead the coil detail. I'll need crewmen: Allistar, Novak, Sandyman, Flora, and Turkaluu to assist me."

"And I'll come with you," Taara chimed in. "We'll pop the covers and pull the plugs on coils 6 and 13—that should give us the optimum use of the reduced power output."

Gwendolyn marveled at Taara. "And, you say you've no engineering experience?"

"Not a bit."

"I'll be happy to learn how you have access to such detailed and accurate information. I agree with your assessment."

Stenstrom was pleased for Taara, that Gwendolyn offered her a compliment. "So it's done. Gwen, you wrangle the coils from the *Demophalon John*, and, Taara, you get the *Seeker* ready."

"Bel, how are we going to lift the coils? They weigh several tons each."

"The robotic arms. We'll commandeer some."

"Are we going to be able to operate the robotic arms?" Gwendolyn asked.

"I'll do it," Taara said. "I should be able to make something out of them."

"And I'll lead everybody else onto the ship," A-Ram said. "Where should I take them to?"

"Take them to the frontal section, decks four or five, and put them in various quarters. That area of the ship should be easy to defend from attackers and give the people a wealth of places to hide should hiding places be needed," Stenstrom said.

Morgan put her plate down. "If someone could get me to the ship's dispensary, I might be able to create a salve which will help ease the civilian's pain. And, when we get back to the League, we in the Ephysians have learned that the damage to skin elasticity and oil levels caused by prolonged exposure to a Kestral *Killanjo* Tank can be mitigated and reversed with a carefully treated soda bath infused with various salts. I'm confident these poor souls can be fully recovered and made whole provided we get them to the League soon."

Stenstrom nodded. "Good—well, I see no reason to delay. As soon as we finish up our meal, we're leaving. Let's not give the Druries time to mess up our coils. We can expect a minimum two mile walk ahead of us. Additionally, we'll need to descend three levels via the pipe holes I described earlier, cross the gangway into the dock area, and make quick entrance to the *Seeker.* The port frontal gangplank was down. When I was last there, the *Seeker* was empty. With any luck, that's still the case.

Taara finished up her meal. "What are you going to be doing, Bel?"

"I'm going to be diverting the Druries. I am going to create a fiasco and force them to come to me, giving you, with luck, time to move the coils."

"How are we going to recover you?" Gwendolyn asked.

"I'll recover myself. Don't worry about me. Get the ship working and get these people out of here, that's the main thing."

Taara got mad. "Bel, don't be stupid! We're not saving everybody else just to leave you behind. Think up another plan because that's not acceptable."

"It's all right, the docks must be a little closer to the surface. I got all my stuff back while I was there. I'll be fine."

Taara was skeptical. "I think you're lying, Bel. I think you're just saying what I want to hear."

"What 'stuff' are you referring to, Bel?" Gwendolyn asked.

"Never mind. And, I've no intention on marooning myself here—I'll get back to the ship on my own."

Stenstrom stood. "All right, it's near time. Let's get finished up. We're moving out."

Stenstrom led the group down the corridor, moving as quickly as they could. The Merians had made rudimentary slings out of their robes and from parts of the insta-meal boxes and were bringing the civilians along, dragging them mostly on the shiny surface of the floor—Stenstrom's pink Holystones keeping them as comfortable and quiet as possible. He was quite pleased by their progress. Taara trailed the group, with A-Ram and Lady Alesta shuttling back and forth making sure everybody stayed together.

Stenstrom carried Morgan-Jeterix. Though weak, rest and her meal seemed to be working wonders. She was smiling and alert.

"I think I rather could get used to this," she said as he carried her. "You're such a strong, handsome fellow."

Gwendolyn, walking nearby, rolled her eyes.

"How is your wound, ma'am?" Stenstrom asked.

"Please, call me Morgan, and it's fine. It's itching somewhat, which is a good sign. After nearly killing me, Gwendolyn did a good job of patching me back up."

Stenstrom looked back to see how the group was coming along. "If I may, you said your name is Morgan-Jeterix. What is 'Jeterix'? Does that mean something?"

She smiled. "It means 'I'm available'… in Thompson." She took one of her braids and waved at him with it. She looked at his collar. "Hmmm, HRN—what does that stand for I wonder—no, no, let me guess. 'H', is certainly for 'handsome', 'R' I'm guessing must be for 'ripped', and 'N' must stand for 'naughty'… Am I right?"

He laughed. She noticed his mask. "What is that mask you're wearing—I'm intrigued." She gently touched it with the tips of her fingers. "Oh, it would be like unwrapping a present. Ladies of Thompson are very forward, therefore, I'll ask you—Paymaster, are you spoken for?"

Gwendolyn interceded. "All right, Morgan, I believe the Paymaster has carried you long enough. He needs his hands free—we might be beset upon. Put her down, please."

"What for?" Morgan cried as Stenstrom put her down.

"I'll carry you, Morgan. As I nearly put one between your eyes, I owe it to you."

Gwendolyn knelt down and picked her up fireman-style, slinging her over her right shoulder, Morgan's rear-end sticking up in the air.

"I don't like this," she said into Gwendolyn's coattail. "I would like the Paymaster to continue carrying me. I'm going to get sick."

"Feel free to vomit, Morgan," Gwendolyn said, moving on at a brisk pace.

Sometime later, they reached the break in the wall to their left. Stenstrom called Gwendolyn, Taara, and A-Ram to look.

"Down there, through that round glass window, that's where the ships are currently berthed."

Gwendolyn peered over the railing. "I see the prow of the *Demophalon John* at dock."

"The *Seeker* is directly to her right. Now, see that gantry way a few levels beneath us?"

They saw it.

"That's how we're getting in. I shall precede the group, enter, and create a diversion. A-Ram, the port gangway is down, so get these people in and scatter them in the frontal area as quickly as you can. Gwen, how long do you think it will take to get the coils transferred?"

"Not long, assuming we can get those robotic arms working in our favor. Just a few minutes to swing them over and install them, and then about thirty minutes to get them calibrated. As soon as I finish, I'm joining you, Bel."

"No, Gwen—no. I'll be fine. You need to get yourself aboard."

Stenstrom resumed walking. "Come on. We've a bit farther to go."

They made it to the end of the corridor, and, after a great deal of effort, made it down three levels moving through the holes. Finally, the gantry way awaited.

"Here's where I leave you," Stenstrom said. "Remember, I'm depending on you to get these people safe, A-Ram. That's the main thing."

Gwendolyn wanted to say something, then Taara came forward, her little face in tears. She embraced him. "We're not leaving without you, Bel."

Alesta came forward, and he took her small hands. "How blessed we are," she said. "Just when my faith was at its lowest, our Star sends us you three. May the Star walk with you, Lord Belmont."

"And with you, Lady Alesta."

Gwendolyn approached.

"Paymaster Stenstrom, "Morgan-Jeterix said, grabbing his attention. He smiled and knelt down. "A moment, please."

"My Lady," he said.

She reached up, took him by the cheek, and kissed him on the lips. Then she whispered into his ear. "When I see you again, I'll tell you what 'Jeterix' means, okay?"

"It's a deal."

With that, Stenstrom withdrew and allowed the group to pass by and get into position. He watched them as they passed, looking intently at their faces, studying their features. He mused his mother once did the same thing as he and his sisters filed out of the grand dining hall every day, she would stand back and watch them all pass, saying nothing, just watching them go by. He always wondered what she was doing.

Now he understood. All these people, strangers only hours ago, now were his to keep safe. He drew his weapons and faded into the shadows, ready to go forth and defend them with his life.

Gwendolyn spun around, trying to see him in the shadows.

10

—"Hallo, Boys!"—

Stenstrom easily made his way back to the dock area. He climbed up to a high perch with a commanding view and assessed the situation.

Down below, he saw the two vessels. Many of the robotic arms he'd damaged around the *Demophalon John* still appeared to be down—several Lemmuels in attendance at the far end of the dock labored to fix them. Stenstrom noted they were having significant issues opening the maintenance panels—a few had been greatly mangled. Some were scorched by hot flames.

In front of the *Demophalon John*, the treaded cart carrying the coils had toppled over—they were stacked up four high nearby, and a Lemmuel was lying on his back trying to fix the cart, a surly Clem watching.

Chance Drury and the Kestrals were not in sight, and the *Seeker* appeared to be rather forgotten for the moment.

Well, he thought, no need to delay. He drew his NTHs, cocked the hammers and lined up a shot on Lemmuel.

Stenstrom hit him in the chest. He kicked out with his legs once or twice, dropped his tools, and went still.

Clem appeared to take no notice. He kept right on yelling at the now dead Lemmuel.

Stenstrom cocked again and got Clem in the back. He dropped into a sort of kneeling position and then fell into full prayer before the feet of the dead Lemmuel.

Two Druries down—at this point, the docks were fairly clear. He saw Taara, Gwendolyn, and several of her crew sneaking toward the *Demophalon John.* He saw two people Waft onto the port wing of the *Seeker.*

Good Creation, an Innocent was walking in their direction! They saw him and tried to take cover near the water's edge. He stopped and turned, having heard them.

Gwendolyn somehow got behind him and, with weapon drawn, sliced his head off with her rapier-like FEDULA—a weapon that appeared to do a lot more damage than a light rapier-like sword should be able to do.

Innocent pranced around headless, his array of antennae sprouting from his neck cavity. Stenstrom lined him up and fired, getting him in the chest where he fell. Gwendolyn and her team then, together, worked to hide his dead, heavy body. They roughly rolled him into the water with a plop.

Looking around, he saw the going clear as Taara began on one of the working robotic arms—good thing he didn't sabotage them all. They had the panel open and Taara was plunged into it, her red Marine coattails and the butt of her SK sticking out of the panel as she worked. He could see the lofty arm overhead swinging about in little, jerky stages as she fiddled with it.

The action on the docks so far had been an anticlimax. Stenstrom had expected nothing less than a chaotic melee on the docks. He had been anticipating slaughtering the Druries wholesale, and had readied himself for it. So far, the Druries were completely taken by surprise.

Taara appeared to have success. The robotic arm swung about under full control, extended and descended to the rear hull of the *Seeker*. Working in concert with the crew standing on the wing, the arm opened the Stellar Mach vent coverings. (the genius of the Straylight design allowed the vents to be opened from outside in a dry-dock situation, or be shut, locked and accessed from within). The vents swung open like the cover of a book. It took only a minute or two.

Next, Taara swung the arm down to dock level. Gwendolyn, still holding her FEDULA, approached the stack of coils and inspected them. She turned and said something to Taara.

The huge, towering arm came gently down. Per Gwendolyn's direction, Taara lifted off the coil stacked on top and set it aside. She then picked up the one that had been underneath it and turned it around, showing it to Gwendolyn, who carefully looked it over. Approving, Taara then hoisted it up, swung it over, and carefully placed it into position in Stellar Mach 6. She then gently closed the SM vent.

It was that easy. One down, one to go.

Taara brought the arm back to the dock. Gwendolyn dismissed the next coil, settling on the bottom one. Taara lifted it, showed it to her, and then hoisted it up.

"Whas' goin' on?" came a loud voice from below.

There was Innocent Drury on fast approach—Creation, Stenstrom had become mesmerized with watching the loading of the coils.

"Who're you?" he cried as Gwendolyn faced him with her FEDULA.

Stenstrom aimed and fired.

Missed.

Three Lemmuels appeared from their work and proceeded to that area of the dock at a run.

Stenstrom cocked and fired, getting one, and then another. They fell hard, one tumbling into the water with a rough splash.

Taara, using the robotic arm, swung it over and, still holding the coil, squashed the third Lemmuel roughly to the dock, little blue squares skittering away from his flattened body.

Gwendolyn and Innocent were in close quarters, and Stenstrom couldn't fire without possibly hitting her. She dropped her FEDULA and got behind him, using wrestling holds and grappling techniques to neutralize his considerable strength advantage.

They fell to the floor. Such a mismatch couldn't last, and Innocent managed to pry her off of him. He got her down and raised his arm to hit her. Such a blow would be her death.

He was knocked back a few steps—Taara unloaded a silenced burst from her SK into his chest and he toppled away from Gwendolyn. Clear, Stenstrom fired and got him in the back, dropping him. Some of the crew came out of their hiding places and helped Gwendolyn while Taara quickly swung the coil over to the *Seeker,* dropped it into SM position 13, and closed the vent.

That done, Taara brought the arm back down to the dock and positioned its massive fingers into a loose fist, where the crew climbed in and secured themselves. Gwendolyn and Taara joined them. Taara looked up and motioned for Stenstrom to come down and join them as well.

They froze.

Chance Drury appeared, followed by five Clems and an Innocent. They looked at the group huddled in the fingers of the robotic arm.

Stenstrom acted. "Hallo', boys!" he shouted loudly. "Did you miss me?"

All heads turned to him. Chance smiled a bit. "I assume I am speaking to Paymaster Stenstrom of the *Seeker*. *Je suis correct?*" Chance said in a clear voice.

"Aye!"

Chance considered his response. "What are you hoping to accomplish here, good sir? You must know you are in a desperate situation. For you and your people here, this docking bay is the pit of hell. *Usted quemará en ello.*"

"Is it? You were good enough to pay me a visit, so I thought I'd respond in kind."

Out of the corner of his eye, Stenstrom thought he could see a line of people moving toward the *Seeker*. They were difficult to see—invisible almost. The Merians' belt—they must be able to move invisibly when they wish and their faith was untested.

Stenstrom had to keep the Druries occupied—this was the critical moment.

"You feel like dying today, Chance? You know I am going to kill you, right?"

He laughed. "You do not seem to understand. We are eternal. We cannot be put to ground. Our hearts cannot be stopped, our voices cannot be silenced. *Besser als Sie haben versucht.*"

"But, you already are put to ground, dust-eater. You are dead, long dead, tainting the earth somewhere with your foulness—and I'll wager all the worms that had the misfortune to feed upon your carcass probably died of a stomach ache. You and your three uncouth brothers died four hundred years ago, and, even when you were alive, you weren't really men, were you—you were cowering jackals, feasting on the weak and the helpless while tucking tail and running full flight from anyone who showed an ounce of strength. Now, look at you—nothing more than a bit of bad data, imprinted and downloaded. You are four tin cans playing at being men, dreaming of foul things, and I am going to see you to an end once and for all!"

Chance had a good chuckle. "A-heheh. *C'est un fait?* That bipedal, flesh-and-blood lung sack you're wearing is overrated in my mind. And, let's be honest, you are just as much a robot as I am." He glanced at the people in the robotic arm. "Are these your fellows here, your devotees—they must be. I am going to order them abused, *viole*, and then order them slain … right now, all while you watch. Clem, fetch that lot!"

The robotic arm suddenly began moving by itself—Taara apparently prepared a pre-recorded sequence for the arm to follow. The arm lifted them high into the air and swung them over the *Seeker*.

Chance, quick as could be, worked his hands and created a long lance of yellow squares. Before Stenstrom could react, he hurled the lance at the robotic arm, its tail fire lighting in midair. The people cradled in the arm's fist jumped out and fell onto the *Seeker's* wing just as the lance struck the arm and exploded like a missile, rocking the arm on its long mount.

Stenstrom lined his guns up and fired.

Missed, Chance ducked away. He fired again, going for Chance as the Clems and Innocent moved about in confusion. Chance was a slippery customer, and appeared to guard his existence carefully. He ducked, moved away, and ducked again, allowing Clem to take one in the chest for him.

Ah!—Chance was cornered by a pier—his head swiveling in fright. Stenstrom cocked, aimed and fired.

The hammer fell. Nothing happened!

Damn! The cinnabar striker was cracked. He aimed with the other pistol and fired, getting Innocent. Chance made a break for it. He ripped out of his clothes on the run, assuming his blocky robotic form, his cluster of yellow squares buzzing about in an agitated state on his robotic frame.

Stenstrom replaced his striker with a fresh cinnabar from his coat and resumed firing. He hit Chance in the arm, and again in the shoulder—yellow squares fell away. Again, in this decentralized form, the NTH couldn't kill him at a shot.

Chance stopped, and formed two long lances of yellow squares. He then hurled them in Stenstrom's direction. He could see the tips of the lances blinking and their heat trails as they honed in on him.

He hauled himself over the side and plummeted as the lances exploded above him.

"He's there, he's there!" Chance yelled in a robotic voice. Clems, Innocents, and a horde of Lemmuels poured onto the dock from all quarters.

Stenstrom returned to the shadows. He gunned down one Drury after the next, the dock becoming quickly littered with their fallen bodies. Colorful squares of red, green and blue, like children's blocks, mingled.

"Where'd he go?" Clem cried.

"Use your antennas, you ponderous slugs!" Chance roared in his robotic voice. "Find him! Kill him!" Of all the Druries, Chance seemed the most at peace with being a robot, while the others appeared to prefer to stay man-shaped, as if to convince themselves that they really were men, not robots.

Several Innocents expanded into pulsating green masses, their head screens unfurling and antennas popping out.

"Thar' he is!" Innocent screamed, his cluster of antennae turning in Stenstrom's direction.

Stenstrom fired at his head screen, where it immediately went dead. Innocent staggered about and fell, his green squares abandoning his body frame like rats from a sinking ship.

Behind them, Stenstrom saw, just for a moment, the main sensor on the *Seeker* light up and then snap back off.

Come on, Gwendolyn, get that ship working!

He continued his barrage. Druries were falling like lead weights.

There was an angry clamor from behind him.

Druries were now pouring out of the assembly area, some were clothed, others nude, and some were in their robotic shape. Additionally, the tiny squares fleeing the Druries whom he'd blinded were coming together in a colonial fashion, forming rudimentary, inchworm-like constructs of red, blue, and green squares. Stenstrom saw several of the inchworms forming on the dock.

"Hay, chingado! Do not allow the rogue cells to form together, they might create an Intelledrone!" Chance cried.

Some of the Druries ceased their attack and began stepping on the inchworms or pulling them apart. A Clem picked up a particularly large one, its tail wrapping around his neck.

Stenstrom fired, killing Clem, where he and the colorful, wormlike robot fell into the water.

The caustic scene Stenstrom had envisioned had finally arrived. Druries were everywhere, and they were all spoiling for his hide, the dock filling with the sounds of cursing, splashings, slapping metallic feet, and booming explosions.

But, as he had hoped, all eyes were on him—the *Seeker* was clear, and his people were aboard.

Chance and ten Clems appeared to be directing the action from the rear. The Clems were creating a steady stream of red, lance-like missiles and were firing them off in quick style. Explosions blossomed.

Stenstrom could not stay where he was. He gunned down two naked Clems and made his way toward the *Demophalon John*.

He climbed the side and got on top of it, raining shots down on them. Fired lances came up at him in answer, where they exploded against the side of the *Demophalon John*, the sturdy ship able to ward off the brunt of the explosion. Lemmuels climbed up after him—he gunned them back down. They stubbornly clung to their man-shape, which he could kill with a shot. Several robotic Clems came up, all blocky and red, and he shot their head screens, blinding them, their squares scattering off and falling into the water.

Stenstrom was cornered. Druries everywhere, a steady barrage of missiles incoming. There wasn't much left for him to do but plunge into the water and start swimming.

He jumped, seeing a long fall in front of him.

Something seized him by the coat. He was hauled back, spun overhead, and slammed to the hull.

Things spun around. He thought he could see a Lemmuel standing over him, the hem of his coat in his hand.

Stenstrom raised and fired, hitting Lemmuel in the gut where he dropped. A Clem fell on him. He raised his fist and rocked Stenstrom in the right shoulder blade. He dimly felt and heard a number of bones break with the hit. He wretched blood.

Innocent stood over him. "Oh, whas' the matter, Gov? Thought you was strong?"

He reared up and brought his foot down on the back of Stenstrom's leg.

His knee collapsed and his thigh bone splintered.

"Bring him to me!" Chance squealed from below. "Bring him here! Bring him here now!"

Clem picked the shattered Stenstrom up and threw him down to the dock, where he fell into the water.

Two Lemmuels roughly fished him out. Dripping, he was thrown down on the dock.

Chance approached, a buzzing collection of yellow squares. Now that Stenstrom appeared to be hopelessly quelled, Chance compressed back into man-form. His head screen rolled up and descended into his chest. The myriad of yellow squares flipped around, sliding compactly into place. Flesh oozed. Soon, a scrawny, naked Chance stood there. A Clem came to his side and draped a coat over him, which he held shut with his right hand.

Overhead, two golden crow-like creatures flapped down and landed on his shoulder. The Kestrals.

"Good Paymaster," Chance said in a soft, almost tender voice, "well met, again." He took a deep breath. "Oh, dear, you made a good showing of it, I'll say." He looked around at the piles of fallen Druries. He moved his hands and created a long barb from yellow squares.

"Better watch him, Chance," Innocent said. "He was real strong on his ship."

"Yes, I recall that, a-heheh. He tore my hands clean off, didn't he? You say we're robots—you looked rather robotic yourself as we battled. I clearly recall another fellow who once did the same thing. You may have heard of him, his name was Darius Jones. I can remember his face, plain as day, and you say I'm a robot, for I have my memories just like you have yours. The thing of it is, as I recall, on the surface Darius Jones could do a number of remarkable things—however, way down here, under the sea, under the stone, he couldn't really do much of anything, except cook, for which he had a delicate touch, ah-hehehe. Something about the stars gave him power. I'm assuming it's much the same with you. Too bad."

He glanced back at the *Seeker.* "Clem, take a group to the *Seeker.* Board her, scour her, and kill any you find. I've a suspicion our friend here has freed our Trogs."

"What about the crew for the *Seeker?*"

"We'll hook-in others. No, no, this current lot dies. *Entiendo?*"

"Aye!" Clem turned to Stenstrom and drove his arm down on his shattered shoulder. "I'll save ya' a leg or two, Gov! Camon', boys!"

A group trundled off in a laughing gaggle, spitting on Stenstrom as they passed.

Chance smiled. "So then, Paymaster, I must consider this carefully. What can I do to cause you the maximum distress? *Les choix.*"

He took several steps forward, using his yellow barb as a walking stick. He poked Stenstrom once or twice with it. "What say you? Any thoughts?"

He hauled back and chopped Stenstrom's right hand off at the wrist. "There, a hand for a hand, seems only fair, wouldn't you say?"

Stenstrom reacted very little. He just lay there, spewing blood. His fingers twitched.

Chance continued. "I suppose the gratuitous spectacle of letting you watch your fellows aboard the *Seeker* die holds sway—has the maximum shock value. Then, I think I could do with putting you in the tank and turning you into my own personal *Killanjo* slave. That has great appeal, I must admit—though you shall be of limited use with only one hand."

Chance's eyes lit up. "Ohhhh, *je l'ai!* I know. We'll set up a little ring here on the on the dock, and force your fellows to fight each other to the death—that always makes for great sport. You'd be surprised how life-long friends turn on each other when confronted by such a quaint topic as death. It is really quite a thing to see."

Chance turned to several Lemmuels. "Clear a space for these people. We're going to have a show. Clem!" he barked.

"Aye!" came a response.

"On, second thought, bring any you find to me!"

"We're not findin' nobody!"

"They're there. Keep looking. *Chcę ich przy życiu!*"

As several Lemmuels began clearing a squared-off space on the dock, the Kestrals took flight.

They transformed into two, toga-clad females. They strode up to Stenstrom. One of them picked up his trembling body and closely examined him.

"In fells he come, we?" one of them said. The Kestrals spoke in gibberish.

"I detect he has a destroyed collarbone and shoulder, along with a shattered right knee and femur-bone, and he's missing a hand. He is no longer a threat," Chance answered.

"Tatters and whey?" the Kestral said in their usual incomprehensible manner. The Kestrals mumbled something else.

"Yes, Elders are rather fragile," Chance replied. "Very poor construction."

The Kestral picked up his severed hand and ate it whole, crunching it up and then swallowing. She then began digging about in Stenstrom's broken shoulder. He squirmed slightly, in muted agony.

The Kestral found a large piece of shattered bone, and began trying to pull it out of the wound.

He stifled a pain-clogged shriek.

From the tower of the *Seeker*, a bullet-shaped ship came blasting out. It circled, overhead. A Clem fell headless from the ship and splashed into the water.

The *Westminster!* Stenstrom could see A-Ram's large hat through the front glass.

"Pour l'amour do Dieu! Destroy that vessel!" Chance cried, ducking for cover.

Lances of red, green, and blue went up. The tiny ship rose and fell to avoid them.

The hatch opened, and a figure came leaping down. Steel flashed and the Kestral fell, quickly dissolving into amber goo.

Stenstrom weakly looked. It was Gwendolyn and her FEDULA.

She came to Stenstrom's side and tried to pull him up.

The other Kestral reacted badly. *"Puddling,"* she said. She raised her hand and a red cone of light shot out, bathing Gwendolyn in it.

She dropped her FEDULA and screamed.

Chance watched with glee. "Burn her, burn her up! Ah-hehehe!!"

Gwendolyn dropped to her knees.

Then three silver daggers entered the Kestral's arm and chest.

Three MARZABLES from Stenstrom. He let three more fly, getting her in the trunk.

The Kestral stood there looking at the daggers sticking out of her.

He shook his good hand and three more MAZARBLES appeared. He threw them, piercing the Kestral three times in the forehead.

She appeared a bit puzzled, then fell apart into an amber mess.

He crawled to Gwendolyn's side. She was slightly smoking.

And there was Chance. He reached down and picked them both up by the scruff of the neck. "I really didn't like them anyway," he said shaking their bodies. "You have done me a nice favor, actually. Now, with that lot gone, we can truly lay some terror on the League, can't we? We'll raise an army of skinless demons and sail out in ghost ships. We'll hit Kana hard and split the League in two, fading back to the shadows whenever we like."

The *Westminster* came around and dropped height, skimming the docks and plowing into a host of Druries, flattening some, knocking others into the water. Chance raised up Stenstrom and Gwendolyn and presented them. "I have your people, here! I'll kill them nice as you please!"

The *Westminster* banked away, and was struck by a red lance. It smoked, was hit again and crashed into the water.

11
—The Star's Revenge—

Chance gave a cry of victory. Stenstrom was thrown to the floor, surrounded by a gallery of Druries who whooped and laughed. Innocent stepped forward and gave him a hard kick to the midsection sending him flying.

"Yeah, mate… this is gonna' be jus' grand. I've got lots a' plans for you. We're gonna' be real chums `fore long."

He kicked him again.

"Leave him alone!" Gwendolyn screamed, reaching out for him. Several Lemmuels held her down, and one kicked her smoking FEDULA away.

They laughed. "Oh, I hear a lady cryin' out for a little attention! You feelin' hungry, Paymaster?" Lemmuel asked.

"He looks real hungry," Clem said.

Lemmuel brandished a small knife. "Well then, let's feed `im!"

Gwendolyn struggled, but they held her down. Lemmuel pulled her coat and shirt away revealing skin. He began cutting, Gwendolyn screamed.

As the army of Druries closed in, something caught their attention high above.

"What in the name of Green Grass is that?" Chance said, leaning back, mouth open.

High above, something floated. It was some sort of round globe, yellowish, wreathed in an undulating column of hissing red smoke.

Stenstrom glanced at it—it looked, from his sister's frequent description, like the Star of Merian.

They looked up at it, incredulous.

"For my children…" an ethereal voice said. *"whom you so cruelly murdered…"*

The chamber filled with a twisting funnel of fog. The Druries were making a terrible racket, yet the whole place fell into an unnatural calm as the fog took hold.

It's the road, the Merian's Road, Stenstrom thought.

High above, through the fog, four gleaming points of bluish light appeared.

Four stars in a rectangular constellation shone down bathing in dock in starry light.

Camalopardus.

Stenstrom was filled with starlight, and his smashed body became whole once again with the Sisters' Power. His bones were mended, his hand regrown. With the Sisters' might, he threw off the Druries and knocked them away from Gwendolyn. He took Innocent to the ground and utterly destroyed him. Alone, he flew into their ranks, toppling them blow after blow.

He tore at them, pulling them apart, smashing them to bits.

He ripped the manufactured flesh from their bodies and hung them with it.

Robotic arms and legs, sculpted heads, and colored squares piled high on the dock in a mountain of metal and wire viscera.

The Druries had never known such terror.

Chance went running. He headed down the dock moving as fast as he could. "Kill the woman! Kill the woman!" he shrieked.

The Druries came at Gwendolyn, trying to get to her. Stenstrom stood over her, smashing, destroying.

A Clem created a lance, reared back and threw it. It sped toward Gwendolyn.

Stenstrom caught it in flight, spun it around and threw it back toward Clem. It exploded.

There was a rumbling from the water. A towering creature made of a patchwork of red, green, and blue squares burst into the air. Metal tentacles reached upward, grasping the remains of the *Demophalon John* and the pole-mounted robotic arms mounted on the dock.

"Good Creation! Intelledrone!" a Clem yelled. "It's a big one! Get it, kill it—It'll be the end of us all!"

The Druries turned their attention to the robotic beast and made to engage it in battle. Tentacles came down, screaming Druries were lifted and pulled into the water.

Two crewmen Wafted onto the dock near Stenstrom in a cloud. He picked Gwendolyn up and handed her to them. "She's wounded. Get the lieutenant and any in the *Westminster* back into the *Seeker!* Get the ship out of here by any means you can!" he shouted, and they bore her away.

The battle at the water's edge was desperate and near hopeless. The raging robotic monster in the water was rapidly getting bigger. It reached up and snapped the poles mounting the robotic arms like twigs. It then consumed the arms, adding them to itself, the huge fingers of the arms opening and closing, infused with a new colonial consciousness.

The Druries assailed it with exploding lances, blowing large pieces of it off, only to have those pieces replaced almost instantly.

It seized the bullet-shaped hull of the *Westminster* and set to work on it. Stenstrom thought he saw the expansion of a Waft cloud in the cockpit as the robotic monster incorporated the ship into itself, the hull being plopped on like a rudimentary head.

The giant Intelledrone reached out with its metal tentacles and seized the flailing, screaming Chance Drury. Stenstrom stood and watched with pleasure as it commenced to beat his body roughly against the hull of the *Westminster*. It reminded him of Lt. Kilos from his *New Faith* days, and how she had a bad habit of cracking walnuts with her forehead in the mess.

Bang, bang, bang! Chance Drury's robot body fell apart into a host of yellow squares instantly absorbed by the Intelledrone.

Explosion after explosion rocked its growing body. With flailing metal tentacles, it seized one Drury after another and pulled them apart, taking the tiny robots making up their bodies and adding them onto itself.

Through the chaotic din of shouting and monstrous bellowing, another sound came to the front, a great whistling roar from nowhere growing louder and more throaty with every passing moment threatening to deafen all on the dock. There was only one thing that made such a terrible, glorious sound.

It was the *Seeker*, its engines spinning up, its dormant systems coming live and proud. Its main sensor came to a dim but steady glow lighting up the dock. It strained against the shackles the Druries had thrown across it, throwing them aside, freeing itself. The *Seeker* had been mute and silent since the

Admiralty had scuttled her, now she would roar.

Stenstrom listened and watched the ship break free. Now, whatever happened to him on the dock didn't matter. He had done his job, his people were safe.

He found his lost NTHs and put them back into his sash. Let these monstrosities consume each other. Good riddance in any case, and he could only hope the Druries suffered mightily in the process.

He saw something come running back out of the assembly room. It was a boxy, funnel-breasted robot with the word DUNCE painted on its torso. It was running fast on spindly legs, sort of high-stepping, knee-kicking as it ran.

It was Chance Drury, back again, wearing the DUNCE body, it had to be him, for it carried itself like Chance did. Apparently no other bodies were left for him to wear.

"To the *Heade!* Get to the *Heade!*" several Clems screamed.

"No!" Chance yelled in a panic from the DUNCE's latex mouth. "You stand here and fight this beast! I shall go to the *Heade!*"

He was carrying four metal tablets, each one stained red, blue, green, and yellow, which he clutched to his soup-can breast as though they were precious. He headed for the levels above at a high-stepping run.

Those tablets must be the source code information for reconstituting the Druries.

"Chance!" Stenstrom roared, following at a run. Climbing a ladder, Stenstrom saw him standing at a large control panel. Pressing buttons, he opened a set of doors somewhere high above and a wall of water at high pressure came rushing into the docks, ready to wash away any standing in its path. He then turned and ran into a long corridor.

Stenstrom was hot on his heels. He entered the corridor just in time to see a door closing at the far end. He charged, covering the distance quickly, and crashed through it. Through the door was a small control-room with a chair and numerous monitors. There was a hinged, yellow device sitting on the floor. As Stenstrom entered, it came to life and sprang shut, like a loaded mousetrap and then exploded, devastating the room. When the smoke cleared, the room was destroyed, the door had been blown off its frame, the control desk melted to slag and was on fire;, however, Stenstrom appeared fine and unfazed—even his clothes seemed untouched.

He could hear the powerful rushing of water behind him. The place was rapidly flooding.

There was a burning staircase at the far side of the room. Stenstrom ran up them. Atop the stairs was a short hallway paneled in silvery metal.

He topped the stairs and ran down the hallway. The hallway opened up into a dock, similar to the one below, only it was much smaller.

There, mounted on a robotic sling, was the *Heade-on-the-Hearth*. He saw DUNCE-Chance clattering up the gangway, arms and legs flailing as he ran, carrying his tablets. His blonde wig fell off and floated on the water.

The gangway closed and quickly, the strange ship coiled and came to life, like a rank warhorse confined in a tiny stall.

He saw a bank of guns mounted on the *Heade's* port side rotate in his direction. He dove out of the way as a hail of explosive fire splintered the doorway.

Behind him, a surge of water came rushing in as the dock quickly began to flood. He thrashed through the water. He reached out and found the girders of the *Heade*. He locked on and gripped hard as a set of doors opened ahead. With a clank, the ship surged out of the flooded dock and soared down a tight, twisting tunnel. The tunnel suddenly headed upward as Stenstrom held on for dear life. He became vaguely aware that the *Heade* was consistently smashing against the side of the tunnel in an obvious attempt to scrape him off. He could feel the pressure of the ship against his body and the roughness of the tunnel wall.

Ahead, a pressure hatch opened with a dark stain of water suspended high above via containment. At speed, his coat flapping like a flag in a stiff breeze, the *Heade* surged through the containment into the pitch black of the water.

The lights went out, and Stenstrom felt the crushing squeeze of hundreds of feet of water on top of him. He could see the occasional flash of strobe lights mounted on the *Heade* and the bluish glow from the engines. The water felt rather warm as he surged up through the depths. Warm blackness turned to gray, to a greenish-blue, to an eruption out of the water into the stormy sky.

The *Heade* quickly gained altitude as Stenstrom hung on. Having no issue maintaining his purchase on the ship, he began hand-over-handing to make his way to the crew capsule about seventy feet ahead.

He could hear the rush of wind and the roar from the engines as the ship rocketed skyward. He pulled off several large pieces of girder and tossed it down into the intake of the nearest engine.

The engine sputtered and flashed. He tore off more metal and tossed it in.

The engine exploded.

The vessel leveled off at several thousand feet and descended a bit. Stenstrom pulled more pieces off of the ship and threw them aside as he climbed forward, ripping off a thruster and other assorted bits.

The *Heade* lowered to about a hundred feet above the water and slowed to a near stop, the damaged engine smoking in an inky manner.

Something in the water below caught his attention.

A huge, dark mass formed in the water. Something leapt out, spanning high into the air. It was coal black, streaming with water. It was long and tubular, like a massive earthworm about ten feet wide and an unknown length long. It had a round, flattened head with a circular, tooth-ringed mouth like a hagfish, and its serrated, ivory-white teeth stood out from its dead-black body. It had an unbroken ring of red, beady eyes placed in a line just behind its mouth.

That's a Cronyn, Stenstrom thought as the nightmare creature approached, mouth open. *I'm about to be eaten by a Cronyn!*

The Cronyn came up quick, gurgling, and it took Stenstrom and a fair portion of the *Heade* in a single bite.

12

—Words with the Cronyns—

He felt a commotion of deforming metal and sucking innards as he slid into the deep belly of the Cronyn.

He saw an image of his father and his sister, Lyra, sitting in his study.

The NTHs can slay anything… no matter how huge and powerful… his father had said.

In the slimy mess, he reached down and found his NTHs. He pulled them, cocked and fired. Surely such a vast beast would not be harmed by his tiny pistols, LosCapricos or not.

After a minute or two, he decided to try and crawl out. He moved past the bitten-off girders of the *Heade* and moved into what looked like a tooth-lined gullet. He saw gray light and a row of impressive-looking triangular teeth ahead. He was able to stand and he splashed through the ankle-deep water.

He emerged at the Cronyn's mouth. The thing was dead—it had to be. It floated at the water's surface like a long, slack balloon, its black body, hundreds of feet long, bobbed with the indifference of death.

He was impressed. *The NTHs can slay pretty much anything.*

He climbed up and stood atop the creature. He was all alone, the ugly sky threatening to storm overhead. He looked around. The *Heade* was nowhere to be seen.

He checked himself out. He seemed fine—his destroyed shoulder and knee were completely repaired. His hand, regrown, looked just like his hand should. Even his HRN coat, having been blown-up, smashed and scraped against the tunnel wall, appeared unharmed.

Off in the distance, he thought he could see something sticking out of the water, something wing-like and metallic.

Wait …was that the wing of the *Seeker?*

Yes, yes, it was the *Seeker*, and by the angle it was protruding from the water, she was rolled over to her starboard side, mostly flooded and submerged.

He looked down at the water, there was debris everywhere, flotsam from the now flooded Kestral tank far below.

And, there were bits of the *Seeker* too, pieces of metal … and bodies.

There were bodies everywhere.

No, no …what had happened?

He saw a Pilgrim of Merian floating face down, and some crewmen. There was a blue coat mixed in and a dead face. Was it … Gwendolyn?

He dropped down into the water. He pulled her up, her face white and puffy, her eyes sullen in the rectus of death.

"Oh, Gwen," he said stroking her drenched hair, "what happened? I saw the ship, you had her ready to go. I saw it light up."

He embraced her dead body, as water slopped out of her lolled mouth. Her drenched hair was a mess. She wouldn't like that—she'd want to be presentable. He smoothed her hair with his hand and straightened her lieutenant's collar. He arraigned the beaded Merian necklace hanging at her throat.

Her necklace.

Wait …

He looked down. He was still wearing the necklace she had given to him. Alesta was going to give him a Merian necklace to put on, but Gwen wanted him to wear hers.

Wear mine, Bel, she had said, offering it to him as a gift.

Here it was around his neck.

And there it was around hers as well. She hadn't gotten another one yet—she didn't have one as they departed.

Thunder and lightning …

Alesta said the Merian's necklace can protect one from the unreal.

Pelting rain …

"This is a trick;, it isn't real." He held Gwendolyn to him. "This isn't real!"

Illusions …

Bobbing on the water.

He reached up and took the necklace into his hand. "Get out of my mind, Cronyns …"

He gripped the necklace hard. "Get out!"

CRACK!

He was standing on the dead body of a Cronyn, that was rapidly sinking into the storm-tossed sea. Thunder crashed and long strokes of lightning lit up the bloated sky at frequent intervals. Huge waves pounded into its black body. Its mouth, open in death, was filling with each passing wave.

Stenstrom was hanging onto one of the dead Cronyn's teeth. Around him, black masses moved through the water.

One approached. It broke the water and reared up, towering overhead—the black, wormlike segments, the open mouth. The teeth. The eyes.

Stenstrom aimed and fired both his NTHs. The shots hit the gigantic Cronyn. It immediately gave a deflating sort of groan and fell back into the water with terrifying slap, creating a huge wave that nearly pitched him into the torrent.

Another Cronyn came out of the water, this time showing only the crest of its back.

Stenstrom killed it just the same.

The storm raged, causing the dead Cronyn bodies to nudge against each other in the whitewash.

Suddenly, he was no longer floating on the wind-whipped water. He was a little boy, back in the middle of his old dream—back in the sand pit behind the Belmont Manor with Lady Vendra's spring-loaded trap.

His sisters, Lyra and Virginia, were there, staring at him.

"What is this?" he said in a boy's voice, hardened a bit with maturity.

Lyra looked at him and spoke. *"We wish to talk …"* Her mouth was full of row after row of serrated teeth.

Cronyn teeth.

"Why have you brought me here? Why this dream?"

"Because you have never left this place. You remain here to this day. You should have died in this sand pit."

"Yet, I did not. Are you trying to frighten me?"

"We simply wish to talk," Virginia said. The image looked like her, but

it didn't act like her in any way. And, there were her teeth, off-color, serrated, rowed.

"There is nothing to talk about! I am going to slay every one of you, as you see I can easily do!"

"Why do you wish to kill us?"

"Why? Because you are evil. Look what you have done? You just tried to kill me three times."

"You were attacked, you defended yourself. We bear you no malice for that. We are not evil, nor are we unreasonable. We live here in this place, we raise our children in the depths. We love our children. We simply wish to survive. We must eat too—our children must eat. Do you deny any living creature the right to exist, to fairly hunt for food?" Virginia said.

"Is this the lament you gave to Darius Jones centuries ago, when he came to kill you as well?"

"It is not a lament, it is simply the truth—it was true then and it is true now. Darius Jones understood. Here we exist as sentient beings, with bellies that need filling, just as your belly needs filling. We have harmed no one in centuries, save for what was brought to us as fair game," Lyra said.

"You invaded our minds, tortured us with vivid dioramas."

"Aye, that is an aspect of our feeding, true enough. We give to those we feed upon what they want most to sustain them."

"What about the people on Bazz whom your illusions killed? What about the crew of the *Demophalon John*—I could hear them screaming."

"We cannot know how beings shall react when confronted with their greatest wants. We attempt to be kind, however, we do not overly concern ourselves with it. Are you not humane to your cattle as well? We shall offer you fair trade..." Virginia said.

"Trade, what do you have to trade? I have you by the hip, and I'll chase you into the depths if I have to."

"Your ship, and the lives nurtured within—we have it 'by the hip', as you say. We will give you your ship, and you may take it and go. And then we will vanish, and you shall not find us again."

"My ship?"

"Yes, even now it is struggling to the surface. We could easily sink her,

a mispressed button here, an opened airlock there—the odd necklaces they wear will not protect them from all of us in concert," Lyra said.

They stood there looking at him standing in the sand.

"What say you, 'Man like Darius Jones'?" Lyra asked. *"Our lives for their lives, an even trade of goods."*

Stenstrom thought about it. He looked behind him, to the soft sand where he knew hiding just beneath the surface was a deadly trap. "Shall I walk away, knowing there is death lurking beneath the sand just waiting for the unwary to spring it? Will I have blood on my hands if I let you go?"

He thought some more. "I do hear validity in what you say, and I do not actively try to be a hypocrite. You do have the right to live."

He took a step back into the pit.

SNAP!! The trap lurched out of the sand. He held the trap open with his tiny hands, slowly mangling the metal. "And we have the right to resist being hunted, and to know of the dangers that exist. I shall alert my people what lurks here, and I cannot predict their response."

"Do what you will—that is your right. Then it is agreed. Take your ship and be away. Be at your guard, however, for we shall continue to hunt and you shall not find us here again."

Virginia smiled, and it was hideous. *"Perhaps one day we shall play again, 'Man like Darius Jones', and perhaps it shall be you making the bargains next time, and not we."*

The dream ended. Stenstrom was back in the stormy sea. Not much of the dead Cronyn remained above water. He leapt to one of the nearby dead ones and stood on top.

The black masses moving through the water came up for a moment in dripping, towering lines, and then dove deep and were gone.

Stenstrom stood there for a few minutes as the dead Cronyn steadily became waterlogged.

In the far distance, he became aware of a small but growing pool of light on the storm-battered surface of the water. A circle od dim, green light appeared, strengthening to gray and then white as the *Seeker* crashed nose first from the water about a thousand yards away, its brightly lit main sensor making a long, rain-clogged beam in front of it. The nose splashed back down in a cascade of white water as the wings surfaced and settled. He could see lights glittering in the tower section and the running beacons strobing on the wings. He could hear the engines screeching as they came up to compression—even so far away the noise it made was considerable. The nose of the ship came about and caught Stenstrom and the bobbing bodies of the Cronyns in its powerful beam. Scanning laser lights came on.

The *Seeker* turned and approached, plowing through the water, getting bigger by the moment. Stenstrom then launched himself from the Cronyn's body and soared into the air. He landed on the soaked hull in the frontal section, found a hatch and banged on it.

The hatch opened a few minutes later and there was Taara, Gwendolyn and a few crewmen.

"Elder's Balls!" Taara cried. "Bel!"

She came forward trying to grab him. "I'm all wet, Taara," he said, dripping as he climbed down.

"I don't give a shit!" she cried, throwing her arms around him with a splat. "Holy Gallicons, it's good to see you!"

Gwendolyn too came forward. "We thought you lost! Oh, we thought you lost!" she said hugging him around the neck. She gave him a soft kiss on the cheek. "Welcome home, Bel."

"You were wounded, Gwen, on the dock. Are you all right?"

"I'm fine now, Bel. I'm fine."

They made their way to the bridge. It was utterly strange for Stenstrom, seeing lights and crewmen walking about the corridors after the lightless, silent journey they'd had so far.

"Taara and I have tried to assign the crew to places where they might serve best. They're not overly familiar with a *Straylight* vessel, but they should do fine. I'm assuming you'll be wanting to conscript them aboard at once."

"Sure will. What's the status of the ship?"

"We were able to gen up some power while at dock, enough to run the gas compression engines and escape the depths, however, we still need to properly calibrate the coils—we'll not make orbit without the coils in calibration," Gwendolyn said.

"How long before we can make sail?"

"About half an hour. I've several crew working on it even as we speak."

"Sounds good. Go ahead and take whomever you need to help you. I'm to the bridge."

Gwendolyn looked like she wanted him to follow her for a moment, and then ran off, grabbing a few crewmen along the way.

Stenstrom continued to the bridge, Taara following.

"How did you get out of the docks?" he asked.

"It was rough, Bel—that big monster down there was ripping things up hard. It ate just about all of the Druries and then started working on the remains of the *Demophalon John*, pulling it down and eating it too. Then, the big bastard turned to us."

"What happened?"

"A-Ram drove the ship backwards out of the docking bay, smashing through a few a retaining barriers along the way. The monster started chasing us through the water but got smashed up as the place began to collapse. That was a Bazz-sized monster. He's probably still down there making a mess."

They got to the lift and Stenstrom went to pry the door open.

"What are you doing, silly?" Taara asked as she pressed the button and the door opened in an easy slide.

"Sorry, old habits die hard."

They arrived at the bridge and the doors slid open. On the bridge was a soft layer of chatter. A-Ram was standing at the helm, and several crewmen were manning the various sensing positions, there were even a few Merians present lending a hand. The odd screens Lemmuel had installed were still there on the Missive's panel, only now they were lighting up with data—several crew were leaning over the panels trying to figure out what was being displayed. Someone stood at the Com, trying to get familiar with it. Lady Alesta was sitting in the captain's chair, looking back at A-Ram.

Just like Countess Sygillis used to do ...

Taara walked out of the lift. "Captain on the bridge!" she said proudly.

All eyes turned to Stenstrom.

"Creation, it's good to see you, Bel!" A-Ram said.

Stenstrom clapped him on the shoulder. "And you. Well done getting the ship out of there in one piece, A-Ram."

"It was touch and go for a bit, but here we are. This is one tough old bird."

Stenstrom turned to the crewmen and addressed them. "Well, I don't know your names, as of yet, but you all are most certainly welcome here. If you don't know who I am, my name is Paymaster Stenstrom, Lord of Belmont-South Tyrol. I am the captain of this ship. I have conscripted Lt. Gwendolyn to the position of ship's engineer, and she's working at this moment to get the ship operational. I would like to dully conscript all of you as well—if any have issue with the conscription, you may disembark once we get back to the League, but I would like to make it clear that I could use every one of you, and if you wish to be conscripted, then your service shall be most appreciated."

"I wish to serve, sir," one of the crew said.

"That goes for me too," someone else said.

"And me as well!"

Stenstrom quieted them down. "I know you have all been through a great deal, as have we all. We've wounded and our clear task is to return to the League as quickly as possible to get them the immediate medical aid they so desperately need. If I had my druthers, I'd rather hunt down Chance Drury, sink his rotten carcass and be done with him. However, that task is for the Fleet—we have to look to our own here first."

Stenstrom looked around. "So, let's set to it!"

The crew shouted in unison.

"Right! As soon as Lt. Gwendolyn gives us the go ahead, we're making sail."

The crew resumed what they were doing. A-Ram leaned forward and whispered to Alesta. "You're sitting in his chair ..."

She looked startled. "Oh! Oh, I didn't mean to—"

Stenstrom put his hands on her shoulders. "You're fine where you are, my lady. Sit. Be comfortable."

She smiled up at him. "I'm not surprised you are returned to us. I knew the Star would keep you safe—I told Rammy, he was frantic for your safety. I told him."

Stenstrom made his way around the bridge, meeting each of the crew, shaking their hands. He got to the Com. "So, who do we have here?" Stenstrom asked.

"Crewman Clement, sir," the brown-headed man said, shaking his hand. "This is a great pleasure, Captain. We all have heard so much about you, and, I must admit, I felt relieved being with you in the Tank. I was certain you would successfully lead us out. I am a gentleman of Mystery. I was the junior Com aboard the *Demophalon John*, but, the Com on a *Straylight* is much different, more complex. I'm doing my best to get up to speed."

"I'm positive you'll do just fine. Do we have any communications at present?"

"Aye, sir, that we do."

Stenstrom was taken aback—still used to nothing working. "Wow, well then, please send to all Pledged ships at sea: Flash, MFV *Seeker* advises *Heade-on-the-Hearth*, a heavily modified *Webber*-class vessel is at roam in the wildlands between Kana and Onaris, and has been terrorizing this region for some time. It is imperative the *Heade* not escape the area as she is crewed by Kestral-based robotic personages of the Drury Brothers. The *Heade* has been damaged, though the extent of the damage is not known. Advise *Seeker* is unarmed and bearing wounded and shall require immediate assistance to sink or take her a-prize with all speed. That is all."

"Aye, sir, sending message."

He shook his head. "Just that easy, eh?"

"Sir?"

"Never mind."

He turned to Taara. "Taara, where is Morgan-Jeterix?"

"She's down in the dispensary trying to help the civilians."

"We have coils, a crew, communications, and a Hospitaler to boot. I don't know what to do with myself."

13

—BAY 15—

"Would you just look at that piece of man! Come here, you!" Morgan-Jeterix said as she leaned over the patient on the table. She was getting around by using her Jet Staff as a crutch. Stenstrom and Taara were standing in the door-way to the dispensary.

She threw the staff aside and hobbled up to Stenstrom where she put her arms around him and held him tight. "Creation, I missed you!"

Stenstrom laughed. "That's a fine sentiment, Morgan, but you only just met me a few hours ago."

"So? I feel I've known you forever. And just look how handsome, I'm going to have that mask off you before long."

He took a good hard look at her—Morgan was certainly a beautiful woman. And, something else: she transformed before his eyes her skin turning a distinct shade of blue, her smooth skin painted in fanciful strokes from an invisible brush. On her left check and brow was a golden crest depicting a burning globe—the crest of the Sisterhood of Light and, orbiting her head was a single word: Vida.

"What is 'Vida'?" he asked.

Morgan was astonished. "You see that?"

"I see the word 'Vida' circling your head. I also see your skin has been painted blue and the official Crest of the Sisterhood of Light is tattooed on your right check."

"The word 'Vida' is Vith for: 'Empath'. My House is branded Certified Empaths by the Sisters and they mark us in a 4-D tattoo so they may easily recognize us, the blue skin, the crest, the word, but only the Sisters should be able to see it."

"I see it now just fine."

Morgan smiled in a seductive fashion and pulled him in close. "Do you like it?" she whispered. "It covers my body. I can show you more ..."

Stenstrom was finding his thoughts addled, the furnace of his passions just beginning to stoke. This 4-D tattoo covering Morgan's body was the most seductive thing he'd ever seen.

He quickly pulled away and changed the topic. Morgan and a few Merians had the civilians laid out on the tables, and some were on the floor. Several Merians were leaning over them, applying a thick, brackish-looking ointment to their blackened skin. "How are these people doing?" he asked.

"They need the League sure enough," Morgan said, "but they're doing as well as can be expected. I found the stores here in the dispensary nearly empty except for a few sacks of dry soda. The Merians, though, found a quantity of lard in the galley, some salts, and a case of grape brandy which they mixed into a simple but effective salve. With it, their skin is moistened and somewhat refreshed. They should rest easy until we return to the League."

A case of brandy? The brandy he was supposed to deliver to Bazz or else??

Taara spoke up. "That brandy? Did they use all of it?"

One of the Merians looked up, the green sleeves of her robe pushed up to her elbows, her hands covered in salve. "We did, as there were only a few bottles and there are so many here to treat. Were we wrong in using it?"

So, his appointment was cost at last. Not by ruse and stratagem, not by a dead ship, Drury, Kestral, or Cronyn, but by a kind-hearted Merian seeking to help those in need.

"Is it helping?" he asked.

"Oh yes, they seem much better, and many have at last fallen to sleep and are resting easy. They were so desperate for sleep."

"They've got a fighting chance now," Morgan said.

"Are they out of danger?"

"For now, yes."

"If it has helped them, then it was well used. Well, we should be underway soon, and then we'll get them all the help they need in a matter of hours."

Morgan smiled at Stenstrom. "So, you wanted me to tell you what 'Jeterix' means?" she said, approaching him. Her eyes were like pristine lamps glowing bright on a field of blue.

"I did."

She hobbled into his personal space. Though he had just met this secretly painted woman, he could feel a distinct tension forming for her—a maddening, distracting tension. He wanted to touch her, to savor the feel and, as she was a certified empath, she probably knew all that too. "Well, let me tell you …"

"It means 'I'm a blithering, unwashed idiot' in Thompson," came Gwendolyn's voice from behind.

Stenstrom turned. Gwendolyn was standing into the doorway, her arms crossed. "Gwen, how are the coils doing?"

"They're small and under-powered, but they're coming along. Should be ready to make sail in another few minutes."

Stenstrom was amazed. "Excellent work."

"Would you care to inspect them?"

The Com buzzed in. "Captain Stenstrom," came Crewmen Clement's voice.

"Aye?" Stenstrom replied, still not used to hearing such a thing.

"Sir, we have a fix on the *Heade-on-the-Hearth*. A vessel matching her description is besetting a passenger liner just off the shipping lanes. We're receiving an uncoded distress signal begging for help."

"What is a passenger liner doing off the shipping lanes?" Gwendolyn asked.

"Apparently she's full of Xaphan refugees. They were fleeing to the League," the Com replied.

"Inform the Fleet. Gwen, we need to make sail, immediately."

"Are we going to engage the Druries?"

"We are."

"We have no weapons—we can't fight!"

"No, but we can divert the *Heade* from the liner and hold her here until the Fleet arrives."

✶ ✶ ✶ ✶ ✶

Stenstrom and Taara returned to the bridge.

"What is our status, please?"

"We are reading minimum power reserves required to launch and make orbit," Crewman Allistar said, looking at screens on the Missive's panel.

Stenstrom turned to A-Ram. "Are we ready?"

"Bel, that we are. The helm is available and ready for travel."

He looked up. "Com, Engineering—Lt. Gwendolyn, we're making sail."

"Aye," her voice came back. "Watch the redlines and don't expect a record dash out of the gates."

"All right, A-Ram. Take us up and get us into orbit."

Stenstrom stood there, with Lady Alesta still sitting in his seat. She was turned around, watching A-Ram work. In his heart, Stenstrom was sure nothing was going to happen. The *Seeker* would sit there stranded on the turbid waves of Cronyn World, forever.

He heard a slight rise in noise.

"Thousand feet," A-Ram said.

"We're at a thousand feet already, A-Ram?"

"No sir, now we're at two thousand. Pitching up and accelerating to standard parking speed."

"How's it feel?" Stenstrom asked, not feeling the motion at all.

A-Ram looked at him. "Like a dream."

"Sensing, are we still reading the *Heade*?"

"Aye, sir."

"How far?"

"She's at 3:45AM, mark 7:17PM, 800 thousand miles. She seems to have stopped."

Stenstrom addressed the bridge. "We've a slight change in plans. The *Heade* has attacked a civilian liner full of innocent souls. We have called the Fleet, however, they are still yet to arrive. We don't have anything to fight with, but, with luck, we can hold them long enough to protect the liner and await the Fleet."

"Creation, Bel, we can hold those fools all the damn lived-long day!" Taara said.

The bridge agreed—after all they'd been through at the hands of the Druries, they were spoiling for a fight.

"So be it, when we arrive, we'll … think of something."

Crewman Clement looked at the Com. "Sir, he said. "I don't think we're completely unarmed."

✳   ✳   ✳   ✳   ✳

They stepped into the darkened bay. The place smelled of old shot blasts and cordite.

Gwendolyn carefully stepped into the bay and stood near Stenstrom. She looked around in the dark. Crewmen Clement and Allistar also entered.

"I thought you'd want to see this right away," Clement said.

Stenstrom took a breath. "Ok, crewman, what are we looking at here?"

In the dark was a gangly, Z-shaped robotic assembly. "This, sir," he said, "is Battleshot Battery number 15, starboard."

Stenstrom took in the sight. It was a large robotic arm about twenty feet tall mounting a sturdy armature and a circular cluster of fifteen rotating barrels mounted at the top, ten feet long, each. There was an empty belt feeding the armature and what appeared to be a well-worn track leading out toward the closed doors.

Gwendolyn looked at it. "Please go on, crewman."

"It's an old-style HArM-6 long barrel Battleshot battery. They used to be the Fleet standard for short-range, ship-to-ship combat until the Sar-Beam sort of put them out to pasture."

Though big and looming, the gun looked quiet, asleep.

"This baby can unload upwards of 200,000 rounds a minute."

"Taara, I thought all the Battleshot batteries aboard the *Seeker* had previously been removed for retooling," Stenstrom said.

"They were, all except for this one," Clement said. "This gun has been used so much over the years that the bolts holding it to its run-out platform are fused in place. The craftsmen who removed all the Battleshot batteries previously couldn't get it out, and they were going to cut the gun out of the position with laser torches during the *Seeker's* refit. It's all in the Com report."

Gwendolyn ran a finger up the length of its armature. There was a red label affixed to its housing. She scowled. "No, no, Clement look at this—this gun has been condemned by Fleet Engineering."

Clement was a little embarrassed.

Stenstrom studied the towering, silent gun. "Oh, come now, Gwen," he said. "Let's think creatively for a moment. Has this gun been branded defective because it's actually broken, or simply because a regulation in a manual says it's defective due to some time limit being met and expired? Do we have any ordinance for it?"

"I found a drum containing two-hundred, fifty-four rounds in a bin marked DEFECTIVE," Clement said.

"Defective?" Gwendolyn replied.

Stenstrom winced. "Two-hundred, fifty-four rounds? At the rate of speed these long-barrel Battleshot batteries fire, two hundred, fifty-four rounds will last about a fourth of a second."

Taara gave the battery a rap. "Yeah, but that'll be a fourth of a second of pure hell. If we line it up right, we can saw the *Heade-on-the-Hearth* in two."

"Provided the ammunition works and doesn't explode in the chamber," Gwendolyn said, shaking her head.

"Yes, of course. Have a bit of faith."

"It won't do that," Allistar said. "This is a great gun—a classic. My father was an armorer aboard the *Grayfox*. He used to tell me that the old long barrel was a gun you could count on. It was a gun that would get you home."

Stenstrom looked up. "Navigation, what is our ETA to the *Heade*?"

"Fifteen minutes."

Stenstrom smiled. "Let's load her up and run her out."

14

—Chance Drury—

The *Seeker* covered the distance fast. Clearing the debris field surrounding Cronyn World, she sprinted into a vast area with Onaris' star, Ole Scrub, shining dead ahead.

Far off, tumbling slightly, was the *Heade*.

She was grappled onto the boxy, ribbed form of a rickety Merci liner, holding it in the manner a praying mantis would hold a dying fly. The robotic armature mounting the cassagrain cannon was pointed that the liner's belly.

Stenstrom took in the scene in the holo-cone. "Looks like he's gripping her tight."

"Sir," crewman Clement said. "Incoming message. It's Chance Drury."

Over the Com came a sinister voice.

"Paymaster Stenstrom, you are full of surprises, a-heheh. *Vous m'ennuyez beaucoup.* But, look what fate brings us? Looks to be 400 hundred souls on this wretched tub, all miserable Xaphans seeking to change their fortunes in the League. I've got my cassagrains aimed right at their keel. One or two shots and the ship will break in half and all those screaming souls will be spaced. *Fácil viene, fácil va, no?*"

"What do you want, Drury?" Stenstrom replied.

"I want their engines, as you saw fit to damage mine."

On the ovular monitor screens, a pair of eyes appeared—Chance's eyes. "And," he said, "I want you as well. Put yourself out into space and I shall collect you—as you are a robot as I am, you shall survive without issue. I wish to keep you near me, as a dangerous attack animal. Or, maybe I'll just kill you, stuff you, and keep you in wardrobe as a hated Auto-Icon, getting you out on days when I feel like yelling at something. I shall inform my reconstituted brothers what an inconsolable bore you were. *Vous êtes une maladie sur mon âme bénie!*"

"We are unarmed, Drury. Let the liner go. What have you to fear from us?"

"I am not going to the let the liner go, Paymaster. I am going to hold it here, take its engines, and kill everyone aboard as slowly as I can. I see you put a call out to your nurse-maids in the Fleet. I see quite a few ships en route at this moment. Too bad I shan't be here when they arrive. Disappeared into the dark, as I do so well. *Wie Spaß das ist?"*

Stenstrom made a cutting motion across his throat.

"Com muted, sir," Clement said.

"Com, what is the ETA of the Fleet?"

"We have the *Exody, Tempest,* and *Coober Peedie* coming in through Kana and the *Danner* en route via Olgolvy. ETA two hours, approximate."

Stenstrom thought a moment. "Two hours—that's enough time for him to up and vanish sure enough. A-Ram, get me a bit closer and give me a full, unobstructed view of the *Heade's* cassagrain assembly. We're going to get close, and I am going to take it out with my NTHs. On my signal, I want you to Slap the Drury-ship hard enough to knock the liner free. Then, we can be ready to deal with them."

He looked around. "Everybody ready?"

The bridge crew nodded.

"Unmute, please."

Crewman Clement pressed a button. "If you want me, Chance, those people aboard the liner are to be set free immediately. It's not negotiable."

"They shall be free, sir, once they're dead—free to float in space. *Leurs morts jetteront des détritus les cieux.* Now, here is how we are going to proceed. In a few minutes I am going to kill a few passengers just to demonstrate my good intentions. To prevent the further killing of passengers, you, Paymaster, shall then exit your ship—you need not don a pressure suit either, sir. Just pitch yourself out. At that time, the *Seeker* shall retire, and I shall take the engines of this liner and be off, well ahead of the party the Fleet shall soon be throwing for me here."

Stenstrom walked into his office. In the distance, he could see the *Heade* with its robotic grapples tied up around the boxy, primitive-looking liner. The *Heade* kept the liner out in front of it, rotating around and presenting it to the *Seeker* like a hostage.

The three ships slowly swirled around each other.

A-Ram skillfully got the *Seeker* in closer, bit by bit.

There! There was the robotic cassagrain assembly mounted underneath the *Heade's* nose.

Just a little bit closer.

"So, Paymaster, what's it going to be? *Fait ils vivent ou mourront-ils?*"

He was now close enough to see the rounded nodes and housings of the robotic assembly. He could see the silvery connectors and servo motors, like a musculature of metal. He drew his NTH's and cocked them.

"I have an alternate proposal for you."

"Do you?" came Chance's voice. "You just cost thirty people their lives. I don't have time for games, Paymaster …"

There!! There was the control housing.

He fired both NTHs. "Nor do I," he said.

Two hits. He watched the cassagrain gun go dead, stuck in position, pointing at the liner. Not firing.

"Now, A-Ram, now!!"

A-Ram spun the wheel and the nose of the *Seeker* quickly came around, the ship moving like glass. Desperately, the *Heade* tried to free itself from the liner.

The *Seeker* and the *Heade-on-the-Hearth* collided hard, the superstructures of both ships momentarily tangling. The passenger liner was released, and the long, clunky ship trundled away as fast as it could, leaving the two warships to battle.

The robotic grappling arms of the *Heade* moved to made to seize the *Seeker* like an octopus reaching out to grasp a crab. With a bang it locked on.

"A-Ram, evasive!" Stenstrom shouted.

"Everybody hang on!" A-Ram said as he spun the wheel and rolled the *Seeker* in a maneuver Captain Davage himself would have been proud of.

The *Heade* was thrown away with the force. She turned her remaining guns to the *Seeker* and blasted away, trying to pierce her armor.

But, this time, the *Heade* wasn't facing a mostly dead, depowered Warbird. This time, Chance Drury was facing a fully functional ship.

Gwendolyn fired the newly installed coils into overboost, and the ship jumped to additional life. The Cyclops eye of the main sensor lit up to near blinding full strength.

A-Ram turned the wheel and the *Seeker* smashed into the Drury ship, caving-in a good portion of its gantry-laced superstructure. Several pieces of odd technology fell off and spiraled away.

The *Seeker* was far too heavy a vessel for the Druries to contend with in a shoving match, and Chance Drury knew it. He tried to disengage and get away but the *Seeker* would not allow it, and, with her coils glowing, she was much faster than the damaged *Heade*. They rammed her full astern, sending her spiraling. The crew capsules began to vent, spewing jets of vapor into space.

The *Seeker* pulled up a-starboard and Slapped her again; more bits of gantry and hull plating careened away. Grapplers fell off and tumbled.

The *Heade*, in a panic, aimed her small caliber, rim-fired guns at the *Seeker*—the same guns that they mercilessly fired at the doomed men in the water on Cronyn World. In this case, nothing happened, as the guns were far too small to dent the *Seeker's* armor. In some instances, the shots reflected back and punctured the *Heade*.

Locked together, the *Heade* was finally in the correct position.

"Fire!" Stenstrom roared.

The solitary Battleshot unit in Bay 15 came to spinning life and laid a one second barrage full on the broadside of the *Heade*, a galaxy of blinking explosive ordinance dancing on its skin.

The *Heade* fell apart in a cascade of debris and deformed metal. The bridge capsule shot away from the doomed vessel, containing the Druries and their last remaining shards of foul programming.

"Another day, Paymaster, another day," came Chance's sinister voice over the Com. "*Ce n'est pas le dernier tu vas entendre a propos de moi, diable! Au revoir, salaud!*"

The bridge capsule sped off into the night of space.

Nothing doing. The *Seeker* fell on it, like a hawk pouncing on a squirrel. The capsule burst open, revealing the struggling occupants. Eventually, either by flattening against the unbending hull of the *Seeker*, or by aimed NTH shot, Chance Drury and his brothers met their apparent end.

With luck, he and his brothers would never rise again.

15

—Under the Table—

Stenstrom sat in his office. He still wasn't quite used to lights and the breathing sounds the living ship made. He'd gotten used to the dark and the mumbling quiet. He sat there absently holding Lilly's locket, feeling the smooth gold in his hand. Sticky-fingered Taara had rescued it from the Sisters' domain, and he was glad. Despite the Sisters' magic, he missed her.

In a few hours, they'd be back at Kana, and he would give up the ship and face whatever charges awaited him at Fleet. The charges didn't bother him much. Just like a stout pair of handcuffs, he could get out of those easily enough. He had friends in the right places, he belonged to the right organizations, and he had lots of money to finance his defense.

What he couldn't get away from was the disappointment.

What was he going to say to Captain Davage and to his father? He promised Captain Davage he would make something of this lady again, this old Warbird *Seeker*. He promised him. Being an optimist, he guessed Captain Davage would see the positives and would happily support him again in the reappointment to another vessel.

Davage was always good for that.

And, his father—what would he say to him? *Sorry, father. I annoyed just about every Admiral I could find, I found out I'm some sort of 'It Man' as well and I belong to the Sisterhood of Light—oh, by the by, Lillian of Gamboa, whom we all liked so much back at the manor, isn't really a woman—she was the Sisters' construct made of sand, and I discovered a world full of hideous creatures that actively feed upon us, both mentally and physically. Oh, and I let them go, too. Also, I got into a big fight with the 400 year old Drury brothers, and they were a bunch of robots being controlled by their Kestral masters. Just like me ...*

And then there was the *Seeker* herself. What would become of her—as

Captain Davage had promised, she stood tall against all that had been arrayed before her. She still had all kinds of fight in her—it would be a shame to let her go.

There was a knock at the door and Gwendolyn came in.

"Ship's engineer," he said. "How goes it?"

"We're making good time, Captain," she said with familiar emphasis. "The small coils are holding up quite well. I'm very pleased."

She sat down. "You look a little sad, Bel. What's on your mind?"

He smiled at her. "You know, Gwen, we've only been acquainted for a short time, yes, and we're already probing each other's thoughts?"

"Neat, isn't it? So, spill it, Bel, what's got you down?"

"Oh, it's nothing. I'm just sitting here wondering what's it's going to be like to give this lady up. Looks like I blew my first mission and my time on the *Seeker's* chair is done."

She smiled. "Well, I suppose 'blew it' is a subjective term. Look at all the people you've inspired along the way to blowing your first mission. A-Ram would still be polishing silver at the Fleet, Taara would still be guarding nothing down at HQ, the Druries would still have free run, and I would still be a miserable, grouchy person without a friend in the world. I seem to have learned that I'm a pretty mean person when I'm in charge—I don't handle it well. I am much better as an important follower. This mission, I think, was a grand success. Feel like hitting something? Come on, let's head to the gym. Care to go a round or two with the Grizzly Bear? You'll feel better."

"Is the gym in pieces like the rest of this ship?" he asked.

"Don't know. I suppose we'll find out."

Stenstrom laughed. "Maybe later."

Gwendolyn left her seat and sat down on his desk. She took his hands. "This isn't an end, Bel, it's just the beginning. The place doesn't matter, and the ship doesn't matter. Wherever you go, I'm coming with you, or you're coming with me. It's a big Fleet, and I'm happy to tackle it knowing you're nearby. I sound like Morgan-Jeterix, don't I? She's always had a knack for saying things that I was thinking or feeling—but that's over. I'm going to say what's on my mind myself from now on—and guess what's on my mind right now?"

"What?"

"You, face down on the mat, tapping out of a rear naked choke hold that's won me so many tournaments. Come on, let's go let some steam off. Kana and all that can wait."

Stenstrom stood and grabbed his coat. "Ok, I'm told I'm pretty tough."

"I'll bet."

Gwendolyn put her arm around him and they headed for the door. There was another knock. Taara, A-Ram, and Lady Alesta came in.

"Come on in, everyone, there's plenty of room," Stenstrom said, bading them to enter.

Taara stepped in. "Were you two going somewhere?"

"The gym," Gwendolyn replied.

"The gym? You were going to the gym to fight, weren't you? Were you going to get me, so I could watch? You weren't, were you?"

"Good sir," Alesta said, "I wanted to offer you a present, one that you have well earned."

"Something for me?"

A-Ram spoke up. "I took Lady Alesta to the mess to see if we could scrounge up a snack before we put into Kana."

Alesta smiled and held out a black bottle of brandy. "I found this rolled under a table in the dining area. I'm told that you need this, that it will help you. Please, take it."

Stenstrom took the bottle of Admiral Derlith's brandy, the last remaining bottle. "Well, what do you know?"

"The Star works in wonderful ways. There are no martyrs, and all will be rewarded. None are left behind," she said.

Taara spoke up. "A-Ram, we still headed for Kana?"

"That we are."

"Then let's come about—we've got a party on Bazz to get to, and I think we can just make it."

A-Ram ran out of the office to the helm.

"Thank you, Lady Alesta," he said marveling at the bottle.

Alesta bowed and followed A-Ram out.

Gwendolyn grabbed Stenstrom by the collar. "Come on, Bel,"

"Are you still going to the gym?" Taara asked, tagging along.

"We're going to engineering, Taara, to see if we can squeeze a little more speed out of these coils, as Bel has an important date to keep on Bazz. Then we're going to the gym and you can watch me beat him up."

Several hours later, Stenstrom and Gwendolyn returned to his office. They were both mussed up and sweaty.

"That was fun," Stenstrom said. "You really can wrestle, Gwen, no kidding."

She smiled and seated herself. "What, did you think I'd be a pushover or something? We need proper attire next time—it's too hard to move properly in what we're wearing now." Gwendolyn took a deep breath. "Ah, the first thing I'm going to do when we get a moment on Bazz is change. Goodness, how long have I been wearing these same clothes?"

Stenstrom looked out the window. "How long until we get to Bazz?"

"Seven or eight hours if we can hold this speed. We'll be cutting it close, but I think we'll have a little time to spare."

He seated himself. Lilly's golden locket was missing from his desk. He wondered where it had gone to when Gwen spoke up.

"What's this, Bel?" she asked.

"What's what?"

"This."

Propped up against the bulkhead was a huge package, at least seven by four feet wrapped in gray paper. Its size and general shape indicated that it was a large, framed painting.

There was a tag. Gwendolyn pulled her gloves off and read it. "It says: To Paymaster Stenstrom, Lord of Belmont. From: An Admirer."

Gwendolyn appeared a little jealous. "Got an admirer I don't know about, Bel, do you? I didn't know Morgan painted."

He looked at the canvas. "I don't know ..."

"Well, you needn't wait until Nether Day, Bel. Open it."

He pulled away the paper. Exposed, he recognized the frame—it was the portrait Lilly had been working on years ago, the one she had never let him see.

Had he not been wearing his mask, he would certainly have been in tears.

"I friend of mine painted this for me, Gwen," he said.

"Where did it come from?"

"I've no idea. The Sisters, perhaps."

Gwendolyn stood there holding the tag. "Well, can we look at it?"

He put his hands on the sides of the frame and turned it around. They looked at the vast face of the canvas.

There he was, standing tall: Lord Stenstrom of Belmont-South Tyrol, masked, in his green HRN coat. Gwendolyn stood in the background, wearing her Fleet uniform and FEDULA, a tiny scar on her cheek. A-Ram and Taara were there too, as was the *Seeker*, peeking through the clouds. He could also see the Merians milling about in the farther reaches of the garden.

He gave the frame a tap, and heard the slight hiss of sand falling away.

"Hey, is that me?" Gwen asked, looking at the canvas.

"Looks like you."

"How is this possible?

Stenstrom took a deep breath. "Ask the Sisters. They seem to know everything."

Gwen leaned close to the canvas. "Who's that back there?"

Stenstrom was lost in thought.

"Bel?"

In the far recesses of the painting, was a figure crouching behind a tree. It was a slender figure, garbed in red.

"It's Knife," he said in reply.

"Who's that?"

"My enemy."

16

—THE BALL—

They arrived at the wonderful Fleet complex at Dyson-Boorman, near the calm waters of the Endax Sea, the evening sky a typical Bazz greenish-gray. They landed the ship at Fleet dock and got the civilians and any others who needed medical attention to The Jones at once. The rest, Fleet and Merians alike, headed to the Fleet ballroom at the heart of the complex. It didn't occur to anybody that the Merians were civilians—they, as a group, had become very close in their shared experience on Cronyn World.

The well-dressed attendants at the door saw the odd gaggle approaching and turned their noses up. "Have the lot of you been invited to this private function?"

"Indeed," Stenstrom said. "We are here under the orders of Admiral Derlith and have been commanded into his presence."

The attendants appeared unconvinced. "Have you a paper invitation or a code to offer?"

Gwendolyn stepped forward. "Ajax, Ajax, Endecar-two. That is his current personal code."

The attendant checked a nearby terminal. "Aye, that's his current code. Very well."

The attendants parted and Stenstrom and his band entered. As Lady Alesta approached, the attendants halted her. "You may not enter the ballroom, ma'am."

"And why not?" A-Ram asked, incensed, taking her by the shoulders.

"Because she is not properly shod as is required," he replied dryly, noting Alesta's bare feet.

Stenstrom returned to the attendants. "These people are part of my party. They are worthy of all honor. She and her lot shall have entry to the ball."

The attendant thought about it, and then stepped aside, the rest of the group piling into the busy ballroom.

Stenstrom and Gwendolyn strode through the posh crowd and approached the vast dining table.

There was Admiral Derlith seated amongst his Admiral friends.

They arrived and stood there a moment.

The Admiral looked up at him. "Gwendolyn, are you all right? What is your business, Paymaster?" he asked, knife and fork in hand.

"You should know, Admiral," Stenstrom replied. "I'm here at your pleasure."

Derlith smiled. "Yes, sorry about that," he said. "Losing your chair and all."

"Lose my chair? On the contrary …"

Stenstrom waved his hands and produced a dusty bottle of brandy which he thumped down on the table.

"What's this?" Derlith asked.

"Your brandy. You should recognize it. I have fulfilled my mission, at your pleasure. And, with several hours to spare, I might add."

The Admiral scoffed. "One bottle? You had a whole crate to bring."

"Apologies, you didn't say how much brandy to bring to Bazz. Some bottles got smashed in my rough upload to the *Seeker,* and a few were used to comfort a group of civilians from Mallets who were in desperate need of aid. But please, enjoy the final bottle with your peers."

"What shall we do with one bottle? There are over a hundred admirals in attendance here."

"I suggest smaller snifters."

"Balderdash—your Appointment is cost. Gwendolyn, please take this fool into custody, under my orders."

Gwendolyn spoke up. "Uncle, you know I love you very much, but this fine man has fulfilled his mission and is, as of now, the bonded captain of the Main Fleet Vessel *Seeker,* and I will attest to it under tribunal. Along the way, he showed remarkable pluck, great ingenuity, and great courage. He saved not only my life, but the lives of my crew and those of the Merians, who are heroes by any measure, and he put an end to a scabrous band of outlaws operating right under the Fleet's nose. I am proud to stand here at his side."

"Gwendolyn!" Derlith yelled, "you are under orders—arrest this man!"

"I'm sorry, Uncle. I have been duly conscripted by the commander of a Main Fleet Vessel and am in his charge. I am currently not subject to your orders."

"Doing what, if I may ask?"

"Ship's engineer," Stenstrom replied. "By hook or by crook, Admiral."

Stenstrom waved his hands and produced a silver dagger. He gently took the bottle from the Admiral and began slicing away the wax. "You are to be commended, sir," Stenstrom said. "You helped raise a fine young woman, if Gwendolyn vouches for you—which she does—then you must be a good fellow. I'm sorry I offended you and I'm sorry this lone bottle is all that's left of your crate. Be comforted, the rest helped save the lives of League citizens and, therefore, was put to good use."

Stenstrom got the wax off and uncorked the bottle. He took a whiff of the contents. "I was wrong about this as well, it smells wonderful, truly a product of fine tending and skill. I shall take my leave, sir, and bid you good night."

Derlith stopped him. "Paymaster, a moment, please. I have been known to be judgmental, and rather stubborn. You inspired my adjutant to insurrection. Josephus ..."

"He prefers to be called A-Ram, sir."

"Yes, Lord A-Ram then, has never shown that sort of style before, and you have won over my niece, whom I love very much and whose judgment I trust. I may have misjudged you and given ear to bizarre things not of either of our makings. So be it, I hereby acknowledge that you have fulfilled your mission at my pleasure. You are, as of this moment, the bonded captain of the Main Fleet Vessel *Seeker.* I will take care of the pending charges against you, and bade you return the *Seeker* to Dry Dock 186 to begin her refits as soon as you are able to get her there. And please, enjoy the ball, stay and be refreshed, be entertained. I would enjoy a dance with my niece at some point this evening. And, please, ask Lord A-Ram to join me when he can. I would like to congratulate him on his appointment. I shall greatly miss him."

Stenstrom and Gwendolyn bowed. They turned to make their way from the table.

Stenstrom's special white Holystone, the one that detected the Astral Plane, began to make noise. Carefully he surveyed the table.

Seated a few place settings down was a black-haired woman in a green gown. She sat there looking at him. "Good sir?" she said, eyes big and round. "I am pleased you made it. I was hoping … praying."

Stenstrom stopped, his stone rattling in his hand. "Madam, do I know you?"

"But of course you do," the woman said. "I once promised myself I'd never return to Bazz, yet here I am. It's a different world than it was before, and so am I."

He stood there regarding her for several moments. Finally: "I believe I do know you. I thought you a phantom of my own imagination for a long time. You have tried to kill me several times, as an infant, as a helpless boy, and again as a bewildered young man. Do you deny it?"

She shook her head. "No, sir, I do not."

"Are you here to kill me now?"

"No, I came here to congratulate you for accomplishing something I never could, to offer my thanks for the example you've shown me, and, most importantly, to ask for your forgiveness."

"My forgiveness?"

"For everything, for everyone. We are in a Closed Circle, the Bazzers say. Time to end it. Time to let old hurts heal."

Stenstrom thought a moment. "I will say that an injustice was done to you once. What you must have felt for my father to be so angry for so long. To put an end to this, to break this curse, I will say that I forgive you and hold you no further malice. Additionally, I must inform you that I intend to escort you to the authorities and inform them of everything I suspect regarding your former activities, both here on Bazz and in the Calvertlands of Kana. I am also going to inform the Sisters that you have breached their thoughts."

The woman sat there. She considered her response, then spoke. "I was ready, ready to atone for my sins and to face justice. But then …"

She pulled a small envelope from her bag. It was new, freshly written in familiar handwriting; looked like his father's distinctive hand in Belmont stationary.

"Then, I discovered it's never too late to begin living again," she said. "We all deserve that, don't we?"

"A fine sentiment, but regardless. Shall we?" he asked, motioning for her to take his hand.

She pulled something else from her bag and set it on the table. "First, please accept this gift," she said. "I have no further use for it."

Stenstrom looked down. Sitting on the table was a large garnet on a burnished chain. His Astral Plane detectors went wild: it was a Planar Bridge, the key to opening a gateway to the Astral Plane. He'd never seen one up close before.

"Please take good care of my niece," she said.

There was a brief commotion of uncorking bottles out on the ballroom floor. He glanced away for a moment.

When he looked back, she was gone. Her chair was empty.

Gwendolyn was confused. "Who was that, Bel? Where'd she go?"

He looked at the now empty chair and sighed. "Nobody. I don't know where she went, but I wish her luck and wish her my best." He picked up the Planar Bridge and made it vanish.

They walked away from the table and made their way across the busy dance floor to where Taara, A-Ram, and Lady Alesta waited. Morgan, still weak, was sitting nearby, alert but a little tired. Taara was standing there with a plate of something. A-Ram fetched a glass of punch for Morgan and for Lady Alesta, who took it and smiled at him, holding her cup. She was so lovely when she smiled—look how pretty, and clearly in love.

Good for you, A-Ram. Well done.

Several of the crew stood around, some holding plates from the buffet line, while others had waded out onto the floor, testing the waters, some dancing with other crewmen, others with robed Merians. The bond that had formed between them was clear and well earned.

They waved, and A-Ram and Alesta waved back.

The music picked up and the dancers parlayed about. Stenstrom and Gwendolyn found themselves jostled and pushed in the tight reaches of the floor. Lace and confetti landed on their shoulders and got in their hair.

Soon, they were arm in arm, swirling across the floor, Gwendolyn's eyes locked with Stenstrom's eyes.

He tried to pull away but she held him. She was so strong.

"We've our ship to return to, Gwen."

"Must we, so soon? You heard my uncle—we've the night. The ball is ours. This is our celebration, Bel—we've earned it. If I may make a suggestion, as acting Ship's Engineer, the crew's been through a lot, and they've earned a few days of fun, to relax, to put on some clean clothes and get their heads back on, and I'm sure Taara would like to visit her folks while we're here, to show them what she's become. And, I wouldn't mind trying some of this hot Bazz food that I've heard so much about, provided I've good friends to share it with. Now that the ship has a real set of coils, albeit small ones, it'll only take us a day or two to get back to Kana and begin its refit. Let's not be in any hurry. We've much hard work ahead of us, all in due course."

She stood there a moment. "I'm sorry, I forgot myself. I'm only an acting Ship's Engineer."

Stenstrom smiled. "There shall soon be an appointment available for Ship's Engineer aboard the *Seeker*—want the job, for good? I know you wouldn't be in command anymore, but think of the name you could make for yourself …"

Gwendolyn stared at him. Stenstrom continued. "And A-Ram … I know A-Ram would miss the daylights out of you if you weren't there, and …"

Gwendolyn didn't say anything. Instead, as the music grew, she reached up and slowly pulled the mask from Stenstrom's face. As she did so, he felt no pain, no rush of anguish for his lost Lilly. Rather, he felt the thrill of possibilities with this beautiful Lady of Prentiss who stood at his side in the pit of hell. She stood there looking at him with unforgettable eyes. She pulled the mask away. Letting it go slack at her side, the hermelin fell from the folds of cloth and clattered to the floor, forgotten.

"So handsome," she said. For the first time, Stenstrom and Gwendolyn—the man in the HRN coat and the Grizzly Bear—kissed.

Apparently, she did want the job.

Epilogue

Up on the bluff overlooking the grand Fleet complex, a solitary figure crouched down and listened to the sounds of the ball drift up to the heights.

The figure was clad in red and black, wearing wrappings and robes. She listened to the music, and allowed herself, for just a moment, to long to go down and join the rest.

Lights and music. Dancing and fellowship—none of it was to be for her. It was soon time to move on, to renew the chase.

Knife stood and made to make her way back to her little Shadow tech vessel. Time to walk her lonely road once again.

As she walked, a storm picked up, and wind and bits of grit flew into her face. Though masked, she covered her eyes and quickened her pace.

Something lifted her up and threw her down. Knife flipped to her feet and whirled around. Something hiding in the wind had attacked her.

She slashed out with her hands sending out invisible, micro-beams of Shadow tech, deadly and cutting.

She heard something cry out. Not understanding what she was fighting, Knife slashed again and again, sending her Shadow tech into the maelstrom, hearing her unseen adversary wail in misery.

Knife thought she saw something slump to the ground ahead. She formed a Shadow tech harpoon and advanced to plunge it into her opponent's heart.

She fell upon the form, rose up and plunged the harpoon into its chest.

There was a scream, and the maelstrom of wind and sand got more and more fierce. Her mask was blown away, and the wrappings around her arms began to tatter. She felt the wind-driven sand scouring into her bare flesh, rending it to the bone.

She dropped her harpoon and tried to get away as quickly as she could.

Hands of sand grabbed her from behind.

Knife was lifted into the air, struggling and kicking, micro blades of Shadow tech shooting out in a deadly fan.

She was savagely bent backwards with a sickening crack, her head was suddenly wrenched back to her legs, her pelvis snapping in two. Folded up and scoured clean, Knife died in agony.

The storm of wind raged for a minute or two more, soon, not even Knife's bones remained.

The winds calmed. A figure formed.

It moved to the edge of the bluff and looked down on the Fleet complex, just as Knife had done only minutes earlier.

The figure lifted a parasol over her head, twirled it about, and sighed. *"I'm coming for you, Bel..."* came a soft voice.

FIN

RDG

2012, 2013, revised August 2018

MAPS AND APPENDICES

Paymaster Stenstrom's Office

1: FEDULA (Gwen's Sword)   2: Vith Artifact (Magravine Chasm)   3: MOLLY (A-Ram/Taara)   4: Marine SK Pistol (Taara)

5: Hospitaler Jet Staff   6: Merian Invisibility Belt (Alesta)   7: Portrait of Countess Sygillis   8: Belmont/Tyrol Coat of Arms

9: Portrait of Captain Davage   10: Portrait of Lt. Kilos of Tusck   11: Fleet Tremblar Hat (Gwen)   12: Hoban Royal Navy Coat

13: Anatameter (Arcane device)   14: NTH Pistol (Stenstrom's gun)   15: Stone Knife (Tempus Findal)   16: MARZABLE (Stenstrom)

The Known Universe--as seen from Camalopardus
To: Gelt
To: Kestral Oligarchy
Wayreth (19)
Tubruk (10)
Bustoke (14)
BloodStein (2)
Woodward (10)
Enseladus
(The Keel)
Gothan (11)
The Bell Nebula
Grith (11)
Charn (11)
Marilith Nebula
Hoban (8)
Two-Pitch Nebula
Planet Fall (7)
Mallets (5)
Poteete (1)
Sorrander (12)
Trimble
Apex
(The Angle)
Codis
Corvus
(The Crow)
Seetac (5)
Wunderland (4)
Bell (12)
Gioma (3)
Xaphans Holly (9)
Conwell (4)
Carina (3)
Mertens
(The Cat)
Mirendra (3)
The Xaphan Nebula
To: Ming Moorland
Kana (4)
Blackmoore (7)
Cronyn World
Xandarr (7)
Onaris (4)
Baaz (4)
Tammerak Cluster
Heron Nebula
Burgon (7)
KEY
Serpens
(The Snake)
Heron (1)
Midas (11)
Zoran (9)
Planets AU (Astronomical Unit) distance from Camalopardus
The Kills
1 = Closest
19 = Farthest
Hydelyde (9)
Crux
(The Black Cross)
Caroline (12)
Brindval (9)
Terrabus
The Compass
Everything goes back to the planet Kana
Olgolvy (12)
Shade Church (7)
PM
AM
Star of Merian
(In Dispute)
AM = East/West longitude
PM = North/South latitude.
LEAGUE
SPACE
XAPHAN
SPACE

Map Of Kana
Barrow
Tuk
Saga
Cotten
Dare
Dare
Rhoda
Mt. Holly
Holly
Burgos
Westron
Tardy
Blanchefort
Durst
The Gaston Way
Griff
Clovis
Charn
Pithnar
Stanton
Atalan
Arden
Provst
Bern
Atalea
Shirster Point
Bloodstein
Bell
Midas
Hannover
Minz
Xandarr
Telmus
Valenhelm
Zary
Vith Land
Hazards of the Old Ones
Tartan
Cithmus Lake
Tartan
Maqravine
Kronos River
River Seven
Bodice
Vincent
Hala
Wayreth
Killbane R.
Hala
Caroline
Thirkill Bay
Horace
Feren
Bern
Straight of Elder
Falz
Sea of Atalea
Champion
Caprinar
Kelt
Prentiss
Tela
Sorrenson
Brynthia
Pitcock
Howell
Jacarta
Remnath
Wiln
Rostov
Want
St. Paris
Sammarcand
Mercia
Twilight 4
Deep 7
Woodward
The Great Blue Pierce River
Zenon
Mystery
Blue Pierce
Kentaro
Lake Monama
Lyra
Sea of Elder
Green Sabre
Rustam
Esther
Effington
Haitathe
Herman
Bert
Veltro
Armenelos
Kurtis
Mystery
Barton
Dee
Witchelwelt River
Waddle
Gamboa
Tardn
Tyrol
Conwell
Dee
Calvert
St. Edmund's
Bezzel
Calvert
Pais
Pattern
Hiei
Hiei
Giants Walk
Sea of Esther
N
S
E
W
Key
City
Ruins
Sisters
Castle
1000 Miles
500 Km

Map of Tyrol
Tyrol Town
Tyrol Rd.
Fox Park
Lady Vendra Captured
Sand Pit
Chalk House
Belmont Manor
Sea of Esther
Lady Jubilees Grave
Gwendolyn's Stone
Merian Hermitage
Merians Hill
Culvert Entrance
Gamboa Rd.
To Gamboa
Tyrol Rd.
To Conwell
Hidden Culvert
(Place of Magic)
1 MI
1.6 KM
N
E
S
W

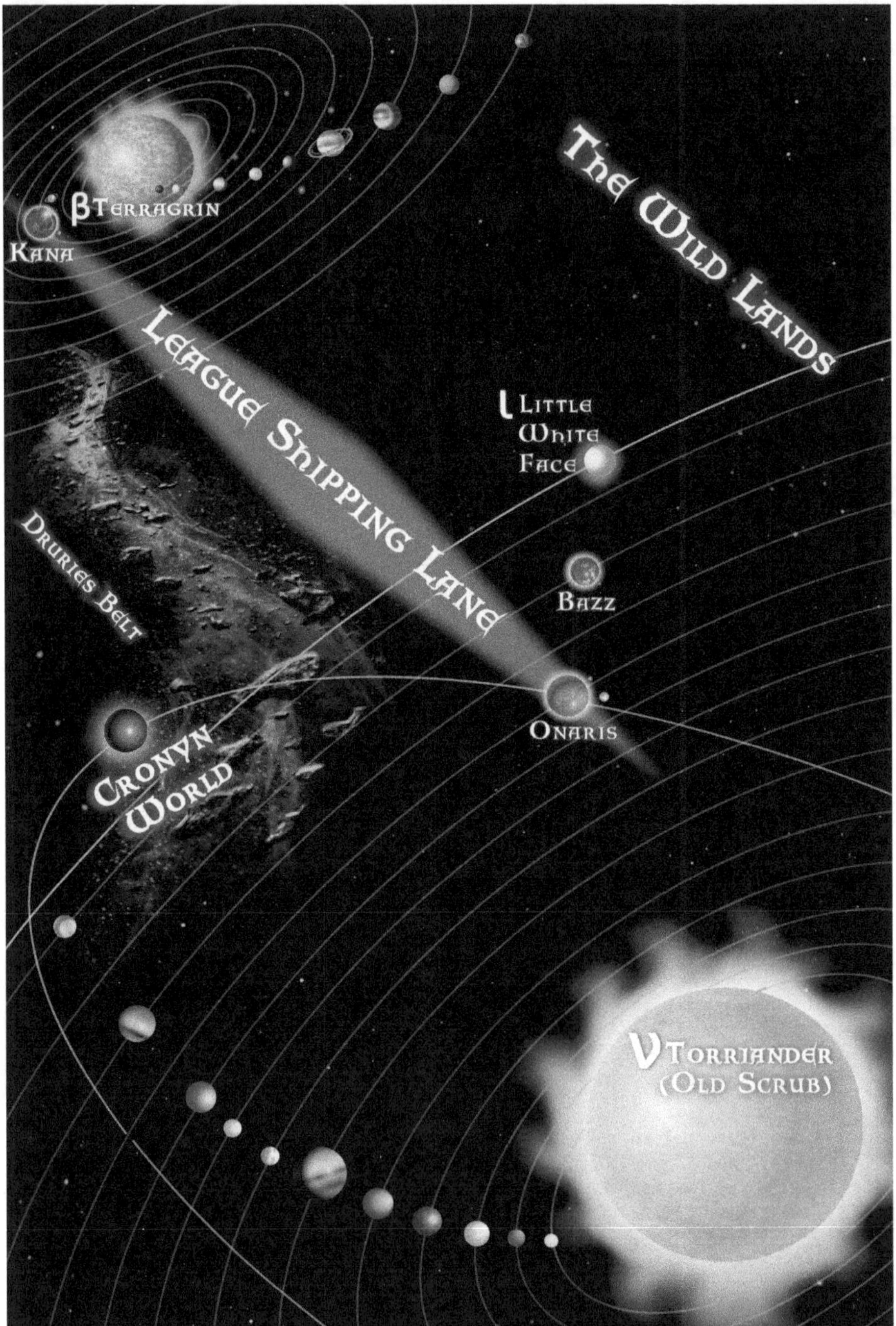

The Wild Lands
βTerragrin
Kana
League Shipping Lane
Little White Face
Bazz
Druries Belt
Cronyn World
Onaris
νTorriander
(Old Scrub)

League Shipping Lane
To: Nu Torriander (Onaris, Bazz)
DRURIES BELT
CRONYN WORLD
Seeker's path as laid out by the lantern
Windward
Seeker intercepted by Demophalon John
Path of Demophalon John
Edam (Hell)
Merian Lookout Point
The Solar Wind
Seeker traveling by the stern
Path of Seeker
The Swarm
To: Beta Terrigrin (Kana)
Seeker returned by Sisters
Leeward
CRONYN WORLD MAP

THE
Fiend of Calvert
MURDER TOUR
Spanning two cities
(Bezzel, St. Edmund's)

*See all of the most notable locations
where the Fiend plied his trade from
the mobile comfort of your seat.

*Witness his escape route across the
rooftops of St. Edmund's.

*Pick from a list of notorious suspects and try to guess who did it!

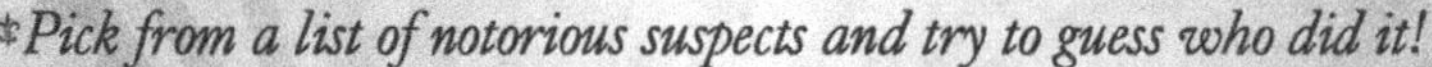

Calvert's Best Guided Tour given by

Grand Dame Lady Miranda of Rosel,
A noted authority on the Fiend and author
of several acclaimed books on the subject.
Lunch served.
Midnight Lantern tours available during Summer months.

Key Tour Sites

1: Empire Hotel: *Calvert's finest hotel tucked on the picturesque corner of St. Edmund's Warf and Marne Grandway was the scene of no less than ten known Fiend murders, the most famous of which was Lord Commadus of Plaid who was murdered in room 322. The hotel throws an annual Fiend Ball on July 32nd, the date of Lord Plaid's death which is a well-attended event.*

2: Bexley Square: *The heart of the Bexley township of St. Edmunds, Bexley Square was the scene of several Fiend murders, all left out in plain sight.*

3: George Yard: *A decrepit alley off of St. James Road, George Yard was a frequent Fiend dumping ground.*

4: Buck's Run: *A trap was set for the Fiend at Buck's Run by the Mad Lord of Walther.*

5: Beasley Canning: *The largest single Fiend murder site with twenty-two victims discovered on the morning of August 19th, 3153AX.*

6: Pitcairn Alley: *Site of the first official Fiend killings in 3114AX, the Night of Unheard cries.*

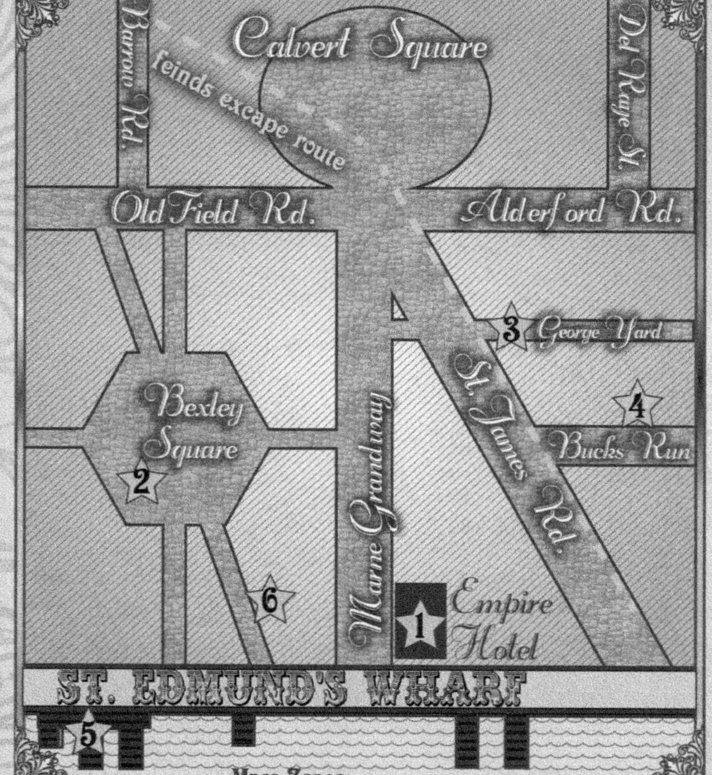

Lord Commadus of Plaid:

A notable Examiner from St. Paris in Remnath, Lord Plaid was brought in at great expense to the city to examine the various crime scenes. Lavishly set up in the Empire Hotel, Lord Plaid seemed more interested in relaxing than investigating the Fiend. Noting the lack of genetics at the various Fiend crime scenes, Lord Plaid's description of the Fiend as a man wearing a bio-suit and a gas mask became an iconic image of the killer. While entertaining friends at the Empire, he boasted he had discovered the identity of the Fiend and would reveal it to the League the following day. He was found dead in his room the next morning.

The Mad Lord of Walther: A vigilant from the east, the Mad Lord of Walther put an end to the Fiend's doings in Calvert. Setting a trap for the Fiend in Buck's Run, he defeated the Fiend and pursued him down St. James Road across the rooftops.

Calvert Square: The locals, tired of living in fear from the Fiend, took to the streets and rioted in Calvert Square, demanding justice in 3164AX. The riot got the attention of the Sisters and help would soon be sent. After the riot, the Fiend's activities would be greatly diminished.

THE FIEND OF CALVERT

is the name given to a killer who roamed the streets of several Calvert cities for nearly seventy years. The Fiend visited all of the major cities in Calvert but mostly concentrated his efforts in St. Edmund's and Bezzel. All of the known victims of the Fiend were vagrant or transitory men and sailors. His usual method of killing was strangulation, though on select occasions he used an edged weapon of unknown configuration. He also had a propensity for breaking arms and legs.

The Fiend left no genetic trace of his passing in the execution of his crimes, making him difficult to catch. How the Fiend was able to accomplish this is not known.

THE Fiend of Calvert
MURDER TOUR

Spanning two cities
(Bezzel, St. Edmund's)

‡ See all of the most notable locations where the Fiend plied his trade from the mobile comfort of your seat.

‡ Witness his escape route across the rooftops of St. Edmund's.

‡ Pick from a list of notorious suspects and try to guess who did it!

Calvert's Best Guided Tour given by

Grand Dame Lady Miranda of Rosel, A noted authority on the Fiend and author of several acclaimed books on the subject.
Lunch served.
"Midnight Lantern tours available during Summer months."

HOUSE OF BELMONT-SOUTH TYROL

Stenstrom, 8th Lord, House of Belmont   Jubilee, 3rd Lady, House of Tyrol

(Key B: Black, P: Pewterlock, H/P: Half Pewterlock, Bl: Blonde)

Beryla	03117AX	B
Wisteria	03119AX	B
Antonia	03122AX	P
Celesta	03125AX	P
Munni	03127AX	B
Solona	03130AX	P
Sabra	03133AX	H/P
Andromeda	03135AX	P
Phaedra	03139AX	B
Ione	03141AX	BL
Io	03144AX	B
Miranda	03147AX	P
Calami	03149AX	P
Persephone	03152AX	B
Lenta	03154AX	P
Deneba	03158AX	P
Jonnia	03160AX	B
Kormandia	03162AX	P
Deserae	03164AX	B
Elma	03167AX	B
Nathalie	03169AX	B
Embeth	03172AX	B
Constance	03174AX	P
Willia	03176AX	P
Nylar	03179AX	H/P
Xantrope	03182AX	H/P
Lucile	03184AX	H/P
Virginia	03187AX	H/P
Lyra	03189AX	B
Stenstrom (M)	03192AX	B

LIST OF ILLUSTRATIONS

About the Author

Ren Garcia is a Science Fiction/Fantasy author and Texas native who grew up in western Ohio. He has been writing since before he could write, often scribbling alien lingo on any available wall or floor with assorted crayons. He attended The Ohio State University and majored in English Literature. Ren has been an avid lover of anything surreal since childhood, he also has a passion for caving, taking pictures of clouds, urban archeology and architecture. He currently lives in Columbus, Ohio with his wife and their four Dachshunds.